GIDEON'S CHILDREN

OTHER BOOKS BY THE AUTHOR:

An Irish Experience:
Travel Tales Flowing from History, Humor & the Search for Home

GIDEON'S CHILDREN

a novel by

HOWARD G. FRANKLIN

Copyright © 2015 Howard G. Franklin

Cover and interior design by Masha Shubin

Buisness People © Nevenasusu. BigStockPhoto.com
Balance Scales of Justice © ClipArtBest.com

This is a work of fiction. The events described here are imaginary. The settings and characters are fictitious or used in a fictitious manner and do not represent specific places or living or dead people. Any resemblance is entirely coincidental.

All rights reserved. No part of this book may be reproduced or transmitted in any form or by any means whatsoever, including photocopying, recording or by any information storage and retrieval system, without written permission from the publisher and/or author.

Publisher: Chamberlain Press | ChamberlainPress.com

Paperback 978-0-9908398-0-4

Printed in the U.S.A.
All paper is acid free and meets all ANSI standards for archival quality paper.

1 3 5 7 9 10 8 6 4 2

To George, Holley, Don, Carl, and Carolyn,
the *children* who made it happen,

For Amy, Matt, and Nick
that they might know,

And for Patty and Linda
whose love and steadfast encouragement
helped make its writing possible

*Injustice anywhere is a threat
to justice everywhere.*

     Martin Luther King, Jr.
       1963

*Power tends to corrupt, and absolute
power corrupts absolutely.*

         Lord Acton
          1887

The price of liberty is eternal vigilance.

          John Charlton
           1809

IT WAS A HOT, HUMID MORNING IN LATE July, 1968, when I turned off the Harbor Freeway and drove in an easterly direction toward the city of Solina. After several miles I entered its outskirts, then slowed the car to take my first glimpse of what had been described to me as the hellhole of Southern California. And while at that particular moment I did not have in mind a precise conception of what hell looked like, what I saw slowly stirred my imagination in that direction.

For several blocks, I passed through a business district composed of a myriad of differently sized shop buildings, often separated at random by a church. They were, for the most part, old and dilapidated. Broken windows, some of which had been boarded over, appeared frequently, and several of the largest storerooms, their interiors having been entirely gutted by fire, were without roofs and stood hollow with the blackened remnants of their charred intestines bared to the rising sun. Occasionally, a fast-food restaurant, housed in a clean and brightly colored habitat, would gleam into view and contrast garishly against the surrounding forest of lonely-looking companions. And outside, beneath this grotesquely configured jigsaw puzzle, the sidewalks lay dirty with fragments of glass from broken bottles, scraps of torn paper, and empty beer cans.

Feeling somewhat more comfortable when I reached Hester Street and turned north into a residential area, after three short blocks brought me to the courthouse, I parked, then eased my lean, five-foot-nine frame out onto the pavement. For a moment, I just stared at the large, off-white frame-and-stucco structure. Then, after noting that the gold letters which spelled out JUSTICE high over the entrance were chipped and faded, I turned and walked across the street in search of the Public Defender's Office. Finding it open, I entered and approached a counter framed by steel bars that rose to the ceiling every four inches or so from its top. Setting down my briefbag, I peered in through the small window in the center, and as I did so, a young woman carrying a cup of coffee entered the room from behind the counter and greeted me.

"Good morning. Can I help you?"

"Yes, thanks. My name's Matt Harris, and I'm supposed to report here for work."

She shrugged her shoulders slightly and started to smile. "So you're the new man, huh. Well, welcome to Solina, Mr. Harris, and may the good Lord help you!" bounced her response through a now widening smile, causing me to nervously return it. "I'm Marilyn Boyd, the secretary here. You want some coffee?"

I don't drink coffee, but answered yes anyway.

"Well, c'mon around here, and I'll get you some." Nodding, I passed through a door to my left, then slipped into the offered chair. "Cream or sugar?"

"Both, please," squeezed off my tongue distractedly, my eyes now enjoying a full view and instantly inhaling her stunning beauty. Her hair was styled in a medium Afro, which further softened the delicately sculpted cheekbones and nose lying beneath large, luminous eyes, and when she smiled, two rows of miniature ivory pillars shined brightly to accentuate the smooth, chocolate-brown skin. Dressed in a white silky blouse and a pair of tailored navy-blue, bell-bottom slacks, she was simply a portrait of loveliness, flashed a thought as she handed me a mug, then a question.

"Been with the PD long?"

"Well, almost three months now."

"Three months? ... Boy, you must be good!"

"Why? What do you mean?"

"Well, Jordan's a crazy man, but he knows his deputies, and he wouldn't have sent you to a place like this unless there were some real smarts behind those soft brown eyes!"

The oh-my-God tone of her voice added to the uneasy feeling I had harbored since learning of my assignment to Solina several days ago, and I reached into my coat pocket for my pipe and the comfort it represented.

"Say, would you like a tour of the place?" she offered as I lit up. Nodding yes, I arose and followed her down a narrow corridor, slowly passing partitions that formed several small offices. Just over a minute into our look-see, the back door flew open and two men burst inside, boisterously laughing and teasing one another. Stopping abruptly when they spotted us, one broke off and entered an office to his left, allowing Marilyn to then introduce me to the "boss of this here place, George Meyerstein." And years later, I could still recall every detail of that first meeting. Standing there in that narrow corridor feeling awkward, I stuck out my hand and was greeted with a firm handshake and a staccato "Glad you're here. C'mon into my office and we'll rap for a few minutes." Then, quickly covering the few feet into his cubicle, George launched into an explanation of how it was hell to be a Public Defender in Solina before I was fully seated opposite his desk.

"What you've got to understand for openers, Matt, is that there's a war going on here—a regular, goddamn war!" he shot out, a slight New England accent punctuating his rapid-fire delivery as I carefully studied him. About thirty, five-foot-ten, thick-framed and heavily muscled, he was dressed in a gray, double-breasted, pin-striped suit that he wore with a faded orange shirt and a thin, outdated, orange-and-green striped tie. His rust-colored hair, curly and uncombed, hung down loosely over his narrow forehead, where below, his chiseled but strong facial features left him just short of being pretty, and radiated forth an energy that could be felt with a single glance. In sync with this vitality, his message arrived in torrents, the words tumbling off his tongue in electric tones as if there would never be enough time to fully discharge them. And as he continued, he twisted and turned in his swivel chair and intermittently threw his hands into the air or slammed them down onto the desktop to accentuate the point he was makitng.

"Now, when I arrived here a few months ago, the pigs owned this place and they still think they do. The court calendar is absolutely jammed. You've never seen so many cases, and the judges don't want to work to begin with, so they deal deal deal!" rattled the machine gun. "Hell, the place was a regular cop-out artist's heaven, and our office was helping by just going along with the system. But that's all changed now. Robbie Gibbons showed up awhile back and demanded a trial. It was funny, the damn fools across the street almost forgot what one was. Why it took them an hour to find the jury interview sheets, and another one to dust them off—and to make a long story short, Robbie won the damn thing and eight more since, and now we're all trying them and the pigs are starting to go crazy!" cascaded his conclusion, George then hesitating momentarily for oxygen, a faint smile creeping across his face as he studied mine to insure I was on board.

"But don't get me wrong," he picked up, satisfied by my rapt attention. "We're not winning the war, just a few battles here and there, and damned few at that. Lose a case and you're going to get the maximum sentence. Your client's going to serve it all right, but you're the one being punished for having the audacity to turn down the pigs' deal and waste their precious time going to trial. Ohhh, you'll love the judges here, j-u-s-t love'm!" spewed his thickening sarcasm. "Funny-man Gelman handles the arraignment court. He thinks he's a comedian, but outside of his lousy jokes, he's not too bad. Next is Lacy, who presides over the preliminary hearing calendar in Division Three and is the worst we've got, although Steiggerman's always trying hard to take over first place. Old Lacy's an Uncle Tom who hates blacks and shows it, while Burroughs, our other black judge, equally favors the prosecution, but at least offers-up a little heart occasionally. He does court trials, and we don't do any anyhow, so outside of overflow Prelims we don't see too much of him. And that," George emphasized with a wink, "brings us to the wonderful world of jury trials, which are handled by Austin and Steiggerman. Now Austin's the one grace-saving factor we've got. He doesn't like trials lousing up his calendar, but he'll dismiss a lot of the garbage cases and he hates sentencing people to jail. Steiggerman, on the other hand, thinks everyone should be in jail, starting with us! Ohhh, he's a smooth talker all right, such a gentleman. But underneath, he's all pig, mean and vicious—and smart too, which makes him even more dangerous than Lacy!" grumbled the indictment into a second's pause, the solid fist-slam onto the desktop then instantly propelling it onward.

"And if the judges aren't enough, we've got the DA's Office to boot!" escalated frustration's tone. "They outnumber us two to one, and file every piece of shit the cops ask them to. Which means, that if somehow you don't wear yourself out completely fighting the cops, DAs, and judges, which you will, then for exercise you can fight your own clients, who aren't exactly in love with us either. Hell, our predecessors here did such a good job of kiss-assing the pigs and copping out the whole world, that our image now ranks favorably only against George Wallace's!"

For a fleeting second after George finished with another firm fist-slam, the mischievous gleam in his eyes advertised the possibility of an encore, an incubating idea abruptly foreclosed by the ring of the phone and the funneling of his attention to a more pressing problem. Both stunned and strangely amused, I just sat there listening to him jabbering about how someone couldn't do something to his client and that he'd be over to the courthouse soon to straighten matters out. Feeling as if I had somehow fallen in with some kind of crazy man, still, I liked him and knew it on both first and second thoughts. There was something, not readily identifiable, in the enormous energy reflected in his face and the tense tones of his voice that hinted of a deep sensitivity lying just beneath the churning exterior. Something subtle, that slowly seeped its secret to the surface. A warm undercurrent cored by an essential empathy and genuine goodness that smoothed the jagged edge of my discomfort and caused me to smile to myself.

Upon concluding his conversation, George then introduced me to Ron Sindel, Leon Schwartz, and Robbie Gibbons, the remaining members of the office. I judged Sindel, a six-foot-tall, well-built fellow with handsomely set features, to be in his mid-twenties like myself. Blond and curly haired, he wore aluminum-framed glasses over his light-blue eyes and appeared the most friendly and outgoing of the group, contrasting sharply with Schwartz, who though also mid-twentyish, carried twenty pounds of excess weight on his medium-sized frame and whose finely formed facial features were clouded sad and gloomy beneath the surrounding curtain of shoulder-length black hair. I noted that even when he smiled, he still looked as if he were brooding about something, unlike Robbie Gibbons, whose amiable air and warm welcome further diminished my sense of being a stranger in a foreign land. Black and also in the vicinity of six feet in height, his impeccable dress, Ivy League–style, failed to mask the fact that he was thin almost to the point of appearing emaciated. And though his easy smile and free-flowing banter projected a youthful, carefree attitude, his graying temples hinted that his years numbered close to forty, and like George, his jet-black eyes, set deep inside his small, round face, reflected both a serious purpose and an energy seemingly without limits. For several minutes, the five of us chatted, the casual conversation bouncing round the circle before following us as we walked together across the street to the courthouse, where George entrusted me to the care of Lester Smith, the deputy I was replacing. For an hour I watched him try an armed-robbery preliminary hearing. Then I spent the remainder of the morning wandering alone up and down the crowded hallways and edging in and out of the other four courtrooms, all the while studying the endless variety of careworn faces found amongst the numerous groups of people huddled in the shadowy corridors.

After lunch, which consisted of a dried-out tuna fish sandwich that I had dutifully prepared the night before and which I ate while reading an arrest report seated at the small desk assigned to me, I returned to Division Three and tried my first Prelim in my new judicial home. It lasted about forty minutes, proceeded uneventfully, and ended like most Prelims, in a loss. My client was held to answer in Superior Court on the charge of possessing marijuana, and after the bailiff led him away, Judge Lacy inquired cordially as to whether I had ever appeared in Solina before.

"No, Your Honor. First time," I answered.

"Well, very nice job," flowed his compliment through a broad smile. "You certainly made the most out of very little to work with. What firm are you with?"

"Actually, Your Honor, I'm replacing Mr. Smith."

"Ohhh ... I see," he drawled with surprise, the smile now thinning, his eyes darting to his errant clerk before returning to me. "Well, it's good to have you with us, Mr. Harris. Do enjoy your weekend now," he squeezed out as he departed the bench.

"You too, Your Honor," I nodded back through the air of uneasiness which now dissolved as he disappeared into his chambers.

'Cause we'll be seeing each other again come Monday morning, won't we? followed a thought energized by eager anticipation, then toned down by a touch of anxiety as I walked slowly back to the office. It was empty except for Marilyn. And after we chatted for a few minutes, we closed the office together, and day one of change's newest challenge ended.

It was slightly more than an hour's drive from Solina to my apartment in West Los Angeles, and as the miles glided by I settled back comfortably against the seat and allowed my mind to gradually drift back over the events of the past several months. Glancing at my watch, which read five-thirty, I pictured the secretaries jabbering at one another as they scurried about closing down the offices of the Kellco Real Estate Investment Company where I used to work. Having bade farewell to the oak-paneled walls and plushly furnished surroundings of the real-estate world just eleven weeks ago, I harbored the feeling that it seemed more like eleven months as I recalled the maze of courtrooms I had wandered through those first few weeks in the PD's Office. Unsure of myself, and uneducated in the intricacies of the criminal law, I had struggled through long, tiring days, with only the butterflies that lived in my stomach from dawn till midnight for company. Slowly, however, with ever-increasing effort, I had learned what a preliminary hearing was all about and begun to confidently grasp the various complex aspects of courtroom procedure. I had even managed to relax a bit, when a small, yellow piece of paper entitled Memorandum had appeared in my office mailbox and notified me of my transfer to the Solina Judicial District. Now, after a brief but eye-opening glimpse, I had the distinct impression that I had been extended an invitation to a war being conducted by a group of likable maniacs against an enemy which to them was clearly defined, but which to me was as hazy as the smoke that billowed forth from my pipe and vanished quickly into the smog-filled air outside my car window. And to make matters worse, I mused, this war was being primarily fought in front of juries where I had always wanted to be, but where to date I had never been. A weak smile emerged as the latter thought settled, then provoked me into soliloquy. "Matthew, my man," oozed my sarcasm, "what you know about trying a jury trial can be placed on either the left or right side of a pinhead! Or put another way, pal, you don't know your ass from first base, let alone second or third. So put the butterflies on red alert, counselor, 'cause your life is certainly going to get interesting all right, and that's with a capital I!" boomed my conclusion, instantly inspiring me to flick on the radio and change the subject.

It was six-thirty when I finally arrived in front of my apartment. Stella, my next-door neighbor, was standing on the sidewalk waiting to be picked up, I assumed, by one of the numerous men she went out with. I had met her about three months ago when I was moving in. She had been waiting then too, and after I had made several trips between my car and the apartment, she had smiled and introduced herself.

"Hi. I'm Stella Charles, and you must be the new tenant." Grinning back at her, while wishing I had shaved and didn't look so grubby, I had set down the box of books I was carting and nervously answered: "Yeah, that's me. My name's Harris, Matthew Robert Harris, and I'm pleased to meet you."

"M-a-t-t-h-e-w R-o-b-e-r-t H-a-r-r-i-s, huh? Well that's a mighty important sounding name," had flowed the reply, the letters rolling off her tongue slowly, spiced with her amusement. And renewing her smile, she had extended her hand and I had shaken it gently and just long enough to feel the soft coolness of her skin. I was about to attempt some witticism in response when a horn had sounded, and after glancing over her shoulder she had dropped a quick "See you around," and strode toward the waiting car. As she was entering, she had paused, looked back at me, and added: "Stop up sometime for a drink. I'm in number three, in the back." The car had begun moving away while she was still closing the door, so it was to myself that I had murmured, "I will sometime ... I will." And while I was most definitely intrigued by the possibility of knowing her better, somehow *sometime* had never arrived. After my move to the PD's Office, I had spent every free moment after court studying criminal law and talking about it with more experienced colleagues. Then too, whenever I had seen Stella around the triplex, she was either climbing into some fancy car driven by a handsome, successful-looking guy, or walking arm in arm with one toward her apartment, which led me to the conclusion that she was not long on spare time. But the real reason, the one that nagged at me when my eyes were so tired that I couldn't read another line in a casebook and the thought of a gin and tonic in the company of a woman appeared just one step short of heaven, was that something about her raised my basic level of shyness with women to new heights. I don't know why exactly, whether it was because she had so many suitors, or the fact that she was older than me, or that she was so extraordinarily attractive while others opined that I was just nice looking, my slightly too large nose preventing the finely formed mouth and subtly defined cheekbones from reaching a deeply desired higher ranking. But whatever the cause, the effect persisted, and *sometime* remained in the future.

A future whose hazy arrival time was further delayed, when after I closed down memory's merry-go-round and exited my car, once again Stella's current date arrived, and once again I returned her smile and waved hello as she departed. Then as I walked slowly to my apartment, I squelched the mesmerizing image of her that trailed alongside, turning my thoughts instead to what Chef Harris was going to prepare for dinner.

THE WORDS *HELLHOLE OF SOUTHERN California* never left my mind as I staggered through my first full week in Solina. As planned, George assigned me to Judge Lacy's courtroom to handle felony preliminary hearings for a week or so until I "sort of get the hang of things." By Thursday, I was just hanging, period. The caseload was simply unbelievable. An average Prelim calendar consisted of fourteen cases, and of these, two would be continued to a later date for a multitude of reasons, leaving the brontosaurean balance of twelve to be split between private counsel with four and the Public Defender's Office with the grand-prize-winning eight. His Honor believed that by nine o'clock, the PD should be prepared on all of his cases, which generously allowed you an average of seven minutes per case to pull a copy of the arrest report from the court files, read it, and then interview the client. And to assist you in following his timetable, Lacy detailed both his clerk and bailiff to constantly remind you to "Get ready. Don't you know there's still a hell of a lot of cases left on calendar!" Or more succinctly: "Boy, the Judge is really getting pissed off!"

The sheer volume of cases made compliance with a reasonable timetable difficult, and obedience to Lacy's totally impossible, if the goal was a fair hearing with the defendant receiving legitimate representation. And since I had decided long ago that the Sixth Amendment's right to counsel required not one iota less, when I so informed His Honor in the face of his unrelenting demands for speed, an atmosphere of active hostility was born, then steadily accrued until it permeated the ensuing proceedings. Featuring Lacy's surly attempts to intimidate me, which instigated frequent snickering by the audience at my expense, after his fusillade of sarcastic brow-beatings failed to change my conscientious course of action throughout a Monday that lasted two hours beyond the Court's desired five o'clock adjournment, by lunchtime Tuesday His Honor had abandoned his tactic of disparaging me in open court, in favor of transferring as many of my cases as possible to whichever other courtroom had a temporary break in activity.

For the most part this resulted in my working in front of Judge Steiggerman in Division Four, where in stark contrast to George's warning that he was even more difficult than Lacy, I was pleasantly surprised by the courteous, respectful, and even complimentary treatment I received. A tall, slim, and movie-star-handsome man in his early forties, he so clearly extended himself to make me feel comfortable, that on several occasions I found myself trying to recall George's exact words in order to determine if I had somehow misunderstood. On Thursday afternoon at one-fifteen, I received my answer. Earlier that morning, with a pregnant Prelim calendar showing twenty-one cases, a highly agitated Lacy had once again shipped me upstairs to Division Four where I had tried three Prelims by eleven forty-five, winning two of them, much to my delight. Then, just as we were about to break for lunch, Lacy dispatched a fourth case involving two black defendants accused of having raped a nineteen-year-old white woman. And suddenly, in true Jekyll-and-Hyde fashion, annoyance flash-flooded across Steiggerman's face, then spilled a heavy air of uneasiness into the courtroom. Almost simultaneously, his clerk handed me a copy of the arrest report, accompanied by a brusque request to "see what we've got here." And the second I finished skimming it, His Honor then rushed an inquiry at me coated in a steely toned impatience that was also new to the brief history between us.

"Well, Mr. Harris, think we can knock this one off before lunch?" he asked. Glancing at my watch, which read eleven fifty-two, I shook my head.

"I doubt it, Your Honor. It's already lunchtime, and the case appears to be somewhat complicated."

"Complicated? What the hell's complicated about a rape? Your client either stuck it in her, or didn't. Not much more to it than that, is there?" he pressed, fixing his blue eyes on me.

"Well, Your Honor, there seems to be a little bit more to this one from what I gather. To—"

"Ohhh? ... What?"

"Well, as I was about to point out, for one thing there are two defendants, not one. And even from my brief review of the arrest report, there seems to be a clear conflict between their interests."

"Conflict? ... Are you sure, Mr. Harris?"

"Quite sure, Your Honor."

"Well now, we can't have that, can we?" dripped his sarcasm. Then, turning toward his clerk, he barked a succinct order to call Division Three and see if private counsel was available to accept an appointment, before returning his attention to me and asking whether I would agree to work through lunch.

"Absolutely," I answered. "But I—"

"But what, Mr. Harris?"

"All I was about to say, Sir, is that I would have to insist on interviewing my client before we begin." For several slow seconds he just stared at me, before forcing a smile back onto his face and the prior calmness back inside his voice.

"Well ... of course, Mr. Harris, you'll have all the time you need. But let's get going, and not overdo it, understand?"

After nodding yes, as I exited, the mystery of what possible urgency had triggered such a rapid and total turnaround in the judicial attitude accompanied me. No solution materialized, but by the time I had slowly descended the back stairs to the lockup located in the courthouse basement, me, myself, and I had voted unanimously that regardless of the reason, or the potential consequences of resistance, we would not be stampeded into shortchanging our client's right to a full and fair hearing. A resolution that brightened the dingy atmosphere of the narrow corridor leading to the adjacent cubicle provided for interviewing defendants who are in custody, it further inspired a warm smile as I entered and introduced myself to the waiting Joseph Allen Williams. He blinked back at me, his eyes not having fully adjusted to the light after being held in the windowless, electricity-free holding tank since eight o'clock that morning.

"You my Public Defender?" he asked softly.

"Uh-huh, Joe. I am."

"Ohhh ... well ... do you think you can do something for me?" he queried hesitantly, his voice quivering slightly. "'Cause I didn't do nothing wrong. I mean, man, you just gotta help me, 'cause the cops wouldn't even listen to me. They just laughed and called me nigger. I—" He stopped suddenly, sat down on the small stool opposite me, and stared at the top of the screened counter between us.

"Joe ... Joe, look at me," I commanded, then waited till he gradually raised his head so that I could look straight into his brown eyes, which were seated deep inside his angular-shaped face. "Listen," I then picked up. "I can't make any promises about what's going to happen when we get to court, except that I'm going to do everything I can to help you. Now the first thing we're going to do is make out this interview sheet. Then, I'm going to explain your constitutional rights. And finally, we're going to go over this arrest report together so that you can give me your side of the story. Okay?"

"Sure," he nodded back at me, then leaned forward onto the counter and cupped his face in his hands as he replied to the form questions I put to him. Next, I made sure he fully understood his rights, and just as I began reading him the all-important arrest report, the telephone rang. It was Ted Greene, Steiggerman's clerk, wanting to know if I was "about ready." No, I explained, it would be at least fifteen minutes more because the case was complicated, whereupon he amplified the pressure with an agitated, "Well, okay, but the Judge's getting r-e-a-l-l-y angry." Suppressing my own irritation, I thanked him for the warning, then asked that he inform His Honor that I was doing the best I could. And when he hung up, I slammed the receiver back onto its wall mount with enough force that the noise startled Joe into returning to an upright position.

"All right now, Joe," I resumed, festering frustration leaking into my tone. "I'm going to read this damned arrest report to you, and then you're going to tell me what really happened! But first, let me tell you one more thing. I've already explained to you that anything you tell me can't be used against you, because that's what the law calls a privileged communication. Now I know that you just laid eyes on me about twenty minutes ago, and I can't give you one goddamned reason why you should trust me, other than the simple fact that I'm the only friend you've got in this whole fucking courthouse!" surged my appeal, my eyes fixed on his. "'Cause I'm not the cops, the judge, or the DA. I'm your lawyer, and it's my job to do whatever I legally can to get you out of this mess, which is exactly what I'm going to try to do. So for Christ's sake, help me help you by telling me the absolute truth!" I exhorted, reaching for my pipe and lighting up. "Do you understand, Joe? Can you see why I need you to trust me?" I added between puffs, my voice softening.

"Yes Sir, I do," he answered firmly, the sudden appearance of respect in his tone placing my next thought on hold as I watched a smile begin to form on his lips. It broadened to full as I returned it, and for the first time since I arrived in Solina, I began to feel like I belonged.

The arrest report stated that on Friday evening, the twenty-first of

July, 1968, Louise Petrie, while walking home from work alone, had been accosted by two male Negroes in their early twenties and raped behind some bushes in Willowbrook Park. Joe listened intently to me as I read it to him and waited till I completely finished before responding. His explanation was that he lived about eight blocks from the park, and that around seven o'clock on the evening in question he had walked alone down to Henry's Market to buy some beer. He had purchased a six-pack of Coors, and drank two of the cans while he was in the market "bulling" with Henry, whom he knew quite well. At about eight-fifteen he left for home and was stopped about three blocks from the store by two sheriffs, who held him at the corner of Lemon and Grove Streets until another sheriff's car arrived. Handcuffed, he was then marched over to the passenger side of the second vehicle where a young white woman, who was crying, pointed at him and screamed: "That's him! That's him!" The officers then advised him that he was under arrest and took him to the station for booking. When he had tried to explain his side of the story, they had just laughed and told him: "Nigger, clam up. You're in a lot of trouble!" And since his arrest thirteen days ago, he hadn't spoken to anyone about the case, and until now hadn't really understood what he was accused of.

After pausing to relight my pipe, I explained to Joe that the Prelim about to occur wasn't a trial, but just a hearing to determine if there should even be a trial, and that I was going to use it as a means of discovering as much information about the case as I could. Later on, should there be a trial, I emphasized, that was when he'd have the opportunity to testify, as would his friend Henry and other witnesses. Then I rang the buzzer to call the marshal who would take Joe upstairs to the courtroom, and departed.

As I reentered Division Four, I noticed that the room had become uncomfortably hot. Inopportunely the air conditioning system was malfunctioning, and there were no windows to provide relief from the one-hundred-degree temperature outside. The lights in the audience section had been turned off in an effort to lessen the humid effect, but this served only to create a dark, dingy atmosphere which stopped just short of being eerie. After loosening my tie, I settled into my seat at the counsel table, opened my briefbag, and methodically thumbed through the chapter on rape in my loose-leaf trial notebook. Minutes later, Deputy District Attorney Irene Fisher entered, along with Phil Mason, the private attorney appointed by the Court to represent the codefendant. And as I was exchanging greetings with them, both defendants were led into the room, and after the handcuffs were removed, Joe sat down in the seat to my left. As I leaned over and told him to relax, out of the corner of my eye I observed Steiggerman emerge from his chambers and take the bench. At one-fifteen, ninety knotty minutes after Dr. Jeykll and Mr. Hyde had begun their chameleon-like performance, we were ready to proceed. And as Steiggerman read the formal Complaint to the defendants and briefly advised them of their constitutional rights, I felt the muscles in my stomach tighten.

Upon His Honor's direction, the DA then called the People's first witness and Louise Petrie walked slowly to the witness box. As she was taking the oath, I studied her, noting that she was overweight, and that while she appeared composed, the tightened muscles of her face and her fidgeting hands provided evidence that she was nervous. Simply dressed in a white blouse and brown skirt, and surrounded by an aura of sadness, she instantly evoked sympathy, including from me. Yeah, I understand, flashed my first thought, after having already undergone a horrifying experience, now you're going to have to recount it in a courtroom full of strangers, and then be cross-examined on top of it. Hell, I'd be nervous and upset, too, 'cause rape's the ultimate violation, and whoever did it should be punished big-time, I concluded, a contrasting series of thoughts then arriving with warp speed. Hey, hold on a minute, Matthew, my man, cautioned my fired-up neurons. First off, like in almost all rape cases, there are no independent witnesses here, it's just Louise saying she was raped. Then, most importantly is her identification of Joe, which she made from the back seat of a sheriff's car while hysterically crying, and probably egged on by the sheriffs eager to make an arrest. Add on the fact that the DA has rehearsed her testimony with her more than once, and her ID is not exactly the foolproof evidence on which to lock up Joe for up to twenty years, I reasoned, glancing sideways at Joe, who looked as strained and nervous as Louise. No, counsel, I reminded myself, sympathy or no sympathy, your job is to test her credibility with every weapon at your disposal. And painful as it may be, your duty is to defend your client and get at the truth, I concluded, nodding my head, my resolve now firmly established.

Taking further note of her shaky toned "I do," after she sat down, I arose and made a motion to clear the courtroom in order to deprive her of the security of the three women she had been sitting with, who I judged to be her mother and either sisters or friends, and upon whom she immediately fixed her eyes. Steiggerman, in a tone that mixed irritation with sarcasm, inquired as to whether I was familiar with the code provision I had cited in support of my motion.

"Yes, Your Honor, I am," bounced my answer.

"Well then, Mr. Harris, you should know that while it does call for a closed hearing, it also provides in cases like these that the victim is allowed to have one female present during the proceedings."

"I'm aware of that, Your Honor."

"Well then, in that the court clerk, the court reporter, the bailiffs, the defendants, and counsel are all male, I'm going to deny your motion and allow this fine young woman's mother to remain," he lectured pedantically, his voice suddenly softening to match the fatherly expression that rushed across his face as he finished, then turned and smiled at the witness.

"Your Honor?"

"Yes, Mr. Harris. What is it now?"

"I would point out, Sir, that the District Attorney is a female. And while the Court is perfectly correct in pointing out that the code allows the victim the presence of one female during a closed hearing, I don't believe that it excludes female District Attorneys from fulfilling that requirement. In fact, Your Honor, Sir, I feel confident that the District Attorney wouldn't argue to the contrary," I jabbed ever so politely, then watched as his smile faded away.

"Very well, Mr. Harris. Very well," he acquiesced begrudgingly. "I'm going to reverse myself and grant your motion. The bailiffs are hereby ordered to clear the courtroom." Then, as the audience filed outside, with a returning drop of honey he added, "The Court certainly does apologize to the District Attorney for its momentary oversight."

The vanquished smile had also been resurrected, and was smugly returned by Ms. Irene Fisher, who fully understood that Steiggerman had not for an instant overlooked her in his effort to protect the prosecution's witness by attempting to exploit my inexperience and force me to commit a serious tactical error out of ignorance on the point of law in question. A few short weeks ago it would have worked, and as I reseated myself to listen to the victim's forthcoming testimony, I mentally patted myself on the back for having prodded my tired eyes over endless pages of case and code books during my self-imposed, nightly study sessions, then vowed to push even harder in the future.

Louise Petrie's direct examination was classic bare bones. With hardly a trace of emotion, she recounted her experience of walking home from work through Willowbrook Park and being accosted by two male Negroes who dragged her behind some bushes, ripped off her clothes, and then had sexual intercourse with her. Her entire story took less than five minutes to relate, and when Irene Fisher confidently stated, "No further questions, Your Honor," Steiggerman's face clearly expressed his approval of Louise's brief narrative as he turned his focus and indicated that I could begin cross-examination.

While still seated at the counsel table, I began cautiously by reviewing with her where she worked, how long she had worked there, and at what time she had left work on the evening of the incident in question. On direct examination she had emphasized under Fisher's skillful guidance that although it was seven-thirty when she departed from her employer's fast-food restaurant, with the attack not occurring until approximately fifteen minutes later, she was nevertheless positive in her identification of the defendants as her assailants because "It was plenty light out—enough to get a clear view of those men who did terrible things to me!" Now, having tiptoed back to the doorstep of this touchy time-of-day/ability to identify issue, I was primed to dissect her prior generalization when suddenly instinct warned "later," turning me instead to the safe subject of her age, height, and weight. And with Louise having been previously alerted by the prosecution to expect being vigorously pressed on the visibility factor, our discussion of such seemingly harmless facts caused her to noticeably relax, and she settled more comfortably in the witness chair, a faint smile even forming in the corners of her mouth. Deciding to further promote this cocoon of security, before continuing I arose and slowly strolled over to the jury box immediately adjacent to where Irene Fisher was seated and about fifteen feet from Louise.

"You feel comfortable here in the courtroom, don't you, Miss Petrie?" I then picked up, my tone sincere and caring.

"Yes, Sir."

"And relaxed?"

"Yes, Sir."

"And I'm not being too tough on you now, am I?"

"No, Sir."

"Well, good. I just want you to understand that my purpose here isn't to annoy or embarrass you—just to ask you a few questions about the terrible things you mentioned so that the Court can understand them better. Do you understand that?"

"Yes, Sir."

"Good, I'm glad. And I'll try to be brief, so that this whole business will soon be over and done with for you. Okay?"

This time her "Yes, Sir" was accompanied by a full smile, which I returned as I resumed my interrogation. "Miss Petrie, will you please repeat what you were wearing on that Friday evening?"

"Well, Sir, I was wearing a pink sweater and a pair of white pants."

"Did you have a coat on?"

"No, Sir, I was carrying it over my arm."

"I see. And were you wearing shoes?"

"Yes, Sir, I was."

"And did these shoes fasten on your feet with shoe strings?"

"Yes, Sir, they did. They were my work boots and they lace up the front."

"This pink sweater, Miss Petrie—did it have buttons or a zipper on it?"

"No, Sir."

"Was it what you ladies call a pull-on type?"

"I think ... you mean pullover, Sir," she corrected after hesitating slightly, her tone shyly sympathetic.

"Well, yes, Miss Petrie, that's exactly what I mean. And thank you for your help, 'cause I'm not too knowledgeable where women's clothing is involved. So is that what you were wearing then, a pink pullover sweater?"

"Yes, Sir, that's it."

"And the white pants you had on, did they have buttons on them or a zipper?"

"Buttons, Sir."

"And were the buttons on the front or the back?"

"On the back, Sir." Having glanced at Steiggerman in between the last question and answer, I found a facial expression that blended boredom with irritation. Sensing that he was about to intervene in an effort to hurry matters along, I quickly prefaced my next query by indicating to Louise that I had just a few additional questions concerning clothing, then continued as she nodded her understanding.

"Now, Miss Petrie, were you wearing a brassiere underneath your sweater?"

"Oh, of course, Sir."

"And were you wearing panties underneath your slacks?"

"Yes ... Yes, absolutely!" she returned with sudden firmness, the coached "Sir" attached to her answers evaporating as emotion jumped into her voice for the first time and a small amount of blush crept into her chalk-white complexion. Steiggerman meanwhile could no longer contain himself.

"Missster Harris!" he growled. "This Court prides itself on its patience, but you've been rambling on for fifteen minutes or so with a bunch of questions which really don't seem related at all to the case. Now let's get down to business so that we can wind this matter up!"

"Your Honor ... Sir," trickled my response slowly. "Do I understand that the Court is telling me that I cannot cross-examine on the subject of what the witness was wearing at the time she says she was raped?" As he was perfectly aware that my line of questioning was totally permissible, the soft, humble tone of my voice combined to spin a look of resignation across his face and lower the decibel level of his reply when he finally stopped shaking his head and answered.

"No, Mr. Harris, the Court is not telling you that. But what I am telling you is that this is a preliminary hearing and not a trial, and the Court would appreciate it if you would keep that in mind. Now continue."

"Very well, Your Honor, thank you for your understanding," oozed my sugar-coated acceptance. Then, returning my attention to Louise, I also thanked her for her patience and immediately offered a series of questions about where she lived, for how long, and the proximity to Willowbrook Park. Designed to reinforce her feeling that Steiggerman had intimidated me away from unpleasant subjects, after two or three minutes had slipped by, my innocent queries had returned her smile to full bloom and she again appeared totally relaxed. I, on the other hand, felt the knots in my stomach reawaken as I paused to lean back against the jury-box railing, then fixed my eyes on hers and launched into my bombing run.

"Miss Petrie," I asked, "prior to the incident you've described, have you ever had sexual intercourse before?" Stunned, she bolted upright as if her behind had been suddenly stuck by a pin, color flooding her face as she stammered "Whhh-a-a-t?"

"Have you, before the incident you've described," I repeated slightly louder, "ever had sexual intercourse before?"

"Nnn-ooo."

"Are you sure, Miss Petrie?"

"Yes … Yes I am!" she mustered, this time with some force, still shaking off surprise, her voice rising in anger.

"There's no need to shout, Miss Petrie, we can all hear you."

"I wasn't shouting, I—"

Cut off sharply by Irene Fisher's objection on the grounds that I was badgering the witness, Steiggerman sustained it so promptly that I was able to continue on almost as if the interruption hadn't occurred.

"Well then, Miss Petrie, let's explore your answer for a moment. Would you please tell us what your definition of sexual intercourse is?"

"Well," she responded slowly after deliberating for several seconds, "that's where a man puts his thing in a woman's thing."

"Things, Miss Petrie? What do you mean by the word 'things'?"

"Well … you know."

"I'm not sure I do, Miss Petrie. Please tell us exactly what you mean." Again she hesitated, this time looking over at Irene Fisher, who tried to reassure her with a smile.

"Well … the man's thing is called a … a …"

"Penis?" I supplied when her voice trailed into silence. "Is that the word you're searching for?"

"Well … uh … yes," she agreed uncomfortably.

"And prior to the incident, had you ever seen a penis before?"

"Yes."

"Okay. Now you told Miss Fisher you were a virgin, so when did you first see a penis?"

"I … I … can't remember."

"Well, did you ever see your brother's?"

"I don't have a brother."

"Okay. Your father's?"

"He died when I was little."

"Well then, whose penis did you see, Miss Petrie?"

"It was a long time ago. I can't—"

"Was it on a date?" I interrupted, pressing her. "Did one of your dates let you see his penis?"

"No, I don't have dates like that. I'm not like that at all!"

"Okay. Then when and where was it that you did see a penis?"

"In a magazine … I saw it in one of those magazines they have at the drugstore," crawled her admission finally, her voice sinking from shame. And having become increasingly upset as the discussion lengthened, as she finished, she lowered her head and stared at her hands, which were clenched in her lap. Slowly, I changed course.

"I see, Miss Petrie. Now, with respect to these men you say did terrible things to you, isn't it true that before the incident you hadn't ever seen them before?"

"Yes."

"You're sure of that?"

"Uh-huh, I never saw them before."

"Okay, let's go back to that Friday evening. Now you were walking along through the park, and all of a sudden two men grabbed you—Is that right?"

"Yes."

"Did you notice where they came from?"

"No, it happened so fast, I didn't see."

"Now let me get this clear, Miss Petrie. As I understand it, the very first time you were aware of these men was when they touched you—Is that right?"

"Yes."

"And you didn't see either of them come toward you?"

"No."

"Okay. Did you see one of them first, or both together?"

"I ... I don't remember."

"Well, tell me what they were wearing. Describe for us what type clothes they had on."

"I didn't get a good look at their clothes."

"Well, were they wearing coats?"

"I think one of them was."

"What color was it?"

"I can't remember."

"All right. Did they have on shirts?"

"Yes."

"What type of shirts? Describe them for us please."

"Well, I don't remember exactly, I ... uh—"

"Were they dress shirts?"

"No."

"Sports type, or tee-shirts, or what?"

"I ... I can't be sure."

"What color were they?"

"I don't remember. I think one was blue, but it was hard to see."

For an instant I was tempted to press her as to why it was hard to see, but decided that I might open the door for her to take the statement back. So moving on, I asked: "How tall were these men, Miss Petrie?"

"Well ... uh ... pretty tall," she answered with consistent vagueness.

"Okay. Was one taller than the other?"

"I think so."

"And how tall would you say he was?"

"I don't know, but he was way taller than me."

Joe was only five-foot-six, so I pursued the point with a confirming, "You told me earlier that you were five-foot-five—Is that correct?"

"Yes."

"So if the taller man was way taller than you, would you say that he was at least six feet tall?"

"Yes."

"Maybe even a little taller than six feet?"

"Uh-huh, I think so."

""And the shorter one, was he almost as tall?"

"Yes."

"So he was also about six feet tall, right?"

"Yes, I think so."

"And how much would you say the taller one weighed?"

"I don't know ... that's sort of hard to say."

"Well, more than you, right?"

"Oh, yes, much more than me."

"And the shorter one, did he also weigh much more than you?"

"Yes."

"All right then, both men weighed much more than your previously testified to one-hundred-fifty pounds—Isn't that right?"

"Yes."

"And were these men wearing pants?"

"Yes."

"And can you describe the pants for us?"

"Well, I ... uh ... think ... I—"

"Miss Petrie, you don't seem able to recall many details about these men who grabbed you. Isn't the reason for this that you became frightened?" I quickly suggested when she once again floundered, suddenly softening my tone to sympathetic. The switch, coupled with the proposed explanation for her shaky memory, surprised her and she paused for several seconds before answering.

"Why ... yes, yes, that must be the reason," she then offered with visible relief.

"In fact, Miss Petrie, you became very frightened, didn't you?"

"Well, yes ... I suppose I was."

"It's quite understandable. I mean there you are walking along, and out of nowhere two strange men grab you. Why, anyone would become very frightened, don't you think?"

"Yes, Sir, absolutely!" she emphasized, growing confident.

"And when you were grabbed by these men, they immediately dragged you over behind some bushes—Is that correct?"

"Yes, that's right."

"And this happened in a flash, didn't it?"

"Yes."

"I mean there wasn't any conversation, was there?"

"No, no way."

"And when all of a sudden you were grabbed, that's when you became very frightened, right?"

"Yes."

"And even more frightened when they started to drag you toward the bushes, correct?"

"Yes."

"Did you scream out at this time?"

"No, I ... uh ... uh ..."

"And wasn't that because the whole grabbing and pulling occurred so fast, for a few moments you didn't really know what was happening?"

"Well ... uh ... yes, that's sort of the way it was," she answered after hesitating to allow the agreeable suggestion to register, then adding her concurrence when it seemed the proper fit.

"So, Miss Petrie, wouldn't it be fair to say then, that the only thing you were really aware of was of being extremely afraid?"

"Uh-huh, I guess so ... yes."

"And after these men then dragged you behind the bushes, they threw you on the ground and began undressing you—Is that right?"

"Yes," she mouthed, her tone suddenly softer, almost tearful, her reply in conflict with her direct testimony that they had begun removing her clothes while she was still on her feet.

"So now you found yourself lying on your back, with your clothes starting to come off, right?"

"Uh-huh," she confirmed.

"And now you were even more frightened, isn't that true?"

"Yes."

"In fact you began to cry, didn't you?"

"Yes ... yes I did."

"And this is because you were terrified about what was going to happen to you, right?"

"Sure! Wouldn't you be if you were a woman?" she sobbed, finally unable to muffle her emotions, the now surfaced tears raising her volume.

"Absolutely!" I agreed instantly, emphasizing my sympathy by nodding my head, then pausing for a full fifteen seconds while she dabbed her eyes with a piece of tissue from her purse. His Honor glared at me from the bench, but said nothing as he knew my line of questioning was allowable. And after Louise raised her head and blew her nose, I continued.

"Now, Miss Petrie, what clothing did they take off first?"

"I ... I can't remember."

"Well, try, Miss Petrie. Was it your sweater or your pants?"

"My ... my sweater."

"Are you sure?"

"Yes, I remember now. It was my sweater."

"Okay. And you were still lying on the ground?"

"Yes."

"And they were holding you there?"

"Uh-huh."

"Was one of the men on each side of you?"

"Yes."

"Holding you down by your arms?"

"That's right."

"And they pulled your sweater off?"

"Yes, up over my head."

"And did they pull off your brassiere too?"

"Yes."

"And did they touch your breasts?"

"Yes."

"Right then, before removing any more of your clothes?"

"Yes, I ... I think so."

"And how did they touch your breasts?"

"H-o-w?" she rolled back incredulously, her emotions rising again.

"Yes, how, Miss Petrie? With their hands?"

"Ohhh ... well yes."

"And were they also still holding you down with their hands?"

"Uh-huh."

"But also touching your breasts with them?"

"Right."

"And did they also put their mouths on your breasts?"

"Oh, yes, both of them did!" she stressed, her eyes beginning to tear again.

"Could you feel their tongues on your breasts?"

"Yes."

"And on your nipples?"

"Uh-huh."

"And did you feel your nipples get hard?"

"I ... I ... can't remember. I ... uh—" dribbled her answer slowly before she trailed off into renewed tears. This time however I didn't pause, but instead returned to an earlier subject.

"Miss Petrie, when you first entered Willowbrook Park, you were walking along a path—Is that right?"

It took a few seconds for her to collect herself, but the relief of an easy question helped, and gradually she raised her head. "Yyyes," she stammered, still dabbing her eyes.

"And were there trees alongside the pathway?"

"I ... I can't remember."

"Flowers?"

"I can't remember."

"A fish pond off to your left?"

"I ... I just can't remember," echoed her reply, causing a sudden flash of neurons inside my brain. Twice before I had strayed from the visibility issue in order to establish suddenness of attack, extreme fear, and tear-choked eyes, and now, gamble-time had finally arrived.

"You can't remember this, and you can't remember that! You can't remember anything, can you, Miss Petrie?" exploded my question with the full force of feigned anger. And while Irene Fisher jumped out of her chair like an uncoiling spring, Louise's answer bolted forth a split second before Irene's objection could sprint off the tip of her tongue.

"Well it was dark, and I couldn't see good!" Louise mustered defiantly in defense, then slumped in her chair and resumed dabbing her eyes.

The damage was done. Big Time! But unable to restrain her frustration, for the next several minutes Fisher filled the airwaves anyway with her ranting and raving about my alleged improper conduct, complete with a list of supporting authorities that stopped just short of including the Ten Commandments. When she finally concluded her tirade and sat down, I started to respond but never received the opportunity due to Steiggerman quickly declaring a recess and requesting counsel to meet with him in chambers. Once we were assembled, with Bailiff Wally Roberts trailing in to stand watch at the door, His Honor immediately turned his attention to me.

"Well, Mr. Harris, I suppose you're very proud of yourself," began his icy-toned lecture, "taking this poor girl and making her cry with your stupid questions that haven't gotten you anywhere anyhow. Well I've had enough, and I think you know what I mean!" he emphasized, boring his eyes into mine as he continued. "Now this Court has tried to be fair with you. I've allowed you all kinds of extra time to prepare, and then listened patiently to your arguments no matter how cockamamie they seemed. Hell, I've been more than fair, I've even kicked a couple of Prelims for you that could've gone either way, and all I get for thanks is this dragged-out nonsense. Well the honeymoon's over, Mister Harris, and if you want to stay on the right side of this Court then you have to play ball—do you understand me?" he ended, resolve reinforcing the ice in his tone.

I don't know whether it was the fact that I was feeling the enervating effects of the stifling heat, or had simply reached my limit of frustration from having been battered about in various courtrooms for the past three months, but as I looked across at Steiggerman's face, which featured an arrogant, all-knowing authority that bullied obedience, I felt the squirming, pain-produced anger that arrived at similar times well up inside me. Slowly, in order to maintain tight control, I answered him, my tone firm but reserved.

"Your Honor, I'm sorry if you have been offended by the questions I've asked the witness. They don't seem improper or stupid to me, and I also don't share the Court's opinion that they haven't gotten me somewhere. Up to now, this Court has treated me and my clients fairly and with respect, and I've tried to show my appreciation by returning that respect and cooperating with you whenever possible. However, as for playing ball, as you put it, I don't know what that means, and I don't want to!" I ended, my voice having hardened.

"Now you listen here, Mr. Virtue!" he blazed back at me, his prior frost now flooded over with an anger that could be felt as well as heard. "I thought you were different, but I can see now that you're just like all the rest of the goddamned Public Defenders—just sitting on your lazy asses and feeding out of the public trough! And because you're nothing but a bunch of left-wing malcontents with nothing better to do, you make trouble. Well you just better learn, starting right now, that this Court doesn't intend to put up with you or your kind. Now you get back out there and wind this thing up. You've got five minutes, understand? Five goddamned minutes!" he thundered to a close, then dismissed us without waiting for my acknowledgment by standing up and heading toward his private bathroom.

As I strolled slowly back outside and over to the vicinity of the jury box, I couldn't help but snicker to myself at Steiggerman's exposed hoax. Did he really think that he could butter me up into giving short shrift to a major felony by dismissing a couple of lighter-penalty possession of marijuana cases that should've been dismissed anyway? I wondered, shaking my head in disgust. Then, as I watched His Honor emerge from chambers and take the bench, two more serious and conflicting thoughts suddenly flashed into mind. While I had absolutely no desire whatsoever to be held in contempt of court, the urge to extend my cross-examination beyond the prescribed five minutes, thereby possibly provoking Steiggerman into putting something like his remarks in chambers on the record, seemed irresistible. And as His Honor then indicated that I could resume my questioning of Louise, the beads of perspiration which had formed in my armpits slowly slid down over my ribcage.

"Now, Miss Petrie," I picked up, forcing a thin smile, "before counsel conferred with the Judge, we were discussing the removal of your clothing in the park near the pathway. After your sweater and bra had been pulled off, did the men then remove your pants?"

"Yes," she answered in an even tone, having regained her composure during the twenty-minute recess.

"And you were still lying on your back on the ground?"

"Uh-huh."

"And the two men were still holding you down by your arms, one on each side of you?"

"Yes, that's right."

"And they were still putting their hands and mouths on your breasts?"

"Yes."

"And you were enjoying this, weren't you?"

This time Fisher reacted with lightning speed, her rifled "Objection, Your Honor," stilling Louise before she could open her mouth. And with like alacrity, Steiggerman issued a "Sustained," before Fisher could even state her grounds, then resumed his in-chambers lecture to me almost without pause.

"M-i-s-t-e-r Harris!" he cannonaded down at me. "This Court is rapidly losing the last of its patience. I've already advised you that this is a preliminary hearing and not a trial, and requested that you treat it as such. Now if you can't understand this simple distinction, then this Court will have no choice other than to take appropriate action. Do you understand me, Mr. Harris?"

"Your Honor ... Sir," I returned cautiously, mustering exaggerated humbleness into my carefully chosen words. "As the Court is aware of, I am not nearly as learned in the law or courtroom procedure as the Court is, and I very much appreciate the patience and understanding of the Court and certainly wish to cooperate with it. Therefore, I appeal to the Court for guidance. Is the Court telling me that I cannot cross-examine on the victim's ability to recall the details of the incident before the Court, including her feelings and state of mind?"

"No, Mr. Harris, I'm not telling you that!" he almost shouted at me, before hearing himself and lowering his voice. "But I am telling you that the cases which allow cross-examination in this area do provide limits, which I urge you to adhere to. You may continue, but I certainly do hope that you will heed my warning."

"Thank you, Your Honor, I'll do my best," oozed my assurance before I severed eye contact and returned to Louise.

"Now, Miss Petrie, as we were discussing, you have told us that you were lying on the ground while these men were undressing you—Is that correct?"

"Yes."

"Were you lying on bare dirt, or on grass?"

"I ... I don't remember."

"And is that because you couldn't see the ground 'cause you were lying on your back?"

"Yes ... that's right."

"All the time that your clothes were being removed, you were lying on your back?"

"Uh-huh."

"Flat on your back?"

"Yes."

"You weren't ever on your side or your stomach?"

"No."

"Well didn't you try to resist these men, by twisting and turning your body and trying to pull away?"

"Nooo, I was too afraid."

"I see. You thought that if you resisted, they might hurt you—Is that right?"

"Uh-huh ... right."

"And your pants, they came off quickly, didn't they?"

"Yes."

"All the way off?"

"Uh-huh."

"And did they then pull off your panties?"

"Yyyes ... yes they did," spilled her answer, this time more hesitantly, her voice trembling slightly as tears threatened to return.

"Well then, Miss Petrie," I probed, inching closer to her, "in view of the facts that you were at all times lying flat on your back, weigh one hundred and fifty pounds, and each of these men was holding you down with his hands, would you please explain how they quickly and easily slid your pants off?" No reply issued. She just stared back at me, so I pressed her. "Don't you have an answer?"

"Well ... I ... uh ... yes," she finally stammered out after several more uncomfortable seconds had passed. "I mean ... uh ... they must've just pulled them off."

"Just pulled them off?" I pressured, inching still closer.

"Well ... you know ... they just unzipped them and pulled them off."

"But didn't you tell us," I jabbed even harder, "that the pants you were wearing had buttons on them?"

"Well ... y-y-yes, I did," she stuttered, surprised.

"So are you now telling us they didn't have buttons, but a zipper instead?"

"Nooo, there were buttons. I mean I ... uh—"

"Well then, how did they pull your pants off quickly with the buttons still fastened?"

"I ... I don't know, but they ... uh ... just ... uh—"

"Somehow unfastened them?"

"Uh-huh ... I ... uh ... suppose."

"How, Miss Petrie? By reaching underneath your one-hundred-fifty pound body with one hand, while holding you down with the other?"

For the second time there was no answer, just tears as Louise slowly shook her head from side to side while again pulling tissue from her purse to dab her eyes. Fisher, pressured to protect her increasingly confused and non-responsive witness, seized upon Louise's upset to move for a "brief, five-minute recess," which Steiggerman granted over my strenuous objection "that a question was presently pending, and it was highly prejudicial to allow time for the alleged victim to compose an answer." With herculean effort I managed to stifle the almost irresistible impulse to point out that it was Fisher, assisted by His Honor, who was extending the proceedings and not me, then hurried outside into the corridor for a quick smoke before rage could resume its debate with reason. And when the hearing resumed, a full ten minutes after the requested five, I further decided to allow Louise's failure to answer to stand as such, rather than listen to her mouth Fisher's resurrected rationale, and moved instead into truly touchy territory.

"Now, Miss Petrie," I picked up in as casual a tone as I could manufacture, "after your panties were removed, did these men touch you between your legs?"

"Y-yes," she answered haltingly, still shaky despite the fifteen-minute respite.

"Where between your legs—on your thighs?"

"Uh-huh."

"And in your vagina?"

"Uh-huh."

"And you were still afraid, right?"

"Yes."

"Even more afraid than before, correct?"

"Yes."

"And you were still crying, right?"

"Uh-huh," she articulated with a sigh, her eyes beginning to moisten once again.

"So there were tears in your eyes, correct?"

"Uh-huh."

"And you were still lying on your back?"

"Yes."

"And they were touching you in your vagina?"

"Yes."

"You're sure that their fingers were in your vagina?" I pressed, keeping my tone as gentle as possible while trying to set her prior answer in stone.

The reward however, proved minimal. For although her "Yyyes," emerged as I intended, it did so through a loud sob, and she then stunned me by blurting out, "And their penises too!"

I had wanted one more yes answer so that I could then surprise her with questions on how she could distinguish between the feeling of a finger in her vagina and that of a penis in view of her testimony that she had never before experienced either. And while this avenue of exploration remained open, in an instant the hoped-for element of surprise had vanished, and I was left instead with an answer that now cried for clarification from a witness who was on the verge of coming totally unglued, and a glowering judge who was primed to use her condition as reason to terminate my examination and do God knows what else! Unsure of whether to proceed immediately, or allow Louise to recover her composure, once again I followed instinct and remained silent. To my further amazement, so did His Honor and Fisher, each of whom was apparently relying on the other to control the situation. And when thirty slowly stretching seconds had finally elapsed, and Louise had quieted down, I began again, carefully and in a tone just barely above audible.

"All right, Miss Petrie ... When these men were touching you in your vagina with their fingers, which one touched you there first, the taller one or the shorter one?"

"I ... I don't know," she responded, still recovering, and apparently helped by the soothing softness in which the question was clothed.

"Well, did they both touch you at the same time?"

"I ... I don't know."

"Well, could you please describe how these men touched you in your vagina?"

"Nooo ... I can't remember."

"All right. Did they slide their fingers in and out of your vagina?"

"I don't remember, I ... just can't."

"Okay. Can you remember what your vagina felt like when they were touching you there?"

"Nnn-o," she stuttered back, tears suddenly reappearing in her voice.

"Well, were you touched on your clitoris?"

"I ... I ... can't remember," she choked out, once again beginning to shake her head from side to side.

"I see ... Now isn't the reason you can't remember because you were extremely upset by this touching?"

"Yes."

"And you were crying even harder, and were even more frightened than when your clothes were coming off?"

"Uh-huh ... right."

"In fact, isn't it true that this touching so upset you that you became sort of hysterical, and that's why your mind can't remember, 'cause it went blank?"

"Why ... why yes, that must be what happened," she agreed after a slight pause to consider the sympathetically toned proposal, her head-shake replaced by a nod, her voice suddenly steadied by relief.

"So, isn't it also true that you don't really remember being touched in your vagina by anything other than a finger?"

"Objection!" Fisher shouted, intervening before Louise could even consider answering. "Your Honor," she followed with exaggerated outrage, "counsel's question is obviously too vague in that it does not specify what was touching the witness in her vagina—either a finger or a penis. And as the Court can clearly see, the witness, having already been subjected to a terrible experience, is exhausted from answering an overabundance of questions calculated to place her in an emotional state so that she can be easily confused!"

"Your Honor, that's absolutely false!" exploded my retort like a heat-seeking missile. "If the Court will have the reporter read back the record, it will easily be seen that my question was not at all vague. I specifically asked the witness whether she couldn't really remember being touched by anything other than a finger, and the District Attorney is perfectly aware of it!" charged my frustration-fueled indictment. "In fact, her objection and subsequent speech was made only to suggest an answer to the witness—an answer Miss Fisher wants the witness to give, whether it's true or not. Which is just plain unethical, Your Honor, because a District Attorney is supposed to be concerned with the interests of justice, not just trying to convict someone by any means whatsoever. Miss Fisher should be ashamed of herself, instead of sitting there so nice and smug, smiling like the proverbial cat who swallowed the canary!"

"Missster Harris!" Steiggerman snarled in return, deflecting my angry argument with his own. "This Court would remind you that it is your client who is on trial here, and not the District Attorney! Miss Fisher has appeared before this Court on countless occasions, and has always conducted herself properly—which is a great deal more than I can say for you!" he steamed, then paused for a second or two to steady himself. "Now, to clear this matter up," he added sternly, but in a much lower tone, "the Court will inquire as to whether or not the witness understood your question." Then, forcing a fatherly smile onto his face, he turned toward Louise and launched his carefully camouflaged ploy to assist the prosecution. "Now, Miss Petrie," he began, summoning sugar into his delivery, "the Court wants you to understand all of the questions asked of you, and doesn't want you to be influenced by anyone. The Court merely wants you to tell the truth. Do you understand, Miss Petrie?"

"Yes," Louise answered softly, still looking confused while smiling weakly back at him.

"Okay ... good, Miss Petrie. Now, do you remember being touched in your vagina by something other than a finger?" floated His Honor's subtly distorted version of my query, like the Goodyear Blimp advertising the right answer in blinking lights.

"Yes, Sir," replied Louise to absolutely no one's surprise. "I remember their fingers and their penises touching me."

"Any further questions, Mr. Harris?" Steiggerman then inquired, returning his attention to me, his smirk reflecting the pleasure of his accomplishment.

Choking off the anger that had now flowed up the sides of my neck and lightly flushed my face, in a voice that almost cracked I informed him that I most certainly did. Reluctantly, after mixing a look of disgust with a heavy shrug of his shoulders, His Honor then indicated that I could proceed. And with his contemptuously toned "Very well, Mr. Harris" ringing in my ears, I took a deep breath to further stabilize my control, then channeled the pain from my injured sense of fair play toward Louise, challenging her like a wounded lioness trying to protect her cub.

"Miss Petrie," I jabbed, "you told the Judge that you remember being touched in your vagina by a penis. Previously you stated that you couldn't remember how your vagina felt when it was touched by a finger, so can you now tell us how it felt when it was touched by a penis?"

"No, I ... can't remember exactly."

"Why not, Miss Petrie? Why can't you remember?"

"Well ... it's hard to remember exactly."

"Okay, let's see if I can help you. Now you were still lying on your back when the penis touched your vagina—Isn't that correct?"

"Yes."

"And you were still crying from being afraid, weren't you?"

"Yes."

"And your fear and crying had increased considerably after you were touched on your breasts and vagina by hands and fingers, right?"

"Uh-huh ... yes."

"And while their fingers were in your vagina, you thought that these men were going to touch it with their penises too, didn't you?"

"I ... uh ... guess so," squirmed her answer, emotion again creeping into her tone.

"And you became even more frightened, didn't you?"

"Yyyyes.

"And cried even harder, didn't you?"

"Uh-huh."

"Miss Petrie, during the events you've described, isn't it true that at no time did you actually see a penis?"

"Yesss," leaked her answer after a moment's pause to think, her eyes again filling with tears.

"And isn't it also true that you never actually saw a finger touch your vagina?"

"Well ... yes."

"You assumed it was a finger in your vagina, didn't you? Because just before it was touched, you felt hands and fingers on your breasts and thighs—Right?"

"Well ... I ... guess so."

"But you can't tell us how the finger felt in your vagina?"

"No."

"Well then, Miss Petrie. If you were lying there on your back, hysterical, with your mind blanking, and didn't actually see a finger inside your vagina, can't remember how it felt there, didn't see a penis at all, can't remember how that felt either, and by your own testimony never felt either before, would you please explain how you were able to tell the difference?"

"I ... I ... uh ... just can't say exactly. I mean ... uh ... it's just too hard," escaped her answer slowly as she began to cry.

"Too hard, Miss Petrie?" I hammered. "Isn't the real reason you don't remember and can't say exactly, because none of what you've told us actually happened?"

"Noo ... Nooo!" sobbed her denial.

"And isn't it also true that you're pregnant, and made up your whole story to explain it to your family?"

No answer arrived, as almost simultaneously with the conclusion of my question, Steiggerman erupted. "Mr. Harris, this Court has had enough!" he chastised, his anger in full bloom without benefit of warm-up. "You have refused to follow the Court's advice and conduct yourself in a proper manner, and you're not going to abuse and torture this young woman anymore. Now sit down at the counsel table!" When I was sure that he had finished, I moved several feet away from the jury box in the direction of the counsel table, then stopped and cautiously replied.

"Your Honor, Sir, is the Court telling me that I cannot cross-examine the witness on the issue of her possible motives for lying? It appears to me to be highly relevant to her credibility, Your Honor, Sir," I offered, loading my query with respectful appellations on both ends so as to establish a solid record for my possible hearing on contempt charges.

"I have told you, Mr. Harris, that I've listened to all I'm going to from you! You may not cross-examine any further! Now do you understand me?"

"Yes, Your Honor, I do. And in that case, Sir, I would move to strike all of the witness's testimony on direct examination, on the ground that my client has been denied his right through counsel to confront and cross-examine the witness against him as guaranteed by the Sixth Amendment to the United States Constitution. And Your Honor, Sir, I would cite to the Court the case of Jennings versus the Superior Court, which holds that—"

"Your motion is denied! Now shut up and sit down, Mr. Harris, or

I'll be forced to hold you in contempt!" Steiggerman bellowed, his face quivering with rage.

Promptly covering the remaining distance to my chair, I sat down, and for several long seconds stared through the stony silence as His Honor struggled to regain control of himself.

When he spoke again, his tone had dropped from fire to ice as he inquired of co-counsel whether he desired to question Louise. Without hesitation, Mason quickly expressed his feeling that I had "more than adequately covered the situation for both defendants," and after Irene Fisher indicated that she had nothing further to add, Steiggerman then shifted his focus back to me and asked perfunctorily if the defense had anything further to present. Rising slowly to my feet, I indicated that I did, which reply in turn mapped a mixture of incredulity and resignation across His Honor's face, coupled with a terse "Very well. What is it?"

"Your Honor, Sir, I would move the Court to dismiss the charge against my client on two grounds," opened my argument calmly in pursuit of protecting the record so that our Office could overturn Steiggerman's rulings with a like motion when Joe's case reached Superior Court. "First, he has been deprived of his Sixth Amendment right to confront and cross-examine the witness against him through his counsel, and I would again respectfully cite to the Court the Jennings case in support of my motion. And secondly, Your Honor, the District Attorney has failed to establish that the crime of rape even occurred in this instance—and moreover, even assuming for argument's sake that she did, she has also failed to show that my client committed it," I emphasized, warming to the task, my voice filling with sincerity founded upon honest belief as I continued. "A review of all the evidence, Your Honor—not just the direct testimony of the alleged victim, but her testimony on cross-examination as well—indicates that Miss Petrie was grabbed while walking alone through Willowbrook Park and immediately dragged behind some bushes where her clothes were removed and her vagina was touched by a finger, which touching does not constitute rape. That, Your Honor, requires a penis, and her testimony on that subject was that she never saw one, couldn't describe what it felt like when it allegedly penetrated her vagina, and couldn't even distinguish between the finger and penis touchings. Your Honor, Miss Petrie couldn't even remember feeling pain, and I would strongly suggest, Sir, that a virgin—and a very frightened one at that, with her muscles tightened out of fear—would certainly have remembered to tell us about having experienced pain if, in fact, a penis had actually been brutally thrust into her virgin orifice!" tailed my trail of reasoning into a three-second pause, during which I mentally shrugged off Steiggerman's steely stare.

"Further, Your Honor," I resumed, conviction flooding my tone, "even assuming that a rape occurred, the victim's identification is unbelievably weak. It consists simply of a physical description of two male Negroes, approximately six feet tall and weighing more than one hundred fifty pounds—a description, Sir, that would fit approximately fifty percent of the adult male Negro population of Los Angeles County! When we look for specifics, Miss Petrie couldn't remember what her attackers were wearing, and didn't testify to one single distinguishing feature about them. In addition, she openly admitted to never having seen them before, getting only a brief look at them as they grabbed her, and the crucial fact that it was dark so that she quote, couldn't see all that well, end quote—not to forget that thereafter she became hysterical from fear and her mind went blank!" streamed my summary into conclusion. "Your Honor, the evidence that a rape even occurred is extremely weak, and the identification of the alleged perpetrator is so weak that it is virtually no identification at all! And for these reasons, I urge the Court to dismiss the charge against my client."

"Your motion is denied, Mr. Harris!" knifed His Honor's ruling without benefit of a moment's deliberation. "And I would add for your edification, as well as your education, that if this hearing had been a trial, this Court would find your client guilty beyond a reasonable doubt! In fact, the evidence against him is so strong that I am raising his bail from five thousand dollars to ten. Now what do you say to that?"

"Well, Your Honor," I fired back, sincerity masking my sarcasm, "my client is so poor that he couldn't post bail if you reduced it to a hundred dollars. And as far as the Court's would-be verdict of guilty beyond a reasonable doubt, I would hope with my whole heart, Sir, that before you reached such a sad judgment, you would at least hear the defendant's side of the case first!"

The hearing then ended with Steiggerman forwarding the case on to Superior Court for trial. Joe looked confused as he was re-handcuffed and led out of the courtroom. As he passed through the doorway to the lockup, he jerked his head back over his shoulder and smiled goodbye to me. He vanished from sight before I could respond, and I just sat there, soaking wet and exhausted, and stared out into the vacant hallway for a full minute. Then, after a heavy sigh, I dragged myself to my feet, turned to leave the courtroom, and found myself staring into the grinning faces of George, Robbie, Ron, and Leon. As I approached them I smiled sheepishly back while shaking my head from side to side, causing George to chuckle out, "Feel like going for a beer?"

"Yeah, sure. I think I could use one," I dribbled tiredly after glancing at my watch, which surprisingly read a quarter to five.

After a brief stop back at the office to deposit our briefbags, we walked the short block north to Belmont Boulevard and wandered into a small, seedy-looking bar named the Black Onion. Orders were quickly placed, and as we crowded around a tiny table near the entrance, the conversation about the Prelim and Steiggerman continued. "Don't think I ever saw that pig quite that mad," Robbie opined, laughing heartily.

"Uh-huh, for sure," George agreed, "even Smitty never pissed him off that bad, and Steiggie hated him worse than any of us. Ruined his afternoon off is what you did, Matt. You spoiled the damned pig's fucking golf game!" he rumbled through a smile, with Ron and Leon nodding their full concurrence between sips from their mugs as Robbie punctuated the point.

"Damned inconsiderate is what I'd call it, just ... plain ... innnn-considerate, Matthew, my man!" he drawled with thick sarcasm.

Even though I didn't fully understand what they were saying, I surmised that in their opinion I had performed well, and earned bonus points for raising Steiggerman's blood pressure, which in combination with the loosening effect of alcohol, allowed me to relax further and join in the laughter.

Leon, who had already finished one beer and was a quarter of the way through another, quickly added to the informal critique. "Did you see the expression on Steiggie's face when Matt asked her about her nipples getting hard?" he posed rhetorically. "Hell, you'd think the asshole never sucked on one."

"And what makes you so sure he ever did?" Ron jeered. "I mean we all know he's sucked a lot of ass, but nipples? ... Christ, that Puritan putz probably thinks they're just for feeding babies!" growled his insult, instigating another round of commentary interspersed with alcohol-enhanced frivolity. Steiggerman wasn't the sole target however, for as the collective conversation continued, an assortment of other judges, DAs, cops, and various court personnel were also spotlighted, the lively examination of their flaws and idiosyncrasies effortlessly carrying the cathartic discussion into the dinner hour. At six-thirty, Ron announced that he had to "split for a date," and when Leon offered to walk back to the office with him, I was left alone with George and Robbie. Prudently, we replaced our beer steins with mugs of steaming coffee, and after several moments of awkward silence, George engaged me in a more serious dialogue.

"We're glad you're here, Matt," he opened casually. "I don't think you realize what you've walked into, and I don't really know where your head's at, but that was some kind of show you put on this afternoon—some kind of show, for sure," he emphasized, his eyes searching mine. Complimented, I smiled back at him until it suddenly dawned on me that I was still a question mark.

"What did you think you were getting in me, a cop-out artist?" I blurted, suddenly a bit anxious.

"Well, we didn't know exactly. Rumor had it that we were kicking up too much of a ruckus out here, and while it was okay with the higher-ups downtown, Harold Keyes, who runs the Long Beach Office to which we're attached, was upset and wanted to replace Smith with a more conservative type."

"Well if I'm conservative, then the goddamned Pope is an orthodox Jew!" chuckled out my response, drawing a smile from Robbie, but not from George, who waited instead for more from me. "Okay, you're right when you say that I don't really know what's going on here," I picked up. "But what I do know is that what I've seen of the Solina Judicial District so far, I don't like—and that goes for downtown too! Hell, since I joined the Office three months ago, I've been eating shit ten hours a day, and I don't much like that either! I'm new at this goddamned game, and I'm ignorant as hell, and even more scared. I don't even know why exactly I had to come and do this kind of work, but I did—and while I can't exactly call myself a real lawyer yet, I'm not some ass-licking, cop-out artist either!" I steamed, the left-over anger from the day's earlier encounter combining with the remnants of the beer to cause a warm flush to sweep up the sides of my neck and spill across my face. Reaching for my pipe, I lit up and was about to add a choice comment or two when I spied the twinkle in George's eye, suddenly realized how defensive and hostile I was sounding, and closed my half-opened mouth.

For several seconds there was silence, a heavy silence that gained weight with each puff on my pipe. And then George began to laugh, softly at first, but when Robbie joined in, it grew louder and deeper and then contagious. Inside half a minute, the three of us were roaring at one another, and the more we laughed, the greater the river's flood. We laughed, and laughed, and laughed till tears formed in our eyes and our bodies shook. We laughed till we were weak, and weakened, surrendered to something undefined that spun a thin thread of unity, propelling us forward till we were lost completely in the uncontrolled pleasure of the moment.

On the walk back to the office, we chatted further about Solina, its people, the serious problems surrounding them, and the judicial jungle we worked in. I asked questions, and George and Robbie took turns answering them. And when the conversation inevitably focused on jury trials, and I confessed to them that I had never participated in one, George smiled at me and said that they knew this but not to worry about it. He and Robbie would teach me and I would learn, and when I was ready, I would learn the rest the hard way—by trying cases. Finally, in the parking lot behind our office, we said good night, and as I drove toward the freeway, the warmth of their voices stayed with me and played amongst the myriad of thoughts that tumbled through my mind.

My God, but what a year 1968's turning out to be, and it's just over half finished, entered first as I settled into the journey, mental snapshots streaming into view to accompany the neurons now working overtime. Hell, right off the bat in January, the Viet Cong's Tet Offensive spiked up the never-ending war in Vietnam, with the protests against the conflict rising right alongside. No way would JFK have ever let this mess happen, I mused, wondering for the zillionth time if that's why he was killed—'cause the military-industrial complex needed to flex its muscles and boost profits. Who knows? But old LBJ sure hurried to place a seventy-five-year lock on a ton of records for some strange reason! argued conjecture, Brother Bobby's sad but determined face popping into view to blot out the assassination scene in Dallas. "Hello there, Mr. Attorney General," I quipped out loud, recalling how while I was still in law school at Berkeley I had begun writing letters in pursuit of a staff position when he ran for President. "Yeahhh," followed through a heavy sigh, "and now he's gone too, and Martin Luther King before him." And like the trigger pulled by Oswald, Sirhan, and Ray, the image of MLK lying crumpled on his Memphis hotel balcony unleashed a bullet-point review of the Civil Rights Movement: Rosa Parks refusing to relinquish her seat on the bus ... the lunch counter sit-ins and the Montgomery Bus Boycott ... the Freedom Riders, Selma, and I Have A Dream ... the Ku Klux Klan and White Citizens' Councils, CORE, SNCC, and the NAACP, with angry, hate-filled faces on both sides of the barricades ... the Civil Rights Acts of 1964 and 1965, the terrifying race riots in Newark, Detroit, and Watts—a poignant parade of tragic, triumphant change rushing through my mind to crash headlong into the bloody rice paddies eight thousand lonely miles from home, drowning the War On Poverty and LBJ's hope for a second term. "Fuuuck!" I growled out to brake memory's merry-go-round, my mind's eye again flashing back to Dallas and the crimson stains on Jackie's pink suit, before returning to today and the pained confusion on Joe's face as the marshals led him back to jail. "Yeah, fuck, all right. Fuck, fuck, fuck!" I snarled, George's "that was some kind of show you put on," then echoing into ear to ease the ache in my chest as I fell silent and listened also to his and Robbie's soothing promise of assistance, the peals of delicious laughter we had shared returning for a cameo and forcing a smile.

When I finally reached home, it was approaching nine o'clock. Too tired to eat, after an hour spent surveying *Sports Illustrated* with my pipe for company, I dressed for bed and fell into sleep while once again mulling over the events of the day and wondering what indeed I had gotten myself into.

III

THE NEXT SEVERAL WEEKS WERE MORE difficult than I had imagined possible. Awakening at six o'clock, I showered, dressed quickly, and left immediately for the office in order to arrive there no later than seven-forty-five. For an hour or so I interviewed clients who wandered in early, or read cases on the rare occasions when the office was empty. At nine the day began officially with Judge Lacy calling the calendar in Division Three, and thereafter I tried one preliminary hearing after another until the day ended between five and six. Even lunchtime was a working affair, with the menu consisting of a homemade sandwich or a box of chicken from the Jim Dandy take-out stand on the corner, and eaten while I interviewed clients from the incessant stream that poured into the office. By the day's end, I was so tired that the short walk from the courthouse back across the street to the office caused me to recall the last mile of the forced marches I endured when I was in the Army. And if it's true that there's no rest for the wicked, then I was surely an early favorite to win the year's Satan Seal of Approval Award, at least in the rookie division. For with my mind reeling from the day's battles in court, and my body aching for some rest and hot food, the earnestly desired downtime was postponed indefinitely due to my enrollment in the George Meyerstein–Robbie Gibbons School for Prospective Trial Attorneys, as night after night the three of us assembled in Robbie's office with our cups of coffee and talked law, law, and more law. Judges, juries, and *voir dire*, followed by crimes, possible defenses, and trial tactics, leading to cases, statutes, and plea bargaining. Seemingly without end, I asked questions and they supplied answers, their wealth of knowledge and experience pouring forth hour after hour into my already tired mind, till like a river swollen by torrential rains to the point of bursting, it would hold no more.

Driving home, I would wonder out loud if it was worth it, conclude with a burst of profanity that it was not, and promise myself that I would quit the next day. Somehow, however, the hour spent alone on the freeway listening to the radio never failed to quiet my frayed nerves, and by the time I reached home, my heightened insecurities had retreated for the day, and after a plate of scrambled eggs or a steak, I would settle comfortably onto my couch, light up my ever faithful pipe, and read still more cases till sleep overwhelmed me around midnight. Often I would awaken in the wee hours with something George or Robbie had taught me pressing on my mind, and lying there in the darkness, I would wince, then smile wryly to myself before slowly drifting back to sleep. And even though the next morning arrived far too early for a full restoration to have occurred, the carefully camouflaged but always present demon that drove me was already dressed and barking orders. "Get going, counselor," it commanded loud and clear as I scrambled to comply, "there's work to be done and lessons to be learned!"

As noon approached on September's third Friday, Graduation Day arrived unexpectedly courtesy of Robbie's casually toned "I don't know about you, George, but I kinda think it's time for Matthew to start pulling his own weight around here." A motion that was instantly seconded by a grinning George, my hastily mustered but smilingly rendered objections were quickly overruled as the office schedule for the balance of September was amended to reflect my appearance for two successive weeks in the jury trial divisions. The good-natured kidding that accompanied my promotion was still in full regale when Ron and Leon returned from court and readily added a chorus or two, including Ron's query to Leon as to where we should adjourn for lunch to properly celebrate this momentous occasion. "Well, this is a very serious issue, and we should not act too hastily on it," Leon opined with mock soberness, carefully stroking his recently acquired beard. "I mean it's not every day that one is presented with the opportunity to lunch with a real, honest-to-God, genuine trial attorney, and—"

"But that's the question, isn't it, oh bearded one," Ron interrupted, his head shaking side to side for emphasis. "I mean, how do we know?"

"Well, Mr. Four Eyes," fired Leon's response. "The court was about to address that very question regarding qualifications, when you so rudely interrupted. Now if that happens again, I'll be forced to take action of a nature similar to that often employed by my disgusting colleague, the Most Dishonorable Arlen James Steiggerman, and ram the court's over-sized gavel up your rosy red ass!" Feigning fear, Ron took two steps backward, then leaned up against the wall as Leon rambled on. "Now, if I may continue," he intoned sternly, in that the court has carefully reviewed all of the evidence, to wit, the fact that the subject in question is possessed of a law degree, has amply demonstrated a penchant for hard work, and has exhibited an unusual propensity for unlimited orneriness, the court finds that this plethora of evidence easily overcomes his obvious deficiencies of styling his hair on the short side and wearing pin-striped suits. And as a result, I hereby declare that if he will but venture forth into the courtroom, and get his fucking ass knocked off like the rest of us, that he's likely to become one hell of a trial attorney! Moreover, in that the court is the only person present with a proper appreciation of the finer things in life, namely food, I also order all of you assholes to get into your cars and proceed forthwith to Alessandro's for a proper celebration of Matt's impending loss of virginity!" he closed, clicking his heels, then bowing, four laughing heads nodding their agreement.

A large Italian restaurant, featuring roomy leather chairs and red-and-white checked tablecloths, Alessandro's warm, family-friendly establishment was conveniently located in the neighboring community of Brynhurst. Famous for its fine food and heaping portions, its onion soup, Caesar salad, veal with spaghetti, and warm sourdough rolls, washed down with mugs of beer and followed by fruit, cheese, and steaming cups of cappuccino, leave one stuffed like the proverbial Christmas turkey and harboring thoughts of a long afternoon nap. A sweet idea, turned actually possible by the afternoon's calendar having been cancelled due to a Judges Conference—instead the six of us chose to remain in each other's company, conversing drowsily over a second round of cappuccinos on whatever subjects happened to wander into mind. Sports, music, and the promising weekend ahead shuffled into view alongside books, art, and politics, and were gradually passed around and shared like fine after-dinner liqueurs. And seated between George and Marilyn, with my stomach so full that there was no room for butterflies, I drank in fully the warm camaraderie of the moment, let it settle inside me, and then drank some more. Even the dark events that intruded from the outside world couldn't fully pierce the cloak of contentment that had settled softly around me, though the group discussion of the Soviet invasion of Prague grew animated, and the nomination of Nixon and Agnew, combined with the ugly riots and savage police brutality at the Democratic Convention in Chicago, roused us into a harsh and sardonically humorous colloquy that energetically expressed both our fears and total disgust, before music haphazardly reentered to restore the previous harmony, the arrival of Herb Alpert's lullaby, "This Guy's in Love With You," in the background soothing our ruffled feathers and returning the conversation to more light-hearted topics.

Around three o'clock, the party ended with hugs, handshakes, and parting good wishes for an enjoyable weekend. And when I finally reached home an hour or so later, I quickly shed my tie, lay down on the bed, and with thoughts of how Solina might just turn out to be my long sought-after home slowly filtering through my mind, fell into the first relaxed sleep I had enjoyed in months. Relaxing, indeed. No dreams. No interruptions, not even a bladder break. In fact, my siesta was so serene, that when I suddenly awakened into total darkness, it took me several seconds to figure out where I was. Glancing at the nightstand clock, which read nine forty-two, familiarity finally registered and birthed the realization that I was at home and it was the weekend's Friday night. After rubbing my eyes, I sluggishly flexed the muscles of my body till they stretched taut, then let them gently collapse as I eased back onto the pillow, where for several minutes I just lay there, enjoying the pleasant ache left over from exhaustion's partial satisfaction. Then, noting that the room had become uncomfortably hot and that I had heavily perspired, I slid lethargically to the floor, undressed, and after a cool shower, slipped back into a tee-shirt and a pair of light-brown corduroy pants. Refreshed, and now moving more nimbly into the kitchen of my non–air-conditioned apartment, I poured some white wine into a coffee mug, grabbed up my pipe along with the unread morning paper and a casebook, and wandered outside, where I sat down on the small porch atop the steps leading to and from the front door. For a short while, I just sat there rubbing my bare feet slowly back and forth on the cool cement while watching the traffic flow up and down Doheny Drive to my front. Every so often, a car would park, and young people would emerge laughing and jabbering at one another, causing me to speculate on who it was they were going to see at the Troubadour, a celebrated night club about a block away. Several of the young women I spied were very attractive, and I gazed at them wistfully until arm in arm with their dates they turned the corner onto Santa Monica Boulevard and disappeared from view.

After a few more minutes had passed, I turned off the overheated engine of my imagination, which had managed to travel where my eyes couldn't follow and well beyond, and opened my *Los Angeles Times*. Lighting up my trusty pipe, I luxuriated in the time I gave myself to lazily turn the pages, my eyes jumping in and out of the various news events until an editorial bemoaning the ever-rising tide of violence in U.S. society captured my full attention and sent my mind on a roller coaster ride. Three weeks ago, Huey Newton, the leader of the Black Panther Party, had been convicted of manslaughter in the death of an Oakland police officer, informed the lead sentence, inducing my memory to flash back to my law-school days in Berkeley when the Panthers had first entered my consciousness. Patrolling the streets of nearby Oakland with their guns prominently displayed for the stated purpose of protecting the black community from police brutality, they occupied the opposite end of the civil rights continuum from Martin Luther King's nonviolent approach, I recalled. Yeah, and scared the holy shit out of everybody too, like they still do! rushed my next brainwave, my mind racing onward. Hell, I don't blame them. If I lived in poverty and faced discrimination every single day everywhere I looked, with white society telling me to just be patient and things will change when an undefined future time happens along, I'd be pissed off too. Big Time! Truth is, little old white me can't even begin to really feel what it must be like to be black, and poor, and afraid, without any hope of a different tomorrow. Remember recently when you stayed up all night to read *Soul on Ice* by Eldridge Cleaver? Remember how passionately and eloquently he argued from prison about the emasculation of black men, of how desperately they needed marijuana just to maintain their sanity?

Uh-huh, I answered myself, my head nodding ever so slightly in silent agreement. And now Huey's going to join his old Panther buddy in prison, not that it'll stop the Panthers from doing their thing—Say, didn't Robbie mention something about them having a large and aggressive branch in Solina? surprised the next question, its echo heavy with possible future implications. "My God, is there no end to the opportunities for violence?" I whispered into the light breeze that had suddenly surfaced, my mind's eye racing over scenes from the race riots in Newark and Detroit to settle on the six days of hell that had exploded right next door to Solina in Watts, before bouncing back to Chicago and the Democratic Convention. "Jesus, fucking-A Christ," I groaned,

Mayor Richard Daley's fat face floating into view on a split screen, the police cracking heads, blood flowing on the other half, "all the protestors wanted was to support the minority platform plank calling for an immediate end to the bombing of North Vietnam. But no, Mr. Corrupt Establishment himself, Mr. I Know What's Best For Everyone, Mr. Arrogant Iron Fist had to show those Commie-Hippies who's in charge!" paused my spontaneous indictment while I relit my pipe, wondering what this would cost Hubert Humphrey in the race against Nixon. "And that's not even the worst part," I shrugged out, calming down as I picked up my train of thought. "Now the violence has moved from the ghetto streets to the floor of a convention, a so-called civilized activity taking place on national TV. So what's next?" I posed, falling silent again as the picture of CBS's crack reporter Mike Wallace getting punched in the face by a security guard faded slowly from view. "Yeahhh ... What's next?" ran the voiceless replay in the continuing silence that quickly grew stony from failing to offer an answer.

"Well, how about a riot in neighboring Beverly Hills?" floated a frustration-inspired creation after several lead-footed seconds had trudged by. "You know, the Panthers show up to protest the unwarranted rise in jewelry prices at Tiffany's, and all hell breaks loose," injected my sense of humor with sardonic flair, my eye catching the name of Arthur Ashe as I replaced the Metro Section with the Sports Page, my memory then pulling up Chief Justice Warren's quip that that's where one goes if you want to focus on man's successes rather than his failures. "Well right on! Mr. Chief Justice," I chuckled to myself as I read the review of how Arthur had risen from segregated Richmond, Virginia, to star at UCLA on a scholarship, then served his country as an Army First Lieutenant, before recently becoming the first black man to win a major tennis tournament, the inaugural U.S. Open. Now how about that! I ruminated optimistically, still smiling at the nugget of hope that had fortuitously floated into view when Eldridge's careworn face reappeared. Okay, I know, it's only a small beginning, rumbled reason, my smile dimming, then returning bright, but still, here's one black man who's not emasculated, and a damn good example of what's possible too. And take a look around, 'cause the schools aren't segregated anymore either, at least not legally, nor are the public restaurants, drinking fountains, and bathrooms. And don't forget, my militant friend, that blacks can vote, even in Mississippi, so there's some progress going on in the here and now, and there's good reason to hang in there, okay? I concluded, folding up the paper, then picking up the case book and ordering myself back to school so that maybe, just maybe, I could contribute a little something to the cause.

Having failed to put my watch back on after my shower, I soon lost sight of time's track as I then immersed myself in reading the latest California Supreme Court cases, and I don't know whether it was still Friday night or the first hour of Saturday morning when I was jarred from my studies by a voice calling out, "Well, hello there." Unable to make an identification after peering through the darkness at what appeared to be the willowy figure of a woman standing thirty or so feet away to my left, I managed a befuddled "Uhh ... hi," then watched carefully as the shadowy figure stepped over the small hedge that ringed the front yard and strolled slowly toward me.

"Matthew ... Robert Harris, isn't it?" teased my neighbor Stella when she reached me, a faint smile on her lips.

"Yeah, that's it all right," I grinned sheepishly, surprised at her precise recall of our first meeting several months ago and embarrassed for a second time.

"Well how about having that drink I offered you? You sure look like you could use it."

"I do?" I issued reflexively, further surprised by her bluntness.

"You just better believe it. Your eyes are all red and puffy, and those dark circles underneath make you look like you haven't slept in a year— Not to mention that your face is pale and drawn, you been worried about something?"

"Nooo," I chuckled, beginning to find my bearings as I stared uncomfortably into her lavender-blue eyes, "I've just been working sort of hard lately, that's all."

"I see ... Well how about that drink, 'cause you deserve it?" she tossed back, her tone warmer.

"Sure," I nodded, climbing to my feet. "Sounds good."

With an economy of movement, in short order I shoved the newspaper and case book back inside my apartment, slipped on a pair of sneakers, pulled the front door closed behind me, and followed Stella across the front yard, over the hedge, and down the narrow path that led to the rear of the triplex and the stairs up to her apartment. For a moment I stood just inside the doorway till she found a lamp and turned it on. Then, after she dropped her coat over the back of a rocking chair, murmured "I'll be right back," and disappeared into a hallway to my left, I sat down on a couch and slowly canvassed the living room. It was not at all what I expected. Having imagined that her apartment would be sleek and sophisticated, like my image of Stella, instead of an ultra-modern swinger's pad, I discovered walls whose hue was a soft, pale-yellow, and thick beige carpeting that accentuated the rich dark woods of the various antique pieces that composed the majority of the room's furnishings, contrasted nicely by the occasional contemporary piece like the brushed velvet couch I was seated on and the glass-topped coffee table to its front.

"Do you like it?" Stella asked as she returned, the dressy housecoat rustling slightly as she walked.

"Yes, very much. I don't know anything about antiques, but I like their look."

"Isn't that all you have to know?" she quipped, a smile forming.

"Yeahhh, you're right. I guess that's what counts."

"For sure," she agreed, strolling over to the large buffet that she had converted into a bar by surrounding a large silver tray containing cut crystal glasses with five exquisitely shaped crystal decanters. "I'm having brandy. What would you like?"

"A gin and tonic would be just great, thanks."

"Okay, one gin and tonic coming up," purred her reply. And collecting several pieces of ice from the covered cooler, which I speculated was already present courtesy of her date earlier that evening, she quickly mixed my drink and joined me on the couch.

"Now, what's so important about this work you're doing, that it's got you looking like death warmed over?" she asked, her voice smooth and rich, and containing a hint of laughter. Noting that up close her lavender eyes appeared even larger, and cast a mesmerizing glow, I dropped my eyes to sip at my drink, then settled further into the well of the couch before answering.

"Oh, I don't know how important it is exactly. I'm working as a Public Defender in a ghetto court, and ever since the Civil Rights Movement got going, I've wanted to help. I didn't march, or ride a freedom bus, so it's my way of doing my share, and that's why it's so important to me."

"Okay ... But if you've always wanted to do this kind of work, and now you're getting to do it, why all the worry?"

"Well, 'cause it's new to me, and sometimes a bit terrifying. I want to be good at it—not just all right, but real good! That doesn't come easy, for sure, so I've been working at it night and day for the past four months, and slowly but surely I'm beginning to know my way around the courtroom. So if I can just outwork the DAs till some experience kicks in, then—"

"Is there a time limit?" Stella interjected, causing me to smile out of embarrassment at how my insecurity-infused enthusiasm might be perceived as immature.

"No ... of course not," I chuckled, taking care to modulate my tone. "It's just that the people I represent depend on me. Most of the time they don't even fully understand what's going on, and if *I* don't, they don't have a chance. They've never had a fair chance at life to begin with, so while I don't get paid to solve the world's inequities, I know that if I were standing in their shoes, the very least I would want is that the person who was representing me gave a good goddamn. Wouldn't you?"

"Yeahhh ... I certainly would," Stella acknowledged after several seconds of consideration. Then, setting down her drink, she reached for a cigarette and lit up. With the gin having mixed nicely with the previously consumed Chablis and the law-centered conversation to dull the edge of the uneasiness I felt at being with Stella, I immediately seized upon the opportunity for the further comfort that smoking represented, lighting my pipe, then continuing on in the same vein.

"Uh-huh, right," I confirmed, puffing away. "And here's the cruncher. Older guys who've been at this game for a while tell me that you have to get used to losing if you're going to sit on the defense's side of the table, and I know enough to know they're right. But I don't ever want to get comfortable with losing, and I sure as hell don't ever want to feel the pain of knowing that I lost a case for want of trying—because I was too tired to learn something I needed to know."

"Okay ... I understand— and that's all good and well," Stella acknowledged, her tone tuned maternal. "But you've got to have a life too."

"All work and no play makes a dull Matt?"

"Uh-huh, that's what they say. What about women—got any time for them?"

"No ... I mean I like them well enough. But in a week or so I'm going to do my first jury trial, with many more to follow—and with so much stuff still to learn, my love life will just have to remain on hold. Besides, from what little I've seen, you're balancing the scales for both of us."

"Oh, I do okay," she shrugged with quiet confidence. "Can I freshen your drink?" I nodded yes, and when Stella returned from the bar, I turned the spotlight in her direction.

"Now, how about you—what's your line of work?"

"Me? ... Oh, I dabble a bit here and there in interior decorating. I don't have a lot of clients because I don't work hard enough at finding them, so I don't actually make a living at it. But it's very satisfying helping others find a décor that they're comfortable with, and my husband left me some money, so I do what pleases me," she explained, pausing to light up another cigarette. "When work's available—and I get a referral here and there—I take it seriously and get involved. But when it's not, well ... I go out a lot, and I travel some, and all in all, it's a good life."

"Uh-huh ... right," I returned, thinking that we lived in different universes, my curiosity piqued. "When did you lose your husband?"

"Oh, a long time ago—a very long time ago."

"I'm sorry."

"Don't be. It wasn't good," she shot back, the rapidity of her response and the slight edge in her tone surprising me. She noticed, immediately softening and slowing her delivery as she added details. "I was young, just seventeen, when we were married. Pete was older, and a lot more worldly, at twenty-five, but definitely not ready for a baby. And when Vicki then happened by accident, well ... the parties and the traveling all had to stop, and my swelling belly certainly wasn't a turn-on, and neither was responsibility—for either of us really. So gradually, he lost interest, and after Vicki actually arrived, well, family life most definitely wasn't his thing—and to make a long story short, after a couple of months, he just took off and I never heard from him after that. He came into big money when his parents passed on shortly afterward, and joined the jet-set until he was killed in a drunken car crash later on," she ended, reaching for her brandy. For an instant, she thought about adding something more, decided not to, and after stubbing out her cigarette in the ashtray, took a deep swallow from her glass. I waited until she had reseated the tumbler on the coffee table before inquiring further.

"Does your child live here with you? I've never seen her around."

"Child? ... Did you say child?" she laughed loudly. "Why Vicki is almost as old as you are, she'll be twenty-four this October."

"Ohhh, I see," I muttered feebly, feeling awkward, and chuckling in a failed effort to hide the remnants of disbelief still marking my face.

"How old do you think I am?" she asked, laughter still coating her voice.

"I don't know," crawled my confession, "but certainly not old enough to have a twenty-four-year-old daughter."

"Well, I thank you for the compliment, you're very kind."

"And I thank you for the drinks, and for the very interesting company," I rolled out in return, still feeling a bit stupid, "but I better be moving along. The clock on the wall over there says it's almost two-thirty."

"Okay ... God knows you could use some sleep—might do wonders for those circles under your eyes."

"Uh-huh, I hear you," mumbled my agreement as we shuffled slowly toward the door, both of us further agreeing "to do it again sometime soon" by the time we reached it and I passed outside into the hallway. "Matthew?" she then asked as I was about to turn away, her tone suddenly sober. "Do I make you feel uncomfortable?"

"No ... Why do you ask?" I lied.

"Oh, I don't know, it's just a feeling I got—you sure?"

"Well ... okay," I squeezed out, "I'll tell you something, Stella, if you promise not to laugh too hard."

"I promise."

"Well, the truth is ... pretty ladies make me nervous, that's all."

For several slowly shuffling seconds, there was silence, pure silence, as we just stood there looking at each other. Then, as a faint smile curled out of the corner of her mouth, she took a step forward, whispered, "That's sweet, Matthew," and kissed me tenderly on the cheek, adding "Good night" as she withdrew.

Surprised yet again, "Good night, Stella, and thanks," managed to find their whispery way off my tongue on their own while I was busy freezing the softness of her lips and the smile inside her oceanic eyes into memory. Then, carefully carrying it with me back to my apartment, I tucked it in beside me and collapsed into sleep.

Morning arrived far too soon, I concluded, when I awakened just after nine o'clock to find myself still tired. For a minute or two I just lay there and focused on the shafts of sunlight that slithered through the narrow openings at each end of my bedroom drapes to bounce a slim smile off the carpet and onto my lips. Triggering Stella into mind, thoughts about last evening's encounter quickly placed breakfast on hold, as I nestled back against the pillow and watched her face form on a canvas just above me, my eyes scrutinizing each of her fabulous features. The creamy white skin, silky smooth and without lines except for traces underneath the lavender pools of her eyes. The high, exquisitely formed cheekbones that complemented her delicately sculpted nose and the lips of her sensuously shaped mouth. The perfectly proportioned ears set close to her head, whose visibility was partially obscured by the mane of jet-black hair that softly caressed them on its journey downward to her slender shoulders. "My God, but she's beautiful!" I marveled, my smile widening as I lifted the fingers of my right hand and lightly stroked the spot on my cheek where her kiss had landed. The replay on my mind's screen caused me to wonder just how incredible a real kiss would feel, in turn instantly inspiring a fantasy to form that undoubtedly would have spun the romantic scenario well beyond kissing if the ring of the telephone hadn't interrupted.

Frustrated for a second, I quickly waved away the preying delusions of grandeur, and with my smile transformed sheepish, picked up the receiver. Ironically, it was my mother calling, and after quickly flashing on the fact that she was only a few years older than Stella, I chatted with her for several minutes, ending up by accepting her invitation for dinner. I didn't truly want to go, because however well intentioned when they began, visits with my parents were always pockmarked with prying questions about my life as a Public Defender. Although couched carefully in subtle tones of disapproval, still, Gertrude Stein's observation that a rose by any other name was still a rose proved true, and their disappointment in me and my chosen occupation could not only be seen, but heard and felt as well. A good son, according to Fred and Rosalie Harris, one who properly appreciated the numerous benefits he had received courtesy of their wealth and social standing, would recognize his duty to assist the family in the never-ending pursuit of greater wealth and an even higher social status, instead of wasting precious opportunity in an idealistic, foolhardy attempt to help even society's playing field. An offshoot of their Great Depression–based philosophy that bigger is always better, and bolstered by the Jewish tradition of supreme parental authority, enforced by the legions of guilt, this ideology had clashed with my natural instincts to the contrary as far back in childhood as I could remember, though the friction didn't graduate into actual conflict until I was in college and law school and fully realized that I couldn't and wouldn't live by my parents' rules, no matter how hard the feelings this decision produced, or the frosty distance it created between us. Still, they were the only parents I was ever going to have, I had reasoned while my mother was rattling off several different menus that I could choose from, and coupled with the facts that we hadn't been together in over seven weeks, and I had no other plans for the evening ahead, the argument for acquiescence seemed compelling, and our conversation had concluded with the further agreement that I would arrive at seven o'clock.

After returning the receiver to its home on the adjacent nightstand, for a moment I lingered on the edge of the bed, smiling as I pictured my mother scurrying about her kitchen cooking up enough food to feed the proverbial army because her poor, undernourished little boy was coming to dinner. Fading after I hoisted myself to my feet and shuffled down the hallway into the bathroom, my grin quickly renewed itself when thoughts of Stella suddenly resurfaced, then shared my mind's stage alongside those participating in an evaluation of my physical condition, the sighting in the mirror of my pale, puffy-eyed, unshaven face contrasting sharply with my phone-interrupted vision of a romantic encounter. And although this striking contradiction between fantasy and reality forced me to chuckle good-naturedly at my ability to magnify a simple kiss on the cheek into full-fledged sex inside one neuronic flash, even the lottery-sized odds against such a possibility failed to stop a closer survey of my features, the faint hope being that while I was sleeping, magic had miraculously transformed *nice looking* into *handsome*. No luck, however. Not today, I told myself, scrutinizing the bumpy ridge and rounded tip of my nose, a product of my Hebraic heritage that detracted from my otherwise above-average attributes. Oh, well, it could be a lot worse, I consoled, moving back from the mirror to take inventory of my physique, the well-developed muscles from my tournament-tennis playing days in high school still present to accentuate my lean frame. Not bad, I judged. Not bad at all, floated the appraisal contentedly until my eyes drifted back to the heavy, blue-black smudges underlining my eyes and reflecting upwards to illuminate the offending nose.

"But not exactly great, either," followed my overall evaluation out loud, disappointment sinking into my voice. "And you need great if you want to play in the big leagues, Buster Brown—remember?" I chided, anger suddenly exploding inside me, fueled by the storehouse of frustration and pain from years of fighting against the feelings of inadequacy that life lessons had taught. "Yeahhh, dream on, lover boy, 'cause that's where everything happens for you, isn't it. You dream about this, and you dream about that, and then you dream dream dream some more!" steamed my tirade, seemingly operating under its own power. "But I gotta hand it to you this time, you stupid sonofabitch—Stella, huh? Yeah, sure, she's just the kind of woman to go for you all right. I mean, didn't you see the movie-star looks on the guys she dates? And what about the super-class cars they drive? Hell, you'd miss the next payment on your little Mustang if you had to pick up the tab at one of those restaurants she's always trotting off to. Not to mention, you silly-ass, that she's forty-two, and has a daughter who could be your sister!" I roared, then stopped suddenly, short of breath.

"Yeahhh ... you're right," I answered myself in whispers after a ten-second pause, stunned by my unexpected outburst, rage having disappeared underneath a wave of shame that forced tears into my eyes and a dull ache inside my chest. Turning slowly away from the mirror toward the shower stall, I reached in and twisted the knob, then climbed inside and directly underneath the streaming head. For several minutes I just stood and let the warm water bounce off the top of my head and trickle down over my body, listening to a voice inside my head repeat over and over, "No one can make you feel inferior, without your permission," until finally a thin smile emerged and I murmured, "Yeahhh ... true all right. But it sure helps if you've got Eleanor Roosevelt's strength of mind and unlimited supply of guts."

A half hour later, refreshed, but still mystified by the strength of my anger, and sadly disappointed by my loss of control, I dressed, skipped breakfast, and left the apartment to run my Saturday errands, the visits to the cleaners, the shoe repair shop, and the market slowly sanding the prickly edges off the hub of doubt that lingered. No matter how hard I tried, however, I couldn't free myself completely from the nagging sense of uneasiness that accompanied me for the balance of the weekend. Even when the dinner with my parents proved surprisingly enjoyable, courtesy of the conversation centering on my dad's enthusiasm for an upcoming shopping-center project, instead of me, still the jittery feeling persisted. And though I attempted to perpetuate the prior evening's relaxed atmosphere by forgoing my Sunday study session in favor of watching football games, still the lifelong questions of *Why was I so different?* and *Where did I fit in this foreign world?* surfaced at intervals to agitate and annoy. Only when I returned extra early to Solina on Monday morning, and dove headlong into the stream of cases that cascaded at a frantic pace through its overloaded court system, did the Nettlesome Twosome disappear, and by Friday, even the sporadically invading thoughts of Stella had ceased as I busily began final preparations for my now impending new assignment.

With my schooling having incubated in slow motion over nine long weeks, now time seemed to accelerate as I rushed my eyes over notes and cases in one, final, weekend warm-up. Tick. Tick. Tick, tick, tick, it sprinted, whisking me to Milestone Monday, where at ten minutes to nine I found myself entering Division Two to handle my first jury trial calendar. No bands were playing. No crowds were cheering. Only eager anticipation and its older brother apprehension welcomed me as I exchanged nods with the various court personnel, seated myself at the counsel table, and began browsing through my copy of the court calendar. When my eye caught the September 30 date at the top of the page, a thought flashed. Well, Mr. September, you're coming to an end now and get to rest, bounced the brainwave, but I'm just beginning, like your brother will tomorrow. "So how about wishing us both good luck, 'cause we're sure as hell going to need it," I muttered quickly in afterthought, before resuming my search of the calendar's columns for the most serious cases. A few minutes later, Ray Cline, the resident bailiff, tapped me lightly on the shoulder and informed that the Judge wished to see me in chambers. Laying aside the court files I was reading, I arose and followed Ray as he ushered me down a short hallway and into a room whose vaulted ceiling made it appear larger than it actually was. Judge Thomas E. Austin rose from the chair behind his cluttered desk as we entered, and surprised me with the warmth of his "Hello there!" as well as the considerable strength of his grip as I shook his outstretched hand. "Sit down—sit down and make yourself comfortable," continued his greeting. "Would you like some coffee?"

"Yes, Your Honor, I would, thank you."

"Well there's a whole pot over there. Fix yourself up a cup the way you like it, and then tell me a little something about Matthew Harris."

Feeling myself breathe a little easier, I poured myself a cup from the small green coffee pot located on a tiny table in the corner to the left of his desk, added some cream and sugar, and while stirring my breakfast together, glanced back over my shoulder at him.

"No, but thanks," he smiled, having read the question in my face. "The doctor says I'm not to drink that stuff anymore—seems it's not good for us older folks." The lively twinkle playing in the center of his blue eyes as he enunciated "us older folks" clearly denied that there was anything old about the man, though I judged him to be in his middle to late sixties. And his voice carried the same vigorous energy as he renewed his earlier request. "Now c'mon and tell me about yourself," he urged. "I know that you're new to us here in Solina—been with the PD long?"

"No, Sir—only about five months, including my time here in Solina."

"Are you enjoying it?"

"Well, to tell the truth, I haven't had a free moment to figure that out yet, or at least it seems that way."

"Well, now, isn't that the truth," he responded, his empathetic tone causing me to settle more comfortably into my chair. "Some days it seems like all the cases in the entire country somehow got set here in Solina. Why I can remember trying cases when I first started in the District Attorney's Office—back before you were even born—and we had time to try them all. In fact, we had so much time on our hands, that it's amazing we didn't get ourselves into more trouble than we did. For example, one time I ... uh—" he braked to a stop, catching himself and breaking into a wide grin before picking up. "Now that's something you'll have to learn, Mr. Harris, if you ever want to get anything done around here. Never let this old goose start rambling on about yesterday, or first thing you know we'll all have two calendars full of cases to worry about instead of one."

"Okay, Your Honor," I chuckled. "I'll try to keep that in mind."

A task which proved easy enough, at least in the short run, for as our amiable chat continued, it stayed firmly rooted in the present. And as the topics bounced from law schools attended, to hobbies and sports, to service in the armed forces, I studied him, arriving shortly at the conclusion that if ever a man looked like a judge, Thomas Austin did. Everything about him was large. From his massive head, the top of which sat a good six feet-three inches from his toes, and was covered with thick, neatly combed, snow-white hair, down through the broad, heavily muscled trunk of his body, every part of him appeared large and powerful. Even the individual features of his face were large. The forehead and cheekbones, the ears, nose, and deep-set eyes, all seemed as if they had been masterfully sculpted so that they could be observed as clearly from a distance as up close, their fine-tuned definition providing him with a ruggedly handsome, almost regal countenance.

When our conversation gradually worked its way back to the extremely high caseload bedeviling the Solina Judicial District, and I explained that no one appreciated this problem more than a newcomer such as myself, His Honor was quick to indicate his understanding, and express sympathetically that "with a small amount of experience and a great deal of patience," I would learn to live with it as had everyone else. At this point I took a final swig of coffee, and rising to my feet, suggested that I had better start tending to one of those overcrowded calendars we had been commiserating about. Readily agreeing, still, he was reluctant to end our encounter. "Say—is there by chance a Mrs. Harris?" he inquired as I took a step away from my chair.

"No, Sir, not yet."

"How come?"

"I don't know. I suppose it's because I've never found anyone dumb enough to want me."

"Yeah, I know what you mean," he chuckled, the twinkle in his eye glittering with amusement. "I don't really know how Mrs. Austin has put up with me for all these years. But then seeing as how you're footloose and fancy-free, do you read much?"

"As much as possible, Your Honor," I smiled back at him.

"Well, good! We'll have to have some discussions about that real soon."

"That's a deal, Sir, I'll look forward to it."

Still smiling upon my return to the courtroom, a whispery "Wowww" tiptoed off my tongue as I discovered a buzzing crowd that easily exceeded the forum's capacity. People were literally everywhere, having readily filled the one hundred fifty available seats, then spilled over into the center aisle, where, standing and jabbering at one another, they stacked up solidly to the double-door entryway and pushed outside into the corridor. Every so often, I observed as my eyes scanned the assemblage in amazement, a latecomer would push, shove, and squeeze his way through the morass of bodies to the wooden railing that separated the court working area from the audience and check-in with the bailiff, who, after searching his copy of the court's three-page, forty-one case calendar, would note the person's presence, then advise him to wait outside till he heard his name called. Recovering quickly from my surprise, I noted that of the forty-one cases set for today, twenty-eight belonged to the Public Defender, and as I walked toward the wooden barrier to call out the first name on my list, I was approached by the DA, a pleasant, pudgy fellow wearing glasses named Randy Johnstone.

"Good morning, Matt, and welcome to Misdemeanorland!" he chirped cheerfully, appearing as calm as he had on the several prior occasions we'd opposed each other during preliminary hearings.

"Misdemeanorland? Is that what they call this zoo?"

"Uh-huh ... charming, isn't it?"

"Yeahhh, sure," I chuckled.

"Listen, I'm going to talk to private counsel first, which will give you some time to interview your clients, which I know you need. Then, in a couple of hours we can get together and see what we can dispo, okay?"

"Sure, that'll be fine," I nodded back, turning again toward the audience.

Dispo is legalese slang for the disposal of cases by plea bargain. The procedure, as George and Robbie had taught me, is very simple in theory. You read the arrest report, then interview your client. If you have a defensible case, you proceed to trial. And if not, which is most of the time, you confer with the DA and the judge in chambers, and try to negotiate a reduction of the alleged crime to a less serious offense and/or obtain a lighter sentence in exchange for your client's plea of guilty, thus eliminating the need for a time-consuming trial and consequently relieving the court's overcrowded calendar. Recalling George and Robbie's general distaste for the process, I also summoned into mind their tempering axiom that "it's heaven-sent when you've got no defense at all, and your client's ass is about to visit the cozy confines of the county jail." The trick to plea bargaining, they instructed, was in knowing when to engage in it. And with their admonition that "unfortunately, the only way you really learn when, and when not to, is by trial and error" dancing squarely in front of my eyes, I nervously cleared my throat, then called out the name of Hattie Connors.

I had to repeat it three times, before a short, emaciated black woman, wearing a faded green dress underneath a black sweater sporting several holes, finally emerged from the center of the chattering crowd and painstakingly made her way forward to the wooden railing. Promptly introducing myself, I asked her to follow me to the jury room so that I could interview her, and once we were seated, I advised her of her constitutional rights and explained to her that she was charged with having committed the crime of petty theft. Her response was a slow, respectfully toned indication that she understood me, which did not appear to be fully true judging from the blank expression covering her face and the hazy stare emanating from her eyes. Deciding that to read her the arrest report verbatim would only confuse her further, I lit up my pipe and tried talking to her like a friend.

"Hattie, the officers say in this report that you picked up some steaks in the Safeway Market, and left without paying for them. You want to tell me about it?" I asked gently.

"Well, that's right, Sir," she nodded after a slight hesitation.

"What do you mean by 'that's right,' Hattie? Are you telling me that you took the meat without paying for it?"

"Yes, Sir ... I did."

"You just walked into the market, picked up six steaks, put them in a shopping bag and walked out?" I probed, continuing my hopeful search for some mitigating factor.

"Yes, Sir."

"Why, Hattie? Didn't you know that it was wrong to do that?"

"It's not wrong to feed your babies, is it?"

"Well, no, Hattie, of course not. But you know you have to pay for food when you shop in a store, don't you?"

"I ain't got no money, Sir."

"None—no money at all?" I asked, my education in surprise growing.

"No, Sir, none at all. I ain't been working since I got sick almost seven months ago."

"What about welfare, Hattie? Don't you know about that?"

"Well, Sir," she responded slowly, her voice sounding tired, her eyes welling with tears and her lower lip quivering. "I'm going on fifty-nine years now, and I've done give birth to eleven children—and buried two, and a husband besides. And all the while, I've worked as best I can, and never had to go on the county—and I never will," she ended sadly, lowering her head onto her folded arms.

Her attorney, wondering how even Clarence Darrow could escape from this noose, just sat there looking at her while sucking on his pipe. Somehow, George and Robbie had neglected to tutor me on what to do when faced with an old, worn-out, undernourished and unemployed mother of nine, who had no prior criminal record, an equivalent amount of money, and a sense of morality that told her it was shamefully wrong to take a handout, but all right to steal food if it was to feed her children. Hell, I reasoned, reviewing options between puffs, poverty, no matter how sympathy inducing, simply doesn't appear on the very short list of known defenses to the crime of petty theft. Intoxication does, in that it negates the ability to form the criminal intent to steal, but that hope was quickly dashed when Hattie responded to my further inquiry by advising that she "never, ever drinks." So, after silently forming the prayer-based plan of talking Johnstone into accepting a plea of guilty to simple trespass, with a minimal fine and time to pay it as the penalty, I instructed Hattie to return to her seat in the audience and wait until I had spoken to the judge about how this unfortunate problem could be resolved.

George Jackson was next on my list. And his self-formed defense to having spit in the face of the white officer who stopped him for a traffic violation was his hostility-infused "I didn't run no goddamned red light! You know how those pig cops are, man—us blackies are just a bunch of niggers to them, just a bunch of jungle-bunny niggers waiting to be hassled!" Like poverty, prejudice, real or imagined, doesn't qualify as a legal defense to battery. And after several minutes of intense discussion, during which my pronounced sincerity finally managed to convince him that I was on his side, but the law wasn't, we finally reached agreement that if possible, a plea to disturbing the peace, with a small fine attached, would be the best solution to our problem. Glancing at my watch as George retreated to the outside corridor, I noted that it was almost ten o'clock, and that twenty-six clients still remained to be interviewed. At my present pace, I quickly calculated, I would be finished in roughly thirteen hours, which realization promptly inspired the butterflies in my stomach to begin multiplying. Resolving to shorten my interviews, while overlooking the issue of *how*, I turned next to Miguel Berrendo, who faced a drunk driving charge. In addition, Miguel presented one other slight problem: he didn't speak English, and I didn't speak Spanish. Having just vowed to become more efficient, I now watched fifteen frustrating minutes waste away while I waited behind a collection of private attorneys to inform the Court Clerk that an interpreter was needed, then resumed waiting with ever growing impatience till Van finally stopped frantically scribbling in various court files and placed a telephone call, only to be rewarded with the unhappy news that none were immediately available. Somehow, using a creative combination of mangled Spanish and sign language, I managed to communicate to Miguel that we would have to wait for an interpreter to arrive, then returned him to his seat in the audience and substituted Miss Alicia Parker.

Charged with prostitution, Alicia's physical appearance alone would have sufficed to convict her. Gifted with considerably more than an ample bust, she was braless underneath the undersized, kelly-green sweater she wore unbuttoned halfway to her waist, which further highlighted the neon-blue hip-hugger pants that stretched tightly over her stick-thin legs till they touched the tops of her gold-laminated, three-inch, high-heel shoes. Forget reasonable doubt, I thought. Even if we use beyond a shred of a doubt, we're got big trouble here in River City. A conclusion that was quickly reinforced when we reached the jury room, and Alicia cheerfully chirped, "Hi, there, honey! You my lawyer man?" while slinging her suitcase-sized shoulder purse onto the table and sliding into her seat. Replying with a simple yes, while struggling to keep my eyes off her almost fully exposed breasts, I pulled my eyes downward onto the file lying in front of me and quickly continued.

"Now this complaint, Miss Parker, charges you with having violated Section 647-b of the California Penal Code," I advised in a business-like tone. "Which means that—"

"I know what it means, honey," she interrupted calmly. "It means that I'm supposed to have been selling my pussy for some bread, right?"

"Yes, that's right, Miss Parker," I nodded, returning her smile.

"You can call me Alicia, if you want, honey."

"Okay, that's fine," I blurted, lighting my pipe and letting the smoke slowly seep out through my lips. "Now you want to tell me about what went down?"

"Well ... what did you say your name was, honey?"

"Matthew Harris, Miss—I mean, Alicia."

"Well, Matthew-honey, there's really not much to tell. I did it, and that's all there is to it."

With the thought that I wasn't ever going to handle a case where someone hadn't done it running through my mind, I pressed her for the details in the hope that the defense of entrapment might raise its welcome head.

"Look, honey," she returned, shrugging her shoulders. "I hustled this dude in this bar, took him to my motel room, took his ten bucks and was about to fuck him when the prick pulls out his badge and busts me. Now I appreciate your help and all, but I don't want no trial or anything. I just want to make a deal and get back to work, okay?"

Caught offguard by her candor, accentuated as it was by her earthy description of what had occurred, and delivered in such a calm, matter-of-fact tone of voice, I unwarily lost control and turned over the case to her. "Did you have something particular in mind?" I asked, then watched a bemused smile spread across her face.

"Sure, honey—I'll cop to disturbing the peace for a fifty-dollar fine."

"Okay, Alicia," I agreed, feeling embarrassed. "I'll see what I can do when I meet with the DA and the judge."

"Thanks," she answered, twisting out of her chair. At the door, she paused and looked back at me. "You new at this game, Matthew-honey?"

"Yeah ... sorta," tiptoed my confession.

"Uh-huh ... I thought so. But no problem, honey. No problem at all," she soothed before vanishing through the doorway.

What a beginning, I thought, as for the second time I found myself just sitting there sucking on my pipe and contemplating what the hell I was doing in a courtroom. My pity-party was soon interrupted however by Bailiff Cline, who stuck his head into the room and informed me that Judge Austin had gone to lunch and that the afternoon session would begin at one-thirty. Nodding my understanding, I closed my briefbag and slowly strolled downstairs and back across the street to the office, where I seated myself at my desk and tried to eat a peanut butter and jelly sandwich that tasted like finely ground sand. As I tossed the uneaten half into the wastepaper can, Ron entered our cubicle swearing at the top of his lungs.

"That fucking Steiggerman! You want to hear what that mother-fucking sonofabitch tried to pull on me?"

"Sure, lay it on me," I offered, settling back in my chair as he pulled off his coat and slammed it down onto his desk along with his briefbag, which promptly tumbled onto the floor and spilled out its contents. Viewing this further catastrophe, he whirled and burst out of the room, down the hallway and out the back door without uttering another word. When he returned about thirty minutes later, I was readying myself to return to court. Having calmed down to a point where he appeared depressed, Ron slumped into his chair, put his feet up onto his desk, and lit a cigarette while staring at his shoes.

"Hey, Matt," he finally muttered, breaking the uneasy silence as I was about to leave, "thanks for putting my shit back in my briefbag."

"Anytime, Ron ... anytime," I answered, watching as he inhaled, then let a perfectly formed smoke ring escape off his tongue.

"How's your first day as a trial attorney going?" he then queried.

"Trial attorney? What trial attorney? I feel like a stupid schmuck stuck in the middle of a goddamned three-ring circus!"

"Enjoying yourself, huh?"

"Oh, yeah, you've hit it right on the head, all right. I'm just having a ball!" I shot back with heavy sarcasm. "First off, I interviewed a pitiful, old woman who stole six steaks out of a market to feed her children 'cause she's too goddamned proud to go on welfare. Then I got hold of a wise-ass who spit in the face of a cop who had the audacity to stop him for running a red light—and whose only hope is that if I can seat him close enough to the jury, his body odor might cause them to pass out before they reach a verdict. And if that isn't enough for starters, next I had a whore on my hands, who has forgotten more about plea bargaining than I know, and a guy charged with drunk driving who I can't even talk to because he doesn't speak English! Why I can hardly wait to get back over there and meet the twenty-four cases still waiting for me. I mean where else could I go to spend such a pleasant, fun-filled day? I already checked with Dante's Inferno, and they're booked solid!" I closed, then smiled when he burst out laughing.

"That's great," he managed between chuckles.

"Yeah, well at least I'm good for something. Listen, if I ever get finished over there, maybe we can grab a beer?"

"Sure," he nodded as I turned to leave, and I could still hear him chuckling to himself as the front door closed behind me.

The afternoon wound away in much the same fashion as had the morning, but at an even faster pace. By five o'clock I had interviewed eleven more alleged transgressors of the law, and my head throbbed from the conglomeration of diverse facts and circumstances that had seemingly flowed inside on a conveyor belt, and in turn onto a Ferris wheel—Drunk in Public, Drunk Driving, Disturbing the Peace, Under the Influence of Heroin, Assault, Battery, Resisting Arrest, and Failure to Provide all passing in and out of the jury room until I felt as if I were an official observer at a Penal Code parade.

At five-fifteen, I wearily proceeded into Judge Austin's chambers to meet with Johnstone, who appeared only slightly less frazzled than myself. Seated to my right on a couch in front of Austin's desk, Randy began by listing the cases in which he needed a continuance to a later date in order to subpoena witnesses that had failed to appear. When I pointed out that in several of these cases my clients were in custody and I therefore couldn't agree to the proposed continuances, he promptly moved to dismiss them "in the interests of justice," and Austin acquiesced with a simple "All right" as he noted and initialed his agreement inside the specified court files. Next up was a series of cases in which Randy offered to reduce the crime charged to a less serious offense in exchange for pleas of guilty. Thumbing through my pale-green interview sheets like a deck of cards, I glanced hurriedly at my notes and quietly agreed to several of the suggested plea bargains, then moved to continue other cases in which my clients had posted bail to a later date so that I could subpoena necessary witnesses. On two occasions Randy protested, pointing out that the Public Defender had already had one continuance, and that his witnesses were present and had been waiting patiently all day. Austin quickly overruled his objections, and we plodded onward through the seemingly endless list of cases to a further series of dismissals, some on Randy's motion and some by Austin acting alone, and all made in the "interests of justice." To my absolute amazement, Hattie Connor's and Alicia Parker's cases fell within this framework, Hattie's sad situation being dismissed because Randy had become irritated with the Safeway security officer who had witnessed the theft, and having become tired after waiting in court for eight hours, had left without even consulting with him—while in Alicia's matter, it was decided that the court's crowded calendar simply did not permit the time necessary to try the case this week, next week the arresting officer was scheduled to go on vacation, and as Randy philosophized, "Why waste any more of the County's money on a common whore anyway."

In twenty minutes it was over, and with a feeling of numbness spreading slowly through my body, as if I'd been administered a shot of novocaine, I wandered back outside into the courtroom to advise my clients of the outcome of their cases. Their reactions were as mixed as the varied dispositions that had occurred. Those that had their cases continued groaned and bitched their disapproval at me, while those whose cases resulted in guilty pleas to less serious offenses, with small fines attached as punishment, smiled indifferently and quickly departed. And sprinkling an ounce or two of happiness into the otherwise gloomy atmosphere, those whose cases were dismissed, laughed and thanked me. Hattie cried, and murmured, "God bless you" a dozen times or so, while Alicia kissed me on the cheek and said, "You done a hell of a job for a virgin. I owe you fifty bucks, lawyer-man—Why don't you come see me and collect it sometime soon, okay?" Embarrassed, I blushed deeply, attempted to muster an appropriate reply, and failing, simply smiled at her, then focused my attention back onto my interview sheets, shuffling through them as if I still had business to complete. Laughing, she finally departed, and I stood alone and listened to the silence while staring at my now crumpled copy of the court calendar, the numerous notes and arrows making it look like a neurotic roadmap. After several moments, a wry grin formed as I slowly shook my head in disbelief at what had transpired. Out of twenty-eight cases, ten had been continued for trial, seven by Randy and three by me. Five more had been disposed of by plea bargain, leaving nine that had been outright dismissed for reasons having nothing whatsoever to do with the law, justice, or any other seemingly rational thought process my weary mind could conjure up. My smile widened as my eyes inched up and down the crowded pages, then suddenly disappeared as I realized that there were still four cases unaccounted for. Glancing about quickly, I found the courtroom vacant and hurriedly made my way back into Judge Austin's chambers where I found him laughing and chatting with Randy and a surprise visitor, my colleague Ron. Greeting me warmly, His Honor asked me to sit down, then continued on with the story he was telling when my appearance had momentarily interrupted him. Settling onto the edge of a black leather chair adjacent to his desk, I waited for him to finish, which soon occurred to the accompaniment of a fresh burst of laughter from Randy and Ron. Forcing a thin smile onto my lips, I waited until Austin's began to fade before attempting to catch his attention.

"Your Honor?"

"Yes, Matthew?"

"Well, Sir, I don't know exactly how to put this, but according to my calendar I've still got four clients that I haven't even spoken to yet—and I don't even know where they are!" I rolled out with concern, then watched as his smile suddenly broadened again just as it was about to disappear.

"Haven't you had enough for one day, Matthew?" he answered, his voice retaining a tinge of his prior laughter.

"Yes, Sir, I certainly have, but—"

"Relax," he interrupted with a chuckle. "Your compatriot here, Mr. Sindel, has already handled the situation." The expression of relief that instantly crossed my face seemed to pique his sense of humor as he continued. "Now I can't say that Ron did as well for his clients as you did for yours, Matt. But for a young fellow who doesn't read much because he spends all of his spare time getting into trouble with womenfolk, I guess he came out all right," traipsed his tease, His Honor tacking on a wink for emphasis. "But in all seriousness, fellas, I certainly do appreciate everyone's help today, it was one hell of a calendar for sure, even for Solina. And speaking of hell," he quickly added, standing up and slipping out of his robe, "I suppose that I better take these tired old bones on home to the missus, or I'm going to really catch some. But then you fellas wouldn't know about that, would you?"

Ron and Randy attempted witty responses to his good-natured jibe, which His Honor easily countered with a fatherly toned "Uh-huh, I've heard that excuse before." I just smiled and nodded my head at him as we left his chambers and strolled downstairs to the street. After a brief discussion, Ron and I decided to forgo our planned beer in favor of arriving home earlier and getting some rest. As we climbed into our cars, I called out to him in afterthought: "Hey—Ron?"

"Yeah, Matt."

"Thanks for the help this afternoon."

"Anytime, Matt ... anytime," he smiled, echoing my words to him at lunch.

"Okay ... see you in the morning," I grinned back at him across the twenty feet of parking lot that separated us.

"Yeah, sure," he chuckled, "I can hardly wait to get back to this hole."

Nodding, I swung my car door closed after his and followed him toward the freeway. A minute or so later, as I was about to turn on my radio, an ancient Talmudic aphorism suddenly entered into mind. "All beginnings are difficult," it whispered, "especially one you make by yourself alone." Steering more cautiously as I considered the message and its mysterious appearance, when I reached the freeway and turned north, an answer finally formed. "Difficult this is, for sure," I mouthed slowly, the trail of my twenty-week PD experience flashing across the windshield. "But the good news is, you're not alone—not really. You've got George and Robbie to teach you, and Ron's beginning to be an okay buddy too. So just hang in there, Matthew, my man. Just hang in there, and all can yet be well," I encouraged, smiling as I watched the sun sink further into the horizon.

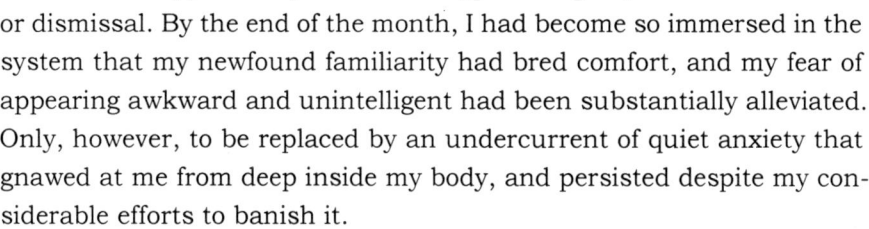

IV

TUESDAY PASSED IN MUCH THE SAME mode as had Monday, and in like manner Wednesday crept into Thursday, which by that time without separate personality slowly slipped into Friday. And linked to one another like elephants in a circus parade, the days then stretched into weeks as case after case disappeared by continuance, plea bargain, or dismissal. By the end of the month, I had become so immersed in the system that my newfound familiarity had bred comfort, and my fear of appearing awkward and unintelligent had been substantially alleviated. Only, however, to be replaced by an undercurrent of quiet anxiety that gnawed at me from deep inside my body, and persisted despite my considerable efforts to banish it.

When time permitted occasional glances outside Solina, the wider world did little to assuage the river of unease, often threatening to add tributaries and force a flood. The war in Vietnam slogged painfully onward, with ever mounting military and civilian casualties, while in neighboring China, late October brought the news that the army was now firmly in control as Mao's Cultural Revolution, which sought to purge his enemies and renew revolutionary zeal, had resulted in such widespread chaos and violence at the hands of the Red Guards that the army was the only force capable of restoring order. And what did this portend for China? For Vietnam? For America and the rest of the world? No one seemed to know. Just wait and see, was the word from the analysts. Meanwhile, in Czechoslovakia, after more bloodshed Alexander Dubček, the Czech Communist Party leader, was forced by the Soviet Union to retract his democratic reforms and agree to have Soviet troops stationed indefinitely inside Czech borders. So almost everywhere one looked on the international horizon, people were being slaughtered and harsh, all-knowing, and inflexible authority was ruling the day, I mused gloomily late at night when I couldn't sleep and thumbed through the *L.A. Times* and *Newsweek*, or stared with bleary eyes at the late-late news on TV. Even my beloved *Sports Illustrated* offered up mixed tidings. The good news: Bob Gibson, one of the first black players to integrate the St. Louis Cardinals, twenty-one long years after Jackie Robinson broke baseball's racial barrier, struck out seventeen Detroit Tigers to set a World Series record while winning the opening game. A triumph, however, followed just two weeks later by bad news from the Mexico City Olympic Games, when Tommie Smith and John Carlos, also black, and America's Gold and Bronze Medalists in the two-hundred-meter sprint, were expelled for raising their black-gloved, clenched fists in a black power salute on the victory stand in silent protest of American Society's treatment of blacks.

"One step forward, two steps back," I moaned morosely, tossing the magazine aside as another new day dawned and I renewed my search for sleep. My moan, however, soon graduated into a full-fledged groan when on November fifth Nixon, Mr. Tricky Dick himself, edged Hubert Humphrey, champion of the little man, and won the Presidency. "Can we never get rid of that mealy mouthed sonofabitch!" I squealed painfully at Robbie the morning after the returns were in. "I mean after lying about Voorhees to win a seat in the House, then imitating Joseph McCarthy in the Alger Hiss case and slandering Helen Gahagan Douglas to snake his way into the Senate, Mr. Slimeball was on a roll!" steamed my venom. "But we had'em stopped, Robbie. We did! The conniving bastard was finally dead and buried after losing to JFK in 1960 'cause on TV he looked like the shyster he is, and then losing the governorship to Pat Brown in sixty-two when Californians finally figured the asshole out—and now he's President?" I whined with incredulity mapped across my face.

"Better get used to it, Matthew," Robbie answered, shaking his head. "And you better get used to some heavy lifting in Nam too, 'cause the bombs will soon be dropping nonstop in the North—and probably in Cambodia too."

"You got that right," George chimed in, overhearing the commotion in the hallway and exiting his desk to join us. "And that's just for openers. Don't forget Civil Rights, and the permanent damage he can do with appointments to the Supreme Court!"

Instigating a fresh chorus of condemnation a second after George's posed catastrophe had sunk in, when Ron and Leon then arrived and instantly joined the confab, the vilification of Nixon, complemented by some creative cussing, swelled to new heights, only to quickly dissipate into a funk when our stream of adjectives finally ran out of steam and the morning's calendars called for our attention.

It rained the entire first week of November, and the weather matched my continuing mood of mild depression as I returned home on Friday evening around eight o'clock. I had been drinking at a topless bar with Ron, and the gin and tonic I had poured into an empty stomach had left me flushed, with a slight headache behind my right eye. As I approached the front door, I turned my face upward into the light drizzle that was falling, then shook my head and ran my hands over my face, stopping to massage my aching eyes. When I reached to insert my key into the lock, my hand brushed against a piece of paper fastened to the doorknob, which I assumed was one of the innumerable throwaways I received from local chicken and pizza vendors. Switching on the entry hall light, I glanced at it and noticed what appeared to be handwriting on a plain white piece of paper, and after forcing my glazed eyes to focus, I slowly turned the individual words over in my mind. "I'll be home alone tonight, and I eat late," they informed. "So if you're hungry, and can tear yourself away from the law for a couple of hours, come up for dinner—Stella." Turning on the living room lights, and without removing my raincoat, I sat down on my couch and reread the brief note several times before the chill draft entering my apartment reminded me that I had forgotten to close the front door. Arising, I hurriedly slammed it shut, and after draping my coat over a dining room chair, entered the kitchen and dialed information, then Stella. The phone rang three times before she answered it with a softly toned "Hello."

"Stella, it's Matt Harris," I chirped cheerfully, now alert. "How are you?"

"Fine, thanks. And how's Matthew Robert Harris getting along?"

"Okay, I guess—Listen, I got your note, and dinner sounds great if it's not too late."

"Late?" she chuckled. "Why it's only eight-thirty. Why don't you change into comfy clothes and give yourself a chance to unwind for a few minutes, then come on up." Not wanting to spend another evening alone, I was so pleased that for a moment I forgot to reply, forcing her to inquire as to whether I was still on the line.

"Yeah, sorry—a thought just flashed, that's all."

"No problem. But you ought to stop thinking so much, and try relaxing a little bit."

"You got that right, Stella. I'll be up around nine, okay?"

"Sure ... bye for now."

With the soft lilt of her voice echoing in my ear, I replaced the receiver on the wall, smiled happily for the first time since I had arisen, and strolled toward the bathroom to enjoy a hot, steamy shower. Afterward, with one eye on the clock, I slowly dressed in a sky-blue, crew-necked sweater and gray slacks. Then, after slipping into my favorite pair of boots, I pulled myself up off the edge of the bed, stretched to my full height, and carefully made a final inspection. Convinced that nothing more could be done to improve what Mother Nature had wrought, I stuffed my pipe paraphernalia into my pockets, withdrew a bottle of wine from a kitchen cabinet, and headed for Stella's apartment.

She interrupted her cooking to answer my knock, and greeted me warmly with a kiss on the cheek and a gentle squeeze of my shoulders. "C'mon in," she smiled. "Dinner's cooking, and will be ready in a few minutes." Following her into the kitchen, I set the wine down on a counter near the sink, then seated myself on a wooden stool adjacent to the stove. "Ahhh, Côtes du Rhône," Stella quipped, renewing her smile. "You have very good taste in wine, Mr. Harris."

"Well thank you, Miz Charles. I'm glad you like it." Reaching inside a drawer, she handed me a corkscrew.

"Here, open it and we'll have some before dinner—unless you want something stronger?"

"No ... wine's fine with me, Stella," I answered while beginning to open the bottle.

When the cork was freed, she produced two hand-painted goblets from a cabinet over the sink, which I carefully filled. And after toasting "To happy times," Stella quickly turned back to the pots on top of the stove, leaving me to lean back against the wall and study her as she stirred, then added pinches of spices, then stirred again. She was dressed in beige slacks that tightly hugged her long legs and firmly tucked behind, and a tee-shirt–thin lavender sweater that fastened down the front with tiny white buttons. Her long straight hair fell loosely to her slender shoulders, where it gently swayed to and fro as she leaned back and forth between the several pots, sniffing and tasting and fussing over her meal. And though I enjoyed only a profile of her face from my angled perch, it was more than enough to reaffirm my original assessment that Stella was one extremely beautiful woman.

"So, Matt, tell me what's new in your life," Stella resumed the conversation after covering one pot, then lifting the cover off another.

"Well, to tell the truth, not a hell of a lot?"

"Noo? ... I would have thought that by now you would have become the greatest, most famous criminal lawyer alive."

"Hardly," I chuckled. "But I certainly appreciate the vote of confidence, it's nice to have a fan club, even if there's only two members."

"You sound a bit down—problems?"

"Nooo ... Actually, the great awakening to which you alluded is scheduled to occur next week. AP and UPI are sending top-flight representatives to cover the event, and Walter Cronkite is going to cover the revelation live, with Eric Sevareid standing by at anchor control to analyze every minute detail for an audience estimated to be upwards of—"

"All right, Mr. Comedian," Stella intervened, grinning. "If you'll carry this dish into the dining room for me, I'll serve you dinner, and we'll just forget the law for now—okay?"

"Sure, Stella—glad to," I nodded, rising to meet her outstretched hands.

And seated at the oval-shaped mahogany table, I then watched with growing amazement as she proceeded to fill its surface with bowls and platters of various sizes and shapes until there was almost no space left. Magically, as if straight out of a King-Henry-the-Eighth banquet, there appeared paper-thin slices of lightly seared veal piled high upon one another and smothered in a creamy, white-wine sauce laced with onions and mushrooms, followed by candied sweet potatoes oozing butter, baby green peas mixed with corn and seasoned with pimento, a large green salad topped with tiny shrimp, and finally, thick slices of crusty French bread with sweet butter. For several moments I just sat there trying to take it all in, until Stella, having slipped into her chair, interrupted my trancelike stare.

"Something wrong, Matt?"

"Nooo ... There's nothing wrong at all except the way I'm dressed. Had I known, I would've come in black tie." Smiling, Stella took my plate, quickly filled it, and set it back down before me in one smooth motion.

"Now, eat!" she ordered sweetly. "Every time I see you, you look thinner and thinner."

"Yeah? ... You sound like my mother," I chuckled, reaching for my fork and tasting the veal. Stella matched my laugh, but I noticed that the smile in her eyes flickered, and I quickly added, "God, but it's delicious!

I mean if I could lawyer like you cook, great and famous would really be possible!"

"Surprised?" she asked, focusing her eyes directly into mine.

"No, not really," I trickled back. "I have the feeling that you can do anything well that you want to. I just wasn't expecting such a feast, that's all—and thanks for being such a good friend and brightening my day."

"Well you're very welcome," she smiled. "More wine?"

"Yes, please," I nodded, wondering as I reached to take the bottle from her if I might possibly tumble into those light-filled lavender pools. "How about you?" I managed to mutter reflexively.

"Sure," she purred, her eyes still fixed on me as I almost over-poured, then returned the bottle to its cradle.

"Matt?"

"Uh-huh?"

"You want to tell me about what's bugging you?"

"No ... I don't think so, Stella," I answered slowly after shifting my weight.

"Why not? Sometimes it helps to talk things out," she countered encouragingly.

"Yeah ... I know, and I appreciate it, honest. But you don't need to hear about my bullshit problems, and besides, I don't really understand myself what's bothering me."

"You sure?"

"Uh-huh. I'm feeling much better now anyway, and there's an ocean of delicious food to eat, and a lovely lady to talk with—so to hell with the law, and the poor troubled souls in Solina, and Matthew Harris too if that's all he can ever think of."

"Okay ... Okay, Mr. Matthew Robert Harris," she smiled broadly. "No more talk of law tonight, and this time I promise."

A promise that was kept, by both of us, as the rest of dinner was eaten leisurely amidst laughter and lighthearted conversation centering on Stella's recent trip to Mexico City. In fact, the chatter was so steady that we finished the Côtes du Rhône, and half a bottle of Burgundy for good measure, before we adjourned to the living room for dessert and coffee, which by that time I was sorely in need of. Seated next to Stella on the couch, I rested my head on its pillowy top and inhaled the faint scent of her perfume as we continued conversing, then drifted in and out of silence before picking up again, the sounds of the Doors' "Hello, I Love You" mixing with Bobby Goldsboro's "Honey" and the Beatles' "Hey Jude" on the FM station playing softly in the background.

"What did you think of Jackie marrying Onassis?" Stella interjected when the Supremes began crooning "Love Child" and the current silence had grown heavy.

"I don't know," I answered lazily. "I'm glad for her—not having to be alone, and having lots of security. But on the other hand, it just makes me miss JFK more."

"Yeah … me too," Stella murmured, her tone serious.

"You liked him too?"

"Uh-huh, Big Time, as you would say," she chuckled softly. "And speaking of not being alone, you been going out lately?"

"Oh, every once in a while," I fibbed, figuring that my visits to topless bars with Ron prevented me from being classified with Nixon.

"Anyone special?"

"Nooo … Why do you ask?"

"Oh, just curious—you know how women are." There was something undefinable hidden in the soft timbre of her voice that penetrated my stupor and gently nudged my defense system awake without actually triggering an alarm. Stalling, I stretched my arms out in front of me till the muscles were taut, then pulled myself up to a sitting position before answering.

"Stella," I smiled self-consciously, "the list of things that I don't know much about runs from here to hell and back, and women most definitely top the list. Sometime, when we both have a free year or two, maybe you could enlighten me a bit."

"Really?" she teased, arching an eyebrow.

"Uh-huh. At the risk of breaking our promise, it's the truth, the whole truth, and nothing but," I jested, reaching for my coffee cup, the movement of my head causing me to catch a glimpse of the clock on the far wall. "Hey, you know what?" I picked up. "It's almost one o'clock, and I promised to give you a hand with the dishes."

"Well, if you're going to do the dishes," she smiled after rising into a stretch of her own, "you're going to do them all by your lonesome 'cause I'm going to sleep—How about you?"

"Okay, you win," I nodded as we shuffled to the door. "And thanks again, Stella, for the lovely evening and the fantastic meal."

Gideon's Children | 73

"You're more than welcome, Matt, we'll do it again soon, so I can give you those tips you're looking for," she returned as we reached it and I stepped outside and turned to say good-night. "Now sleep tight, and pleasant dreams."

"You too," I whispered, then smiled with surprise after Stella suddenly leaned forward and kissed me lightly on the lips before squeezing the door shut. With the magic having seemingly occurred inside the space of a single second, as I meandered back to my apartment I wasn't sure it had actually happened, the only proof being the smile that lingered on my face till I slipped into bed and collapsed into sleep.

Awakening with a start just after six-thirty later that morning, I found myself lightly bathed in perspiration. Lanie had returned in my dreams once again, and I slowly nodded my confirmation of the reoccurrence as I nestled back into my pillow. She hadn't appeared for quite some time, almost six months, my memory calculated. But there she was again, in all her beauty and sweet innocence, and the whole happy-sad story had painfully played out yet another time in full color and stereophonic sound. Eight years ago, when I was in my first semester at USC, a friend of my sister Karen had fixed me up with Lanie when I needed a date for a fraternity party. A year younger than I, at seventeen she had matured late but fully during her senior year in high school, and like myself, having dated sparingly, was ripe for romance. Possessing a warm, outgoing personality, founded on a core of pure sweetness, along with a pretty face and a *Playboy* body, she was readily drawn to my curious mixture of shyness and burning intensity, as well as my collegiate status and future plans for law school and politics. Inside a month, love bloomed, and thereafter deepened steadily over the ensuing three years into a shared dream of a life together, nurtured as it was by an innate compatibility and the wondrous adventure of sex. Until, that is, the sacred socio-economic objectives of my domineering parents drove a serious spike through love's marriage plans—Fred and Rosalie objecting to Lanie's family's low economic standing, along with the sordid reputation of her entrepreneurial brother, and categorically refusing to supplement Lanie's prospective earnings while I attended law school. Only twenty-two, and having been raised to respect parental authority like God, I floundered in the face of dilemma, eventually capitulating by obtaining Lanie's agreement to work and wait while I was attending Boalt Hall in Berkeley. An arrangement which was doomed by Lanie's deep-rooted need for security, further heightened by long periods of separation that allowed doubt to magnify, it dissolved a year later when Lanie, having been introduced to and thereafter enthusiastically courted by a thirty-year-old engineer from one of the wealthiest Jewish families in Mexico City, persuaded herself that love could be celebrated more fully amidst comfortable circumstances—marrying her adoring beau and moving to Mexico City, where today she is already the mother of two sons.

Devastated, and wracked with shame, I had tucked the painful loss into the reservoir of guilt deep inside me and renewed my vow to work even harder to make myself into someone so special that the world would be forced to allocate a proper place for me. Fearing pain, during the remaining two years at Boalt, I retreated from the women I met at parties when their interest in me appeared serious, the only exception being Ronnie, whom I met in my last semester. An auburn-haired cutie, her high intelligence and active sense of humor overwhelmed my defenses, and a long-term relationship stood smiling on the horizon until this time religion intervened, Ronnie's devout Christianity making union with a Jew impossible.

Rules, rules, and more rules, marched a taunting thought as I twisted uncomfortably against the pillow, provoking guilt to visit next. "Is that why Lanie visited?" it queried in a razor-sharp tone. "'Cause Stella's tiny kiss triggered the fantasy of romance, and she needed to remind me that I don't deserve it, 'cause I can't stand up against authority? Is that why, Mr. Public Defender? Huh?" Mr. Blame chastised forcefully, causing me to grimace, then watch as the tortuous trail of recent courtroom experiences paraded into view. Slowly, the cases, interspersed with fragments of conversation, pranced past my wary eyes till the room became crowded with talking faces wearing expressions that were as varied as their voice tones, all finally blending together into a chorus of emotion that steadily grew louder and louder and louder. Pulling myself upright as a chill swept over the upper half of my body, I rubbed my hands up and down my forearms to warm the goose bumps away. Meeting only mild success, I climbed out of bed and made my way quickly down the hallway and out onto the front porch, where clad only in my pajamas, I dropped down onto the top step and began poring over the newspaper. For several minutes I read with maximum concentration, forcing a firm focus on each and every word to prevent thinking about anything else, and only when my feeling of extreme apprehension finally dissipated into one of simple uneasiness did I return inside for a steaming hot shower and a bite of breakfast.

An hour later, when my reading of the latest Supreme Court decisions failed to further alleviate the lingering anxiety despite the accompaniment of soft music from my stereo, I tossed my books and notes aside, and after quickly walking to my car, drove east without any designated destination. On LaCienega Boulevard, a large art show set up in a vacant parking lot caught my attention, and stopping, I accepted a free cup of coffee from a pretty teen-aged hostess who smilingly bade me welcome, then began browsing up and down the long rows of paintings. Halfway through the fifth row, my eyes were drawn to an enlarged black-and-white photograph bordered by a thin, black-wood frame. Focusing intently on the old man and woman, who, bent and bowed by age, were walking arm in arm up a narrow winding path through a forest, for several minutes I just stood and stared at the aged couple and allowed my mind to wander into their lives. Where had they met, and how had their love begun? I wondered. And how, through life's innumerable ups and downs, had they managed to nurture it? clicked my curiosity into high gear, rolling on to ask: What country did they live in? And were they farmers? Or merchants maybe? How about family? Did they have children, grandchildren, perhaps even great-grandchildren? And where, after all the years, still together and arm in arm, were they walking to? Finally, after sentiment seconded imagination's motion, I removed the prize from its stand and smilingly purchased it with only a fleeting thought as to how it would fit within my budget. Then, striding briskly to my car, I carefully cradled my treasure onto the passenger seat next to me, and drove eagerly south toward the home of my grandparents, whom I suddenly missed very much.

Grammy Esther greeted me at the front door with hugs and warm, wet kisses. "Matty, oh Matty!" she enthused. "How wonderful it is to see you—and just wait till your grandfather hears you're here!" The pure joy emanating from her reminded me that I had now entered the land of unconditional love, the one place where I was safe from judgment, where my strengths were emphasized and my weaknesses overlooked as if they didn't exist. And wrapping my arm around her waist as we walked toward the breakfast nook at the rear of the house, I happily chirped, "What's the old character up to anyway?

"Eating lunch—what else?" she quipped. "You know how he's always complaining about me starving him, don't you?"

"Oh, yeah, seems I've been hearing about that for some time now—like all my life. You know what, Grammy? He's been saying it for so long, that I think he's actually convinced himself into actually believing it."

"Oh, he does, Matty—he does!" she agreed with mock effrontery, smiling up at me as we reached the breakfast room, then stopped and stood silently in the doorway.

Grampy Max was seated in his favorite spot next to the window overlooking the garden, totally engrossed in the Sports Page that was spread out on the table in front of him. Oblivious to our presence, he was poring over the fine print of baseball box scores with a magnifying glass, interrupting himself only to reach for a piece of herring or bagel, which he slowly placed in his mouth while searching for the precise spot where he had left off. It was a sight familiar to me since I was a small child living next door, and I smiled as my eyes told me how good and well he looked as he neared his eighty-fifth year. When Grammy cleared her throat loudly to attract his attention, the gravelly noise startled him. Looking up at the two of us, he was momentarily puzzled, then broke into a broad grin.

"Well, well ... look what the cat drug in!" he offered through a deep chuckle. Returning his wide grin while noting how happy he was to see me, I slipped my arms around his neck and kissed him several times on his soft, smooth cheeks.

"Sit down, big boy—sit down and tell your old Grampy how you are. I haven't seen you in ages," he encouraged, motioning to the seat on his left where I had always sat to share countless meals and conversation with him.

"Ages, Grampy?" I teased, sliding down beside him.

"Well ... it seems like ages. Say, do you want something to eat? We've got herring and bagels, and eggs and peaches, and—"

"Hey, I thought that Grammy never gave you anything to eat—so where did all this food come from?" interrupted my query, a twinkle slowly forming in his eyes as he realized that I was poking fun at him.

"Well, even a blind chicken finds a worm sometimes," he grinned. "You just listen to your old Grampy, and watch out for women. 'Cause they rule with an iron hand, I tell you, and some of them with two iron hands. You gotta do this, and you gotta do that, and you can't ever do anything at all that you really want to, not even eat!" he mustered with mock outrage, looking at Grammy out of the corner of his eye to make sure that her face held the proper amount of disapproval, then winking at me. And when I returned it, his smile broadened and he slammed his fist down to emphasize how happy he was with his own humor.

"Listen, Grampy," I continued the repartee, shaking my head to feign concern. "Aren't you a little bit afraid that airing your accusations publicly is going to cause one of those iron hands to clamp down on you?"

"Nahhh ... I've got my lawyer here to protect me. You'll defend your old Grampy, won't you?"

"Uh-huh, you can bet on it," I assured him. "And with you as a star witness, no jury would ever convict you, 'cause you're way too cute!"

"Exactly," he nodded with satisfaction. "We're a team."

"That's for sure," I fed his widening grin. "Always have been, always will be!"

Having disappeared into the kitchen during our fun-filled chitchat, Grammy now returned carrying three Cokes to wash down the bagels and herring, and after parceling them out, slipped into a seat across from me. Grampy, who was just finishing up a sizeable bite, took a long swig, then reached for his pipe as he turned the conversation in a more serious direction. "Say, Matty," he inquired as he lit up. "Are you still enjoying your new job?"

"Yeah, Grampy, I am," I squirreled back after swallowing a final mouthful, then reaching for my own pipe to join him. "I've got an awful lot to learn, but I'm working hard, just like you always taught me, and I'm getting better at it. I haven't made anyone forget Clarence Darrow yet, but if I keep at it, you'll see—I'll be good enough to make you proud."

"I'm already proud of you," he shot back between puffs, "and I always have been ever since you were a little boy. You've grown into a fine young man—and smart too. And if you turn out to be half as good a lawyer as you are a grandson, you'll be the best there is—you hear?"

"Yeah, I hear you," I answered, smiling at his burst of affection for me, then widening it further when Grammy's added her approval. "But you wouldn't by chance be just a little bit biased, would you?"

"Well ... maybe just a little," he acquiesced. "But I'm right all the same. You'll see, you just listen to your old Grampy—I've never steered you wrong yet, have I?" My reply remained frozen on my tongue, when Grammy jumped into the conversation.

"No, you haven't," she answered for me, then resurrected her prior reservation. "But I don't see why he has to be the best criminal lawyer. What's wrong with being the best real estate lawyer, and making a living too?" she mouthed forcefully.

"Because Matty wants to be a criminal lawyer, that's why," Grampy trickled out slowly, measuring his words carefully out of respect for the sincerity of her concerns. "He's told you that a dozen times, and if you'd only listen, you'd understand what he's—"

"I listen," she insisted. "But a lawyer's a lawyer. What's such a big deal about being a criminal lawyer? I tell you, I worry about him down there—in whatever the name of that place is—working for a bunch of shvartzehs when he could have a nice safe job with lots of money in the business," Grammy rolled out fretfully, gathering steam. "And you know you worry too, and that it's just killing his parents!" she picked up after a second's pause to take in oxygen. "And what do you do? You encourage him! Why if anything happens to him—"

"Now, now," Grampy soothed, "don't get all worked up. Take a look— you see anything wrong with him? He's fine, and you're worrying about nothing, and so are Rosalie and Fred. You all just don't understand that—"

"And you do, huh?" Grammy interrupted, her voice filling with emotion. And before Grampy could reply and really stoke her fire, I went to his rescue.

"Grammy, listen to me, please," I mouthed sweetly. "You know that I tried hard to make a go of it in Dad's business, and I've explained to you before that he and I just don't see eye to eye on things—namely me. Now I realize that you only want what's best for me, but you also know all the trouble I had with him—and Mom too. So can't you see that I just can't be part of their world anymore?" The concern echoing from my voice and mapping my face instantly melted her resistance.

"All right ... okay, I see," she acquiesced. "You know that I don't really care what kind of lawyer you are, all I want is for you to be happy. It's just that they worry so about you, and it hurts me to see it," she offered, her green eyes beginning to tear as they looked at me, searching for some sign of possible compromise.

"Grammy, I understand—and I'm really sorry that you're worried and upset," I soothed, trying to make her feel better. "I'm sorry too, that Mom and Dad have to be upset because I do love and care about them. The problem is," I strained to explain, "that while I know they love me,

I also know that they don't like me. You see, Grammy, my values and goals are different than theirs, and like most people, they don't like what's different. You know I've tried to make them understand this, why, I've talked to them till I'm blue in the face. But Dad doesn't even really listen, and Mom just believes whatever he tells her. To them, their way of life is the only way of life—so I have to do what's best for me, and if that upsets them, then they'll just have to be upset. They'll get over it one of these days, and everything will be okay—you'll see, so please don't worry," I ended, smiling at her and nodding my head for emphasis.

Knowing deep down that she and Grampy had always encouraged me to be myself, and having previously expressed her observation that "the folks are putting on airs" after financial and social success had begun arriving, when both these facts emerged from her brain's cellar, Grammy had no choice but to accept them, and a confirming smile slowly curled out of the corners of her mouth. Then, still nodding her understanding, she arose from her chair, gently patted me on top of my head, and after collecting the dirty dishes, carried them into the kitchen. Returning shortly with coffee, she departed again to work in her garden, leaving Grampy and me to while away the remainder of the afternoon, schmoozing, smoking, and laughing about sports and whatever else happened into mind.

Around five o'clock, my announcement that I had to leave was met with a chorus of arguments, Nanny Lou, who had returned from her bus ride to MacArthur Park, joining in. Grammy and Grampy's housekeeper since my mother was seven, if one looked up the adjectives good and kind in the dictionary, Lena Louzader's sweet face would pop up, surrounded by exclamation points. Seated atop her slender frame, it featured sky-blue eyes that twinkled from behind her wire-rimmed glasses and accentuated the omnipresent smile advertising the warmth bubbling forth from her loving soul. A wonderful cook, whose specialty was the best apple pie in history, she asked little, gave a lot, and was universally beloved by all who were fortunate enough to know her. "So you can't stay for dinner, huh—what's her name?" she teased after tightly hugging me, adding that she had baked a fresh pie that very morning. But after I had assured her that she was my best girl, and always would be, and that I really did need to return to my studies since I had taken the day off, she relented in view of my promise to return soon, and my instant agreement to carry a heavy box out to the garage.

After placing it carefully in the designated storage cabinet, as I returned inside, I spied the large avocado tree standing to the right of the garage, in the corner of the backyard farthest from the house. And breaking into a smile, I turned, walked over to it, and gently patted its trunk. "Hello, old friend. How's life been treating you?" I inquired, then patted again as my eyes slowly scanned upward from its base to the branches where I had retreated so often as a child. Instantly picturing how the little boy, troubled and frightened, had climbed as far above the earth as he could reach, then lay hidden amongst the leafy branches and dreamed of whatever would soothe the terrible hurt of the moment, with equal speed, the distant memory stirred my current anxiety awake and turned my smile sour. Surprised, for several seconds, I toyed with the idea of climbing to the top, wondering if that would soothe my present pain as it had when I'd suffered a bloody nose in my first fist fight, or received poor grades in school and had planned to run away from home, or on numerous occasions when I'd fled the house seeking refuge from the harsh words of my father who seemed always to be reprimanding me for something I had done or failed to do. And stretching my arms upward in symbolic gesture, my fingertips grazed the lowest branch, before falling back alongside my body as I dropped my arms in disgust and bitterly chided myself.

"Matthew, old boy, are you ever going to stop being afraid?" I growled, feeling my stomach begin to shake with anger as my mind flooded with additional images of the little boy lying up in his tree, wiping away tears with his small chubby hands and crying to himself about how when he grew up it would be different. "You haven't answered, counsel," I taunted as the anger increased. "What's the problem, no defense? Or are you just so damned afraid that you can't even face up to what you're afraid of?" screeched my indictment, my father's face suddenly sliding into view. Searching it as I had on countless other occasions, I found the same steely strength, the same haughty pride born from a steady stream of successes, and the same unalterable cocksureness that silently bespoke an arrogant, all-knowing certainty about everything. Shuddering, and clasping my arms together across my chest as I peered deeper into the image floating before my eyes, some strange force pushed me to find something that I hadn't seen before. "What is it? What's new and different from that which you've known ever since you could remember? Huh, little boy?" I sneered, narrowing my eyes to focus my full power of concentration on the haunting features and reflected attitudes that filled me with such apprehension and abhorrence. Sixty silent seconds slowly passed as I stood there shivering in the deepening dusk, before a blue jay settled onto an overhead branch and the rustling of the leaves jarred me from my trance. Glancing upward, almost simultaneously the icy toned words that Steiggerman had hurled at me during the heat of the Williams Prelim echoed into ear. "Well, I suppose you're very proud of yourself, Mr. Harris," replayed the lecture, growing louder as it progressed, "taking this poor girl and making her cry with your stupid questions that haven't gotten you anywhere anyhow. Well, I've had enough, and I think you know what I mean!" sounded the diatribe, flowing onward as I now also watched His Honor's eyes bore into mine in an attempt to intimidate. "Now this Court has tried to be fair with you. I've allowed you all kinds of extra time to prepare, and then listened to your arguments no matter how cockamamie they seemed. Hell, I've been more than fair, I've even kicked a couple of Prelims for you that could've gone either way, and all I get for thanks is this dragged-out nonsense. Well, the honeymoon's over, Mister Harris, and if you want to stay on the right side of this Court then you have to play ball—do you understand me?" thundered the tirade to a close for the second time. And not content with a single reappearance, the stinging words echoed over and over again till they seemed to swarm about me like hornets from a disturbed nest, until suddenly, astonishingly, they floated over and surrounded my father's matching visage, now mocking me with full approval. Jesus, fucking-A Christ, that's right! roared enlightenment like a rocket, it all fits together: the intimidating words, the unalterable cocksureness, the arrogant, all-knowing attitude. And clenching my fists, I shook them furiously at the now smugly grinning merger of my father and Steiggerman, then mustered my defiance.

"Okay, you're right: I am afraid of you—and everyone and everything that's like you!" I growled. "'Cause you have all the answers, while I have only questions and feelings—which you, wallowing in your omnipotence, laugh at and call stupid and weak. So, afraid? You just bet I am. 'Cause when you guys group together to run the world, your power dishes out a whole lot of pain! Ohhh, yeah, you've got Big-Time money, and social networks, and political influence—and you're really good at using them to frighten and bully us lesser beings into submitting to your authority and doing what you want. You make the rules, and it's your way or the highway—right? Well, you just listen to me for a change, and listen good!"

I threatened, rage rushing each word at the glowering image. "Losing to you scares the holy shit out me. But guess what? Eventually the pain of surrender outweighs the fear, big as it is—And someday soon, somehow, someway, I'll manage to climb up off the mat and beat the living hell out you and everything you stand for! You hear me, assholes?" rumbled my fury to a close, oxygen suddenly in short supply.

Grammy, wondering what had delayed my return, finally investigated, her call out of "Matty? Where are you?" sharply cutting through the heavy silence that had descended. And after sucking in one final deep breath, I exhaled quickly, then ambled out of the shadows cast by the backyard lights she'd switched on and quickly assured her that all was well, that I'd just been visiting my old friend, Mr. Avocado Tree. Returning my smile, she motioned for me to follow her back inside, and after turning to wave good-night to the faithful companion who had rescued me once again, I trailed after her, then alongside till we reached the living room where Grampy and Nanny Lou were waiting. For a minute or two, the four of us traded goodbyes and urgings to "Take care" near the front door. Then, after hugs and kisses had been exchanged, along with my promise to each of them to return soon, I departed, feeling better than I had in days. Having finally focused on my failure to try a case out of fear of losing, as I steered my car toward home, the words *continue, dismiss,* and *plea bargain* spun round and round inside my head like records on a turntable, till finally I regurgitated them out loud, then burst out in sarcastic laughter. "Sounds like the Father, the Son, and the Holy Ghost—a regular, goddamned, unholy trio!" rumbled my wisecrack. Well, get ready, Solina—good and ready—'cause old chicken shit here is going to try some cases! And when he learns how—really and truly learns how—you're going to have one hell of a problem on your hands," bellowed my pledge into the traffic outside my window.

Still chuckling to myself after I had parked the car, as I approached the triplex I glanced up at Stella's window and noticed that her lights were on. For a moment I entertained the thought of knocking on her door and offering to buy her a drink. Rejecting it in the next instant, I tightened my hold on the new but already prized piece of art, and quickening my step past the pathway that led to her door, hastened up the one leading to mine. "One problem at a time, little boy," I nodded out in approval of my decision to resume reading cases as I pulled the door closed behind me. "One problem at a time."

On Wednesday of the following week, I was working the trial calendar in Division Five when the opportunity to honor my recently formed vow unexpectedly arrived. The Office's position on trying cases before a judge was that it amounted to legal suicide, "the equivalent of slowly pleading your clients guilty," as succinctly summarized by George and Robbie. "I've met damn few judges who even attempt to understand what reasonable doubt is," George opined, "and those few who actually do, wouldn't apply it in a courtroom with a cop and a DA present if their lives depended on it!" Robbie concurred wholeheartedly, and consequently, when handling misdemeanors in Judge Benjamin Burroughs' courtroom, our duties consisted of plea bargaining the cases that called for it, and withdrawing the jury waivers on the remainder and resetting them for jury trial.

Having worked for five consecutive weeks amidst the continuous chaos of Divisions Two and Four, I was thoroughly enjoying my vacation from their depressingly overcrowded calendars. And having fulfilled my responsibilities within half an hour after the afternoon session opened, when no Prelims trailed upstairs from Division Three, I took my leave and was strolling back toward the office to spend a relaxed afternoon reading cases, drinking coffee, and chatting with Marilyn, when I bumped into Roberts, Steiggerman's bailiff, in the hallway outside Division Four. Looking as if he could use a Valium, when I inquired as to why, he offered a machine-gun summary whose bullet points consisted of a calendar from hell designed by the Devil himself, the fact that Judge Austin had a trial under way in Division Two and couldn't assist, and the exacerbating problem of "that damned Sindel who's taking advantage of the situation by stalling every which way possible!" Nodding my head in feigned sympathy, after he rushed away toward the stairs leading down to the Clerk's Office, for several moments I just stood there puffing on my pipe while debating with myself. The tipping point arrived in short order, when my recently formed vow to try cases suddenly began vibrating and forced the conclusion that in my case discretion was most definitely not the better part of valor—and after quickly tapping out my pipe, I entered the courtroom in search of Ron.

When I found him in the jury room, he appeared remarkably relaxed, and in no hurry to address the crisis that Roberts had so artistically described. Introducing me to his client as "my dear friend and fellow Public Defender, Mr. Matthew Robert Harris" while lighting up a cigarette, he proceeded to put his feet up on the corner of the table and inquire as to how my day was going. The way my name sounded rippling off his tongue flashed a picture of Stella into mind, and I smiled at both of them as I advised that I was free, understood that he had a few problems, and was available to help out. "It's the pig sitting on his arrogant ass in chambers that has problems," he responded matter-of-factly, breaking into a grin. "But I do, ever so humbly, accept your kind offer, Sir—Here," he tacked on, pushing a stack of files toward a seat to his right, take a look at this pile of shit the DA's filed." And sliding into my appointed chair as Ron returned his attention to his puzzled client, for about an hour I read over five arrest reports and interviewed the corresponding subjects. Then, at five minutes to three, the window of opportunity occasioned by the chance meeting with Roberts, slowly began to open when Steiggerman, through his still frazzled bailiff, summoned us into chambers to plea bargain. Expecting only Ron and the DA, David Ludlow, His Honor was surprised to see me. "Well … well, my old friend, Mr. Harris," he dripped sarcastically. "And what, may I ask, are you doing here?"

"Well, Your Honor," I answered while slipping down onto the edge of the couch to the right of his desk, "when I ran into Roberts in the hallway, he advised that the calendar was unusually heavy today. And having finished up in Division Five, I thought that perhaps I could be of service here."

"Ohhh, I see … Well in that case the Court thanks you for helping out, Mr. Harris."

"The Court's welcome, Your Honor," I nodded, then watched as he relaxed backward into his cushiony chair and turned his attention first to Ron's cases.

Almost immediately, the battle between the two of them—which had been steadily growing more acrimonious since nine o'clock that morning—resumed, instantly raising the temperature to new heights.

Ron was not only being difficult in his plea bargaining negotiations, but obnoxious as well. Respectfully obnoxious, I noted from my observer's seat, but obnoxious all the same. And infuriated before the session was even five minutes old, Steiggerman alternated between sternly suggesting that Ron "be reasonable," and in an even louder voice threatening him with contempt if he "didn't settle down and watch his language!" In the midst of this turmoil, David Ludlow, the DA, sat glued to his chair like a disinterested third party. No trace of emotion appeared on his heavy, square-shaped face, and when prodded, he responded to Ron or Steiggerman by mechanically interjecting the "People's position" into the debate on a given matter, but without actually entering the fray. Speaking in his usual monotone, and so slowly that the words seemed to crawl off his tongue, his contribution did little to settle the cases under consideration or infuse the hostile atmosphere with further fire. Recalling that I had first been introduced to Dave after the conclusion of a Prelim during which Robbie had systematically chewed him and his case into little pieces, the impression that lingered was one of amiability mixed in equal parts with immobility, as everything about him conveyed slowness. He walked slowly, talked slowly, got in and out of a chair slowly, and even shook hands slowly while nodding his massive head at the same sluggish rate. Watching him for a protracted period of time, I had concluded, left one with the feeling of having observed a large, prehistoric snail. Since that time, however, I had learned from my brethren that while Dave was by far and away the most conservative of the DAs stationed in Solina, he was also the only one who was utterly devoid of viciousness—and both George and Robbie had further informed that it was unwise to underestimate him, because underneath that tortoise shell lay a high level of intelligence.

My brief mental meandering was suddenly aborted, when Ron and Steiggerman reached agreement on a case and Ron headed back outside to obtain his client's approval. Turning his attention to me, His Honor asked what I had in mind on the Cedeno case. During his interview, Joseph had admitted to me that he had imbibed too much in a local bar, and thereafter during a disagreement with a fellow patron had broken a table and three chairs, as well as struck the bartender who had intervened. So, without any plausible defense available, I suggested that in exchange for dismissing the more serious battery and malicious mischief charges, my client would plead guilty to the lesser charge of disturbing the peace, and pay a small fine along with making total restitution for the damage he caused. Because Joseph was employed and could make payments over time, Steiggerman reluctantly agreed, and when Dave nodded his assent, the Cedeno case quickly passed into history. Three others followed in similar fashion, before Ron returned and informed Steiggerman that his client had refused the plea bargain. Instantly, color flushed up the sides of His Honor's neck and flooded into his face as he leaned forward to glare at Ron. Without speaking to him however, Steiggerman suddenly directed his attention back to me, fuming, "All right, Mr. Harris—Let's finish up your cases before I deal with Sindel here. Now, what do you want to do with your drunk case?"

"Well, Your Honor," shuffled my answer, "I feel that this case ought to be dismissed."

"Dismissed?"

"Yes, Sir."

"What the hell do you think you're doing, pulling some of Sindel's shit on me?" rocketed his response, the matching volume causing me to hesitate before replying.

"Your Honor, as far as I know, Mr. Sindel has nothing to do with this case. I, alone, represent Mr. Ginther, and it is my opinion, alone, that the case should be dismissed for the following reas—"

"Alone is the right word, Mr. Harris!" he exploded, shaking a finger at me. "'Cause you're the only one here, with the exception of Sindel, who's crazy enough to suggest such a damn fool thing! Now you listen to me, and you listen real good: Your drunken bum of a client has already done twenty-six days in jail, so if you cop him out, I'll sentence him to forty-five days and give him credit for the time he's already served. Now take it or leave it!"

"My client elects to leave it, Your Honor," marched my answer in a firm tone. "And, Your Honor, Sir, I'd like to advise you that I'm not hard of hearing—so in view of the fact that I'm sitting approximately six feet away from you, I think it's totally unnecessary, as well as equally unbefitting, for the Court to yell at me. I would remind the Court that as an attorney I'm an officer of the Court, and as such, am entitled to at least some small measure of common courtesy. Moreover, Sir," I tacked on without a pause for oxygen, anger seeping from the well deep inside me to harden my tone, "it's not a crime, or any other form of misconduct, to respectfully disagree with a judge, especially in chambers during a plea bargaining conference—so there's absolutely no justification whatsoever for your abuse, and everyone here, including you, knows it!"

Stunned by my response, Steiggerman unconsciously nodded as amazement slowly spread across his face, the fury he discovered in my eyes doing little to diminish it. Five full seconds of heavy silence slid by before he settled back into his chair and forced a grin onto his reddened face.

"Well ... well ... a bit sensitive, aren't we?" oozed his response finally. When I failed to reply, but just sat there meeting his eyes head on, he gradually sat up and leaned forward onto his elbows. "Okay" he nodded. "Now what does the Public Defender suggest that I do to soothe his hurt little feelings?"

"Nothing, Your Honor, since you've stopped shouting," I fired back at his sarcasm. "But on behalf of my client, I will accept the Court's apology for calling him a drunken bum when the Court's never even laid eyes on him—and moreover, hasn't been presented with a single shred of evidence as to his guilt on this or any other charge."

"Well, Mr. Harris, this Court isn't in a very apologetic mood at the moment," he rushed at me, straightening up, the bullying tone suddenly returned. "But I tell you what we're going to do—we're going to try the case. Now how does that sound?"

"Just fine, Your Honor—just fine," rolled my reply reflexively, butterflies surfacing, but fear of failure no longer in control.

"Well, good! And let me tell you one more thing, Mr. Public Defender: If you lose, I'm going to give your client ninety days! Now how does that sound?" tramped his final threat.

Deciding to not even acknowledge it, I asked instead if I could be excused so that I might confer again with my client before the trial commenced. His "Certainly, Mr. Harris—by all means" was delivered with a notable loss of steam, and as I departed I noted also a tinge of surprise creeping across his face as he instructed Roberts to order up the jury panel.

When I reentered the courtroom, I immediately headed for the drinking fountain to relieve the dryness pervading my mouth and throat. As the water settled into my stomach amidst the now multiplying butterflies, my mind flooded with assorted bits and pieces of information I had learned from George and Robbie. And wondering if I could even remember to put into actual practice all of my relatively small storehouse of knowledge, I pulled my trial notebook out of my briefbag for security's sake, then decided to attend to more pressing matters and headed for the men's room where I relieved my aching bladder, then slowly massaged my flushed cheeks with cold water. As I dried them, Grampy Max's smiling face suddenly appeared in the mirror, his wise words simultaneously echoing into ear. "Just do your best," instructed the lesson I had first learned at age seven while learning baseball: "Always give it your all, and if you don't get a hit the first time at bat, think how to improve your best for your next chance. And remember—as long as you try with all that's in you, you'll never have to be sorry," trailed the teaching I'd adopted, then pursued all my life. "Okay, Grampy," I whispered back, a thin smile emerging on my lips, "I remember. Win, lose, or draw, Fred Ginther will get everything I've got. And thanks again," I tacked on with a wink as I turned and ambled back to the courtroom to pore over my notes on picking a jury.

Ten minutes later, the entryway doors swung open and the jury panel methodically filed into the courtroom. Studying them from my seat at the counsel table as Bailiff Roberts steered them into the section of the audience nearest the jury box, I noted that they appeared to be a predominantly middle-aged group, and one that featured more men than women. Turning back to my notes before they noticed that I was observing them, as I switched to the arrest report and began rereading it for the third time, a vague uneasiness settled inside me, and halfway down the first page I paused to ponder what it was about the panel that disturbed me. It wasn't until Fred Ginther was led into the courtroom and seated next to me, however, that it struck home: Not one member was black. In a judicial district whose citizenry was seventy-five percent black, not one single solitary member of the panel was! thundered a thought, Well I'll be goddamned! following so closely it could be cited for tailgating. So what do I do about it? entered next. And as Steiggerman emerged from chambers, took the bench, and greeted the jury panel, I furiously searched through the large black binder holding my case notes for help.

Nothing jumped up and waved a red flag, but the many hours I'd pushed tired eyes over countless Supreme Court decisions weren't entirely in vain either. So when Roberts then directed the first twelve members of the panel to be seated in the jury box, I rose to my feet and advised Steiggerman that I had a motion to make, best heard out of the presence of the jury. The look of suspicion which jumped onto his face deepened as he contemplated what kind of mischief I was up to. But after explaining to the jury in an overly apologetic tone that "occasionally unusual matters occur which unfortunately cause some slight inconvenience," and expressing his hope that they would understand, His Honor directed Roberts to transfer the panel back to the jury assembly room.

"Well, now, Mr. Harris," flowed Steiggerman's next directive sharply after the entryway doors closed, "let's hear your motion."

"Thank you, Your Honor, I appreciate it. And my motion, Sir, is combined with a challenge—which is to say, Your Honor, that I am moving this Court to dismiss the entire jury panel on the grounds that as it is presently composed of only members of the Caucasian race, it cannot and therefore does not afford my black client a jury trial as prescribed by the Sixth and Fourteenth Amendments to the United States Constitution." Whatever it was that he possibly expected from me, it wasn't the proposition that I had presented. Inside a second it registered that I had raised a valid issue, with sensitive political overtones to boot. And as the realization fully settled, consternation replaced condescension on Steiggerman's face, the sudden shift causing him to delay for several more uncomfortable seconds before inquiring as to whether I had any authority in support of my motion.

"Yes, Your Honor, I do," ambled my answer as my brain hummed into overdrive trying to weave whole cloth from the threads of my various readings. "I feel confident that this Court is aware of the large number of U.S. Supreme Court Cases that interpret the Sixth Amendment to the Constitution, so I won't waste the Court's valuable time by listing them all, but would instead call your attention to one highly interesting fact that is crucial to the issue facing us here today. Consider if you will, Sir," I mustered with conviction, "that approximately seventy-five percent of the populace that comprises this judicial district are members of the black race, and yet not one, single, solitary member of the jury panel is! Now, as your Honor knows, the Sixth Amendment, which guarantees my client the right to a jury trial, also provides that this jury be comprised of his peers—which the Supreme Court has defined as a representative cross-section of the community. Now that being the law, Your Honor, I would submit that as my client is black, and lives in a community where three out of four residents are black, it is obvious that the representative-cross-section-of-the-community requirement compels the jury panel to contain a significant number of black peers for my client to choose from in selecting the jury that will try him. Therefore, Your Honor, in that our panel, which is one hundred percent Caucasian, clearly fails to meet the Constitutionally prescribed jury of his peers, it should be dismissed!" I concluded, then paused for added emphasis.

"Not only that, Your Honor," I picked up when the frown mapping Steiggerman's face told me I had him pinned in a corner, "but the long line of Supreme Court cases I previously referred to also held that where a clearly defined and recognizable group of persons is systematically excluded from the jury system, then invidious discrimination occurs—which not only further violates the peers provision of the Sixth Amendment, but also the equal protection and due process mandates of the Fourteenth Amendment as well!" I padded my argument, fixing my eyes directly into Steiggerman's as I zeroed in on the target panel.

"Your Honor, it seems to me, and I submit to you, Sir, that in Solina, where seventy-five out of every one hundred persons are black—I repeat, seventy-five out of every one hundred—that it's inconceivable for it to be a mere coincidence that on our jury panel of more than one hundred persons, not one, single, solitary one of them is black! But that being most definitely the case, Your Honor, it's quite clear that it fails to satisfy the Sixth Amendment's requirement that a jury be composed of a representative cross-section of the community—and on that ground alone, as well as the two fundamental violations of the Fourteenth Amendment, I ask this Court to dismiss the subject panel! Thank you, Your Honor," I tacked on quickly before falling silent.

There was no immediate reply, and for a full fifteen seconds we just stared at each other across the soundless gulf, which seemed to grow more hollow with each time-tick. Still searching for a way out, Steiggerman chose to focus on my reference to invidious discrimination—which I'd added only to worry him—rather than my cross-section of the community argument. "Mr. Harris!" he finally responded with great indignation. "Are you accusing this Court, or some other part of the Solina Judicial District, of tampering with the jury panel selection process?"

"No, Your Honor, I'm not," crawled my answer carefully. "While in my opinion, the composition of this panel is strange indeed considering the population make-up of Solina, and while I believe that the overwhelming odds against such a selection occurring naturally would allow the Court to find invidious discrimination at work, no concrete evidence exists to prove it. However, Your Honor, it doesn't matter—because whether the jury panel was properly or improperly selected, it doesn't alter one iota the simple fact that as presently constituted in its one hundred percent

Caucasian form, it deprives my client of his Sixth Amendment right to a jury composed of a representative cross-section of the community, and therefore should be dismissed!"

"Very well, Mr. Harris," His Honor returned in a more tempered tone, a thin smile playing on his lips. "You've made some strong arguments on behalf of your client, which are now on the record. However, since the Court Rules for this judicial district require that pretrial motions be submitted to the Court and opposing counsel a minimum of one week prior to trial in order to allow a thorough hearing, and since you've failed to comply with these rules, your motion is denied for that reason."

"Your Honor, Sir!" exploded my response, deep-seated anger surging to inflame my tone before I could exercise control. "Until approximately one hour ago, I had no idea whatsoever that I would be charged with the responsibility of trying this case, and no one knows that better than you! So in view of the circumstances, and the absence of any objection to my motion by the District Attorney, I think it's grossly unfair of the Court to deny my motion on a procedural technicality when justice demands otherwise!"

"All right, Mr. Harris, that's enough!" Steiggerman punched back. "This Court does not consider its rules mere technicalities, and I'm warning you that if you address this Court again in a similar tone of voice, I'll hold you in contempt. Your motion's denied, and that's final! Do you understand?" he blazed then waited impatiently for several seconds till I replied.

"Yes, Your Honor—It was not my intention to offend the Court, but only to impress upon it to the best of my ability how deeply I believe in my motion. I do apologize, however, if the Court construed my conviction otherwise."

"Very well, Mr. Harris, I accept your apology," he nodded, his anger defused. "Now, is there anything else before we continue?"

"Just one item, Your Honor," I assured calmly, "I would respectfully request that the record reflect my client's continuing objection to the prospective proceedings in its entirety on the previously stated grounds and argument in support thereof."

"Very well, Mr. Harris, the clerk will so note the Defendant's objection on the docket," he shrugged, a smug smile slithering onto his face. "And now we will proceed to trial."

Aware that I had created a solid record for appeal purposes, it was small consolation when contrasted against the reality that if I lost the trial, Fred Ginther would have finished serving his ninety-day jail sentence at least nine months before an appeals court would rule on the matter. And hiding my disappointment behind a thin grin as I reseated myself at counsel table, I reminded myself to focus forward so that I could improve at my next at-bat.

Five minutes later, the panel returned to their seats in the audience, and twelve members—ten men and two women—were seated in the jury box. Facing them, Steiggerman, wearing a fatherly smile and speaking in a matching tone of voice, proceeded to introduce both counsel and the various other court personnel, then carefully presented his preliminary instructions. Concluding his remarks in a sugary tone, it carried over to his "You may now *voir dire*, Mr. Harris," and in a single, transformational moment, the second inning had softly but nervously begun.

Nervously, indeed. For with my anger having retreated to a safe distance, the vacuum allowed the application of CPR to the butterflies in my stomach—and buoyed by new life, they promptly proceeded to test their wings with a flight pattern that would do justice to a stunt flier in an aerial circus. True, I had managed to harvest fragments of knowledge from my brain's backyard and cobble them together into cohesive arguments in support of my defeated motion, but the procedure was similar to that involved in a Prelim and the familiarity had allowed some degree of comfort. Now it was Novice-Time, and although thirty-five feet is not a very long distance, the forty-mile trip to my apartment seemed much shorter as I shuffled over near the railing to the jury box and smiled at the twelve persons who instantly morphed into the most important people on earth. To my amazement, words emerged from the desert inside my mouth when I opened it to reintroduce myself as Fred Ginther's attorney, and thereafter flowed smoothly for several minutes as I began my inquiry by focusing on the traditional subjects of age, education, occupation, and family. Then, having momentarily grounded the butterflies, I turned to matters closer to the focal point of the trial.

"Mr. Haskins—Do you ever take a drink, Sir?" I asked as casually as I could muster. Lawrence Haskins, a forty-six-year-old currently unemployed aeronautical engineer who was married with three children, blinked several times before answering "Yes, Sir," while breaking into a faint smile that I immediately returned.

"And would it be fair, Sir, to describe your drinking habits as that of a social drinker?"

"Yes, Sir."

"Do you ever have a cocktail when you come home from work?"

"Yes, Sir ... occasionally."

"What does occasionally mean to you, Sir?"

"Well ... I guess maybe two times a week."

"All right ... And do you ever enjoy a cocktail at lunch?"

"Well, I have, but very rarely, Sir."

"Okay," I nodded. "Thank you, Mr. Haskins, I appreciate your candor. Now how about you, Mrs. Lippitt? Do you ever take a drink, ma'am?" I continued, now focusing on the silver-haired grandmother of seven, who appeared uncomfortable with the question.

"Only at parties," she answered without hesitation in her naturally soft tone of voice, her facial expression still reflecting unease.

"Do you see anything wrong with a person taking a drink more often?" I then explored, my mind flashing on several reasons for her discomfort, but unable to come to any conclusion.

"No, Sir."

"Then you wouldn't think it improper for a person to have a couple of martinis for lunch?"

"No, Sir—but I wouldn't myself."

"No, ma'am, I didn't think you would," I smiled at her. "But how about if you got some seriously bad news that made you extremely nervous—might you have a couple of drinks to ease the tension and make you feel better?"

"Well, no ... but I could understand it."

"Me, too, ma'am—thank you. And how about you, Miss Reese?" jumped my interrogation to the second row, bypassing a stone-faced Peter Thatcher in favor of the only other female currently in the box. "Might you take a couple of drinks to ease extremely strained nerves from receiving terr—"

"M-i-s-t-e-r Harris, let's hold off here, please," Steiggerman intervened, cutting me off in mid-syllable. "I can't see the relevancy of you exploring the personal drinking habits of every prospective member of the jury, so unless you have an explanation for your overly curious and embarrassing questions, I think it would be best if you moved on to other areas."

Slipping out slowly, His Honor's carefully camouflaged reprimand was delivered in the same sugar-coated, overly concerned tone of voice that he had used to comfort Louise Petrie and assist the prosecution's case during her testimony in the rape Prelim, and inexperienced and unsure of myself as I was, I immediately understood that his suggestion was calculated to make the jurors dislike me for improperly prying into their private lives. Squelching the anger that instantly resurfaced, I decided to see if two could play the prejudice game—and after turning halfway around so that I could face him and still maintain contact with the prospective jurors, I responded humbly but firmly.

"Your Honor, Sir," I opened unhurriedly, "I'm a bit confused by your implication that my questions to the prospective jurors are not relevant and somehow improper by way of being too personal and therefore embarrassing. My client, Mr. Fred Ginther, is charged with appearing in a public place so intoxicated by alcohol that he couldn't care for his own safety and welfare, and in that these ladies and gentlemen are going to decide whether that was true beyond a reasonable doubt, their attitudes and experiences in connection with alcohol seem highly relevant to me. In fact, if I didn't ask them about it, Sir," I opined with swelling sincerity, "I wouldn't be representing my client, which you know is my sworn duty. And while I can't speak for them, I'm fairly confident that if any one of these fine citizens found themselves in Fred's place, that they'd want and expect me to check out the attitudes of the people who are judging them. What if a juror was a member of a temperance organization? Would that be fair?" I posed, pausing briefly for emphasis, and noting that three out of the twelve prospects were shaking their heads in agreement, while the others appeared neutral, but listening carefully.

"Now as for my questions being overly curious and embarrassing," I picked up, "I didn't ask them about their sex lives, Your Honor, that would be highly improper in this case. However, I only asked about their attitudes on drinking, and as nicely as I know how. So I don't understand how there's any problem at all, 'cause I'm just representing my client to the best of my ability, Sir. But if the Court is ordering me not to inquire further on this subject, then I will, of course, comply." I ended, my eyes joining those in the jury box to collectively fix on Steiggerman while awaiting his response. It arrived only after he cleared his throat, then forced his best smile to appear.

"Now … now, Mr. Harris … You misunderstood me," he oozed unctuously in retreat. "I'm not ordering you not to pursue the subject—merely suggesting that you not belabor the point, that's all."

"Very well, Your Honor, I thank the Court for making it clear that

I wasn't doing anything wrong," I oozed right back at him, feeling that for the moment I was holding my own in the Battle of Bias, but still concerned that the prospective jurors were learning that the judge was suspicious about my tactics. It was only a tiny seed of distrust that His Honor had planted, but I needed to be careful not to nourish it, I reasoned. So, when I resumed my examination on the drinking issue, I continued along the same line but reduced by half the number of questions I put to the various prospects—and a half hour later, after I'd thoroughly explored with them the issue of whether or not anyone would have a problem applying the concepts of presumption of innocence and reasonable doubt, I felt that a good rapport had been established between us. Then, buoyed by that positive development, I strayed from the safe ground of traditional subjects and wandered into territory that was sensitive and therefore dangerous, but also necessary.

"Ladies and gentlemen," I began with a smile. "We've discussed quite a number of issues here this afternoon, and I only have one more to present to you. I feel that it's an important one, so I hope that you will all bear with me for just a few minutes more," I soothed, moving up to where I almost touched the jury railing. "Mr. Waylie," I then probed gently. "Have you noticed that my client, Fred Ginther, is a member of the black race?" Tall, lean, and graying heavily at age fifty, Donald Waylie snuck a quick glance at Fred, then raised his eyes to meet mine.

"Yes, Sir, I have," he nodded.

"And, Sir, do you feel that you can give him the same open-minded and fair hearing that you would give a member of the Caucasian race?"

"Yes, Sir."

"Okay ... Now do you feel that black people's drinking habits and their attitude about alcohol in general is different than say ... yours or mine?"

"No, Sir, I don't."

"Mr. Waylie—have you ever heard the expression, you can't give firewater to an injun, or words to that effect?"

"Yes, Sir, I have," he nodded, a thin smile creeping onto his lips.

"You know, Mr. Waylie," I pursued, returning his nod, "that phrase is generally considered to be an expression of the white man's prejudice against people of a different color—Do you really feel free from this type of feeling?"

"Yes, Sir ... I ... think so," he answered more deliberately after first hesitating for three or four seconds to think.

Noticing that Gloria Reese, seated in the upper row and three seats to the right, had shaken her head ever so slightly in a negative fashion during Waylie's answer, I followed up from a different angle. "Miss Reese, just like Mr. Waylie, most of us don't consciously think of ourselves as being prejudiced—but being human, sometimes a bias sneaks into our subconscious without our intentionally placing it there. So with that in mind, do you feel that you can give Mr. Ginther the same open-minded and fair hearing that you would give a member of the Caucasian race?"

As she parted her lips to answer, Steiggerman intervened before a single word emerged, and this time the sugar had disappeared from his voice. "Mr. Harris!" he reprimanded in his customary steely tone, his blue eyes shooting daggers. "I've tried to be patient with you and the manner in which you've conducted your *voir dire*, but you have simply gone too far! Race has nothing to do with this case, and I feel confident that you realize that. So if you'll stop and think about what it is you're trying to do, I believe you'll move on into other areas without my having to order you to do so! Do you understand?"

For a fleeting instant, I considered approaching the bench and punching the sonofabitch in his fucking mouth. Instead, having glanced at the prospective jury and noticed an air of apprehension settle over them, I considered my options at warp speed. Feeling that to refuse His Honor's directive, and allow him to threaten me with contempt, would seriously injure the just established rapport with the prospective jurors, yet not wanting to back off the race issue and have them believe I'd buckled because I knew I'd committed a serious wrongdoing, I decided to walk the tightrope of compromise.

"Your Honor, Sir," I returned in a voice that quivered from the mixture of anger and anxiety that coursed through me like electric current. "I sincerely regret that the Court feels the way it does. I have been conducting my *voir dire* to the very best of my ability, and while race may not be directly involved in this case, indirectly it may well be the single most important factor giving rise to it!" I offered, my voice cracking ever so slightly. "Moreover," I continued after a moment's pause, "it's my understanding of the case law on the subject, that it is perfectly permissible for counsel to explore this area on *voir dire*—So would the Court be so kind as to explain why, for example, *Stephenson versus the Superior*

Court, and companion cases, are not applicable here today?" I posed ever so politely.

"Because I don't read them the way you do, that's why!" Steiggerman replied confidently, knowing that while he would be reversed on appeal, as was the case with my jury panel motion, it was highly unlikely that the PD's understaffed Appellate Department would even bother in view of the fact that if I lost the trial, by the time the Appellate Court handed down its ruling, Fred Ginther would have long since served his sentence.

"Well, that's most unfortunate, Your Honor. But in that the Court has indicated that if I pursue the subject of race it will order me to cease, I will defer to the Court—requesting however, that defendant's continuing objection be noted on the Court's docket for purposes of appeal!" I tacked on with feigned confidence, hoping that the prospective jurors might consider the acerbic give-and-take to have resulted in the proverbial Mexican standoff.

"Very well, Mr. Harris, so noted. And I'm sorry that you don't see the error of your ways, but the Court appreciates your cooperation nonetheless," Steiggerman returned, getting in the last word, and still trying to camouflage his effort to discredit me by coating his voice with a thick layer of sincerity.

Whether or not His Honor's actions were fooling the prospective jurors, or might instead have placed me in a sympathetic light, were questions the answers to which I couldn't glean from reading their faces as I returned my full attention to them and discovered a virtual blank slate. No hostility showed. But no smiles, or a hint of friendliness either. Pure Switzerland is all I could discern. And already toying with the idea of concluding my *voir dire* in view of the fact that I hadn't elicited any answers that would allow me to challenge any of the prospects for cause, and was precluded from probing further on any meaningful subject, I decided that for the time being, neutrality was the best I could hope for, thanked the group for its willingness to serve and their careful attention, and informed Steiggerman that I had no further questions at this time. Pleased, his smirky smile quickly disappeared when I then added that I was exercising two of my peremptory challenges and excusing from service Mr. Peter Thatcher and Miss Gloria Reese. Although concerned that the latter choice left me with only one woman on the prospective jury, still, Gloria's head-shake while I was discussing the racial issue with Donald Waylie stuck in my memory and filtered into instinct that compelled such a decision, limited as it was by my lack of experience.

The hour that followed featured an exercise full of futility. Beginning after two new members of the panel were seated in the jury box, for thirty minutes, Ludlow, in his characteristic methodical monotone, droned an air of somnolence into the proceedings by failing to ask a single question that I had not previously presented—the only factor preventing his *voir dire* from being a total waste of time being the surprise ending wherein Dave utilized two of his peremptory challenges, visibly irritating His Honor. With four new prospects now at hand, for the next twenty minutes I slowly and deliberately re-explored the areas of age, occupation, and education for the sole purpose of seeing if I could provoke Steiggerman into cutting me off from inquiring about even safe subjects so as to further expose his bias to the panel. When he failed to swallow the bait, however, I then unleashed the final two arrows from my arsenal and exercised my remaining two peremptory challenges. Exasperated, His Honor constrained himself to glowering at me as I returned to my seat at the counsel table and glanced at my watch which read five minutes past five. Next up in the batter's box, Ludlow, taking an obvious Technicolor cue from Steiggerman's reddened complexion, asked only three or four perfunctory questions before advising him that he accepted the jury as presently constituted. In that the last two additions, Mssrs. Herman Sears and Carl Wilkerson, appeared to be more lively and in possession of attitudes less starchy white and conservative than the others, I also indicated my acceptance. And after breathing a discernible sigh of relief, Steiggerman immediately had the clerk officially swear the jury into service, then promptly trailed the case to nine o'clock the following morning.

After saying good-night to Fred Ginther, who thanked me for "trying so hard," I quickly stuffed my notebooks into my briefbag and hurried from the courtroom in search of a consultation with George and Robbie. To my considerable dismay, they had already left the office, as had Ron and Leon, so unfortunately had only myself to confer with on the long ride home. For the first ten miles, I just listened to music on the radio and allowed the flow of adrenaline to slowly ebb and finally cease. Then, relaxed and suddenly drained all at once, I carefully replayed the events of the afternoon. Reasoning that as amateurish as my performance had been, Ludlow's lackluster personality hadn't hit a home run either, I concluded that if Steiggerman's efforts to turn the jury against me had been less than totally successful, which seemed to be the case, well then ... maybe, just maybe, there might be some hope in spite of the fact that the jury was all-white. That considerable handicap however, instantly caused Mr. Worry to reappear, and I was about to run the arrest report back through my mind for the tenth time in search of some weakness in it, conversely adding some strength to Fred Ginther's radically different version of the incident in question, when I caught sight of Stella as I turned onto Doheny Drive. Dressed in a pale-lemon pants suit that accentuated the lines of her lovely body, she was standing where she always stood when waiting to be picked up—and all thoughts about analyzing anything instantly evaporated in response to her wave as I hastened to park so that there might be time for a brief chat before she departed.

"Hi, there! ... What's new?" she smiled warmly as I crossed the street.

"Not too much, pretty lady—what about you?" I bounced happily back when I reached her, grinning widely as my eyes inhaled her like a suddenly sighted oasis. Hers faded slightly as she got a closer look at me.

"You look exhausted!" she emphasized with a head-shake.

"Well ... I got this here thing called a trial going on, and I—"

"The first one?" she enthused.

"Uh-huh, Numero Uno, all right."

"So, are you very worried about it?" she followed, concern now lapping over the edges of her prior excitement as she studied my face.

"Who ... me?" I gibed. "Now why the hell would I be worried? You don't think that I let little things like the fact that I don't have the faintest idea of what I'm doing bother me, do you?"

Accompanied by an exaggerated expression of mock horror, my self-deprecating reply pierced the momentary air of seriousness and caused Stella to burst out laughing. I quickly followed, and we were still enjoying it when the beep of a horn interrupted. Still chuckling as she walked to the waiting car and opened the door, as she was about to enter, Stella turned back, and with only a faint trace of smile left on her lips, uttered, "Good luck!" in a low, serious tone of voice, her facial expression sober as well. Nodding my acknowledgment as she slowly pulled the door closed, in the suddenly loud, lonely silence that followed her disappearance, I added softly, "Bye, pretty lady—have a nice time."

The remainder of the evening passed away as quickly as the five fast minutes I had enjoyed with Stella. After dinner, which consisted of a steak that I over-broiled because I was still daydreaming about her and forgot I was cooking, I settled onto the living room couch to plan tomorrow's strategy. For the first hour, thoughts about pretty lady lingered to sporadically interrupt my preparation. But gradually, The People versus Fred Ginther permeated my mind and I pored over my notes until midnight, when I went to bed and tossed and turned till morning.

VI

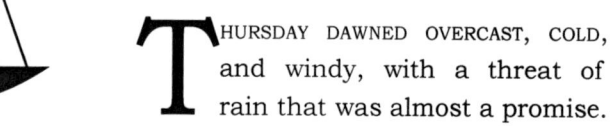

Thursday dawned overcast, cold, and windy, with a threat of rain that was almost a promise. Arriving at the office at seven-thirty, I poured down two cups of Marilyn's steaming hot coffee while pacing up and down in front of her desk waiting for George or Robbie to arrive. Neither had by eight forty-five, so with Marilyn's smilingly delivered, "Hang in there, lawyer-man!" ringing in my ears, I made my way across the street and upstairs to Division Four. As I entered, all twelve members of the jury were already seated in the jury box chatting with one another. When Dave Ludlow greeted me, I seized the opportunity to demonstrate my amiability and walked over and shook hands with him, then returned the "Good Mornings" of four of the jurors whose attention the event had drawn. At precisely one minute after nine, Steiggerman took the bench, and after formal greetings were exchanged, he directed Ludlow to call his first witness.

In response, Officer Glenn Hardy—white, forty-one, and married with two children—rose from his seat in the rear of the courtroom and strode forward to take the stand. Of medium height, barrel-chested and heavily muscled, his broad face and large facial features matched his physique well, I noted as he was seated and sworn in.

"Would you please state your name, occupation, and current assignment?" Ludlow asked matter-of-factly, opening his direct examination.

"Glenn Hardy, Deputy Sheriff, LA County Sheriff's Department, Solina Division— currently assigned to patrol," marched the response firmly. And as I was getting to my feet, I noticed that when Hardy had answered, he turned his head slightly toward the jury.

"And calling your—"

"Your Honor," I interrupted, "begging the pardon of the District Attorney, I move to exclude any other witnesses from the courtroom while Officer Hardy is testifying."

"Very well, Mr. Harris. Mr. Ludlow, would you please read off the names of your other witnesses."

"Well, Your Honor ... there will only be Officer Buxton, who is serving as my investigating officer—and the exception to the general rule of exclusion allows him to remain."

"All right, Mr. Ludlow, that's correct. So, Mr. Harris, based upon the District Attorney's representation that the only other witness he will call is his investigating officer, I'm going to deny your motion because it's become moot."

"Your Honor, if the Court please, may I be heard further on this issue?"

"Yes, Mr. Harris, you may. But please be brief and to the point."

"Thank you, Your Honor, I'll try. And what I want to argue to the Court, Sir, is that the code provision exception which allows an investigating officer to remain in the courtroom during the testimony of other witnesses was designed to afford help to a District Attorney trying a complicated case involving numerous pieces of physical evidence tied to testimony by several witnesses. In our case, however, no such set of circumstances exists as the prosecution has only two witnesses and no physical evidence. So, in that the purpose for the exception to the general rule has no application here, I submit to you that it's patently unfair, and highly prejudicial to my client, to allow Officer Buxton to listen to Officer Hardy's testimony before he himself testifies in support of it."

"Thank you, Mr. Harris. Your motion is still denied."

"Very well, Your Honor. I then move that the Court order the District Attorney to have his investigating officer testify first, which eliminates the problem." Feeling that logic, plus his desire to appear in favor of fair play, had him cornered, I was unprepared for the stream of vitriol that immediately flowed my way.

"M-i-s-t-e-r Harris," rolled Steiggerman's reply sternly, "this Court listened to your original motion and was prepared to grant it. It was denied only because the investigating-officer exception made it moot. Now thereafter, you fed the Court a lot of phony-baloney, hocus-pocus nonsense in an effort to trick the Court into taking your side despite the clear provisions of the law. And when that failed, you now ask the Court to tell the District Attorney how to run his case. Now you know better than that, Mr. Harris, so you ought to be ashamed of yourself! And once and for all, your motion is denied!" concluded his reprimand, his eyes emitting a cold stare.

"Your Honor," I returned slowly, squelching the trigger that outrage wanted to pull and replacing it with as much hurt as I could muster into my voice, "I'm sorry that you see it that way. 'Cause I didn't try to trick anyone, and I don't believe at all that I have to be ashamed for attempting to protect my client's rights from prejudicial testimony. In fact, despite the Court's anger at me, I'm proud to represent Mr. Ginther, and I have a new motion to make, which is—"

"Mr. Harris, if you don't sit down and be quiet immediately, this Court will have no alternative other than to hold you in contempt!" knifed His Honor's interruption. Having already turned halfway toward the jury so that they could clearly hear my attempted refutation of Steiggerman's insulting remarks, I cast a hopeful, see-how-unfair-he-is? look at them, then slowly sat down. After a moment's pause to lift his glare, Steiggerman indicated that Ludlow should continue, and as he shuffled his notes, I decided to see if making life difficult for him could provoke His Honor into a course of conduct that the jury couldn't possibly misinterpret.

"All right," Ludlow resumed, "calling your attention to the date of October eleventh, 1968, around eight o'clock in the evening, were you on duty at that time?"

"Yes, Sir, I was," Hardy nodded.

"And did anything unusual occur on that date and at that time?"

"Objection, Your Honor," I intervened. "The question calls for a conclusion with respect to the word unusual, and in addition calls for opinion evidence without any proper foundation having been laid by the District Attorney."

Steiggerman instantly overruled the objection, shaking his head as if I had once again committed some grievous error, and Officer Hardy answered "Yes."

"And what was the unusual occurrence that you observed?"

"Well, my—"

"I'll object to that question too, Your Honor, it calls for a narrative answer."

"O-v-e-r-ruled, Mr. Harris! And just what do you think you're doing?" he growled, anger reddening his face. Feeling beads of perspiration forming on my chest and shoulders as I climbed to my feet, I continued my objection in a tone that put a capital H in humbleness.

"Your Honor, Sir, I don't understand. The evidence code clearly provides that counsel has the right to object to improper evidence being introduced before the jury, and if a witness is allowed to give a narrative answer, counsel is effectively prevented from objecting to improper testimony until after it has already occurred. Therefore, I respectfully implore the Court to reconsider its previous ruling."

For a full ten seconds, we stared at each other across the hostile silence. Then, just as the hush began to supersede uncomfortable, a quizzical smile suddenly flickered across his face, softening its mask-like hardness and stifling his urge to shout at me. In fact, when he finally responded, full control had returned, as well as his usual attitude of honey-coated condescension.

"Mr. Harris," he advised, "the Court understands fully the argument that you have outlined, I simply don't agree with it. Now your objection is overruled, and the witness is advised to answer Mr. Ludlow's question, so let's continue please."

"Very well, Your Honor. But in that case I would request that the record and docket reflect my client's continuing objection to every single word of the officer's answer, along with the accompanying motion to strike it."

"All right, the record and docket will so reflect."

"Thank you, Your Honor," I nodded, silently adding, For nothing, you slimeball! as I sat down and prepared to take notes on Officer Hardy's testimony.

"And what was the unusual occurrence that you observed?" Ludlow then repeated.

"Well, around eight o'clock in the evening, my partner Officer Buxton and I were on patrol—and as we turned onto Belmont Avenue from Olive Street, we observed the—"

"Objection to the word, we, Your Honor. The witness can testify only as to what he observed—he's speculating as to what anyone else did or did not observe."

Surprising everyone involved, Steiggerman uttered, "Sustained," and directed Officer Hardy to relate only what he himself observed, with such speed, that Hardy, after nodding his understanding, was able to proceed almost as if nothing had transpired.

"Well, as we proceeded eastbound on Belmont Boulevard, I observed the defendant staggering down—"

"Objection, Your Honor, and a motion to strike the word, staggering, as being a conclusion. The witness should simply describe what he saw and not tell the jury his conclusions!" I argued.

"Overruled, Mr. Harris. Staggering is not a word of art, and is commonly used by us all as a descriptive term—and I'm sure the members of the jury understand its definition perfectly," Steiggerman countered. "Please continue, Officer Hardy."

"Well, I observed the defendant staggering down the sidewalk in front of Martin's Hardware Store. Officer Buxton and I then pulled over to the sidewalk to investigate the situation, and upon approaching the defendant we—I mean I—observed that he had bloodshot eyes, his clothes were soiled and disarranged, and he had an odor of alcohol about his person and on his breath."

"And what happened next?" Ludlow asked, simply seeding the ongoing narrative.

"Well, I asked the defendant for some identification, and he fumbled through his wallet for a few minutes and then handed me his driver's license."

"And then what happened?"

"I asked him where he was going, and he said—"

"Objection, Your Honor—calls for hearsay."

"Overruled, Mr. Harris," Steiggerman snapped. "You may answer, Officer."

"Well," Hardy picked up instantly, "he said that he didn't know where he was going, and I noticed that his speech was thick and slurred."

"And what happened next?" Ludlow monotoned.

"Officer Buxton and I administered a field sobriety test to the defendant—He was asked to walk a straight line placing one foot in front of the other so that the heel of one foot touched the toe of the other."

"And how did the defendant perform on the test?"

"Very poorly—He staggered and almost fell down several times!" Hardy stated emphatically, once again angling his head in the direction of the jury.

"I see. And what did you do next?"

"Well, having formed the opinion that the defendant was intoxicated to such an extent that he was unable to care for his own health and safety, I placed him under arrest for 647(f) of the Penal Code and Officer Buxton and I transported him to Solina Station, where he was booked."

"Thank you, Officer," nodded Ludlow, who then advised Steiggerman that he had concluded his direct examination.

"Very well," acknowledged His Honor, glancing at the clock, which read ten minutes after ten, before adding smugly: "All right, Mr. Harris, you may inquire now."

As I stood up and slowly shuffled toward the jury box, I realized fully that I was in serious trouble. Not only was there the highly prejudicial effect of Steiggerman's unwarranted assistance to the prosecution, but the case itself presented considerable problems, not the least of which was Officer Hardy. For having testified in hundreds of cases, he was not only a professional witness—who knew what to expect on cross-examination, and who had further demonstrated his expertise by subtly playing to the jury during his direct testimony—but one armed with the additional security of having his partner to back him up. And because Steiggerman had ruled that Buxton could listen to Hardy's answers on cross-examination, he would then be in an excellent position to correct and/or clarify any inconsistencies I might elicit. Then, just to make the hill even steeper to climb, there was the additional problem of Fred Ginther's conflicting story. Fred had leveled with me and confided that after losing his job late in the afternoon, he had consumed four scotch and sodas between six and eight o'clock on the evening he was arrested, leaving him "pretty tipsy" when he was walking from the bar to his home three blocks away. However, he had also been adamant about having been placed under arrest and searched without being questioned or administered any tests whatsoever, and had pleaded with me to believe him. I did. But that left me with the call-the-cop-a-liar defense, and as I stopped two or three feet past where Ludlow was seated and turned to face the witness box, Robbie's admonition that "it was the worst defense in the world" gnawed at me. Glancing down at the arrest report, I ran my eyes over it to buy a few more seconds of time. Then, having decided to work around the edges of the disfavored defense so as to buttress the more plausible one that Fred was not unable to care for his own health and safety, I shifted my gaze from the arrest report to the round, heavy face of the confident accuser, and in a neutral tone of voice began my cross-examination.

"Officer Hardy, who was the driver of your vehicle on the evening in question?"

"Officer Buxton."

"And when you first observed Mr. Ginther, was your vehicle traveling in an easterly direction?"

"Yes, Sir."

"And Mr. Ginther was traveling in a westerly direction, wasn't he?"

"Yes, Sir."

"Would you say that Belmont Boulevard is a heavily trafficked street?"

"Yes, Sir."

"And at the time you first observed Mr. Ginther, there was traffic traveling in both directions, wasn't there?"

"Yes, Sir."

"So, would it be accurate to say that when you first observed Mr. Ginther, that in order to make your observation from the passenger seat you had to look through the windshield across two or three lanes of traffic moving in both directions?"

"Yes, Sir," he nodded after hesitating slightly.

"Were the lights on in the windows of Martin's hardware store?"

"Yes, Sir."

"And the lights of the vehicles traveling on Belmont Boulevard were also on, correct?"

"Yes, Sir."

"Approximately how many feet away from Mr. Ginther were you, Sir, when you initially observed him?"

"Ohhh, I'd say ... approximately one hundred twenty-five to one hundred-fifty feet."

"Okay ... And how wide was the sidewalk where Mr. Ginther was walking?"

"About six feet."

"All right ... .Now drawing a line down the middle of that six-foot sidewalk, Officer Hardy, on which side, north or south of the center line, was Mr. Ginther when you initially observed him?"

This time he thought for three for four seconds before answering, "I don't remember."

"I see ... Well, would it then be a fair statement to say that you observed Mr. Ginther to travel more than twenty-five feet before the decision was made to pull your vehicle over to the sidewalk?"

"Yes, Sir—more like fifty feet."

"All right, Officer Hardy, thank you. ... Now having observed Mr. Ginther to travel approximately fifty feet, how many times would you say he crossed over the center line and back during the first twenty-five feet?"

"Several times, Sir."

"Several?"

"Yes, Sir."

"Within twenty-five feet?"

"Yes, Sir."

"Well, tell me, Officer—how many times, exactly, is several?"

"Well, I can't remember exactly." Noticing a slight tinge of irritation had crept into his tone, I decided to gamble early and press him.

"Officer Hardy, on direct examination you accused my client of quote: staggering. Are you telling us now that you did this without being able to tell us how many times you saw him move back and forth over the center line during a twenty-five foot distance?" Frowning in response to the accusation inside the question, he answered quickly, as if even the slightest delay in defending his veracity might be construed negatively.

"No, Sir, I'm not," he rifled, his voice rising. "I saw him weave back and forth several times, but I didn't count them."

"Weave? ... Did you say weave, Officer?"

"Yes, Sir."

"Well, on direct examination you used the word staggering, and now you use the word weave—Do they mean the same thing to you?"

"Yes, Sir, sort of the same," he returned, his tone hardening, the frown furrowing deeper.

"Officer, I'll repeat the question. Do the words staggering and weave have identical meanings to you?"

"Well ... yes Sir ... they do," arrived his begrudging admission slowly. And instantly sensing that he was vulnerable on this point, yet not wanting to present him with the opportunity to clarify his previous admissions and take away the few little Brownie points I'd scored, after a moment's pause, I decided to gamble further, instinct outweighing reason.

"Officer Hardy," I pressed, "would you please define the word weave for us?"

My concern proved unnecessary, as Steiggerman, also sensing trouble brewing, stopped me cold. "Mr. Harris," he interjected, "this line of questioning seems to be highly irrelevant at this point. Please move on to other areas."

"Ir-relevant?" I boomed back at him, surprised by the intervention because I was concentrating so intensely on the witness that I'd forgotten about His Honor. "This witness used a word—and a conclusive type word at that—to describe my client's conduct. How can his definition of that word be irrelevant?"

"Mr. Harris, I must warn you to lower your tone of voice when addressing the Court!" returned his admonition instantly. "And for your information, the Court believes that the witness has adequately described what he observed, and that any subtle distinctions between the words staggering and weave are best left for the linguists and are irrelevant for our purposes!"

Rocking up and down on my toes, I could feel my shirt stick to my back as I tried to decide what in God's name I was supposed to do now. Feeling that his rebuke had destroyed the mood of the moment anyhow, I reasoned that it was better to pay lip service to his authority and seek a new avenue on which to expose Officer Hardy's lack of veracity.

"Very well, Your Honor, if you insist. And I apologize to the Court if my tone gave offense," I offered with feigned sincerity, "I was just very surprised, Sir, that's all—because the District Attorney didn't object to my line of questioning."

Deciding not to further emphasize to the jury the fact that Ludlow had remained silent, Steiggerman ignored the jab I'd slipped inside my explanation, instead reinserting his all-knowing smile and directing me to proceed. And after nodding my acquiescence, I again turned and faced Officer Hardy.

"Officer," I queried in a now less threatening tone, "after you made your initial observation and your police vehicle pulled over to the sidewalk, would it be a fair statement to say that you apprehended Mr. Ginther by jumping out of your car and grabbing him?"

"No, Sir, it would not."

"Well, you didn't just call out to my client to stop, did you?"

"Yes, Sir, that's exactly what I did."

"What exactly did you say to him?"

"I called out to him to halt."

"And Mr. Ginther complied with your order?"

"Yes, Sir ... of course," he responded smugly, angling his head toward the jury once again. The moment after Steiggerman had performed his rescue mission and foreshadowed his witness protection program, Hardy's face, which already reflected a solid self-assurance, increased that level to where it bordered on arrogance. Now, as I played to his sense of power and self-importance, his voice engendered a matching tone, while mine by design retained its mixture of humble harmlessness tinged with mild surprise.

"Well then, Officer Hardy," I picked up. "Isn't it true that when you approached my client, the first thing you did was shine your flashlight in his eyes?"

"No, Sir."

"Well, you did shine your flashlight in his eyes at some point, didn't you?"

"No, Sir."

"Well then, how about your partner, Officer Buxton—did he do so?"

"No, Sir, no one shined anything in the defendant's eyes."

"I see. ... Well, did you ask Mr. Ginther whether he'd been crying?"

"No, Sir."

"Or when was the last time he'd been to sleep?"

"No, Sir.

"Did you ask him whether he wore glasses?"

"No, Sir."

"Did your partner, in your presence, ask him any of these questions?"

"No, Sir."

"Are you sure?"

"Ab-so-lutely ... Sir!" he rolled out, condescension coating his tone.

"Okay," I continued, forcing a sheepish smile onto my face to support his feeling that he was destroying me with his testimony. "Now you stated on direct examination that you smelled an odor of alcohol on Mr. Ginther's breath—is that correct?"

"Yes, Sir—and about his person, too. He really ree—"

"I see—And could you identify that odor as being of a particular type of alcohol?"

"Yes, Sir, I could."

"And what type was it?"

"Bourbon, Sir."

"I see ... And are you sure of that?"

"Yes, Sir, I am."

"And is that because you consider yourself to be an expert in such matters?"

"Yes, Sir, absolutely—After ten years in the Department, you get to know these type of things extremely well," he readily agreed, tacking on a smile for emphasis.

With some effort, I stifled my urge to ask him why, after ten years of service during which he achieved such expert status, he was still assigned to patrol, and instead nodded: "Yes, Sir, I imagine that with that amount of experience you'd be very sure indeed." Then, after pausing for a moment to glance again at the arrest report, I shifted subjects.

"Officer Hardy, you previously stated that you asked Mr. Ginther for his identification, correct?"

"Yes, Sir."

"And he produced his driver's license for your inspection, didn't he?"

"Yes, Sir."

"Did you inspect it?"

"Yes, Sir, I did."

"And do you remember the address shown on that driver's license?"

"No, Sir, I don't."

Turning away from him, I walked hurriedly over to my briefbag, and after withdrawing a sheet of paper and an attachment returned to my station opposite the jury. "Your Honor," I picked up, "I have here the original and a copy of what appears to be a California Driver's License Number G671865—may they be marked defendant's number one for identification?" After briefly hesitating to consider what I was up to, Steiggerman granted my request, as well as permission to approach the witness. And after placing myself on the side of the witness box that allowed both me and Officer Hardy to face the jury, I handed him Fred Ginther's driver's license to inspect, then stepped back several feet and waited till he raised his eyes to meet mine.

"Officer Hardy," I then continued, "have you reviewed the item which I just handed you?"

"Yes, Sir."

"And would you please tell the jury what it is?"

"It's a California Driver's License issued to the defendant."

"And is there an address shown on that license?"

"Yes, Sir."

"Would you please read us that address?"

"Five Seventeen North Cedar Street, Solina, California."

"Thank you, Officer. And what, approximately, is the distance from Martin's Hardware Store to Five Seventeen North Cedar Street?"

"Approximately ... three blocks," crawled his answer after he first hesitated for several seconds to carefully think.

"In which direction, Officer?"

"That would be westerly."

"I see ... And if I recall correctly, you testified that Mr. Ginther was traveling in a westerly direction when you ordered him to halt—Isn't that true?"

"Yes, Sir, it is." A trace of his previous frown reappeared as he began to sense what I was driving at, and I hurried my next question to him.

"And, Sir, isn't it true that Mr. Ginther told you that he was headed home when you inquired as to where he was going?"

"No, Sir, it is not!" he snapped, his voice rising. "As I said before, the defendant stated that he didn't know where he was going!"

"All right, Officer, now let me see if I understand the overall situation. You have told us that you called out to Mr. Ginther to halt, and that he complied with your order—correct?"

"Yes, Sir."

"And you have further told us that you requested Mr. Ginther to produce some identification, and that he also complied with this request—right?"

"Yes, Sir."

"And lastly, you have shared with us that when you stopped Mr. Ginther, he was traveling in the direction of his home just three blocks away—true?"

"Yes, Sir."

"Okay, Officer Hardy, we're both on the same page. So now I ask you: In view of the facts that you ordered Mr. Ginther to stop, and then requested him to produce identification, and that he complied with both your order and your request—all of which presents strong evidence that he had a clear understanding of what was occurring—do you still insist that he stated he didn't know where he was going, especially since he was just three blocks from home and traveling in that direction?"

Suddenly flushed with anger from my implication that he was a liar, Hardy leaned forward till he grasped the railing to his front with both hands before growling, "He certainly did!" In an instant, the professionally polished "Sir" attached to his previous responses had vanished, as had the falsely respectful tone of voice, and his glare reflected fully the anger seething inside him. Returning it with a head-shake that silently accused, "You naughty little boy, you," I followed verbally only after three or four electric seconds had passed.

"A-m-a-z-i-n-g, Officer Hardy ... simply amazing!" I oozed with thick sarcasm. "'Cause it makes absolutely no sense whatsoever, in that it's just not logical human behavior! But you know what?" I posed, turning toward the counsel table. "I'll just bet Officer Buxton here, who's been listening very carefully, heard the same illogical thing you did—so I guess we should move on to the next line of the script. Officer Buxton was standing close by during this conversation, wasn't he?"

For a moment, I thought Hardy might climb out of the witness box and strike me. But after several seconds spent struggling to control his expanding anger, he restrained himself and was about to answer when Steiggerman once again intervened.

"M-i-s-t-e-r Harris!" he boomed out in his all too familiar lecture tone. "Once again this Court feels compelled to advise you that the line of questioning you are pursuing is objectionable, and requests that you move on to other areas."

"Your Honor, might I inquire as to what grounds the Court bases its objection on?" I asked, hoping to lure him into again displaying his bias to the jury.

"Asked and answered, Mr. Harris—You're repeating questions which the witness has already answered."

"But that's allowed, Your Honor. On cross-examination, counsel's permitted to examine and reexamine on a given point—Why won't the Court permit it here?" I posed, mustering hurt into my voice.

"Because at some point, Mr. Harris, mere repetition constitutes badgering the witness," he countered instantly, his firm tone edged with anger. "And in that you've reached that point in the Court's opinion, I'm directing you to move your inquiry along into other areas!"

"Very well, Your Honor, I will of course comply with the Court's order," I acquiesced. Then, still hoping the jury was paying careful attention, I added: "However, Sir, I would have the record reflect that while the Court has seen fit to object to my questioning of Officer Hardy, once again the District Attorney, at whose request he's testifying, has not!"

For several seconds, silence returned while Steiggerman decided whether or not to counter a second time. Electing not to, instead he formed a disdainful smile and simply instructed me to proceed. And after reminding myself that it was still my turn at bat, I returned my attention to Officer Hardy.

"Officer, you mentioned that you administered a field sobriety test to my client—is that correct?"

"Yes, the walk-the-line test."

"And, Sir, is there more than one type of field sobriety test?"

"Yes."

"What are the other types?"

"Well, counsel, there's the touch-the-nose test and the balance-on-one-foot test."

"I see. And you didn't give either of those tests to Mr. Ginther, did you?"

"No, I did not."

"And, Sir, isn't it also true that you didn't administer to Mr. Ginther, or have administered to him, any type of scientific test to determine how much alcohol he'd consumed?"

"Yes, counsel."

"No breathalyzer test was given to him—correct?"

"Correct."

"No blood test or urinalysis was performed—correct?"

"That's right."

"Now, Officer Hardy, isn't it also true to say that during all the time you observed my client, you never actually saw him fall down onto the ground?

"Yes, counsel."

"And did you at any time observe him to be wandering in the street?"

"No."

"Did you at any time observe him to disturb, annoy, or molest any other citizen?"

"No, counsel."

With my planned cross-examination now complete, I was about to so notify His Honor and take my seat, when Hardy's smug expression suddenly united with my lingering frustration from Steiggerman's assisting the prosecution to fuel further inquiry. I had noted that after His Honor's second rescue mission Hardy's anger appeared to have subsided, but the fact that his rehearsed reference to me as "Sir" had been replaced by the more antagonistic "counsel" argued that it still seethed just below the surface. So, as I set my notes down on the counsel table immediately adjacent to Ludlow, I decided to see if I couldn't provoke an additional display of that anger for the jury's consideration.

"Officer Hardy," I asked, fixing my eyes directly into his, "isn't it true that the real reason you stopped my client was so that you could search him for drugs or narcotics?"

Blinking noticeably as the accusatorial question sunk in, Hardy's professional tone never wavered however as he answered, "Absolutely not, counsel!"

"But you did search Mr. Ginther, didn't you?"

"Yes, but just a cursory pat-down search for weapons."

"Just a pat-down search?"

"Right, that's all."

"Officer, you did place Mr. Ginther under arrest while he was still standing on the sidewalk, didn't you?"

"Yes, counsel."

"And you do know that it's legal for you to search someone as incidental to a lawful arrest, right?"

"Yes, counsel."

"Then why is it that having placed Mr. Ginther under arrest, you didn't search him?"

"Well, in cases like this," dribbled his answer after a slight hesitation, his delivery slow and measured, "we usually prefer to perform a thorough search of the defendant at the station during booking."

"Officer Hardy, isn't the real reason you didn't search Mr. Ginther because you knew that the arrest was without legal grounds and therefore unlawful? And isn't it also true that you—"

"Your Honor, I must object. I—" Finally heard from, Ludlow's objection was sustained by Steiggerman before he could even state his grounds. Shaking my head at Hardy while sharing my best you-know-that-I-know-what-really-happened grin, I moved several steps closer to him and perched on the edge of the counsel table to the right of Ludlow.

"Officer Hardy," I resumed, "I've noticed that throughout your testimony, you've consistently referred to my client by the term 'defendant'—isn't that correct?"

"Yes, counsel."

"Why is that exactly?"

"Why?" he shrugged, almost laughing in amazement, "'Cause that's what he is."

"Is that all he is to you, Officer?"

"Yes, of course," he fired confidently back at me.

"Then what you're telling us, Officer, is that when you stopped my client, you already viewed him as a defendant—isn't that correct?"

Realizing that he had answered the last question too quickly, Hardy now twisted uncomfortably in his chair while planning his current reply. Smelling blood, I pressed him.

"Didn't you hear the question, Sir?"

"Yes, counsel, I did."

"Then answer it please."

"Well ... I ... didn't place the defendant under arrest until after he had failed the walk-the-line test."

"That's your answer, Officer?" rocketed my attack in a tone laden with disbelief. "You've already told us that from the moment you first saw him, Mr. Ginther was already a defendant, 'cause that's all he is to you. So are you now changing your prior testimony to—"

"Mr. Harris, this Court has tolerated all of your nonsense that it's going to!" Steiggerman cut in angrily, jumping to the rescue yet again. "You ought to be ashamed of yourself!" he added more slowly for emphasis, then paused to allow me to respond.

"Very well, Your Honor," I acquiesced with sugar-coated sincerity. "I won't press this issue any further, since Officer Hardy can't explain anyway why he sees only defendants and not human beings. And, Your Honor, with the Court's permission, I only have one additional question to ask him."

"Okay ... all right, Mr. Harris ... Ask your question," he returned, his tone matching the disgust mapped across his face.

"Thank you, Your Honor ... Now, Officer Hardy," I resumed, once again fixing my eyes directly into his, "if my memory serves me correctly, you've told us that you've been a deputy sheriff for ten years or so. And that being the case, Sir, would you please explain to the jury how it is that after ten years of service, and being such an expert as you say you are, you're still just an ordinary patrol officer?"

Ludlow instantly objected in what for him would be considered an angry tone of voice, and Steiggerman sustained it in a distinctly louder and more angry one. Officer Hardy just sat still as a statue, radiating hate in my direction, and for several serious seconds I maintained contact with his fiercely belligerent stare in the hope that it would become indelibly impressed in the minds of the jurors. Then, shaking my head, I broke it off and slowly returned to my seat, leaving Steiggerman to finally interrupt the thirty seconds of stony silence that had prevailed since he last spoke.

"Will there be any redirect examination, Mr. Ludlow?" His Honor inquired, his tone clearly indicating that he did not feel there was any need for it. And acccpting Steiggerman's judgment, Ludlow promptly waived redirect, whereupon Steiggerman immediately declared that court stood in noon recess until one-thirty.

Waiting until the courtroom had cleared, I then reviewed my notes on Fred Ginther's upcoming testimony. Sitting there alone in the silence, the only sound being the occasional jingle-jangle of the motor regulating the air-conditioning, I carefully sifted through Fred's version of what had occurred while mentally comparing it to Hardy's testimony. Satisfied after ten minutes or so that the differences were firmly embedded in my mind, but still fretting about whether the jury would give enough credence to Fred's story to raise a reasonable doubt, I then left Division Four and slowly walked down the rear stairway leading to the lockup.

When I arrived, lunch was being passed out to those in custody, courtesy of the County of Los Angeles. In no hurry to visit Fred, for a full minute I stood in the entryway and watched as the prisoners silently filed one at a time out of the holding tank, shuffled over to a nearby desk where each one was handed a cheese sandwich and an orange, then disappeared back into the total darkness of the tank to eat, still blinking from their eyes' failure to adjust to the contrastingly harsh light. After this procedure had finally run its course, Sheriff Moorehouse, who was in charge of the lockup, glanced up and greeted me with a smile.

"Well, hi there, counsel. You want to see Mr. Ginther?" he queried warmly.

"Uh-huh," I nodded, returning his smile. "I'd appreciate it."

"How's things going for you upstairs? Roberts says you and the Judge got a regular war going on."

"Well ... you got that right."

"You holding your own?"

"I don't know, Sheriff," I shrugged, slumping down into a chair next to his desk. "I'm sorta new at this game, so it's hard to tell how the hell I'm doing." He chuckled softly in response to the weary head-shake accompanying my reply.

"Say, you want a sandwich?" he offered, trying to lift my flagging spirits. "It's lunchtime, you know, and you gotta have fuel to do battle."

Edward Moorehouse's reputation for being an exceptionally good human being, as well as the most competent and fair-minded of deputy sheriffs, was already legendary within the Solina Judicial District when

I was still in high school. When I had first arrived, George had advised that he was unlike any other cop anywhere, and since that time I had found that to be totally the case in my contacts with him. Now, as I sat there opposite his small desk on an uncomfortably hard chair in the stifling hot anteroom of the lockup, feeling tired, discouraged, and more lonely than I ever had in my entire life, and wishing to God that I could climb once again into the comforting arms of my leafy friend in Gram and Gramp's backyard, his kind offer of a stale cheese sandwich truly touched me. For an instant, I wanted to hug him. Instead, however, I mustered a gratefully toned "Thank you, kind Sir," that matched my accompanying smile, and took two oranges from the cardboard box on the corner of the desk.

"Okay ... good!" he grinned broadly, standing up. "Now, I'll get your client for you, Mr. Public Defender."

Several minutes later, he led Fred Ginther into the interview room from the opposite side of the steel grate that separated lawyer and client. I had just finished eating the first orange and was peeling the second when the door opened and a surprised Fred entered.

"Hey, man," he jerked out, puzzled. "What you doing here? Something wrong?"

"Not a thing, man ... not a thing," I assured him, chuckling. "I just missed you, that's all."

"Yeahhh ... I'll bet," he grinned, and I was glad to see that he still could after the way the morning's proceedings had gone down.

"Listen, Fred ... you're going to testify this afternoon, and I just dropped by to make sure that you tell the jury exactly what you've told me—okay?"

"Yeah ... sure," he nodded slowly.

"Okay. Now you just relax, and while you're finishing your sandwich, tell me exactly what happened the night you were arrested."

Complying in detail in between bites, when he was finished, I again encouraged him to tell his story to the jury exactly as he had related it to me, then ended our discussion by advising him that I would see him upstairs shortly. As I was halfway through the doorway, he called to me.

"Mr. Harris—"

"Yeah, Fred?"

"I just want to say that whatever happens ... well, I want to thank you for caring about me and for fighting so hard for me. I appreciate it, man."

Stunned, followed by a flood of emotion, I nodded, then smiled, and finally managed to say, "Thanks, Fred. 'Cause I do care, and it makes all the fighting worth it." Then, turning away quickly before he could see the tears welling in my eyes, I brushed them away with a swipe of my hand as I hurried back to the first floor and outside the courthouse to grab a breath of fresh air and a smoke before the afternoon's proceedings began.

His Honor was detained at lunch, and it was not until two forty-five, and after he had made an ingratiating apology to the jury, that the afternoon session finally began. Fred took the stand and was sworn, and for several stiff seconds I let him sit there in silence in the hope that he would loosen up and convey a moderately relaxed appearance to the jury. It didn't work, and after asking him to state his full name and address for the record and receiving his halting answer, I altered my initial examination of him.

"Are you nervous about testifying, Fred?" I queried, smiling.

"Yes, Sir ... I'm very nervous."

"Well, that's normal, but there's absolutely nothing to be afraid of. I'm a little nervous too, and so are most of the jurors probably, 'cause it's a new experience that we're all sharing here together. So you just try and relax some, and listen carefully to my questions—and if all of us show each other a little understanding, then everything will be just fine, okay?"

"Yes, Sir, I understand," he nodded, a faint smile forming.

"Okay, now ... Are you employed, Fred?"

"No, Sir, not since I got laid off about four weeks ago."

"I see. Well where did you work?"

"At the Reeves Paper Manufacturing Company here in Solina. I worked there for almost thirteen years."

"That's a long time, Fred. How come you were laid off?"

"Well, Sir, business had been falling off for some time, and at the end of September, Mr. Jensen, the owner, told us he might have to close down."

"All right ... And do you remember exactly when it was that you were laid off?"

"Yes, Sir. It was on October eleventh, a Friday afternoon."

"And what was your feeling at that time, Fred?"

"Well, Sir, I was very upset and worried."

"That's understandable. Would you please tell the ladies and gentlemen of the jury why you were so upset?

"Well, Sir, I have a wife and four children to take care of—and jobs are hard to get these days, and I don't have much savings to help us get by on."

Keeping watch on the jury out of the corner of my eye as Fred's story unfolded, I noted that his soft, sincere tone of voice combined with his humble mannerisms was having the hoped-for effect. Every single member was giving him his or her undivided attention, and as I continued, long dormant optimism began to slowly bubble toward the surface.

"Okay, Fred. What did you do after you learned of your layoff?" flowed my next question.

"Well, Sir, I gathered together some of my belongings in my locker, and then drove home."

"Did you tell your wife about the layoff when you reached home?"

"No, Sir ... I was going to. But after I parked and started into the house, I don't know what came over me exactly, but I just couldn't go on in and tell her."

"Okay ... so what did you do at that time?"

"Well, Sir, I decided to go have a drink with my friend Sam Luther."

"I see. So you went on over to Sam's house?"

"No, Sir. I walked over to his bar on Belmont Boulevard. It's called Sam's Place."

"All right. And what time was it when you arrived at Sam's Place?"

"About five-thirty in the evening."

"And was Sam there?"

"Yes, Sir."

"And did you talk with Sam?"

"Yes, Sir."

"And did you have a drink, Fred?"

"Yes, Sir, I did."

"Okay, Fred, now this is very important, so please listen carefully and then tell the members of the jury: Did you have more than one drink?"

"Yes, Sir, I did."

"All right ... How many drinks did you have while you were at Sam's Place?"

"Well, Sir," he answered softly after a slight hesitation, "I had four drinks."

"Four, Fred?"

"Yes, Sir ... four."

Gideon's Children | 121

"Okay ... How long were you at Sam's Place having these four drinks?"

"A little over three hours, Sir."

"I see ... And did these four drinks have any effect on you, Fred?"

"Yes, Sir, they did."

"All right. Tell us please: What effect exactly did they have on you?"

"Well, Sir, they made me a little high and relaxed me some."

"A little high, you say?"

"Yes, Sir."

"And by the expression, a little high, do you mean that you felt intoxicated?"

"Yes, Sir, I did feel intoxicated some."

"And did you continue to talk with Sam while you were having your four drinks?"

"Yes, Sir, I told him about losing my job and how upset and worried I was."

"And did Sam have any suggestions for you?"

"No, Sir ... He just felt bad for me, that's all."

"I see ... Now, Fred, do you usually have four drinks when you visit with Sam?"

"No, Sir."

"And do you feel that the four drinks you had were a little too much for you?"

"Yes, Sir, they were."

"How do you know that?"

"Well, Sir," Fred said sadly, shaking his head ever so slightly, "'Cause I sort of let my feelings slip and started to cry."

"While you were at Sam's Place?"

"Yes, Sir ... in front of everybody."

"And did the drinks cause you to do anything else unusual?"

"No, Sir. But when I started to cry, I knew I was high, and I felt ashamed."

"Ashamed? ... Why?"

"Well, Sir ... Thirty-seven-year-old men ain't supposed to cry, even if they lose their job and don't know how they're going to care for their family."

"I see," I nodded sympathetically. "Well tell us, Fred: Did you have any other alcoholic beverage to drink earlier that day?"

"No, Sir."

"You didn't have a beer or two for lunch, did you?"

"No, Sir ... no way."

"But you did have lunch, didn't you?"

"Yes, Sir. I had a sandwich and some fruit and cookies that my wife packed for me."

"Okay. By the way, Fred—what type of drink were you drinking at Sam's Place?"

"Scotch and soda."

"All four drinks?"

"Yes, Sir."

"You're sure you weren't drinking bourbon?"

"Yes, Sir. I never drink anything but scotch, 'cause that's what I like when I'm drinking."

"I see: All scotch ... no bourbon," I summarized slowly, emphasizing for the jury Officer Hardy's fallacious testimony. And glancing over at them as I turned a page of my notes and prepared to conclude Fred's testimony, I smiled inwardly upon finding expressions of sympathetic understanding creasing several of their faces. Then, focusing on the details leading to his arrest, I proceeded as carefully as if I were indeed walking on the proverbial egg shells so as to allow Fred to contradict Officer Hardy's account without unnecessarily exposing him to Ludlow's upcoming cross-examination. "All right now, Fred," I picked up, "at some point you left Sam's Place, right?"

"Yes, Sir."

"And what time would that be?"

"About eight o'clock."

"Did you say goodbye to Sam?"

"Yes, Sir, I did."

"And as you left, did you have any trouble walking?"

"Yes, Sir, a little."

"What do you mean exactly when you say 'a little'?"

"Well, like I said, I did have a little too much to drink and was sort of high—and when I walked, I wasn't as steady on my feet as usual."

"Okay. Did you weave a bit?"

"Yes, Sir, I did."

"Slightly, from side to side?"

"Yes, Sir."

"I see ... And where were you going, Fred?"

"Home, Sir—to my wife and kids."

"So you were fully aware of where you were going?"

"Yes, Sir—home."

"And was there any doubt in your mind that you could walk home safely, even though you were not as steady on your feet as usual?"

"No, Sir. Like I said, I had a little too much to drink, but I wasn't drunk so that I didn't know where I was, or what I was doing. And home was only three blocks away." No objection spilled forth from either Ludlow or His Honor, and relieved that I could proceed without interruption, I headed for the crux of the conflict.

"Fred, do you remember being stopped by Officer Hardy?"

"Yes, Sir."

"And were your eyes bloodshot?"

"They might have been, I couldn't see. But I had been crying a bit."

"And were your clothes soiled and disarranged?"

"Well, Sir, they were a bit dirty from work ... I don't really understand what dis ... arranged means."

"It means out of place, Fred—all messed up."

"Well, I wasn't real neat, if that's what you're getting at."

"That's it exactly," I smiled, causing him to faintly return it. "Now, Fred, this is quite important," I picked up. "After you were stopped, were you searched?"

"Yes, Sir. First thing they did was search my pockets and everything—and they kept asking me where the stuff was."

"They? Who were they, Fred?"

"The officers, Sir."

"And did you know what they meant by stuff?"

"Well, I guessed they meant dope, and I told them I didn't have any."

"Did they believe you?"

"No, Sir. They just laughed at me and kept searching through my clothes."

"I see ... And did you tell either of the officers that you didn't know where you were going?"

"No, Sir. I told them that I was on my way home, which was the truth."

"Thank you, Fred. Thank you for being so open and honest," I nodded, then turned toward the bench. "Your Honor, I have no further questions at this time."

"Very well, Mr. Harris," Steiggerman acknowledged, then followed by directing Ludlow to commence his cross-examination. Not knowing what to expect from him, but fully aware that a nervous Fred Ginther would be vulnerable to a forceful attack, I inched up onto the edge of my chair, pushed my alert button to full, and sat waiting to protect him with timely objections whether justified or not. Much to my surprise, Ludlow only asked Fred a half dozen or so meaningless questions, which produced corresponding answers, and the total interrogation strangely took less than three minutes.

Also surprised, His Honor promptly ordered a ten-minute recess, which lasted twenty, and at five minutes after four we were once again ready to proceed. Having exhausted his storehouse of shockers, as expected Ludlow called Officer Jerry Buxton to the stand as his rebuttal witness, and over my strenuous but futile objection he was allowed to reiterate Officer Hardy's testimony. Having already decided that I would deal with the details of his testimony by ignoring them so as to not further reinforce them in the minds of the jurors, on cross-examination I asked him precisely five questions.

"Officer Buxton, you were present in the courtroom at all times during Officer Hardy's testimony, were you not?"

"Yes, Sir."

"And you listened very carefully to his testimony, didn't you?"

"Yes, Sir."

"And you were allowed to do this, because you were assisting the District Attorney by serving as his investigating officer—right?"

"Yes, Sir."

"Officer Buxton, approximately how much time did you spend in preparing this case as the investigating officer prior to the commencement of the trial?"

"Time, Sir?"

"Yes, officer—time. You know, minutes, hours, days," I machine-gunned. "Who did you interview? Did you take any photographs of the scene? Analyze any laboratory reports? In other words, what service exactly did you perform in your role as investigating officer?"

Several uneasy seconds ticked slowly into the silence as he twisted in his chair, then shifted his weight forward while still searching for an answer. And sensing that Steiggerman was about to attempt yet another rescue mission with the next tick of the clock, I frustrated him by terminating the brief exchange.

"Never mind, officer, I withdraw the question," hurried my foreclosure of Steiggerman's impending intervention, lecture undoubtedly included at no extra cost. "Your silence speaks for itself anyway!" I tacked on, summoning maximum disgust into my voice and giving him my naughty-boy head-shake before striding briskly back to my seat and turning my focus to Steiggerman. "I have no further questions for this non-investigating investigating officer, Your Honor. Thank you."

"Very ... well ... Mr. Harris," leaked his reply, his irritation clearly visible. "Anything further, Mr. Ludlow?"

"No, Your Honor, the People rest."

"Mr. Harris?"

"The defense rests also, Your Honor."

"Very well, gentlemen," Steiggerman advised, closing his notebook. "In that it's getting along toward five o'clock, I'm going to put over final arguments and instruction of the jury till eight-thirty tomorrow morning. Court stands adjourned until that time."

After saying good night to Fred before he was led away, and then being informed by Bailiff Roberts that the Judge requested the presence of Ludlow and myself in his chambers at eight sharp to discuss jury instructions, I slowly made my way out of the courthouse and back across the street to the office. Leon was the only one present. Seated at Marilyn's desk with his feet propped up on top of her typewriter, he was surrounded by clouds of smoke billowing from his pipe as he jotted notes in a well-thumbed copy of *Das Kapital*, appropriately housed in a bright-red dust cover. Glancing up from his intense seminar with Karl Marx as I dropped heavily into the chair opposite the desk, he greeted me with a warmly toned, "Good evening, counsel. How the fuck are you?" the playful sarcasm inside his welcome spilling out through a spreading smile.

"Ohhh, just wonderful, you commie Jew bastard!" I cracked while reaching for my pipe, suddenly an urgent need. "How's your left-wing, hippie ass—comfortable?"

"Oooooh," he gurgled with feigned alarm, his smile growing wider in response to mine, "I see we're a bit touchy this evening."

"Absolutely, not, dear sir! In fact I'm surprised that an experienced PD like yourself can't recognize a warmhearted compliment when he hears it—Say, where the hell is everyone?"

"Over in Division Two. It seems like some little asshole who fancies himself to be a trial lawyer is kicking up quite a ruckus in Division Four—a little problem that caused the transfer over the last two days of some seventy-three cases to Division Two, which was already blessed with sixty of its own to deal with. So can you dig, man?"

"Holy ... Christ, I've fucked up the whole courthouse!" rushed my reply when the full import of his explanation slipped through the screen of exhaustion numbing my mind. "Shhhit, I feel bad for the other guys, Leon, I better go—"

"Why? They're loving every minute of it," he interrupted. "The pressure on the DAs to deal is unbelievable, and we're stealing the courthouse. Feel bad? ... Hell, you ought to feel fucking terrific!—Speaking of which, how's your trial going anyway?"

"Which one?" I snickered. "I'm doing fine against Ludlow, but Steiggerman is fucking me over something fierce."

"Yeahhh, I know the pain," he shrugged, commiserating through a fresh grin.

"Listen, do you think the guys would mind if I split early? I want to work over my closing argument and some jury instructions."

"Get out of here, will you," he answered, shaking his head disbelievingly. "You're making me and Mr. Marx here nauseous with all your bullshit worrying."

"Okay, thanks, man—I'll see you tomorrow."

"Right on. And good luck, you hear?"

"I hear. And I'll need it too," I chuckled, then headed for the back door.

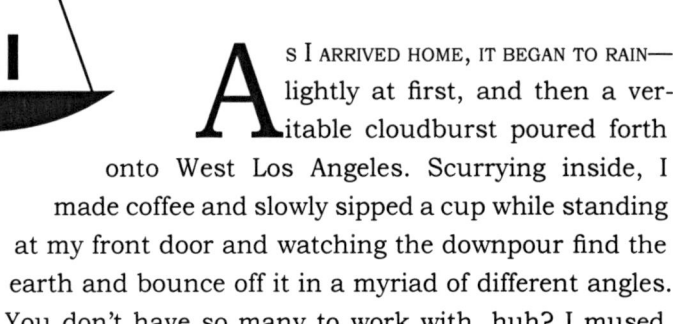

VII

As I arrived home, it began to rain—lightly at first, and then a veritable cloudburst poured forth onto West Los Angeles. Scurrying inside, I made coffee and slowly sipped a cup while standing at my front door and watching the downpour find the earth and bounce off it in a myriad of different angles. You don't have so many to work with, huh? I mused, listening as the rain finally slowed to a relaxing pace, my mind's hyperactive motor following suit. No, reasonable doubt is the only angle you've got, so how about we go cobble a set of facts together that can't result in anything else but? I posed, a thin smile forming as I closed the door. And shuffling over to my comfy couch, for the next several hours I reviewed my notes line by line, forming my closing argument as I ground along. Finally satisfied that it was clear and cohesive, I turned next to a perusal of the jury instructions prepared by the Office's Appellate Department, noting in detail the California Supreme Court Cases that supported them. Around midnight, exhaustion arrived. And greeting it with a wan smile, I carefully repacked my briefbag, then shuffled down the hallway and undressed, set both of my alarm clocks for five-thirty, and slipped into bed. Too tired even to read *Sports Illustrated*, I turned off my nightstand light, and after silently mouthing my prayers, fell into sleep. A troubled sleep, to be sure, as every so often I would awaken with Fred's words, "I want to thank you for caring about me and for fighting so hard for me," ringing into ear, each time triggering a replay of some scene from the trial, with thoughts of what I could have done differently marching alongside. Forcing them from view by summoning forth a picture of Stella's lovely face to smile at till sleep returned, I was unfortunately treated to a continuous repetition of the cycle until finally, at five o'clock, I surrendered and arose.

Forty-five minutes later, after sipping a fresh cup of coffee while I shaved, showered, and dressed, I drove unhampered by traffic to the office. Fortifying myself with two additional cups of caffeine as I surveyed my notes one final time, when the rest of the crew arrived I put them aside and attempted to relax by participating in the usual good-natured banter until it was time to leave for Steiggerman's chambers.

Already dressed in his robe when I entered at ten minutes to eight, when Ludlow followed five minutes later, His Honor promptly settled down to the business at hand and immediately rejected all of the jury instructions I submitted for his consideration. The reason proffered was that they were unnecessary because the ones he customarily gave incorporated the essence of those which I proposed, although couched in somewhat more neutral language. Neutral, my ass, I thought, then for a full five minutes argued, pleaded, and cajoled in a determined effort to at least obtain a compromise. To no avail however, as my articulation of the Supreme Court's logic in the numerous cases I cited in support of a more balanced approach failed to move him one iota from his rigid position. Cutting me off when he determined that I wouldn't take no for an answer, he indicated that my objection would be duly noted by the clerk in order to further protect the appellate remedies I had "already preserved so vigorously." Then, bolting to his feet, he summarily dismissed us with a steely toned "That's all, gentlemen!" before heading to his private bathroom.

Yeah, that's where you belong all right, in the toilet! flashed a thought as I exited, Ludlow trailing surprisingly fast on my heels. "I only wish I could flush it!" I hissed to myself, hurrying to the men's room where I relieved my coffee-filled bladder and washed my flushed face with cold water.

When I returned to the courtroom, Fred was seated at the counsel table, and all twelve members of the jury were assembled in their proper places. Five minutes later, at precisely the called-for eight-thirty, His Honor took the bench, and after quickly greeting the jury and various court personnel, indicated to Ludlow that he could make the opening phase of his final argument. Not wanting to present me with any points to counter, Ludlow waived it, and without uttering a single word Steiggerman nodded to me that it was my turn. "Thank you, Your Honor," I replied as I rose slowly from my chair, then shuffled toward the jury. The journey seemed shorter than it had on Wednesday, but if possible, the burden I carried felt even heavier as reality fully registered that this was it, the ninth inning, the last say-so, the final hope for Fred—and it was all up to me!

Hey, now—relax, whispered a familiar voice. Even with two strikes against you, it only takes one good swing to hit a home run. So take a deep breath, concentrate, and give it your best, coached Grampy Max as I reached the railing of the jury box and the warmth of his smile coaxed one out of the corners of my mouth. "Good morning, ladies and gentlemen," I opened amiably, "I want to begin by thanking you on behalf of both my client and myself for serving as jurors, and for giving me and Mr. Ludlow your undivided attention. It's very much appreciated, and as a small reward, I'm going to try very hard not to bore you with a long and flowery speech. So if you'll grant me just a few minutes more of your valuable time and attention, my job will be finished, and I'll leave you alone to complete yours," I explained while swiveling my head slightly so as to make eye contact with each juror. Pleased that each set was steadfastly fixed on me, I turned to the issues at hand.

"Now when this case began, you and I discussed numerous matters on *voir dire*, and of these, I want to briefly review two with you, the first being presumption of innocence. All twelve of you agreed with the principle that a person charged with a crime is presumed innocent until proven guilty—and I want to point out to you, that that presumption is still fully in effect, and will remain so unless each one of you chooses to overcome it," I tutored, my voice gentle, but serious. "Which, of course, raises the question: What burden of proof is necessary to convince you to make that choice and overcome this presumption of innocence? And that, ladies and gentlemen, is evidence of guilt beyond a reasonable doubt, the second principle I referred to, and one which you all also agreed to apply in determining the outcome of this case. Now, His Honor is going to instruct you on the legal definition of reasonable doubt, and I hope that you will listen very carefully when he does—because he'll tell you that it's not just any doubt, but instead a doubt that a reasonable person would form after looking carefully at all of the evidence presented. And is that an easy task, to weigh all of the evidence and see if it raises a reasonable doubt? ... No, it's most definitely not. In fact, it's very hard work—and before I review with you the evidence in our case, and ask you to do that extremely hard work, I want to first explain why little old me, a stranger to you, has the raw nerve to ask you to do it. And the answer is, because if you don't do it—if you don't search your minds and hearts and struggle with all that's in you to actually apply both the presumption of innocence and beyond a reasonable doubt principles, then the American criminal justice system simply ceases to work," I emphasized with a slight pause, before adding: "Because, ladies and gentlemen, these principles didn't accidentally become the heart and soul of our system. No, they were placed in our Constitution and laws by very wise men to make sure that if you or me, or Mr. Ludlow, or Fred Ginther is charged with a crime, that before our freedom can be taken away, an impartial group of our fellow citizens must be certain beyond a reasonable doubt that that's called for. In fact, we Americans so value our freedom, that our system says it's better for ten guilty persons to go free rather than one innocent one be wrongly convicted. And while that theory of justice is truly magnificent, ladies and gentlemen, in the reality of everyday life in which we all live, it only comes alive and works if each of you actually does that terribly hard work of presuming innocence and applying reasonable doubt," flowed my train of thought into another brief pause, my nodding head being matched by several jurors.

"Okay," I smiled, breaking the momentary silence. "Let's try it together. Right this second, Fred Ginther is an innocent man—and he's going to stay that way unless the evidence in this case convinces each of you otherwise beyond a reasonable doubt. And what is that evidence that requires you to work so terribly hard to sift through and evaluate? ... Well, the way I see it, there's basically two piles of evidence: Officer Hardy's pile, and Fred Ginther's pile. So how about we start by examining Officer Hardy's pile," I suggested, my tone turning conversational. "Now you'll recall that each of you promised you wouldn't give greater weight to an officer's testimony, merely because we've all been raised to believe that law enforcement officials are our protectors and a symbol of honesty. In general, they are of course. But like you and me, they're also human and therefore subject to making mistakes—and being human, they also have a hard time admitting they made a mistake when they do. For example, I'll bet all of us have received a traffic ticket that we honestly didn't think we deserved, and even went to traffic court to tell our side of the story. And can you remember how very difficult it was to get the judge to believe you instead of the officer, 'cause he's a professional law enforcement specialist and you're only an ordinary citizen? Hey, the officer's not biased, runs the reasoning, but you are 'cause you don't want to pay the fine—right? ... Well, not always, correct?" I advanced, then smiled back at several of the jurors who were grinning faintly in acknowledgment.

"Okay, let's examine what Officer Hardy told us," I picked up. "Now for openers, he said that when he first observed Fred from his patrol car, already referring to him as the defendant, Fred was staggering down Belmont Boulevard. However, on cross-examination, Officer Hardy admitted that his observation was made from a distance of no less than a hundred twenty-five feet, through a windshield, in the dark of evening, and across two lanes of oncoming traffic whose headlights shone directly into his eyes—which explains first, why he couldn't say how many times Fred crossed over the center line of the sidewalk over a distance of twenty-five feet, and secondly, why he later changed his word, staggering, to weaving in describing Fred's walking ability," I contended, now beginning to stroll from one side of the jury box to the other as I continued.

"All right, what did we learn next? ... Well, that Officer Hardy ordered Fred to halt—and he did. And that he asked Fred for identification—and he produced his driver's license. Evidence that Fred couldn't function? That he couldn't care for his own safety and welfare? No, no way, ladies and gentlemen—in fact, exactly the opposite!" I stressed, my voice rising slightly. "So what further symptoms did we then receive? Was Fred falling down on the sidewalk? ... No. Was Fred wandering into traffic? ... No. Was Fred causing a disturbance, or molesting other citizens in the area? ... Again, no. Officer Hardy clearly stated that none of these events occurred—so at this point, what evidence do we have that Fred couldn't care for his own safety and welfare? ... Absolutely none, ladies and gentlemen. Absolutely none!" I repeated after slowing to a stop at the center of the jury box and once again swiveling my head to make eye contact with each juror, their facial expressions varying, but appearing to signal they were in agreement.

"All right, now," I picked up, "that leaves us with two final pieces of Officer Hardy's pile to examine. First, there's the field sobriety test, that in connection with, we were told that Fred almost fell down. Well, ladies and gentlemen, almost falling is not the same as actually falling—just like staggering is not the same thing as weaving. Moreover, it's really not important that Fred couldn't place one foot tightly after another on a straight line, 'cause that's an impairment test to determine whether a person can drive safely, not walk safely! ... Now Fred openly admitted to you that he was unsteady on his feet, but the reality is that he didn't actually fall down even once either before or during the sobriety test—so there's absolutely no reason to believe that he couldn't safely continue to his home just three blocks away!" I emphasized strongly by slowing my delivery, then pausing for a second or two.

"Which leads us, ladies and gentlemen, to the very last issue," I resumed, still speaking slowly, "which concerns Fred's alleged statement that he didn't know where he was going. And here's where a little common-sense logic can help us, the question to be carefully answered being: Does it make sense that a man who clearly understood and followed orders to stop and produce identification suddenly became so foggy that he didn't know where he was going, especially when he was headed correctly in the direction of his home just three blocks away? ... Well, ladies and gentlemen, I would strongly suggest that that makes no sense at all, 'cause it's just not logical, it just doesn't figure. I mean, a man can clearly understand and comply with two orders, so one plus one equals two. But add a request for just one simple piece of information to the equation, and all of a sudden, he answers two and a half? ... No, common sense says, absolutely not!" I concluded firmly, shaking my head and pausing to let my argument sink in.

"All right, ladies and gentlemen," I picked up after several seconds had passed, "in that most of the evidence shows that Fred was clearly able to care for his own safety and welfare—the exact opposite of the charge against him—and because when analyzed the remaining sobriety test and alleged statement are heavily clouded, our previously formed reasonable doubt remains strongly in place unless weakened by the second pile of evidence. So let's see," I advocated, resuming my stroll, "and let's look first at Fred's credibility in order to learn whether we can believe him. Probably the most important test relates to the subject of drinking—and in this regard, did Fred deny that he had been? ... No, he didn't. In fact, he openly and honestly admitted to you that he had four drinks during the roughly three hours he was at Sam's Place. Not only that, he further admitted that they had made him a little high, and more unsteady on his feet than usual," I recounted, coating my tone with sincerity. "So, is this evidence of Fred hiding the truth? ... No, ladies and gentlemen, the exact opposite—total honesty. In fact, Fred even confessed to you that he was ashamed about having cried over losing his job and being unable to care for his wife and children. That certainly wasn't easy for him, but he did it because he was totally leveling with you—and that's why he's equally believable when he told you that he was a little high, but not so much so that he didn't know what he was doing, which was going home. And you know what, ladies and gentlemen? A little high makes darned good sense, if you stop and consider that during the three hours Fred was in Sam's place, the effects of two of the drinks would have in large part worn off, leaving him influenced by only two drinks, not four," I stressed, stopping once again at the center of the jury box.

"Okay," I nodded, heading into the homestretch. "The two piles have been examined, and I thank you for listening so patiently. In closing, I want to remind you, ladies and gentlemen, that you are the trier of fact, that you are the ones who decide whether or not the evidence goes beyond a reasonable doubt. Not me. Not Mr. Ludlow. Not His Honor. But you, and only you, have this responsibility. And you, and only you, have the opportunity to make a judgment that honors justice," I informed, emotion having seeped inside my voice, my pace quickening. "Now in a minute or two, the District Attorney is going to have the last word with you, and I won't have the opportunity to respond. So while listening carefully to Mr. Ludlow, I urge you to also carefully remember what we've discussed together—especially the fact that the state has the burden of proof, not Fred. That's why the only verdicts are guilty and not guilty. You don't have to find that Fred was lily-white innocent. No, instead your sole duty is to judge whether the state has proved guilt beyond a reasonable doubt," I underscored one final time, then exhaled slowly before making my final plea.

"Ladies and gentlemen, the charge here is not being intoxicated, but instead being intoxicated to such an extent that one is unable to care for his own safety and welfare. And the overriding question is simply this: When the evidence shows that Fred was absolutely able to understand and comply with orders to halt and produce identification, never once fell to the ground, didn't wander into traffic, wasn't disturbing anyone, and was walking, albeit unsteadily, toward his home just three blocks away, how can the state claim in view of all these factors that he was unable to care for his own safety and welfare beyond a reasonable doubt? ... And the answer I trust you'll find is that they can't!" I urged strenuously. "Because simple common sense says: Hey, wait just a minute. There's clearly a doubt here. A reasonable doubt. And that means Fred's not guilty!" I concluded confidently, then added through a faint smile: "Thank you, ladies and gentlemen. Thank you very much."

Slipping back into my seat after an absence of nine minutes, I felt myself gradually begin to relax as I listened to Ludlow quietly deliver his closing remarks. Unsurprisingly, the entire focus of his argument was that Fred Ginther could not be believed because he was the defendant and obviously had something to lose, whereas the officers, who were mere servants of the people and had no axe to grind, could be believed beyond a reasonable doubt—thus leading to only one possible conclusion: that Fred Ginther was guilty as charged. When Ludlow finished, after having spoken deliberately and unemotionally for just over three minutes, Steiggerman, in his most fatherly tone of voice, painstakingly instructed the jury, and at ten minutes after nine they retired to the jury room to deliberate.

After a second, urgently needed visit to the men's room, I spent the remainder of the morning interviewing clients whose cases appeared on today's calendar. At noon, when the jury hadn't reached a verdict, His Honor declared an unusually long luncheon recess, the extra thirty minutes allowing me to join Robbie and Leon for a visit to the nearby Sizzler Steak House. Feeling considerably more relaxed, but still without appetite, I played with a mixed green salad and sipped two cups of coffee while bantering with them about events in the morning newspaper, photography, a hobby they shared in common, and plans for the coming weekend. Then I returned to Division Four and the unholy trinity of dismiss, plea bargain, and continue, until at three thirty-five, Roberts appeared in chambers and announced that the jury had reached a verdict.

After I promptly returned to my chair at the counsel table, an eternity seemingly passed before Fred reappeared in the courtroom through the side door and was seated next to me. Steiggerman had already taken the bench, and at three forty-five the jurors slowly and silently filed out of the jury room and took their places in the jury box. Studying their faces for some indication of what they had decided, I was unable to glean even a trace of a clue as one stressful second crept into another. Finally, His Honor interrupted the heavy silence that hovered over the courtroom like a nimbus cloud, and inquired as to whether the jury had selected a foreman. "Yes, Your Honor," announced Herman Sears after standing. And when his reply to the follow-up question of whether or not the jury had reached a verdict was identical, a brief bustle of activity occurred wherein Roberts obtained the written form and handed it to Steiggerman, who glanced at it without changing expression, then handed it to the Court Clerk, Ted Greene, with instructions to read it aloud. And rising unsteadily, my heart quickening its beat, I stood alongside Fred as he faced the jury and Greene quickly sped over the form introduction, then slowed his delivery upon reaching the actual verdict.

"And we, the jury, having heard all of the evidence presented, and having duly deliberated thereon," he pronounced without a trace of emotion, "do hereby find the defendant, Fred Ginther ... guilty as charged!" droned the conclusion, the final three words seeming to hang suspended in the warm, moist air for several slow-motion seconds before then exploding into my consciousness. Feeling as if I had been soundly struck in the abdomen, I raised my right hand to my chest and gently rubbed it as breathing resumed, then glanced at Fred who appeared as thunderstruck as I was, his large brown eyes having filled with tears. Strenuously fighting off the desire to cry myself, when Steiggerman then followed up by inquiring whether I'd like the jury polled, I squeezed out a weak "Yes," and stared numbly as each juror replied "guilty" when Greene called their respective names.

Recovering from the shock as Steiggerman thanked the jury profusely for having fulfilled their civic duty, then dismissed them, I remained standing alongside Fred as they filed silently out of the room without any one of them casting a glance in our direction. And when His Honor then asked whether the defendant was ready for sentencing, his face absent the triumphant smile I had expected, my "Yes, Your Honor, we are," was delivered with a restored firmness.

"I would, with leave of the Court, point out to you," I picked up, sincerity, fueled by heartfelt hurt, flooding into my tone, "that this is my client's first and only transgression against the law—and that he does have a wife and four children who depend solely upon him for their support. These are truly mitigating circumstances, Your Honor, and I deeply hope that you will give them full consideration. Thank you, Your Honor."

Surprisingly, his grim expression softened, and for a fleeting second, I thought that my brief argument might have penetrated the hard outer shell and touched on a reservoir of sympathy that lay hidden deep inside him. Wrong again, however. For while no I-told-you-so-grin emanated from his mouth, payback remained firmly centered in his mind as he rendered his decision.

"Very well, Mr. Harris," shuffled his acknowledgment, his delivery then picking up speed as his tone hardened. "The defendant having been found guilty of violating Section 647-f of the California Penal Code, and the Court having heard from his counsel on the issue of sentencing, it is the judgment of this Court that Fred Samuel Ginther be placed on one year's summary probation, upon the condition that he serve the next ninety days in the county jail!" drummed the decree remorselessly. "The bailiff will please take charge of the defendant and deliver custody of him to the sheriff forthwith! And this Court stands adjourned," Steiggerman tacked on without pause, then rose and exited into his chambers with a speed ordinarily reserved for Olympic sprinters.

Drained, I slowly sank back into my chair and watched helplessly as Fred was led away, his head bowed to hide the tears trickling down his face. When he disappeared through the doorway, for several moments I just sat there alone and concentrated on the large lump in my throat. Then, the hurt seemingly renewing with each beat of my heart, I quickly shoved my notes into my briefbag, and without knowing exactly where I was going, left the courtroom. As I emerged, I almost bumped into Ludlow, who was apparently looking for me. Shaking his hand, I congratulated him on his victory, then attempted to move on. He wanted to talk, however, and began by complimenting me on the "outstanding" job I had done. "Best closing argument I ever heard," he nodded out before I interjected that I was in a hurry to head home, thanked him for the sentiment, added my congratulations again, and walked away without looking back. When I reached the first floor and was halfway to the large double doors leading outside, a voice called out to me from a dimly lit corner. "Mr. Harris—wait please," sounded a request softly. And turning to my left, I observed a pleasant looking but shabbily dressed woman in her mid-thirties rise from the wooden bench where she had been waiting and walk toward me.

"Yes, ma'am, that's me—or what's left of me anyhow," I replied as she drew near, causing her to smile.

"My name's Ann—Ann Ginther. I'm Fred's wife, and I'm pleased to meet you."

"Well I'm pleased to meet you too," I nodded, returning her smile faintly. "And I can't tell you how sorry I am about what happened to Fred."

"Ohhh ... you couldn't help that. You did the best you could, and I could see how hard you tried," she replied soothingly. "Now I know you must be tired and have things to do, so I don't want to keep you. I just wanted to thank you for trying to help us."

The lump in my throat, which had disappeared only minutes before, returned suddenly and swelled even larger as the soft, humble tones of her voice trailed into silence. "Thank you, Ann, I really appreciate that," I returned, my voice almost cracking. "Say, can I offer you a ride home?" I added as we stepped outside into the early evening air.

"That's so nice, Mr. Harris, but I have the car with with me—it's over there with the kids," she answered, her eyes moistening as they focused on the hurt showing in mine. "You take care now—and thanks again for everything," she added, then turned and hurried away.

When I crossed the street and reached the front door of the office, I found it locked. Time to go home, announced a thought wearily as I glanced at my watch and learned it was five-fifteen. The week's over, and it's time to go home, I nodded to myself as I walked around the side of the building to the parking lot. The only problem is, I mused as I entered my car and drove toward the freeway, I don't want to, the prospect of being alone in an empty apartment with only painful disappointment for company causing me to shake my head as I reached the freeway and turned north. "So, don't!" I declared defiantly, switching on the radio and searching my mind for options. None surfaced. Absolutely zero. So when it began to rain heavily, I concentrated on listening to its steady beat on the roof of my car until a medley of Beatles tunes captured my attention, and singing along to "Hello, Goodbye" and "Hey Jude" proved successful in forcing flittering thoughts of the trial, along with the sweet, sad faces of Fred and Ann Ginther, out of mind. Slowly, as the miles sped by, numbness settled over me like a heavy blanket and combined with the warmth from the car's heater to create a snug-as-a-bug feeling that was so highly pleasing it fostered a smile. In fact, so momentarily content was I that when I reached West Los Angeles and Jeannie C. Riley was thumbing her nose at the Harper Valley P.T.A., suddenly an appealing possibility materialized. How does a nice drive up the coast sound to you, Matthew, old boy? danced an enticing idea onto center stage, then dangled before my eyes like a lollipop offered to a crying child with a skinned knee. "Sounds good to me," I chuckled in response, switching back to the middle lane and accelerating. "And tell you what," I added, "if by some strange and miraculous event you should get hungry, I'll even throw in dinner."

It was a good plan, and one that gained luster when at eight o'clock I reached the outskirts of Santa Barbara and the warmth of her twinkling lights beckoned to me. Only it didn't work. Finding a cozy-looking coffee shop, and purchasing an evening newspaper as I entered, I spent the next hour drinking coffee and poring over the sports page. Then, unable to eat much of the eggs and sausage I'd ordered, and after my stomach refused more than two bites of my favorite pecan pie, I wandered back outside and lit up my pipe. It tasted delicious, and together we considered what to do next, a hopeful process that quickly proved futile during a ten-minute discussion. So, after rejecting once and for all the recurring idea of driving on through the night to visit San Francisco, I was forced to accept the reality that home and bed was the best place for a half-depressed, totally exhausted young man with unacceptable ideas of what to do with himself. And climbing back inside my Mustang, affectionately nicknamed Old Greener for long and faithful service, I dutifully headed her due south.

As I reentered the San Fernando Valley, the skies that had been rainless for a hundred miles suddenly exploded with lightning that reoccurred with sufficient frequency to cast an eerie glow over Los Angeles. In combination with the accompanying thunder that clapped and rolled across the somber sky, they created a spooky atmosphere that was sadly suited to the return of my prior mood. For on the return journey, slowly but steadily, the veil of numbness which had sheltered me wore thin, allowing the pain of loss to worm its way back inside my chest, where it formed an ache that seemingly churned inside itself to grow larger. And with the music from the radio no longer able to suppress thoughts of the trial, snapshots of Hardy's arrogance and Steiggerman's abuse of authority now flashed in sync with the lightning bolts, and the crushing sound of the jury's "Guilty as charged!" echoed afresh with each thunderclap, until finally the dam broke and the pain rushed upward and flooded my eyes. Suddenly, I couldn't see clearly, and swerved dangerously, the blare of car horns warning me back into the center lane where I swiped away tears, then with trembling hands steered off the freeway at the next exit and braked Old Greener to a halt.

Exiting in search of fresh air, I stumbled and fell when a wave of nausea swept over me, followed by swirling dizziness. For half a minute, I just lay there, trying to understand what happened. Then, recognizing fatigue and famine as the culprits, I dragged myself to my feet and back inside the car just as the heavens unleashed a full-fledged monsoon. Resting my head on the steering wheel, I chuckled softly as the driving rain fiercely assaulted Old Greener, my ever faithful sense of humor asking: What? Did you drive all the way to India? And somehow the unlikely combination of falling down, coupled with the truth of trying to escape contained within my gibe, acted as correction fluid applied to a typing error—leaving the hurtful ache in place, but overlaying it with a new and stronger resolve. "Okay, you won this game, motherfucker, 'cause my best wasn't good enough to overcome your evilness," I whispered, raising my head to stare with cold anger at the image of Steiggerman pronouncing 'ninety days in the county jail!,' my father's face sliding into view alongside. "But you only half won at that, 'cause you want me to quit, and that's not happening," I nodded, too tired to yell, but emotion infiltrating nonetheless. "Not only that, you cocksucking sonofabitch," hissed my follow-up, "but I've got news: The World Series is the best out of seven, so the game's still on. And I'm going to make my best better and better, until somehow, someway I'm going to break your balls, then dance on your fucking grave!" I ended, smiling at how much better I felt.

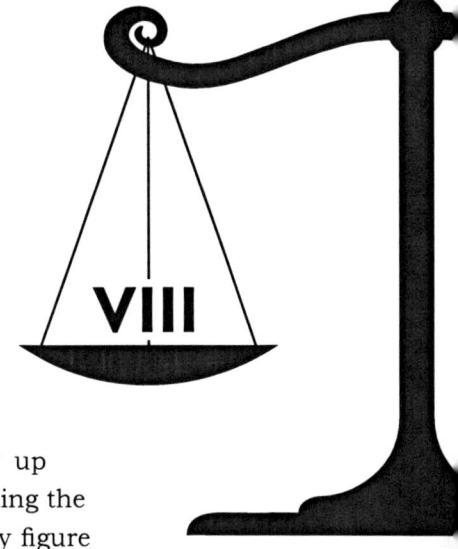

VIII

WHEN I REACHED HOME AROUND eleven-fifteen, the rain had finally ceased. And after patting Old Greener good-night, I slowly strolled down the sidewalk and part way up the path to my front door, luxuriously inhaling the chilly night air. Surprised to find a shadowy figure underneath an umbrella standing on my porch, I approached further and inquired as to whether I could be of assistance.

"Matthew? ... Is that you?" replied the umbrella-draped figure.

"Uh-huh," I answered unsurely, then recognized Stella as she lowered the umbrella.

"Are you all right?" she quizzed, seeming slightly irritated. "When you didn't answer my note or calls, I thought maybe I should check."

"Yeah, I'm okay—and that's very nice," I responded, stepping forward to open the door and flip on the entry hall light. "I just got home, so I didn't know. But it's good to see you as always. C'mon in."

For several seconds she just stood there staring at me as if she couldn't gather all of me in with a single glance. Then, stepping inside, her expression indicated that better light hadn't improved my appearance. "My, God, what in the hell happened to you?" hurtled her query, concern replacing her prior irritation.

"Well, I had a little accident," I explained, too tired to feel fully embarrassed. "But I'm okay—honest."

"Well, you'd never know it to look at you, that's for sure. Your clothes are soaking wet, and your pants have mud on them, and a tear over the knee—and they look good next to you!" she expounded forcefully. "I mean, you're so pale you look like a ghost, and your eyes are so bloodshot that I can hardly make out any white at all. You look like you haven't slept in a week, and haven't eaten in a month. Why, you'd think you just fought World War Three and lost!"

Emotionally drained as I was, the adjective "lost" still struck a nerve and caused a sour taste to pool underneath my tongue, a defensive response collecting on top. But as I looked at her standing there in her raincoat, concern mapped across her lovely face, I choked off the harsh words that had formed and, after sinking onto my couch, simply muttered softly: "I did Stella ... I did."

Shuffling over to the sofa, she sat down beside me and smiled. "Listen, why don't you come up to my place," she suggested, her tone suddenly comforting. "A little brandy and some hot food will make you feel better, and then we can talk. C'mon now, try it and you'll see."

Nodding my okay, I followed her up off the couch and toward the front door. As we neared it, Stella added: "Say, why don't you grab a pair of jeans and a shirt to slip into. Your clothes are soaked, and you could catch one hell of a cold." Hearing my mother, I smiled, then walked into the bedroom and returned shortly with the suggested items. Half a minute later we reached her apartment, and once inside, Stella flicked on several lights and proceeded immediately into the kitchen where she hastily poured something into a pan, placed it on top of the stove, then returned to me.

"Listen, I've got a great idea. While the brandy is warming, how about you slip into the bathroom and take a hot shower?"

Never argue with someone who's right, unless you're getting paid to, was another of Grampy Max's axioms. And in that I wasn't, my "Sounds good" instantly seconded the motion, the natural appeal of her proposal combined with her gentle hold of my right arm as she led me toward the bathroom further assuring me that I had made the correct decision. Setting my fresh clothing down on the pink tile counter that supported the wash basin, Stella quickly produced a matching set of large, chocolate-brown bath towels, and after chirping, "Now get warm—and take your time," disappeared back into the living room.

Reprocessing the unexpected sequence of events that had occurred since I arrived home as I undressed and carefully folded up my soiled shirt and suit, I began to hope that perhaps the needed shower could also lessen the fog of exhaustion that seemed to have my brain functioning in slow motion. And pursuing the idea hopefully, I twisted the knob to On, climbed inside, and stood underneath the steady stream of hot water for several soothing minutes. It was a huge success, as slowly but surely a degree of clarity returned. And when I noticed that I was beginning to feel like a boiled lobster, I celebrated by soaping myself and studying the suds as they cascaded downward off my body onto the tile floor. If I needed any further proof of the return of my faculties to full function, the uninvited thought that I was showering where Stella took hers clearly convinced me—accompanied as it was by imagination's vision of how incredibly sexy she looked with soapy water tumbling down over her naked body. "Beyond a reasonable doubt," I chuckled sarcastically, quickly turning off the shower, then hurrying to dry myself off and slip into my shirt and jeans.

When I reentered the living room, Stella was seated on the couch sipping a drink. "Well, now, that looks more like the Matthew Robert Harris I know," she smiled. "Come sit down, I've got your drink all ready for you." And arising, she entered the kitchen, poured my drink, and returned just as I settled onto the sofa. Sitting down close to me, she stared into my eyes as she handed me a large, dark-green mug that was warm to the touch.

Wrapping both hands around it, I took several long sips before settling back against the cushions and drawing my bare feet up underneath me. "That's good, Stelle—what is it?"

"Stella's secret mixture of brandy and a few spices. Drink some more, and tell me what you want for dinner."

Taking another swallow, I smiled wryly at the thought. "Would you believe that I'm not hungry?"

"Well, you need to eat something. How about some cheese and fruit to go along with Stella's brew?"

"Okay," I nodded. "I can handle that."

Rising a second time, she returned shortly with an assortment of cheeses and apple slices, which surprisingly tasted delicious. "Maybe the drink sparked my appetite," I speculated between mouthfuls of Gouda and Edam, sipping steadily at my refilled mug to wash them down.

"Don't analyze it," she smiled, "just enjoy."

I did. And it wasn't until half an hour of idle chatter had passed, during which I consumed most of a third mug of Stella's brew, that our conversation finally returned to the events which fostered our little get-together. "All right, you're looking a little better now," she smiled encouragingly as the closing strains of Paul Mauriat's "Love Is Blue" faded away on the stereo. "So tell me what happened."

"Well," I shrugged, taking a deep breath, then exhaling slowly, "the whole terrible truth is, I lost the trial, Stelle. I gave it everything that was in me, but no matter," I explained, the alcohol having dissolved my built-in resistance to discussing failure. "And while it hurts a lot, that's okay for me, but it isn't for my client, Fred, or his sweet wife and kids," I added, emotion creeping into my voice. "They shouldn't have to pay 'cause I wasn't good enough to beat the odds."

"Ohh ... I see ... I'm sorry," trickled her response cautiously. "But I'm sure you did everything you could, right?"

"Uh-huh, that I did," I nodded, meeting her gaze. "It's the only grace-saving factor—that they know how much I care about them. They even thanked me for it, both of them. Fred's doing ninety fucking days in jail, and can't even try to earn money for food and rent, and what does his wife do? She waits outside the courtroom to tell me how much she appreciated my fighting so hard," tumbled my explanation sadly, flashing images of Fred being led away mixing with Ann's sweet-sad smile to recoil the pain inside my chest and squeeze tears into the corners of my eyes.

Searching my darkened face carefully for a clue on how to respond, and finding no answer, Stella didn't say anything. Instead, after four or five seconds of awkward silence had gained weight, she slowly leaned forward and kissed me lightly on my lips.

"Hey, what's that for?" I smiled with surprise.

"For being you," she said softly, wiping away my tears. "For caring so much that it hurts."

Feeling my face flush as she remained close, and with her brew having also dissolved my inhibitions, my tongue took on a life of its own. "Did I ever mention that you're incredibly beautiful?" I listened to my subconscious interject, apparently unwilling to listen to any further pity-party complaints from the overloaded upper chamber.

"Nooo," she chuckled, "I don't think that ever came up during our little chats."

"Well, for the record, you are—and beyond any doubt, reasonable or otherwise," I assured, joining the conversation's new subject through a fresh grin.

"Well ... thank you, kind sir. But if I remember correctly, pretty ladies frighten you. So are you scared?" she teased, leaning in even closer.

"No, that's not the right word exactly—terrified would be far more accurate," I squeezed out, inhaling the sweet scent of her perfume and feeling fully the weight of her breasts pressing against my chest.

"Well, we can't have that—brave warriors shouldn't be terrified. So come with me, I've got the cure," she quipped encouragingly, taking me by the hand and guiding me up off the couch and toward the hallway leading to her bedroom.

Stunned by the filtering realization that my long-stored fantasy had somehow suddenly and mysteriously come to life, and with the third mug having coaxed my defense mechanisms into early retirement, I followed without uttering a single word. When we reached the bedroom, Stella quickly lighted a candle seated on a nightstand adjacent to the telephone, which she disconnected, and then after returning to where I was standing transfixed, slowly unbuttoned my jeans, followed by my shirt, which she slipped off my shoulders, the touch of her long, slender fingers sending a wave of excitement coursing through me. Smiling in response, and still half disbelieving, when she then unzipped and stepped out of the high-style housecoat she had changed into while I was showering, for several seconds I had to force myself to breathe. "Stelle," I managed to murmur as she gently pulled me down onto the bed next to her, "I was wrong—incredibly beautiful doesn't do it. Perfect comes closer, but that could leave you wide open to being sued for being a monopoly. So how about—"

"How about you stop talking, and kiss me?" she interjected, smiling and opening her arms to me.

"You got that right, pretty lady ... for sure," I whispered, nestling closer and cupping her face in my hands, then drawing her lips into mine. Velvet heaven, flashed a fleeting thought as I lost myself completely in her sweet softness, kissing and kissing and kissing her lovely face. Nothing escaped my exploring lips and tongue as I kissed her mouth, her eyes, her cheeks, the tip of her nose. Up and down, and from side to side I moved, not even pausing to fully breathe for fear that the crystal magic of the moment might shatter into tiny pieces and scatter away, never again to be fastened whole.

Seconds later, we separated only long enough for her to guide my hands to her breasts. Kneading the full, firm, creamy white mounds gently, I followed by moving my parade of kisses to their pink tips till they hardened, then downward over her ribcage and across the perfectly flat stomach to the heavy triangular shadow covering the ultimate cathedral. Returning upward after a pleasurable moan escaped off her tongue and she reached forward and caressed my stone-hard member, suddenly I hesitated, memories of Lanie flashing into view. Sensing a flare of anxiety from the shadow that flittered across my eyes even as they searched her shimmering shades of lavender, Stella curled a sweet smile out of the corners of her mouth and softly squeezed out, "Just let go, Matty ... let go of everything ... and just make love."

Nodding ever so slightly as she gently pulled me toward her, I kissed her lips tenderly as I slowly slipped inside her, the warm, wet welcome foreclosing thought and memory. Time then took a holiday as the sparks of heat fomenting deep inside our bodies broke into open flame, and glowing ever brighter as we moved rhythmically against one another in our insatiable drive to the summit, finally rewarded us with an exquisite explosion of pure ecstasy.

When I could finally breathe again, my eyes searched for her face and found it radiant, pink-flushed cheeks highlighting the pale-yellow light that flickered off the textured wallpaper to peacefully bathe both of us. Kissing the tip of her nose tenderly, I whispered, "God, that was wonderful, Stelle."

"You got that right—Big Time, as you would say," she returned softly, pulling me closer for a tight hug that lasted for several seconds, until finally I gently withdrew and lowered myself sideways onto the pillows where I smiled contentedly at her.

"I don't think even Shakespeare, on his best day, could capture that," I offered when the silence finally seemed to summon sound. "I mean—"

"Sshhh," Stella whispered, "there'll be lots of time to talk in the morning—you need to sleep. You're safe, Matty ... totally safe—so just close your eyes and sleep."

And I did, the lullaby inside her voice massaging me into dreamland almost instantly, then guiding me to long and sound. No dreams. No nightmares. No interruptions of any sort. Just eleven blessed hours of repair, restoration, and rejuvenation.

When I awakened, I was alone. Stella had thoughtfully left an extra robe on the foot of the bed. And climbing inside its pale-blue terrycloth softness, I smiled at myself in the mirror above the dresser before shuffling down the hallway into the living room.

"Well, good morning," Stella smiled from her seat in the nearby dining room, putting down her cup of coffee. "How do you feel?"

"Like I've been born all over again—thanks to you," rushed my reply, my eyes surveying her with equal speed. Having already showered, she remained in her pink bathrobe. And underneath the dark hair that she had twisted into a bun atop her head, the scrubbed ivory skin of her face, absent even a trace of makeup, gleamed like fine porcelain, accenting the deep purple pools of her eyes, and painting a portrait of such perfect beauty that it almost hurt to look at her.

"Well, good," she bounced back at me, her own flash inspection having confirmed some improvement in my appearance. "How about some coffee, then breakfast? You must be starved by now."

"Coffee sounds great—especially with some conversation. Then we can talk breakfast, okay?"

"Sure," she nodded, rising, then returning in seconds with a large mug.

"Now, what's on your mind that pushes food onto a back burner?" she queried through a fresh smile.

"Well, for openers, why last night?"

"Well, I promised I'd give you some tips about women—they worked pretty good, don't you think?" chirped her good-natured tease.

"Absolutely, positively, divine. But the question still remains why? I mean, I'm not complaining, and if I may quote Lou Gehrig, I consider myself the luckiest man alive. But still, what did I do to deserve being so lucky?"

"Lots of things, but mostly 'cause I like you."

"You like me—that's it?"

"Alll … right, all right—serious time, huh?"

"Uh-huh."

"Well, the truth is, I like you a lot, Matty—a real lot," she replied, her eyes meeting mine, her voice filling with sincerity. "You're just such a curious mixture—so kind, and gentle, and caring, yet so intense and angry, and hard on yourself. I've never known anyone like you—with all those elements somehow mixed together. But the bottom line is, you're filled with goodness and honesty—and that's hard to find, trust me," she finished, her smile fading slightly.

"Wow, that's a mouthful," skipped my response. "I don't know exactly what to say."

"You don't have to say anything, Matty, but know that it wasn't just a gift. Oh, you needed to be hugged and kissed all right, but I needed to be hugged and kissed by that good heart of yours, too—understand?"

"I … think so," I replied after a slight hesitation, feeling more satisfied, but still finding her explanation hard to fully accept.

"Then everything's okay?"

"Sure," I nodded. "And to prove it, let's do breakfast."

"Okay. How does some hot cereal, eggs, sausage, and toast sound to you?"

"That'd be great—thanks."

Promptly reheating the oatmeal and pouring herself a second cup of coffee, Stella rejoined me at the table, sliding her chair closer to mine so that we could read the paper together, in particular a follow-up article on the election of Shirley Chisholm to the House of Representatives that she'd pen-marked a star by. "How about that!" shot out my exuberant response. "First time in history that a black female will serve in the House! Here's to the little lady from Brooklyn's worst ghetto!" I toasted, raising my mug in salute.

"Yeah, I thought you'd like that—me too," she added, smiling.

"Hey, looky here," I said, pointing with my finger. "Yale's announced that it's planning to go co-ed. So score two more big points for the Women's Movement as well, and thank God for some good news to balance out the election of Tricky Dick. You know, the eggs and sausage are going to sit one whole hell of a lot better."

They did, too, interlaced with our speculative discussion that maybe, just maybe, President Johnson's halting the bombing of North Vietnam would lead to real progress at the Paris Peace Talks, the North Vietnamese response of allowing the South Vietnamese Government to participate giving rise to reasonable hope. Then, over more coffee, our attention turned to how to spend the remainder of the afternoon. The renewing drizzle ruled out a long walk, the football games on TV weren't of particular interest, so very quickly we decided to take in a movie.

Funny Girl, starring Barbra Streisand, was easily first choice, and the four o'clock showing found us snuggled into cushiony seats with an unobstructed view, holding hands. Unexpectedly happy to begin with, and quickly enthralled by Streisand's once-in-a-lifetime voice, I soon found myself completely relaxed for the first time in months, Solina and all its problems blessedly banished for a couple of precious hours. A jealous mistress, however, on the drive back home after we grabbed a bite of dinner at Hamburger Hamlet, she once again raised her irksome head. "Matty, I don't mean to bring up a sore subject," Stella prefaced cautiously in response to my offhand comment that I wished I could lawyer half as good as Streisand could sing, "but can I ask you something about the trial?"

"Sure ... what?"

"Well, did you make some particular mistake that you blame yourself for?"

"No ... I don't think so—maybe I screwed up in who I kicked off the jury and who I left on, but I didn't really have all that much to work with. Robbie taught me to stay away from the call-the-cop-a-liar defense, so I tried to show that they were simply biased, and focus instead on the facts which led to a reasonable doubt that Fred was intoxicated to such an extent that he couldn't care for his own safety and welfare," I explained calmly, tuning back in to the trial's sequence of events. "However, it still boiled down to the fact that Officer Hardy insisted that Fred told him he didn't know where he was going after they stopped him, and even when Fred testified opposite, and Hardy agreed that he was walking in the right direction toward his home just three blocks away, my all-white jury rejected common sense in favor of not calling Hardy a liar."

"All white? In Solina?" she questioned disbelievingly.

"Uh-huh. I fought that issue too, before the trial started. But Steiggerman, the pig judge that he is, shot me down on the technicality that my motion wasn't timely or in writing, even though I didn't see the jury panel until they were ushered in," I answered, emotion beginning to creep into my tone. "Then for a bonus, His Arrogance spent the rest of the trial discrediting me in front of the jury at every opportunity. Stelle, I swear I'm going to get that sonofabitch, if it's the last thing I do!"

"Well, I'm not a lawyer," soothed her response, "but it sounds as you were pretty damn good—especially considering all the handicaps, along with the fact that it was your first trial."

"You wouldn't be just a little bit biased now, would you?" I smiled, turning my head to peek at her. "I mean the fact that I consider you to be the most beautiful woman on earth wouldn't influence you, would it?"

"No," she chuckled, "'cause I know I'm not. But thanks for thinking so, I like it coming from you, 'cause I know you mean it, even though your eyes need a check-up. And besides," she tacked on as we reached home and parked, "that's not really important, is it?"

"No ... no it isn't, and I know it. I'm not shallow like that sounds," I answered as we strolled back to her apartment. "Still, somehow part of me needs to know that if I can appeal to someone as beautiful as you, then somehow I deserve it. I can't help it, last night was really special for me, and extremely meaningful. I don't even have words to properly express it," I ended as we entered inside.

"You don't need any, Matty," she stressed, taking my hand and turning me so that our eyes met. "As I already told you, it was beautiful for me too—and as for meaningful ... well, it's not over you know, it wasn't a one-night stand, at least not for me."

"You can just magnify that to infinity for me, pretty lady," bounced my reply through a fast spreading smile.

"Well, I can't speak for infinity," she shot right back at me. "But in order to prove our mutual feeling beyond a reasonable doubt, I think that more experience is needed—how about you?"

"Did I fail to mention that you're also a genius?" I chuckled, this time taking her hand and leading toward the bedroom.

What followed was even more special than our prior coupling. With both of us more relaxed, and the absence of alcohol leaving us more alert and receptive to each and every tender caress, tiny seeds of true intimacy seeped into play and raised the level of our enjoyment to a new height. In fact, afterward neither of us even attempted words, the feeling in our eyes doing all the speaking necessary. Even the long, deep sleep that followed was better, my prayer of gratitude collapsing into dreamland in sync with my closing eyes.

Arising nine halcyon hours later, this time I found Stella sitting on the living-room floor surrounded by a semi-circle of sketches, color swatches, and paint and tile samples, scribbling in a notepad. "What have we here?" I chuckled, dropping down beside her and kissing her on the cheek.

"Hi, there, sleepyhead," she smiled. "Just a project I'm working on."

"Looks complicated," I nodded, having noted that the sketches were precisely drawn and included much detail. "Did you go to school for this, Stelle?"

"Uh-huh. But only for two years—I had the baby to take care of, and work, and after a while I couldn't keep up with it all so I dropped out."

"Well, it looks very professional to me, especially the sketches."

"Thanks for noticing, 'cause drawing's special to me. It's my little gift, and really helps me think through coordinating room color, carpet, and furnishings—after, of course, learning what my clients' tastes and preferences are to begin with. I get to be creative, but within boundaries naturally."

"Yeah, I see. But what about your family, couldn't your parents help out with the baby, and some bucks, so you could finish?"

"No," she shook her head, "the school was in Dallas, and they still lived in the small town where I was born and raised, about a hundred miles away."

"I see ... Well, no matter, you obviously learned enough to put your super creativity into action Big Time!" I enthused.

"I don't know about super or Big Time," she grinned, "but I'm pretty good at what I do, and my clients seem to be satisfied—this project here is a referral. You hungry? I am!"

I was. Stella cooked. And once again we ate seated close together, this time sharing the front section of the overstuffed Sunday Edition of the *Times*. Afterward, the afternoon drifted slowly away with us leisurely reading the special sections while an NFL game droned by on the TV. Perfect, I thought, when I occasionally interrupted my reading to glance over at her, or she discovered an item she felt would interest me and casually called for my attention.

It wasn't until after we shared a macaroni and cheese dinner that the veil of total relaxation and comfort was disturbed by the creeping realization that the weekend was coming to a close, birthing an uncomfortable silence. When I could no longer stand the swelling ache that arises when a treasured time has visited and all too swiftly passed away, I entered the kitchen where she was emptying the dishwasher and pulled Stella into a hug. "Listen, pretty lady, I know it's time for me to go, but I really don't want to," I whispered over her shoulder.

"It's okay, Matty—it's not over," she replied softly, stepping out of the hug and kissing me lightly on the lips.

"God, I hope not. It's just that I don't know how this works—when I can see you again."

"No problem," she smiled. "No rules—you can see me whenever you want, just call. I know you've got a lot on your mind, and so much to do, so don't overcrowd your schedule and run yourself into the ground. Let's just take it slow and steady, okay?"

"Uh-huh ... sounds reasonable—and I'll call soon, I promise."

"You just better, Mr. Public Defender, or I'll get that pig judge to bug you," she teased as we walked to the front door.

Hugging her tightly again in response, just in case, my subconscious warned, when I finally released her, I turned and hurried down the stairs, not trusting myself to look back.

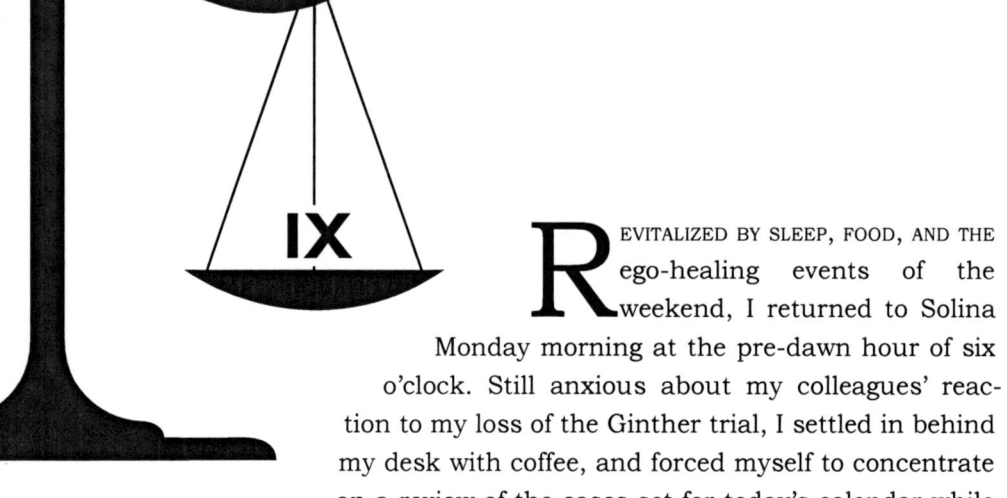

IX

REVITALIZED BY SLEEP, FOOD, AND THE ego-healing events of the weekend, I returned to Solina Monday morning at the pre-dawn hour of six o'clock. Still anxious about my colleagues' reaction to my loss of the Ginther trial, I settled in behind my desk with coffee, and forced myself to concentrate on a review of the cases set for today's calendar while awaiting their respective arrivals. Much to my surprise, not a word was uttered about the sore subject as they drifted in, then bustled about the office bantering at one another intermittently while preparing for their various assignments. Only Marilyn acted differently, bringing me a second cup of coffee while I was poring over a mass of arrest reports, then patting me ever so lightly on the shoulder as she hurried away. And that, I sighed with relief, was that.

At quarter of nine, I walked across to the courthouse with Robbie and Leon, the two of them filling the entire distance with chatter about the use of a particular type of camera lens in bright light. Inspired by the appearance of the sun, their technical discussion was otherworldly to me, but I did note that loss or no loss, the golden globe was indeed still shining, and chuckled under my breath as I swung open the heavy oak doors and entered the courthouse.

Division Three was already in the throes of its customary Monday-morning panic. The audience section had filled to capacity and then overflowed up the center aisle and out into the hallway, so that anyone wishing to enter or leave had to push and shove and squeeze his or her way through a morass of anxious, confused, and heavily perspiring humanity. Doing so, I pushed further through the swinging wooden gates that formed the entryway to the official area of the courtroom, and after setting down my briefbag, stared for several minutes at the various court personnel as they scurried about in their frantic efforts to ready the court machinery for the day's work. Returning several rushed "Good mornings" as I strolled to a side door, for the first time I was struck by the feeling of truly belonging, that somehow I was in the right place and doing what I was meant to do, the sudden awareness surprising me and creasing my face with a smile as I departed the beehive and headed for the lockup to interview my first three clients of the new week.

To my continuing surprise, my relaxed mood and quiet sense of confidence remained as I plunged into the heavy workload, accompanying me like a shadow as I unconsciously endorsed myself and virtually ignored the frenetic pace of the morning as it rushed away. Trying my Prelims carefully and creatively, with each one receiving the time and attention it deserved, I could feel renewed strength flowing through my veins as I hammered at whatever weaknesses in the prosecution's case my cross-examination was able to uncover. Fully energized by the middle of the first case, a burglary wherein my client was caught inside an industrial plant stuffing tools into a suitcase he had brought along for the ill-conceived occasion, later, when opportunity unexpectedly shined its promising face, I pounced greedily, winning both the second and third Prelims, a possession of marijuana and grand theft auto duo, and watching with masked glee as Judge Lacy stormed off the bench in disgust after declaring the noon recess.

Basking in the sunshine of a little success, I rewarded myself by lunching with George and Robbie at the Jim Dandy chicken stand up the street from the office. And amidst chatter about the morning's problems, along with the wonder of the Fourth Amendment to the U.S. Constitution, whose application had resulted in the only two successive dismissals by His Honor, William Lacy, in recent memory, I hungrily gobbled my chicken, fries, and corn on the cob. Even the conversation suddenly tasted delicious, and upon our return to the office we extended it over coffee, adding sports and politics to the colloquy's menu, with Robbie and I enjoying our pipes and teasing George about his nasty habit of inhaling cigarettes. Several minutes later, Ron wandered in and asked if he could switch calendars with me because he had specialed two of the Prelims set for the afternoon session to himself and was already prepared on them. "No problem," I returned instantly without even a glimmer of a thought that the switch would return me to Division Four and my dear friend, Arlen James Steiggerman. In fact, it wasn't until I was making ready to return to court and hastily surveyed Ron's interview sheets that I noticed the number four appearing in the upper left-hand corner. "Well I'll be goddamned," I murmured, smiling wryly as a twinge of anxiety stirred in my stomach, then served up an encore as I departed the office.

Strangely, however, Mr. Uneasiness took a nap as I returned to the courthouse and began climbing the stairs leading to Division Four, unexpectedly lulled into slumberland by the lyrics from a Stephen Stills folk song I'd listened to on my early morning trek to work. "There's something happening here/What it is ain't exactly clear," echoed into ear, slowing my ascent as the message repeated and repeated, then grinding my progress to a halt when I reached the second floor. "Yeahhh, I whispered in reply, "something's going on all right—especially if you toss pretty lady into the mix—and God knows I'm not clear on what it all means. So what do you say we walk up the path a little further, and see what we can find out?" I posed to myself, chuckling as my adrenal gland received its subconscious order from my brain to prepare for battle.

Roberts seemed both surprised and a bit disappointed to see me. And after quickly explaining that Ron and I had switched calendars for the afternoon, I abruptly adjourned to the jury room and began interviewing Emanuel Garcia, who was charged with petty theft. It wasn't five minutes later that he stuck his head into the room and notified me that "the Judge," as he was wont to call Steiggerman, wished to confer with me in chambers immediately. Interrupting my interview, I slowly gathered my notes together, and even more slowly followed Roberts into His Honor's den. Seated behind his desk reading a newspaper when I entered, Steiggerman frowned, and ignoring common courtesy greeted me sharply with, "Roberts tells me that you and Sindel traded places. Are you ready on any of his cases?"

"Yes, Your Honor, I am," bounced my reply. "In fact, if you'll give me another thirty minutes or so, I'll be ready on all of them."

"Well, now, that's certainly good news," he returned, the frown instantly chameleonizing into a smile. "Ready on the entire calendar, huh?"

"Yes, Sir—that is, after I finish interviewing one client outside in the jury room and one more who's in custody. I'd say that in half an hour or so I'll be ready for trial on all eight of the remaining cases. May I be excused to finish my preparation, so that I don't hold up the Court?"

There was a slight hesitation as his smile began to fade, followed by my question being answered with one of his own. "Did you say ready for trial, Mr. Harris?"

"Yes, Sir, I did."

"I see ... Well it would appear that your little experience of last week didn't teach you much, did it?"

"I wouldn't say that, Your Honor, I feel I learned a great many things from it. May I be excused now, Sir?"

Surprised by my firm refusal to be cowed, for a second or two Steiggerman just stared coldly at me, the remnants of his smile disappearing into a look of disgust. "Oh, by all means, Mr. Harris," he oozed sarcastically. "I'll expect you back here by a quarter of two for a meeting with the District Attorney."

"Very well, Your Honor—thank you," I nodded, then exited.

With nervous energy propelling me, I returned to Emanuel Garcia in the jury room and completed his interview, then hurried downstairs to the lockup and launched into the final case on calendar. Completing my consultation in fifteen fruitful minutes, and ten less than His Honor's deadline, I promptly notified his clerk, Ted Greene, that I was prepared to proceed, and after lighting up my pipe, seated myself at the counsel table to await the next call to confrontation.

I didn't have to wait long, as it arrived at five minutes after two. And within ten minutes thereafter, Steiggerman's anger was in full bloom as he ranted at me over my calm, overly polite, but rock-solid refusal to accept any of the District Attorney's plea bargain offers on the various cases. In fact, the calmer I grew in the face of his bullying outbursts, the more intense his anger became, until finally the inevitable threatening challenge was made, then promptly accepted. Unexpectedly, far sooner than I had planned, I was back in trial. And smiling cantankerously as I reviewed what I considered to be my most damaging mistakes in conducting the Ginther trial, my grin grew wider and warmer as my vow to improve was bolstered by the knowledge that while Steiggerman believed he had chosen my weakest case for trial, a surprise witness, who had appeared with my client at the time of her interview, had turned it into my strongest. Now don't get cocky, my man, I cautioned, chuckling under my breath as I returned to my seat at the counsel table. Just be patient, and fight like hell!

Steiggerman took the bench as the hour turned to three o'clock. And the war between us began almost immediately. For even before the all-white jury panel was fully seated, I requested that they be removed, and then commenced arguing vigorously in support of my motion to have a court reporter present for the proceedings, and then even more strenuously on behalf of my motion challenging the entire jury panel—tailoring the arguments which I had made in the Ginther case to fit the fact that my client was a Mexican American rather than a black one—His Honor promptly denied both motions, then thundered down at me that he expected no further waste of the Court's time. Thereafter, in rapid-fire order, the jury panel was seated, formally welcomed by the now smiling Steiggerman, and immediately pressed into service when the first twelve members were summoned for *voir dire*.

My client, Consuelo Martinez, an attractive twenty-three-year-old Chicana who was employed as a checker in a Lucky supermarket, was charged with disturbing the peace, resisting arrest, and two counts of committing battery on a police officer. Her defense, as she explained it to me, was that she was simply protecting herself. On the evening of October ninth, she had returned from a date with her boyfriend to her small, one-room apartment where she lived alone. Retiring around a quarter of eleven, about a half hour later she was jarred awake by a loud crashing noise coming from the direction of her front door. Sitting up in her bed, she was further surprised, then alarmed by the light from the hallway that suddenly flooded into her eyes. And seconds later, when she was able to make out two shadowy figures approaching her bed, fright turned into panic and she immediately began to scream and call out for help. Grabbed by the arms and dragged from her bed totally nude, she instinctively began to struggle with her attackers, hitting and kicking at them as best she could while continuing to shout for aid. For her efforts, she was rewarded by being placed under arrest, handcuffed, and transported to jail. Now, free on bail, she smiled sweetly at me as I arose, then approached the jury box.

With her story firmly in mind, I spent only a bare minimum of time covering the subjects of presumption of innocence and reasonable doubt. Focusing instead on obtaining as young a jury as possible, and one containing a like number of women, I geared my questions to these ends and explored in considerable detail the areas of occupation, education, and family. Lulled into a state of inertia by my series of harmless questions, His Honor remained remarkably quiet, even when I touched on the seemingly irrelevant area of religion, and I was therefore able to complete my initial inquiry without interruption in less than half an hour. And satisfied so far with the jury's composition, I then leaned back in my chair and carefully studied Mr. Stephen Shafer as he inquired on behalf of the People of the State of California, a reference to his hallowed authority that he repeated no less than four times as he progressed.

Smiling inwardly at his opening remarks, I mused that in a nutshell, they accurately summed him up. Short, at five-foot-three, and slight of build with thinning hair, Shafer took his job as Deputy District Attorney more seriously than anything else in his life. Accustomed like most DAs to winning a high percentage of his cases, he hated with a furious passion to lose even a single one, and unlike most of his colleagues, he was always thoroughly prepared and equally charged up to do battle. Smart, and eager to try cases, he offered the bare minimum when engaged in the plea bargaining process, and could rarely if ever be budged by intellect or emotion from a given position once he had formed it. This stubbornness combined with his generally bellicose attitude and a subtle but nonetheless clearly discernible arrogance to earn him the reputation of being the most vicious and thoroughly disliked DA in Solina, surpassing even Irene Fisher in his ability to engender the enmity of his opponents. I had come to respect his abilities, in particular his combativeness, soon after I arrived in Solina. And showing him respect, while at the same time assuming a friendly but standoffish stance with regard to his efforts to engage me in personal contact outside of court, I had slowly developed the best rapport with him of anyone in the Office, which in turn had resulted in my being able to draw from him reasonably good dispositions when the necessity arose. Now, as I watched him almost casually inquire of the respective jurors, I debated whether or not it would be to my advantage in this case to exploit his one glaring weakness—his temper. Several times I had managed to use it effectively against him during Prelims, but this was trial, and its effect upon a jury incalculable. So, shelving the potential asset midway back in my mind, I tabled for the moment any deliberate action to provoke him into explosive conduct.

Two hours later, after the mutual exercise of peremptory challenges, seven women and five men were accepted by Shafer and myself, and promptly impaneled by Steiggerman, who with equal speed then trailed the case to nine o'clock the following morning. Pleased with the sexual composition of the jury, but wishing that its average age was five years closer to thirty than my quickly calculated forty-three, I was about to leave the courtroom when His Honor's clerk, Ted Greene, informed me that I was urgently needed in Division Three. Glancing at my watch, which read five-thirty, I nodded my understanding, grabbed my briefbag and hurried down the front stairs and into Lacy's lair.

When I reached the counsel table, I found Ron seated on the defense-side corner, serious concern mapped across his face. Glancing up at me, he managed a faint smile, accompanied by a weak "Hi."

"Hi, yourself, big fella—what gives here, anyway?"

"Trouble—what else? Lacy's in chambers considering whether or not to hold me in contempt."

"W-h-a-t?"

"Yeah, we really got into it, man. He sent for you because everyone else is gone, and Mr. Prim and Proper thinks I need a lawyer—funny, huh?"

"Yeahhh, sounds hysterical. You want to tell me what happened?"

Shifting his weight, then reaching down inside his jacket, he pulled out a cigarette and lit up, and without taking my eyes off him, I pulled out my pipe and joined him. "What happened, was this," trickled his explanation through a cloud of smoke, "I'm trying this armed robbery—one of the Prelims I specialed—and it's going along pretty well, Matt. I had the only eyewitness so damned confused that he couldn't identify himself, let alone my client, and then shithead got into it. First, he called us to the bench so that he could discuss with Irene Fisher how to shore-up her fucked up case, and when the stupid cunt couldn't rebuild her witness to the asshole's satisfaction, he took over the redirect examination himself. Now I've heard some leading and suggestive questions before—Fisher's not bad at it herself," Ron emphasized with maximum sarcasm. "But Lacy put every goddamned single word in the witness's mouth, so I started objecting, and kept at it question for question."

"Hey, I'm no authority on contempt," I interjected when he paused to inhale, "but so far you haven't described anything that even brings the subject to mind."

"Well," he smiled sheepishly, "I'm coming to the sticky part. When I kept objecting to the pig's questions, he got upset and told me I was acting improperly."

"Yeah? ... So? ..."

"Well, I ... uh ... blew my cool a little, and told him that he was too."

"H-o-l-y ... shit!" I returned, chuckling despite the seriousness of the situation.

"Yeahhh, I was afraid you'd say that. What do you think we ought to do?"

"Pray, but I don't think anybody would listen to us," I replied, my jest pulling a thin grin onto his face, which then instantly disappeared as Lacy emerged from his chambers, assumed his seat on the bench, and addressed himself to me.

"Thank you for coming, Mr. Harris."

"You're welcome, Your Honor."

"Has Mr. Sindel explained to you what has occurred, and why I asked for you to be present?"

"Yes, Your Honor, he has."

"And are you prepared to assume the responsibility of representing him?"

"Yes, Your Honor, I am."

"Well, then, what do you have to say on behalf of your client?"

Studying Lacy's face, and listening carefully to his tone as he inquired of me, I was struck by the absence of the expected hostility, finding instead that his sober countenance seemed tinged with sadness, something I'd never observed in him before, and an element that instantly tailored my response.

"Your Honor, from what Mr. Sindel tells me, the Court has every right to be upset with him," I began slowly and sincerely. "However, Sir, because of the special circumstances under which we work here in Solina, this is only one of innumerable occasions that he has appeared before you, and I'd like to suggest, therefore, that you evaluate his conduct in this particular instance against a backdrop of his overall conduct before this Court over a considerable period of time. And, Your Honor," I continued, now making direct eye contact, "knowing this Court's reputation for hard work, I feel confident that you appreciate the fact that Mr. Sindel is the hardest working Public Defender in your court, and that despite the pressures that build up from overwork, he ordinarily conducts himself in a manner perfectly consistent with the highest possible standards. I think that what happened here today, Sir, is that Mr. Sindel, exhausted from a long day's work, and struggling in the heat of combat to protect his client, committed a human error in judgment. But knowing him, Your Honor, I feel quite sure that no willful disrespect for this Court was intended, and would on his behalf tender the sincerest of apologies if this impression was somehow mistakenly created in the Court's mind," I ended humbly, then watched as a smile slowly softened Lacy's solemn expression.

"Your point about overall conduct is well taken, Mr. Harris, and I'm going to go along with you," Lacy nodded out calmly but without firm conviction. "But I'd feel better about it, if I also heard from Mr. Sindel himself."

Glancing at Ron out of the corner of my eye, I watched him fidget with a stack of papers, then look up at the expectant Lacy, and with common sense prevailing, offer a subdued, "I apologize, Your Honor. I meant no disrespect for the Court."

Several strained seconds passed before Lacy, satisfied that Ron's repentance had restored him to his proper place, uttered a terse, "Very well," then promptly trailed the interrupted Prelim to tomorrow morning's calendar, and exited as abruptly as he had entered. As the door to his chambers closed, Ron jerked his right hand into the air and awarded him the middle-finger salute. Pulling his arm down before any of the court personnel observed his gesture, I grabbed both his briefbag and mine, then prodded him in the direction of the hallway and onward outside and toward the office. Fuming the entire distance, his prior anger having resurfaced to flush his face, when we reached our cubicle, he exploded.

"Lacy, you motherfucking, cocksucking sonofabitch!" he screeched, "I hate your fucking guts, you Uncle Tom asshole! And I'll get you for this, you can just bet on it, you shit-eating prickhead! You'll see, before this is over, I'm going to tie up Irene Fisher in little knots and shove her white-worshiping ass up yours till the both of you choke!" he growled to a halt, gulping oxygen. "And what the hell are you laughing at, you little wart on the ass of justice!" he tacked on, having turned toward me as I slumped into a chair, my laughter increasing as the rant continued. "Ohh, I know, you think you're pretty goddamned smart 'cause you just saved my ass by licking his, don't you? Well, you just listen to me, you little ... you little—"

His anger finally dissipating in mid-sentence after his brief but intense tirade, when I then managed to gurgle out, "Hey, tell us what you really think," he suddenly switched gears and burst into laughter which soon rivaled mine in heartiness. Howl after howl escaped for a full minute, until finally our aching diaphragms demanded that we quiet down. Then I made coffee for us, and amidst a mixture of pipe and cigarette smoke we leaned back in our chairs and chatted in softened tones.

"Matt," Ron murmured, blowing a smoke ring.

"Yeah?"

"Thanks."

"Hey, no problem. But if you don't mind my asking, what got you so extra angry?"

"I don't know. I guess I'm just tired of groveling before pigs like Lacy—you know, always having to plead with them to treat us and our clients with the respect they demand as a God-given right, then begging their arrogant asses to actually follow the law and kick the truly shit cases the asshole DAs file. And speaking of assholes, I hear that you started another trial in front of Steiggie."

"Yeah, I did. Sorry about stealing one of your cases, old pal."

"No sweat. Which one's going down?"

"As your friend and mine, the Honorable Arlen James Steiggerman puts it: The People of the State of California versus Consuelo Martinez," I rolled out with exaggerated formality.

"Honorable, my ass," Ron snickered. "Steiggerman's a bigger prick than Lacy ever thought of being—and a whole lot smarter too. Boy, do we ever have some sweethearts to do business with in this shithole."

"Uh-huh, that's a for sure."

"But that case has possibilities, don't you think, Matt? I mean, what with the priest and all, you could win it."

"Yeah," I nodded back at him, smiling at his sudden tone of concern. "And I assure you, I have every intention of achieving that result if at all possible."

"Who's the DA?"

"Shafer."

"Congratulations—you've got two pricks to deal with."

"Yeah, I know. But the priest might just surprise the holy hell out of both of them."

"Yeahhh, right," Ron returned, still weighing the prospect. "And let's hope so, 'cause that's all you've got—one priest and your big mouth."

"You got that right," I agreed, then joined in another chuckle before we lapsed into five minutes of silence, during which we made some final notations on our various interview sheets, then dropped them into the wire bin atop Marilyn's desk as we departed the office. As we approached our cars, Ron suddenly muttered, "You know, Matt, that was some damn good fly-by-the-seat-of-your-pants lawyering. Thanks for bailing me out, I won't forget it."

"Anytime, friend ... anytime," I shrugged, smiling. "Besides, tomorrow it'll probably be your turn to rescue me from the monster of Division Four."

"I'll be there. You can bet on it," Ron replied, emotion swelling into his tone. And for several moments, we just stood there grinning at each other. Then, mutually embarrassed at the feeling of closeness that suddenly overtook both of us, we quickly withdrew from the mood, traded wishes for a restful night, and headed our cars toward the freeway.

The drive home was the easiest I could remember, the buoyant feeling swimming around inside me sweeping the long miles away effortlessly. Two Prelim victories back to back was a highly unusual occurrence in itself. In front of William Lacy, it was special indeed, and combined with the successful rescue of Ron, and the fact that the jury trial was off to a promising start, unquestionably constituted the most satisfying day's work I had experienced since the great experiment of becoming a trial attorney had begun nine mystifying months ago. And smiling as I glanced into the rear view mirror, my grin widened full, then turned sheepish as I realized how overly pleased I was with myself. Following suit, my mood soon turned to mild puzzlement when I then addressed the suddenly appearing question of why Lacy had allowed Ron to escape so lightly? An interrogative no more easily answered than the overriding query of who or what was William Lacy? the tricky triumvirate hung in front of my eyes like a jigsaw puzzle with missing pieces—especially in view of my colleagues' varying shades of opinion about the man who always seemed so closed-in, so iron-clad tight-assed, even when angrily chastising PDs and anyone else threatening his reputation for running an efficient courtroom.

When I first arrived, I recalled, George had cautioned that Lacy was "an Uncle Tom who hated blacks," a position that Ron certainly seconded, and with which Leon also agreed, but on the grounds that "he's too stupid to be a real bigot." In contrast, Robbie, while affirming the Uncle Tom indictment, had also pointed out that Lacy's life experience was different from the vast majority of African Americans of his generation, this knowledge acquired from having been introduced to Lacy when Robbie first moved to Los Angeles, and thereafter remaining tangentially acquainted with him through mutual friends during the past fifteen years. First, off, Robbie explained, Lacy had never personally known poverty, being born to parents who had migrated to Los Angeles from Maryland and started a small restaurant that grew successful enough to provide a decent standard of living, including a neighborhood that was racially mixed, and not populated by gangs, drug dealers, and prostitutes. With his parents' example instilling a strong work ethic during his formative years, Lacy was employed while attending college and law school, but only part-time, and not in menial positions. Clerking in the office of a local Sears Roebuck store, courtesy of an offer from the white manager who frequented the family restaurant and was catered to by his parents, Lacy learned early on that blacks who ingratiated themselves could get ahead in the white man's world—a lesson that was further reinforced through successfully courting favor with his law school professors by routinely visiting them during office hours, impressing them with his thirst for knowledge, and eventually seeking their counsel on what field to specialize in and how best to get started therein. A wise investment that paid large dividends, it resulted in the dean using his connections to secure him a position in a previously all-white firm where during the next ten years Lacy honed his socio-political skills into an art form, his also polished work ethic pushing him day and night to perform fruitfully for his clients, as well as join various church and community organizations—always steering clear of controversy so as to make no waves, and carefully massaging egos located both higher and lower in whatever organizational structure he was involved in. Eventually, he made junior partner, and when a judgeship opened up in the ghetto, "Well," as Robbie put it, "who better to help keep the blacks under control than a black judge who thinks like a white man. Now I don't know if he hates black people, like George says," Robbie had added. "But there's no question that he takes it personally when blacks do anything that denigrates his hard-earned position in the world—and that includes the Civil Rights Movement, 'cause confrontation's totally opposite of what he learned growing up, and rigid as he is, he's not about to change."

"Hell, I don't really know what makes him tick," I muttered out loud after the clutter of thoughts had bounced around inside my brain. He's just a strange man, 'cause he could've easily put contempt on Ron's record, but didn't—yet he still has that arrogant attitude that says, I'm authority, I know what's right, and don't you dare challenge me," I concluded, unable to further fathom the who? or what? make-up of the man, but still clearly aware that though Lacy was less truculent than Steiggerman, he was nevertheless part and parcel of the same abusive power structure, and therefore the same enemy. And shaking my head at the confusion so easily sown by shades of gray, I pushed the latest installment into a rear compartment of my mind, content for the moment to let it slide away in favor of settling back and relaxing to the music on the radio, the bouncy strains of Dionne Warwick's "Do You Know the Way to San Jose" soon drawing me into a spontaneous duet.

A half hour later, as I strolled up to my front door, Stella entered my mind for the zillionth time during the seemingly longer than twenty-four-hour stretch of time that had passed since we parted. Feeling suddenly antsy as I opened the door and stepped inside, I tried pushing her out of consciousness by settling onto my couch and browsing through the latest issue of *Newsweek* that had arrived in the day's mail. To no avail, however, as every few pages she returned and interrupted my reading by raising questions. Where was she? ... What was she doing? ... And what was she wearing—something blue perhaps, to accentuate those magnificent eyes? they posed innocently enough, before rushing forward with, Was she thinking about me? Maybe even missing me, as I was her? before then slowing down to spotlight the inevitable, anxiety-instigating, Was she alone? Or with someone—maybe one of those handsome, wealthy guys who were always calling for her in their fancy cars and whisking her off to some exotic place of entertainment? Even in the past, when Stella was only partly real, and mostly fantasy, the thought of her being with other men produced a strange feeling inside me—one composed in large part of envy, but nourished also by a wistful longing from a reservoir deep inside me. Now, however, after the miraculous events of the weekend, longing had developed a sharper and more defined appetite, and envy had transformed into jealousy—newly born to be sure, but still strong enough to empower anxiety. Counter-balanced, as it was for the moment, by the lingering effects of the days' triumphs, an overall sense of peace and tranquility managed to prevail, and I was easily able to resume reading the article I had begun about a breakthrough discovery for the treatment of ovarian cancer.

Not for long, however. For though I was soon so absorbed in the layman-oriented details that it took five or six beeps of a car horn to crack my wall of concentration, the longer and heavier sounding duo that followed penetrated fully. And lifting off the couch, I parted the living room drapes slightly and peered through the small aperture just in time to see Stella enter a pale-blue Cadillac that sped off before I could observe who the driver was. "Awww, shit," escaped off my tongue after several seconds passed and I remembered to breathe. "Now, what?" followed like a right cross after a left hook, my slow exhale tipping over the counterweights and freeing a wave of tension to sweep across my chest, then settle in my stomach where it knotted into a dull ache. My response consisted of turning away from the window and heading into the kitchen, where I pulled a bottle from the fridge and poured myself a glass of Chablis. Then, returning to the couch, I sipped steadily while attempting to finish the hopeful article—an evasive tactic that quickly proved futile, as Stella's face soon drifted back into view and refused to depart, even after I climbed off the couch and poured myself a second glass.

"Alll ... right, all right," I finally nodded out, a smirky smile creasing my face. "Let's just settle down here, and get hold of ourself—okay?" floated common sense's suggestion, my reflexive reply a sarcasm-coated, "Uh-huh, sure ... great idea. Got any others on how you do that?"

I didn't. So slumping into a chair at my kitchen table, I took another healthy swig of Chablis, then leaned forward and cupped my face in my hands, and after slowly releasing a heavy sigh, lapsed into a submerged dialogue with myself, neurons flashing, and feelings swimming to the surface. First, off, Buster Brown, began truth's painful lecture, honesty striding center stage to occupy the spotlight, let's get clear on the fact that pretty lady doesn't owe you a damn thing! She's listened to your problems, offered encouragement, cooked delicious meals for you, and even made love with you—so what's the problem, that she's not sitting at home waiting for you to call?

Nooo, slinked my answer, I just didn't think she'd be out so soon. I mean, I know she has every right to, it's just that she said she liked me a lot, and that the lovemaking wasn't just a gift, that she needed to be hugged and kissed by my good heart too, traipsed my defense dejectedly. So it makes me wonder, that's all—especially since Lanie also said that good was hard to find, but didn't wait anyway. Hell, tacked on memory's lesson, I'm just trying to learn, that's all, 'cause I sure don't need more hurt.

Okay, fair enough, reason returned. But how about we not jump to any conclusions, but instead gather up some more experience before deciding what's going on here? And in the meantime, how about employing some of that presumption of innocence you're so sold on—hasn't she earned that?

"Uh-huh ... sure," I drawled out loud, breaking the silence that had grown heavy, Stella's "it wasn't a one-night stand" echoing into ear to produce a thin smile that matched my slowly improving mood. "And speaking of ye olde presumption, and its sweet sister, reasonable doubt, how about we go tend to business?" I then urged somewhat more cheerfully.

And nodding my head in agreement, I successfully brushed away recurring thoughts about Stella, broiled a small steak, sliced some tomatoes, and ate a quiet dinner while finishing the hopeful article. Then, this time accompanied by coffee, I returned to the couch and carefully reviewed my notes on the Martinez case until midnight arrived and sleep called.

TUESDAY DAWNED CRYSTAL-CLEAR AND cold. Eager to resume trial, I matched yesterday's early arrival in the office, and quickly settled in for a final review of my notes. Satisfied that I was fully prepared by the time Marilyn arrived around eight-thirty, for fifteen minutes I relaxed with her over coffee and chatter about a play she and her boyfriend had attended last evening, before heading off to Division Four. Having previously proclaimed an early start, at nine o'clock sharp, Steiggerman took the bench, and after quickly dispensing with the routine courtesies, directed the District Attorney to call his first witness.

Shafer promptly complied, and Officer Paul Richard Tison, an eight-year veteran of the Brynhurst Police Force, took the witness stand, and in less than five minutes, presented the prosecution's case. On the evening of October ninth, flowed his testimony, he and his partner, Officer Neil Reese, were on patrol when at approximately fifteen minutes after midnight, they received a radio report of a loud disturbance occurring at 16001 Wheeler Drive in the City of Brynhurst. Responding to that address within ten minutes, they first surveyed the perimeter of the subject apartment house, and having satisfied themselves that nothing was amiss there, then entered the building to further investigate. As they did so, loud screaming was heard coming from the second floor, which they immediately ascended to by way of the rear stairway, and as they approached Apartment Number Twelve, the screaming grew louder and was accompanied by what sounded like breaking objects. Knocking on the door, Officer Tison identified himself as a police officer, and stated that he was present to investigate the report of a disturbance on the premises. No reply was received, and when the noise inside then increased further, he and Officer Reese formed the opinion that a fight was in progress and that it would be necessary to make a forcible entry to quell it. Accomplishing this by kicking the door open, upon entering, Tison observed the defendant to be out of control, manifested by her stomping about and breaking various furnishings by throwing them on the floor and against the walls, while alternately laughing hysterically and screaming at the top of her lungs. Vocal attempts by both officers to calm her down were met with a steady stream of obscenities, and when they then attempted to restrain her, she hit, kicked, and spat upon both officers, "whereupon we arrested and handcuffed the defendant," Tison concluded, a confident Shafer nodding his approval, then smiling as he made eye contact with Steiggerman before reseating himself.

Having surprised both His Honor and Shafer by failing to object even once to Officer Tison's testimony, my brief cross-examination, which also lasted less than five minutes, pushed them to the brink of pleased amazement. Tailoring my inquiry only to the heart of Consuelo's defense, I carefully explored the physical aspects of the arrest scene, establishing that the individual apartments in the building faced each other across an approximately five-foot corridor that was well lighted, that the front door to her apartment had not been removed from its hinges during the forced entry, that she was not in bed when first observed, and was fully clothed at all times during the subject incident. Thereafter, I obtained Tison's admission that while he had heard several other doors open and shut, neither he nor officer Reese had observed or spoken to any other person during their visit to the premises, then closed my interrogation with a simple "Thank you, that's all."

Hiding his considerable pleasure from the unexpected gift of my brevity behind a thin smile, Steiggerman declared a ten-minute recess after Shafer indicated that he had no further witnesses. And when we resumed, the time had arrived for Consuelo to deliver her version of what had occurred. Admitting that she was "a little nervous" because testifying was a totally new experience for her, she managed a smile, and the sincerity mapped across her face and flowing from her voice combined with the natural warmth of her personality to make her instantly likable. Both attractive and bright, she listened patiently to my introductory questions, then humbly but firmly detailed the sequence of events exactly as she had to me during her initial interview.

Sensing that the jurors had responded favorably to her, on cross-examination Shafer smartly managed a tone that was amiable but nevertheless stiff. And handling herself beautifully, without need of a single protecting objection from me, Consuelo kept her answers short and on point, and grew stronger and more confident as Shafer's careful but still relentless interrogation continued, until finally he was forced to take off the velvet gloves. Pouncing suddenly with the harshly toned, "Are you calling Officer Tison a liar?" his glare radiating contempt, Consuelo retained her composure, and answered him exactly as we had rehearsed.

"I'm telling you the truth, Sir, which is all I know how to do," strolled her reply slowly with some emotion seeping into her tone. "If the Officer says something different than what I've told you, then he's not telling the truth, Sir."

Satisfied that he had openly exposed the almost always fatal call-the-cop-a-liar defense, and not wishing to create any sympathy for Consuelo in the eyes of the jury by pressing her on the issue, Shafer terminated his cross-examination, once again smiling up at Steiggerman after he reseated himself. Apparently in a hurry to attend to some other pressing matter, His Honor failed to return it, instead declaring noon recess even though it was only a quarter of eleven, and rushing off the bench into chambers.

Must be he needs to confer with his stock broker, I mused on the walk back to the office, recalling George's comment that "if the bastard had a heart, it would belong to Wall Street!" "Well, you just enjoy your nice business lunch, while thinking that it's closing arguments time," spurted a spontaneous reaction, "'cause I have a little surprise waiting for you and your buddy Shafer," I concluded, chuckling softly as I reached the front door. As I entered, Marilyn was hanging up the telephone, and happily surprised to see me at the early hour of eleven o'clock, asked if I would watch the office for a few minutes so that she could go shopping before the noon rush. "Sure," I answered, and after returning a smiling, "Thank you, kind sir," she disappeared down the hallway, calling out over her shoulder that she had left several telephone messages on my desk.

In no hurry to work, I poured myself a cup of coffee, and after slipping into a chair behind Marilyn's desk, lazily scanned the pages of the local newspaper, the *Solina Bugle*. Around noon, the office began to fill with clients who were seeking appointments, and I assisted them until Marilyn returned a few minutes later. Wandering back to my desk to eat half a sandwich and think over the concluding phase of Consuelo's defense, as I settled into my seat, I noticed the stack of pink-colored telephone messages that Marilyn had mentioned and began thumbing through them, my eyes freezing on the next to the last one. The pink slip didn't actually contain a message, just the name Stella, with check marks appearing in the boxes labeled *phoned* and *call back*, but judging from the smile that swept across my face, you would have thought that I had just received official notification that the jury had found Consuelo not guilty without even hearing the rest of the case. Grabbing the phone, I dialed the number and waited, excitement keeping me company. When there was no answer after six rings, I slowly replaced the receiver, then picked it up again and dialed more carefully to insure I hadn't made a mistake by rushing. The result was the same, so stuffing the slip inside my breast pocket next to my pipe, I forced Stella out of mind and returned to my notes. I was going to try one more time before returning to court, but Leon popped in to consult with me about a new case limiting an officer's authority to stop and detain that I had noted on the interview sheet for a Prelim he was scheduled to try that afternoon, and after we had conferred, it was quarter of one and I departed for Division Four.

Within ten minutes after my arrival there, Steiggerman had taken the bench, disposed of the formalities, and inquired as to whether the defense had any further witnesses. Confident that I did not, His Honor's face clearly reflected his surprise and consternation when I announced that I had one additional one, and called Father Caesar Rodino to the stand from his seat outside in the corridor where I had carefully hidden him from view. Stifling my urge to chuckle at the success of my private witness protection program, I permitted myself a thin smile as Father Rodino, dressed in his priestly accoutrements, was sworn in, during which time Shafer busily conferred with his investigating officer. Hesitating for several moments before I began my examination, in order to allow his pious appearance to fully impress the jury, I then asked him to state his full name and address.

"Caesar Ricardo Rodino, 16001 Wheeler Drive, Brynhurst," he replied in the deep baritone that was his natural timbre.

"And would you please tell the Court your occupation, Sir?"

"I'm a priest in the Catholic Church."

"And how long have you been a priest, Father Rodino?"

"For about seventeen years, Sir—the last ten at St. Joseph's, right here in Brynhurst."

"I see," I continued, noting out of the corner of my eye that he had drawn the full attention of every single juror, and that their collective expression clearly showed a proper respect. "And Father Rodino, in which apartment do you reside at 16001 Wheeler Drive?"

"Number thirteen, Sir."

"And, Sir, do you know the number of the apartment directly across the hallway from yours?"

"Yes, Sir. It's number twelve."

"And, Sir, do you know the occupant of apartment number twelve?"

"Yes, Sir. I have met Miss Martinez on four or five occasions while coming and going in the building."

"Then she isn't a close friend of yours—is that correct, Father?"

"Yes, Sir. I don't know her well at all, we're just casually acquainted neighbors you might say."

Having completed laying the foundation for the critical part of his testimony, I now struck at the heart of the prosecution's case. "Father Rodino," I asked, moving a step closer to him, "prior to today, when was the last time that you saw my client, Consuelo Martinez?"

"Approximately five weeks ago."

"And Father, where was it that you saw her?"

"Well, Sir, both inside her apartment and in the hallway outside."

"I see ... And where were you located, Father, at the time you observed her?"

"I was standing in my apartment, looking through my slightly opened door into her apartment, which is directly across the hallway."

"You said your door was slightly open, Father. Had you previously opened it?"

"No, Sir," he answered, smiling faintly. "I opened it to see what had caused the loud, crashing kind of noise I heard in the hallway."

"All right, Father ... Would you please tell the jury what you saw and heard after you opened your door to investigate the loud, crashing noise in the hallway?"

Yes, Sir ... When I first looked out, I noticed that the front door of Miss Martinez's apartment had been knocked off its hinges and was lying flat just inside the entryway. Then, I heard a female voice cry out for help, and saw Miss Martinez being dragged out of her bed by two men who looked like police officers. I—"

"Sorry to interrupt, Father," I cut in, "but why did you say looked like police officers?"

"Well, Sir, I wasn't sure until they turned around and I saw their badges and guns."

"I see … that's very clear," I nodded back at him, glancing again at the jury and smiling inwardly upon noticing that several members had leaned forward in their chairs, and all appeared to be hanging on his every word. "And Father," I picked up after a slight pause, "when you observed Miss Martinez being dragged from her bed, what was she wearing?"

"Nothing, Sir. She was naked."

"Naked?" I repeated more loudly.

"Yes, Sir. Completely!" he stated emphatically, emulating my louder volume.

"I see … I see … And did either of the officers say anything to Miss Martinez?"

"Yes, Sir. They were both asking her questions about drugs, and where she kept them."

"Okay … And were—"

"And, Sir," he intervened, "they were also asking her about a man named Fred, and his whereabouts."

"All right, Father, thank you," I smiled, recovering quickly from my surprise, as he hadn't been able to recall the specific name the officers had used when I had interviewed him yesterday, and because I had planned to use this piece of information on redirect examination. Not a problem, you can use it twice, flashed a thought as I continued mining gold from the same vein by asking, "Now, Sir, did Miss Martinez answer any of the officers' questions?"

"No, Sir … At first, she just tried to pull the bed covers about herself. Then, after she was forced out of the bed, she just kept screaming for help and kicking and struggling with the officers."

"And, Father, what did the officers do in response to Miss Martinez's behavior?"

"Well, Sir, they just laughed between themselves, and the one sitting at the table over there made a remark about her breasts."

Pausing for two or three seconds to allow his statement to fully sink into the jurors' minds, when I resumed, I played it to the maximum. "About Miss Martinez's breasts?" I asked, inserting shock into my tone and facial expression. "Is that what you said, Father?"

"Yes, Sir. His exact words were that she's got real nice titties for a Mexy!"

Shafer was going to object, but the words spilled off Father Rodino's tongue so rapidly that his statement was completed before the word "hearsay" had formed on his, and not wishing to further impress it on the jury, he remained silent. Shaking my head to emphasize my dismay at the outrageous conduct just reported, I turned to my last two subjects.

"Father Rodino, approximately what time was it when the events you've described occurred?"

"Around twelve-thirty, Sir. I had returned home around midnight, and was preparing for bed about twenty minutes later when I heard the loud, crashing noise."

"And, Father, prior to this loud, crashing noise which you've told us about, had you heard any other loud noises?"

"No, Sir."

"No sounds of screaming, or fighting, or objects breaking?"

"No, Sir ... absolutely not!"

"All right ... And one last question, Father ... In a peaceful manner, of course—why is it that you didn't intervene in the events you've described?"

"Well, Sir, I didn't understand what the officers were doing, and I certainly didn't approve of the way they were treating Miss Martinez—but they were police officers, and I assumed that they must have a good reason for arresting her, so I didn't interfere."

Thanking him for his testimony, I scanned each juror's face as I slowly turned away from the witness box and returned to my seat next to Consuelo, who patted me on my knee underneath the counsel table. Shafer, with worry furrowing his face, then requested a brief recess, which Steiggerman granted without even glancing in my direction.

Shafer never did really recover from the devastating effect of Father Rodino's testimony, nor in retrospect, did the People's case. The opportunity to confer with Officers Tison and Reese generated no help whatsoever, and despite Shafer's stubborn attempt to rescue the People's case when we resumed, resuscitation proved utterly futile. Faced with the totally unfamiliar, and therefore excessively uncomfortable situation of having to cross-examine a witness who was not a defendant, or a presumably biased friend or family member, but instead confronted by of all things unimaginable, a priest who was telling the truth, his cross-examination of Father Rodino can best be described as short. Unable to elicit any evidence that would cast doubt on the Father's ability to see and hear, his questions regarding the wearing of glasses or a hearing aid being met with a polite but firm, "No, Sir," he surrendered inside of two minutes, in favor of launching a counterattack during rebuttal by placing Officer Reese on the stand to testify in support of his partner, Tison.

Analyzing his move as being based on the prosecution's time-honored strategy that it was essential for the People to remain on the offensive at all times, and feeling that the best way to convey to the jury the defense's total disdain for the credibility of the evidence presented was to not even respond to it, I remained seated when Steiggerman indicated that I might cross-examine, and answered politely but positively, "Thank you, Your Honor—but the defense, not wishing to waste the Court's time, has no questions for this officer."

Shafer had no further witnesses on rebuttal, and in that my choice to ignore Officer Reese's testimony negated the need to summon back Father Rodino for an encore, closing arguments promptly became the next order of business. Wanting to hear my argument first, Shafer waived his initial opportunity to influence the jury, and sat back in his chair with pen and legal pad in hand as I ambled toward the jury box. Once arrived, I made eye contact with each juror before I uttered a single word. Then, in soft, amiable tones, I thanked them for serving, and after quickly reminding them of their promise to apply the presumption of innocence and reasonable doubt principles, I dispensed with caution, and with steadily increasing emotion argued the heart of the case to them.

"Ladies and gentlemen," I opened slowly. "In the early morning hours of October ninth, something happened inside the apartment house at 16001 Wheeler Drive. And this case presents you with a choice of two opposing sets of facts as to what actually occurred and why: the prosecution's version of events, and the completely different account offered by the defense. Now I think it's fairly obvious that what you decide will depend totally on which witnesses are to be believed, and which are not. That, of course, is for you, and you alone, to determine. And while I have every confidence that you possess the intelligence and human sensitivity to make this decision, without any assistance from me or Mr. Shafer, I nonetheless feel compelled to briefly comment on the credibility issue to you, because it is a highly unusual case for the defense.

"Why?" I posed after a slight pause. "Because even in my short career as a Public Defender, I've learned that the believability issue almost always boils down to a confrontation between the testimony of police officers versus the defendant's. And, ladies and gentlemen, time after time I've listened as District Attorney after District Attorney has argued long and loud that police officers are public servants without any bias whatsoever, while the defendant cannot be believed because he or she has a clearly identifiable stake in the matter, and therefore automatically becomes a liar and a perjurer, and a person that cannot be trusted for a single instant."

"Well, ladies and gentlemen," I continued, a slim smile playing on my lips, the volume of my voice rising, "this is most definitely not the situation in this case! No, not at all. You have heard the testimony of Father Caesar Rodino, and it is one hundred percent supportive of Consuelo Martinez's version of what occurred! Moreover," I emphasized by holding my hands out to the jury, "Father Rodino is neither a friend nor a relative of my client, but merely a neighbor. And not only that, he is, of course, a practicing priest in the Catholic Church, and has been for almost seventeen years! So do I think that you can safely believe him?" I posed, pausing for a split second. "Absolutely!—and I urge you to do so," emoted my plea as I dropped my hands gently onto the jury-box railing, then paused, this time for a full five seconds. All twenty-four eyes were fixed on me, and as I read agreement in them, I felt a wave of excitement course through me, accompanied by a never-before-experienced feeling that I would later recognize as power. Desiring to steal the last vestige of Shafer's thunder, I closed on the offensive.

"Now I realize that by asking you to accept the testimony of Father Rodino, I am also asking you to reject the testimony of Officers Tison and Reese. And, why? ... Because they simply did not tell you the truth! And if Mr. Shafer tries to tell you that I think all police officers are liars, please, I beg of you, don't believe him, because it's absolutely not true. What I do think, however, is that police officers are no different than you or me in the sense that they are human beings, and therefore subject to making mistakes just like you and I do," I argued, confronting the call-the-cop-a-liar issue head on, my voice rising with emotion, then calming as I continued. "And, mistake, simple human error, is precisely what I want to suggest to you occurred here in our case. Tired and overworked, Officers Tison and Reese, in their desire to protect society from those persons selling drugs, erred in their over-eagerness to arrest someone named Fred, and mistakenly broke into Consuelo Martinez's apartment. Then, very disappointed in their failure to capture bad-guy Fred, and also embarrassed over making a mistake which they realized could result in a possible civil lawsuit against them, they made an even worse mistake and arrested the terrified and quite naturally resisting Consuelo Martinez," I spelled out, anger now creeping into my tone as I flowed onward toward conclusion.

"Now, while I can sympathize with human error, ladies and gentlemen, I suggest to you that like me, you should be horrified that a citizen simply sleeping in her own bed can without notice or justification be dragged naked from that bed, and after being terrified and humiliated, made to suffer the further insult of being arrested for merely attempting to defend herself! And when I then consider the fact that the true reason for Consuelo's arrest was to cover up the officers' mistake, my horror turns to outrage!" I protested vehemently. "And I hope to God that you twelve fellow human beings, having heard my client's testimony, as supported by that of the totally impartial Father Rodino, will recognize how truly tragic and unjust the events of October ninth were for Consuelo, then prevent that terrible injustice from turning into an even greater one by finding her ... not guilty!" I concluded emphatically, then lowering my voice, tacked on, "Thank you ... Thank you very much," my eyes still scanning to maintain contact with each juror, a thin smile forming on my lips.

After resuming my seat at the counsel table, I then listened with cold anger as Shafer allocated ninety percent of his closing remarks to chastising me, "and all those persons like me, for all too readily criticizing and disparaging police officers—who, after all, were only human beings enlisted in the public service, and doing the best they could do to protect society from its vicious, criminal elements." The remainder of his argument was then devoted to the proposition that Father Rodino, "because of his poor vantage point, didn't really see or hear the actions and statements he had in good faith but erroneously testified to."

When Shafer concluded his remarks, His Honor, wearing a look of concern, promptly instructed the jury, and at eleven minutes past three, they filed solemnly out of the jury box and into the adjacent room to deliberate. Inhaling deeply, then exhaling slowly in a partially successful attempt to ease the angry tension that gripped me, I adjourned to the hallway where I smoked and chatted quietly with Consuelo, until ten minutes later Bailiff Roberts interrupted with the news that the judge requested my presence in chambers. Expecting trouble when I arrived and found both Steiggerman and a hostilely subdued Shafer waiting for me, instead I was met with a request from His Honor that he be excused for the remainder of the afternoon due to "pressing business of a personal nature," and that Judge Austin be allowed to take charge of the case until tomorrow morning. Still standing, I agreed, signed the written waiver, and without uttering another word returned to my station in the hallway, where I was suddenly overwhelmed with the desire to speak to Stella. Excusing myself from Consuelo's presence, I walked rapidly to the far end of the corridor, entered the public telephone booth, and dialed her number from memory. It rang four times before I heard her "Hello."

"Hi, Stelle," I chirped happily. "It's Matt, returning your call."

"Ohh, good. How are you?"

"I'm okay," I returned, enjoying the warmth of her voice. "How about you?"

"I'm fine. But how come I haven't heard from you?"

Recognizing that the concern in her voice was also tinged with tease, I returned a cautious, "Well, I didn't want to take advantage—then work got in the way. Also, I called earlier, but there wasn't any answer."

"Oooo-kay," she purred. "So could you come for dinner tonight?"

"Uh-huh, I'd love to—say around seven-thirty or maybe even eight, 'cause I might be a little late getting out of court?"

"Sure, that's fine."

"And Stelle—will you do me a little favor, please?"

"You bet—what?"

"Keep a good thought for me the next couple of hours—okay?"

"Absolutely—but are you sure—"

"I'm fine, pretty lady," I intercepted the suddenly reappearing concern in her tone. "Just keep that good thought, and I'll explain later."

"All right, sure ... You take care now."

"Thanks ... And that's a promise, Stelle. I'll see you soon."

"Okay ... bye for now," she ended, the uncertainty in her voice echoing as we hung up.

Having replaced the receiver on its arm, for several moments I remained seated in the booth, carefully replaying the conversation in my mind while also recalling how upset I had been just last evening when I watched her drive away with someone else. Mumbling to myself to watch what I was doing, then answering that I would check out the situation carefully, I was about to devote additional thought to why I was suddenly both excited and fearful, when George interrupted. "Just four and a half measly months, and he's already gone bananas!" I listened to, then looked out to find him and Ron standing in the hallway about ten feet away, with Ron quickly adding his agreement before I could utter a word of reply.

"Uh-huh," he drawled. "It's a real shame to see it happen so soon, and to one so young and innocent. I mean, sitting in a public telephone booth in a daze, talking to one's self when you're supposed to be working, doesn't exactly match up to the image of the aggressive, hard-hitting attorney that characterizes our office, does it?" he ended, shaking his head vigorously.

My attempts at disclaiming their good-natured accusations were met with a chorus of "Oh, sures" and "Uh-huhs," delivered in all-knowing tones of voice, and after the humor of the moment was enjoyed all around, both of them turned serious. "How's things going?" George inquired.

"I don't know," I answered, still smiling. "You're the one that taught me that you never know what the hell a jury's likely to do."

"Yeah, right—that's for damn sure, Matt," he nodded in agreement, then smiled. "Word is, though, that you really laid it on the pigs in your closing argument—sorry I missed it."

"Well, I had to—there was no way to tippy-toe around it."

"Roberts told us that you called them a bunch of goddamned liars—did you?" Ron chimed in, his tone a mixture of disbelief and hopefulness.

"Uh-huh, I did, big fella, but not in those exact words—though they fit perfectly. You remember the priest you subpoenaed, Father Rodino?"

"Yeah ... I never met him, but Consuelo said he could help, so I issued one."

"Welll ... he was absolutely terrific!" I rolled back at him. "I couldn't have asked for a better witness short of Jesus Christ himself! And if those twelve fools, as Robbie calls them, don't believe a man of the cloth, who was in no way related to Consuelo, then the Second Coming better not be too far off, 'cause we're all in one hell of a lot of trouble!" flowed my sarcasm, Ron and George chuckling in response. "Problem is," I added softly when the laughter faded, "I'm scared shitless that they won't."

"Hey, man, just hang in there," George quipped, a sentiment that Ron instantly seconded and emphasized with a hug, before they left for the office. Suddenly alone, I shuffled over to the windows, placed my elbows on the metal railing, cupped my face in my hands, and stared out at the world below. Dusk was already gathering, and for several minutes I remained motionless, gazing aimlessly at the pedestrians walking to and fro on the sidewalk, slow-motion thoughts about the trial mixing with those about Stella, with both quandaries then giving rise to a steady growth of anxiety till finally, the knots in my stomach having turned to stone, I yearned desperately to climb to the very highest reaches of my old friend, still standing patiently in my grandparents' back yard. "Sorry ... but not an option," I muttered softly, tearing myself from my trance and strolling over to the water fountain for a sip. Not today, Buster Brown, it's grown-up time, followed a thought as I turned away and almost bumped heads with Bailiff Roberts, who tersely informed me that "the jury's got a verdict," then hurried down the corridor toward the District Attorney's Office in search of Shafer.

Glancing at my watch, which read ten minutes after five, I whispered a hissing "shhhit" as I recalled the aphorism that early verdicts almost always favor the prosecution. Finding Consuelo waiting for me in the doorway leading to the courtroom, I smiled as confidently as I could muster, then returned with her to our seats at the counsel table. Shafer appeared shortly thereafter, and Judge Austin, substituting for the now absent Steiggerman, then emerged from chambers and began thumbing through the Court's file.

A three-minute eternity then passed before the jury returned. And though I carefully studied their faces as the twelve silently filed into the jury box and settled into their chairs, their sober expressions offered not the slightest indication of their collective decision. What's new? flashed a thought, as I folded my arms across my chest to stem the steadily increasing beat of my heart. And as Judge Austin quickly dispensed with the formalities and instructed Roberts to take the verdict from the foreman and submit it to him, I silently wafted a prayer, then inwardly snickered at the futility of seeking the Lord's intervention after the decision had already been arrived at—not to forget your gall, you selfish idiot, for bothering an already besieged Godperson in the first place! I chided, as Austin, without changing expression, read it and handed it back to the clerk. One second ticked by, then two, three, and four, and finally Ted Greene calmly spoke the two most beautiful words I had ever heard. In fact, not once, but four times, in response to each separate charge, the words "not guilty" marched off his tongue in the methodical monotone that only five short days ago had gloomily delivered into my life the message of defeat, but which now, transformed magically into an instrument befitting angels, sweetly heralded victory.

For a long moment, I sat glued to my chair, amazed. Then, as the last "not guilty" registered fully, a smile exploded across my face, and after first returning Consuelo's warm hug and kiss, then watching her break into tears as her boyfriend reached her side, I rushed across the room, and with tears forming in my eyes, embraced and thanked each and every one of the now smiling jurors as they filed out of the jury box and crowded around me, shaking my hand and slapping me on the back. Drunk with four-hundred-proof joy, for the better part of an hour I remained in the courtroom, thanking the jurors over and over again, and discussing every aspect of the case with them in an effort to learn precisely what had impressed them both positively and negatively. Finally, a custodian asked me and the three remaining jurors if we could continue our discussion outside so that he could lock up the courtroom. And after walking with them downstairs and out into the chill, early evening air, I again thanked them and exchanged handshakes as they departed. Suddenly finding myself alone again, but this time at peace, for several seconds I just stood there on the sidewalk and enjoyed the silence. Then, lifting my eyes to the very top of the courthouse as I turned toward the office, I ran them slowly over the weather-scarred letters which spelled JUSTICE, and smiling at the thought that this time it had occurred, and even more broadly at the idea that I had had a hand in it, I whispered, "Thanks, Adonai ... Big Time," before walking toward my car.

Fifty-five minutes later, as I turned off the freeway onto Robertson Boulevard, I passed a young boy selling flowers on the corner. The long drive home, spent quietly listening to the day's news, then music, had been sufficient to dial down the adrenaline of roaring jubilation to a state of simple euphoria that simmered softly in the sweet juices of success. Now, as I backed up my car, purchased a bouquet of tiny red roses, and then proceeded onward toward the triplex, I felt my nerve endings begin to tingle again as being with Stella approached near reality.

After parking Old Greener across the street, I delayed crossing and meeting her by carefully inspecting each individual rose for hidden defects. Finding none, I looked over at the window of her apartment, and after smiling sheepishly at my stalling tactics, darted across Doheny Drive and strode briskly up the path and stairs to her front door and knocked. After only a moment's delay, it swung open and we stood facing each other, smilingly tongue-tied after saying, "Hi." Finally, after three or four seconds had passed, I pushed my left hand forward and said softly, "These are for you, Stelle. I don't really know much about flowers, but I hope you like'm."

Her smile broadened as she took them from me, then still without speaking, she slipped her free arm about my shoulder and pulled me into a long, tight hug. When she withdrew, I thought that I noticed a faint tearing in her eyes, but before I could look more closely she turned, and taking my hand, led me inside, where she astounded me with, "Now tell me—what kind of a trial was it ... that my favorite lawyer won?"

Only for an instant did I wonder how she knew. "Does it really show that much, pretty lady?" I asked, shaking my head and chuckling.

"Uh-huh ... it's in your eyes," she replied sweetly, then leaned forward and kissed me lightly on the lips before gently guiding me toward the couch. "Now, you want to tell me all about it?"

"Well, if the Pope's still Catholic, I might want to say a few words—nothing more than a million or two," spurted my jovial reply.

"Okay, but hold on a minute and I'll whip us up a couple of drinks. A person should have a drink when discussing such important matters, don't you think?"

"Oh, yeah," I nodded. "Absolutely!"

With her characteristic alacrity, inside sixty seconds, she returned from the bar, handed me a gin and tonic, and nestled close beside me to listen to my tale of triumph. The awkwardness between us had melted, and during the next half hour, together we alternately grimaced and groaned, then gloated and laughed as I acted out for her the various aspects of Consuelo's trial, complete with me simulating the jury's reaction, and slamming my fists down on my knees to emphasize a particularly important point. When she interrupted me with a question, which she did often, I would draw myself out of the role of participant, and amidst her laughter, provide a sober-toned imitation of Eric Sevareid offering an analysis of events "as they were occurring on the floor of the courtroom." Finally, when against all odds, justice had triumphed over the Machiavellian machinations of the wicked police officers and the evil District Attorney, and I announced the quadruplicate verdict of "not guilty!" she burst into applause—and when I then joined her in shouts of "Hurray for the defense!" the sheer ebullience and unadulterated joy of the moment caught us up like a tiny piece of driftwood in a swollen river, tossing and turning us through yet another long-lasting current of laughter, until exhausted from our happy efforts, we sank back into silence and gazed softly at each other.

Stella finally interrupted it, murmuring, "What are we going to do to celebrate your great victory?"

"Could I have a kiss—a real one, please?" I answered, searching her eyes.

"Well, you certainly deserve it," she whispered, sliding closer and leaning in. "And I think I remember how."

"Good ... let's see," trickled my tease an instant before her lips met mine and locked us into warm embrace.

"Pretty lady," I quipped after being gently returned to Earth after thirty seconds of heaven, "did anyone ever tell you that you're the greatest kisser in the history of the world?"

"Uh-huh ... you did," Stella nodded, pulling me up off the couch and toward the dining room. "How about some dinner? You can collect the rest of your reward later."

"My eyes, again?"

"Uh-huh ... dead give-away."

"Boy ... good thing Shafer and Steiggerman can't read me the way you can," I chuckled, shaking my head as I sat down at the table.

Dinner, as always, was positively delicious. Salad, filet of sole with rice, hot rolls with sweet butter, and brownies topped with vanilla ice cream all soon found a welcoming home, the warm, relaxed conversation that governed while we ate serving as the perfect garnishment. Continuing over coffee and smokes after we returned to the living room, for over an hour it centered on music, news, football rivalries and the upcoming USC-UCLA battle, and whatever else happened into mind, till finally it drifted innocently onto the awkward subject of next week's holiday. "Stelle," I broached cautiously after the latest laughter faded, "I was sort of wondering about Thanksgiving, what with your family being in Dallas and all."

"Oh, that's very thoughtful, Matty—and sweet. But no problem, I know you've got to be with your family, and you can't out of nowhere ask to bring me—so I accepted an offer from my new friends, Jean and her hubby Lou. I do have an idea however. How about after dinner, we meet around nine for pie and coffee? It could be our own Thanksgiving together, sound okay?"

"I love it … I absolutely love it!" I enthused, relieved of the worry that she would be alone while I was stuck at my parents' home, and equally delighted that we would actually be able to celebrate together after all.

"Good … I'm glad," she smiled. "Then it's a date."

"You just bet it is, pretty lady. But did you say, new friends?" I asked, curiosity camouflaging last evening's sublimated anxiety.

"Uh-huh … You know the project you saw spread out on the floor last Sunday?"

"Yeahhh—"

"Well, my clients are Jean and Lou. I met them awhile back through an old friend, Samantha, and through working with them we've become friends—especially me and Jean. In fact, I went out to dinner with her last evening, 'cause Lou was out of town on business."

"Ohh … I see," slipped slowly off my tongue as last evening's erroneous assumption suddenly struck home like a sucker punch, forcing a smile to hide my guilt.

"Hold on a minute, Matty," Stella cut in, instantly reading my mind. "Did you think I went out with a guy, the night after our weekend together?" she posed, her expression mirroring the anger flashing into her tone.

"Well … not really," tiptoed my answer. "I mean, I didn't want to. But you're so beautiful, and there's always been all those guys after you, and … well—"

"Well, nothing!" she exploded. "And you just listen here, Mr. Candidate for the Most-Insecure-Person-In-The-World Award, those other men I was seeing were just dates—they don't mean anything to me, but you do! I thought you understood that, but apparently you think I sleep with everybody, and I—"

"No I don't," I interrupted, now instinctively on red alert, and struggling to save the situation. "I think you're special—really and truly special. The problem is that I'm not a candidate for this year's top insecurity award, 'cause I already won it—for the whole fucking century in fact! I was born that way, goddamn it, so I can't help it if it's so difficult for me to accept that I'm important to you—and the last thing in the world that I'd want to do is hurt your feelings, so I'm really really sorry … honest!" I ended, emotion having flooded into my voice, my eyes tearing slightly.

Stella just looked at me as the anger slowly drained from her face, then was replaced by a mixture of frustration and sympathy. "Ohhh-kay," she nodded. "But if we're going to build some kind of a relationship, Matty, you're going to have to start believing in yourself—both in and out of the courtroom, you hear?"

"Uh-huh … I hear," trickled my answer repentantly. "And I'll try harder, I promise."

"You just better," she smiled, sliding back closer to me from her position of retreat and raising her hand to gently caress my cheek. "It's nice that you were jealous, though—probably saved the day for the second half of your reward," she added, her fingertips generating amorous thoughts as they drifted from cheek to neck.

"Eyes, again?" I chuckled, shaking my head.

"Uh-huh," she whispered, drawing close, "dead-bang give-away."

As a foreword, the kiss that followed certainly made me want to read the book, especially because I adore happy endings. And to be sure, the ensuing novel, featuring lovemaking, did contain one—as well as a sweet surprise by Stella, who seized control of the sensual plot after two chapters, then produced an ecstatic ending from her dominant role on top.

"That, pretty lady," I exclaimed when I could breathe again, "was living proof that there is a God!"

"R-e-a-l-l-y?" teased her reply.

"Uh-huh … and a loving one too—one-upping what was already special-plus."

"Listen, you silly person," she whispered, kissing me, then rolling softly onto her side and smiling. "It was great, for sure. But don't sell short what you accomplished today."

"I'm not, Stelle. I know how extraordinary it was, and I'll never forget it—ever. I mean, if you could've seen the expression on Consuelo's face when the verdict was read, it made all the worry and effort worthwhile and then some," I smiled out at her, the recollection warming excitement into my tone. "And the jurors, Stelle—they really liked me. In fact, one of the ladies, an older one, told me that I was wonderful, and kissed me and said God bless. I know that it must all seem silly to you, sometimes it seems that way to me too. But ever since I was a little boy, I've had this need inside me to help people," I shared, opening a deep well, my tone suddenly straining with purpose, "and that's why I've just got to be good, Stelle—maybe even the best. And I think I could be, if I work hard enough, and sacrifice enough," I added, a lifetime of concern for the underdog channeling my message. "And I'm not afraid to make that commitment, and struggle to meet it, that's all I've ever known—and it's so important to me, so deep-down-inside-me important, that I don't think I could change it even if I wanted to," I confessed, slowing my words, then raising myself up on my elbows to ask, "Can you understand that, Stelle? ... Can you?"

"Yes ... I think so," she answered slowly after a thoughtful moment's hesitation. She was going to add something, but stifled it, and instead softly slid her arms around my shoulders and drew me into a tight hug that lasted for a full minute.

When we parted, our eyes affirmed the deeper intimacy that had developed. Good-night kisses followed, along with smiles that said, sleep well. Then finally, the curtain fell on what had truly been a magical day.

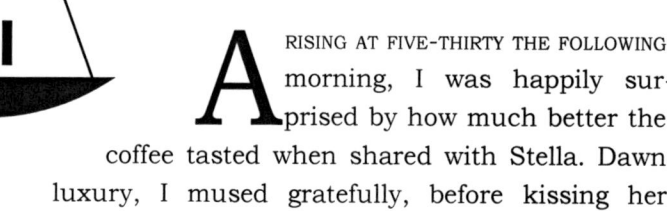

XI

A RISING AT FIVE-THIRTY THE FOLLOWING morning, I was happily surprised by how much better the coffee tasted when shared with Stella. Dawn luxury, I mused gratefully, before kissing her goodbye and whispering "Thanks again" as I hugged her, then hurried to my car. Arriving in Solina under darkly overcast skies, I spent an hour studying the stack of previously prepared interview sheets on my desk while sipping a second cup of coffee, then stuffed them into my briefbag, and after kissing Marilyn on the cheek in response to her warmly articulated "Congratulations!" scurried across the street to the courthouse.

With Ron still tied up in Lacy's court in the third day of a murder Prelim, I again took his place in Division Four, which was by this time fast becoming my home away from home. Roberts congratulated me upon my entrance, as did Ted Greene, and acknowledging their felicitations as I set my briefbag down and withdrew my interview pad, I then adjourned to the jury room and began interviewing my first client of the day. Around ten-fifteen, Steiggerman called a plea-bargaining conference. And thereafter, the remainder of the morning passed by quietly and uneventfully as I traveled back and forth between the jury room and chambers, conferring with my clients, then with Steiggerman and the District Attorney, a pleasant, mild-mannered fellow named Neil Maddern, before decisions were finally arrived at and cases pled-out, dismissed, or continued. His Honor remained silent with respect to the Martinez case outcome, but I detected in his manner toward me the faint outlines of a newly formed respect, begrudged though it was.

Returning at noon to the office, I was unexpectedly mobbed by my cohorts, all of whom crowded into the small cubicle I shared with Ron to shower me with congratulations on yesterday's triumph. Amidst the boisterous conversation that ensued, which quickly turned both humorous and profane, I managed to catch George's eye, and his slow wink added the final stamp of approval. A moment or two later, Leon suggested lunch at a small Chinese restaurant a few blocks away, and after we arrived, the lively conversation quickly resumed, with much of the dialogue centering on Steiggerman and Shafer, what asshole pigs they were, and how very good indeed it was to have defeated them. Later, when I returned to court for the afternoon session, those harsh words swung heavily back into mind when I unexpectedly discovered Shafer seated in Division Four, eagerly awaiting Steiggerman's return and the resumption of the day's business.

Greeting me coldly, he softened enough to shake hands and offer a perfunctory acknowledgment of my recent success, before quickly returning his attention to the case files he had been reading when I entered. Upon His Honor's arrival several minutes later, the afternoon's first plea-bargaining session began, and though operating in an atmosphere of quiet tension, managed nevertheless to progress quite well for the better part of an hour. Then, however, as we reached a series of cases growing out of a single incident, Shafer steadily stiffened his penalty demands until there was little to no room left for negotiation. Seeking to break the developing impasse, Steiggerman placed them momentarily on hold and skipped instead to the last case on calendar, a maneuver which soon proved futile when Shafer agreed to drop the charge of prostitution in exchange for a plea to disturbing the peace, but insisted on a sentence of six months in the county jail. Realizing that this would be unacceptable to me, His Honor pressured Shafer into agreeing to a hundred-twenty-day sentence, only to have me firmly reject the offer without even leaving the room to present it to my client, thereby shifting the burden of bargaining back onto me with split-second speed.

"Now, Mr. Harris," Steiggerman oozed, "you can't take every case to trial. And even if you do, you know that you're not going to win them all—so why not be reasonable and settle this matter, so we can get back to the more important cases."

"Your Honor, I don't recall having expressed a desire to try this case," I returned politely, fully aware from the arrest report that I had no viable defense to work with, but unwilling to have my client serve additional jail time on such a minor offense. "However, Sir," I tacked on in an attempt to shift the pressure back to Shafer, "if the District Attorney insists on exacting a pound of flesh, I don't see that I have any alternative."

"Well then, let's just try it," Shafer suddenly interjected before

Steiggerman could reply. "He can't have a surprise priest to rescue him in every case, Your Honor!"

"What Mr. Shafer means, Your Honor," I shot back, smiling inwardly at how suddenly his wounded ego had surfaced, "is that I won't always have one-hundred-percent truth on my side. But what's really disturbing, Sir, is that while he's outraged by the heinous crime of my client allegedly selling her body, which harms no one except herself, he's not bothered one iota by the fact that just yesterday Officers Tison and Reese committed perjury in this very courtroom!" flowed my indictment as I turned my head toward Shafer. "Unless, of course, you filed charges against them, and I missed the news. Did you, Mr. Guardian of the Public Trust?"

"That settles it, Your Honor!" Shafer exploded. "The People are ready to proceed to trial!"

Uttered with the full force of the vindictiveness that infected him, Shafer's steaming pronouncement short-circuited any further effort by Steiggerman to dissuade either of us from our polarized positions, and shaking his head, he instructed Roberts to summon the jury panel. Exiting chambers, I was surprised to see Ron hurrying through the entranceway in my direction, and craving a smoke, I quickly motioned for him to retreat back outside into the hallway.

"What's up, big fella?" I chirped as the doors closed behind us.

"I need the citation on that new case dealing with torture that you were telling me about."

"Okay—hold on a minute and I'll get it for you."

Returning to the courtroom, I withdrew my notes on the case from my briefbag, then smiled and nodded my head at various members of the jury panel whom I passed while making my way back outside. Handing them to Ron, I pointed to several underlined quotes and turned to leave after he thanked me, stopping short when he added: "Hey, what the hell's going on here?"

"You aren't going to believe this," I smiled, shaking my head, "but I'm back in trial again—and this time I really have my tit in a wringer!"

"Yeahhh ... what kind of case?"

"Prostitution."

"Not Laura Salero?"

"That's the one, big fella," shrugged my answer, causing his grin to vanish.

"That's a dead-bang loser, Matt."

"I know. Like I said, my tit's in a wringer, but I had no choice. Steiggie wanted to give her a hundred and twenty days, and he was doing me a favor, you understand—Shafer wanted six months!"

For a second or two we just stood and stared at each other. Then, suddenly, his smile reappeared, and it was his turn to shake his head. "Well, little guy," he mustered slowly, "don't ever let anybody tell you that you don't have balls—and solid brass ones at that!"

"Yeahhh, I hear you," I returned, squeezing a grin back onto my face. "Problem is, though, that I've got a matching brain to go along with them."

Chuckling, he turned away and walked toward the stairway, stopping to call out "Good luck!" as he turned again, then headed downstairs. Muttering underneath my breath, "Good luck, hell, I need a fucking miracle," I smiled at my nervously inspired attempt at humor, and with butterflies beginning to multiply in my stomach, I returned to the courtroom and took my seat at the counsel table.

The remainder of the afternoon was spent in jury selection. And with the laborious process still not finalized by a quarter of six, it was a highly irritated Steiggerman who halted the proceedings at that time, announcing brusquely that tomorrow morning's session would begin at eight-thirty instead of the usual nine o'clock. Without experience to guide me in regards to what type of juror was best suited to the defense in a prostitution case, and armed only with a gut feeling that I was somehow better off with men than women, I had thus far plodded routinely through my *voir dire*, using five of my twelve peremptory challenges in support of instinct's strategy, while trying to establish a warm rapport with each individual juror. Now, with the trial in recess, I was pleased to have several hours free to evaluate the entire, seemingly hopeless situation.

Employing Robbie's "There's always a hole in the DA's case if you look hard enough" technique as I revisited the arrest report on the way home, I drew a complete blank. And when Roger Williams' keyboard began wafting "The Impossible Dream" as I parked the car, my growled, "Ain't that the whole fucking truth of the matter!" seemed to sum up the depressing situation perfectly. "Well, almost perfectly," I chuckled sardonically, turning off the radio. "I mean, at least there's no death penalty involved."

Still shaking my head in disgust as the front door clicked closed behind me, I immediately dialed Stella, but was left alone with my hopeless predicament when she failed to answer. Without appetite, I skipped dinner in favor of settling onto the living room couch with coffee and pipe to carefully read and reread the arrest report in a desperate search for some weakness, some slight opening in the prosecution's case that I might be able to widen into a reasonable doubt. But mirroring my failed attempt on the ride home, my intensified scrutiny served only to present the proverbial goose-egg, staring vacantly back at me until finally, frustrated, I dropped the arrest report onto the floor, then retreated to the kitchen where I redialed Stella. When her failure to answer also repeated itself, I grabbed my jacket and headed out for a walk in the cool evening air to relieve the tension that was steadily mounting into a full-fledged headache.

Returning to the apartment just before nine, I tried to reach Stella for a third time and again listened to no answer. "Okay. Three strikes and you're out," I snickered sarcastically, concern nudging my mind in the dangerous direction of *Where is she?* and *Who's she with?* "Not this time, Buster Brown," I ordered instantly, strolling back to the couch, "it's Trust Time, remember? ... And besides, if you want something to worry about, I've already got it for you in spades!" I trumpeted, a wan smile forming as I picked up the arrest report off the floor and plopped back down onto the couch's cushiony surface. Lighting up my pipe, I once again began to inch down the first block of the dead-end street, when suddenly Shafer's fatuous face popped onto my mind's screen, causing me to grimace, then slowly reverse gears and break into a grin as the germ of an idea floated into view.

You've got no defense, dribbled the sluggishly stirring neurons, *so how about we try and turn Mr. Angry into one?* posed the second half of the thought. "Yeahhh, why not?" I answered out loud, chuckling as enthusiasm climbed aboard. "You considered using that anger against him in the Martinez trial, but worried about how the jury might react to a provocateur. But this time," I opined, "you've got nothing to lose, 'cause the best offer was a hundred and twenty days in the pokey, so you're only gambling an extra sixty versus the possibility of a hung jury if just one juror dislikes Mr. Wrath-Rage enough to hold out for acquittal," rambled reason to a close, its hopeful message widening my grin as I climbed off the couch and began to pace up and down the living room. "Yes! ... That's it!" I screeched mischievously after a careful review confirmed the plot's viability. "And you don't have to play the part of the bad guy, either. Unh-uh, that's Shafer's role. All you've got to do, Mr. Nice-Guy-Trying-to-Defend-Your-Poor-Client, is humbly insert a little salt into that wounded ego, then patiently rub-a-dub till the arrogance and anger mix into a venomous vessel that explodes like a Hydrogen Bomb!" I postulated, stopping my stroll to relight my pipe, its taste suddenly delicious as my mind's screen now played a Technicolor film-short featuring Shafer's enraged actions, followed by co-conspirator Steiggerman chastising the holy hell out of poor little me, whose pain and bewilderment from just trying to defend his damsel-in-distress client from the big bad wolves then wins the sympathy of the outraged jurors and carries the day!

The ring of the telephone jarred me from my reverie, and its second and third summons hurried me into the kitchen where I grabbed up the receiver and smiled at the sweet sound of Stella's voice. "Matt?" she asked warmly.

"Uh-huh. You were expecting Robert Redford maybe?" I teased, relief widening my grin to full.

"No, I already passed him over in search of bigger game," she shot back. "How are you?"

"I'm okay. But I miss you."

"Me, too. But listen, Matty—I'm fine, but I'm not in L.A. I had to fly to Seattle due to an emergency, 'cause my dear friend Lea was seriously injured in an automobile accident. The doctor's now say that she's expected to live, but she's still in really bad shape."

"Jesus! I'm sorry, Stelle," reflexed my reply. "Is there anything I can do to help?"

"No, sweetie. Just take care of yourself—and eat, okay?"

"Uh-huh, sure."

"And you don't have to worry that I'm all alone. Lea's sister is on the way from Chicago, and should be here at the hospital within the hour."

"Okay. That's good, glad to hear it."

"Yeah, for sure. Listen, you take care of my Matty, and I'll call you tomorrow when I know more. I'll try and leave a message for you at the office, and I'll call for sure tomorrow night when I know I can get you—okay?"

"Uh-huh, that's great. And you take care of my pretty lady—and tell Redford to piss off if he calls back, okay?"

"It's a deal. Now bye for now."

"Bye, Stelle," I answered softly, hanging up, then savoring the replay of her "my Matty" for several suspended seconds.

In fact, the charming concept of belonging to her so buoyed my spirits that I floated back to the living room. Then, recalling my pledge to eat, I retraced my steps back into the kitchen, pulled from the freezer a pint of Haagen-Daz vanilla, added a pint of chocolate for a chaser, and treated myself to a creamy sugar-feast while browsing the Sports Page. Gradually, thoughts about tomorrow's trial filtered back into mind, and after returning the ice cream cartons, I lit up a fresh pipe and reevaluated my recently hatched and still bubbling plan. "It ain't much, Laura," I reflected out loud, recalling how unconcerned she had appeared during our meeting in the lockup when she confessed that she "earned her keep" as a streetwalker and was guilty as charged, "but it's all we've got—so here's hoping," I toasted with the remnants of my coffee, before ambling off to bed.

Aroused at five forty-five by the seemingly roaring ring of my alarm clock, after a shave and an extra-long steamy shower to bring me fully alert, I headed for the office, eating a large orange and hoping that it would nourish both me and my cockamamie strategy during the long day that lay in wait. Supplemented by two cups of coffee and some idle chatter with Ron and Marilyn after I arrived, when time soon ticked to eight-thirty, it found me reseated at the counsel table listening to Shafer resume his *voir dire*, while awaiting with mixed feelings of eagerness and apprehension the first opportunity to inject Operation Piss Off, as I had aptly nicknamed my plan, into the proceedings.

My wait wasn't long. For Shafer, in a sanctimonious tone that would have done justice to a fully warmed-up Jerry Falwell, quickly launched into a series of questions dealing with society's need for law and order, complete with references to the underlying moral values that supported this urgent necessity, and further propped onto a pedestal by repeated statements to the effect that the People of the State of California had seen fit to do this or that, and that in so doing, had expressed their feelings in such and such a manner. Adding that he hoped the jurors understood that as a representative of the People, he was duty bound to enforce these codified moral values of society, he then homed in on the statute making prostitution a crime. That is he started to, until genuinely repulsed by the steady stream of hypocritical Silly Putty that he was pedantically feeding to the jurors, I climbed to my feet and interrupted him.

"Your Honor," I eased out in my most humble tone of voice, "I'm sorry, but I feel compelled to object to Mr. Shafer's line of inquiry, which at this point is calculated solely to mislead and prejudice the prospective jurors against my client, Miss Salero."

Annoyance flashed across Steiggerman's face, but before he could fully express it by stoutly overruling my objection, Shafer intervened with: "Your Honor, my line of questioning is perfectly proper, and the PD knows it!" Accustomed to quirky behavior from me, the sheer volume of Shafer's razor-toned reply caused surprise to overlay Steiggerman's irritation and further delay his response, an opportunity I instantly seized to further bait Shafer.

"That's not really true, Your Honor," I retorted, acting hurt. "My objection is taken most earnestly, and respectfully, Sir, because for the past ten minutes or so, Mr. Shafer has been suggesting that the prosecution's side of this case somehow has the individual support of every single person residing in this state, the so-called People. And not only that, Sir, he has also insinuated that because Miss Salero has been charged with a crime, she's no longer one of the persons who comprise the People—no longer a human being, no longer a member of the society which he has referred to," I argued underneath an umbrella of sadness. "And that's just not true, Your Honor, even though Mr. Shafer may feel that when a citizen is charged with a crime and the label defendant attaches, that simultaneously that individual becomes some kind of strange animal that's separate and distinct from the People he has so laboriously referred to. It's simply not true, or fair, and the District Attorney ought not to be trying to create the misleading impression that it is," I ended, shaking my head slowly to emphasize my deep concern.

In a voice now quivering with fully aroused anger, but still within the bounds of control, Shafer once again responded before Steiggerman could enter the fray. "Your Honor," he shot back loudly, "it's the PD who's trying to mislead the jurors, not the People—and I'm outraged at his insulting behavior, and request the Court to immediately cite him for his misconduct!"

His Honor, looking perplexed, now found himself in a strange position. Angered by my attack on his favorite District Attorney's integrity, but equally disturbed by the furious expression on Shafer's face, and the even more surprising disrespectful tone of his voice, he hesitated, unable momentarily to choose which of us to censure. Then, having assessed that Shafer's history of loyal service outweighed his unintended breach of proper decorum, Steiggerman promptly launched his customary program of discrediting me in the eyes of the jurors.

"Mr. Harris," he delivered in a cold, cutting tone, "your ill-advised objection is overruled! And, further, you should be aware that this Court is perfectly capable of determining when a participant is acting improperly, without any help from you. So in the future, you will please confine your efforts to trying the case, and leave the conduct of the trial to me—do you understand, Mr. Harris?"

"No, Your Honor, with all due respect, I'm confused," crawled my sincerity-infused reply after a few silent seconds had elapsed. "All I've done, Sir, is to object in the customary fashion to the District Attorney's attempt to mislead the prospective jurors into believing that the entire population of our state is personally supporting his prosecution of this case, while my client, merely because she's been charged with a crime, has automatically been divorced from society and is no longer considered a human being. I'm deeply sorry, Your Honor," I stressed, honey dripping from my every word, "if the Court has formed the opinion that I was trying to advise it on how to conduct this case. I assure you, that that was not my intent. In fact, Your Honor, I was merely appealing to the Court for its help in stopping what I felt was unfair and improper behavior on the part of Mr. Shafer, and nothing more, Sir."

The soft, apologetic tone of my voice momentarily disarmed him, and a thin smile formed on his lips as I picked up after a second's pause to allow my apology to sink in. "Actually, Your Honor," ambled my expanding explanation, "if you'll examine Mr. Shafer's last statement that quote, 'It's the PD who's trying to mislead the jurors, not the People,' you'll be able to see exactly what it is that I'm objecting to. Notice, Sir, that Mr. Shafer has the PD—that's me—set off and distinguished not from Mr. Shafer, but instead from the People, illustrating perfectly his desire to create the false image that he is part and parcel of the goodness that the People represent, while me and my client are some lower specie associated with being bad. Now that's simply not a true and accurate portrayal of the operation of our legal system, Your Honor," I continued, my honeyed tone thickening, "and I think that Mr. Shafer knows it, and is deliberately creating a misimpression anyway in order to prejudice the jurors against my client. And that's exactly why, Sir, that I most sincerely and respectfully object to it."

As I finished speaking, the smile disappeared from Steiggerman's face and was replaced by a fresh flush of anger. Having assumed that I was merely going to explain my actions in the course of apologizing for them, and then allow the confrontation to die, my defiance, even though subtle and couched in humble terms and tone, now provoked full hostility.

"Mr. Harris, I have warned you once, and I'm now doing it a second time. But I'm not going to do it again!" cascaded his thunder. "If you continue to argue this issue with me for one second longer, I will hold you in contempt of court! Now, do you understand that?"

"Yes ... of course, Your Honor," tiptoed my reply plaintively, my face masking mock hurt and confusion. "But does that mean that you are ordering me not to object to anything for the remainder of the trial?"

Still glowering at me, he started to answer quickly, caught himself and stifled the word, yes, on the tip of his tongue, then shaking his head in disgust as full control returned, replied in a softened tone of voice: "No, Mr. Harris, I am not telling you that. ... Now sit down, and let's proceed."

Satisfied that Steiggerman had emphatically put me in my proper place, Shafer, wearing a wide grin, turned back to the jurors and resumed his *voir dire*. It vanished almost instantly, when I objected to the first question out of his mouth, His Honor overruling it with like speed. And once established, this purposeful pattern of punch and counter-punch soon settled into a wriggling, writhing war of attrition, as with Steiggerman having acknowledged that even in his courtroom objections were permitted, as long as they were not contested at length, during the next three hours I interrupted Shafer an additional sixteen times with carefully worded objections, each based on a recognized legal ground and delivered to His Honor in a soft, totally respectful tone of voice—all of which were disdainfully overruled by Steiggerman, whose face mirrored increasing levels of frustration, and whose voice steadily hardened until his responses were low, gravelly growls. Holding my own despite being outnumbered two to one, I clung steadfastly to my strategy in the face of the increasingly heavy body blows hurled my way in the form of derision and ridicule. Recalling Tolstoy's hopeful aphorism that the strongest of all warriors were time and patience, as the tension mounted and nerves began to fray, I gleaned the strength to steel myself, then waited for my trusty allies to take their toll.

Finally, just before noon, the ground shifted, when as I meticulously phrased my last objection to Shafer's pending question, he whirled around from the jury box and exploded at me. "There's absolutely nothing wrong with my question, and you know it, you stupid, obstructionist idiot!" he shouted, turning purple with rage.

"Mr. Shafer—please!" His Honor boomed out, hurtling to the rescue before Shafer lost the last semblance of control and added to his outburst. "The Court sympathizes with you, but you must address your grievances to me and not to the Public Defender." Then, satisfied that he had halted the stream of invectives forming on Shafer's tongue, Steiggerman turned his attention to me.

"Mr. Harris, you ought to be ashamed of yourself!" he admonished, fuming. "In all my years on the bench, I have never experienced such foolish conduct on the part of counsel, and if you have an ounce of decency left in you, you should apologize, and then shut up!" he concluded, the fire in his voice matched by his blazing eyes.

Having at last succeeded in evoking from Shafer the exact display of intense animosity I desired the jurors to view, and noted the varying degrees of dismay etched across their individual faces, I hesitated before replying, watching the muscles in Shafer's narrow face continue to twitch in response to his still seething anger as my answer formed. Then, smiling inwardly at the bonus Steiggerman had gifted me with, his "shut up!" still echoing in the electrically charged atmosphere, I responded in the same soft, conciliatory, and pained tone of voice that I had adopted since I placed my desperately designed scheme into operation.

"Your Honor, I sincerely regret that I have offended the Court," I began cautiously. "I assure you that such was not my intention. In fact, Sir, all I did was object to Mr. Shafer's question, and it was him, not me, that shouted insulting language—so I'm sorry, but I just don't understand why I should apologize for being called ugly names. Moreover, in that the Court has sanctioned Mr. Shafer's reference to me as stupid, by indicating that I am a fool, I would like to move the Court to declare a mistrial on the grounds that these remarks have unduly prejudiced the prospective jurors against my client, and I—"

"Your motion is denied!" Steiggerman barked, cutting me off, then announcing in the same breath that the trial stood adjourned until two o'clock, prior to rushing off the bench and disappearing into chambers before the ice in his echo had fully melted.

Sinking slowly back in my chair, I carefully studied the faces of the jurors as they filed silently out of the jury box and followed Bailiff Roberts to lunch. Detecting perplexed expressions on most of their faces, I wondered if maybe, just maybe, my desperation-crazed strategy might be having the desired effect. One of the few optimistic thoughts to surface on an otherwise hopeless horizon, it wasn't allowed to entertain me for long, as Shafer, on his way out of the courtroom, stopped in front of me and rudely interrupted it. "You really are an asshole, Harris—you know that?" he snarled.

"Well, thanks for the compliment, Steve," I shot back at him, breaking into a smile. "Or should I more properly address you as the People?"

Whatever response he was expecting, my gibe failed to coincide, and when his stony stare failed to diminish my grin after several uncomfortable seconds had passed, he broke off his gaze and walked away without uttering another word. Returning to the office by way of my friendly neighborhood Jim Dandy chicken outlet, I searched my pile of messages while munching on a tasty thigh, happily discovering the sought-after one from Stella second from the bottom. "Lea improving, will call you tonight," it read succinctly, and after tucking it carefully inside my shirt pocket, I relaxed by picturing her lovely face and taking a large bite of chicken to show her that I was following orders, then drifted down the hallway to share smokes and conversation with Robbie and George.

Two o'clock soon arrived, and after Steiggerman took the bench, the morning's hostilities promptly resumed, with an increasingly bellicose Shafer leading the charge. With the jury finally impaneled, the People now presented their sole witness, Officer Dennis Hill of the Brynhurst Police Department Vice Squad. And amidst the virtual hailstorm of objections that I raised, and His Honor instantly overruled, he staggered through his simple story of having been seated in a bar on Leale Street, sipping a scotch and soda, when he was approached by the defendant, who after engaging him in conversation for several minutes, then proposed "having some fun." Departing from the aptly named Action Express, he had driven her in his unmarked police vehicle to her apartment several blocks away, where he gave her twenty dollars and then arrested her when she undressed and lay down on the bed to perform the bargained-for act.

Knowing full well that Hill was telling the truth, I cross-examined him with the sole objective of arousing his anger, and in turn engendering further displays of malice from Shafer in concert with the acerbic criticism from Steiggerman that was certain to follow. Focusing on issues such as whether Hill hadn't in fact sampled Laura's allegedly offered wares before effectuating her arrest, and bluntly asserting that what had actually occurred was a pickup date followed by sex, with the arrest merely an afterthought to justify his evening's work, I readily produced the desired results. For inside ten minutes of my inquiry, Shafer, in a tone that grew more obnoxiously pedantic with each occurrence, one-upped me in the raise-an-objection contest, with His Honor sustaining him with religious regularity, before finally terminating my efforts by once again threatening to hold me in contempt if I uttered so much as another single word. Falling silent, as pain painted a portrait across my face, I emitted a deep sigh that silently screamed HELP! before turning slowly away from the witness box and returning past the jurors to my seat at the counsel table.

His Honor then declared a ten-minute recess, during which I remained in my chair next to the thoroughly confused, and now equally frightened Laura Salero, due to her ringside seat at the Histrionics Horror Show. Chatting casually with her in an effort to ease her newly arisen anxiety, I forced a smile onto my face, even while failing to squelch the nagging worry about the disastrous effect her inability to testify on her own behalf was almost certain to have on the jury. Having long ago shelved this concern in the far recesses of my mind, I now felt it resurface in full force as Steiggerman returned to the bench and indicated that the defense could call its first witness. Mustering confidence into my voice, so as to at least hide from the jury the sinking feeling in the pit of my stomach, I responded by firmly announcing that I didn't have any witnesses to present at this time, then dropped back into my chair and smiled at Laura so as to convey the impression that we planned it this way. However, when Shafer, wearing a cocky grin, promptly rested the People's case, I was forced to follow suit, and after he waived the opening phase of his closing argument, time continued to rush forward, and with the game on the line, it was my turn to step into the batter's box.

Having no alternative other than to deliver a final plea that was consistent with the zany defense I had concocted, and see if I could somehow stretch a walk into an inside-the-park home run, as I slowly climbed out of my chair, I bolstered myself with the counter-arguments that while Laura couldn't testify, nevertheless, she was only charged with a crime that had no real victim, and if I could just get one juror to hold fast to the idea that something smelled fishy in the case due to all the commotion I'd created, then a hung jury resulted. And as I strolled toward a spot in front of the jury, I could hear Grampy Max whispering, "Yeah, that's right, so just keep your eye on the ball, and take your best swing." Smiling sadly when I reached the railing, for several sober seconds I just stood silent and motionless before the twenty-four eyes that fastened upon me. Then, in a soft, sincere tone of voice, I began to speak.

"Ladies and gentlemen," trickled the words off my tongue, "I deeply regret that there is very little that I can say to you at this time, other than to sincerely thank each and every one of you for serving on this jury. As you have undoubtedly observed, His Honor, Judge Steiggerman, is highly displeased with me, and if I have also offended any one of you, I want to take this opportunity to apologize and assure you that that was not my intention. All I have tried to do," I explained, battle fatigue suddenly leaking emotion into my tone, "is defend my client to the best of my ability—so, please, I beg of you not to hold my efforts, and the ugly names shouted at me, against Laura Salero," seeped my plea into a brief pause, my eyes carefully sweeping left and right to make contact with each juror.

"As for the case itself," I picked up, a wry smile faintly forming, then fading away, "well, you've got eyes and you've got ears—and each of you has seen and heard all that has gone down in this courtroom over the past two days. So all I can add is, that when you're alone in the jury room trying to decide on a verdict, I hope and pray to God that you'll ask yourselves one question ... Why?" I ended, my voice cracking ever so slightly as I tacked on a "Thank you," then turned slowly away and returned to my seat at the counsel table.

As expected, Shafer then proceeded to lambaste both Laura and me from the proverbial pillar to post. Moralizing first about the mores of society and the evils of prostitution in a feverish tone of voice, he closed with a ringing denouncement of me as a "rebellious radical" and a blistering warning to the jury to not be fooled by the "stupid, obstructionist tactics offered in place of a real defense," but instead to concentrate on the valid evidence presented by the People, which would lead them to the only possible verdict, guilty as charged.

Leaning forward in my chair as His Honor then droned out his instructions to the jury, I slouched backward after he finished and the jurors silently filed out of their box and into the adjoining room to deliberate, then noted that time had ticked forward to four forty-five. Suddenly tired as the adrenaline ebbed, I wandered outside into the corridor for a puff on my pipe and bumped into George, who was checking up on me after learning from Sheriff Moorehouse that I was "taking quite a hammering upstairs." For half an hour we chatted together over smokes before he finally left for home and I settled onto a bench and took up my vigil, first watching the faint shadows of dusk slip softly into the darkness of early nighttime, then reading a discarded newspaper. Fortunately, His Honor had a dinner engagement, so when the jury had not reached a verdict by six-thirty, the proceedings were trailed to nine o'clock the following morning, and I headed home to wait for Stella's call.

It arrived after I'd sipped several glasses of Chablis during a two-hour sojourn through the carefree pages of *Sports Illustrated*, and it was a thoroughly relaxed and slightly inebriated me who exuberantly answered the third ring. Our ensuing conversation was short but sweet, like Lincoln's old lady's dance. Lea was improving, thank God, though she had a long slog ahead of her to full recovery. Stella was holding up well, and to demonstrate just how well, she promptly read me over the phone as expertly as she did face to face by correctly intuiting that I was once again engaged in trial. When I explained that "this one was way too crazy for a phone discussion," but promised full details upon her return, she acquiesced, and after assuring me that she'd received "no further advances from that Redford guy," she indicated that she'd probably stay till Saturday, but would let me know tomorrow. And just like that, short faded sweet into silence. Hanging up the receiver, I smiled at the echo of her parting, "Take care, and I'll give you a hug and kiss soon," then followed with a rolling chuckle as I recalled my succinct summary to her of Laura's trial. "Way too crazy for a phone discussion?" I reiterated. "Hell, it's so fucking nuts that it would take a whole panel of shrinks to explain it!" I grumbled, refilling my glass with wine, then retrieving *SI* from the couch, and strolling a bit unsteadily toward the bedroom, hoping that in combination they would manufacture sleep.

At nine-fifteen the following morning, the jury resumed its deliberation, and after uttering a silent prayer, I commenced work on Friday's calendar. The Chablis-*SI* sedative had worked, and refreshed from a full night's sleep, bolstered by a cup of coffee that Roberts had for some unknown reason provided, I sat outside the courtroom on a small bench at the end of the corridor and slowly but steadily interviewed the long list of persons whose names appeared in blue ink on the legal-sized sheet of paper dated November 22. Between interviews five and six, it suddenly dawned on me that it was the fifth anniversary of JFK's assassination, and as my mind merry-go-rounded the tragic events surrounding it, from first learning of the shots fired in Dallas as I left a ten o'clock torts class at Boalt Hall to three-year-old John-John saluting his father's casket, an ache crawled up through my chest to mist my eyes. "I miss you, Mr. President. God bless," I whispered as I wiped away my tears, then stood up and called out the name of my next client. And just as I introduced myself to Samuel White, Roberts interrupted with the news that the jury had reached a verdict.

Excusing myself from Samuel, I returned to my seat at the counsel table and waited for the arrival of Laura. Focused on the fact that Roberts had reported "reached a verdict," not that the jury was hung, I nevertheless forced a smile onto my face when Laura slid into her chair next to me and we exchanged good-mornings. Then, glancing up at Steiggerman as he directed Roberts to take possession of the single folded sheet of paper from the foreman, I struggled to bolster my drooping spirits as Steiggerman quickly eyed it and in turn passed it to his clerk. It seemed forever until the Scottish-accented tones of Ted Greene's voice droned toward the end of the paragraph he was so carefully reading. And pausing for seemingly an eternal second when he finally reached it, his firm articulation of "Not guilty!" exploded into my brain with such a force that I went momentarily numb. Focusing on Steiggerman's face as my heart skipped several beats, then jack-hammered back into motion, I gleaned from his sour expression of disbelief that I had not misheard the verdict. And after darting my eyes in Shafer's direction, the anguish I observed digging deep furrows throughout his narrow face conclusively confirmed the miracle, its magic instantly blowing away the remnants of the fog that had enveloped me, and allowing the faint smile that had cautiously formed to broaden over my entire face until it fairly glowed. Feeling like a condemned convict whose impending execution has just been stayed, then expunged forever by a last-second pardon, I listened gleefully as Steiggerman chastised the jury with words to the effect that their verdict was the greatest miscarriage of justice he had witnessed in his ten years on the bench. Then, rising to my feet as he stormed angrily into his chambers, I rushed over and warmly embraced each and every one of the jurors.

Four hours later, after the unrestrained exultation of the moment had been tempered by the afternoon's tiresome business of continuance, plea bargain, and dismissal, made less distasteful only by Steiggerman's sudden departure due to illness, and the transference of my calendar to the far more peaceful chambers of Judge Austin, I stood alone outside the courthouse and reflected on what had earlier transpired. As I peered up through the gently dropping dusk to the weather-worn letters that spelled out JUSTICE high on the building's facade, the upper-cased characters blurred like the curious mixture of thoughts and emotions coursing through me. And while my gaze remained fixed, time slipped into suspension as I struggled to separate happy from sad, and exhilaration from fright, so as to glean some semblance of truth and meaning from the strange sequence of events that over the past three days had carried me like a rollercoaster from the depths of depression to the heights of jubilation, and had now finally settled into a nagging string of perplexing questions.

Though different in nature, the thorny interrogatives were all connected, like quarrelsome but nonetheless chummy members of a debating club—each with its own personality and life purpose, but united by the common thread of the central roles they played in the administration of criminal jurisprudence. And fittingly, since she had chafed at my conscience all afternoon long, it was Lady Justice who stepped into the spotlight first, absent her blindfold so that she could look me straight in my mind's eye when she asked, "How do you feel, Mr. Public Defender, to have ushered a guilty person out of jail and back into proper society?"

"Well," I breathed slowly into the twilight after a deep sigh, "I know what you're getting at, and I certainly do believe in rules, and punishment for breaking them. But on the other hand, I also believe in our legal system, which holds that moral guilt and legal guilt are separate issues, and you're only guilty of a crime if the evidence convinces a jury of that guilt beyond a reasonable doubt," I espoused softly, struggling to balance reason and feelings, and pausing for several seconds to further reflect before continuing. "Now, as you know," I picked up, a faint smile forming as logic began to soothe my nagging sense of having done something wrong, "under that system the prosecution presents its evidence, I defend against it, and the jury decides guilty or not guilty. My job wasn't to judge Laura Salero, my sworn duty was to do all I legally could to defend her!"

"Alright, I hear you," Lady Justice drawled. "But since you knew she was guilty, didn't you pervert the system by baiting His Honor and Mr. Shafer with your obstructionist tactics?"

"Hell, no, I didn't!" I fired back without hesitation. "I didn't ask for the trial, Shafer did, 'cause he was sure he had a winner to punish me with for having defeated him in the Martinez case. And all Steiggerman had to do was overrule him on the extra jail time, and I'd have taken the plea bargain," streamed my argument, now fueled by remnants of my original anger, my words flowing faster. "But instead, Mr. Kiss-Ass backed the DA's Office as usual, like they're some kind of gods, and then instead of performing his job of being a neutral arbiter and insuring a fair trial, he acted like a second prosecutor. Hell, talk about perverting the system?" I growled, pausing to catch my breath, then rolling to conclusion. "And as for Shafer, it's not my fault that the fucking egomaniac can't control his temper. Moreover, where were you, oh Queen of Honor and Fair Play, when the slimy sonofabitch put on two police officers who clearly perjured themselves, and instead of being outraged, and dismissing the false charges against Consuelo, instead tried to discredit an honorable priest who was telling the truth? You want to talk perversion of the system, do you?"

No answer. Just several seconds of silence rubbing together like sandpaper, before another query sallied forth in response. "So, is justice just a game?" needled her namesake, a sour smile twisted onto her lips.

"No, not for me it isn't," rifled my return. "My clients are real live human beings to me, not some DA statistic rolled into their record of convictions, or a number on a court calendar. I care about them, 'cause most them are poor, uneducated, and never had a fair chance in life—not to forget that they're scared to death and desperately need a friend," flowed my words with growing conviction. "And all I did, when pushed into a trial that only Shafer wanted, was give him and Steiggerman the opportunity to show the jury just how ugly with prejudice the system can be when arrogant power-mongers are running a closed shop!"

"I see. And that justifies your helping turn loose a prostitute back amongst us?" intervened Mr. and Mrs. Proper Society, now substituting for Lady Justice.

"Listen, if you're talking murder or armed robbery, I see your point. But the truth is, that serious charges, with major punishments attached, just means that we've got to be even more vigilant in insuring that the accused receives a fair trial, so as to safeguard against an innocent person being wrongly convicted," rolled out my reply. "But here, we're dealing with a victimless crime. And the only ridiculous reason that prostitution is even on the books is 'cause the Catholic Church, which believes that sex is only for procreation purposes, pressured the state legislature into putting it there—along with oral sex, by the way, even between a husband and wife!" I steamed out into the cool night air, pausing again to gather in oxygen, then generate more steam. "And as for that lily-white innocence you cloak yourself with, oh Goody-Two-Shoes Guardian of Right and Wrong, let me ask you a question: Is that community you so cherish the same group that enters into war, and cheats in business, and commits adultery, while also holding down the poor, and discriminating based on skin color—all while fervently espousing the virtues of Christianity? Hell's bells, if the dream of that second coming ever actually occurs, a high percentage of that prim and proper society better run for cover, 'cause Jesus is going to kick ass Big Time!" I ended, shaking my fist at so much of what was wrong in the world that needn't be.

"Ohhh, I see ... But I didn't know you were so perfect," interjected Mr. Power-User, stepping into the spotlight as Lady Justice and Mr. and Mrs. Proper Society yielded center stage. "In fact, didn't you abuse the power developed from your skills to intentionally inflict pain on your adversaries?"

"Yeah, I did—and it felt good," I readily admitted, then paused to concentrate on my accumulated awareness that ever since I'd hammered Louise Petrie into a more truthful account of events during the rape Prelim, deep inside me I'd felt the faint stirrings of possessing a kind of power, a feeling that had grown when I'd surprised Steiggerman and Shafer to win freedom for Consuelo Martinez, and then blossomed fully when I'd feasted with pleasure on their agony resulting from today's verdict. "But," I picked up, "I wouldn't call it abusive, unless it was used against innocent bystanders, and assholes like Steiggerman and Shafer hardly qualify. They're the ones with real power, and they're the ones who abuse it daily by making perceived underlings afraid to stand up against them."

"Oh, really?" Mr. Fear suddenly intervened, squeezing in alongside Mr. Power-User. "You were afraid, little boy?" he oozed, snickering.

"Uh-huh ... for sure," I nodded out, equally aware that I had been terribly frightened—first of giving in to Shafer's piss-poor offer that provided extra jail time for Laura just to avoid losing a trial, then even more so of actually losing that trial once it commenced. "But you know something?" I countered, a fresh smile forming. "In spite of that fearsome weight on my shoulders, I didn't retreat one inch, even in the face of the ignominious insults and bullying tactics hurled against me. So while I'm not half the lawyer I wish I was, I'm not the gutless wonder of the century either!" closed my defense defiantly, a satisfied grin shooting across my face. "And you know something else? It felt damn good fighting back, and watching those bastards suffer—and it still does!"

Five, maybe six, minutes had slipped by. And suddenly very tired from the day's efforts, but still exhilarated from triumphing in trial and wrestling my conscience clear, I pulled my eyes down from the gold-flaked letters overhead, and feeling both stronger and better about myself than I could ever recall having felt in my life, I turned slowly away from the courthouse, straightened my shoulders, and strode briskly toward the office.

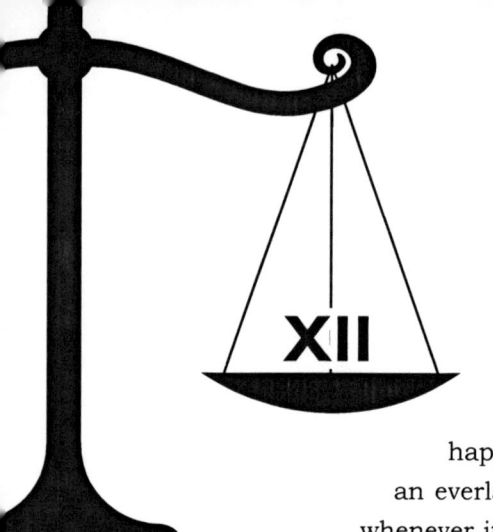

XII

Dame Fortune had already turned Friday special. But sometimes a special day holds two happy surprises, the second seeking to insure an everlasting memory that smiles from the heart whenever it is summoned to the surface. And though already feeling fully rewarded, when I reached the office, the sugar that stitches together such a sweet memory was waiting. For taped to the office door was a note bearing congratulations from George, Robbie, Ron, Leon, and Marilyn, along with the message that there was a telegram on my desk.

Marilyn, who had also taped a copy to the windshield of Old Greener, and was just about to turn off the office lights when I entered, greeted me with a smiling, "Oh, good, I get to say well done in person, and not have to worry you'll miss your telegram," followed by a kiss on the cheek, before rushing off to a date with Will. And still feeling the warmth of her parting, "The guys said to tell you you're unbelievable, Mr. Trial Man. Have a great weekend!" as I hurried to my desk, my grin grew even wider after I opened the telegram and read:

Hi, Matty,

I'll be arriving at LAX tonight at 7:30, United Airlines Flight #99. Pick me up if you're not tied up in court too late. If you are, don't worry, I'll catch a cab and see you when you get home.

Love, Stelle

Glancing at my watch which signaled five after six, for several seconds I just stood there, wondering what I had done to deserve such double luck. Then, quickly stuffing Monday's interview sheets into my briefbag, I locked up the office and hurried to my car, even though LAX was only half an hour away and I'd be arriving an hour early. "That's okay," I hummed happily as I turned the key in the ignition. "When a miracle's already happened, and it's topped off by getting to celebrate with a pretty lady who's seriously special, there's no such thing as too early!"

Seated by a window in the United Airlines Lounge at six thirty-seven, an adrenaline-fueled time-distance record soon to be recognized by Guinness, I reread Stella's telegram a half dozen times before finally slipping it back into the heart-side pocket of my blazer and turning my focus to the sports page of the evening newspaper I'd purchased. But even as relaxed as I was, I found it difficult to fully concentrate on an interesting column about the upcoming USC-UCLA football game, her closing, "Love, Stelle," beaming back into mind every so often to squeeze yet another smile onto my lips. Is that what's happening? Love? I suddenly pondered, lifting my eyes toward the starry sky. And what do you think about that, Matthew, my man? traipsed a following interrogatory into mind, winking, then smiling shyly while I carefully considered the proposition, her use of the L word, accompanied by my personalized version of her name, certainly suggesting that something was changing. "Well," I whispered into the paper, as if it were somehow a participant in the unfolding analysis, "as usual, I can't be sure. But it sounds good, and feels good—real good, in fact. So, I guess we'll just have to wait and see what we see, when we see it … okay, buddy?"

Okay, for sure, I readily agreed, nodding my head as I resumed reading the sports page, this time with somewhat better success. For even though eager anticipation steadily increased as the minutes ticked slowly by, an entertaining interview with SC's coach, John McKay, combined with my intermittent study of the fascinating variety of people streaming to and fro in the concourse to nicely fill them until finally time trickled to the appointed hour and a voice over the loudspeaker announced the arrival of Flight Number 99. Ninety seconds later, passengers began to emerge, and five patience-testing minutes after that my heart quickened with the sight of Stella's lovely face breaking into a smile upon sighting me. A tight hug followed when we quickly converged, accompanied by over-the-shoulder murmurs of how good it was to see each other, animated conversation then flowing as we walked toward the baggage claim area. "What happened with the trial?" Stella instantly zeroed in after my request for a Lea update smiled by.

"We won. It was a fucking miracle, Stelle!" squirted my answer as I squeezed her hand. "Wait till you hear about this nutsiness. I mean, it was way beyond boogie-meshuggie!"

"That's great, Matty. We gotta celebrate."

"I already am. I've got you back, and a whole day earlier."

"Thanks, sweetie, I'm glad too," she smiled. "I'm sorry I couldn't let you know earlier, but the doctors didn't know till late in the afternoon that Lea's head injury wasn't as serious as originally thought."

"I see ... More good news to celebrate."

"Uh-huh, right. And when I learned that, and relaxed enough to realize how much I missed you, I got the first plane I could, and here I am."

"Well, thank you very much for the absolutely perfect gift!" I announced happily as we reached the baggage carousel. "And for a bonus, look what we have here," I tacked on, spying Stella's suitcase and lifting it off.

The chatter continued as we walked to the parking structure and located Old Greener, Stella filling me in on her history with Lea, and getting to know her sister, with me tossing in a question here and there, then assuring her that I had been eating when she expressed some skepticism after a quick survey. "Listen, I have a serious question for you," I tossed at her as we climbed inside the car.

"What?" she answered, concern edging her tone.

"Well ... exactly how much did you miss me? I mean, on a scale of one to ten, where—"

Sliding toward me, Stella's lips interrupted my query by delivering a kiss that lasted long enough to take on a life of its own. No complaint was registered, however, as I responded with equal fervor, then smiled as we parted and she teased me with, "Did that answer your question, counselor?"

"Uh-huh, for sure. But somehow I missed the last few words, so could you repeat them please?"

"Greedy, aren't you?" she whispered, her mesmerizing eyes working their magic as usual.

"Not really, Your Honoress," I teased her back. "Irresistible impulse is a well-recognized defense, and I can't help it if God made you impossibly gorgeous. I mean, it's—"

I'm not sure how exactly, but somehow Stella managed to improve on wonderful, slicing my playful thought in two for the second time, and raising the encore to new heights. Maybe she had the help of the Supreme Being I'd alluded to, I don't know. The only thing that I was certain of was that I didn't want it to end. Ever! And after we finally separated, the only consolation was her promise of more later, if I promised to buy her a drink to celebrate "our victory over those evil bastards, Steiggerman and Shafer."

"I can do better than that, pretty lady. How's dinner at my favorite little French restaurant sound?" I chuckled as I turned on the ignition.

"Perfect. Between worrying about Lea, and then you, I lost my appetite up there in Seattle, and I'm starved," purred her reply as we headed for the exit.

Twenty minutes later, after a freeway drive featuring a full introduction to the Salero trial, fittingly accompanied by Aretha Franklin's "I Say A Little Prayer" on the radio, we parked just off Santa Monica Boulevard in lower Westwood and strolled around the corner to Le Coeur Sucré. With both of us still chuckling over the odds of Aretha's serenade coinciding with the explanation of my wing-and-a-prayer defense when we arrived at the base of a steep flight of red-brick stairs, our attention quickly shifted to the colorful flower boxes that welcomed us, before Stella slipped her hand inside mine and we began to climb. "Oh, how lovely," she murmured softly when we reached the top, her eyes inhaling a cobblestoned square centered with trees wearing necklaces of tiny, sparkling lights that illuminated the cluster of shops hemming the edges. "I'm glad you like it," I returned, steering her to the right. "And just wait till you taste the food."

A promise of full satisfaction made from a mixture of experience and hope, it was soon honored by the romantic atmosphere and Chef Luis' genius. Seated at a tiny table for two next to a window that overlooked the street below, with a cozy fire burning in the brick fireplace a few feet away, for a spellbinding minute we gazed over the gleaming silverware and crystal into the starry night. Vodka Tonics then arrived as if they'd been waiting for us, followed a few minutes later by Caesar salad, Chateaubriand with Pomme Frites and candied carrots, all absolutely delicious, and savored with an equally excellent bottle of Burgundy wine. The perfect platform for conversation, our words flowed as easily as the wine poured, flavored further with intermittent laughter and mock groans as I reenacted the highlights of the "Wicked War of Attrition," my nickname for the bitter confrontation between "Shafer's People and little old me." Wondering if Stella would have a misgiving or two, as I originally had, her answer was, "Absolutely not. You did the only thing you could, and I'm very proud of you for thinking up such a clever defense with nothing to work with—and even prouder of the courage it took to stick with it in the face of such hostility," she added, her eyes glowing with confirmation. Over coffee, and the Baked Alaska we shared, the conversation trailed to softer subjects, what we were going to do with the weekend that was waiting for us centering our focus, our smiles widening over the appeal of the variety of possibilities available.

Fabulous Friday, as I would later label it, wasn't over however. For inside its final hour, lovemaking flowered into a beautiful bow that tenderly tied all of its miraculous minutes together and tucked them into our hearts for safekeeping. Afterward, snuggled close together in the soft, surrounding silence, our eyes did all the talking, saying sweetly, "Yes, that's right. What's between us is good, and growing better." And when we finally did speak, it was only to whisper good-night, as sleep closed the curtain on our exquisite evening.

As was the case on prior occasions, Stella awakened first the following morning, and an hour later, it was the tempting aroma of fresh coffee that finally roused me from her bed. Greeting me with a kiss and a hug when I shuffled into the kitchen wearing a sleepy smile, Stella eased me toward alertness with the good news that Lea was continuing to improve, then asked if I had enough energy left to root my Trojans to victory over the big, bad Bruins. "Ohhh, yeah," drawled my assurance. "But to tell the truth, Stelle, after the win yesterday in court, and all that goodness last evening, I'm almost afraid to ask for anything more."

"Okay," she quipped, "no more sex for you until something bad happens."

"Hey, now, hold on a second, pretty lady, let's not jump to any hasty conclusions," I shot back, chuckling. "I mean, I'm still ready to help kick the Bruins' butt."

"Good. That's more like it. Now how about some coffee to fire you up?"

"Okay ... That, and a hot shower, and I'll be ready Big Time!" I mustered, affixing a firm hold to the mug she handed over, then strolling toward the bathroom.

And half an hour later, magically, transformation had occurred. For as it turned out, Saturday, somewhat jealous of its predecessor's success story, was harboring a sweet surprise or two of its own. So even though I had learned long ago to never underestimate the combined power of strong coffee and a hot shower to revive and rejuvenate, nevertheless I was seriously surprised by the sock-it-to'em level of energy surging to the surface as the final notes of "The Star Spangled Banner" faded into the roar of the crowd anticipating the kick-off. And with Stella then joining me in popping up and down off her living room couch to shout encouragement, chastise the referees, and boo the enemy, over the next three hours the mighty Trojans handily defeated their arch rivals by the tidy score of 28–16 and solidified their nationwide number-one ranking. Expert analysts, of course, would attribute this glorious victory to Troy's stout defense and explosive running game, but we knew better. In fact, so great was our caffeine-hyped enthusiasm, and the warm flush of camaraderie that flowed from sharing an electric experience, that fused together they fostered the delightful delusion that we actually helped produce the triumph we celebrated so joyously, the afternoon floating by like a bright balloon filled with the helium of pure fun.

Afterward, the feeling of being alive, truly alive and grateful for it, didn't disappear, but instead settled around us like a soft shawl as we relaxed over a snack of wine and cheese while recounting the game's highlights. Then, still energized, we opted for a long walk over running errands, before settling into a dinner of spaghetti, crusty bread, and more wine. More magic appeared also, as the Merlot somehow harmonized perfectly with the music flowing from the stereo, and soon we were dancing barefoot to Jose Feliciano's "Light My Fire" and Stevie Wonder's "For Once in My Life," then pressing even closer to the sweet strains of Sergio Mendez's "The Look of Love," before dreamily shuffling off to bed and the siren call of sleep.

Sunday, an odds-on underdog to match the gifts bestowed by its older brothers, opened by settling softly onto the shoulders of Saturday's success, and after securing an appropriately restful position, welcomed us with a super-sized edition of the *L.A. Times*. And chuckling over how lucky we were to have the luxury of time to fully enjoy it, Stella and I did exactly that over our steaming cups of coffee and cheerful chatter about various news items that caught our attention while we thumbed through its picture-dotted pages. Followed by a brunch of bagels and eggs, a matinee viewing of *The Odd Couple*, and another long walk during which we marveled at the brilliant performances rendered by Jack Lemmon and Walter Matthau, the soul-nourishing weekend of joy and contentment trailed to a close. Not, however, before one final surprise bubbled to the surface of Sunday's sunset. "God, but I hate to leave," I lamented softly to Stella as nine o'clock approached, the sadness of separation mixing with the anxiety of returning to battle to spread an ache across my chest.

"Who said you had to?" Stella returned, smiling coyly.

"Well ... uh ... no one, actually. But I ... uh—"

"But what?" she interrupted, leaning forward on the couch to kiss me lightly on the lips.

"Stelle, you want me to stay too?"

"Of course, silly. You think you've been walking up Relationship Road all by yourself?"

"No ... But I wasn't assuming anything either."

"Oh, of course not, counselor. You deal in facts, huh?" she teased, her smile warming as she shook her head ever so slightly. "Well, try these on for size: I'm just as fond of you, as you are of me—maybe even more. And I miss you, just as much as you miss me when we're not together. Now maybe it's because I'm a little older, but I don't like wasting time when no one knows for sure how much we've got—so why don't we just follow what's natural?"

"You know something?" I smiled back at her. "My Grampy always taught me to never argue with a person who's right, unless I was getting paid a hell of a lot of money to do so. And in that I'm not, and you're wonderful beyond words, case closed," I ended, staring into those luminous pools of lavender that were also smiling, then leaning forward to kiss her.

Monday didn't even bother to try and emulate the weekend's success story. Still, filled as it was with long hours and the grueling pace of plea bargaining, it shined far more brightly than usual, like a tiny piece of the sun had somehow separated from the mother ship to surround it with its own golden haze. And taking its cue from the extra-long hours that characterized a shortened work week, Tuesday then tumbled slowly into Wednesday, which in turn waded patiently through an even more wearisome calendar, until finally the Thanksgiving Holiday called a halt to the grinding regimen and rewarded all those involved with a special reason to be grateful.

After sleeping late, then lazing around the apartment before leisurely dressing, Stella and I kissed so-long just before two o'clock, and in accordance with our previously developed plan proceeded to our separate Thanksgiving Day dinners. While the complicated set of circumstances which dictated that practically it was wise for Stella to celebrate with friends, and me with my family, remained clearly annoying,

I was so truly grateful to have her in my life that I surprised myself at how easily I was able to suppress the negative of not sharing turkey by focusing on the pie and coffee we would enjoy together later that evening, and arrived at my parents' home still smiling over what I had to look forward to.

My mother greeted me like I was a soldier just returning from a long war, and unexpectedly my dad also seemed genuinely pleased with my presence. Over cocktails, which he mixed and served to us at the bar, the three of us engaged in pleasant conversation, which grew more lively in between the first and second round of gin and tonics. "Matty, you look very tired," entered my dad's observation as he refilled my glass.

"Yeah, a little bit," crawled my answer cautiously. "I just finished a difficult trial that lasted three days, and I didn't get much sleep in between," I added, then sipped at my drink while waiting for the inevitable question to arrive.

"Ohhh. How'd it come out?"

"Fine, Pop. I got lucky and the jury came in not guilty."

"Well that's good," he smiled approvingly, nodding his head for emphasis. "What kind of case was it?"

"Prostitution, a really sexy case—you'd have loved it," I tossed back, teasing. And with all three of us acutely aware of his decided aversion to open discussions about anything that even touched on the subject of sex, we all enjoyed a hearty laugh in which he participated fully.

When the laughter died away, however, a silence ensued that lasted just long enough to become awkward. Then, finally breaking it, he looked up from his drink and asked if I was really enjoying my new job. The expression on his face was sincere, as was his tone. But inside the latter, there was also a tinge of sadness, which, although faint, was instantly detectable to my ear, and served as a reminder of the hurt he had felt and still nourished over my departure from the comfortable surroundings of the family business for the risky rewards offered by the Public Defender's Office. Ordinarily, his inquiry would have caused me to become defensive, but as I looked into his handsome face and studied the concern creeping in between the numerous lines which time and hard work had sculpted, not even mild irritation arose inside me. Instead, even though I was fully aware of the hostile history between us, and equally cognizant of the fact that he strongly disapproved of my career choice and was deeply disappointed in me, I suddenly felt like trying yet one more time to communicate to him how truly important my work was to me, and how very much I needed to be personally involved in the changes that were occurring in our society.

"Hey, remember, Pop," I began slowly, "how when I was younger we used to discuss some of the social problems that exist, and you told me about what it was like for you growing up as the only Jewish kid in Union City, and the fights you got into in high school after getting called a kike? Not to forget, of course, being refused admittance to certain clubs when you got to college," I tacked on, pausing for a second or two as he nodded his acknowledgment. "Well, that's what it's been like for blacks in our country, only much much worse—until finally, in 1948, a few poor blacks in Greensboro, North Carolina, said, enough, and sparked a revolution by somehow summoning the courage to sit down at a whites-only lunch counter and order a meal. They didn't have a big voice, Pop," I continued, shaking my head for emphasis, "but their cry for social justice contained so much pain from the outrageous wrongs being committed that it echoed right on through Rosa Parks refusing to give up her seat on a Birmingham bus and all the way to the riots in Newark, Detroit, and Watts," rolled my explanation, now picking up steam. "And as a result, the increased energy for change that's been flowing through our country since the early sixties has turned into an extremely important movement—one that keeps growing, and that offers the real possibility of new attitudes that make a more fair society possible. You remember, Pop, how when I was a kid I used to hole up in my room alone and read books about history and politics, and my heroes, Lincoln and FDR—and you were proud of my appetite for learning, and asked what I was going to do with all that knowledge I was accumulating?" I posed, waiting for a response before I launched my closing argument.

"Yeah, I remember," he answered, smiling. "Sometimes I didn't think you were ever going to come out, even to eat."

"Uh-huh, right," I chuckled. "But Mom's great cooking always got me to the table, just as that knowledge I accumulated finally spoke to me," I tacked on, then zeroed in on the heart of my argument. "And what it said was, that I should use my learning and my skills to help that movement forward, with my heart adding that I needed to help. Now I'm not an important civil rights leader, or a powerful senator. But there's a huge battle going on in the courts over legal justice, and that's where

I can add my little drop of water to the river that's been growing from little drops ever since those brave guys sat down at that lunch counter. And if one by one, enough people add their drops, then slowly but surely a better society will come about," I ended, then waited for his response.

It didn't come quickly. For several moments he just stared down into his drink and stirred the ice cubes with his index finger. Then, finally, he raised his head and nodded ever so slightly as he replied. "Well, Matty," he dribbled out, "I think that I better understand your feelings ... and they're very good feelings, very commendable. Not only that, but if you argue as well to a jury, you're going to win a hell of a lot of cases—and I'll drink to that, and I'm sure your Mom will join me," he finished, raising his glass.

I don't know if he truly understood, or if the passage of time had simply diminished his angry stance, but his response led me to believe that for the first time I had made some small degree of progress in obtaining his acceptance of my goals. Full-fledged approval was something that realistically I had long ago crossed off as possible—our fundamental differences in make-up were too great for that—but the opportunity to gain his respect still existed, and I made a mental note to foster that procurement whenever the opportunity presented itself. Even that wouldn't be easy to acquire from such an oversized ego in a man who had been a frightening stranger to me since childhood, but it seemed as if a foothold had been secured, and I was happily surprised to learn how much less frightening he appeared to me than last Thanksgiving. Yes, indeed, there was much to be grateful for, I mused as our glasses clinked, and the prior air of uneasiness began to dissipate.

It disappeared entirely when the doorbell then rang to announce the arrival of Grammy Esther and Grampy Max, along with my oldest sister, Karen, and her husband, Jay. And when five minutes later, Kay, the baby of the family, followed with her boyfriend, Michael, the family assemblage was complete. A round of greetings and good wishes promptly ensued, followed by an hour of cocktails and casual chatter, before my mother proudly announced that dinner was ready and we adjourned to the dining room. A truly great cook, and a devout believer in the concept that food was love, Mom was true to form and dinner was indeed a feast. And beaming as we showered her with compliments between delicious bites of the traditional turkey, accompanied by her famous dressing and a lavish array of side dishes, from her perch at the head of the table nearest the kitchen, Rosalie, the Red-headed Wonder, as her children had long ago nicknamed her, enjoyed herself more than anyone as second and third helpings were served amidst a wellspring of conversation.

Composed for the most part of the latest gossip, supplemented with questions and answers about my dad's latest shopping center projects, the most recent happenings at Jay's CPA firm, and Michael's progress in architecture school, I was delighted with the harmless nature of the flowing chitchat. Only once did it stray into dangerous territory, when, as dessert was being served, Kay inquired about whether there were any young women in my life that were noteworthy. Passing on the pie, while smiling inwardly at the thought that the hour for reuniting with Stella was beginning to approach, I explained that my duties in Solina had kept me far too busy to do much dating. Hey, I chuckled to myself as we withdrew to the family room a few minutes later, the question didn't ask about older women.

The last hour of the get-together easily earned the title of best, as its minutes were meaningfully spent sharing conversation, coffee, and a smoke with Grampy Max. To say that he was excited about my latest two victories in trial would be an understatement of significant magnitude. "That's my Big Boy!" he enthused, the smile in his eyes even brighter than the one lighting his face, Grammy, who was seated nearby, also nodding her approval. "I'm proud of you, Matty—and don't you ever forget it for one minute," he added, filling my heart with yet another reason to celebrate the holiday. And with the clock now having ticked to eight-thirty, my collection of blessings grew exponentially when Jay announced that tomorrow being a workday for him, he and Karen had best be heading home, thus freeing me to join them in exiting the festivities after a round of hugs and kisses was exchanged.

"Thank you, God," I whispered as I climbed into Old Greener and gunned her down Sunset Boulevard toward home. "And thank you again, Big Time!" I boomed out gleefully upon arriving at the triplex just as Stella was parking her car. "Happy Thanksgiving, sweetie. And now it is!" gushed my greeting as I hugged her on the sidewalk, then felt her hand slip inside mine as we crossed the street and strolled to the apartment, the adrenaline-infused rush of excitement dropping a notch, from through-the-roof to simple exhilaration. "How was your dinner?" I asked more casually, calming further as we began climbing the stairs.

"It was fine. And yours?"

"Miracle of miracles, it went surprisingly well," flowed my answer as Stella opened the door and flicked on the lights. "I got along okay with my folks, and surprisingly, no one else bothered me either—or each other, come to think of it."

"That's good," she smiled, heading for the kitchen to warm up the pecan pie we had chosen for our private celebration.

And a truly meaningful celebration it was, too, with peace and contentment serving as overseers. In minutes, the pie was warmed and crowned with ice cream. And cozied up facing each other Indian style on the couch, we savored each and every bite while sharing lighthearted conversation interspersed with gentle kisses and hand-pats, our dialogue dotted with tidbits from our separate dining experiences. Jean and Lou had been cordial hosts, and wanted to meet me, as did Samantha and a further-improved Lea who surprised with a call—and yes, of course I would secure the recipe for my mother's dressing that had no equal, spun the highlight reel slowly over the sweetness of the pie and the pungent smell from the coffee. A collage of fresh memories, knitted together by strands sheared from the simple joy of our sharing, it cast a warm glow over the growing feeling of closeness that hugged us as tightly as we did each other before finally shuffling off to bed, wholehearted gratitude for all our blessings nestling in on both sides of us as we kissed good-night and happily drifted into sleep.

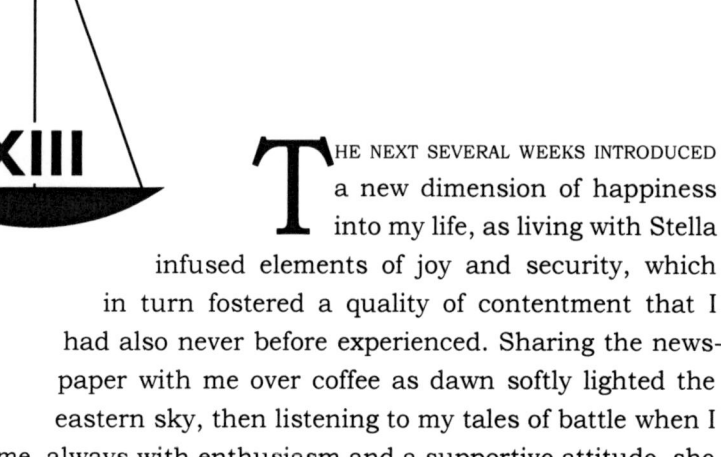

THE NEXT SEVERAL WEEKS INTRODUCED a new dimension of happiness into my life, as living with Stella infused elements of joy and security, which in turn fostered a quality of contentment that I had also never before experienced. Sharing the newspaper with me over coffee as dawn softly lighted the eastern sky, then listening to my tales of battle when I returned home, always with enthusiasm and a supportive attitude, she showered me with attention and affection. And caring for my every need, from cooking meals to sewing a button onto my blazer, in a manner so subtle as to almost go unnoticed, as time ripened episodes of daily life into intimacy, she seeped into the very center of my life, becoming both my anchor and refuge.

In Solina, my work life also continued its upward trajectory. In fact, as November faded into December and the year headed toward conclusion, I tried my first murder Prelim and three additional jury trials, the latter all in front of Judge Austin. The two-day murder case produced a weighty transcript, which growing confidence allowed me to feel would be of considerable help to our trial deputy in Superior Court, and I won the first trial outright, and another in the sense that the charges were dismissed after the jury was unable to reach a verdict. The third one resulted in a loss, which in the face of a maturing outlook that no longer judged performance solely by the outcome, quickly paled into memory's bank of experience after I carefully scrutinized my performance and determined that there had been no let-down in effort, and that I had in fact presented the best possible defense under the circumstances.

In mid-December, as Christmas loomed on the horizon, the courthouse virtually closed down due to the judges' attendance at a statewide judicial conference being held in Anaheim. Dividing their duties, and rotating the performance thereof, only two of the five were present daily each of the last two weeks of the year, thus allowing only the Arraignment and Preliminary Hearing Divisions to operate in usual fashion, with all trials postponed until January. In that all five of us were now available to staff just two operating courtrooms, this resulted in routinely overloaded calendars instantly shrinking to extremely reasonable caseloads, which by working as a team we were able to easily dispose of by mid-afternoon. Coincidentally creating some unofficial vacation time for us too, most unexpectedly this resulted in setting the stage for the surfacing of an explosive idea that would permanently alter the operation of the Solina Judicial District, and indelibly change our lives as well.

Fatefully, on Friday of the first week of the holiday hiatus, our teamwork had peaked, and by one o'clock we had all finished our cases and returned to the office. Robbie and Leon left several minutes later to visit the neighborhood camera shop in search of a special lens for taking close-up photographs, while George joined Ron and me in our office for a bull session over coffee and smokes. Our conversation was totally lighthearted for the better part of an hour, but turned more serious after George returned from taking a telephone call at his desk. "Hey, what's wrong?" I inquired when he growled, "Goddamnit!" then sank heavily back into his chair.

"Ohhh, I don't know, Matt," he answered, concern furrowing his forehead. "You'd think after five years of this crap, a person would get used to the shit that happens here, but I never seem to. That was a call from the wife of a guy I tried to represent earlier today."

"Tried to represent?"

"Uh-huh ... tried. Just before lunch, I ran over to Division One. Some guy who was appearing before Gelman on a traffic warrant asked to see a PD, so Gelman's clerk called Division Three, and as soon as I finished the Prelim I was doing, I hustled my ass over there," he explained, his pace increasing. "Only problem was, that by the time I got there, Gelman had convinced the poor idiot that he didn't really need an attorney, and after taking his guilty plea to failure to appear on a fucking speeding ticket, sentenced him to five days in jail!"

"Jesus, that sucks."

"Yeah, right. I tried to get the case recalled of course, but Gelman had already declared noon recess, and the county jail bus had just left with the morning custodies for downtown. Now, he's lost his job according to his wife, who wanted to know if I have any advice for her," he ended, shaking his head dejectedly.

"I told you that Gelman's a fucking prick, George, but you won't listen to me," Ron responded the instant George quieted. "We're taking it in the ear in his courtroom, worse than anywhere else."

"I know, Ron ... I know," George shrugged, nodding his head. "But if you're so goddamned smart, you tell me how we can cover six courts—seven, if you count the commissioner—with only five PDs?"

"Hey, I'm not blaming you," Ron shot back, realizing he'd added a ruffle to George's already roiled feathers, "you've done one hell of a job running this office and everyone knows it! We just gotta get a sixth deputy, that's all I'm saying."

"Have we really tried hard to get one?" I floated innocently into the surrounding fumes of frustration, silence prevailing for several seconds while the two of them stared at each other in disbelief, then over at me after failing to decide whether to laugh or cry.

"Is the goddamned Pope Catholic?" Ron chuckled, finally tipping the scale in favor of amusement. "I mean, is there a little bit of traffic on the fucking 405 Freeway during Friday's rush hour? And, ladies and gentlemen of the jury," he squeezed out as George and I joined the gigglefest, "does the big brown bear still shit in the north woods? Or upon sober reflection, has he decided to dump his odoriferous offerings in the Palace of Injustice across the street in order to answer beyond any doubt why it smells so rotten?"

"Okay ... Okay ... I'm sorry I asked," squirmed my apology as the mirth died down. "But in all seriousness, guys, what I'm really sorry about is what goes on over there that screwed George's would-be client today, my man Ginther a short while back, and God knows how many other poor souls in between. And that's just the tip of the iceberg," I rambled on, suddenly inflamed by the painful thought of another lost job and another struggling family placed in a precarious position over trifling offenses. "Hell, we can sit here and bitch forever about the shit we take, from having the judges openly insult us so that our clients don't think we're real lawyers like private counsel, to trampling their constitutional rights, to punishing them and us with harsh sentences for daring to go to trial. I mean, those arrogant assholes don't even fake having respect for us, let alone treat our clients like human beings!" I steamed through the smoky atmosphere. "And that utterly disdainful attitude they lay on us is quickly soaked up and put into action by the clerks and the bailiffs too—not to forget the damned DAs who already think their shit smells like perfume! Christ, I'm still new to this game, so I sure don't have a solution to the stinking situation. But sixth deputy, or not, something inside me just refuses to believe that there isn't something we can do to change it!" I ended, suddenly surprised at the depth of my angry outburst, and smiling sheepishly at having preached so strongly to the choir.

In the silence that followed, George and Ron grinned back at me, nodding their heads as their grins widened full. And all three of us then laughed simultaneously when Robbie suddenly joined us, carrying a chair as he entered, and drawling, "Well ... well, Matthew's certainly waxing eloquent this fine afternoon, isn't he?"

"Yes, he most certainly is," George replied as the sounds of our laughter softened before fading away. Then, after an inquiring glance at Robbie, which was returned with a wink, he asked where Leon was, and learned that he was out in back cleaning his car.

"Ron, would you go get him, please," followed George's request. "Tell him I've got something to say that he needs to hear. Tell him it's important," he tacked on, a twinkle now appearing in his eyes.

"Sure, no problem," Ron replied, climbing to his feet from his seat nearest the doorway, then returning with Leon in tow less than sixty seconds later. During the brief interlude, Robbie had asked if I could loan him some tobacco, and as the smoke billowing from our combined ignitions drifted away, Leon dropped into a chair next to George and broke the brief silence with a quizzically toned, "What's going on that's so damned important?"

A pregnant question, to be sure, George allowed it to hang in the smoky air just long enough to insure our full attention. "Well," began his answer, the twinkle in his eyes now dancing, "we've been discussing the many problems that we face across the street, and Matt expressed himself rather strongly on the subject, as well as stating that he was unable to accept the proposition that there wasn't something we could do about it," sallied his preamble calmly into view, like the *Enola Gay* before it dropped the first atomic bomb. "Which raises the precise point I want to discuss with you, namely that there is something we can do to change it. Absolutely, positively, and best of all, right now! However, what I'm about to propose is not only radical, but carries an extremely heavy load of risk—so listen, and listen carefully!" George instructed, pausing for effect, electricity now riding the airwaves alongside our cigarette and pipe smoke.

"Now, as you already know," George picked up, "Robbie and I have been here a lot longer than you three characters, and have always dreamed about making the system work correctly. We've had to go slowly, taking baby steps away from the cop-out heaven that we inherited from the old-school PDs before us. But we've never lost sight of our ultimate goal, which was to turn the fucking courthouse upside down and shake it until the corruption falls out like counterfeit change, then set it right side up and make it work fairly, the way it's supposed to! And we've devised a plan for doing exactly that!" rolled his explanation, the twinkle in his eyes now turning to fire. "However, we've known from the start that we can't execute that plan alone. To make it happen requires the cooperation of all five deputies. Three, or even four, isn't enough, what's required is a totally united effort, and I do mean totally united! Robbie and I were waiting until after the holidays to discuss it with you, because we finally feel that all the right men to do the job are finally here. But in that Matt happened to raise the subject today, now's an even better time, 'cause we're not too busy and have the time to seriously consider all of the possible ramifications before taking action. So if you're open to our idea, what I propose now is to detail the plan for you, with time-outs along the way for open discussion. Then, after you've had the weekend to think things over, we'd meet again Monday afternoon and vote on whether or not to put the plan into action. What do you think?" George posed, then ground out the butt of his cigarette and waited for a response.

For several seconds I just listened to the supercharged silence which had suddenly filled the room, conscious all the while of Robbie's large brown eyes softly searching the three faces in question for an answer to George's proposal. When they met mine for a second time, a thin smile curled out of the corners of my mouth. "Hell, I'd stay here all night to hear such a plan, no problem," I replied firmly. And when Ron and Leon then echoed my sentiments, smiles grew contagious, as did the wave of excitement that also swept round the circle.

"Alllright, now, you grinning bunch of hyenas, here's the way Robbie and I see it," George picked up, his tone stern. "First of all, let's get one thing clearly understood, and that is that what we're about to discuss doing amounts to starting a war with the entire system! And once we start it, we damn well better be prepared to see it through, or all of us are finished as PDs in Solina, and probably everywhere else as well! So we've got to win—understand? A hung jury is no good for our purposes. Either we win outright, or the power of the system will crush us like little bugs underneath a very large boot!" George emphasized by banging his fist on the desktop, then fixing his eyes on us.

"Okay, now as you already know, within the system the DAs and the judges have all the legal power, 'cause it's the DAs who file the cases, not us, and it's the judges who hold the power over bail, whether to trust a defendant to appear and release him from custody on his own recognizance instead of bail, what evidence is or is not admitted during trial, and punishment via sentencing. But, and it's a very big but, an easily overlooked fact is that we hold the practical power. Not the pigs, but us. And we hold it totally, too, all by ourselves, so that's precisely the tool we're going to use to knock their fucking asses off and turn this shithole around!" George boomed out, his voice hardening with an anger fueled by a storehouse of prior wrongs he'd witnessed helplessly, his eyes now blazing.

"So, fine," he steamed onward after the briefest of pauses. "Let the DAs continue to file every shit case that the cops drop on their desks, and let the judges just keep sitting back on their lazy asses and offering the same standard plea bargains. The plan is for us to stop buying, and I do mean stop! As in totally and completely! Now on an average day, there are thirty cases set for jury trial in Division Two, and thirty more set in Division Four, ninety percent of which are PD cases. So let's just see what they do with them all when we categorically refuse to deal and announce ready for trial on all fifty-four of them, because that's exactly what we're going to do! Fortunately, they've got exactly thirty days to give our client a trial if he's in custody, and forty-five if he's not—and any one trial will take from one to three days to try. So let's just see what those assholes do with fifty-two cases a day piling up day after day, until the time periods run out and they have to dismiss between fifteen hundred and two thousand cases—not a single, solitary one of which can they refile!" George growled, pausing to suck in oxygen, a sarcastic smile forming. "Christ, ever since I've been here I've been listening to the judges moan and groan over the heavy calendars, and bitch at us to hurry up and get ready, as if we somehow caused the ridiculous situation. Well, we don't arrest people, and we don't file cases, and the damned calendar belongs to the fucking court, not us. So the problem is theirs, not ours, and all we have to do is politely inform their dumb asses that such is the case! It's the only major weapon we have to use against them, but if used uniformly it has unlimited fire power, believe me! I can—"

"Your idea is fantastic, George," Leon cut in. "It warms the cockles of my tender little heart just thinking about the chaos those fuckers would find themselves in. But how in the hell can we be ready to try anywhere near twenty-five cases by nine o'clock in the morning? We don't have a deputy in Division One, interviewing our clients and preparing their cases for trial after their arraignments, so how can we possibly be ready to try a bunch of cases, when in the vast majority of them we won't even have met our clients by calendar call, let alone discussed their cases?" Having been interrupted, George listened carefully to Leon's question while pulling another cigarette out of his shirt pocket, then answered without hesitation when Leon finished speaking.

"Obviously we can't, Leon, but we don't have to be," flowed his answer smoothly. "One of the things we must face, of course, is that we can't pick which of the cases will go to trial. We can try, but most of the time we simply won't know which case will go on a given day until the asshole in the black robe tells us. However, even if he picks a case that you are totally unfamiliar with, it still takes from ten to twenty minutes before the jury panel arrives, and that gives you enough time to read over the arrest report. Then, you can *voir dire* the jury until the noon recess, when you'll have a full hour to interview your client and get his side of the story. If there are any witnesses, you can call them on the phone, and if you can't reach them immediately, well, additional *voir dire*, plus the fact that the prosecution puts on its case first, will get you into the second day of trial and allow you the evening in between for contacting them, as well as for further preparation of the case," streamed George's explanation, his head nodding slightly as he paused for a second. "Now I realize that this is far from the ideal way to try a case," he resumed, studying the concern in our faces, "but don't forget that we handle the same type of cases day after day, and as a result we're pretty damn good at quickly analyzing a given situation. Believe me, it sounds far more difficult than it actually is, and once you overcome the psychological feeling of not being as thoroughly prepared as you'd ideally like to be, you'll discover that in almost every case extra preparation time wouldn't really help, and you'll be able to try your cases to the best of your ability—okay?"

Nodding his head as George's advice slowly registered, a thin smile finally appeared as Leon muttered a hopeful "Yeahhh, I hear you alright," the posed degree of difficulty shrinking, but still hanging in front of his eyes and begging for further consideration. Also still concerned by the fly-by-the-seat-of-your-pants scenario under consideration, Ron stood up and stretched before then raising some further issues.

"What about the case that's a dead-bang loser, and shouldn't be tried in a million years?" he asked. "I mean, I hate those bastards across the street as much as anyone. But how do you try a case that you know damn well should be dealt out, especially when the client is going to get clobbered with extra jail time because the judge is pissed off at us for trying to fuck him over?"

"That's probably the very toughest situation that we're going to face," George responded, his tone fully empathetic. "And the only answer is, that you'll just have to try the case anyway and suffer the consequences, hard as that is. But for every case of this type that you lose, and for every client that goes to jail, we'll get a hundred dismissed and our clients set free!"

"Yeah, that's good and all," Ron countered, "but Georgie, we don't represent a hundred clients at a time. Our obligation as lawyers is to represent the client we have in a particular case, and to serve his best interests, not the best interests of a whole group. I mean, who appointed us to judge that a particular person go to jail, so that a larger group of people can reap the benefits? I don't know if I can do that."

This time George didn't answer immediately. Instead, he twisted around in his chair so that he faced Ron directly, then drew heavily on his cigarette and leisurely exhaled. And when he did finally reply, a tone of sadness had crept into his voice. "Ron, I agree with you completely when you say that you don't want to have to judge your clients," he began slowly. "But have you thought seriously about what your position is every single time you enter into the plea bargaining process? Let me tell you something, I have, and it makes me more than uncomfortable, it makes me sick to my stomach! Now I'm not telling you that there isn't a time to deal, we all know better than that. But for Christ's sake, don't you realize that every time you analyze a case and decide to deal, that you're judging anyway?" George contended. "It may be on an individual case-by-case basis, as you say, but you're still judging nevertheless. And I don't give a fuck what name you call it, it still boils down to the fact that you, all by your little self, are deciding guilty or not guilty to something—and that's not a defense lawyer's obligation either!" he emphasized with another fist slam, then caught himself and lowered his voice. "Hell, it's supposed to be the job of the so-called impartial third-party trier of fact, and there isn't anyone, anywhere, who really knows what a jury will do with a given case, no matter how bad it appears—just look, for example, what Matt pulled off in the Salero case. So, while sometimes you can be pretty sure of the outcome, you can never be absolutely positive, and yet every single one of us, day after day, in spite of that uncertainty, makes that judgment and cops out the majority of his cases," George ended, then drew again on his cigarette.

"Okay ... that could be," Ron nodded, the argument still sinking in. "You've certainly got some good points, Georgie. I never thought about it quite that way."

"Uh-huh, sure ... no problem. 'Cause it's damn complicated, and we're always stuck in the fucking middle, trying to decide what's best for our clients," George empathized, the deep distress furrowing his forehead clearly reflecting his long struggle with the knotty problem of plea bargaining, and reminding me of the countless times I'd already faced the judgment process in question and resolved it, only to have its haunting moral and ethical complexities return to gnaw at my conscience like a festering sore. Now, spotlighted once again, the thorny dilemma intensified my concentration even further as George continued.

"Now I'll admit that if we put our plan into action, all of us will end up trying some cases that should have been dealt out in the client's best interest," marched his reasoning. "But on the other hand, all of us are also far less likely to cop out someone who ought not to have been, and let's face it, it happens more often than we'd all care to admit. And why? ... Because gradually over a period of time, without even thinking about it, plea bargaining becomes an altogether too comfortable way of doing business, especially when you consider the terrible pressure from the overcrowded calendars that we operate under, and our natural human desire to ease it whenever possible. Just remember, guys," George implored soberly, "how many simple drunk-in-public cases the damn DAs file, knowing that most of them will get bargained out for a sentence of time served, so as to conveniently bolster their hefty roster of conviction statistics to show the public what a great job they're doing. And just ask yourselves, how many of those simple drunk cases we've all copped out. Ohhh, sure, I know," he nodded, his pace picking up, "it was a good, safe deal. Hell, the case looked lousy, our client had a rap sheet filled with priors, and he'd already done ten to twenty days waiting for trial, so for a little old guilty plea he received no further sentence and was immediately set free, as opposed to risking doing an additional ninety days if the jury said guilty. But goddamn it, what if he wasn't guilty on this occasion? And worse yet, how many of those harmless little pleas were made by first offenders, who weren't in jail but were simply afraid, and therefore listened to our safety prone advice and ended up with a permanent criminal record, even if it isn't a serious one?" George argued strenuously, again sucking in oxygen before rolling to conclusion. "Look, we could argue the pros and cons of plea bargaining versus trial till hell freezes over, and the only fucking thing we'd ever agree on is that there's no perfect solution to the problem. But let's not forget one extremely important fact, and that is that before our clients met us in the trial court, all by themselves they made a decision to plead not guilty and go before a jury for judgment. So if we just follow their decision, and try their cases to the utmost of our abilities, then we'll end up judging one hell of a lot less than if we deal those cases out even for the highest of motives!"

"Okay, Georgie ... I see what you mean," Ron interjected after several seconds had passed, finally acquiescing. "I never thought about the pros and cons that way. But I still have one additional problem with the plan. You know that I feel the judges here are first-rate pricks, but with one big exception, Judge Austin. He's a horse of a different color, and I don't think anyone here will disagree with me," Ron expressed earnestly, concern reappearing in his eyes. "He treats every single one of us with respect, and our clients likewise—from pressuring the DAs into fair plea bargains, to rarely handing out jail time, to giving small fines and lots of time to pay them. And the way our plan operates, we're going to fuck him over just as badly as Lacy, Steiggerman, and the other assholes who really deserve it!" he ended, sadness edging his tone of conviction.

"Ron ... once again I agree with you," crawled George's reply, his words being carefully chosen, "Austin is a good man, and he does treat us and our clients fairly. However, let me remind you that his deals weren't so great before we started trying cases and putting some pressure on the system. And the way I see it, our job is to make all of the judges treat our clients fairly, not just those lucky enough to end up in Austin's court, and the only way to accomplish that is to get off our asses and try cases until the rest of the asshole pigs are forced to fall in line! Then, and only then, will anything even approaching justice come to Solina!" George asserted, passion flaring into his tone, then dialing back after he heard his echo and paused to light up again.

"Look," he picked up more calmly, seeking to ease the subtle tension which had surfaced, "I prefaced this entire discussion with a warning that if we went to war across the street—and a war is exactly what we're talking about—that it wouldn't be easy on any of us. And I also suggested that we talk the idea over, and think about it long and hard before actually acting on it. Well, that's where we are now, and let's not forget it," George nodded out, breaking into a reassuring smile. "Nobody's jumping into the water yet, we're going to discuss it and discuss it until we're blue in the face, and then we'll discuss it some more if necessary. Because if we can't all thoroughly understand and truly believe in what we're setting out to do, then we can't act like the iron fist that's necessary to make the plan work, and we'll just have to continue along as we have in the past," George stressed, then again made direct eye contact with each of us.

"I'll leave you with one extra thought to seriously consider," he then added, his tone now soft and humble, but underlain with emotion. "This is our chance to contribute to the momentous change that's occurring all around us. We didn't sit in at the lunch counter in Greensboro, and we weren't on the bus with Rosa Parks or those ridden by the Freedom Riders. We didn't face the fearsome fire hoses or Bull Connor's vicious dogs in Birmingham, or march to Selma with Martin Luther King and get arrested or have our heads cracked open by the pigs' batons. So this is our chance to put our asses on the line for change and a better society. This is our chance to look personal risk squarely in the eye and work within the system to stamp out discrimination and inequality and corruption as best we can," George ended, his voice beginning to crack. "Christ, but I could use a cup of coffee," he tacked on after a second's pause. "Anybody else?"

Before the pin-drop silence could even consider aging, the offer was instantly and unanimously accepted. But before any one of us could even climb out of his chair, Marilyn, who had been sitting at her desk on the opposite side of the partition listening to our every word, appeared in the doorway carrying a pot of coffee in one hand and a stack of paper cups in the other. "Did I hear you revolutionists call for coffee?" she asked, beaming a smile at us that could manufacture sugar to add to the cream.

Though the laughter in her voice hinted that her approval was included in her good-natured tease, nevertheless her reference to a revolution struck me full in the face and caused my smile to fade slightly as I raised my cup and took a sip. Still thinking about the concept several seconds later as she finished pouring the last of the coffee into Robbie's cup, I finally shrugged it off without resolving in my mind whether or not it validly applied to the proposed course of action. Revolutionary or not, however, additional support for putting the plan into actual operation soon surfaced, when as she departed, Marilyn stopped in the doorway and volunteered her opinion.

"Fellas," she drawled, "I'm not a lawyer, but I've been here in Solina almost nine years now, and what George said about the way this office used to be run is the absolute truth and then some! Nobody here gave me a vote on what you've been talking about doing, and I don't mean to be butting in, but I've seen so many wrong things done here in this office, and seen the pain it caused, that I just feel I have to tell you that what you're talking about doing is as right as anything human can be! And if you decide to go ahead with it, which will take a lot of guts, I want you guys to know that I'm with you one hundred percent, and I'll do everything I can to help!" she promised, then turned and disappeared from view as suddenly as she had arrived, leaving the five of us smiling at one another through the silence.

Comfortable, the relaxing stillness lasted through several more sips at our coffee cups before George interrupted it and brought us back to the business at hand. Then, for the better part of two hours, he detailed the refinements of the basic plan of attack, carefully outlining the pros and cons of every weapon at our disposal should we elect to go forward with the proposed challenge. The considerable time and thought that he and Robbie had invested in formulating their strategy became readily apparent as he delved into the complexities of the format for doing battle, covering in his narrative, and in response to our numerous questions, the most subtle nuances involved in the varied aspects of the web of actions necessary to parry the power of the structure under assault, then channel that power and its corresponding pressure back against the very source from which it originated.

Driving home after we finally adjourned around five-thirty, my mind was abuzz from the myriad of thoughts that streamed into view. Both practical and philosophical in nature, they swarmed feverishly about while vying for the limelight of center stage, till like the rush-hour traffic, they slowed to a bumper-to-bumper pace that allowed me to sort them into a quasi-logical sequence for examination individually, then finally together as a whole.

Having arrived first, and steadily clamored for attention, Will the plan work? jumped to the head of the line. And turning off the radio so that I could focus without distraction on its foundation, the elimination of the plea-bargaining process, my initial conclusion was that it was sound. "It has to work," I reasoned out loud. "There are only two courtrooms available for jury trials, and with a combined fifty to sixty cases a day to be disposed of, any one of which would take from one to three days to try, the judges would have no choice other than to trail the waiting cases to the next day if we categorically refuse to deal, and hold fast to it—knowing with certainty that the following morning's calendar would already contain sixty cases of its own, just lying there nestled comfortably in the court folders waiting to raise their ugly little heads and cry to be attended to. Why, within just a week, if we tried two cases in each division, there would already be a backlog of between two hundred and fifty and three hundred cases!" I squealed enthusiastically, then lapsed into silence while I pictured the total chaos that the trailing of so many cases would occasion inside the two courtrooms and the adjoining hallways. Fascinated with the prospect, I studied the scene carefully as civilian witnesses for the prosecution, defendants and their witnesses, along with friends and relatives of both groups, intermingled with virtually a small army of police officers to form a noisy, perspiration-soaked, and thoroughly irritable mob that jammed the corridors, then overflowed back downstairs and spilled outside onto the front lawn. Shaking my head as a new surge of excitement, intertwined with a slight chill, produced goose bumps, suddenly I crowed like a rooster. "Good God! We'll wreak havoc on the bastards!" trumpeted off my tongue. "I can just hear old Steiggie now, calling for a meeting in chambers to discuss what arrangements have been made between us and the DAs on the waiting cases, only to be greeted by the shocking news that there weren't any arrangements to make, that these cases too were ready for trial just as soon as the one under way was completed. Why they'll be able to hear the arrogant pig's screams, all the way downstairs in Division Three. And speaking of pigs, can you imagine the expression on Lacy's face," I then conjured up with considerable delight, "when he takes the bench, all prepared to 'move the Prelims along' to use the shithead's favorite term, only to learn that none of the drug or narcotics cases are ready because we've refused to stipulate to the certified chemistry reports, and the DAs, assuming that we would, didn't subpoena the chemists to court and therefore can't prove that the various items in the evidence envelopes are what the reports say they are? H-o-l-y Christ! The sonofabitch will go absolutely berserk when his sacred calendar gets fucked up!" I screeched, banging the steering wheel with my fist for good measure, then reveling in the renewed silence at the anguish we would inflict.

My ear-to-ear grin didn't last long, however, fading to faint when my own words, born less than three minutes ago, floated back into view, then disappearing altogether as I digested them. "Yeahhh," I muttered, "if we categorically refuse to deal, and hold fast to it. I mean, can all five of us really hold together like fingers balled into the iron fist George called for? He warned us to make no mistake, that what we were starting was a full-fledged war. So what kind of army do we really have, huh? Are our soldiers strong enough, and brave enough to fight not just a battle or two, but a whole war?"

Startled, I felt anxiety suddenly stir awake in my stomach, then squirm upward into my chest, and I quickly pulled my coffee mug from its holder to relieve the dryness in my mouth and throat. "Well," I whispered, beginning to assess our forces, "our General, George, is A-okay, that's for sure. He's as strong and brave as he is smart," ambled my analysis, my voice growing firmer as the fire in his pale-blue eyes reappeared for close inspection. "Uh-huh, no problem with his ability to hold the line," I concluded, falling silent as Marilyn's short biography of George flooded back into mind to detail how childhood poverty had piqued an innately sensitive soul to forge personal and political belief systems based on empathy for the have-nots, then mold a deep-seated anger for social injustice of any type into a steely resolve to foment change that could withstand even the strongest earthquake. Born and raised on a small farm in Connecticut, she had explained, he had watched helplessly as the post–World War II technological expansion had slowly but surely eliminated the ability of the small farm to compete, thereby steadily reducing his family's income until it fractured his parents' lifestyle and forced George to seek a new way of life in the strange environs of the big city, creating grievous wounds that never fully healed as he struggled to work his way through college and law school, and along the way fostering a burning liberalism and intractable desire to help the underdog.

"Yeahhh, no problem there, for sure," I confirmed out loud, nodding reflexively as I pulled out my pipe and lit up. "And no problem with Colonel Robbie, either," I opined, breaking into a smile and now shaking my head side to side in renewed amazement as his history slipped silently back into mind. It was George who had imparted the totally improbable story to me, late one evening after one of my learning sessions when we'd lingered by our cars and chatted amiably for a few minutes before heading home. Coincidentally, Robbie was also born and raised on a farm, this one in rural Tennessee where black skin put you in your place early, and the Ku Klux Klan made sure that you stayed there, George had related in response to my off-hand inquiry, relishing the details as they tumbled off his tongue. Somehow, by gift of God, as he had put it, Robbie, at age seventeen, knew inside that he had to escape, so armed with a sack lunch, and a dollar and fourteen cents that his mother gave him, Robbie hitchhiked to Tennessee State College, where while working nights as a janitor, he earned his degree in engineering. With the job market for black engineers in the South virtually non-existent, he soon migrated to Chicago, where it turned out, prospects in his chosen field weren't much better, leading him to fall back on his irrepressible charm and gift for gab to land a job as a disc jockey for a black radio station, where fate introduced him to Loucille. Bright, as well as beautiful, with family connections in California, it was she who became the motivating force behind their move to Los Angeles, where she worked while Robbie attended law school, a step she considered essential for him to fulfill the potential she so earnestly believed in.

"Jesus, fucking-A, Christ!" I hissed into the surrounding silence. "Talk about 'we shall overcome.' Can you imagine having the guts at seventeen to walk away from all you've ever known, and with a sandwich and a buck-fourteen for reserves, head out into the big strange world to make your way?" I postulated with absolute astonishment. "Hell, Matty, my boy, you think you did something big, just by leaving the family business for the PD's Office, so how about eating a very large slice of humble pie, as in all of it including the tin!" I croaked, shaking my head again, this time more vigorously. "Yeah, no need to worry about Robbie cracking in the face of fear cast by the enemy. He'll just laugh, and keep on fighting, the way he has his whole life," I tacked on, then fell silent as the depth of his courage and accomplishments momentarily overwhelmed me.

"Ohhhkay," I mumbled out a full minute later, returning to my review, "the officers are definitely ready, willing, and able. So how about the troops?" I queried, unconsciously squinting to concentrate my focus. Leon popped onto center stage first, carrying my book on him, which was thin by comparison to George and Robbie's bios due to my more limited personal contact with him. Robbie had confided to me, soon after my arrival in Solina, that no one loved the Fourth Amendment's prohibition against unreasonable search and seizure more than Leon, nor did anyone defend drug cases with as much vigor. "An almost fiendish zeal," Ron had added, stemming, he opined, from Leon's regular use of marijuana. From my own observation, he was bookish, always studying the latest cases or a text in political philosophy leaning toward Marxist doctrine, which Marilyn advised he was drawn to after his father died from a condition resulting from wounds suffered in the Korean War, thereby thrusting him into the role of family breadwinner well ahead of schedule. "He may look like the absent-minded professor, what with his long hippie hair and his sloppy dress," she had shared with me during one of our coffee chats, "but don't be fooled. He cares about average people a lot, and the terrible hurt deep inside him makes him boil with anger and fight like a crazy man when he's in court!"

"Okay," I muttered softly after the reassembled fragments of Leon's background had passed in review. "Crazy men with boiling anger can go a distance—God knows, I can relate to that," I tacked on, a bittersweet smile forming. "And speaking of boiling anger, what about your buddy Ron, can he hold it together?" entered the next quandary, my smile disappearing as I flashed on the rescue mission I'd performed awhile back in Lacy's courtroom. Well, poverty certainly isn't a motivating factor in his case, I mused, recalling that he was the only child of doting, middle-class parents. No, from our chats in the office, and over drinks we'd shared on the three or four occasions we'd visited the local strip club, what I had learned was that while the family's Jewish culture had promoted an active empathy for the underdog, the overbearing influence of his domineering mother, when combined with his lack of success with women, which he attributed to his curly hair and glasses, had somehow twisted into a fierce hostility to any authority which challenged his shaky perception of his manhood. "Hell, I can certainly relate to that too," I shrugged, wincing at the oppressive ways of my father that flashed into mind. "And anger that steams from such a deep well only flows faster in the face of challenge, even a long one," I concluded, nodding as the striking similarity of the source turned the spotlight onto myself, the fifth and final finger necessary to form the desired fist.

So how does your Battle Biography read? pranced the thorniest of interrogatives onto center stage, where it stood stiffly at attention and waited patiently for an answer. Several weighty seconds passed before it slowly began to arrive. "Well," I finally shrugged out, a faint smile forming, "a few months ago I couldn't have answered that question with any degree of certainty. But now, with the Ginther and Salero trials under my belt, there's damn good evidence that you won't run when push comes to shove!" I stressed, focusing on my own storehouse of anger and empathy. Both had formed early in childhood, I recalled, flashing back to age eight when it had suddenly struck me that all the maids on our block were black, and Grampy had explained their struggle upward from slavery. "Besides," I added, my smile curling into a grimace, "where would you run to? The avocado tree no longer works for big boys!"

No, no it most certainly doesn't, I confirmed in the silence that, having renewed itself, now surrounded me and grew heavier as the gears of my brain shifted into overdrive and I struggled to analyze the group as a whole. If ever there was a motley crew, I mused as I pictured the five of us form a circle: We've got one black and four whites, two Protestants who are married and three bachelor Jews, somehow gathered from all four corners of the country. We've got the sons of farmers, a grocery store manager, and a real estate tycoon, all of which are left of center politically in varying degrees, and each harboring from a different source of fearful resentment a deep-rooted anger for absolute, all-knowing authority, while carrying right alongside a paining sadness pinpointed at the social injustices created by a sleeping society that turns a blind eye.

"Boy, but we're all so different, yet oddly so alike," I muttered softly, breaking the silence and shaking my head at the curious, almost strange collaboration cobbled together by time and circumstance. "Yeahhh ... with anger and sadness the glue that binds us together," surfaced truth suddenly from my subconscious, "a white-hot anger, mixed with a quiet but serious sadness—a kind of turbulent melancholy, like the bubbling underneath a volcano before it erupts!" tailed my observation back into silence.

The conclusion, while primarily positive, still troubled me, the rawness of the revelation stunning my mind's forward trajectory to a stop, then forcing it to roll the unexpectedly exposed emotions over and over and over until finally I made peace with them. "Alll ... right, different angles, separate sources, but sometimes a bond formed from unlikely fragments defies geometry, and is strangely stronger than the sum of its parts," I murmured almost prayerfully. "And if you add to the crazy concoction the fact that we like and respect each other, then that glue hardens into cement, and we should be able to hold fast together no matter how difficult the situation becomes," I concluded, then watched carefully as the five-spoked circle folded into a fist, a grin managing to find my face.

Mr. Insecurity, however, when seasoned from birth, is a demon possessing great strength and an equal aptitude for perseverance. And no sooner had my grin widened to full than it began to retreat when his gravelly voice snickered that "Maybe has an opposite twin named Maybe Not," and it disappeared completely when the enemy's weaponry suddenly marched into view behind a solitary figure who stood toweringly tall in the center of the stage, wearing the mask of authority and glowering with rage. "It won't be easy, you hippie motherfuckers!" bellowed his deep voice, "the DAs outnumber you nine to five, and when you add the weight of six judges and all the bailiffs and clerks, you five troublemakers are really alone! In fact, you can capitalize ALONE, 'cause when push comes to shove, you don't even know if your big bosses downtown will support you, do you? There's politics involved, you little shits, and the big bosses have to worry about the County Board of Supervisors and getting their budget approved. Ohhh, yeah, and not only that," thundered the mask's snarling lips, "but just wait till we revoke your clients' bail and OR releases while they wait for trial, and dish out maximum sentences on the dead-bang losers you're stuck trying! Oh, yes, indeed, you little liberal bastards, it's not quite so one-sided as you might think—you'll see!" echoed and reechoed the taunting threat, doubt now bouncing off Old Greener's windshield and swirling all about me till finally I switched on the radio and turned up the volume to drown out its shrieking voice.

Ten minutes later, when I turned off the freeway and steered toward Doheny Drive, I had calmed, and even managed a thin smile as I watched the pros and cons settle onto opposite platforms of a balance scale and teeter up and down before settling, the right side holding a slight edge. "No matter," I told myself as I climbed out of the car. "Believing as we do, if we don't put our asses on the line and try, we won't be able to look ourselves in the eye—so there's really no choice," I nodded out firmly, locking the door, then crossing the street after looking carefully in both directions.

When I entered the apartment, Stella was in the kitchen cooking, and called out to me to join her for a glass of wine. Only too happy to, I instantly complied, and her warm smile accompanied by a kiss gently slid the lingering anxiety from the afternoon's prickly proposal into the far corners of my mind, the chilled sweetness of the Riesling that followed working wonders in keeping it at bay.

Only long enough, however, to enjoy a delicious meal of lamb stew with wild rice, washed down with more wine, enjoyable conversation centered far away from anything remotely legal in nature, and topped off with a sweet hour of lovemaking before sleep. For Saturday morning immediately witnessed the return of Shakespeare's To Be or Not To Be, with Mr. Anxiety doing a tap dance to the tune of "You're Always on My Mind." And by Sunday I had argued both sides of the now seemingly eternal proposition so many times, that neither one seemed right or wrong. Seriously frustrated, and with the knots in my stomach growing heavier by the hour, I grew steadily more quiet as the morning wore away and Monday's hour for decision loomed closer and closer. Finally, just before noon, when Stella noticed that my attention to the Rams-Bears football game was straying, she suggested that we go on a picnic. "C'mon, the fresh air will relax away some of that built-up stress," she chirped, smiling. And while I no more felt like a picnic than I did kissing Steiggerman's bare ass in front of a sold-out crowd in Memorial Coliseum, the guilt from having subjected her to my funk forced my tongue to trickle out, "Sure, Stelle, might just help."

Surprisingly, it did. Stella proudly revealed her "secret refuge," a small, relatively unknown and therefore sparsely populated park nestled into the Hollywood Hills high above Sunset Boulevard. And after we settled onto an oversized blanket in a shady spot, within minutes a cool breeze and the soft sounds from the nearby waterfall smoothed the sharp edges off the gnawing anxiety. "Better?" Stella smiled after I stretched my arms taut, then relaxed them in sync with a long, slow exhale.

"Hey, you got that right, pretty lady," spilled my answer through a yawn. "Now if I can just shake this tiredness, I'll be better company, I promise."

"The company's fine, Matty. But I don't doubt you're tired, you tossed and turned all night, and talked in your sleep too."

"Yeah? ... What'd I say?"

"I can't be sure exactly, something about a scary situation, and you being worried about pulling it off—whatever it is," she returned, sliding me a plate holding slices of my favorite Italian cheese and salami, accompanied by some thick, crusty bread, potato chips, and sweet pickles. "Here," she added, pouring last night's leftover Riesling into paper cups and handing me mine. "Now, while we have a bite, why don't you tell me what's bothering you?"

"Listen, it's not about us, if that's what you're thinking. I just got a bug up my butt about work, that's all, so not to worry."

"Yeah?" she snapped back sarcastically, raising her eyebrows. "Well that must be a bug with a big appetite, 'cause it's been eating away at you for the better part of two days now. So pardon me if I'm not buying, but based on an intimate knowledge of my guy, I'd say there's definitely probable cause to believe that something out of the ordinary's going on!" she teased good-naturedly, her irritation showing at the same time.

"Jesus, Stelle, you sound like a damned defense lawyer," I chuckled.

"Uh-huh ... And guess who trained me?" she nodded. "So better let your best buddy in on what's happening, or you'll just get into deeper trouble. Besides," she smiled, her voice now softening, "last time I checked, you like to share."

"That's right ... I do, especially with you, Stelle. And I was going to tell you, I just wanted to think it through myself, before asking what you think."

"About what, Matty?" she asked, her eyes widening with curiosity, then settling watchfully on mine as I began to explain. And although Stella had already formulated several possible problems in her mind so as to better prepare to be supportive, from me facing a contempt citation to having difficulty with a complex case or with a colleague, she was definitely not expecting the bold blueprint of revolt that I presented for her consideration, complete with all the pros and cons discovered to date. "Wow ... that is a lot to chew on, Matty," she mouthed slowly when I finished and asked her what she thought. "So I certainly see why you're concerned."

"Uh-huh ... it's a bit chancy for sure. But when I look back at the risks other ordinary people took, and the sacrifices they made for what they believed in, like the Freedom Riders, I don't see how we can't step up and put our asses on the line—you know what I mean?"

"I do ... absolutely," she affirmed. "That's one of the things I most admire about you, you don't run when you're afraid, you stand and fight."

"Yeahh ... I've been learning to," I nodded. "But this is different."

"Maybe ... But listen, Matty, I only know what you've taught me, but from what I see, the difference isn't as great as you think," Stella advised, her voice gathering emotion as she continued. "A few minutes ago, you called your plan a war. Well, whether or not you realize it, you've been at war since the first day you set foot in Solinaland, as you call it! I've—"

"I have? I mean, that's the way you really see it?"

"No question. Being a Public Defender isn't just a job to you, and you know it. You've always treated it as if you were right smack in the middle of a crusade! Why I've watched you come home night after night, totally exhausted from having fought your guts out for every single person you represent—and from what you've told me, the other guys do exactly the same. So this war, as you call it, isn't really new to me. It's just that you and your fellow hell raisers finally decided to coordinate your battle plans, that's all—and then send out an official announcement that the group's pissed off with the pigs' operation, and it's time to change it right now!" Stella ended, breaking into a warm smile and reaching forward to squeeze my hand.

"Well, that's certainly a view of the situation I haven't seen before," I nodded back, feeling the fog lift as her message sunk in, then returning her smile. "So I'm a crusader, huh?"

"Uh-huh," she confirmed. "I know you don't see it, but you were born a fighter, Matty, it's in your blood. That's why you've trained yourself, and worked so hard to learn from others, so you can be the best you can at it. And because you believe in your cause with all of your huge heart, and have enough anger in you to fill up the sky, kind and gentle soul that you are, you're a warrior nevertheless! A loving warrior," she tacked on, her voice softening, "but fierce all the same."

"Wow, that's some sort of mixed résumé," I shrugged, further surprised by her view of me.

"Hey, I know my guy, that's all."

"You do, huh?" I teased, leaning forward and kissing her lightly on the lips. "Say, did anyone ever tell you you're delicious?"

"No ... And don't try to change the subject."

"I'm not. I'm still thinking over what you said, 'cause I never thought about me that way. Sort of strange, don't you think?"

"Interesting, is the way I see it—all in all, quite wonderful," she smiled back at me, again squeezing my hand. "Think about it some more, and you'll see what I mean."

"Okay ... I will," I answered softly, returning her squeeze.

And think some more I did indeed. Long and hard, and with all the honesty I could muster. Stella's observations had certainly helped clear away the fog clouding my decision, and later that evening after dinner, two articles in the newspaper further resolved my doubts. Norman Thomas had died at age eighty-four, informed the *Times'* eulogy, then set forth the major risks he had taken along with the considerable sacrifices he had made fighting poverty and injustice. Resigning his comfortable position as a Presbyterian minister because he believed that these problems couldn't be solved within the political status quo, he had helped found the American Civil Liberties Union, then ran for President six times on the Socialist ticket to call America's attention to the pain and suffering of those who had no voice, never retreating, even in the face of defeat and ridicule.

All right, Norman, I mused quietly to myself on the living room couch, I hear you. When the status quo stinks bad enough, a guy's gotta fight to change it! And speaking of fighters, fired my next brainwave as I turned to the Sports Page and perused an article on Muhammad Ali, how about the sacrifice he's making in the name of principle? I mean, I don't agree with the Black Muslims' separatist agenda, but I sure as hell can understand how they'd feel that way after four hundred years of slavery and another hundred and fifty of Jim Crow, and I certainly do admire Ali's courage. Hell, after already being stripped of his Heavyweight Title and losing millions of dollars, now he's willing to risk going to prison for refusing military service in opposition to the Vietnam War.

"And God knows, he's definitely right about one thing," I snickered softly, "no Viet Cong ever called him nigger."

"What are you mumbling about?" Stella interjected, bringing me some coffee and settling alongside on the couch.

"Oh, nothing," I smiled. "I'm just thinking like I said I would."

"Feeling any better about your decision?"

"Uh-huh, actually I do—and thanks for helping."

"You're welcome. But all I did was reinforce what you already knew. Like I said, you don't run when the chips are down."

"Well, we're certainly going to test that, aren't we?" I quipped, lifting my coffee cup and clinking it against hers. "So thanks again for your support, and here's hoping."

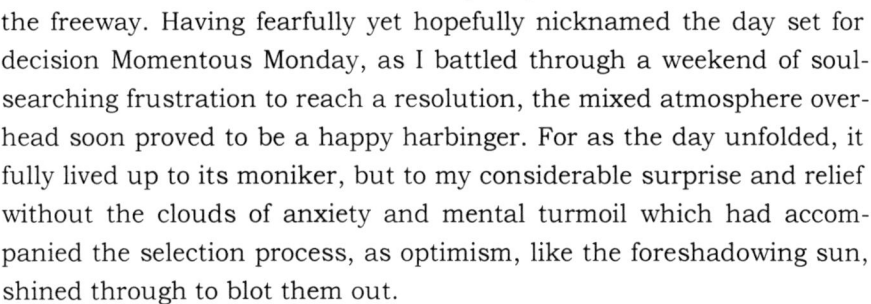

XIV

MONDAY ARRIVED UNDERNEATH A sky painted gray by blanketing clouds. But the sun was also involved, if a bit lethargically, I noted as I drove toward Solina, slanting its warm rays into the overcast to create intermittent patches of goldish haze, and even slicing through on two occasions to cast streaks of bright light onto the freeway. Having fearfully yet hopefully nicknamed the day set for decision Momentous Monday, as I battled through a weekend of soul-searching frustration to reach a resolution, the mixed atmosphere overhead soon proved to be a happy harbinger. For as the day unfolded, it fully lived up to its moniker, but to my considerable surprise and relief without the clouds of anxiety and mental turmoil which had accompanied the selection process, as optimism, like the foreshadowing sun, shined through to blot them out.

After a busy morning, at noon George promptly reconvened our war council. And after two additional hours of animated discussion amidst an air of palpable nervous anticipation, George's call for a vote was answered by each of us, calmly and without hesitation, in the affirmative. Marilyn promptly pushed the unanimous tally to six, then ignited a chorus of laughter by adding, "And may the good Lord help us. Amen!" A round of handshakes followed, with good-natured gibes flowing back and forth, as each of us, pleased with his individual decision, now embraced what had morphed into a collective choice. It was right. Both our brains and our hearts told us so. It wasn't fully real yet, but having wrestled with the knotty issues involved and squarely faced the attendant risks, we had exercised our choice and could feel our tiny circle already drawing tighter even as we chuckled and teased one another.

Following suit, the year also closed ranks, threatening to whirl to an end before we could even take a deep breath. So to stretch December's fast-fading calendar, and put the six work days left to us to maximum use, the five of us readily agreed to use every free minute in preparation to execute our plan. And immediately lengthening our afternoon schedule to six o'clock, we began to carefully dissect our central strategy into separate distinct parts so as to examine and reexamine every known aspect of our joint venture, both offensively and defensively, in order to insure that each and every weapon at our disposal stood reflexively ready, and our ability to coordinate our efforts was perfected as far as anticipation allowed.

Only the holidays would intervene to detour us and provide a joyful respite from our intense preparation. Late Monday evening after our commitment was firmly established, I drove Stella to the airport for her red-eye special to Dallas. Like Thanksgiving, we had agreed that practicality dictated we spend Christmas with our families, with New Year's Eve and Day reserved for our private celebration together. During the interim, we would keep in touch by telephone, and I would be waiting for her when she returned on Saturday, we confirmed as we turned onto the freeway, then switched the subject to the details of the discussion that had led to our noontime decision and subsequent scheme for implementing it. Finishing with a flourish after we reached LAX and settled in the lounge to await the call to board, there was just enough time left to exchange gifts. From Stella I received two intriguing books: *Man's Search for Meaning* by Viktor Frankl, and a collection of poems by Rainer Maria Rilke entitled *Rilke on Love and Other Difficulties*. "I'll start tonight, they'll keep you close," I told her, then watched as she opened the small box from Tiffany's and discovered a thin gold chain bearing the letter S, her eyes tearing as she slipped it on. "I'm going to miss you extra for this, Matty," she murmured, then kissed me. The call to board interrupted it, and our hug before she answered it seemed even tighter than previous ones. In fact, I could still feel it when I reached home and the two of us climbed into bed together to read ourselves to sleep.

Tuesday buzzed by in a frenzy of activity, the five of us working like a souped-up engine to dispose of the relatively light calendar before noon so that we could devote ourselves with even greater intensity to refining our Grand Plan, as we now referred to it, making solid progress. And for a second reward, at eleven-fifty Dallas time, Stella phoned to share Christmas Eve with me, and allow us to welcome Christmas Day together. "Did you see the Apollo 8 astronauts, Matty?" she inquired excitedly. "Wasn't it special, with Lovell, Anders, and Borman reading verses from the Bible while orbiting the moon?"

"For sure, and then some!" I enthused. "Hard to believe that they're two hundred-fifty thousand miles away, and we're watching on TV—amazing! And speaking of which, how's my pretty lady getting along?"

"Fine, in fact better than expected," she assured me, adding that her daughter, Vicki, was more accepting of her than previously, and sister Lauren and her husband David were also welcoming. Then, just after I had provided details of our battle plans, midnight arrived and we wished each other a Merry Christmas, articulated hugs and kisses, and promised to chat again tomorrow.

Christmas Day passed pleasantly. I spent the morning studying special cases that George had provided as authority in support of our prospective actions, the afternoon and early evening at the family celebration at my sister Karen's home, and the remainder, while waiting for Stella's call, reading about how Viktor Frankl survived the horrors of Auschwitz. "Hell, if he could overcome that," I grumbled, "then what we're facing is a piece of cake." And when the phone then rang as if on cue, Stella's warm greeting instantly added to my rising comfort level, as well as swelled my sense of gratitude for how truly fortunate I was.

With only four days now left to prepare, on Thursday and Friday the Fomenting Fivesome, as we jokingly called ourselves, further accelerated our efforts, once again reviewing our expanded list of tactics and obligations, then quizzing each other on the nuances of the various maneuvers available in a given situation, and revisiting for the umpteenth time what to do if one or more of us was held in contempt. Satisfied that we were fundamentally well prepared, with the following Monday and Tuesday still available to add extra polish, as well as address further issues should they surface, nevertheless, "to leave no stone unturned," George requested that we meet on Saturday from ten to four to review case law. Everyone agreed, and the session proved to be a double blessing for me, adding further nuance to my understanding of Supreme Court rulings, while presenting companionship to make the hours until Stella's return pass more quickly.

Pass they did. And nine o'clock that evening found me seated in the airport lounge, preparing to get acquainted with Mr. Rilke. On the drive to LAX, my upbeat mood had unexpectedly been altered when the radio served up Dion's stirring rendition of "Abraham, Martin and John," the melancholy melody and poignant lyrics suddenly striking home, a throbbing ache swelling up inside my chest and tearing my eyes as

I smilingly recalled how much I loved what they stood for, our proposed small role in the continuing struggle for social justice flashing to make me proud yet anxious, then mixing with the already present sad-happy hybrid to churn inside the same strangely expanded moment. Now, fifteen minutes later, with my cheerfulness fully restored, and an undercurrent of anticipation's excitement belying my outward calm, I opened the small volume and discovered on the flyleaf that "If only we arrange our life according to that principle which counsels us that we must always hold to the difficult, then that which now still seems to us the most alien will become what we most trust and find most faithful." Well ... thank you very much, Mr. Rilke, I mused silently, flashing again on the upcoming challenge and smiling at the comfort his words offered, I think we're going to be great friends! A spontaneous prophecy, it was promptly validated by his first poem, "The Lovers," and I was about to enjoy it for the third time when I glanced upward to check the clock and found Stella emerging from the jetway.

An absolute vision in form-fitting beige jeans complemented by a light-yellow sweater, the beauty of her luminous eyes clearly visible from the distance of fifty feet, all of me smiled as I quickly closed both the book and the space between us to collect the hug and kiss she had teasingly promised at the end of last evening's telephone chat. It had only been five days since we had separated, but I returned the promised reward as if it had been five months, and only released her when she chuckled over my shoulder that rationing was not in effect and more awaited at home. "Okay," I smiled, surprisingly unembarrassed as we headed hand in hand toward the luggage pick-up area, "I've got plenty of patience."

It wasn't needed, however. Stella's suitcase was the third one to slide onto the carousel, and in less than fifteen chatter-filled minutes, we had exited the parking structure and steered onto the freeway, our conversation jumping from Christmas dinner menus to the Grand Plan, then bouncing back and forth between details about Vicki's master's degree program and how my grandparents were faring. In fact, I was just about to share one of Grampy Max's vaudevillian jokes with her, when for the second time that evening the radio intervened, this time presenting the beguiling Simon and Garfunkel ballad that had accompanied the seduction of a young man by a mature woman in the film, *The Graduate*, "Coo, Coo, Ca-choo, Mrs. Robinson, Jesus loves you more than you know," warbling forth to surround us like a tightly tucked blanket. And while I had no clue whatsoever as to where Joe DiMaggio had gone, my lonely but laughing eyes turned toward Stella, who while fully appreciative of the irony at work, promptly fixed her sparkling lavender gaze on me while drawling, "Don't even think about going there!"

"Who, me?" I protested. "No way. Hell, I'm so fucking happy to have you back home, I wouldn't say a word. Some other wiseass might suggest that it's our song, but certainly not innocent little me," I mustered with exaggerated sincerity, then instantly lost the battle with self-control and burst out laughing.

With a faint smile already appearing on Stella's lips despite her stern admonition to me, my squeals and the hopelessly feeble attempts to muffle them proved infectious, and within seconds after she joined me Old Greener was filled with our howling laughter. And the more we laughed, the more delicious and addictive it became, roaring to full, then fading, only to ascend yet again, like a runaway rollercoaster that ran out of fuel only when we exited the freeway ten minutes later, our sides aching from the mirthful exercise. "God, but I missed you, pretty lady!" I rolled out after we pulled over to rest and my ache subsided. "Really, that empty apartment was lonely, as in Big Time!"

"Me, too," she nodded back, sliding over to kiss me, then pull me into a tight hug.

Lasting for well over a minute, the warm embrace, in combination with the free fall of laughter that preceded it, set the tone perfectly for the sweet and tender lovemaking that followed when we reached home, which in turn fostered a relaxed sleep that birthed an easygoing Sunday. In stark contrast, Monday was a blur of activity. But pronouncing us "ready at last" when we finally reached its seven o'clock end, George, wearing an ear-to-ear grin, summoned the old year to a cheery close with the news that tomorrow we would celebrate New Year's Eve Day by heading home at noon. No more planning. No more question-and-answer sessions. No more review. We were ready! And eager, too, although years later, hindsight would provide the clear conclusion that despite all the thought and consideration given to our Grand Plan, not a single one of us truly realized the totality of the ramifications involved in the mission we had so fully committed to during those final fleeting days of 1968.

New Year's Eve Day turned up sunny. And wearing a matching bright smile when I returned home just after one o'clock, I quickly slipped out of my blazer and slacks and into jeans and a Polo sweatshirt my parents had gifted me with for Christmas, then settled at the small table in the kitchen nook to share a light lunch with Stella. Afterward, I lit up my pipe and leisurely perused the Sports Page, while Stella began preparing the evening's celebratory feast, every so often entering into a duet with Judy Collins crooning "Both Sides Now" on the living-room stereo, then joining Stevie Wonder's bouncy version of "For Once in My Life" as it floated into ear. And with music and the exchange of casual conversation continuing to fill the slowly ticking minutes, contentment reigned as the afternoon edged steadily into evening.

At seven, we dined on Stella's favorite specialty, lobster ravioli in a sweet white-wine sauce, accompanied by Caesar salad and garlic toast, fittingly complemented by a chilled bottle of champagne. Laughing as we composed humorous toasts to the old year in between bites of second and third helpings, when our stomachs finally cried full, we adjourned to the living-room couch for coffee and smokes, dessert having been reassigned to welcome in the new year. Pausing our conversation when the magnificent "MacArthur Park" poured forth to surround us with its exquisite melody, "God, that Jimmy Webb's a genius," Stella enthused as the final strains faded away.

"Big Time!" I concurred. "It's like a mini symphony, what with its separate parts, some rocking and rolling, some softening into a lullaby. And speaking of geniuses," I added, "how did you get to be such an incredible cook?"

"Well, my mom was a good cook, and I always liked it," Stella explained after exhaling.

"I see. So you and your mom were close?"

"No ... not really. Mom was nice, and always saw to it that Lauren's and my needs were met. But unfortunately she wasn't what you'd call warm and open; in fact she was really private and sort of distant. Lauren and I often wondered about what she really thought about us, or Dad, or a lot of things—like was she happy, or did she have hopes and dreams? But we could never tell; it was all like a big secret."

"Ohhh ... I'm sorry," I returned, noticing a pained expression cross her face, then disappear underneath a fresh smile. "How about your dad, was he warmer and more open?"

"Uh-huh, he was. But the problem there was that he was always working, so we never really saw much of him. He was a plumber, and the hours were long, and he always seemed tired. I could tell he liked me from the way he patted my head, but we never really talked, or worked on a school project together. And you know what?" Stella added, her tone softening with sadness. "He never ever once said to me I love you."

"Well, I'm sure he did. I mean, men from that generation weren't exactly touchy-feely. My dad's the same way."

"Yeahhh, I know. And I think he actually *did* love me," eased out her return, her eyes narrowing as thoughts turned over in her mind. "But, still, he never did say so, and come to think of it, the number of times I heard it from Mom you could count on one hand. I think that's why I was so wide-open vulnerable when Pete came along,"

"What do you mean, Stelle?" I reflexed back at her, suddenly aware that my casual inquiry about her cooking skills had surprisingly turned the conversation serious, and now piqued my curiosity.

"Well, like I said, I felt sorta neglected emotionally, and not really loved. So when this handsome older guy came along and paid me all sorts of attention, and told me he loved me, I sorta sucked it all in like a vacuum cleaner," she clarified, the insightful details adding lifelike color to the pale picture of her early marriage that she'd previously sketched.

"Well, that's pretty natural," I nodded. "But pretty hard to see, too, when you're only seventeen?"

"You certainly got that right, Matty," spurted her agreement. "I didn't really see it clearly for years, until I was in therapy."

"Therapy? ... You never mentioned that before, Stelle."

"Yeahhh, I know," she shrugged, then paused, the pained expression returning as she pondered whether or not to proceed. "Matty, there's actually a lot that I haven't shared with you," she then picked up slowly, choosing her words carefully. "I really wanted to, especially since we've grown very close, 'cause you should know the whole story. I was waiting for the right time to tell you, but first the War came up, then Christmas and Dallas—so I guess a little bit just spilled out of the reservoir when your question about cooking led to my mom. But it's really not the right subject at all for New Year's Eve—we're supposed to eat, drink, and make merry."

"Hey, listen, pretty lady," I smiled back at her. "I happened to have researched the matter thoroughly, and that's not at all what New Year's really supposed to be about. Its true purpose is to stop and reflect, so that we can learn and make resolutions for living better and fuller lives. It's a time for being close with loved ones, and sharing memories, and hopes, dreams, and disappointments, so that we can grow even closer. Besides, sweetie," I added, meeting her watchful gaze, "I want to know everything there is to know about my Stelle. I would've asked before, but I didn't want to pry. And there's still plenty of time left before midnight arrives, so if you want to empty that reservoir and share, let's do it—you and me, together."

"Okay, Matty ... okay," she nodded, a thin smile of relief appearing as she reached for a sip of coffee, then lit a fresh cigarette before picking up. "You remember how I told you about dropping out of design school, 'cause after two years I just couldn't keep up a schedule of working, taking classes, studying, and caring for Vicki too?"

"Uh-huh, sure, I remember."

"Well ... after I dropped out, for the next two years I worked as a sales clerk in a department store, and on the side I added whatever interior design work I stumbled into. I couldn't really promote myself, so it wasn't much, but that's what I really lived for."

"How old were you at this point?"

"Twenty-one, when I started at Davidson's. I couldn't have managed to juggle my schedule as well as I did without Lauren helping take care of Vicki. She and my brother-in-law David had two little girls of their own, so adding one more wasn't a problem," Stella elaborated, a faint smile reappearing. "And they were really great, too, about encouraging me to date so that maybe I could find someone, as well as meet people who might have connections in the interior design field."

"Right, very nice. Makes sense, too."

"Uh-huh, but it never worked out that way. The only break I ever got was over two years later through a friend of a friend, who got me an offer from a design firm in Miami. Lauren and David said I should take it, 'cause it was a chance to build a whole new life. They'd continue to take care of Vicki, and after I got established, Vicki would join me."

"How old was Vicki?"

"Five ... And I couldn't afford child care, so after thinking it over I decided to give it a try," Stella returned, shaking her head ever so slightly. "I was only twenty-four, and I didn't know what else to do to try and make a life, so I went. And the funny thing is, it almost worked out. Work went well, and a few months later I met Paul. He was wonderful—so different from Pete—and when the relationship got serious, I began thinking marriage and—"

"What do you mean, so different from Pete?" I interjected, having noticed that her voice had hardened when she said his name.

"Well," she answered slowly, the wheels in her head spinning again, "when I told you we got divorced because he wasn't ready for family life, I left out a few details."

"Like what, Stelle?"

"Like before he left, he began drinking a lot, and going to parties—which, of course, ended up with him meeting other women and cheating on me," she tacked on, her voice hardening again. "And then, when I tried to talk to him about it, he wouldn't. He just got angry, and yelled, and hit me."

"What?" I rifled back, my voice registering shock.

"You heard me. And more than once, too, a whole bunch of times. He'd yell and scream that I ruined his freedom, and that I wasn't worth it, and then he'd slap and punch me!" she detailed, her tone a mixture of hurt and anger, me finding myself stunned all over again.

"Son-of-a-bitch!" I growled, shaking my head.

"Uh-huh ... no doubt, reasonable or otherwise," she chuckled sarcastically, then shifted her weight before continuing. "Anyway, as I was saying, Paul seemed so different. He was kind and gentle, and hard-working—and very serious about us. So when his company promoted him to vice-president and transferred him to Minneapolis, thinking that we were going to get married, I agreed to follow him, hard as it was to leave my job."

"What year was this, Stelle?"

"Nineteen fifty-one, a big one as it turned out," she shrugged sadly, her face growing taut. "We hadn't been in Minneapolis but about three months when Vicki was introduced into the equation. I thought he knew about her from the friend who introduced us, 'cause he'd asked how long I'd been divorced early on. I thought maybe he was waiting to bring her up until he was sure he was serious about me, and I was also waiting for the right time to fit her into the picture—so when he started talking about getting married, and mentioned how much he wanted children, I thought the time was perfect to tell him all about her."

"And?" I posed after she paused to light up.

"And ... that was the end of us!" rolled her reply, a pinched smile emerging as she revisited the painful memory. "After he got over being shocked and all upset, I tried to reason with him that if he loved me, and wanted kids like he said, what difference did it make? But his only answer was that he was sorry, but it just changed things—and two days later, he told me he wanted me to move out."

"Fucking-A ... sonofabitch number two!" I interjected when she paused again, then smiled sympathetically. "So what'd you do?"

"Not much, I was too devastated. From marriage and family, all of a sudden I was back working in a department store with absolutely nothing going for me—only now I'm twenty-five, and between Miami and Minneapolis I'd really lost contact with Vicki. I didn't know what to do, I just felt so ashamed and so guilty. I guess you could say I kind of had a mini breakdown."

"Jesus, Stelle—and you're all alone. Were you able to get help?"

"Oddly, yes. I mean, I was struggling along, when Pete's lawyer called to tell me that Pete had been killed in a car crash, and had left me and Vicki a sizeable amount of money. So that allowed me to afford some therapy."

"Well, thank God for little favors."

"Uh-huh, for sure. I don't know what would've happened to me without it—my self-esteem was not only in the toilet, but flushed down the drain. I just felt totally worthless," seeped her admission dejectedly, her eyes glazing over, then slowly refocusing to search mine for a reaction.

"Hey, that's understandable," I consoled. "And so damned unfair, there are no words."

"Not so unfair, Matty, but thank you for saying so," Stella replied, forcing a faint smile. "I made a lot of terrible mistakes, and I wasn't through either. After nine months of therapy, I was better, but I still couldn't deal with the Vicki issue. I kept telling myself that I had to get *me* straightened out before I could put her back in my life. I couldn't go back to Miami, and I had to get out of Minneapolis, so I moved to Chicago, figuring that I could somehow start all over again."

"Okay ... That sounds reasonable."

"Nooo ... not really. I was just escaping—refusing to face my responsibility as a mother. True, I'd been through a lot and was scared. But what really frightened me was that I'd lost contact with Vicki, I hadn't even seen her for over two years. So, instead of facing the difficult problem, and going back to Dallas and working it out, I submerged it and ran away to Chicago."

"Well, that's easy to say in hindsight," I offered after she paused to take another sip of coffee.

"Yeahhh, I know, Matty," she nodded. "But it's still true, all I did was set up a pattern of escaping. When all I could find in Chicago was more department-store work, and when my dates went nowhere, after two years I ran again, this time to St. Louis where another three years got wasted the same way. Now, I'm thirty-one, and none the wiser," she pushed out, her words flowing faster, her tone growing emotional. "So I escaped again, now moving west to Seattle. I—"

"Did you see Vicki while you were in Chicago and St. Louis?"

"Oh, sure—on visits. She was going from eight to thirteen during this time, and pretty much looked at Lauren as her mother, not that I blame her."

"I see. But Seattle worked out okay for you, right?" I asked, recalling that she was almost always upbeat when the Emerald City came up in conversation, and hoping for a ray of sunshine to poke through the deep disappointment shadowing her face.

"Yeah, it did, in a way," she responded, nodding, a weak smile forming. "I mean, I was able to hook-on with a design firm for starters, so that was a big improvement. And I made a lot of friends, and one special one in Lea. Then, too, towards the end of my third year there I met Lennie, and for a while I thought our relationship was special and really going somewhere. But," she strained out, the smile disappearing, "after eighteen months or so, when I mentioned marriage, he said goodbye before I could even blink. So ... a few months later, I moved on again to the sunnier pastures of L.A., and the rest you pretty much know. After I landed here, through some contracts from Lea I made a few friends. And over the last six years, through my work and joining an organization or two, both circles gradually expanded. I dated, of course, so as to have some sort of social life, but I gave up any expectations of having a meaningful relationship—until I met you, that is," she rushed to assure, then fixed her eyes on me and waited anxiously for my reaction.

"My God, Stelle ... but that's some story," I offered slowly, the full weight of it sinking in, but without time for me to reflect. "I don't know what to say exactly, except I'm really sorry for all your pain. I—"

"That's okay, Matty," she blurted, forcing a thin smile. "Like I said, I made some terrible mistakes, so I deserve it. But that's really generous of you ... Any questions?"

"Well," I returned hesitantly, a funny feeling stirring awake in my stomach, "have things improved between you and Vicki?"

"In a way, yes," trickled her answer, the words chosen carefully. "The good news is that Vicki grew up loved, well-adjusted, and happy. The bad news for me is that family roles got reversed—Aunt Lauren is Vicki's mother, and I became the visiting aunt. All in all, a wonderful result for Vicki, and I'm eternally grateful for it. But the guilt I felt for abandoning her, which started way back in Minneapolis, never left—it just rooted inside me, a permanent reminder of all my many mistakes."

"I see," I nodded back at her, my funny feeling now having balled into a tight knot. "And I'm sorry to have to ask, Stelle, but am I somehow a substitute child, a way for you to atone by helping me?" I squeezed out anxiously, the contagion instantly jumping the short distance between us to flush Stella's face.

"No ... no, absolutely not!" she rushed back at me, fear propelling tears into her eyes. "I was afraid you'd think that, that's why I didn't tell you more before. But listen, Matty—please listen to me. I think that subconsciously that element was working when we first met. I mean, I saw how shy you were with women, and I did think that I could help you over that by adding to your confidence a little," tumbled her words as she leaned slightly forward toward me. "But once I got to know you, and saw how special you were—how good, and honest, and courageous, and with such a huge heart that had so much love to give—well, I reverted right back to being selfish Stella, with SELFISH in capital letters, 'cause I wanted that love for me!" she gushed, nodding her head for emphasis as the torrent flooded onward. "I needed it, Matty, so so much. Just once, I wanted to be loved—not just a pretty face and curvy body that was nice to cozy up to and fuck, but loved, really and truly loved! So don't you think for a minute that I'm on some sort of salvage mission, 'cause I'm in love with you, Matty, God's truth I am!" she cried, finally breaking to a stop and slamming the floodgates closed, a trickle of spillover occurring when I was slow to respond. "And now that confession time's over, your pretty lady isn't quite so great as you thought, huh?" leaked her postscript slowly to add to the Mississippi River–sized load of information I was attempting to process.

"Nooo ... even better," I finally managed to muster, crawling out from underneath the blanket of overwhelm. "More human, and real, and not so intimidating—so even more wonderful!" I assured her, reaching forward to grasp her hand. "And if my love can make you feel even half as special as you make me feel, then I just might be able to learn to believe that I deserve you," I ended, tears welling in my eyes to match hers.

"Oh, you silly silly man," she returned through a fast-growing grin. "I know you were raised in Beverly Hills, where the culture teaches that money is God, and if you want to get the hot women you better have lots of it. But listen to me, Matty, please hear me. You know all those guys with the fancy cars you saw me go out with, and were jealous of?"

"Uh-huh—"

"Well, they're not good, and honest, and caring like you—they're not real, all they care about is creating the proper image, with symbols of prestige, and they don't even know how to spell the word relationship, all they want is a good fuck. *You,* sweetie, make love! You make me feel like a woman, not a pretty face and boobs. You make me feel special, and needed, and loved!" she ended, the urgency in her tone swimming forth to surround me.

"'Cause you are special, and needed, and loved—and God knows you're a woman!" I choked out, edging forward and pulling her into a hug.

Neither one of us wanted to let go, so for well over a minute we just held each other, feeling safe and secure inside a cocoon of heightened closeness that emerged from enlightenment once the storm of words and emotion had subsided. Finally, after Stella caught sight of the clock and whispered that it was almost midnight, we gently separated. "Sorry I risked blowing us up on New Year's Eve," she tacked on when we had unfolded to a distance of twelve inches. "But after being in Dallas with Vicki and Lauren, I felt you just had to know the truth."

"Hey, all you did was make us closer. What did you think, that I was going to run away?"

"Well, with my history, it certainly crossed my mind."

"Uh-huh, well that's over, I'm not going anywhere. Except," I added, kissing the tip of her nose, "I would like to climb off this couch and celebrate by dancing with you to all the wonderful music coming from the TV."

And dance the old year out and the new one in we did, mixing in several kisses as tight together we swayed gently to the soft sounds of the Troggs' "Love Is All Around" and Bobby Vinton's "I Love How You Love Me." At midnight, as the Temptations, with perfect synchronicity, offered up "Cloud Nine," we stopped for a Champagne toast, then further welcomed in 1969 by adjourning to the bedroom to make love.

Afterward, in the contented moments before sleep arrived, I reflected on the new tenderness that had governed our lovemaking, and when sleep claimed me seconds later, with Stella snuggled up against me, my final thought was that I wouldn't trade the enhanced feeling of intimacy between us for anything.

That feeling of extreme closeness, that reflection of oneness, which occurs when two people, having honestly and painfully exposed all their weaknesses side by side with their strengths, accept both and cherish each other, was also my first feeling and thought when I awakened the following morning. As usual, Stella had exited slumberland before me, and beamed a smile over the newspaper when she sighted me shuffling into the kitchen.

"Good morning, love," floated her honey-toned greeting. "Coffee, sound good?"

"Ohhh, yeah ... And I love you too, Big Time," I returned through a gaping grin, then kissed her before she could climb out of her chair.

"You just better," she teased, sliding the Sports Section toward my spot before heading over to the Mr. Coffee.

When she returned, we began planning our day. First off, we agreed, it was necessary to have a look-see at the Rose Parade, and we promptly adjourned to the living-room floor, where, supplementing our coffee with the new year's first smoke, we watched with childlike awe the magnificent floats and marching bands. Complementing the spectacular flower show with our casual but animated conversation that alternated between commenting on the exquisite intricacies of a given float and the items of interest that cropped up from the newspaper spread out before us, unconsciously we added our contribution to the concept of bliss as the morning slowly smiled by.

At noon, slow, steamy showers were followed by a light brunch of bacon and eggs with bagels, after which we settled onto the couch to attend to the serious business of rooting for USC in their Rose Bowl battle with Ohio State. Sadly, our Trojans went down to defeat by the score of 27–16, and we quickly acted on Stella's suggestion of a long walk in the fresh air to ease the sting of our disappointment. Laughing and chatting while holding hands during our five-mile stroll down Santa Monica Boulevard into West Hollywood, we window-shopped, meandered through two bookstores, and purchased an Aretha Franklin album in a record shop before finding ourselves back home, our Rose Bowl upset long since vanished.

With our holiday now rapidly coming to a close, and purposefully sequestered thoughts of the impending battle in Solina now sliding back into view and looming larger and closer after a tasty dinner of roasted chicken with seasoned noodles was enjoyed, over coffee and smokes our conversation inevitably settled on the quiet elephant in the room. "It's going to work out just fine," Stella encouraged after I commented that tomorrow was Grand Plan Time with less than radiating confidence.

"I know ... I believe," I returned, smiling for emphasis. "It's always hardest waiting, I just want to get going."

"Soon enough, Matty. And you know what'll help? Extra sleep, 'cause you'll be getting up extra early to make sure you're ready, and then some, to quote my favorite PD."

"You are absolutely, positively, right, hon," gurgled my response, my grin widening as I climbed from my chair to help her turn off various lights.

In bed, we read for a full hour. Then, at ten-thirty, when eyelids were finally heavy, we kissed good-night and talked for a few minutes about how truly rewarding the last two days had been. Just before I fell into slumberland, I noticed that for the second time Stella had snuggled up right against me, and smiling sweetly at how totally content this made me feel, I slipped into sleep.

XV

On Thursday morning, at precisely nine o'clock, Arlen James Steiggerman took his place on the bench and began calling 1969's first jury calendar. As he methodically began droning through the list of thirty-three cases, when he hesitated between the named defendants to ascertain who was or was not present, as planned, I began responding in a calm but crisp tone of voice, "Public Defender matter, Your Honor, the defense is ready for trial." By the time he had finished calling the fifth case, his darting, sideward glance in my direction told me that the words "ready for trial" had registered with him, and at the calendar's midway point, he finally stopped and adjusted his horn-rimmed glasses. Then, the monotone quality in his voice having been replaced by mild concern, he endeavored in his characteristically indirect manner to determine the nature of what he now clearly perceived to be an atypical pattern of response.

"Mr. Harris," he intoned calmly through a thin smile, "as I'm sure you are aware of, it is not necessary at this juncture to advise the Court of the status of a given case. There's plenty of time for that at our opening conference in chambers between the first and second calendar calls."

Delaying my response for several seconds while I considered which was the most advantageous time to initially confront him with phase one of our carefully constructed battle plan, and quickly concluding that there was no time like the present, in a sugar-coated tone of voice I then offered him a small bite of the proverbial food for thought. "I apologize, Your Honor, for taking up the Court's valuable time," oozed my reply. "Perhaps it would simplify matters if I just advised the Court now that my review of the calendar indicates that twenty-seven of today's cases are Public Defender matters, and that I am ready to proceed immediately to trial on all of them, Sir."

A quizzical smile flickered across his face, then quickly disappeared after I concluded speaking, and his response was equally brief. "Very well, Mr. Harris," he advised curtly. "We'll discuss this in chambers, later on!"

As Steiggerman then returned to his procedural task, next door in Division Two Judge Austin began his. And patiently, Leon, who was Austin's least-liked Public Defender, and who had been selected for his post for that very reason, proceeded to respond in the identical fashion I had presented to Steiggerman. Despite the fact that Leon shared Austin's voracious appetite for literature, and had spent numerous after-hours occasions with him in chambers engaged in discussions of various authors' works, Austin had never been able to develop a genuine affection for him, even though he had tried continuously for over a year. Leon suspected that the distance between them, evidenced by the fact that Austin treated him with a cold formality both in and out of the courtroom, was engendered by Leon's deep-rooted and heartfelt social philosophy, which if it did not openly embrace socialism, certainly trespassed further into this doctrinal house than the front yard, and gave him the appearance of being an extreme radical. Now, as Austin proceeded to read off the list of cases on today's typically overcrowded calendar, Leon, without raising his eyes from his copy, consistently repeated that the defense was ready for trial. And naturally unaware at that early hour of the rebellion under way, which like the gathering winds of a hurricane now stirred only as a gentle breeze, Austin assumed that during the holiday recess Leon had prepared extensively, and was quite properly, even if in overly formal manner for him, just representing his clients, and calmly continued wading through the calendar.

As ten o'clock approached, and Bailiff Roberts informed me that Steiggerman wanted to see me and the District Attorney in chambers, Ron had just completed his work in Division Five. Judge Benjamin Burroughs, Solina's other black judge who presided there, was a slender, pleasant-appearing, and personable individual. Born and raised in poverty in rural Alabama, like Lacy he had worked his way through college and law school, and having settled in Los Angeles before the outbreak of World War II, had worked hard at his law practice and ridden the post-war wave of growth and prosperity far above his humble beginnings all the way to the Municipal Court Bench. The father of six, and part-time pastor at his church, his demeanor off the bench was characterized by a gentle, almost shy manner, which was complemented by an understated sense of humor. In court, however, he appeared uncomfortable, and possessed of only B-minus intelligence, became rapidly confused and thoroughly flustered when confronted with tense situations. As prosecution oriented as Lacy, but vastly more lenient when it came to setting bail or sentencing, and unlike his colleague, totally ill-suited to presiding over criminal jury trials with their inherently hostility producing environments, he had carefully managed to secure the safest position available to a judge in Solina, that of hearing Court trials, wherein the judge decides innocence or guilt. In that our Office tried cases only to a jury, this resulted in his playing an active role only in a few private counsel cases, or trials involving persons charged with minor traffic violations, wherein our representation was legally precluded, and an occasional overflow preliminary hearing. Accustomed, therefore, to having PDs withdraw jury waivers entered by our clients at time of arraignment in Division One where they appeared without benefit of counsel, and resetting their cases for jury trial, he nonchalantly granted all nine of Ron's motions on this fateful morning, and by nine forty-five, as I was entering Steiggerman's chambers, Ron was already downstairs and striding briskly toward Divisions One and Three, readily available as planned, to aid either George or Robbie.

I hadn't been present in Steiggerman's court since the miraculously successful Salero trial, and as I glimpsed his artificial smile upon entering his chambers and taking a seat, as well the bare nod of acknowledgment offered by Stephen Shafer, the entire sequence of hostile events that had occurred during her trial flashed through my mind and twisted wide open the already loosened valve on my adrenal gland. Having sensed that I somehow represented further trouble for him on this early January morning, consistent with his calculating method of operation, he tried applying sugar first, and leaning forward in his chair, renewed his grin and turned on his unctuous charm.

"Well, well, gentlemen ... here we are again," he opened amiably. "As usual we have a crowded calendar, but it's the first court day of the new year, and I think we should start off with some coffee. Would you like some?" Shafer was quick to accept, and Steiggerman turned his attention back to me.

"No thank you, Your Honor."

"Some tea, perhaps?"

"No thanks, Your Honor, but I will smoke if that's permissible."

"Certainly, Mr. Harris, please make yourself comfortable."

Roberts poured and served the two requested cups of coffee, during which time I lit up and watched the smoke billow forth and fade away into the pervading silence. Realizing that it was reaching an uncomfortable length, His Honor broke it.

"I trust that everyone had a pleasant holiday, right?" floated his small-talk inquiry. Once again, Shafer's "Yes" was instantaneous, with Steiggerman's "And you, Mr. Harris?" then following on its heels.

"Fine, thank you, Your Honor—And you?"

"Wonderful, just wonderful!" he shot back. "After the Judicial Conference ended, Mrs. Steiggerman and I got away for a few days alone and really relaxed. Someday, when you have kids, you'll understand how much fun that can be, and how very necessary."

The adjective, wonderful, when conjoined with Steiggerman, appeared totally incongruous to me, either connotatively or denotatively. That he was married was difficult to believe, despite his strikingly handsome looks, and my understanding that he was the sole heir of a large oil and real estate fortune. That, in addition, he had children, was almost impossible for me to accept, and both surprises produced a fleeting feeling of sympathy for his wife and progeny as they passed quickly through my mind. Silently wondering when the slimy cocksucker was going to terminate his charade of cheerful camaraderie and get down to business, I nodded my head in mock agreement and sucked heavily on my pipe. I didn't have to wait long. After Roberts had elaborated on his holiday camping trip, His Honor settled far back into his chair, and wearing his most fatherly smile, finally addressed my irregular calendar-call response.

"Now tell me, Mr. Harris," he inquired, "What's this business of you being ready for trial on every case all about?"

"Nothing very special about it, Your Honor," I returned in a matter-of-fact tone. "I'm simply ready to proceed to trial on whichever case Your Honor selects, that's all."

"I see," flowed his response, his smile still glued to his face but fading slightly. "But as you are well aware of, usually we dispose of most of our cases. Is there some reason why today you want to try all twenty-six of yours?"

"There are twenty-seven, Your Honor."

"All right, twenty-seven. But you still haven't answered my question, Mr. Harris."

"Well, Sir, let's just say that I don't think any useful purpose would be served by attempting to plea bargain."

"I s-e-e," he said slowly, still smiling while searching his mind to discover what exactly I was up to, the slight inflection of irritation that crept into his elongation of "see" informing me his patience was already wearing thin. "Now, Mr. Harris," continued his response. "I realize that you've enjoyed considerable success in trial recently, and you are certainly to be congratulated on the outstanding job you've done. However, as I'm sure you realize, you can't win every time, so why not reconsider your position and at least discuss the situation with the District Attorney. He's a reasonable person, and so are you, and with my help, I'm sure we can work out some dispositions that would satisfy you."

"Your Honor, I understand what you're saying," I nodded back. "And I assure you that I've never refused to discuss anything with anyone since I arrived here in Solina, and I'm not now. However, I'm well aware of how you feel about wasting time, and therefore have to advise you that in defining what's fair and just, Mr. Shafer and I are about as far apart as the North and South Poles. Moreover, Sir, Mr. Shafer and the District Attorney's Office as a whole take the position that whatever case they file is absolutely ironclad, and that the defense should be extremely grateful for whatever slight compromise they offer out of their kind and generous hearts. My clients, however, beg to differ. All by themselves at arraignment, they pled not guilty and elected to be judged by their peers, and it's my duty to see that they get the requested fair trial and the opportunity to present their side of what allegedly occurred, which is all I've indicated, Sir."

The smile pasted on Steiggerman's face now disappeared rapidly, but before he could respond, Shafer entered the conversation. "Your Honor, me and every member of my Office is sick and tired of the crybaby attitude of the PDs. Just because Harris got lucky and won a case or two doesn't mean a damn thing!" he barked. "Like you said, he can't win'em all, so let's just try the cases. 'Cause the People are also ready, and maybe a few guilty verdicts will put an end to all this whining!"

Expecting cooperation from his ally in softening my position and keeping the plea-bargaining system smoothly functioning, after absorbing Shafer's surprise outburst, Steiggerman instinctively decided to support his bullying tactics in the hope that two against one might sober me back to reality, and turning in his chair so that eye-to-eye contact was achieved, he instantly switched his Dr. Jekyll into Mr. Hyde. "All right, Mr. Harris," he challenged, his tone hardening, "you've heard the Court's position, and now you've heard the DA's. If you want to maintain this nonsensical hard-line position of yours, I'll have no choice other than to call a case and let you roll the dice. If, on the other hand, you want to be reasonable and cut out this bullshit about wasting time, when you waste more than anyone I've ever seen, we'll try to work out some satisfactory deals. Now, what's it going to be?"

"Your Honor, Sir," marched my retort calmly, my emotions under tight control. "I seriously doubt whether Mr. Shafer and his Office even know how to spell the word reasonable, let alone comprehend or apply its meaning. And as far as his whining issue is concerned, and my nonsensical, bullshit position, as you put it, all I have done is respectfully advise this Court of my clients' election to proceed to trial, and that they are ready to defend themselves as best they can. How that is improper in any way is beyond me, as is the need to change it."

Left with no choice, Steiggerman hesitated only long enough to forge his anger into an acid-toned response. "Very well, Mr. Harris, we'll start at the top of the calendar and work our way down! Which, by the way, is where you and your damned clients are going to find yourselves—down, and out!"

"May I be excused then, Your Honor?"

He nodded his permission, and rising quickly to my feet, I exited at a brisk pace. Once outside in the courtroom, I broke into a wide grin, as with twenty cases totally unprepared, Steiggerman, by virtue of his mechanical approach, had selected one of the remaining seven that I was prepared on. Chuckling at my good fortune, I then tempered my sudden flush of optimism with the thought that now all I had to do was somehow win.

Twenty minutes later, as Steiggerman formally announced the case of the People versus Barbara Leyton, followed with his sugar-coated opening instructions to the jury, and then indicated that *voir dire* could begin, downstairs in Division Three a veritable explosion occurred. Robbie had had to wait until ten-thirty to engineer it, but when the flash finally occurred, a scene reminiscent of a hydrogen-bomb blast soon followed. Defending against a possession of dangerous drugs charge in the third preliminary hearing of the morning, over the continuous, condescendingly toned objections of the DA, Irene Fisher, he had performed meticulously minute cross-examination with respect to the only possible defense, an illegal search and seizure by the arresting officers. Then, after forty-five minutes of the battle had elapsed, he had objected to the formal entrance into evidence of the nine Seconal tablets in question on the ground that they had been secured by the arresting officers via an illegal entry into the glove compartment of his client's car in violation of his constitutionally protected Fourth Amendment rights, an objection that Judge Lacy had promptly and curtly overruled before adding his opinion that he considered the police work performed "nothing short of brilliant!"

Smiling like a contented cow, the thoroughly pleased Irene Fisher had then read into the record the standard stipulation to the effect that the offered evidence had been submitted to and thereafter analyzed by a police chemist, and found to be in fact the prohibited drug, Seconal. Beginning with the words, "Counsel, will you for the purposes of this hearing stipulate," the stipulation, including the certified chemist's report, takes a full two minutes to read. And seated at the counsel table, Robbie had waited patiently until Fisher had articulated the last word of it before responding with a simple "No."

Lacy was so stunned that no immediate reaction occurred. Glancing quickly at Fisher, whose smile had instantly disappeared, then back at Robbie, and still believing that he had somehow misheard the response, "Did you say, no, Mr. Gibbons?" crawled slowly off his tongue.

"Yes, Sir," Robbie informed tersely, beginning to enjoy himself.

"I don't understand, Mr. Gibbons," Lacy returned, "the defense always stipulates to these things at the preliminary-hearing stage. What's your problem?"

"I have no problem, Your Honor," shuffled Robbie's answer. "I had no prior agreement with the District Attorney to enter into any stipulation, in fact she didn't even speak to me prior to beginning this hearing."

Still not fully believing that this totally unexpected development could actually happen to him, for several soundless seconds Lacy just sat and stared at Robbie, momentarily immobilized by a situation which he could not recall ever having been faced with. Fisher, however, having recovered from her initial shock, and flushed with anger, boldly interrupted the heavy silence.

"Your Honor, this is just one more bit of outrageous behavior by Mr. Gibbons, who seems to specialize in obstructing justice!" she announced with her usual pomposity. "He knows perfectly well, as does the Court, that by mutual agreement between our two Offices, an understanding exists that in drug and narcotics cases PDs are to stipulate to the chemists' reports at Prelims, and Mr. Gibbons' conduct today is just another example of the lack of good faith that my Office consistently runs into when doing business with the PDs! It is highly unethical behavior on his part, Your Honor, and I hope that you will deal with him accordingly!"

Still baffled by Robbie's refusal, but with Fisher's diatribe jarring him loose from the confusion surrounding it, Lacy instinctively joined the attack. "I understand perfectly what you are saying, Miss Fisher, and I fully agree with your position," he assured her firmly. "Now, Mr. Gibbons, this Court would like an immediate explanation for your behavior!"

None was forthcoming. Instead, Robbie twisted his body deeper inside his chair and returned Lacy's fixed stare, five weighty seconds slowly slipping by before Lacy, his anger further heightened by Robbie's failure to respond, finally hissed, "Didn't you hear me, Mr. Gibbons?"

"Yes, Sir," Robbie nodded.

"Well, then?"

"I was just trying to think, Your Honor ... about how I was going to further explain what I've already explained ... That's all," inched Robbie's reply, baiting the hook. "Is the Court requesting a full history leading up to my refusal to stipulate?"

"Yes, exactly. What about it?"

"Well, Your Honor, in that the Court is insisting, I'll do my best," Robbie answered while rising to his feet, the realization that the era of judicial badgering and bullying was about to close sparking a twinkle in his eye. "Let me begin by pointing out," he picked up, his tone calm and confident, "that like most statements made by Miss Fisher, the one which she just finished is almost totally erroneous. I say, almost, because one tiny part of it was a correct statement of fact—she has offered a stipulation, which I have refused. Other than that, however, there isn't a single, solitary ounce of truth to anything else that came out of her mouth, not that this is unusual for her, Your Honor. In fact, it is standard operating procedure for her to be loud, arrogant ... and wrong!" Robbie suddenly amplified, the quiet rage inside him, forged from having endured almost two years of insults from Solina's judges and DAs, now surfacing, and no longer quiet.

"There has never existed between the Office of the Public Defender and that of the District Attorney any formal agreement with respect to stipulating to chemists' reports," continued Robbie's electric-toned elucidation. "What occurred, in fact, was that many months ago the DAs orally asked us if we would stipulate to them for the purposes of preliminary hearings only, in order to save the DAs and the County the inconvenience and expense of having the chemists testify in person—and in the spirit of cooperation, we agreed. Thereafter, Your Honor, this accommodation was observed so frequently that it developed into a habit—and so much so, that its proper status has been completely lost sight of by the DAs, and the judges as well for that matter. Our consent, Sir, was and is nothing more than a favor! There exists no statutory authority or case law whatsoever which even hints that the defense must enter into such a stipulation!" streamed Robbie's legal history lesson, wisps of steam now escaping as he once again zeroed in on Fisher. "Moreover, Your Honor," he picked up after having briefly hesitated for added emphasis, "nowhere is there a shred of authority for the proposition that the failure by a defense attorney to enter into such a stipulation is a breach of any canon of ethics, let alone constitute the very serious felony of obstructing justice. As usual, Miss Fisher, totally carried away by delusions of her own self-importance and power, has misrepresented both the facts and the law, and in the process slandered a fellow Officer of the Court. My refusal to stipulate is one hundred percent within the framework of those rights guaranteed by the laws of our state, and all I have done is exercise and stand by that right. It is Miss Fisher's conduct, Your Honor, that is not only outrageous, but fraudulent in nature! And while an apology by her would be deemed meaningless to me personally, the one which she owes to this Court ought to be made immediately!" cruised Robbie's seething indictment to a close.

Whatever clarification Lacy was expecting from Robbie, the explosive nightmare of defiance which had poured forth from him most certainly was absent from the list of possibilities, and left him literally dumbfounded. Recovering from the initial turbulence only when Irene Fisher began screeching for recognition, he shouted her into silence, and as the mushroom cloud rose from the initial blast to settle over the courtroom, offered his own contribution to the reverberating shockwave.

"Mr. Gibbons," he snarled, "when this Court needs your advice on how to operate, I'll ask for it! Until that time, however, you can just keep your mouth shut! Your ideas and opinions amount to a bunch of nonsense, and I'm sick and tired of your whining, as the District Attorney called it, as well as your delaying tactics which eat up the Court's valuable time!" frothed his counterattack, which he then paused in order to restrain his anger from jetting out of control. "Now, even though you act like it most of the time, you're not a novice at this game—which makes your intentionally insulting conduct even more inexcusable than it already is," he added more slowly, then further lowered his tone several decibels when he continued. "But, Mr. Gibbons, in spite of your childish behavior, I'm going to appeal to your better judgment one last time before I take other necessary action, and allow you to reconsider your arbitrary position and enter into the subject stipulation. Now, what do you say?" he ended firmly, but without the jagged edge of hostility, trusting that the implied threat of contempt of court would finally procure acquiescence.

Robbie, still standing, but now leaning forward and resting his hands on the counsel table, broke into a thin smile. Easing out through it a soft "No," as he shook his head, he followed it with a polite "But thank you anyway, Your Honor, Sir," and slowly sat down.

Glaring down in disbelief at the still smirking Robbie, Lacy literally choked on his refreshed anger as he attempted to speak. After a moment's respite, when he was still unable to regain control, he suddenly slammed his notebook shut and hurriedly exited the bench, coughing and sputtering like an old, malfunctioning car as he disappeared into chambers.

One full hour passed before His Honor reemerged and continued the entire calendar over to the afternoon session. Fully satisfied that he had Lacy boxed into a corner from which there was no escape, as the law was conclusively on his side, a buoyant Robbie exited the courtroom and headed for the office, only to be stopped outside in the hallway by Irene Fisher, who interrupted her conference with her investigating officer to shout that she wished to speak with him. Perplexed, but having lost little of her bluster, her "Hey, Robbie, what the hell's going on here?" was delivered in her typically arrogant tone.

"Listen, Irene," Robbie countered, more than happy to explain, "dumb as you are—and you are dumb, believe me—you ought to be able to understand the word 'no'!"

Having assumed that Robbie had been employing his delaying tactics in Division Three in order to achieve some favorable compromise he desired upstairs in the trial divisions, Fisher was momentarily stunned by the personal nature of his face-to-face attack, delivered forcefully as it was, her eyes blinking several times in rapid succession, and her half-opened mouth closing without making a further sound. In the several seconds that it took her to recover, Robbie had moved on toward the front door, and when she shouted after him that whatever he was doing, he wasn't going to get away with it, the only response was his laughter as he pushed down on the door's lever and disappeared from view without even a backward glance.

He was still chuckling to himself when he arrived back at the office. Leon and I were seated in my cubicle, drinking coffee and chatting excitedly, and when George and Ron entered just as Robbie was pulling up a chair to join us, they immediately followed suit and the first of innumerable luncheon meetings that lay ahead began spontaneously. As always, George presided, quickly conferring with each of us to determine where we stood individually, then adding his own status to the pile of responses and folding them together into a wide-angle view of our overall operation. In Judge Austin's courtroom, Leon was in trial on a battery case, with twenty-three cases trailing behind, while next door I had just completed *voir dire*-ing the jury, and twenty-six cases were also neatly stacked up waiting for attention. Robbie, in Division Three, had inflicted the greatest damage, with Lacy suffering from acute apoplexy, and his calendar at a total standstill, and in Division One's Arraignment Court, now staffed for the first time, George and Ron had spent a highly productive morning pleading defendant after defendant not guilty and having their cases set for jury trial around the middle of the month, by which time the steadily inflating balloon of backlogged cases would near its bursting point.

The comprehensive assessment that followed was also optimistic, two facts appearing crystal clear. First, we had achieved success with the initial thrust of our attack, as all of the court calendars were already backed up, even though their weight had not yet made its presence felt. And secondly, the judges and DAs were still unaware of the depth and breadth of what was transpiring, which meant that at least for the short-run the element of surprise remained our ally. Thoroughly pleased with our morning's collective endeavor, when Marilyn then returned from Montavani's Pizza Parlor with lunch, the six of us hungrily devoured pizza and salad along with as many details of each other's activities as the crowded conversation permitted. Ducking out of the gabfest for a minute, I also shared a brief summary of round one with Stella, promising full details over dinner and returning her "Best of luck" with a chuckling "Thanks, sweetie, I'll need it" before hanging up. Then, rejoining the group, I steadily inhaled the caffeine from Marilyn's super-strong coffee while reentering the flow of nervous chatter that continued until it was time to return to court, and together the five of us strolled toward the afternoon's waiting encounters.

Upon returning to Division Four and settling into my seat at the counsel table, I recalled that I had first met Barbara Leyton at seven-thirty on a cold, rainy morning several weeks ago. Her uncle had come into the office and explained to me that his niece was across the street in the courthouse waiting to plead guilty to a crime she hadn't committed because she suffered from a nervous ailment and couldn't face the prospect of the pressure that a trial would create. Locking the office, I had hurried across the street to find her seated on the bench outside the Arraignment Court dabbing at her red-rimmed eyes with a piece of tissue. Her uncle introduced me, and after I calmed her down with several minutes of small talk, we discussed the case and I learned that she was accused of stealing a shopping cart filled with food items from a Brynhurst supermarket. With pauses to wipe away fresh tears, she had explained to me that she had been shopping for over half an hour, and when she finally approached the checkout stand, she discovered that she had left her purse in the car with her husband and two children. Thinking that she could motion to her husband to have one of the kids bring her the needed purse, she had wheeled the cart three or four feet beyond the entranceway, then stopped, and was waving to her family when the market's security guard had approached and placed her under arrest. When I then carefully questioned her about the details of her account of the incident, her answers were totally consistent with her original sketch of what had occurred, and as unshakeable as her determination to plead guilty and end the matter without any further turmoil. Having been apprised by her uncle during the walk to the courthouse that she was currently on probation for illegal possession of dangerous drugs, I had then literally pleaded with her to trust me and reverse her position, particularly in light of the fact that her intended course of action would constitute a violation of the terms of her probation and most likely result in her being sentenced to jail. When this sobering consequence fully registered, and I assured her that both she and her version of the events were highly believable, she had finally relented and allowed me to set her case for trial, adding through her first smile of the day that "I trust you. I'm in your hands."

Now, having just indicated my acceptance of the jury, I felt the full weight of that trust, alongside its twin sister, responsibility, even as I casually returned her smile while reaching for my legal pad. The knowledge that I was about to face off against both Shafer and Steiggerman, each of whom would employ whatever dirty trick necessary to force the jury to convict her, did little to lighten the heavy load, and only when my new acquaintance, Viktor Frankl, flashed into view did the tightness in my chest begin to ease. Smiling, he reminded me of the central lesson he had learned at Auschwitz: that the only thing you can control is yourself, and your reaction to whatever obstacles were hurled at you. Nodding my acknowledgment, I instantly coupled the teaching with Grampy's "Just do your best," and resolved to utilize both precepts to their maximum as Steiggerman directed Shafer to call his first witness, and the security officer for Abel's market took the stand.

In direct contrast to the Salero trial, I allowed him to lead his witness through his testimony without objecting even once. Except for the crucial fact that no mention was made of Barbara having performed a waving motion after opening the door leading from the market and stepping outside, the jury listened to a set of facts identical to that which she had related to me during our first meeting. And after approaching the vicinity of the witness box to begin cross-examination, as planned, I proceeded to make a major issue out of that missing fact, knowing that the odds were stacked against my shaking it free from the experienced witness, but desiring nonetheless to firmly implant the subject in the mind of the jurors so as to revisit it at a later time when I planned to introduce a small surprise. As expected, I failed to uncover the absent detail, and after a little less than five minutes I resumed my seat at the counsel table, then pulled out my pipe when Steiggerman declared a fifteen-minute recess.

As the first wisps of smoke drifted upward, and I assured Barbara that all was well so far, and that all she had to do was tell her story and keep telling it no matter how belligerent Shafer became on cross-examination, downstairs a sullen Judge Lacy had at two o'clock, and one full hour later than usual, finally returned to the bench. Advised by Irene Fisher that the police chemist had not arrived, nor was expected to,

Lacy then asked Robbie if reason had finally returned during the noon recess to reverse his previous position, only to receive a second dose of negative news.

"Very well, Mr. Gibbons ... Very well," dribbled Lacy's response. "If you insist on continuing this foolishness, then you leave me no alternative other than to continue this case over to a later date, with your client remaining in jail, of course. Do you understand that?"

"Well, not exactly, Your Honor," Robbie answered. "I feel confident that the Court is familiar with the various sections of the Penal Code which provide that where practicable a preliminary hearing must be completed in the same day in which it has begun—along with the numerous cases that affirm that mandate. So, with that body of law in mind, Your Honor, I move that this case be dismissed."

Lacy's immediate reaction was to raise his body out of his chair and so far forward that for a moment it appeared as if he were going to climb over the top of the bench, so intense was the anger which coursed through him. "Dismiss?" he bellowed so loudly that he was heard in the hallway outside.

"Yes, Sir," Robbie calmly confirmed.

"Have you gone insane, counsel?"

"No, Sir, I—"

"Well you must have, if you think that I'm going to dismiss this case because you insist on acting like a stupid ass! What's wrong with you?"

"Nothing, Your Honor," Robbie informed, "I'm just asking the Court to do what the law requires, and I don't see at all what's insane or asinine about that, Sir."

"Well, you're not only insane and an ass, counsel, but you're also blind!" Lacy shotgunned back. "Your motion is denied! And I am also making a specific finding of fact that the People's expert witness is unavailable because you, Mr. Gibbons, breached an oral agreement without advising either the Court or the DA, and knowing that this made it impossible for him to appear on such short notice—all of which makes it not at all practicable to finish this hearing today! Now, do you have any other tidbits of knowledge to share with us before I continue this case?"

A faint smile had been sliding in and out of the corners of Robbie's mouth as Lacy's anger had steadily increased. And having saved his best ammunition until the final stage of the confrontation, he now banished its faint traces as he opened his trial notebook, then proceeded to fire the proverbial silver bullet. Carefully controlling his choice of words so as to remain well outside the boundaries of contempt of court, he did not however restrict his tone of voice, well aware that the Court Reporter's transcript did not show sarcasm, disdain, or disgust. "Just one, Your Honor ... Just one," Robbie advised, returning Lacy's glare with even greater intensity, his eyes radiating scorn. "Undoubtedly, the Court is also familiar with the Penal Code section which provides that a person charged with a felony must have his preliminary hearing within ten working days from his arraignment. Well, Sir, this being the tenth working day, the continuance of this case would amount to a judicial absolution of the ten-day statutory requirement prescribed by our state legislature—a mandate, which our Supreme Court has consistently upheld, as I'm sure the Court also knows!" rolled Robbie's argument into a slight pause, the defiance mapped across his face clearly evidencing his lack of fear, his taunting tone, soaked with sarcasm in selected spots, perfectly complementing the animosity emanating from his eyes.

"Now, Your Honor," he picked up, "I have during the noon recess checked over the Court records, and determined that not only this case, but six others on today's calendar also require a chemist's testimony, and also fall on the subject tenth day. In addition, Sir, I would like to advise the Court, that in support of my motion to dismiss this case, as well as the six others I will make when they are called, I have conferred with Mr. Lester Smith of my office's appellate department and requested that he prepare seven Writs of Habeas Corpus—which he is to file in Department One Hundred of the Superior Court immediately upon communication from me or one of my colleagues, should my clients' aforestated rights be suppressed by this Court on the grounds that attempting to exercise them is, and I quote, Your Honor, Sir, 'stupid,' 'asinine,' and 'blind'!"

"You've gone too far, Mr. Gibbons!—one step too far!" Lacy shouted the instant that the closing exclamation point stomped off of Robbie's tongue. "Your conduct is not only outrageous, but it's contemptuous! And I hereby hold you in ... in ... in—"

Choking for the second time on his own anger, heightened further as it was by the sudden realization in mid-sentence that the law with the respect to the ten-day requirement was precisely as Robbie had represented, and that a reading of the transcript would indeed reflect his usage of language that was not only highly insulting to defense counsel, but more importantly displayed a bias in favor of the prosecution so blatant that it could qualify for censure by a higher authority, Lacy stammered to a stop, then stormed off the bench in an exact reproduction of his performance earlier that morning. When he reemerged some twenty minutes later, having in the interim conferred with his clerk and personally reviewed the court records in question, he had regained his composure and restored a stony calmness to his voice. Ignoring the fact that in his hasty departure from the bench he had failed to declare a recess in the proceedings, he formally called the court back into session, and then addressed Robbie without actually looking at him.

"Mr. Gibbons," he monotoned, staring downward at his notebook, "I have, during the recess, considered your argument with respect to the ten-day requirement, and on the technical ground you cited, the case before us is hereby dismissed. However, I am at the same time, also ordering the District Attorney to refile this case at the earliest possible time, and am further ordering her to subpoena the necessary chemist to appear at the time subsequently set for the preliminary hearing on this matter."

Fisher promptly interjected that her Office would be "more than willing to comply with both orders," and plodding onward, Lacy then called the next case. And as Robbie, wearing a sweet smile of satisfaction, informed him that the defense was ready, upstairs in Division Four, I likewise advised Steiggerman that I was prepared to present Barbara Leyton's defense, which, with one minor addition, consisted primarily of her testimony.

Watching her closely as she took the oath and then seated herself in the witness box, I was struck by how lovely she looked. I had realized at our first meeting that she was pretty, despite her tear-stained, somewhat bedraggled appearance. But, now, with the jurors forming a first impression, I was most appreciative of what a difference an attractive dress, along with a visit to the hairdresser and a touch of makeup, had produced. Noticing, also, that she was fumbling nervously with the handkerchief she clutched tightly with both hands inside her lap, I began with a series of questions that allowed her to tell the jury exactly how nervous she was, smiling inwardly as the informal exchange also accomplished the added purpose of visibly relaxing her. Then, carefully structuring my succeeding questions so as to allow her to tell her version of the events in controversy in her own words, just as she had consistently related them to me, I returned several times to the critical point of her having been waving to her family to bring her the needed purse at the time of her arrest. Finally, pleased with the favorable impression that she had made on the jury, a judgment gleaned from the sideward glances I stole towards them as she supplied details and twice repeated that she waved with her right hand, I concluded her testimony by stealing the capital T out of Shafer's anticipated thunder on cross-examination.

Priming her first by asking whether she had told the jury the whole truth about the incident in question, without adding or subtracting any facts she thought they should know before making their decision, to which she answered solemnly that she had, I then inquired about her previous conviction. Just as we had discussed, and with a tinge of embarrassment creeping into her voice to lend credibility to her truthfulness, she openly shared how during the time she had been separated from her husband she had become depressed and foolishly turned to drugs as an escape. Turning her head to face the jurors directly as she concluded her admission, she then highlighted her remorse by stressing that she had been convicted, "because I knew that I was wrong, and pled guilty," adding through a shy smile that "I'm still on probation, attending my NA meetings, and have been totally sober for the past year and a half."

Thanking her for having the courage to tell the whole truth about herself to a group of her peers, who were nevertheless strangers, I smiled reassuringly at her, then likewise with a nod of my head at the jury, before returning to my seat to await Shafer's bombastic cross-examination.

And even though I had deprived him of his favorite weapon for disparaging a defendant, he did not disappoint me. For having remained docile during Barbara's testimony, he now found himself, and employing his typical vitriolic style, produced tears inside of two minutes. Objecting continuously to his ugly toned questions, as well as the misrepresentations of the facts they frequently contained, in an effort to protect her, I soon discovered that the more strenuous my protestations became, the louder Steiggerman's overrules and chastisements rained down on me, in the process encouraging Shafer to exercise his hunting license to the fullest possible extent. For fifteen eternally long minutes, he hammered and rehammered at every detail Barbara had previously related, while in between his knife-edged queries and her repeated dabs at her eyes, she stuttered and stammered her answers back at him. However, while her already existing nervous condition made her an easy target to intimidate into tears, because her story was not invented, she remained steadfastly true to her version of the incident down to the smallest detail. And when Shafer finally terminated his torturous interrogation with one final demeaning remark and a shrug of his shoulders, I immediately jumped into rescue-and-rehabilitation mode by meeting Barbara as she stepped down from the witness box, and assisting her as she unsteadily made her way back to her seat at the counsel table.

His Honor, noticing the sympathetic looks the jurors cast Barbara's way during the slow return to her chair, immediately declared a ten-minute recess in an effort to allow their pooling compassion to dilute and then drain away. As usual, it lasted closer to twenty, and when we finally returned to open session, I sprang my little surprise and called Linda Leyton, Barbara's six-year-old daughter, to the stand. Wearing a pale-pink dress, she entered the courtroom after exiting from the side hallway where I had carefully concealed her, and immediately caused the stir which I had anticipated her Dresden-doll looks would produce. And as I had also anticipated, with even greater certainty, Steiggerman declined to allow her to testify due to her age. Arguing vigorously that the legal test for determining the competency of a child witness was first, the ability to distinguish truth from falsity, and secondly, the ability to observe a given incident and to articulate that which was observed, I then made a formal offer of proof that if given the opportunity, Linda could more than adequately demonstrate that she possessed both of these abilities. Without even blinking twice, Steiggerman curtly rejected the offer, then likewise denied my subsequent motion for a hearing on the issue outside the presence of the jury. Knowing that Linda was the only person who saw her mother waving, as Barbara's husband, Leonard, had been reading a newspaper during the subject events, and equally aware from having interviewed her that she was quite capable of testifying, with frustration and anger welling up inside me, I proceeded to risk causing a mistrial, and ignoring Steiggerman's "And that's final, Mr. Harris, period!" engaged him further.

"Your, Honor, Sir," I pleaded in my most humble tone of voice, "I appreciate and respect the Court's ruling, and will of course abide by it. However, in the interests of justice, I would most urgently like to make one further offer of proof—which is that Linda, if allowed, would testify to the fact that she saw her mother waving at her, and being grabbed by a strange man during the incident in question. This, in my opinion is extremely crucial, Your Honor, and I—"

"Mr. Harris, you're way out of order!" Steiggerman interrupted, bellowing at me with the full force of the anger that flushed up the sides of his neck like a rushing river, then burst its banks and flooded his face. "And if you say even one more word about that child, I'll hold you in contempt of court! Do you understand me, counsel?"

Glancing down at Linda, who suddenly grabbed my leg and began to cry in frightened response to His Honor's resounding outburst, I gently slipped her hand inside mine before lifting my gaze to meet Steiggerman's fuming stare. "Yes, Sir, I do," trickled my reply softly, Dr. Frankl winking his approval as I muzzled my anger and led Linda away from the witness box and back to her father. As I returned to the counsel table, I remained fully aware that my assertion in front of the jury of exactly what Linda's testimony would be constituted highly improper conduct, and was clearly grounds for the declaration of a mistrial by His Honor. So, when he then inquired if the defense had anything further to offer, I appeared quite contrite while replying politely, "No, Your Honor, but thank you," before sitting down to wait and see what action he would take, a citation for contempt also still within his purview.

I had had only a nanosecond to make my decision after flashing on the risk of mistrial and contempt versus the possible reward of swaying the jury in favor of Barbara, hoping that His Honor would see that a mistrial didn't benefit the Court's calendar one iota, but in fact only made the congestion worse if the case was retried. Now, in the silence that suddenly enveloped the courtroom, it was Steiggerman's turn, and as he carefully weighed his options while painstakingly thumbing through his notes to buy time, much to his chagrin he discovered that the prevailing circumstances prevented an easy choice. For openers, his reasoning regarding the benefits versus consequences of a mistrial forced him to the exact same conclusion I had hastily formed, and he quickly dismissed it. Next up was the highly appealing opportunity to punish me by holding me in contempt. However, while nothing would give him greater pleasure, he mused, smiling inwardly, logic then dictated that this choice not only led directly back to the already rejected mistrial, but would actually back-up the calendar even further, as with me temporarily sidelined awaiting a hearing on a citation that was unlikely to be upheld in Superior Court anyway, my replacement could validly request a lengthy allotment of time to acquaint himself with the long list of cases which were totally unfamiliar to him. Shaking his head as this disturbing resolution was also discarded, His Honor then found himself forced to the doorstep of option number three, declare a mistrial and dismiss the charges, while leaving me in place, a choice so unsavory that it instantly loomed as a waking nightmare. For while it dispensed with the need for a retrial, and immediately returned focus to the remaining calendar, it also provided that Barbara would be home-free, and worst of all, that that little shithead of a PD would have won, Steiggerman concluded, frowning visibly as he turned over the last sheet of his notes. No, far better to gamble that the jury would believe the security officer over Barbara and convict her, dictated hope and practicality, His Honor then shuffling his notes aside and clearing his throat.

"All right, gentlemen ... All right. Now that we're all calmed down, we'll proceed with closing arguments. Mr. Shafer, you may begin."

Preferring, as usual, to hear what I had to say first, Shafer promptly waived the first opportunity to argue, and after easing out of my chair, I slowly strolled over to a spot in front of the jury. For several seconds I just stood there, searching the sober faces of Barbara's twelve judges. Then, when all twenty-four eyes had fastened securely on me, I cut directly to the heart of the matter, and in a low, conversational tone of voice delivered my entire plea to them for a not guilty verdict in just under three minutes. After briefly summarizing the facts of the case, I asked them first to focus on what I defined as the only issue: Did Barbara Leyton intend to leave Abel's Market without paying for the groceries in her shopping cart? Then, emphasizing that both she and the security officer had agreed that she was stopped and standing in place just a few feet outside the doorway when she was arrested, I argued that from this mutually testified-to fact, one could only draw two logical inferences: First, that she was not hurrying away, because she did not intend to leave without paying. And secondly, that this stopping and standing in place was perfectly consistent with Barbara's testimony that she was waving to her family to bring her the forgotten purse. Both witnesses had a bias, I informed them, drawing to a close. But Barbara, I reminded, had been totally honest about what she felt and did when she found herself in the wrong on a past occasion, and had also offered a witness in support of her version of the events, whom His Honor judged too young to testify. In contrast, however, I suggested, the security officer, having rushed in the heat of the moment to make an arrest, wouldn't want to admit to a mistake in having missed the waving motion due to professional pride. All in all, I concluded, the evidence clearly added up to a reasonable doubt, and after thanking the jurors once again for having served, I returned to my seat at the counsel table.

Shafer, anticipating a lengthy, emotion-filled plea for justice from me, was caught off guard by my sudden conclusion, and fumbled through his notes for over half a minute before finally setting a book down on top of them and climbing to his feet. Once in front of the jury however, he quickly warmed to the task, and in his customarily acerbic style pilloried both Barbara and me. His Honor then instructed the jury, noticeably quickening his pace during his reading of the law with respect to the necessary element of intent, in an effort to prevent the jury from attaching the appropriate amount of importance to what in fact constitutes the very crux of the crime of theft. Trusting that my brief but firm argument that had focused on little else other than this crucial element would remain in the collective mind of the jury, I silently prayed to the god of What Goes Around Comes Around as they slowly strolled out of the box and into the adjoining room to deliberate.

Two hours later, at five-thirty, when the foreman reported that the jury had not yet reached a verdict, Steiggerman excused them till nine o'clock the following morning, then trailed all twenty-six of the remaining cases to tomorrow's calendar and declared court adjourned. Feeling that the facts of Barbara's case were so simple, and therefore expecting a brief deliberation by the jury, on the walk back to the office I was mildly dispirited, though still highly hopeful for a good result. "They'll believe her, you'll see," I muttered softly, summoning a smile for company.

Leon had entered the office just a minute or two before me, and when my arrival brought our strength to full, the day's second strategy session was quickly convened. Nothing overtly had changed since our noontime meeting, and we quickly evaluated that overall our war could not have gotten off to a better beginning. However, in Division Three, one potentially serious side effect had occurred, Robbie reported, his grin fading into a pained expression as he informed us that while he had successfully forced Judge Lacy into dismissing seven of the sixteen cases on the Prelim calendar, the DA's office, eagerly complying with His Honor's order, had immediately refiled all seven, and arranged for all of the defendants to be rearrested before they could be released from custody. So, while Robbie had been totally successful in wreaking havoc with Lacy's obsessively ordered operation, and humiliating him and Irene Fisher in the process, the end result was that seven of our clients, having already spent two weeks in jail awaiting their Prelims, were now faced with rearraignment proceedings and a second two-week wait as guests of the county. Unexpected, in that we had not anticipated that the DA's Office could respond so quickly, as Robbie's remarks sunk into our collective mind and spun around like a spiraling bullet in slow motion, silence collected and threatened to cloud what otherwise had been a triumphant day. Not on our leader's watch, however. Before the potential fallout could significantly diminish our enthusiasm from having successfully established a beachhead, General George jumped to the rescue.

"All right, now, listen to me, you bunch of blockheads," he commanded, slicing through the stillness before it could add another ounce of weight. "We understood from the moment we started planning, that this wasn't going to be a Sunday school picnic—that's why we called it a war! And we also knew that we weren't going to win every battle outright, so we agreed that when the going gets a little rough we'd talk it over and figure out how to counter whatever's being thrown back at us—so let's just do that, okay?" rumbled his suggestion, George then pausing briefly as each of us nodded his approval.

"All right, then," he picked up, his tone upbeat. "The way I see it, this situation isn't nearly as bad as it appears. Sure, today the DAs were able to refile seven cases, and believe me, I'm sorry that those seven clients are stuck with an extra two weeks in jail. But the good news is that the DA's secretaries can't consistently keep up with the extra load of paperwork on top of their already heavy load of bullshit, especially since the load is only going to get heavier and heavier as the list of dismissed drug cases grows. Moreover, and this is extremely important to remember, guys," George stressed, swiveling his head to make eye contact with each of us, "the DAs can't solve this testy little problem either by subpoenaing the chemists to court, because to do so day after day, with some of them already testifying in Superior Court, would drain their labs so short of manpower that they couldn't keep up with analyzing the new shit coming in. So, while it's most unfortunate, for the next few days we'll just have to live with the pain of extra jail time for our clients. But, within two weeks—maybe even shorter—we'll be getting cases dismissed and not refiled—and then the only question facing us will be, which direction do we twist the DA's balls now, clockwise or counterclockwise!" he growled to a close, highlighting the optimistic picture he had painted with a fist slam onto the desk, then breaking into a grin, the rest of us spontaneously mirroring it.

"Okay, I hear you," Robbie nodded back at him. "But that's not all of what's bothering me, George."

"Yeah? ... What else?" George inquired.

"It's downtown. My real concern is that when Huxton and Stone—and even crazy old Jordan—learn that we're backing up the felony calendar and filling up the county jail with our clients, that they'll shit in their pants, and then right on top of our little heads. Fucking up misdemeanor calendars is one thing, but felonies are s-e-r-i-o-u-s business," Robbie drawled to a close, then pulled out his pipe and struck a match when George hesitated for several seconds before responding.

"Well," George finally shrugged, "I'll admit that I don't have an easy answer for that. But I wouldn't underestimate the big boys downtown, not by a long shot. I know Huxton and Stone pretty well, and Jordan too, who's a little crazy and all, but just like the wily old fox—and I'm also fully aware that on top of running the whole Office, they have to cozy up to the County Board of Supervisors come budget time. However, let's not forget that every one of them was a goddamned good trial lawyer in his day, and a first-class fighter, too!" ambled his analysis, George straining to convince himself as well as us. "So, maybe in this case they won't play politics and put the squeeze on us, especially if by the time our war hits home, we can demonstrate to them that we can pull it off if they'll just back us for a short while!" he expressed hopefully, then paused for a split second before continuing. "Anyway, if somehow they won't, and instead transfer us out of here, then they can have my job, because if standing tall and fighting fire with fire isn't allowed, then it's not worth having anyway!" he ended on a bittersweet note, then waited for a response.

Once again, our heads nodded in agreement, albeit a bit more slowly as we pondered the questionable response from the heads of the Office in the returned silence. When George again pierced it to instruct us to turn the touchy subject over to him should a call arrive, his omnipresent sense of humor adding a "Hey, I've been to charm school across the street, so no problem explaining, right?" laughter finally joined the confab, spurting forth despite the prevailing air of concern.

"Ohhh, yeah, no problem at all," Ron replied, chuckling, his echo cut off by Leon's, "Right, none whatsoever. You just tell them, Georgie—nicely of course—that we just got a teensy weensy bit tired of eating pig shit all day long, and decided to teach those fucking cocksuckers a little lesson in civility and proper court procedure, that's all!"

"Uh-huh, you got that right!" Robbie chimed in, "Like to begin with, how to recognize a human being, so our clients could be treated as such—not to forget us hard-working public servants either, of course. Hell, you can sweet talk'em, Georgie, I just know you can," he ended, our laughter swelling to fill the room.

When it finally died down, we gathered up our briefbags and tiredly shuffled down the narrow corridor to the back door and out into the chilly January night. Overhead, the sky was clear enough for us to sight several stars, an omen which momentarily soothed away the lingering remnants of our anxious speculation that had trailed alongside, and after we traded a few additional gibes, and cheerfully chorused "Have a good one, see you tomorrow!" round the circle, car doors slammed shut, engines ignited for the long drive home, and day one finally came to a close.

XVI

Friday morning dawned sunnier than its predecessor, and even the gray clouds dotting the sky to the south seemed to be in a better mood. Me, too, smiled a thought as I reached the freeway and flicked on Old Greener's radio to find Marvin Gaye crooning out "I Heard It Through the Grapevine." And while I had no way of knowing as I hummed nonchalantly along, it turns out that Marvin was also psychic. For just an hour later, at their regular, pre-calendar-call meeting, Solina's judges would be singing their own downbeat version, entitled: "What Does the Grapevine Have to Say About the Odd Behavior of the PDs?"

Chaired by a visibly irritated and perplexed William Lacy, who insisted that "something very strange was going on," the entire forty-five-minute session was then devoted to a careful, courtroom-by-courtroom review of his allegation, which resulted only in our Office being convicted of boorish behavior in the first degree. All that had happened, the judges concluded after due deliberation, was that during the holiday slowdown occasioned by their attendance at the Judicial Conference, the PDs had "gotten a bug up their immature asses," as Judge Steiggerman so eloquently opined, "then used this publicly paid for vacation-time to excessively prepare, so as to make a little trouble in order to get better plea-bargains." And consistent with this finding, it was then decided that the wisest policy they could adopt was to completely ignore the existing provocation, in the belief that the failure to even acknowledge that a problem existed would soon deter us from our erroneous path, in the exact same way that a lack of recognition eradicates the attention-seeking antics of a small, misbehaving child, who when ignored, soon ceases its naughty conduct and returns to its usual pattern of play.

The details of this meeting were, of course, unknown to us. But we soon surmised from their Honors' collective stance of calmly pretending that business was proceeding as usual that this synthetic denial constituted their official response, and having successfully anticipated that such would be the case, smiled contentedly to ourselves while continuing to implement our plan without resistance.

Late that afternoon, as I was *voir dire*-ing the jury in the next case Steiggerman had selected for trial, this time more carefully choosing a drunk-in-public scenario wherein the evidence was heavily stacked in favor of the prosecution, my individual morale received a sizeable boost when jury number one returned a not guilty verdict in the Leyton case. Glancing over Barbara's shoulder as she joyfully threw her arms around me in celebration, I gleefully watched as a sober-faced Steiggerman slowly retired from the bench to his chambers and a thoroughly piqued Shafer stormed angrily out of the courtroom. Then, as my smile swelled huge, I returned Barbara's hug and kiss on the cheek, before together we rushed over and thanked each member of the jury.

When I finally returned to the office an hour later, more good news awaited, as Leon's trial had ended in a hung jury, with Austin having then dismissed the case rather than exercise the alternative of resetting it for a second trial. And collectively buoyed by this double success, heightened even further by the realization that after only two days there were already over two hundred cases backing up toward the dates fixed by statute for their dismissal, the five of us were jovial indeed. In fact, in direct contrast to the sweet-and-sour mood that had prevailed a scant twenty-four hours earlier, this time we laughed without reservation as Robbie related the details of his second tension-filled day of combat with Lacy. And as he artfully mimicked the latter's pained facial expressions and grunts, which had occasionally escaped despite his efforts to stifle his true emotions as he was forced to dismiss every drug case on calendar, the immense gratification infusing Robbie's beaming face proved contagious, instantaneously sparking a second chorus of mirthful satisfaction that featured growling gibes and catcalls when I then capped off the late-afternoon gabfest by recounting the misery that had befallen Steiggerman and Shafer.

Even after the echoes from our laughter had faded into the falling dusk, and the short week ended, we rode our wave of merriment into a weekend that was both enjoyable and restful. A happy highlight, it was short lived, however, as on Monday, with fresh jury trials continuing, and additional drug cases being dismissed from the Prelim calendar, a portentous pattern of pretense was established that during the following two weeks slowly and steadily escalated into a grinding war of nerves. For with the judges continuing to pretend that nothing out of the ordinary was occurring, and the five of us likewise continuing to implement the Grand Plan, as both sides willfully refused to budge an inch in the face of the steadily growing tension and concomitant hostility, taut nerves stretched tighter and tighter with each passing day. And while a casual third-party observer would have been hard put to detect that anything significant was amiss, the grim expressions that intermittently slipped through the combatants' overriding masks of tranquility, and the spurts of bitterness that occasionally squirted forth when one of the actors in cold-war play momentarily lost his iron-like grip on his seething emotions, served well as circumstantial evidence that the constant strain was wearing the false facade thin on both sides of the trenches.

Adding an additional degree of difficulty to our task of fully maintaining our course of action was the fact that as January dragged toward its middle our overall daily schedule grew increasingly longer, and in combination with the smoldering air of animosity that threatened to flare into open warfare at any moment, began to sap our strength. Beginning at six, when we arose to hurriedly shave, shower, and dress, then grabbed coffee and an orange to serve as breakfast as we took the first of our one-hour daily drives, the mornings passed by swiftly with ninety minutes of new client interviews opening the official day, followed by the trial already under way until noon. Lunch, which usually consisted of a hastily swallowed sandwich while searching for a potential witness on the telephone, or handling some other problem that arrived via its interminable ring, was succeeded by our noontime war council. And after a round-the-horn review of the morning's events, if there was still time, we shared casual chit-chat over fresh coffee and a smoke or two, in an effort to do nothing except relax for a few precious minutes.

By one-fifteen, we had returned to trial, and the afternoon hours then disappeared acrimoniously into each other as we alternately examined and cross-examined witnesses, argued for and against objections and motions, orated our reasons for requesting the dismissal of charges at a Prelim, or poured our hearts and souls into a plea to the jury for a not guilty verdict, then prayed silently for at least a hung jury. Upon returning to the office after darkness had fallen, emotionally drained and physically exhausted, for an hour or so we then forced ourselves to make or answer still more telephone calls, or interview yet another new client. Then, finally, we would convene together for a second time to review the day's events, and plan tomorrow as best we could.

Tired as we were, the long drive home quickly developed into a welcome respite from the hectic pace and worrisome problems presented by the day just passed. With the driver's-side window down to allow a flow of fresh, cool air and insure as much alertness as possible, we carefully steered our cars onto the freeway and headed north, then tried to blank our minds to all except the music lofting from our radios, Led Zeppelin's "Whole Lotta Love" and the Rolling Stones' "Gimme Shelter" soothing our frayed nerves as the miles glided by. Then, once one relaxed minute had collected its brothers and sisters into a family, there was time to gather one's private thoughts and calmly greet several minutes of reflection before finally arriving home. Within a week, I had become quite good at temporarily closing the door on the constant tumult we lived with, so as to quietly evaluate how we were performing as a group, then me individually. Overall, I concluded thirteen days after the war had commenced, our little army was performing A-okay, having seriously stalled Lacy's assembly-line Prelim operation, and placed an unmanageable burden on both the DA's Office and the department of police chemists, the proof being that recent drug-case dismissals were not being refiled, just as General George had predicted. And as for myself, I was holding my own, losing the second drunk-in-public case that Steiggerman had handpicked, but winning the disturbing-the-peace scenario that followed, and managing to create just enough reasonable doubt to obtain two hung juries thereafter, with Steiggerman then dismissing the cases in the face of a backlog that had now reached almost three hundred, and was matched fully by Leon's efforts next door in Division Two. True, we had certainly underestimated the physical, mental, and emotional wear and tear that our Grand Plan was producing, but nevertheless, we had managed to remain fully on course, and our spirits remained high. "So, all things considered, not bad," I concluded, pulling up in front of our triplex and parking. "In fact, not bad at all!" I repeated as I exited, my smile widening as I headed toward the pretty lady waiting for me.

Stella had quickly adjusted to the increased tension that I was operating under, and almost without fail was at home to greet me when I shuffled into the apartment and flopped down on the living room couch. Mixing up her vodka-tonic specials, or introducing a new wine that she had discovered, she would swiftly cozy up next to me, and after gifting me with a kiss, listen eagerly to the tale of my day before sharing hers. Magically, within a few short minutes, she would have me laughing and jabbering away over the parade of events we recreated, the free-flowing, unguarded conversation always unwinding me further so that for the most part I could shelve Solinaland in a far recess of my mind and enjoy fully our time together. Happy Hour, we nicknamed our first sixty minutes of reunion, a time for give and take that need made so extra special that it became a ritual, and one that we would both come to cherish more and more as time passed, the bond between us growing thicker from countless words and acts that comforted and nourished, memory adding poignant pages to our history.

During dinner, and afterward over coffee, the outside world that was living multi-faceted lives separate from our own and seemingly at a far distance, was invited to join us for a smoke and some analytical discussion. First up on this middle-of-the-month Wednesday was the startling victory by the New York Jets during last weekend's Super Bowl. Although the Big Apple's entry was a heavy underdog to Baltimore's Colts, stressed the review in *Sports Illustrated* that Stella had earmarked for me, the Jets' talented, brash-talking Joe Willie Namath had made good on his boast and led his team to the upset of the ages, 16–7.

"Ring any bells of similarity?" Stella tossed at me, her sparkling eyes joining in her smile.

"Uh-huh," I acknowledged. "Only problem is, our playing field isn't level. But, still, if Joe Willie could pull off that little number," I speculated with lukewarm optimism, "I wouldn't bet the house against us."

"Neither would I," she affirmed, then joined me in laughter when the radio suddenly streamed the Beatles' "Here Comes the Sun." "See?" she encouraged. "And speaking of underdogs upsetting the old apple cart, how about Adam Clayton Powell only getting fined by the House of Representatives instead of being expelled?"

"Yeah, Robbie and George were crowing about that too," I shrugged back slowly, "and no doubt it's good to have his solid-brass-ballsy voice sticking up for poor blacks from within the system. If he can keep the inside pressure rising, and the civil rights organizations can keep up the pressure from the outside, we just might get the change we're looking for. Hell, the younger firebrands like Stokely Carmichael, with his Student Nonviolent Coordinating Committee, are scaring the shit out of the white power structure. Did you see what our super compassionate Governor had to say the other day," I posed with thick sarcasm. "The sonofabitch wants a specific law to quote, 'drive the criminal anarchists and latter-day fascists off campus.' Well, Mr. Governor, I've got news: Stokely is so full of hate for what you stand for that sometimes he even scares me, so don't count on SNCC and its allies going away. Not today. Not tomorrow. Not ever, you fucking prick!" spewed the answer to my own question, venom suddenly surfacing from the well-supplied storehouse that Dr. Frankl and I had kept so tightly capped these past two weeks.

"Well," Stella teased. "Tell me, how do you really feel about Mr. Simple-Solution-to-Complex-Problems?"

"Yeahhh, I know ... sorry," I shrugged sheepishly, instantly disarmed and returned to a state of perfect calm.

And even though I remained so when Stella then raised the subject of the Sirhan Sirhan trial having opened with its myriad of surrounding questions, from possible conspiracy to insanity, it reminded me that my nightly date with the advance sheets was waving its red flag in my direction. So, after a brief discussion of the media frenzy surrounding the trial, followed by Stella's suggestion that my impending devotion to duty deserved to be rewarded by our going to see the movie *Oliver* Friday night, I smiled at the happy thought of Charles Dickens put to music as I turned my attention to the latest Supreme Court rulings and began to read. Knowledge is your best friend, was the first lesson that Robbie and George had stressed, and subsequent experience had taught me just how critically important a thorough understanding of the criminal law's complexities could be in the heated combat of the courtroom. Now, more than ever, I realized, our army's success depended on the exercise of our wits and the storehouse of favorable appellate rulings on the intricacies of criminal jurisprudence that we had carefully collected. And focusing on this invaluable tool as I lit up my pipe, I pushed my tired eyes over case after case in search of new weaponry that I could utilize in battle until my eyes turned blurry and bloodshot, and Stella gently advised it was time for sleep.

Sound, restful sleep was not possible however. Following in the footsteps of diminished appetite, fitful slumber had quickly joined the list of unsavory side effects birthed from the extreme pressure produced by the war, and stubbornly resisted all attempts to reform its harmful routine. I had little difficulty in falling asleep, but within a week of the opening battle, remaining in slumberland for more than two to three hours at a time became increasingly problematic. Jarred awake by the anxiety-filled thought that I needed to check my notes on some critical point in a case currently being tried, or from a nightmarish defeat in which my client was being led away in handcuffs while Steiggerman gloated and Shafer snickered, and I was drowning in an ocean of doubt over what more I could have done to prevent it, I would just lie stiffly in place for several seconds until the initial shockwave had passed. Then, realizing what had occurred, I would soothe myself with the thought that it was just Mssrs. Fear and Guilt at work, and that in reality all was okay, confirming it by turning my head sideways and finding Stella close by. For a minute, I would simply listen to her slow, steady breathing, then finally smiling at the thought of how lucky I was, I would try to synchronize my breathing with hers in the hope that the peaceful rhythm would hypnotize me back to sleep.

This strategy bore fruit, but only on about half of the attempts. So, when it didn't succeed, I would then try the ploy of thinking pleasant thoughts. My childhood love affair with tennis was often a starting point, with me embellishing my early status as prodigy all the way to the hallowed lawns of Wimbledon. But when that path didn't lead to drowsiness either, and my treasured memories of going to Hollywood Stars baseball games with Grampy Max also failed, I would then detour to revisiting a favorite movie, or speculate about traveling to an intriguing foreign country that I had read about. And when the latter efforts only served to pull me wider awake, in the lull that followed, shadowy remnants of the original disturbance would inevitably summon my colleagues into mind.

Did any of them suffer from the same malady? I posed on this mid-month Wednesday evening as midnight approached. No answer arrived, of course, but as usual, a smile formed when my next brainwave advised how fortunate I was to have them as friends, leading me to visit them. George, whom I instinctively felt closest to, was as always my first stop, the omnipresent energy sparking a twinkle in his light-blue eyes, the smile warming like it always did when we were chatting personally during lunch, or late in the day when we were the last two to leave. Funny, though, I considered, with all we chat about, and as open as he is, he only talks about his wife in passing—I wonder why? formed another enigma, then floated toward the ceiling.

Hell, Robbie certainly does, finally followed, the internal conversation with myself picking up when several seconds of silence was the only response to the hanging question. He's always kidding about Lou being "The Big Boss," and bobbing his head for emphasis when he extolls her professional nursing skills, or her ability to "cook up the greatest ribs you ever tasted!" the love and respect for her easily discernible in the warmth of his smile and gentle tone of voice. And when he talks about his son Huntley, aka "my heir," I recalled as the latest story about the ten-year-old's "terrorist activities" flashed back into mind, Robbie's pride was so evident that it seemed to add a much-needed pound or two to his razor-thin frame. Lord knows he could use it, escaped a gentle jest as I nestled back against my pillow and reflected on the sweet harmony that memory had projected, admiring yet again how, from such disadvantageous circumstances, Robbie had built a successful career while also helping create a warm and loving family.

And seizing this interim opportunity for a repeat performance, Robbie's depiction of Lou's mouth-watering ribs then snuck back onto center stage to trigger Leon's appearance. For no one I knew loved good food as much as he did, and his own considerable culinary abilities were equally well established throughout the Office, though I had yet to sample his creative endeavors. Classical music was the other passion in his personal life, and I soon pictured him sitting at his piano playing his beloved Mozart, Brahms, or Grieg, before his politics suddenly jumped into view to tickle my funny bone. Oh, yeah—right, I thought, beginning to grin in the darkness, that crazy character is far more likely to be pounding out Chopin's "Revolutionary Etude" with one hand, while raising his wine glass to salute Karl Marx with the other!

Uh-huh, I mouthed with my lips only. And with my grin having widened to full, its magnetic pull, fueled by my desire to revisit more humorous memories, now quickly slid Ron into my mind's eye, the hilarious story about the time his mother showed up at his apartment without warning at nine o'clock on a Sunday morning trailing alongside. Having thoroughly enjoyed a Saturday evening of "hot sex" with a lady he'd met in a bar several hours earlier, and desiring a repeat performance the following morning, Ron had left his phone off the receiver, spun the opening to the ticklish tale. This highly practical, but in retrospect, equally hazardous act, resulted in Momma Marlene not being able to reach her only child. And that worrisome failure, combined with not having heard from him for the prior twenty-four hours, quickly produced the extreme stress that had propelled her to rush over and rescue him from whatever terrible fate had befallen him, only to have a totally naked young woman answer her furious pounding on the door. With "stunned out of her gazoo" serving as Ron's official version of Momma Marlene's reaction, no matter how many times I imagined the oceanic depth of the bewilderment that swept over her sweet face, unmitigated as it was by the nude stranger's English-accented greeting of "Hello, love. Can I help you?" it never failed to evoke a spurt of laughter, which on this latest occasion in mid-January I managed to stifle in honor of Stella. Christ! I cracked silently instead through an ear-to-ear grin, a defense team composed of Clarence Darrow, Louis Nizer, and assorted members of the U.S. Supreme Court couldn't have saved him this time. Not from the felonious charges of negligent failure to keep in touch, intentional infliction of mental distress, and murder of a mother's heart in the first degree! concluded my midnight judgment with a healthy seasoning of sarcasm, a fresh smile forming, then fading when my next brainwave caused me to consider what my own mother's reaction would be to my relationship with Stella, a woman only eight years younger than Mama Rosalie herself. Ohhh, no problem, marched my instant analysis. After she crapped in her pants despite your brilliant, culture-based defense of "But Mom, she is a great cook!" she'd just drop those loaded panties squarely on top of your head, that's all! lambasted my conclusion, my smile returning to its prior panoramic setting.

Lingering on my lips as I again glanced over at Stella, it slowly slipped into a yawn, then disappeared altogether into another longer one when several seconds later I realized that I was ready to attempt sleep once again. And after spying the clock on my nightstand, which was set for six o'clock, I hurried toward the three hours of rest left to me, a quip from a law school friend echoing into ear as I closed my eyes. "Sleep quickly, 'cause we need the pillows," Noel Nefsky had shared with me after a late-night study session had ended. "Right on," I whispered, then fortunately failed to complete the sentence forming on my tongue.

Naturally, tomorrow arrived far faster than full rest required. Somehow, though, when that trusty old alarm clock bugled its call to return to battle, partially refreshed by the salutary effects of the comedic episodes that highlighted last evening's insomnia, then juiced by a large dose of adrenaline, supplemented further by fresh coffee and an encouraging kiss from Stella, I was ready, willing, and able to rejoin my colleagues. And as Thursday slipped into Friday, then joined hands with the next week to steadily tick time within striking distance of the thirtieth day mandated by statute for the dismissal of charges against defendants who were in custody, so too were our adversaries on the move, finally altering course, and in turn not only escalating the war, but accelerating its pace as well. For having by this time reevaluated their initial position in view of the impending avalanche of dismissals, and the fact that the naughty children had not been reformed by being ignored, the judges switched strategies and counterattacked, pulling off their gloves and pursuing a solution to their knotty problem by implementing the bare-knuckles game of politics.

On Friday, January seventeenth, the bell to open Round One rang at noon, when our lunchtime council was interrupted by a surprise visit from Harold Keyes, head of the Long Beach Division to which our Office was nominally attached. Keyes, a medium-sized, sixty-four-year-old veteran who was balding and wore wire-rimmed glasses, appeared most amicable upon his arrival. But after exchanging greetings, and being introduced to me, he quickly dispensed with the small talk and launched directly into the purpose for his visit.

"Fellas, I'm here today," he advised, his tone growing serious, "because it seems like a little problem has developed between our Office and the judges here in Solina. I talked it over with them after they called, and they seem to feel that lately our Office has been totally uncooperative, and engaged solely in making trouble. So, I thought that I'd better drop in on you and see what's been going on."

Silence was the only reaction after Keyes finished letting the black cat out of the bag, an instant vacuum into which tension suddenly swelled while the five of us exchanged glances accompanied by smirky smiles. Finally, after first pulling out a cigarette, lighting up, and exhaling slowly, George calmly explained our position in moderate detail. Not having seen the inside of a courtroom as a trial attorney for over fifteen years, and having functioned as one during a vastly different era of the criminal law from the one in which we practiced, Keyes, like many of the old-line attorneys in the Office who now occupied administrative positions, was almost totally divorced by time and change of circumstance from the realities of today's trial experience. So, while he listened carefully to George's explanation, his background left him incapable of actually understanding it at a gut level, and he therefore returned to the only position he knew and tried to negotiate a compromise.

"Well now, George," he shrugged, smiling to try and hide his discomfort, "I understand what you're saying about the judges being prosecution-minded and not giving our clients a fair shake, and I want you to know that I don't like it any better than you do. However, there must be some way to correct that situation without upsetting the entire court system—right?"

"Well ... maybe," George answered politely, focusing his eyes intently into Keyes'. "Like what?" he posed, his taut facial features testifying fully to his steely determination to continue the plan in progress.

And as George's question floated in the short space between them, matching the weight gain of the ensuing silence as the seconds ticked by, Keyes twisted uncomfortably in his chair as he sought to craft an answer that might actually solve the impasse. Unable to do so by either refuting the legality or the effectiveness of the strategy being employed, and faced with George's unyielding stare, he was finally forced to suggest that having already made our point with the judges and established considerable leverage, we were now in a position to back off and take full advantage of the plea-bargaining process. And when that proposal was rejected after less than five minutes of roundtable discussion, which served only to further illustrate the depth of our combined will to pursue our present course of action, he simply surrendered, having already determined the best way to deal with us and the situation we had created. Just nine months short of retirement, after almost thirty years of service in the Office, Keyes was in no form, shape, or manner looking to get caught in the cross-fire of a serious altercation with the Solina Judiciary, let alone a triangular conflict when the DA's Office was added as a combatant. No, this was a matter for his superiors to handle, he concluded, taking his leave with a smilingly delivered, "Well ... good meeting, guys. Now you take care of yourselves, and be careful with what you're doing."

"Okay. We will," George assured him, the rest of us nodding our agreement. Then, having won Round One on points, over coffee and smokes the air quickly filled with sarcastic gibes as we speculated on just how long it would take for Round Two to begin.

Not long, it turned out. On the following Monday, January twentieth, at five-thirty in the afternoon, a telephone call arrived from Tim Stone, Chief Trial Deputy and second in command of the overall operation of L.A. County's Public Defender's Office. Having just concluded our final status review for the day, we were busily engaged in animatedly bemoaning Nixon and Agnew's inauguration earlier that day when the call came in, and now as George reached for the phone amidst the sudden hush that had fallen, we inched forward onto the edge of our chairs in nervous anticipation of what Stone would have to say.

"Hello, Tim, this is George Meyerstein here. What can I do for you?" George opened confidently, then paused to listen. A growing silence followed as he concentrated intently on Stone's message, at first just nodding his head, then interjecting staccato-paced responses of "Yeah, Tim, uh-huh" or "Well, I see—yes" every so often, until finally after two or three minutes had passed, George began a detailed explanation of the problems we faced in Solina, and the plan we had created to solve them.

When Stone responded by pointing out that even assuming our endeavor had merit, we had nevertheless acted without having cleared it with either Long Beach or headquarters, George quickly replied that we most certainly had intended to get his personal approval, just as soon as we had tested the waters to see if our venture would even float, adding further that our operation had only been in effect for a little over two weeks. Then, he proceeded to emphasize that our plan was fundamentally a defensive reaction to the judges' and DAs' trampling of our clients' basic rights, stressing that nowhere in L.A. County was the criminal justice system more in need of reform than in Solina. And as he pleaded our case, growing steadily more emotional as he focused on our adversaries' commission of "innumerable atrocities" and stopping only when Stone interrupted with a question, I tried to imagine the expression on his long, angular face as he sat listening in his large, sparsely furnished office on the fourth floor of the Hall of Justice some thirty miles away, the fragmented pieces of information about him that I had acquired suddenly collecting into a cohesive form.

Tall and rail thin, Timothy Wilkerson Stone had joined the Office over twenty years ago, and had soon decided to make it his life's work. Armed with a brilliant mind and a highly developed work ethic, he had quickly developed into a first-rate trial attorney. Not satisfied to rest on Base Superior, however, year after year he further improved his performance by unceasingly adding layers of knowledge to his already extensive storehouse and relentlessly refining his technique through analyzing each and every case he tried, win, lose or draw, until his courtroom exploits grew legendary both within the Office as well as with the knowledgeable elements of the criminal bar outside the official family. Appearing fiercely hard-nosed, with his gaunt facial features adding to his intimidating aura, in addition to his considerable abilities he also possessed a dry sense of humor whose active employment had combined with the fearsome fighting spirit that dwelled within to support him through the thousands of cases which fifteen years of warring had seen pass by. Having finally retired from the courtroom five years ago, he had proved to be an equally excellent administrator, and was the odds-on choice to become head of the Office upon Huxton's retirement. Most important, however, for our purposes, was the fact that since his departure from the courtroom, it was reported that he had lost none of the warrior spirit that had characterized his performance in trial. And silently, I prayed that this last representation was true as George concluded their conversation and spun round in his chair to face us.

"Well, you bunch of blockheads," he fired at us, "Stone is with us one hundred percent!" And like a balloon that is suddenly punctured, the thick air of tension that had surrounded us evaporated amidst the exploding clamor of our jubilant shouts. Smiling and shaking his head, when our initial outburst had quieted somewhat, George sobered us up a bit further. "Now hold on a minute," he cautioned, "I said that Stone's for us, and that's true. But he still has to talk it over and clear it with Huxton and the rest of the big muck-a-mucks before he can give us the official blessing—understand?"

"Okay," Ron responded. "But Stone carries a lot of weight with Huxton, 'cause they're buddies and he actually runs the daily operation of the Office—so he should be able to convince him, right?"

"Yeah, most probably," George returned. "But Stone's in a tough place here, because first of all, we didn't give him a heads-up so that he could've laid some groundwork with Huxton. And secondly, that no-good cocksucker, Keyes, called Huxton directly and told him that there is a very serious problem with the Solina Office, because the five of us are, and I quote: 'extremely immature, and have as a result abandoned our proper roles of defending clients in favor of stirring up as much trouble as possible with the judges!' Now, based on that rip-roaring report by Benedict Arnold the Second," George added with sour sarcasm, "Stone's got his work cut out for him. However, he does carry more weight with Huxton than anyone, and is extremely persuasive as we all know, so in the end I think it'll be okay. Meanwhile, we're cleared to continue on course, so let's keep a good thought and keep taking it to the assholes with all we've got!"

By the time George concluded by taking a deep drag on his cigarette, then exhaling slowly, full smiles had returned to all of our faces. Further discussion followed for the better part of an hour, with the five of us finally reaching the conclusion that Round Two also belonged to us on points by virtue of the facts that the counterattack had been blunted, and Stone had become an ally. Still, as we departed for home, doubt rode right alongside our reforged optimism as we warily eyed Round Three.

Neither Tuesday nor Wednesday witnessed the opening bell, with both days passing busily by without word from downtown. As we were later to learn, Huxton was ill with the flu, and Stone had decided to delay approaching him with the delicate situation until his return, preferring to discuss it with him face to face when he was in a good mood, rather than broach it with him over the telephone while he was confined to bed. Also unaware of this development, the judges, watching their already bloated backlog of cases swell further, and having received no return communication from Harold Keyes, were seized by a sense of urgency. Meeting briefly for the second time this testy Thursday, just before the afternoon session commenced, they decided to bypass Keyes and place a call directly to Huxton. The Honorable Arlen James Steiggerman was elected to perform this highly important task, which he did promptly and in accordance with his own inimitable style. Informed that Huxton was ill, he graciously condescended to speak with his assistant, and thereafter, in a voice which reflected his annoyance at having to deal with an underling, he proceeded to inform Timothy Wilkerson Stone of our "totally incompetent and ethically outrageous conduct," then demanded our "immediate removal from the Solina Judicial District!"

And suddenly, with the flash of a hammer, the bell had been rung and Round Three was under way, with our newly minted ally having been unexpectedly summoned into the fray. Momentarily surprised by Steiggerman's arrogantly toned attack, which forced him into a corner, once there, Stone quickly kissed his preference for conferring with Huxton goodbye, then proceeded to remove himself from his uncomfortable position. Which is to say that in a bristling tone of voice he informed His Honor that in his opinion the five of us were "not only outstanding young men, but highly competent attorneys as well!" and that for his further information, "headquarters not only knows about the course of action being employed in Solina, but fully approves and sanctions it!" Then, thanking Steiggerman for his concern, he hung up in his ear before he could respond. And being the thorough individual that he was, Stone immediately placed a call to George, informed him exactly as to what had transpired, and requested that he promptly relay his message to the rest of us so that the judges could not bluff us into retreating from our position. A request that George was only too happy to comply with, he quickly excused himself for five minutes from Division Two where he was just about to resume a drunk driving trial, and dashed up and down the hallways and in and out of the various courtrooms on both floors to update us on the latest occurrence, sharing our absolute delight before returning to his trial with renewed vigor.

George's cross-examination of the arresting officer, however, was further delayed when Judge Austin was summoned to an emergency meeting in Steiggerman's chambers. As after recovering from his shock over Stone having hung up in his judicial ear, Steiggerman had quickly called his brethren together to share the news of the latest outrage by the Public Defender's Office, and inside of two minutes his equally astounded colleagues agreed that their next step was to contact the Judicial Council, the foremost organization of Los Angeles County Judges, and its political voice. A call was placed, and after a ten-minute discussion of the various alternatives open to the judges in the face of our defiantly obstructionist conduct, which the Chairman was astonished to learn was endorsed by the top authorities in the Public Defender's Office, it was decided that the urgency of the situation dictated a direct appeal to the County Board of Supervisors. This was then accomplished the following morning, and proved to be the judges' singularly astute strategic move of the entire altercation thus far.

For with January's calendar having now ticked to the twenty-eighth, and ever closer to the thirty-day mandate, when Huxton returned to his domain the following Tuesday, he found that it had become the center of a political storm that threatened to escalate into a full-fledged hurricane. On his desk were messages from the Judicial Council, the County Board of Supervisors, and the Mayor's Office, and for good measure, several requests for interviews from the media, both newspapers and television. Hastily convening a meeting of the entire upper echelon of his Office, he turned the chairmanship over to Stone because he alone seemed to have a complete understanding of what was occurring in Solina, and still retained Huxton's full trust despite having made a policy decision that engendered the current crisis. Beginning slowly, within ten minutes Stone had outlined in detail the sordid history of abuse that had led to the confrontation between our Office and the judges, and after another ten minutes of preliminary discussion, the small audience of ten divided evenly into two groups, one in favor of supporting the stance we had taken and one against.

This division, however, did not center on contrasting legal philosophies, but was instead created by the real-world dilemma dictated by competing interests. For everyone present articulated their firm belief that the five of us were morally right, as well as duty bound, to resist the trampling of our clients' constitutional rights, and had proceeded in a totally legal fashion in seeking to right the wrongs we observed and establish a fundamentally fair playing field. However, as Ellis Fielding, Supervisor of the Special Trials Division, argued strenuously, the potential cost of supporting this highly principled stance, being employed in such a revolutionary fashion, was simply too expensive. Yearly, he noted, each of the various departments comprising the L.A. County governmental structure filed with the County Board of Supervisors its proposed budget and request for funds with which to operate during the following year. And at present, he stressed, our Office's pending request sought not only a ten-percent increase in salaries, but further, the allotment of twenty-five additional attorney positions. This additional staff, Fielding contended, was essential to the Office's ability to continue providing top-grade representation in the face of an ever-increasing caseload. "Now, as we all know," he stated firmly, shaking his head to underscore his point, "unfortunately our Office is viewed primarily as an extension of the seamier side of society which we serve, and is not exactly beloved by the Supervisors to begin with. So if we really piss them off," he concluded bluntly, "they'll not only reject our present request, but will likely seize the opportunity to reduce the number of attorney positions already allocated—particularly if they side with the Judicial Council's view that these positions were being occupied by radicals whose sole purpose was the obstruction of the entire judicial process!"

Stone didn't respond until the head-nodding murmurs of agreement with Fielding's position had subsided. Then, after making it perfectly clear that he fully appreciated the need for the additional twenty-five attorneys, and thanking Fielding for pinpointing the importance of providing top-grade representation, he then cleverly countered by arguing that the very best way we could accomplish this goal was to establish beyond any doubt that our Office was totally independent from the other branches of the County government. Emphasizing emphatically that the most difficult daily problem every one of our deputies faced was obtaining the trust and confidence of our clients so as to gain their full cooperation, a heavy burden that was created and nourished by the widespread knowledge that our Office was funded from the exact same source as the DA's Office and the Judiciary, thereby fostering the image that we were "just a cog in the system," Stone then forcefully opined that "nothing, absolutely nothing, was more critical than maintaining that independence, and clearly displaying it for the whole world to see! I understand fully the risk involved," he argued, emotion crowding into his voice, "but it's totally worth taking when matched against surrendering the freedom to perform our jobs in accordance with the oath we have taken! Moreover, as far as practicality is concerned, let's not forget that the media has already gotten hold of this power-play attempt to blackmail us into submission," he tacked on with cold anger surfacing. "So if our Office backs down in the face of economic pressure, especially when our deputies in Solina have done absolutely nothing wrong, then what little credibility we *do* have with our clients will be totally destroyed! And how the hell do you provide top-grade representation then?" he posed, issuing a challenge and swiveling his head to make eye contact with everyone seated at the conference table.

The air in the conference room had grown humid from escaping fumes of fear and frustration, Stone's echoing question hanging heavily in the sweaty atmosphere, then swinging slowly back and forth from its overhead perch during the hour of roundtable discussion that followed, like a lead weight attached to a metronome that increased and decreased both its speed and volume as arguments heated, then cooled, then repeated and repeated and repeated yet again. In the end, Stone prevailed, his reputation for unimpeachable integrity and time-tested judgment finally swaying seven of the senior deputies to support our stand, with all in agreement to unite firmly behind Huxton regardless of which choice he ultimately exercised. So, now, the entire matter rested with the "man in charge," as Stone so informed George around five-thirty that evening. And reporting these latest political developments to us a half hour later during our regular post-court status session,

George completed his review by reiterating Stone's anxiety-producing conclusion that Huxton had elected not to make a decision until he had time to "carefully think things through."

"How long do you think it'll take him, Georgie?" I asked after the chorus of groans had faded away.

"Well, if I know Huxton, it won't be long."

"Any ideas on which way he's likely to go?"

"Yeah, but I can't be really sure," he shrugged in response to my follow-up. "Huxton's attitude is generally just like Stone's, that's why he relies on him so much. But on the other hand, he's much more of a politician than Tim is—and before anyone here gets bent out of shape about that, let me tell you that he's had to be. No one in our Office has ever fought harder for his clients than Hux did, he's always been the exact opposite of a cop-out artist. And when he was still trying cases, they used to assign him only the toughest ones, the cases nobody else wanted to touch, and he tried them one after the other. That's how his drinking problem started," George tacked on before pausing to sip at his coffee, grimacing, then smiling wryly at its cold, sour taste.

Marilyn jumped up to get him a fresh cup, and after he ran his tongue around his mouth to banish the bad taste, he continued.

"Anyway, since Hux took over as the head honcho about seven or eight years ago, he's busted his ass to make our Office what it is today—which is light years better than what it was when he took over. Let me tell you something, it's not easy getting those asshole Supervisors to give us additional attorney-slots, let alone for investigators and secretaries. It's a piece of cake for the DA, all right, but old Hux has had to fight with the Supervisors year after year to get what we need, and most of the time he's gotten it by somehow pushing the right buttons at the right time. And you know what he got for his trouble? Well, the Supervisors haven't raised his salary in five years, while they've raised the DA's twice, leaving Hux with ten grand a year less than that prick Oulder. Nice, huh?" he posed rhetorically, pausing again to sip at his coffee, then cast an appreciative smile at Marilyn.

"Anyway, to sum it up," he added after lighting up a fresh Marlboro, "Hux will do what he feels is best for the overall Office. I'm sure he sympathizes with what we're trying to accomplish, and Stone's opinion definitely counts for plenty with him, but in the end, he's the one who's responsible for shepherding the overall operation—and we gotta remember too, that we didn't exactly ask him for permission to pull off this little war of ours. So we're just going to have to hang in there and keep taking it to the enemy, while trusting that Hux will decide that the huge risk is worth taking—Okay?"

Nodding our assent in conjunction with our collective "Sure," we then began packing our briefbags as we made ready to depart for home. George's quasi assurances regarding Huxton had dropped the tension's temperature, but only a degree or two. And having risen steadily since it was born right alongside the Grand Plan in mid-December, then climbed up January's spine like English ivy twisting up a tree, it had thickened to a choking point, the continuous gnawing strain of sparring with the judges and trying cases in an atmosphere of palpable hostility combining with the yo-yo–like sequence of events the past several days to spark intense frustration into an angry outburst between Ron and Leon in the parking lot. Robbie had already taken off due to the need to entertain a visiting relative, and while waiting for George to finish the last telephone call of the day, Ron was once again bemoaning the uncertainty of our situation. When Leon then commiserated with a bitterly toned, "God damn all of the politicians straight to hell!" Ron's jocularly intended reply of "What? Our resident commie pinko has asked God to help us? What would Marx say?" was misinterpreted, and in a flash a war of barbs commenced that lasted long enough for each of them to storm away with hurt feelings.

George emerged just as their taillights faded from view, and after I explained, just shook his head while pulling out a cigarette. I lit up my pipe, and for the next five minutes, we chatted and joked as best we could about the stifling pressure, successfully easing it for the moment. When our swirling thoughts inevitably led us back to the sixty-four-dollar question, George confided that while his brain told him that Huxton's decision could go either way, his heart said that he'd end up supporting us. "And God, do I ever hope so," George nodded out as we finally pulled our car doors open, "'cause we're so close to winning, so fucking close I can taste it."

"Well … let us pray," I shrugged back at him. "'Cause you know what they say about the Lord working in mysterious ways, right?" I added with teasing optimism as we climbed inside our cars and turned on the engines.

"Yeahhh, right … and amen!" George returned through the open window, smiling and nodding his head before turning away and leading our tandem toward the street.

Uttered casually, with a vein of humor, but also containing grains of serious hope, my off-hand reference to God's labors soon tripped a wire inside a different chamber of my mind to snake forth a different perspective. For if the Lord does work in mysterious ways as the poets and prophets teach, a few hours later that same evening, I bore witness to the fact that so too does his jealous adversary. Indeed, as after I had shared a delicious dinner with Stella, followed by comforting conversation and another sublime session of lovemaking, a few minutes after midnight the Devil sucked the nightmare from hell out of my subconscious to frighten me awake groaning in pain. Later, I would view the incident as a further outburst from the same perforated valve that had unleashed the sulfuric steam between Leon and Ron. At that moment, however, I just bolted upright and for several seconds tried to shield myself from the bruising blows raining upon my body. Then, realizing that it was only a horrific dream, I just sat there shaking until I recognized Stella's voice as she reached for me. "It's okay, Matty," she soothed after flicking on the lamp, then pulling me into her arms and holding me fast. "Just a bad dream, that's all. You're fine, sweetie ... just relax."

A full sixty seconds slowly ticked by before I finally did, nodding my head slightly in acknowledgment after the trembling stopped, then sliding out, "Boy, that was a bad one," as I gently slipped out of Stella's comforting hold and withdrew a short distance away so that I could see her face.

"Yeah, for sure," she agreed, her eyes brimming with concern.

"I thought I had that fucker beat, but guess again, huh?"

"You've had it before?"

"Ohhh, yeah ... but not for a long time, must be that the build-up of pressure set it off. Sorry to scare you so."

"Don't worry about that. You want to tell me about it?" she asked, the concern in her eyes drifting into her tone. "I think it would help," she added when I was slow to respond, fragments of thoughts spinning round inside my brain.

"All right," I finally nodded out. "I've never told anyone about it before, but all right, Stelle ... all right," I acquiesced, my mind's eye now returning to the lush green grass of my grandparents' backyard on a sunny, blue-skied afternoon almost seventeen years ago, a picture I shared with her as the story opened. "It was a Sunday, and I was playing by myself, near the avocado tree I've told you about," continued my explanation slowly.

"Uh-huh, I remember."

"And my sister Karen came outside and wanted me to walk her to the drugstore. I didn't feel like it, because the drugstore was several blocks away and I wanted to watch a baseball game on TV with Grampy Max that started in about ten minutes or so. I told her this, but she didn't care and began to whine and carry on—and when I promised to take her later, it only got worse, she went into a full-fledged tantrum, jumping up and down like a jumping jack and screaming, 'Now, now, I want to go now!'" spun memory's recording through a forming frown to match yesteryear's. "I tried walking away from her, but she just followed, yelling and taunting me. I should've just climbed up to the top of the tree like I always did when something was bothering me, for years I've wondered why I didn't. But for some strange reason I stayed put, and next thing I know she pushed me, and when I dodged her next attempt, she picked up a small wooden block that belonged to my younger sister Kay—you know, the kind that little kids play with?"

"Uh-huh, sure," Stella nodded.

"Well, she threw it at me and hit me in the chest, then started running for my grandparents' back door when I picked it up and she figured that I was going to throw it back at her. Running fast, while trying to look for the block so that she could duck, she misjudged her turn when she reached the steps and ran into the metal railing and hurt herself. Then, screaming and crying as if she'd been killed, she hurried on inside."

"Did you ever throw the block?" spurted Stella spontaneously.

"No, that's what's so unfair," I said sadly, shaking my head slowly, "I was still holding it in my hand when my father came racing out the door and down the steps a minute or so later. I guess she told him I'd hit her with it, because I never saw him so mad, and later on I saw a black-and-blue mark over her left eye from where she bumped her head on the railing."

"I see. So what happened next?" Stella prodded when my pause lengthened as I scrutinized the slow-motion replay.

"Well, I took one look at that angry face as he came running at me, and started to run myself. I was always a fast runner, and dodged all over the place, so he couldn't catch me in the backyard. In fact, he never did really catch me, 'cause eventually I ran inside our house, then all the way through it and upstairs and down the hallway into the bathroom, where I closed the door and locked myself in. When he finally got there, madder than ever now because he couldn't catch me, he started pounding on the door and yelling loudly at me to open up. I didn't know what to do, Stelle, I was so frightened—I was scared I'd get killed if I opened it, and even more afraid of what would happen if I didn't and he broke it down!" I related, emotion beginning to creep inside my tone.

"I'll bet," she commiserated. "So did he finally stop?" she nudged again when I paused to focus on the small boy huddled behind the bathroom door.

"Ohhh, no, not him. He just kept pounding and yelling, so finally I opened up, and for a split-second tried to explain that I hadn't done anything wrong. I say a split-second, because he started hitting me almost immediately, and when he did I fell down and couldn't talk anymore because I was too busy trying to block his slaps with my arms and protect my face and head. My mother had arrived on the scene, and I could hear her shouts to me asking if I was okay and telling him to stop, but just barely because as he kept pounding on me he was also yelling that I was getting what I deserved for hurting my sister, and this would teach me never to do it again!" I streamed, my tone hardening. "And if I live to be a thousand years old, Stelle, I'll never ever forget his face—it was all twisted up, and red and purple from anger, and his eyes had this wild look in them as he kept yelling and hitting, then yelling and hitting some more!" I growled, then paused as I watched him finally stop on my mind's screen, then turn and leave.

"Eventually, he wore himself out and went downstairs," I then picked up in a softer, sadder tone. "And after a few seconds, I just slid over into the corner next to the bathtub and began to cry. My mom helped me to my bedroom and tried to comfort me, but it didn't do much good. I just lay there on my bed and cried. Then, when the shock of what had happened wore off, I began to ache all over, and I cried some more," I ended, tears suddenly welling up in my eyes, Stella then slipping her hand over mine and gently squeezing.

"How old were you when this happened?" she asked sadly.

"Ten."

"Ohhh, God!" she groaned, disgust now coating the sadness still centering her tone. "Did you ever get to explain to him what really happened?"

"No ... I've never discussed it with him to this day. All I could think of afterward was that he hadn't even given me a chance to explain."

"And he never said anything about it to you?"

"No ... never. But I think he learned the truth and was ashamed. I did explain to Mom, and she probably told him, because later that day when Karen asked him to take her to the drugstore, he sent her to her room. Also, the next day when he saw me, he tried not to notice the bruises on my face and arms."

"Yeah, I'd have tried not to notice too if I were him," Stella offered, cold anger hardening her tone. "Did you get beaten like that often?"

"Unh-uh ... that's what's so odd about the whole thing ... 'cause that's the only spanking I ever got in my whole life," shuffled my reply, my brain wrestling with the anomaly for the umpteenth time. "I don't know, but maybe that's what makes it stand out so much in my mind, and what keeps it coming back. But you know what, Stelle? What I really and truly remember are those awful, ugly names he called me while the pounding was going on, names like *stupid* and *selfish little shit-ass*. That old line about sticks and stones will break my bones, but names will never hurt me, is bullshit!" I hissed, my submerged anger waking up. "'Cause bruises heal, and the mind can't really re-create physical pain. But the hurt from cruel words, thrown at you hatefully by someone important in your life, never ever fully heals! And to make matters worse, that time was just the beginning, 'cause old reliable Dad, Mr. Consistency himself, never missed an opportunity all the years I was growing up to make me feel small and inferior, or weak and helpless! ... And all, just because I'm not like him," I concluded, my sudden flash of anger tailing back into a sad sigh of resignation.

"You want to know what I think?" Stella shot back, a sweet smile forming underneath the tears in her eyes. "I think that the very second that beating occurred without any chance to explain, a defense attorney was born. And not just any kind of defense attorney, but a special type, a Public Defender," she streamed, swiping at her tears, her smile widening. "I think you're familiar with the type, they're the ones that fight with all their heart, and all their smarts, to make sure that no one gets punished without getting to tell his side of the story."

"Uh-huh, I hear you," I tossed back at her. "So what you're saying is that me and my clients are actually indebted to my father—right?"

"Noo ... not exactly," she returned, chuckling with relief that my tease showed I was me again. "That sick fucker should first go pull his head out of his asshole!" she then unloaded, her smile remaining in place, but her tone switching from sugar to acid in a nanosecond. "Then, he should go find a really good battery of psychiatrists to try and fix his outer-space size insecurity problem!"

"Hmmm," I chuckled. "To quote a wise woman I'm sorta close with, 'How do you really feel about the Popster?'"

"I think I've summed up the prick pretty good," marched her reply confidently. "But what do you mean, sorta close with?"

"Well, you've certainly been very nice and understanding about my little problem here, and the hug and the hand-pats were definitely most appreciated and all ... But do you realize that this recently traumatized soul sitting before you is kiss starved?"

"Ohh, is that right?" Stella murmured, leaning forward to gently push me back against the pillows. "Well, luckily I can fix that," she whispered as she drew close, her eyes still searching my face to make sure that all was well.

And fix the alleged hunger, she did. Sweetly and profusely. A minute later, cozied up next to another, we chatted aimlessly in soft tones about movies that we wanted to see but hadn't gotten to yet. At the top of Stella's wish-list were *Romeo and Juliet* and *Yellow Submarine*, while my picks were *Bullitt* and *The Green Berets*. When I jokingly suggested that *War and Peace* might be the perfect compromise, she countered with the proposition that plea-bargaining movie selections proved beyond a reasonable doubt that I seriously needed sleep. And though it seemed to me that the odds of transforming this attractive possibility into actual reality were next to zero, with the Devil momentarily defeated, God was back in charge, and exhausted from my early-hour excursion back into boyhood, I returned to slumber the instant after I honored my promise to close my eyes.

XVII

THE FOLLOWING MORNING, DR. VIKTOR Frankl suddenly appeared as a surprise guest during the journey to Solina. "Hi, Vic! Nice to see you!" I chirped as Old Greener pulled away from the curb, beaming my brightest smile at his shadowy image to try to cover up the guilt from my perceived failure to have staved off the accumulated pressure in view of last evening's horror show. He returned my smile, though without the same enthusiasm, then tilted his head as if to ask, "How're you doing, my troubled friend?" "Well, not so good to tell the truth," I confessed. "Sorry, buddy ... I know I can't control Hux's decision, that I can only control my reaction to it," squeezed out my self-indictment, as I snuck a sideward glance to confirm that he was listening. He was, and I also detected a tinge of disappointment in his slightly furrowed forehead. "But see? I really do understand," began my apologetic defense. "It's just that sometimes, it's difficult to actually apply the lesson—damned difficult in fact! I mean, trial's tough enough, without all this political crap adding to the pressure cooker!" squirmed my all-too-human attempt to excuse weakness. Once again, he didn't say a word. He didn't have to, his steady gaze, silently spelling out "Difficult? Compared to Auschwitz?" was all that was necessary. "Okay ... I get the message. I'll try harder ... much harder," I promised, then placed myself on probation after his smile widened in agreement. "All right, then, thanks for not being too hard on me. Now, how about we share a little music before we head back into battle?" I chuckled, feeling a little better and switching on the radio.

Wednesday and Thursday proved to be interminably long, the silence from downtown adding weight as each hour dragged slowly into its successor, testing fully my recently reinforced vow, as well as my colleagues' already depleted storehouse of patience. True, Round Three had ended in a draw, we concluded as we returned to trial, for even though the judges' vigorous counterattack had placed us in a highly precarious position, still, we weren't without allies at headquarters, and for the time being the Grand Plan was still in operation, with each creeping hour bringing us one tiny step closer to the hallowed thirtieth day mandated for the dismissal of cases now numbering in the several hundreds. On the other hand, though, based on the judges' unruffled countenance, an impartial observer would have been hard pushed to conceive that we were still ahead on points, and that they were counting on a knockout to extricate themselves from this horrific outcome. No, to the contrary, as we labored unceasingly to further backlog their calendars, their Honors' supreme confidence that our annihilation would occur at any moment led them to posture a collective facial expression that smiled: "Enjoy yourselves, little boys, 'cause you're about to be booted the hell out of here!" And responding to their cock-sure grins by maintaining our own uniform facade of tranquility while we continued to try our cases, inwardly we worried as the silence grew deafening and we waited seemingly forever.

Fortunately, though, forever is a highly relative measure of time, and eternity mercifully short-circuited to Friday at twelve-fifteen, when Marilyn shouted out excitedly, "Guys, Mr. Huxton himself is on the phone!" In an eye blink the atmosphere turned electric from our instantaneous outpouring of nervous energy as George slowly picked up his receiver and was warmly greeted, then informed that Stone was also on the line, which led to a request for each of us to also join the conversation. Scrambling for our phones like a pack of starving wolves that suddenly happened across a hobbled prey, one by one we checked in, then listened for a very long moment to the silence at the other end. Finally, after chuckling over our breathless, tension-toned greetings, Hux rendered his verdict.

"Listen to me now, you hellions," he began, the laughter in his voice fading to serious, "You've placed me and the entire Office in one hell of a ticklish position, and that's putting it mildly! However, after thinking it over, I'm going to go along with you, as long as you understand fully the tremendous responsibility you're carrying! Now—"

Despite the fact that the conscious chamber of our minds remained aware that Huxton was still speaking, the subconscious division instinctively pushed the override button and sparked a flash fire of cheers loud enough to jar our clients waiting in the outer office from their lethargic reading of old magazines. For in a nanosecond, Hux's "I'm going to go along with you" had washed away the numbing anxiety that had shadowed us for the past ten days in a sudden flood of joyous relief that simply exploded outward. The clamor ended, however, almost as quickly as it began, when George, having excused himself for a moment, rushed up and down the hallway screaming, "Shut up, you bunch of idiots, Huxton still has something to say!" And quieted by this salient fact, which now fully registered, after we returned to our phones and meekly apologized, Hux instantly sobered us up further.

"Stone told me that I was being represented by a bunch of crazy people," he chastised, "but I didn't think he meant it literally! Now you fellows get a hold of yourselves, and quickly, because I want you to understand me one hundred percent. Are you lunatics listening to me?"

Our affirmative assurances, delivered in totally serious tones, arrived promptly, and after the final echo died away, Hux reengaged. "All right, now," he picked up, his tone softening slightly. "As I was saying, I believe wholeheartedly in what you fellows are trying to accomplish, and I'm prepared to back you all the way. That said, however, I want you to also know that our Office stands to lose a great deal over this altercation, so I'm not handing you a blank check. What you're getting is my complete approval and full support of your basic position, as long as you pursue your objective by the perfectly legal means that you've been employing, and as long as you keep me regularly informed of all developments. Now, do each and every one of you understand me exactly?" he ended, his question flowing to us with palpable force.

Once again Hux received a chiming chorus of "Absolutely!" And when he continued, his tone was now noticeably softer. "Fellas," he picked up more slowly. "Before I turn you over to Tim, who wants to talk things over with you, let me say one more thing. What you're trying to achieve is wonderful, and what you're going through to try and accomplish it takes a lot of guts. So hang in there, and nail those bastards' asses to the hardest cross you can find—and drive a nail or two home for me too, okay?"

"You got it!" George assured, accompanied by our enthusiastically rendered refrain of "Right on!" And smiling in agreement, Tim Stone waited patiently until the echo had totally faded away. Then, after greeting us most amicably, he advised that he really had nothing further to discuss at this time, but wanted instead to inquire as to how in God's name we had managed to obtain such highly favorable and incredibly timely newspaper publicity. When we responded by asking him what in the world he was referring to, he burst out laughing, then suggested that we immediately lay our hands on a copy of Solina's morning newspaper. Which, after signing off, we instantly hastened to do, "forthwith," as General George commanded through a grin forced wide by optimistic curiosity.

Jumping up from our desks, we raced out the back door, across our parking lot, and up to the automated dispenser on the corner, where Robbie then placed a single dime in the designated slot, and five rapacious hands then plunged inside to withdraw copies of the *Solina Bugle*. Eagerly scanning the front page, we didn't have to search long to discover what Stone had alluded to. For directly beneath the headline, just to the right of center, in large, black, capital letters only slightly smaller, appeared the magical words: "PUBLIC DEFENDER'S OFFICE TAKES HARD STAND!" And just below those sweet drops of pure sugar, separated by a thin line, they were complemented by: "PUBLIC SUPPORT URGED AGAINST ANGERED JUDICIARY!"

There followed an article authored by Martin Sills, the owner and editor of the *Bugle*, and, as I later learned, the most respected member of Solina's black community as well as those of her neighboring sister cities. Referring to each of us individually by name, and collectively as "The Solina Five," Sills first set forth in vivid detail the long history of abuses that instigated our altercation with the "dictatorial judiciary," as he referred to the judges. Then, after adding the seamy particulars that provoked the subsidiary fracas with the DA's Office, which he characterized as "an only too willing tool" of the all-encompassing white superstructure, he vehemently argued that this "Caucasian Establishment" had carefully conceived and cleverly implemented a widespread conspiracy to insure that Solina's black population would remain glued to the bottom rung of society's ladder, socially, economically, and legally.

Noting that this conspiracy had achieved its greatest success within the closed confines of the judicial system, where blacks had not only been subtly and systematically denied their constitutional rights and an application of the criminal judicial system consistent with the American concept of justice, but had been in addition been robbed of their human dignity, with equal candor and clarity, Sills pointed out that the Public Defender's Office had historically been part and parcel of this tragic travesty, spelling out in precise detail "the collusive effect of the plea-bargaining process," and our deputies' "surrender of effective representation to expediency!" "BUT, HOWEVER," he then argued strenuously in capital letters, "the five, fine young men, and their secretary, who currently staff the PD Office are a different breed altogether!" Noting that he had personally observed our conduct over a five-month period, both inside and outside the courtroom, he labeled us as "courteous, caring, human beings, as well as highly competent and extremely hard-working attorneys who consistently busted their backsides on behalf of their clients!" Then following up on the latter point, he stressed that precisely because of our steadfast commitment to our clients, we were not only subjected to a relentless stream of venomous denigration by "a group of men who purported to be judges, but were in fact nothing more than prejudice's henchmen!" And concluding his article by indicating that we were "risking highly promising careers by refusing to surrender and comply with the judges' wishes," after emphasizing that "reliable sources" had revealed that their Honors had appealed to the County Board of Supervisors to force our removal, he then passionately urged every member of his audience, both black and white alike, to telephone their representatives on the Board, and further, to send telegrams addressed to the entire agency that not only demanded our retention, but in addition, requested that a formal commendation be issued for our courageous efforts to bring true representation and justice to the Solina Judicial District!

Like a warm hug, silence surrounded us when Robbie stopped reading aloud. For words alone simply couldn't describe the kaleidoscopic mixture of emotions that swirled and churned through each of us as Sills' message fully registered, and the five of us stood mute on that dusty, paper-and-glass–littered corner smiling at one another while tears formed in the corners of our eyes. Finally, after a reflective minute had ticked by, I caught George's eye, and chuckled, "See, He really does work in mysterious ways, huh?"

"Ohhh, yeah, for sure," George muttered in return, still stunned by the turn of events. A condition that continued to linger in all of us, even after the surprise finally dissipated and we celebrated with a round of jubilant shouts, handshakes, and hugs, it was a humble group of young men, who, prouder and more grateful than they had ever been in their entire lives, returned to battle that afternoon.

Around six o'clock, when we had all returned to the office and huddled together over coffee to relive every detail of what had turned out to be a truly momentous day, a second sweet surprise occurred when a tall, slender, well-dressed man wearing a shy smile on his handsome face entered and introduced himself as Marty Sills. To say that he received a warm welcome would challenge the world record for understatement, our exuberant greetings coming close to overwhelming him. Smiling broadly and shaking his head in return, after he settled into Robbie's chair, the only one which contained a cushion, and which was thrust at him along with five outstretched hands, he firmly shook each one, then readily accepted Marilyn's offer of coffee. "With a touch of cream and sugar, please," he added, his smile widening again, his voice containing a melodic quality that made one want to hear more from him. "So, how are you gentlemen this afternoon?" he obliged, his grin widening even further.

"Splendid, thanks to you and your stupendous newspaper!" George answered for all of us.

"Ahhh, yes, gentlemen, the wonder of the press," he hummed. "I take it you've read my little article."

"Little article, hell. Why you fired a cannon right up the judges' assholes, if you'll pardon the expression," bounced George's editorial.

"No pardon necessary, Brother George. I simply told the truth, as one old man sees it, and I'm very pleased if it helped."

"Helped? ... Oh, you just better believe it did! It swayed the head man downtown to let us keep fighting the pigs across the street."

"Yes ... I know. Mr. Huxton was nice enough to call me around noon to thank me."

"Well, I'll be goddamned!" George shot out in surprise. "Is there anything else you'd like to let us in on, Marty?" he tacked on, matching his grin.

"Well, just this," he replied, relighting his pipe before continuing. "I've seen with my own eyes what you fellas are trying to bring to Solina, and I want you to know that both me and my newspaper are with you for the long haul—come hell or high water, as the old saying goes from a time before you were even born. Now, I've got a few connections downtown at City Hall, and I intend to keep on top of the situation and use whatever influence me and my newspaper have to support your efforts. So you just hang in there, as your generation says, and together we'll make life mighty interesting for those pigs across the street as you call them, and all the rest like them too."

Heads bobbed up and down emphatically when George interjected a short but sharply toned, "You can bet on it, Marty," and Robbie tacked on the exclamation point by adding, "And you can risk the whole house, too."

"Good, I'm glad for our mutual understanding. And while I'd love to stay and chat some more, I have a previously scheduled appointment that I'm a little late for, but I just had to drop by and let you know that you're not totally alone in this fight. I'll come back soon for a longer talk. And meanwhile you keep up the good work, and I'll be in touch."

Rising to his feet as he finished explaining his need to depart, Marty paused long enough to accept a handshake and warm-hearted "thank you!" from each of us before striding briskly out of the office. Still under the influence of the ebullient energy flowing from the day's cup of good fortune, the five of us, not wishing to let go, remained together for another half hour or so, sharing, then further evaluating the miraculous events that had transpired. And it was then that objectivity slowly but surely crept back into our collective consciousness and tempered our euphoria. For even though Huxton's vital support and the surprise acquisition of a powerful newspaper ally retained their wondrous halo of hope, having settled into mind and been fully digested during the long afternoon, the explosive surges of emotion that had accompanied them recessed, leaving us drained and pensive. And in the quieted-down, soberly reflective atmosphere that now governed, our close examination also revealed that these positives had resulted from a diverse set of actions and reactions that were both intentional and accidental, a discovery that soon birthed a strain of bemused bewilderment when we then stepped back and observed through a wide-angle lens the patchwork battlefield upon which our war was now being waged. True, we acknowledged gratefully, faith in the possibility of final triumph still occupied center stage, standing tall and shining brightly. But equally true, we realized, was the fact that just outside the spotlight, lurking in the shadows, the Board of Supervisors still huddled, posing questions that only the foggy future could answer.

Finally, weary from trial and taxed further into exhaustion by the afternoon's mental and emotional gymnastics, we concluded our discussion a few minutes after seven and trooped outside together, where Ron sounded one final note to finish the day's Rock-and-Roll Symphony in A-Plus Minor. "Hey, guys," he quipped cheerfully as he climbed into his car. "However this ends, isn't it nice not to be alone anymore?" His answer arrived in the form of tired smiles from slowly nodding heads. But after I turned on Old Greener and followed the caravan out of the lot, I added a firm, "Yeah, for sure," then winked at Dr. Frankl, who had reenlisted for the long trek home. The friendliness emanating from the smile in his eyes indicated that he approved of how we had reacted to the day's promising developments, and was optimistic about the future so long as we remained confident but not cocky, and refused to lose sight of what we could and could not control. O-kay ... no problem, I sighed silently. Now how about some more music, maybe even something more to your taste, like some Chopin or Tchaikovsky? "After all, it has been a classical day," finished my thought out loud, its warm afterglow banishing the chill from the night air.

As usual, Stella was waiting for me when I reached the apartment, and I hugged her so tightly that she laughingly cried out, "What is it, Matty? What?"

"Well, I'll tell you—but no, I've got a better idea," I bounced back at her, opening my briefbag, then pulling out my copy of the *Bugle*. "Here, just read this while I make the drinks for a change," I urged through a growing grin.

Mixing our gin and tonics extra carefully while I watched her face mirror the various emotions that Sills' commentary evoked, when her smile had grown full, I returned wearing a wide one myself. "What do you think, Stelle?"

"God, it's wonderful!" she enthused.

"Yeahhh ... and then some!"

"Does downtown know about it?"

"Uh-huh. It was the tipping point for Huxton and Company to give us the go-ahead at lunchtime."

"They did? For sure?"

"Yeah, absolutely."

"Well, then, how come I had to wait almost nine hours later to find out about it? Like who am I, Miss Nobody?" she asked, her tone teasing, but tinged with hurt.

"Ohh, God, I'm sorry!" I groaned, setting down the drinks. "But first Hux called, then we went racing up to the corner to get a copy and read it, and then we were due back in court, and then Sills dropped by—and in between all the commotion, I fucking-A just forgot to call. I'm really—"

"Good defense—fast, and believable. And you know what?" she spewed. "It's a damn good thing you can read those judges and juries better than you can read me, 'cause I was just kidding. I know you're swamped, it's all right," she assured, her smile flushing back across her face.

"Hey, listen," I countered, dropping down next to her on the living room couch, "first of all, you're my partner, and it won't happen again, I promise. And secondly, I know you better than you think. So if I did overreact a bit, it's just that your friend Dr. Frankl is still working on my little insecurity problem, and your buddy Mr. Rilke warned me to never get cocky and take you for granted—which I don't, 'cause you're so beautiful and wonderful. Hell, even Vic gives me credit for that, he's just trying to solve the million or so other little problems I have, like not being able to sleep and having nightmares strong enough to blow the asshole out of a large bull, and—"

"You're silly, you know that?" she interrupted, then leaned forward and kissed me.

"Yeah, I know" eased out my admission when we separated several seconds later. "So what are you going to do with me?"

"Well, for one thing, I'm going to finish cooking your dinner—you look thinner than ever despite the efforts I make to get food down you," she answered with exaggerated concern, then paused for a fleeting instant as her smile passed to her eyes and twinkled mischievously out at me. "Then, well ... maybe we'll see if you're really as fond of your pretty lady as you say you are."

"Sounds perfectly wonderful," I grinned back at her as she rose from the couch and headed for the kitchen. Halfway there, she stopped and turned around.

"Matthew?" she floated out, then paused till I lifted my eyes from the *SI* I'd picked up. "I really am very proud of you, so don't forget," she added sweetly, then turned and disappeared into the kitchen before her kind words fully settled into mind. God, please don't let this day end, I thought, leaning back against the cushions, and contentedly sipped at my drink while resuming my reading until she called me to the table several minutes later.

The Swiss steak we enjoyed was even more delicious than usual, complemented as it was by the day's spectacularly good news and the fact that I hadn't eaten a full meal since last evening's dinner. "My God, Stelle, but you're a great cook!" I shot across the table at her, dipping another piece in the wine sauce, then plopping it into my mouth and hurriedly following it with a forkful of rice.

"Yeah? ... Well if my food's so great and all, how come you're so skinny?" she teased in return, obviously pleased over my enjoyment.

"Skinny? ... Who, me?" I bounced jovially back, cramming in another mouthful.

"I'm not talking about your friend Steiggerman."

"Hey, listen, Madam Prosecutor, you look a little thin yourself—you know that?"

"Don't try to switch subjects on me, Matthew Robert Harris, I won't let you get away with it, and you know it."

I started to chuckle and form some witty reply, but ended up instead with a weak smile when I suddenly realized that she really did look thinner, and slightly pale too. "I wasn't trying to, honestly, hon. You do look a little thin to me, are you feeling okay?"

"I feel just fine, Matty—just fine," she assured, feigning mild irritation. "If I've dropped a pound or two, it's from worrying about you, so enough of this nonsense. Tell me all about what happened today, okay?"

"Okay ... all right," I acquiesced, letting go of my brief concern and launching into a detailed summary.

Listening with a relaxed but serious expression mapped across her face, when I finished, Stella cut to the heart of the matter. "Do the judges know about what happened?" she asked, her eyes widening with curiosity.

"Good question, Stelle. And we discussed that very point, just before I came home," I answered, grinning at her acumen. "Truth is, we don't know what they're aware of. They certainly could've read Sills' article, which could give them cause to follow up. But Huxton didn't notify the Chairman of the Board of Supervisors until late this afternoon, so we doubt that there was time enough for the Board to thoroughly discuss it, let alone confer with the Judicial Council, who would then get back to our dear friends in Solina. It's possible, but unlikely—so at the moment, the whole ballgame is in limbo."

"Yeah, I see," she nodded. "So what happens next on Monday?"

"Boy, you got me there, hon. But one thing's for sure, though, whatever the judges do, they're going to have to do it in one hell of a hurry because—you remember how I explained to you about the thirty-day period and all?"

"Uh-huh, dismissal times. Thirty days for custodies, and forty-five for bail-outs, right?"

"Exactly, hon, right on the button. And Tuesday is the thirtieth day, so whatever it is that they plan on doing, they're going to have to pull it off wearing sprinters' shoes rather than robes!" I finalized, adding a sprinkle of sarcasm.

"Yeahhh ... right," she drawled, a fresh smile appearing. "Say, do you want some dessert while we're talking?"

"No thanks, sweetie, I'm stuffed. But a little more coffee would be in order, while we get serious and plan out the weekend. As Grampy Max would say, we'll see what we see when we see it—so in the meantime, how about we have some fun?"

"Well, I certainly wouldn't want to argue with Grampy Max," Stella cracked, grinning as she retreated to the kitchen. "Not unless I was getting paid a helluva lot of money, if my memory serves me."

It did. And once again I marveled at the attention she paid to the details of my life, including even Grampy's vaudevillian-style sayings. When she returned bearing two full cups of tasty caffeine, our planning quickly evolved toward simplicity. "Lots of lovemaking for the soul, followed by lots of sleep for the body," Stella suggested, turning on the luminosity in the depths of her eyes with overwhelming effect. "And in between, if you're a good boy with respect to the sleep department," she added, "we could work in a couple of long walks for exercise, dinners out to break with routine, and his-and-her choice movies for pure escape!"

There was no arguing with the sheer brilliance of her uncomplicated but comprehensive plan, for a hell of a lot of money or otherwise. It was perfect, period, as Grampy was also fond of saying. And as Stella then took me by the hand and nudged me toward the bedroom, I wafted prayers of major gratitude the entire distance of the journey, at that moment more certain than ever that the Godperson in fact existed.

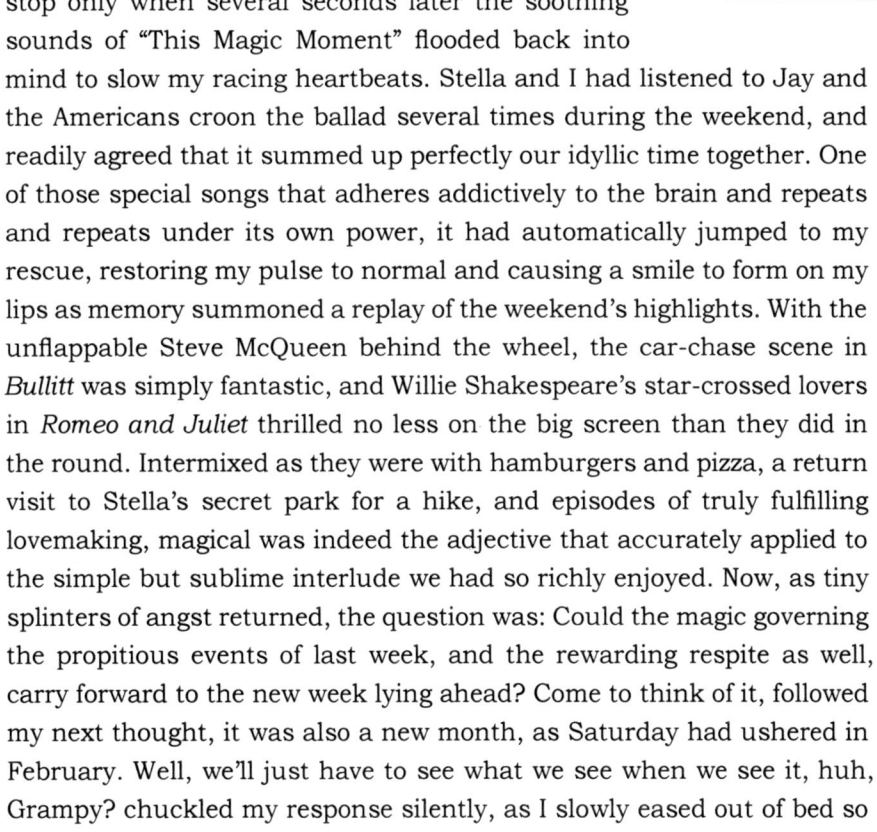

XVIII

ON MONDAY MORNING, ANXIETY PIN-pricked me awake a full fifteen minutes before my alarm clock was scheduled to perform its habitual chore. And almost instantly I rocketed fully alert, the flow of adrenaline choking to a stop only when several seconds later the soothing sounds of "This Magic Moment" flooded back into mind to slow my racing heartbeats. Stella and I had listened to Jay and the Americans croon the ballad several times during the weekend, and readily agreed that it summed up perfectly our idyllic time together. One of those special songs that adheres addictively to the brain and repeats and repeats under its own power, it had automatically jumped to my rescue, restoring my pulse to normal and causing a smile to form on my lips as memory summoned a replay of the weekend's highlights. With the unflappable Steve McQueen behind the wheel, the car-chase scene in *Bullitt* was simply fantastic, and Willie Shakespeare's star-crossed lovers in *Romeo and Juliet* thrilled no less on the big screen than they did in the round. Intermixed as they were with hamburgers and pizza, a return visit to Stella's secret park for a hike, and episodes of truly fulfilling lovemaking, magical was indeed the adjective that accurately applied to the simple but sublime interlude we had so richly enjoyed. Now, as tiny splinters of angst returned, the question was: Could the magic governing the propitious events of last week, and the rewarding respite as well, carry forward to the new week lying ahead? Come to think of it, followed my next thought, it was also a new month, as Saturday had ushered in February. Well, we'll just have to see what we see when we see it, huh, Grampy? chuckled my response silently, as I slowly eased out of bed so as to not disturb Stella, then tiptoed into the bathroom.

Spurred by the genuine excitement that joined with the renewing anxiety to reopen adrenaline's spout wide, I shaved, showered, and dressed in just under fifteen minutes, hurrying to be right on time for the six o'clock meeting that George had requested as we were leaving the office on Friday. As I reached the front door and swung it open, a yellow piece of paper taped to the inside panel flapped in the early morning breeze. Recognizing Stella's handwriting, I smiled, and it grew considerably wider as I read the large printed letters that she'd centered inside the succinct message:

Dear Matt,

FUCK THE PIGS!

Love,

S

Hey, nice touch—short and sweet like the old lady's dance, as Lincoln said—bounced my cheerful response silently as I returned to the bedroom doorway and blew a kiss toward her sleeping form. "We'll do our best, pretty lady. And thanks, sweetheart," I whispered, then quickly wheeled around and hurried outside to my car.

When I arrived at the office forty minutes later, Marilyn already had a fresh pot of coffee waiting to be appreciated. George, Robbie, Ron, and Leon all arrived within the next ten minutes, and underneath an umbrella of steadily growing excitement, we convened in George's office to review one final time the auxiliary plan we had hatched late Friday. Our purpose was to retake the offensive by launching a barrage of multi-faceted tactics designed to further sabotage the court calendars, thereby placing even greater pressure on the judges and forcing them to capitulate. For the first hour, each of us carefully spelled out his responsibilities, and after another spent trading suggestions to maximize coordination of our efforts, General George nodded his approval, and once again we trooped across the street together to the courthouse.

At precisely nine-fifteen, Steiggerman seated himself atop the bench and delivered a stony-eyed glare at me for several seconds before beginning to call the calendar. And as he slowly pronounced each defendant's name in the lordly tone of voice that I had grown to detest, I approached his clerk and politely placed in front of him one sworn statement after another, each bearing my signature at the end of its declaration that my client could not receive a fair trial with His Honor presiding. By the time Steiggerman had completed the initial task of his judicial day, a neat stack of thirty-eight had formed, and together with their accompanying lists of points and authorities, rose slightly over three inches above the surface of Ted Greene's tidy desk. Marilyn had spent several hours over the weekend meticulously preparing them, and now, as Greene handed them to His Honor, whose face first paled, then flushed with anger, I wished that she was present to enjoy the fruits of her efforts as much as I was.

The effect of a General Affidavit of Prejudice is that it compels the judge against whom it's filed to transfer the subject case to the nearest available court. Unlike its sister affidavit, which sets forth in detail the actual prejudice that allegedly exists, and which may be filed in each and every courtroom where the subscriber can prove the charged prejudice, no specifics whatsoever must be provided in the General Affidavit. And while only one of these can be filed per case, the judge charged within it cannot demand a hearing on the matter in front of another judge, but must without delay transfer the case out of his courtroom and into another. Having thoroughly mastered the numerous technicalities of the criminal law in order to viciously employ them to the disadvantage of the defendants whose misfortune it was to appear before him, Steiggerman understood perfectly well what the law required him to do. But with his inherently combative spirit on red alert, he instinctively refused to follow the law's dictates without engaging in an ugly argument calculated to escape its devastating consequences.

"Mr. Harris, do I understand that you intend to file an affidavit in every single case on today's calendar?" he queried angrily.

"No, Sir," I answered slowly, measuring my words carefully so as to insure my message remained respectful, while the sharp edge of my tone implied otherwise. "I am not intending to file, but have already filed thirty-eight General Affidavits of Prejudice with this Court."

"And these affidavits which you say you've filed, they are of course for actual prejudice, are they not?" flowed His Honor's attempt to trick me.

"No, Sir, I believe that both the affidavits themselves, as well as the attached list of points and authorities, clearly refer to Section 170.6 of the California Code of Civil Procedure, the provision relating to General Affidavits."

"I see," he snarled. "And you honestly expect me, Mr. Harris, to transfer my entire calendar to another judge who already has one of his own?"

"Yes, Your Honor, I believe that the command of Section 170.6 is quite explicit on that point."

"Oh, you do, huh?"

"Yes, Sir."

"And if I refuse, counsel?" he challenged in a taunting tone, causing a murmur of apprehension to circle the audience, then hush into a hollow silence as if it had been suddenly swallowed by a sinkhole.

"Well, Your Honor," I answered, still measuring each word carefully. "If what the Court is telling me is that it does not intend to follow the law as clearly set forth by our State Legislature, then I would have no alternative other than to telephone my Office's Appellate Department and have Mr. Lester Smith immediately file with the appropriate court the thirty-eight Writs of Mandamus which at my request he has already prepared. Then, when issued, Your Honor—"

"How dare you threaten this Court, Mr. Harris!" Steiggerman suddenly exploded, cutting me off. "You're in a lot of trouble, you know that?"

"No, Sir. Because I'm not threatening anyone," flashed my reply. "I was merely answering the Court's question, that's all."

"Is that right?"

"Yes, Sir, it is—absolutely!"

"Well, I'm not at all sure, Mr. Harris, that if there were to be a hearing on the issue, that my recollection of what has been said here would be the same as yours, not to forget the District Attorney's of course—and I would also remind you that no court reporter is present. So if I were you, I'd reconsider your position in a hurry, and immediately withdraw your erroneously filed affidavits. Then, you'd do well to make the apology that's owed to this Court. Now, before I take further action, if you want I'll give you a five-minute recess to think things over—interested, Mr. Harris?"

"May I have just a few seconds before I answer your question, Your Honor?"

"Very well."

Turning around so that I faced the audience, I called out the name of Susan Ellis. And immediately, the tall, slender form of Marilyn's best friend arose from the last row of seats on the right side of the audience area and replied, "Yes, Mr. Harris, I'm here."

"And did you get it all?" I inquired.

"Yes, Sir ... every single word."

"Thank, you, Susan—and please continue," I rushed out through a smile, then turned back around to face Steiggerman, whose hostile expression was suddenly edged with concern.

"Your Honor," I offered before he could act on it, "thank you for the brief intermission. As a result, it will not be necessary for me to avail myself of your offer to recess. My affidavits, all thirty-eight of them, stand as filed. And, Sir, as far as the Court's allegation that I threatened it is concerned, there is a record of what has transpired here other than your recollection, or the DA's, or mine, and I will stand on that record in any appellate court you choose to place me in!"

"Record, Mr. Harris? What are you talking about?" he fired back at me, his growing concern now reflected in his tone.

"Miss Ellis, Your Honor, is a fully certified court stenographer of over ten years' experience, and as I'm sure you heard, she clearly stated that she has recorded every single word which has been spoken here today since you took the bench and opened court. So there is indeed a record, Your Honor, and as I previously indicated, Sir, I'm perfectly willing to face any appellate court based on what's reflected in it!"

As I rolled to a stop, a totally stunned Steiggerman paled for the second time, on this occasion without a resurgence of anger-inspired color. Instead, as the shockwave from my surprise revelation reverberated off the walls of his mind and translated into, That little fucker's got me totally trapped!, His Honor just sat there silently glowering at me. Finally, after Irene Fisher, who had been gleefully anticipating my citation for contempt, slumped back into her seat wearing an expression that mixed disgust with despair, His Honor interrupted the thirty seconds of stony silence that had slowly ticked into a tension-packed eternity.

"Very well, Mr. Harris ... very well," he managed to squeeze out in a low, gravelly tone. "The cases in question will be transferred next door to Division Two, and this Court will for the moment stand in recess."

Smiling as I watched Steiggerman hurriedly arise from his seat and descend from the bench, I quickly turned my attention to repacking my briefbag in preparation for my departure to Division Two. So it was my turn to be surprised, when His Honor, having approached the counsel table, then called out to me. "Harris?" he barked.

"Yes?" I answered after looking up.

"I just want you to know that before this is over, I'm going to hang your ass from the highest tree in Solina! And that's a promise, you little shit! You hear me?" he boiled out, startling even his own clerk who had arrived to ask if I would help transport the court files next door.

"There aren't any!" I fired back, flashing a smile to help settle the mixture of anger and anxiety that rocketed through me.

"Aren't any what?" Steiggerman growled.

"Tall trees in Solina," rifled my return. "They outlawed them a long time ago, along with green grass, sunshine, fresh air, and justice!" stormed the words off my tongue, anger having overruled fear as I stared into the ugly face of the all-knowing authority whose powerful and uncompromising rule I had struggled with my entire life.

No retort issued. Absolutely dumbfounded by my unmitigated defiance, and the hatred emanating from my eyes that matched the loathing exiting his, after several seconds had melted into the molten silence, he whirled and headed for his chambers. Taking a deep breath, and exhaling slowly, I smiled as I then slipped the pile of files Ted Greene was still offering under my arm, picked up my briefbag with the other, and headed for Division Two, where I promptly reported to Robbie.

"How's things going, Matthew?" he drawled through a friendly grin from his seat at the counsel table, where he was smoking his pipe and reading an arrest report.

"Quite nicely, actually," I nodded back. "That little gem of an idea Marilyn had for having her court-reporter friend Susan available just saved my ass and fucked over that pig Steiggerman something fierce!"

"That's good ... But it actually went that far?"

"Yeah, it did. And I just wish you could've seen the expression on that cocksucker's face, when I told him that Susan had recorded every single word."

"Well I'll be damned, I never thought the asshole would push it all the way. Never underestimate a pig, huh?"

"Right. But we didn't, Rob, we anticipated perfectly, and were totally ready for his strong-arm tactics. The bully got his balls squeezed real tight!"

"Hey, couldn't happen to a more deserving prick. Good job, Matthew—you did just fine!" he emphasized through a fresh smile.

"Of course, I had good teachers," I chuckled back at him. "So what's going on here?"

"Not too much, as you can see. We've got the usual jammed calendar, but after I filed thirty-one motions challenging the ridiculous makeup of the jury panel, Austin declared a recess and I haven't heard from him since."

"Well, you've got thirty-eight more cases now," I informed, pointing at Ted Greene, who had entered carrying a mound of court files that he placed on the desk of Austin's clerk, Lee Van Arsdale. "And I've got a shitload more here with me."

"Well, how absolutely lovely," Robbie quipped sarcastically. "And since you've become an expert on closing down courtrooms, how'd you like to stay and help me close down this one?"

"You don't look like you're doing too poorly yourself—but sure, I'm in."

"Great. Here, take these extra copies of my motions and start printing in the names of the defendants you transferred over here."

"You got it, teach," I nodded, grinning as I pulled out my pen.

By eleven o'clock I had carefully printed in the names of each of the thirty-eight individuals I had represented earlier that morning, and stood ready to submit them to Judge Austin and then argue in support of the motions' combined objective, the dismissal of the entire jury panel. The heart of the argument was that the all-white panel, selected from a judicial district whose community was seventy-three percent black, could only have resulted from systematic and hence invidious discrimination, a practice which the U.S. Supreme Court had declared was constitutionally prohibited. It was the same, identical argument that the five of us had been making orally for months, totally without success. Now, however, we had prepared formal written motions, together with attached lists of points and authorities in support of our thesis, both of which had been carefully constructed under the expert supervision of Lester Smith, our colleague in the Office's Appellate Department, who was prepared to take the matter up on appeal. On this occasion though, we were deprived of making such a formal argument, because at twelve-fifteen, Austin further recessed his court until the highly irregular hour of three o'clock.

Upon our return to the office for lunch, we learned why when George promptly informed us that "Something's up, 'cause Austin, as Presiding Judge, has called a meeting of all the judges at one-thirty and wants the five of us present too." All of us readily agreed, and George wasted no time in placing a telephone call to Tim Stone to ascertain what, if anything, headquarters knew about further developments in connection with the Board of Supervisors. Chuckling out that he was just about to call us, Tim then had Huxton join the conversation, and after he in turn requested that the rest of us also join in, for the second time in four days we were treated to the wondrous workings of our ally Martin Sills. On Saturday, we learned, Marty had run a second and even more strongly worded article in the *Bugle*, in which he urged the community, as well as organized political and business groups, to support our efforts in every way possible. Then, not fully satisfied with this effort, he spent the entire weekend conferring personally with the leaders of the Los Angeles Divisions of several of the most prominent Civil Rights Organizations, from the more conservative NAACP to the radical and militant Black Panthers, informing them of the details of the altercation that had developed, and applying the full power of his prestige to persuade them to openly declare their support of our actions and initiate affirmative plans to further what he argued was "our joint cause."

Achieving his objective of consensus by noontime on Sunday, he thereafter labored through the night, and in the early morning hours of today delivered to the homes and newsstands of his constituency an edition of the *Bugle* which carried the ringing endorsements of no less than five major Civil Rights Organizations, as well as their united call to the community for action on our behalf. As a result, by ten o'clock, the County Board of Supervisors had received so many telephone calls from irate citizens protesting the Judicial Council's efforts to have us relieved of our duties that overwhelmed secretaries and administrative assistants closed down the incoming lines. And by eleven, the Chairman had received via messenger from each of the five supporting Civil Rights Organizations, as well as three Chambers of Commerce, a formal statement commending our actions and demanding an immediate full-scale investigation of the Solina Judicial District's legal apparatus. Then, to complete the disruption of the Board's planned agenda, telegrams from angry citizens began arriving in droves, and when the number had reached over three thousand by eleven-fifteen, and simultaneously the Supervisors learned that reporters from the *L.A. Times* and all of the local TV stations were now covering the festering altercation, the Board decided to adjourn early for lunch so as to determine informally and out of the public eye how best to deal with the now potentially explosive situation that only four days earlier had seemed so simple and clear-cut.

At this testy point in time, with our Monday afternoon having now stretched to ten minutes shy of one o'clock, this highly welcome information was nevertheless inconclusive. Wonderful news for sure, and clearly cause for optimism. But on the other hand, still not a decisive indicator of our ultimate fate. So, after we concluded our telephone conversation with Hux and Tim, then slowly picked at the fried chicken Marilyn had rushed out to obtain for us, all we could do was wait. Stick to our guns, as we had promised, and anxiously wait.

As we would learn later, during their lunch the Board of Supervisors also had a lot on their collective plate besides food. In fact, the full menu included politics, socio-economic conditions, and a discomforting review of recent history. Los Angeles County, as the Chairman noted, had like the rest of the nation, taken a deep breath, exhaled slowly, and then rested more calmly and comfortably in the peaceful posture that prevailed after the violent upheavals produced by the Civil Rights Movement during the first nine years of the tumultuous Sixties. Nevertheless, however, the mordant memory of 1965's Watts Riots and the fire and blood which they had belched forth still clearly lingered, serving strongly as a reminder that while some efforts had been made to alleviate the social injustices that triggered them, conditions had not significantly improved, and that underneath the carefully constructed exterior of Los Angeles society's tranquil exterior, there still remained a forest whose black and brown trees of hatred and frustration lay bone-dry and capable of being easily sparked into a bonfire of violence if ignited by an aggressive action perceived as personifying the white power-structure's total indifference to their plight.

Each of the Supervisors stored this frightening possibility in a far corner of his mind, and during the course of their animated luncheon discussion in the private room provided for them high atop the Music Center Pavilion, it now stepped forward and loomed larger and larger as the time for decision approached. And even setting aside this serious worry, argued cold, hard reason, practical politics still presented itself, with adverse consequences certain to follow from the highly unfavorable publicity generated by the media should they callously disregard the enormous outpouring of opinion from a sizeable portion of the citizenry they were elected to represent.

Thus, even though the Board personally favored supporting the judges, with three of the five members known to be staunchly anti–Public Defender's Office, in the end it was overwhelmed by the combined effects of both possible reactions to such an unpopular judgment, and it was therefore unanimously decided to quietly reject the Judicial Council's complaint without a full public hearing and move on to the much tamer rapid transit proposal scheduled for the afternoon session. So, highly unpleasant task that it was, as time now arrived at one o'clock, a call was placed by the Chairman to his counterpart on the Judicial Council, wherein he spelled out the "regrettable result" as diplomatically as possible, while also noting that a full public hearing might well reveal certain irregularities in the operation of the Solina Judicial District that were better left out of the purview of higher courts, not to forget the media. Initially shocked and angered, but then upon sober reflection clearly grasping the wisdom in this judgment, the head of the Judicial Council then carried out his own mournful duty and telephoned the sad news of their tragic defeat to Solina's judges, who, lunching together in Austin's chambers, sat patiently awaiting a diametrically different communication.

And that, as the saying goes, was that! Except, of course, that neither Hux and Tim, nor the five of us, had any knowledge of this manna from heaven. And while the judge's dessert of apple pie à la mode turned seriously sour in a nanosecond, we skipped ours altogether, thus creating an exception to the theory that ignorance is bliss. Our increasingly anxious state was soon alleviated, however, when ten minutes later Marty Sills triumphantly telephoned with an update, an absolutely glorious revelation which George profusely thanked him for, then immediately proceeded to share with Tim and Hux while the rest of us celebrated with smiles that could've lighted the Grand Canyon at midnight.

"Well," George squeezed out slowly after he hung up less than a minute later, a vengeful smile sliding across his lips, "I need four sonofabitching pig-fighters to accompany me across the street and help finish those fucking bastards off! Any volunteers?"

"You got it!" Ron pumped back through the smoke from George's exhale of a fresh Marlboro. "But what did Hux say?"

"What did he say? I'll tell you what he said," George chortled. "The main man reminded us that our instructions remain the same. But he also added, and I quote: 'Fuck'em over real good—you've earned it!'"

Unlike prior occasions, the celebratory cheers and jeers which followed were more subdued. Though jovial, and fueled by the electric excitement from realizing that Sills had silenced the judges' last best hope, at the same time we understood that Round Four had witnessed a total turnaround and that now it was our turn to seek a knockout, the companioning knowledge that that objective had yet to be accomplished tugging tightly on the reins of restraint. And while Hux's battle-cry hung before our eyes and resonated in our hearts, the storm clouds overhanging the final confrontation tempered our upbeat mood, and it was an emphatically determined but sober band that trudged silently across the street to attend the scheduled meeting.

Arriving in Division Two at thirty-three minutes after one, we were warmly greeted by Ray Cline, Austin's bailiff, who promptly ushered us into chambers where the judges and every single member of the DA's Office were assembled. Despite the fact that Judge Austin, wearing a friendly smile, quickly rose to his feet and shook hands with each of us, one could not help but feel the chilly atmosphere that pervaded the room. The seating arrangements had been planned so that the five of us would not be grouped together, but instead interspaced with the DAs, and as I settled uncomfortably into my chair between Randy Johnstone and David Ludlow and nodded hello, I wondered which of our adversaries had created this cozy arrangement. A thought that my colleagues shared, judging from the winks I received when my eyes darted here and there to meet theirs, I also wondered if the judges and DAs were as uncomfortable as their solemn faces reflected. The stony silence that followed the moment after cursory greetings had been randomly exchanged answered my question, and Austin, also sensing it, quickly interrupted it.

"Gentlemen, and of course, Miss Fisher," he smiled, "let me open this little meeting by thanking each of you for coming. Now I'm not going to beat around the bush about the little problem which exists here in Solina, because everyone present is intimately familiar with it. I do, however, want to make one point perfectly clear, and that is that I called us all together not to put pressure on anyone, or any faction, but instead to see if we can discuss our little problem amicably and work out a mutually satisfactory solution. Now it may not appear easy to do," Austin added through a fresh grin, "but I believe that if we keep this objective firmly in mind, and put our personal differences aside, we can freely exchange our ideas and arrive at a suitable compromise that will make our little problem disappear."

Pausing to clear his throat, then swivel his head to ascertain from various facial expressions how his opening statement had been received, he was encouraged by the thin smiles and head nods of several of his colleagues, as well as three of the DAs. What? jumped into mind. Now that they've lost, they want to negotiate a compromise? I flashed on incredulously, glancing over at George, who winked back at me as Austin picked up.

"Now, Mr. Meyerstein, I think that you should start our discussion, in that you're the head of your Office, and it seems to have some grievances over how things are run here in Solina. So, to set the table, why don't you tell us, George, exactly what your complaints are?"

"Well, Your Honor," George replied slowly, "that would be difficult to do in a short period of time, because the little problem you referred to, isn't little."

"That's all right, George, we're not in a hurry," Austin coaxed amiably. "So please, go ahead and tell us what's on your mind."

"All right, Your Honor, I'll give it to you straight. And I trust, that everyone here will remember that I was asked—I repeat, Sir, asked—to answer your question."

"Okay ... We understand, George."

"All right then ... Now I've been here in Solina a long time, for almost two years," trickled the preamble to George's explanation. "And during that time, I've both observed and felt first-hand the total disrespect which the judges here, along with the District Attorneys, have subjected us and our clients to day after day after day," he rolled out calmly. "In fact," he continued, his tone now hardening as anger began to gradually seep to the surface, "month after month the members of my Office and our clients have been deliberately demeaned, embarrassed, and humiliated by the persons assembled here, whenever and wherever possible! We've been insulted at will, joked about in open court, ridiculed in chambers, and generally treated as if we were some lower form of animal life whose sole purpose for existing was for your pleasure and amusement—and while it's hard to believe, our clients have been treated even worse!" George stated emphatically, emotion now pushing his words to flow faster.

"Because we've been unable to staff Division One, we've been helpless to prevent our clients from being subjected to the whimsical humor and judgments of Judge Gelman, while their constitutional rights are ignored! Worse yet, we've had one OR release after another revoked by Judge Lacy, as well as bail raised to ridiculous levels, just because his precious calendar was delayed by our having the audacity to really defend our clients during Prelims, something he apparently thinks we're not entitled to do! And for a bonus, we've had to attempt honest plea bargaining in front of Judge Steiggerman, who's almost always in an ugly mood, and specializes in attempting to coerce, badger, and blackmail us into entering into deals which heavily favor the prosecution!" George steamed out, then realizing that his voice had risen dangerously close to a shout, paused for a moment to lower both its level and rate of speed.

"And, Your Honor, that's just for openers," he picked up, red-hot anger having suddenly been reduced to a choked, gravelly sound, "there's also a sizeable problem with the DAs, who seem to have been born with gigantic egos and a matching arrogance to boot! In fact, with the judges treating them as their little darlings, they act like they're some kind of gods entitled to have their asses kissed from morning to night—an attitude which we find personally intolerable, and which makes any attempt to engage in a fair plea-bargaining process absolutely impossible! Moreover, this judge-DA partnership has directly created problem number three, in that the vast majority of court personnel have picked up on and joined their conspiracy of disrespect by showing us and our clients the bare minimum of common courtesy, while bending over backwards to do favors for the DAs!" rolled George's indictment toward a close.

"So, to sum it up, in a nice, neat, little nutshell, Your Honor," he pumped out, his words once again picking up speed, "the entire legal apparatus around here, for no good reason that I can think of, has been shitting on our heads and enjoying every goddamned minute of it! And to put our position very simply: Eee-nough!" George declared, then stopped and slid back off the edge of his chair.

Austin, whose face had reddened slightly, started to reply, when Steiggerman, who had somehow contained himself during George's torrent of complaints, suddenly exploded.

"Goddamn it! I've never listened to such bullshit in my entire life, and I'll be damned if I'm going to sit here for one, single, solitary minute more and listen to a bunch of stupid, communist-infested, ignoramuses who don't know their asses from a hole in the ground slander us!" he raged. "For Christ's sake, let's not forget that we're judges and DAs—that we represent the superior, elite class, while they're just a bunch of idiot nobodies who couldn't even feed themselves if we didn't create a society that gives them jobs and a livelihood! Hell," he thundered, "just because these maniacs have had a little temporary success by taking advantage of a few provisions in the legal system and using them for perverted purposes never intended by their creators, let's not lose sight of the fact that they're nothing more than a little group of low-life vermin who think they're entitled to smash down what's civilized! So listen to me, we're the rulers—we're in control of this situation, not these crazy bastards. I say, let's go to the Board of Supervisors and teach them, and all the animals like them, a lesson they won't ever forget!" he bellowed, thrusting a clenched fist forward for added emphasis, his face having flushed blood-red.

Once again the storm clouds had rolled menacingly overhead. Only this time, they were no longer dangerous, and we knew it. George jumped to his feet a split-second after Steiggerman's diatribe ended, with Robbie close behind, and the rest of us following right on his heels. The muscles in George's face began to twitch as he opened his mouth to speak, and when words followed, the quivering guttural tones of his voice fully evidenced the battle transpiring inside himself to maintain control.

"Judge Austin," he squeezed out, "we came here, Sir, at your invitation, only out of respect for you and you alone! And I answered your question regarding our bitch list, only upon your repeated request," twisted out his response slowly, his sideward glance at the sneering Steiggerman then terminating his internal battle in a nanosecond. "Now what you've just seen and heard from that motherfucking pig over there is simply one more example of the piss-poor attitude I just finished describing—and which I clearly stated we would no longer tolerate! I'm not going to waste one precious second of time by answering the devil's drivel, but before we leave, I will tell you this," George declared, turning slightly to look directly at Steiggerman, a lifetime of accumulated hatred for all he represented pouring out of his eyes, then amplifying the venom in his voice as he continued. "We are thoroughly aware of the actions you've already taken with respect to the Board of Supervisors, as well as the fact that they politely told you to go straight to hell! Which, is exactly where you belong, you sick ... patrician ... scumbag!" George growled with a frightening ferocity that is usually reserved for physical violence. "And the only lesson that's going to be learned is by you—the judges and DAs!" he concluded, glaring at an absolutely astonished Steiggerman for several searing seconds before returning his gaze forward to Austin.

"Here's the deal, Your Honor," he picked up, his anger now reeled in after having been vented, his tone still heated but respectful. "This is the thirtieth statutory day from arraignment for six hundred and twelve cases presently pending before your combined courts, and we respectfully demand that they be dismissed now, today, or our Office will run writs and compel compliance with the law! Also, we further advise you that the forty-five-day time limit for non-custody cases is only fifteen days off, at which time there will be an additional one hundred and thirty-one cases pending for which we will seek the identical remedy!" George stated succinctly, then tacked on: "We're going to leave now, Your Honor, so that you can confer with your colleagues and reach a decision. We'll be available to learn your choice—and should the judges wish to speak further with us about improving our relationships, we'll be pleased to do so, but only with you, Sir."

Initially shocked into remaining silent by Steiggerman's vulgar outburst, a condition instantly bolstered by George's crazed-toned response, and concluding that the entire incident was easily the most bizarre, if not actually insane experience of his entire judicial life, Austin was perfectly content to continue speechless as the five of us filed silently out of his chambers. Bumping into his bailiff as we emerged into the courtroom, George instantly noted that Cline, who had not been present in chambers but had nevertheless heard much of what had transpired, appeared equally stunned, and simply nodded his acknowledgment of our advisement that we would be outside on the front lawn if needed.

Once we reached it and flopped down on the cool, slightly damp grass, for a long minute we remained silent, each of us lost in his private thoughts, until finally George chuckled and broke into our reverie. "Well ... not exactly Hux's style—more like Attila the Hun's," he rolled out, shaking his head slowly from side to side. "But, still, we got the message home, didn't we?" tumbled the balance of his thought, his smile widening in reflexive response to those that flashed across our faces. Followed by a mixed chorus of "You just better believe it!" and "Right on!" this animated confirmation was engineered not only by our wholehearted agreement, but also in part by our relief over George's return to his normal state as evidenced by his poking fun at himself. Still fully alert, even while cooling off, he immediately sensed the latter factor. "Sorry, guys, for going crazy on you, but I just couldn't help it," he grinned out a bit sheepishly. "I hope I didn't blow it, and goad those pricks into some off-the-wall, face-saving effort that'll make more work for the appellate people."

"Blow it?" Robbie responded. "All you blew, my man, is the hottest stream of lava I ever saw, right up their pig assholes! And if anyone ever had it coming, they did! In fact, Georgie, great as you were, there are a few things you left out, like the fact that that cocksucker Lacy wants to be white so badly that he hates his own kind worse than any white man I've ever met! Not to forget, of course, that Burroughs thinks the Fourth Amendment is some kind of strange fairytale, and wouldn't recognize reasonable doubt if it walked up and punched him in his dumb face. Which brings me to the little matter of—ohhh, hell, I could go on forever, but the truth is you laid it on those bastards real good, and I'm glad. The only thing that'd make me happier would be if the whole damned lot of them dropped dead!"

For a moment or two the five of us just exchanged searching glances. Then, when George began to laugh, Robbie followed, and as a cool breeze whipped across the lawn and dried our perspiration-soaked shirts to our backs, it became contagious, and conjuring up images of the various degrees of bewilderment that had crossed our enemies' faces, we howled gleefully till our energy banks emptied and our sides ached. Idle chatter followed, flowing effortlessly forth on subjects ranging from sports to music, and food to photography, with the inevitable speculation about what was transpiring in Austin's chambers cropping up every so often, until after an hour had passed, at ten minutes past four Ray Cline arrived to deliver a message.

"Hi, fellas," he chirped upon reaching our circle.

"Hi, yourself, Raymond," George responded. "What's up?"

"Well, Judge Austin asked me to tell you that the six hundred and twelve cases have all been dismissed. He said that it'll take a little time to catch up on the paperwork, but that George can inspect the court files tomorrow morning at nine o'clock when he wants to meet with him alone—okay?"

"Uh-huh, for sure!" George fired back. "You tell Judge Austin that I'll be there, and that I feel confident that the two of us together can work things out for the future."

"I'll tell him, George," Cline assured. "And by the way, congratulations to all of you, you've got one hell of a lot of guts!"

"Okay ... thanks," George nodded out through a smile. Then, as Cline walked rapidly back inside the courthouse to report to Austin, the five of us jumped to our feet and began celebrating. As spontaneously inspired by triumph, an adrenaline-spurred surge of energy recharged our drained batteries, and we hugged and slapped hands and pounded each other on the back with such vigor that it's another miracle that no one was injured. No bells rang out. Nor did any cannons echo down

Hester Street. But we didn't need them, because we had won! Big Time! And as we shouted and screamed that fact at each other while bouncing up and down like a bunch of school children at play, the reality of victory, the wonderful, glorious, intoxicating reality of success seeped into our psyches, the warm glow then spreading outward to drape around us like a toasty blanket in the growing chill of late afternoon.

After our almost-totally drained energy banks finally mandated that we quiet down, we half-walked, half-ran to the office, where, bursting in upon Marilyn like rain from a monsoon, we showered her with shouts of the wondrous news accompanied by hugs and kisses. Just as delighted as we were, when several minutes later order had once again been restored, Marilyn, who had sobered more quickly, remembered that we still hadn't notified Huxton and Stone, teasing that "they might just be a teensy bit interested," while smiling and shaking her head at us in mock disapproval of our negligence.

George immediately placed the call, with the rest of us listening in on our extensions, and after he shared the fabulous outcome to the altercation, in short order each of us took turns exchanging congratulations with Hux and Tim, and once again expressing our gratitude for their support and trust, receiving in return their generously worded commendations for "a dirty job well done!" Then, to insure that no further allegations of neglect arose, the second we hung up, George instantly placed a second call to our valued ally, Marty Sills. And after a similar exchange had occurred, while George continued to converse with Marty about future plans, I telephoned Stella, whose response was so enthusiastic that for a moment I seriously entertained the idea that she was going to climb through the phone to hug and kiss me.

A few minutes afterward, Leon popped his head into my cubicle and mouthed his latest brainstorm to the four of us, who were busily engaged reliving the day's highlights over coffee and smokes, having already devoured the doughnuts which Marilyn had scurried to a nearby bakery and fetched for our suddenly ravenous appetites. "We've gotta have a party!" he announced with a gleam in his eye that appeared only when he harbored thoughts of a culinary feast.

"Now? ... Tonight?" I shot back at him.

"Absolutely!" he affirmed, his tone radiating zeal.

"Schwartzy, you're crazy, you know that?" Ron chuckled, adding his two cents to the growing colloquy.

"Of course, my dear colleagues and fellow conspirators. But it's a great idea anyway, don't you think?" he rolled back nonchalantly, totally undeterred. "I mean, you tell me: When are we ever going to have a better reason to have a party? And when can triumph be better celebrated, than when it's smiling the widest right in your face?"

Attractively attired as it was, and aided further by the sea of euphoria that surrounded us, after three or four seconds had scooted by, Leon's inspired logic overwhelmed any and all well-reasoned objections that strolled into mind. In fact, so much so, that they remained unarticulated as the five of us hurriedly formed a plan for a pot luck dinner at George's house, then hastened to gather together our belongings and noisily depart the office, excitedly jabbering additional instructions and suggestions at one another all the way till we reached our cars and rushed off toward the freeway.

XIX

GEORGE LIVED ON A BROAD, TREE-lined street in Canoga Park, in the San Fernando Valley section of Los Angeles. He had moved there just three months ago from an apartment in West Los Angeles, and as Stella and I searched for his house amongst the modern, ranch-style tract homes dotting Lee Street, each fronted by a neat, well-manicured lawn, I wondered what George was doing living in suburbia. It didn't make sense to me—it just simply didn't fit his make-up or background. The question lingered, and after the numbers 2031 finally appeared, and Stella and I parked and began walking up the red-brick pathway toward the front door, it trailed along behind my long-stored and now piqued curiosity about his wife.

Only later would I learn how suburbia and George formed a relationship. But introductory information about his wife soon surfaced, when several seconds after our knock, it was answered by a strawberry blonde with a strikingly pretty face, and an even more impressive figure. Immediately identifying herself as Marie Anne while forcing a nice but weak smile, after relieving us of the cheeses, wine, and oversized chocolate cake that we were carrying, she quickly ushered us into the living room where George, Ron, and a young woman I assumed was his date were seated on a couch opposite a blazing fire, chatting over drinks. Both George and Ron rose instantly upon sighting us, and Ron hailed our arrival warmly and in character. "Hey, Matt, baby!" he cried out, then turned his head and gushed to his lady friend, "You gotta meet this little mother—he's the one who started the whole damn thing we were telling you about!" Smiling, I introduced Stella while shaking both of their outstretched hands heartily, and in turn, we were introduced to Ellen, who appeared tall and slender, and whose slightly too wide nose caused her to fall just short of being beautiful. George started to introduce Marie Anne, but was stopped short by her staccato, "We've already met. Why don't you fix them a drink, while I check on Leon and Carla in the kitchen."

Turning sideways, she swiftly strode away, and as George shuffled over to the card table in the corner to mix our drinks, his eyes followed her until she disappeared through a doorway. As I had gotten to know George well, I had often wondered why he failed to refer to his wife around the office, except on those occasions which commanded it. Now, as I watched him raise the bottle of gin and pour some into two paper cups, the thought once again flashed into mind, this time triggering the feeling that Marie Anne didn't fit either. I wasn't sure why exactly, and quickly emphasized that fact in an effort to assure myself that all was well between them, and lessen the uncomfortable feeling that she gave rise to. But there was something, albeit indefinable, in the stiffness that edged the tones of her voice, and the somewhat starched quality of the smile beneath the porcelain-like skin of her lovely face, that continued to argue otherwise, causing me to conjecture that something was amiss. Vaguely troubling, my mental meanderings washed away when George returned with our drinks and I quickly lifted my cup to toast him. "To our trusty leader, and host!" I bounced out jovially.

"Thanks, Matt," he replied humbly. "And to you, for lighting the fire with your angry outburst, what seems like a very long time ago."

"And also, for bringing a lovely lady to help us celebrate!" Ron chimed in, occasioning yet another sip from our drinks. God bless his big mouth! I thought, a tinge of color creeping into my face as I lipped the cup.

"Good Lord, I think he's blushing," Ron picked up, letting well enough alone never his strong point. "Uh-huh, it's true—the man who singlehandedly destroyed Division Four is blushing!"

"If you don't shut up, big fella," I returned, smiling despite my discomfort, "it won't be the only thing I destroyed!"

"All right, little guy, all right," he squeezed out, joining in the soft laughter that had spurted forth. "I didn't mean to touch a nerve. Problem is, you're just too sensitive."

"And you just won this century's award for calling the kettle black," interjected George good-naturedly after he and I traded are-you-kidding-me? looks, then directed our best accusatory stares at Ron. Three, maybe four seconds elapsed before his snicker evidenced his plea of guilty as charged, causing the three of us to then burst out in a fresh round of laughter, which Stella and Ellen participated in without fully understanding why.

Robbie and Loucille arrived as our laughter was dying away, and all attention was immediately focused on them as George facilitated another round of introductions. Grateful for the diversion from me and my flushed face, I began to fully relax as the liquid refreshment took effect, and promptly took a booster swig when George refilled my empty cup. Leon and his live-in girlfriend Carla soon emerged from the kitchen to join the lively conversation, and when Marilyn and her boyfriend Will arrived fifteen minutes later, round three of our gin-and-tonic festival was quickly dispensed to celebrate the collection of the entire family. Several minutes afterward, I found myself standing alone near the fireplace, watching the ice cubes bob up and down and clink together in my cup as I jiggled it ever so slightly. Stella had volunteered to help Leon and Marie Anne put the finishing touches on dinner, leaving me to share chit-chat with Carla, who a few minutes later had excused herself to visit the powder room. Raising my eyes when the two larger cubes finally allowed the tinier one equal space to float, the picture that greeted me caused my smile to widen full. Ron and Ellen were engaged in a highly animated gabfest with Robbie on the couch across the room from me, with Ron laughing raucously at some point Robbie was illustrating with a pointed finger, my ears and lip-reading skills combining to inform that Judge Lacy was the centerpiece of the episode. To their left, and a few feet forward, George, Lou, Marilyn, and Will were seated in a small circle on the floor, also jabbering and smiling happily at one another over a mixture of subjects. For a full minute, I turned my eyes back and forth between them, savoring the warmth and laughter that bubbled forth from the center of their merry mood. Searching their faces, I nodded ever so slightly at the enjoyment of each other mapped clearly in their attentive expressions, their eyes sparkling in salute to the special moment they were sharing. But it was the unmistakable peace and contentment I read in the faces of George, Robbie, Ron, and Marilyn that I treasured most, and which I freeze-framed into memory. A portrait of fulfillment, hard won and now thoroughly enjoyed, in later years I would summon it to the surface whenever need dictated.

As my eyes suddenly misted, and I broke my gaze, Marie Anne reentered and summoned us to dinner. Stella followed behind her, and when she took my hand and led me toward the dining room, I whispered, "You okay?"

"Of course. Why wouldn't I be?" she smiled back at me.

"No reason. Just checking, sweetie," I murmured, then was promptly rewarded with a kiss on the cheek, a gesture that the omnipresent Ronald, walking behind us, failed to miss.

"Hey, hey, none of that now," arrived his tease, "not before dinner anyhow."

"Ron, my man, with all due respect, you're getting to be a royal pain in the ass!" I tossed over my shoulder at his smiling face, only to watch his grin widen further.

"You mean after being together for over seven months, you just discovered that?" he shot back. "Christ, and I've been telling everyone just how bright you were, too."

My slight irritation with him disappeared as rapidly as it had arisen, overwhelmed by the genuine goodness of his nature now radiating through every pore of his glowing face to force a smile onto mine. And shaking my head at him in mock disgust as my smile widened, I tried turning the tables on him. "Nooo ... I knew it, all right, it's just that Ellen's pretty face made me forget, that's all—something, by the way, that you should be paying more attention to, instead of me," I needled, chuckling as he glanced sideways just in time to catch Ellen's wink that seconded the motion. Then, taking the plate that Stella handed me while also winking her approval, I eagerly began filling it with assorted delicacies from the array of trays and bowls neatly arranged buffet style around the dining room table.

Slowing, when I realized that the magnitude of the culinary layout before me rated the label of feast, I smiled at the image of King Henry VIII that flashed into mind. Yeah, he would approve all right, I mused as my eyes swept over the absolutely amazing assemblage of appetizers, entrées, and side dishes. For openers, there was a cheese platter harboring Gouda, Havarti, and Brie seated adjacent to bowls of baby carrots, celery sticks, radishes, and olives. Next, there appeared a seriously oversized bowl of Caesar salad, nestled against a basket containing several kinds of bread. And for the main course, there was a beautiful baked salmon garnished with raspberries, and pan-fried chicken breasts smothered in a creamy mushroom-and-onion sauce, both of which were complemented by wild rice with diced almonds and garlic-seasoned asparagus. Dessert, for those with football-player-sized appetites, consisted of several types of cookies and the chocolate cake Stella and I had purchased from the Fairytale Bakery.

Uh-huh, "fairytale" is the right adjective to describe this banquet, I opined as I piled my plate high with goodies, then carefully carried my teetering treasure-trove while following Stella back into the living room, where we seated ourselves in front of the fireplace. The room soon filled with ravenous diners, and thereafter the better part of two hours passed deliciously by between bites of Chef Leon's marvelous food and a continuous stream of cheerful chatter, until finally the combined effects of too much food and wine downshifted our exuberant celebration into neutral. Coffee then replaced Merlot as the drink of choice, and within minutes a fresh wave of energy recharged the flow of lively conversation and companioning laughter. "Hey, little guy," Ron quipped, sliding down next to me on the floor where I was peacefully smoking my pipe. "I didn't mean to bug you earlier, you know that, right?"

"Sure ... of course," I nodded.

"I was just trying to give you a compliment, but you know me."

"Yeah, I do. No problem," I assured, watching Stella out of the corner of my eye abandon her seat on the couch across the room to huddle on the floor with Robbie and Lou.

"If you don't mind me asking, how long have you known Stella?" Ron continued, unable to contain his curiosity.

"About eight months. We live in the same triplex, that's how I met her."

"I see. Do you get together often? I mean, you never mentioned her."

"That's true, big fella," I shrugged. "'Cause up until a short while ago I wasn't sure what was happening. Then, casual grew into close, then very close, and now we're living together. I'd have shared with you, but with all that's been going on in our little war, there didn't seem to be a right time to talk personal stuff."

"Well, I'll be goddamned!" he enthused. "Here you've got your old buddy all worried about you 'cause you never rap much about ladies, and all the time you're shacked-up with the most gorgeous creature I've ever laid eyes on! Hot damn, Vietnam—talk about a little injustice in the world!" he rolled out, admiration mixing with surprise to fashion a gleam in his sea-blue eyes.

"And what about Ellen? I suppose she's ugly or something?" I returned, fully aware that shacked-up was a positive term to Ron, but seeking to steer the conversation in a different direction nonetheless. My complimentary styled question seemed to turn the trick, but unexpectedly also opened the floodgates of Ron's insecurity.

"Nooo ... I didn't say that," he grinned, shaking his head. "As a matter of fact, Matt, she's got the best body of any girl I ever fucked.

But to tell you the truth, and share a little secret with you, now that you've shared yours, I have a hard time getting beyond the sex. I mean, Ellen's nice, real nice in fact—and smart, too, she just got promoted again at the advertising agency where she works," Ron nodded out, then paused to search for the right words. "But I don't feel close, I can't talk to her about anything really important. I mean, I've tried, but letting out what's inside is ... well, scary," he confessed meekly. "So, we just talk about fun things like movies and concerts and restaurants, then fuck our brains out. She really likes that," he trailed off, sipping at his coffee and pulling out a fresh cigarette.

"Hey, give it a chance, and don't be too hard on yourself," I soothed, empathizing fully, but equally cognizant of the fact that I wasn't exactly an expert in such matters. "Just take baby steps, and be open to what happens," I eased out in the most non-advisory tone I could muster.

"Yeah? ... Well ... sounds reasonable. Is that what you did?"

"Uh-huh. One tiny step at a time," I answered, then smiled. "And, hey, I'm here for you, we can talk about it some more anytime you want—okay?"

"Yeah, sure. And thanks, Matt."

"Hey, as a very good friend of mine once said: 'Any time ... any time.'"

With the bond between us then underscored by our soft chuckles, we lazily drifted into a short silence during which Ellen, who had been chatting with Carla, strolled over and sat down beside us. Kissing Ron tenderly on his cheek, she then inquired as to what we had been discussing "so seriously and all."

"Hey, how timely," Ron supplied in return. "I was just telling Matt about what a wonderful person you are, and that I was beginning to miss you."

"Uh-huh ... right," she responded through a forming smile, her sweetly sarcastic tone hanging in the air just long enough for me to interject that I, too, was missing a certain lady as I hoisted myself to my feet and went in search of Stella.

I found her in the kitchen helping Leon clean up. Thanking him again for the magnificent meal he had prepared for us, after lighting Stella's cigarette, I grabbed a towel and joined them until we reached spick-and-span a few minutes later. It had grown late, considering the fact that tomorrow was a workday. And when Tuesday then arrived some twelve minutes later, everyone readily, but sorrowfully, agreed to end our joyous celebration, though no one hurried to make ready to depart. Finally, however, after a round of lingering goodbyes, complete with promises to "do it again soon," alongside pledges of "See you later this morning," we divided and went our separate ways.

Late hour or not, Stella remained fully energized and top-of-the-scale upbeat about the evening as we hummed along on the freeway back towards West L.A. "I'm so glad you enjoyed getting to know them, Stelle," I responded when she told me how special she thought the guys were.

"How could you not?" she exclaimed. "They're so warm and good-hearted, and vibrant and bright—not to forget their backgrounds, which are downright fascinating. Why Robbie alone could fill up a big book on how to overcome a shitload of obstacles! I mean, it's just incredible that he didn't even know what roast beef was until he was eighteen!" she poured out, smiling, but shaking her head.

"Yeah, hon, I know. He didn't learn what it was until he worked a summer job as a waiter on a railroad after his freshman year in college. It's amazing, all right, but really sad, too."

"For sure. But still, I think the key word is amazing, 'cause it sorta summarizes his whole life. I mean, can you imagine being born black on a little farm in Nowhere, Tennessee, to parents who don't have a thing in the world except three other children, and working your way out of that and all the way up to being a lawyer?"

"I can imagine it, sweetie, but that's all," I answered. "I couldn't have done it."

"Well that makes two of us—want to form a club, as you would say?"

"Right. And we could get a whole lot of other members, too," I chuckled. "Did he tell you, Stelle, how he finally got off the farm?"

"Uh-huh. He said he left home when he was seventeen and enrolled in some college outside Nashville."

"Okay. But did he tell you why he decided to leave? And how?"

"No, tell me."

"Well, about three or four months ago, I heard him talking with George in the office late in the day. When I entered, he was explaining how he finally just got tired of being afraid. He said that he had a wonderful father and mother—she's still alive and lives with Rob's sister in Milwaukee, and he goes to visit her twice a year," I related, pausing to light my pipe before continuing. "But getting back to the main point, Rob told us that while his folks were super, and loved him a lot, they'd been trained by their parents to be white man's niggers and couldn't ever change 'cause inferiority was just too ingrained. He said that they were so afraid of the white man, and so used to being just a cog in his wheel, that they accepted it because that's all they knew and couldn't see that anything else was possible. So, as a result, they were just doomed to live out their lives in poverty and boredom."

"Okay ... I see why he felt he had to leave ... 'cause he didn't want to end up the same way," Stella mouthed slowly, thinking heavily about what I had just told her.

"Yeah, right, that's exactly what Robbie said," I confirmed. "But ask yourself this, Stelle: Operating in such a culture of inferiority and submission, how the hell did a seventeen-year-old kid figure this out all by himself? When George and I asked him, he said that somehow he just knew, that's all. But to me, it's beyond amazing, it's just mind-boggling!" I boomed out, the unlikelihood of such an accomplishment actually occurring once again filling me with absolute awe.

"You got that right," Stella flashed in return. "And the only answer I've got is that his natural-born brilliance came out and saved him."

"Well ... you're probably right," trickled my response, "that, and a large dose of divine intervention. But was he also born with a natural supply of guts? 'Cause when he took off for college in the big city, he left with the clothes on his back and one change, a sack lunch, and a dollar and fourteen cents that his mother slipped into his jeans—which to me is mind-boggle number two! I mean, I thought it was a big deal when I left the family business for the big, bad PD's Office. How the fuck was he not paralyzed with fear?"

"I don't know, Matty, I don't know," Stella said softly, shaking her head. "With all my problems, I still had it a whole lot easier, and I didn't come close to functioning as well as he did. But how did he survive, with only a buck-fourteen?"

"Well, are you ready for mind-boggle number three? After he hitchhiked to the school, an all-black college called Tennessee A&E, he immediately marched over to the custodial department and talked his way into a job as janitor. By luck, a guy had just quit two days earlier, and Rob convinced them that he could go to school and work nights all at the same time."

"Jesus," Stella groaned, shaking her head again.

"Uh-huh, I hear you, and you're right on the button. Rob says it was the hardest job he's ever had. Every day, after going to class, he worked for nine hours sweeping and mopping hallways, emptying trash cans, and cleaning bathrooms, including the toilets. He couldn't start till night classes ended, so sometimes he didn't finish till four or five o'clock in the morning—which left a whole four or five hours for sleep till his first class, and then the whole fucking cycle started all over again!" I growled, anger suddenly crowding into my voice. "And he did this for four fucking years, too!"

"Hey, take it easy, Mr. Fighter Man," Stella soothed. "You're off duty, remember?"

"Yeah, you're right … Sorry," I replied, instantly defusing.

"You wanna hear mind-boggle number four?" she chuckled.

"Uh-huh, sure."

"Well, from what I can tell, you're more pissed off about it than Robbie is."

"Yeah … well … guilt's an extremely powerful animal," seeped my defense as a smile curled out of the corners of my mouth. "Say, listen, I didn't get to really talk with Lou one on one—how'd you find her?"

"Ohhh, she's a sweetheart, Matty!" Stella reported, matching my grin. "And smart as they come, too!"

"Yeah, I thought so, there's a look that comes into Robbie's eye when he mentions her that spells out SPECIAL in capital letters."

"That's funny, but that's exactly what Jean says happens to me when I mention you."

"Well, thank you, sweetie. And you know something?" I chuckled, "I'm really starting to like that lady, and I haven't even met her."

"Well, I can arrange that easily enough, she's mentioned several times that the four of us should get together for dinner," Stella mouthed nonchalantly, then turned the conversation back to the party. "But she's not the only one who noticed, so did your friend Ron," she added as I steered off the Ventura Freeway and north onto the San Diego.

"What's the matter, didn't you like him?" I asked, noting the slight tone of disapproval that crept into her voice when she pronounced his name.

"Oh, he seemed nice enough, Matty—very warm and friendly. It's just that I never had anyone undress me with his eyes the way he did, I felt as if he were almost touching me. I don't mean to sound paranoid, but—"

"Oh, you're not, hon," I interjected, beginning to shake my head, "that's just Ron's immaturity shining through. He's very young acting where women are concerned, and extremely insecure because of his curly hair and glasses."

"Why? He's nice looking, and has a good physique."

"Uh-huh. You know it, and I know it, but guess who doesn't?"

"I see ... But that's really silly."

"Yeah, no doubt. But let me tell you something, so you'll understand better. While you were talking with Robbie and Lou, Ron slipped down beside me to apologize for teasing me earlier in the evening," I explained. "We started talking, and after I shared with him how close we had grown, and how happy we were, for the first time ever he actually confided in me that where ladies are concerned, he just can't get by the physical element and enter into a real relationship. He's so damn busy trying to prove that he's a stud, despite his curly hair and glasses, that sex has become everything, and he's missing out on what's truly meaningful."

"Ohhh ... Well that's very sad then."

"Exactly. And that's just how he sounded when he was telling me how much he liked Ellen, but just can't open up and really talk with her, and share thoughts and feelings. I could tell he really wants to, but he's just too confused and scared—in fact, that's the word he used, scary."

"What did you say to him?" Stella asked, a touch of sympathy creeping into her voice.

"Well, I tried to downplay the problem by telling him not to be too hard on himself, and to just take baby steps and be open to what happens."

"That's good ... that's perfect," she agreed, breaking into a smile.

"Yeah, look who's talking, huh, Mr. Pretty Ladies Make Me Nervous, himself," I chuckled.

"Well, not so much anymore—not the last time I checked anyway," teased her return, a compliment squeezed inside, her smile widening.

"Uh-huh. Well I just got lucky, hon, that's all. And you know what's really sad? I think that Ellen truly likes the big dummy, and wants a relationship—while he's hiding all the good stuff he has to give, his kindness and loyalty, and his big heart. You'll see, when you get to know him better, you'll like him."

"Hey, I already have a different picture, believe me. He's got a great lawyer, and you turned me around, just like you did Judge Lacy that time his ass was in the wringer."

"Okay, good ... that's better," I nodded out, shaking my head over how she remembered everything. "And as long as we're on the subject of hazy pictures," I tacked on, "what's your take on Marie Anne?"

"Hmmm ... I don't know," Stella shrugged. "I can't really come up with very much, 'cause we didn't really have a conversation. She stayed so busy with the preparations and all, that she didn't really share with anyone as far as I could see. So ... very pretty, but kinda standoffish is all I can say."

"Yeahhh ... that's pretty much what I thought—that, and that she doesn't fit with George."

"Well, he's certainly the proverbial horse of a different color all right," Stella responded instantly, her face brightening, her voice filling with enthusiasm. "He's warm and welcoming, and honest and open—and what a mind, it feels like it's electric, you know what I mean?"

"I sure do," I affirmed as I steered off the freeway and headed east along Santa Monica Boulevard. "And I'm glad you liked him, 'cause he's the best friend I've got, except for you of course."

"Well, thanks for the P.S., Mr. Harris," she chuckled. "And I did like him, a lot in fact. How couldn't I? He reminds me so much of you, especially in the warrior department. He may be coming from a different place, but he cares the exact same way you do, with his whole being. He's something else, for sure! ... And so is Leon by the way," she tacked on after a split-second's pause.

"Yeah, you're right, Stelle, in his own way, he's a piece of work all right. I mean, who else is a first-rate philosopher-revolutionary, a virtuoso pianist, a gourmet cook, and a die-hard defender of the Fourth Amendment all at the same time?"

"Uh-huh ... And also in his own way, he's a warrior, too. Not in the same fiery way as you and George, but he still cries for all that's wrong in the world, and he's just as committed to trying to fix it!" Stella emphasized, then paused to choose her words before continuing. "There's a deep, deep sadness in him that I could feel even though he often uses his dry sense of humor—he really cares about people, and he's very loyal and responsible. Did you know that he's taken care of his mother ever since his dad passed away during his last year in high school?"

"Uh-huh, George told me."

"Well, that's pretty special in my book," Stella opined, as we reached home and parked. "And, I might add," she postscripted as we climbed outside and strolled toward the apartment, "special is the one word I'd used to describe all the guys! You're lucky, Matty ... very lucky."

"Yes ... yes I am," I returned as we entered inside and flicked on the hallway lights. "And doubly so, 'cause I've got you."

For the second time that evening, I was rewarded with a kiss, this time though on the lips. And when we separated, several sweetly passing seconds later, we reluctantly agreed to make ready for bed. One question kept buzzing around inside my head, however, so when Stella emerged from the bathroom, I allowed it to escape. "Hon," I asked casually, "remember awhile back you said I was a born fighter, a warrior?"

"Uh-huh, sure ... in the park, when you were wrestling with the idea of starting the war. Why?"

"Well, earlier tonight when I got pissed off about how hard Robbie had it, you called me Fighter Man, then later added that George had warrior in his blood, just like me. So ... I just wanted you to know that that thing inside me, what I call an animal, is something I'm trying real hard to learn to control. In fact, I think if you'll look back a ways, I'm a lot better than when you first knew me—don't you think?"

"Yes ... yes I do, absolutely," she responded positively, concern then suddenly flooding her face. "But Matty, I never said or implied that the animal, as you call it, is something evil, 'cause it's not, it's good, it's from love. You look out at the world and see all the terrible pain and injustice, and you want to help fix it. That's wonderful, the very best part of you," she argued, emotion now crowding into her voice. "But fixing sometimes requires fighting, and that requires a special kind of strength, so the same God that put the need to cure inside you also placed warrior right alongside. There's no problem, Matty, you don't need to change for me, or anyone," she urged, tears suddenly swelling into her eyes. "You just have to learn to accept that it's not your fault that there's so much wrong, and lose the guilt so that it doesn't eat you up, that's all. You understand?"

"Yeahhh ... I see," trickled my answer. "I've got Dr. Frankl teaching me, and as long as I've got you, I'll be fine, just fine."

For a long moment her smile widened as she brushed away her tears. "Listen to me," she then said softly, "just sit down on the bed and listen to me, okay?"

"Sure, Stelle ... sure," I nodded, slipping down close to her.

"Okay, here's what I want you to remember," she began, a fresh smile forming, but her tone serious. "I may not know very much about a lot of things, but I have learned a great deal about you. And the truth is that the Matthew I know is fine right now, and always will be, all by himself!" she asserted strenuously, fixing her eyes on mine. "And you know why, Matty? 'Cause I've watched how when serious shit hits the fan, and you're sometimes confused and frightened, you never give in to it. Instead, you use your smarts to figure out what's best to do, and then suck up the guts to do it!" she gushed. "Oh, sure, it's nice to have a sounding board and some support, but you don't need me or anyone else to be fine—you'll always be fine 'cause you have your huge heart and mind, and your unbelievable courage and work ethic. They make you special, and you've earned that by making yourself the best you can be! So don't you ever forget it, okay?"

"Yeah ... sure, no problem," I returned, my surprise at the feverish insistence behind her words then giving way to a wave of exhaustion that suddenly swept over me. Constructed from the accumulated efforts and emotions from the day's turbulence, triumph, and celebration, it had tsunami-size strength, and quickly drowned the desire for extended discussion. No need, anyway, flashed a thought, 'cause she'll be here to remind me just in case I accidentally forget, it comforted as I pushed myself backward toward the bank of pillows and squeezed in between the sheets. Then, after she joined me, I leaned over and kissed her tenderly. "Good night, sweetheart, see you later this morning," I whispered, smiling faintly as she returned the sentiment while reaching to turn off her lamp and tumble us into darkness.

Nestling my head deeper into the well of my pillow, for several slow-motion seconds I tried to briefly scan all that had occurred since I had awakened. My eyes ached, and the top of my head throbbed to the beat of my heart as faces, places, and bits and pieces of conversations floated into mind, then paraded around till they intermingled and flowed before me like a whirling reel of film on a projector that has suddenly gone out of control. Quickly closing my eyelids, I dammed the flooding river, and with my last ounce of strength murmured silently, "Thank God, the fucking war is over ... at last the fucking war is over," before instantly dropping into sleep.

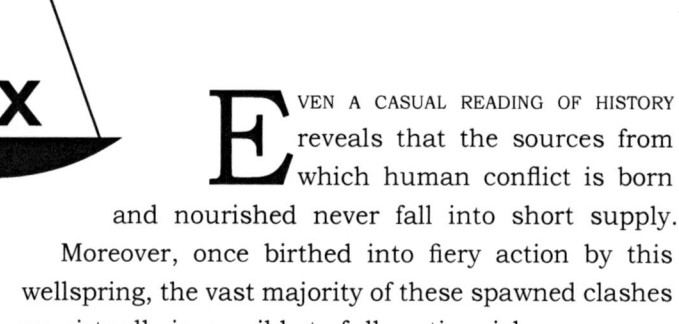

EVEN A CASUAL READING OF HISTORY reveals that the sources from which human conflict is born and nourished never fall into short supply. Moreover, once birthed into fiery action by this wellspring, the vast majority of these spawned clashes are virtually impossible to fully extinguish.

Delve a layer deeper, and corollaries emerge. One reminds that power corrupts. Another teaches that those who hold power strenuously resist its loss or diminishment, and that should same occur, they will immediately apply all available energy toward seeking its repossession or restoration to full strength. And just to insure that you're paying attention to this age-old account of rueful acrimony, like a climactic exclamation point, yet another warns that those who do not learn and remember history's lessons are doomed to relive it.

Thus, without special dispensation from these immutable laws of human nature, our war did not end and was far from over. Victory, triumph, and the like are ephemeral. And in the months that lay ahead, we learned this lesson only too well, and several more for good measure. Some were welcome. Others exposed the most hideous and painful facets of life, and were resisted with all of our strength collectively, and in some instances separately, alone. In the end, by command of a power neither seen nor heard, we were shaken like a tiny leaf clinging frailly to a branch in the face of a fierce storm. Tossing us up, down, and around, it finally forced us into our proper place within the governing scheme of order, and though initially uncomfortable with our reduced stature, we survived, and grew, and went on about the very serious business of living, difficult as it was.

Tuesday had been born well before any one of the five of us had closed his eyes to capture a few hours of much-needed rest. When it had aged to the point where the sun's rays peeked over the tops of the trees to the rear of the courthouse, then filtered through the front window of the office to cast soft shadows onto the brown-and-white flecked linoleum floor, the Solina Five, looking as tired as they felt, limped to their desks with a cup of Marilyn's coffee in hand. Three or four swallows lifted the film from their eyes, and amidst smiles and grumbled greetings we then assembled in George's cubicle for a brief conference prior to departing for court.

With priorities firmly in mind, our first order of business was to affirm that despite its obvious debilitating effect on us, the party had been extremely worthwhile, a cheery conclusion that spontaneously sparked a unanimous call for more, and soon. Then, during a second round of caffeine, it was agreed that there would be no deviation from our previous course of action until George reported the results of his meeting with Judge Austin. Most fortunately, by ten o'clock this had been accomplished, and the further realization that the judges' capitulation was both factual and total served well as a substitute for lost sleep, the accompanying adrenaline hype propelling us pell-mell through the remainder of the morning. In fact, at lunchtime, we were so buoyed that we even allowed the outside world to encroach on ours, Leon instigating its return with a profanity-laced summary of how yesterday in the Middle East the various Palestinian political factions had united under the Palestinian Liberation Organization headed by Yasser Arafat. "Isn't that just great," he growled. "We win a small one for freedom and justice, and at the same time a group of blood-thirsty motherfuckers get together behind an evil sonofabitch so as to coordinate a second Holocaust! I mean, give me a rest, world, will ya?" he groaned, slumping down into a chair.

"Hey," Robbie answered, "don't let it get you down. The world's like the Shondells' new song on the radio, 'Crimson and Clover'—that's the way it is, both at the same time."

Fortuitously, we were spared the serious discussion that was brewing in the seconds of silence that followed by the sudden appearance of our esteemed ally, Martin Sills. Taking a break from the endless rounds of appointments he maintained to personally congratulate us on our "great accomplishment," he was quickly persuaded to share in our mixed repast of chicken and pizza. Then, over coffee, and the cigars which Marty had brought along to celebrate our success, George recounted the details of his meeting with Austin and itemized the changes which His Honor had assured him were genuinely acceptable to the judges and were therefore to be implemented immediately.

Adding a layer of icing to our triumph, all that we had demanded had been agreed to. First off, no longer were we to be subjected in open court to being identified in ignominious tones as PDs. Instead, in a manner indicating respect, we were to be referred to as attorneys from the Public Defender's Office. Further, no longer were our clients to be subjected to an en masse arraignment procedure in Division One, wherein they were advised of the charges against them, along with their constitutional rights, in a rapid-fire approach calculated to deprive them of any real understanding and actual exercise of those rights, so as to lead to pleas of guilty with respect to the allegations. Instead, it was stipulated that the admonition of rights would be administered to no more than ten individuals at a time, thoroughly explained in lay terms, and the offer of our services repeated yet a third time when the formal charges were then read and clearly defined for each person before the court. Still further in this vein, it was also agreed that no judge, and in particular, Judge Gelman, was to exercise his sense of humor at the expense of any defendant.

Next, the focus was shifted to the "congestion difficulty which had arisen," as Judge Austin phrased it. And while we conceded that there would be a resumption of the plea-bargaining process, attached was the proviso that this procedure was to be conducted in a manner that was utterly devoid of the strong-armed, extortion-type tactics previously employed by the judges, most notably by Judge Steiggerman. No longer would the demand for trial, the legitimate exercise of a constitutional right, result in the arbitrary and capricious revocation of OR releases previously granted to our clients at arraignment, nor would bail be increased. Further, no longer would trials, or any other matters conducted in open court, transpire without benefit of a court reporter, nor would any case proceed to trial without there first occurring in chambers a full discussion of the jury instructions to be delivered upon completion of the proceedings, with a court reporter also present at that time in order to provide a complete record for purposes of appeal should that procedure become necessary. Then, too, and still within this same vein, it was agreed that the system for selecting the jury panel would be modified with all deliberate speed so that a valid cross-section of the judicial district's community was reflected in its composition no later than the following Monday, with no trials commencing until that time.

Finally, and we all broke into a hearty round of derisive laughter at its enunciation, Austin, in his capacity as Presiding Judge, had agreed to issue a written memorandum to the supplementary court personnel. To be distributed to every department within the judicial structure, and each member thereof, it would serve to advise and instruct them that the members of our Office were fully qualified attorneys, as well as Officers of the Court, and as such were entitled to their full respect and cooperation at all times, as well as every courtesy extended to private counsel and the staff of the District Attorney's Office. Robbie squealed with delight as George concluded his review of the peace conference. "Can you see the expression on uppity Andrea's face when she's told that she's gotta be nice to us?" he chortled. "Why the old bag will choke!"

"Yeah?" Ron chipped in. "Well, she can ram a red-hot poker up her ass and rotate it around a bit for all I care!"

Harsh as their fantasized revenge was, it accurately reflected our extreme dislike for Judge Lacy's clerk, Andrea Colari, whose contempt for us and our clients was almost as obvious as that which we generated for her boss. Having crossed swords with her over matters large and small for years, our hardened feelings instantly elicited a chorus of hearty "Amens!" along with a matching spurt of laughter. When it finally faded away, we again thanked Marty for all his efforts on our behalf, and after promising him that we would "keep the lid on our friends across the street fastened down tight," in turn we extracted his pledge to visit us again soon, and often.

However, as we confidently returned to court that afternoon, energies were already flowing into action against us that would make honoring our promise to hold the high ground every bit as difficult a task as originally achieving it. For even as the ink was drying on the peace treaty, the judges, humiliated and sick at heart over the diminishment of their power, and that of the ruling structure they served, began channeling their bitterness into formulating a strategy to fully reclaim their prior position of total dominance. Simple in nature, it required no immediate overt action. Instead, borrowing a lesson from the Russian Army at Stalingrad during World War II, they firmly clung to the remnants of their control, and while subtly resisting their reduced role whenever possible, exercised a newfound patience while waiting for our over-extended supply lines of energy to gradually strangle us into submission.

Easily employed and operated, like the Russian winter, this strategy of attrition slowly but surely inflicted the desired results. By mid-March, the frantic pace at which we rushed through our days began to take its toll. Trying case after case, and adding to the incessant pressure produced by this responsibility the additional burdens of preliminary hearings, arraignments, and the resumed process of plea-bargaining, produced a steadily increasing weariness, even more so mentally than physically. Aware of this continuing energy drain, and seeking to correct it before it became acute, we vigorously petitioned headquarters for an additional deputy. And though the powers downtown appeared to fully understand the seriousness of our predicament, they were faced with similar demands from every one of the Office's subdivisions, and mixed into the hopper with the myriad of other problems they had to deal with on a daily basis, the urgency of our request was lost sight of, so that while promises of "soon" were made, no help arrived.

Joking that we needed to "beware the ides" as March turned an eye toward April and we sought a self-help solution, our daily conferences proved to be an exercise in futility. For regardless of from what angle we viewed the problem, and despite numerous efforts to devise and apply alternative methods for handling our daily workload, we always ended up face to face with the stark realization that there were simply more cases than the five of us should be handling in view of our steep standards. So, the day-to-day grind continued, and even when we sought encouragement from the outside world, the news was mixed, and did little to bolster our dwindling energies. In February, the National Guard had been called in to oust protesters who were occupying buildings at the University of Wisconsin, though the administration, after harshly condemning the Students for a Democratic Society for stirring up the unrest, did agree to include more black students and faculty in the future. "Hey," Robbie gibed, optimism mixing with sarcasm, "at least they got a promise. Down in old North Carolina, all the protesting students got was a crack in the head from the cops' battle sticks! They didn't discriminate though, the pigs cracked white heads too—gotta give'm that," he opined to an audience of shaking heads.

March didn't do much to improve on February's news. True, for us sports fans it offered up the return of baseball and an NCAA basketball title for UCLA, but it also brought the sadness of Mickey Mantle's retirement and the end of an era. Then, turning away from pleasant diversions to serious matters, mixed was once again the key adjective involved as while Golda Meir at age seventy-one became Israel's fourth Prime Minister and boldly offered face-to-face talks with the Arab nations in pursuit of peace, former President Eisenhower passed away at age seventy-eight, thereby depriving the world of a highly respected voice of experience and reason at a tumultuous time in history. In fact, to accentuate the need, just as the Concorde flew across the Atlantic in three and a half hours to bring the world closer together, Chinese-Soviet relations reached their highest level of strain due to cross-border attacks by both poised armies. "Yeahhh," Ron muttered, summarizing our feelings with a tired sigh, "the whole damn world is struggling just like us."

How true, I thought, as we made another withdrawal from our energy bank's reserve account, and continued the fight into April. And just to stamp my observation with an exclamation point, as I spun the dial on the radio to and from the office, Tommy Roe was belting out "Dizzy," a new number one song that captured just how we felt most of the time. Two favorable incidents, however, momentarily recharged my depleted battery, the first being a not guilty verdict on a driving under the influence charge, which brought my record since early February even at three wins, three losses, and provided an overall standing of five wins since two trials had ended in a hung jury and the charges were then dismissed. "Not bad, Matthew, my man," I muttered to myself as I exited Division Two and lighted my pipe. "Especially since trying cases helps us get much fairer plea-bargains, and that's no joke, either," I grinned, noting that the jury had reported happy returns on April Fool's Day. Then, on a purely personal note, there was the celebration of my twenty-seventh birthday just five days earlier. Even though it fell on a workday Thursday, Stella made a dinner reservation at Tony Roma's, where we feasted on baby-back ribs, chicken, and a mountain of the world's most delicious onion rings, followed at home by the chocolate-fudge cake Stella had baked earlier. Then, over coffee Stella presented me with a handsome new watch, an Omega chronometer that she said would remind me to think of her often. "As if I already don't, huh?" I teased, hugging her tightly, feeling like the luckiest man on the face of the earth. "Wow, what a wonderful, wonderful day!" I enthused drowsily as we headed off to bed, recalling that earlier, with my parents conveniently vacationing in Hawaii, I had been free to visit Grammy, Grampy, and Nanny Lou on my way home. As always, it had been a good visit, brief, but filled with warm laughter, excited chatter about the opening of baseball season, and topped off with a birthday check that Grammy slipped inside my hand amidst a round of robust hugs and kisses as we were parting. Ohhh, yes, wonderful indeed! I mused as my head nestled into the pillow and found the perfect spot, a smile forming as I fell into sleep and rested more soundly than I had in several weeks.

In the middle of April, I was scheduled to try my fourth murder Prelim. A complicated case, it involved the death of a male child just over two years old, who the DA's Office charged had been willfully, deliberately, and with malice aforethought starved to death by my clients, Louise and Robert Bankman, the child's parents. Desiring to view the apartment where the alleged crime had occurred, as well as the surrounding neighborhood in order to further develop a feeling for the poverty-stricken environment in which the defendants lived, I persuaded Robbie to accompany me on a drive through the Oakbrook area late in the afternoon two days before the hearing was scheduled to begin. When we returned to the office, it was dark, but there were lights burning to the rear, and checking inside, we found George asleep at his desk. Our entry awakened him, and after determining that he was fine, just too tired to drive home, I made a pot of coffee and the three of us chatted for a while.

"Find out anything helpful, Matt?" George inquired while stretching his arms overhead.

"No, Georgie ... nothing. It's the usual situation, a shit-hole of an apartment in a run-down neighborhood. And as for the neighbors, well, as usual they don't know anything about anything—they just plain don't want to talk to you. They don't disappear, they just stand there and answer no, or shake their heads no, and won't tell you anything that might actually be on their minds. I don't know, maybe it's me. Maybe I just don't know how to ask questions anymore?"

"They're just frightened, Matthew, that's all," Robbie interjected, settling far back into his swivel chair and putting his feet up on the corner of George's desk.

"Of me, Rob? Why the hell should they be scared of me?"

"Because you're white, Matthew, that's why," he answered, then shook his head knowingly at the frown of surprise crawling across my face. "I know you find that hard to believe, because you don't see color. In fact, I don't think I ever met a white man who was as blind in that area as you are, unless maybe it's old George here," he added, breaking into a smile.

"Well, thanks ... unless you're just being kind?"

"Absolutely not," he responded instantly. "But let me tell you something else. Just because you see things right, don't think that they understand that, and don't ever think that you know how they feel because you don't—believe me, you don't!" he stressed, emotion now creeping into voice. "You're white, Matthew, and while you may work here in these parts, you don't live here. You didn't grow up in this filth and stink. And your father didn't split from home when you were a baby, 'cause without skills he couldn't get a job and wanted you and your momma to be able to get welfare so you could eat!" streamed his words faster and faster. "And that's just for openers, 'cause you didn't go to school here either, in overcrowded classrooms inside old buildings that a strong wind could knock down, and you didn't have to fight a bully to keep your lunch if you were lucky enough to have one. Not to forget, of course, that you didn't meet any dope pushers in your neighborhood, or have your sisters raped and knocked up by the local gang who just felt like having a little fun!" Robbie ended, catching himself and braking to a halt when anger jumped into his voice, then pausing further to squelch it.

"No, Matthew," he then picked up, his head shaking ever so slightly, "you didn't live that. And you didn't learn to fear walking the streets of your own neighborhood either, 'cause white cops stop and search you any time they feel like it, then plant shit on you and haul your ass off to jail if you look cross-eyed at them—or maybe instead, break down your front door in the middle of the night and take away your brother for stealing a car, or your mother or sister for whoring. No, your streets had trees and flowers, not guns and pimps. They were clean and safe, not infested with trash and every kind of crime you can think of!" he spun to a close, pausing again, this time to look me straight in the eye.

"Now don't get me wrong, Matthew, please," he then continued more slowly, his voice now suddenly soft and tinged with pain. "You're one hell of a good guy, and there wouldn't be an Oakbrook anywhere if it were up to you ... All I'm trying to say is that while you know about these things I've said, you didn't actually live them or feel them. You're white, not black, and you just can't know what that's like no matter how hard you try—you see?"

"Yeah ... sure," I responded, nodding my head for emphasis. "You're right, you're absolutely, one hundred and twenty percent right. It's just that sometimes it gets so goddamned frustrating, I think I'm going to explode. I'm busting my butt just trying to help, and it seems as if they're fighting me just as hard as the pigs."

"I know ... I know. Listen, I'm black, and they look at me the same way, 'cause they think I'm just a token—just something the white man put into his system to fool them into thinking they're getting a little justice when he's really fucking them over. They just don't understand, but would you if you were them?"

"No, no way. But didn't Marty Sills' articles help change that a little bit?"

"Sure they did," Robbie nodded. "Marty told them to back us, and 'cause they trust him, they did, one time. But that doesn't mean they trust us across the board, just 'cause Marty says we're okay. They're opening their eyes, and they're a tiny bit hopeful, but that's a long way from trust—that takes time, Matthew, a lot of time, understand?"

"Yeah, of course, that makes sense," I readily acknowledged, shaking my head. "I'm just so damn tired that I'm dumber than usual, that's all—thanks for setting me straight," I tacked on through a forming smile.

"Well, if we stay here any longer, we're all dumber than usual," bounced Rob's reply, his grin adding to the collection as he stood up. "So I'm going to mosey on home to Lou and my son and heir, how about you?"

"Not for a while yet, Rob," George answered, "I gotta get caught up on my paperwork. I'll catch you in the morning."

"And you, Matthew?"

"Well, sounds good, but I think I'll keep George company. I want to read over the coroner's report again, there's still something about it that bothers me—guess I'm looking for that hole, like you taught me to."

"Ooookay ... I'll see you two fools later," he shrugged, then shuffled to the doorway, where he stopped and turned around. "Matthew?"

"Yeah, Rob?"

"You do understand what I was trying to get across to you, right?"

"Yeah, sure, Rob ... except for one thing."

"What's that?"

"Well, if I'm so white like you say, why is it that my skin is all black and blue?" I teased, rolling up my sleeve and lifting my left arm so that he could see several large and very dark bruises I had collected when a heavy box fell on me several nights before while I was helping Stella store luggage in the garage.

"Hmmm," he nodded out, pretending to study the situation carefully while a smile formed. "Must be your black blood, brother ... seeping right to the surface," oozed his answer.

"Yep, I thought so ... that must be it, all right," I chuckled.

"Good night, Matthew."

"Good night, Rob—and thanks for your help this afternoon, brother."

Before he turned and walked away, our eyes met for an instant, and his were smiling, too. When I heard the rear door close, I turned toward George, my grin still full. "That's some kind of a man, you know that?" I opined.

"As he would say: For sure, M-a-t-t-h-e-w, for sure!" George returned, doing his best impression of Robbie's drawl.

"You want another cup of coffee?"

"Uh-huh, I could use it."

Walking to the front of the office, I refilled both of our cups, then started a fresh pot brewing before returning. "You as tired as you look?" I muttered, setting George's cup down carefully and dropping back into my chair.

"Uh-huh ... that's why I didn't jump into the conversation. Besides, you're both right—our clients, and their friends and neighbors, could certainly be more cooperative, and we could try even harder not to forget where they're coming from."

"Yeahhh ... for sure. Fact is, I don't forget when I'm not so tired I can't see straight. Hell, I know I'm not black, and I'm not disappointed either. I'm already Jewish, and one minority group's plenty enough for me!" I rolled out, then watched a grin form on George's lips. "I'll tell you something, though. I may not really know all that much about that jungle out there, but what I do know is that the five of us, and Marilyn too for that matter, are about to fall on our asses from this fucking marathon we're in. Christ, we've discussed it a million times or more, but isn't there something we can do to get help?" I tossed out in frustration.

"If I recall correctly," trickled his response slowly, a twinkle suddenly appearing in his eyes, "didn't this little spat start with an almost identical question from you?"

"That's your answer? To hold a little slip of the tongue against me?"

"Well, I'm seriously considering it, yeah," he replied, nudging the needle a little deeper.

"You know what?" I jabbed with mock outrage. "You'd make a good judge. I mean, here I am, a friend and all, breaking my ass, or at least what's left of it, in the name of justice, while struggling against overwhelming odds to overcome evil and aid the underprivileged and downtrodden, and going without food, sleep, and even sex—and what do you do? You hang me with a few feeble words I once spoke that don't prove anything other than the fact that I'm out of my fucking mind—which isn't exactly news to begin with, and is probably the only reason I took this Godforsaken job in the first place! I mean, you show me one sane person that would get involved in this lunatic asylum. Go ahead, show me, Mr. Smart Ass!" I challenged, then stopped to enjoy George's grin as it widened even further, expanding across the tired lines in his face, then upward to crinkle the corners of his eyes, before finally evolving into a chuckle. When I matched it after an instant's hesitation, the two sparks quickly flamed into full-fledged laughter that lasted for a magnified minute.

"Thanks, Matt," George squeezed out after our hearty echoes tailed away and he reached for a Marlboro, "I really needed that."

"Yeahhh ... You, me, and that dumb sonofabitch in the ad on the boob tube," I confirmed, pulling out my pipe to join him.

"I'll be goddamned, but this one's really got me stumped," he slipped out slowly after exhaling, his forehead furrowing as he approached our knotty predicament for the umpteenth time. "The only answer to the fucking volume is a sixth deputy, and I just can't figure out how to make Stone and Huxton see that our need is more important than everybody else's."

"Yeah, I know. But there must be some way to convince them that our tight-zoog situation should be number one."

"A tight what?" he reflexed back at me.

"A tight-zoog situation. That's yiddish for when your ass is turning to grass and the other guy is revving up his electric lawnmower—you dig?"

"Yeahhh, I'm digging all right. But unless we figure out how to get help, the only thing we're going to dig is a hole just big enough for us to fall into, and there's a waiting line across the street for who gets the honor of covering us over!" George sarcasmed out through a weak smile.

For several slow seconds I didn't respond, listening instead to the echo of my own gibe about the lawnmower, the refrain of "ass turning into grass" somehow triggering the formation of an idea. "Hey, hold on a minute," I finally dribbled out, studying my thought as if it were someone else's. "What saved our ass in the first place?"

"Well ... uh ... a lot of things," George stammered. "What do you mean?"

"What, in particular?" I replied, reaching for my pipe, then holding it up to my lips and imitating playing a bugle. For a split second, George looked even more perplexed. Then, as the wrinkles in his frown disappeared, an inkling of a smile crept into the corners of his mouth.

"S-i-l-l-s?" he spilled out in surprise.

"Uh-huh ... Sills."

"Go on."

"Well, he helped us once. And I was just thinking that if he juiced up his newspaper again, and started a campaign to get us more manpower, that might just grab downtown's attention long enough to make us Numero Uno. I know it would take some time, but we can hold on for a while yet—a hell of a long while if necessary, 'cause you and I both know that tired, frustrated, or whatever, they'll carry all five of us out of here in boxes before we give the courthouse back to the pigs, right?"

"You can just bet your sweet ass on it!" George confirmed, the dormant grin now pouring onto his lips, electricity jumping into his voice, the wheels in his head spinning rapidly. "And you might just have something, Matt. I mean, if it were done just right, so that it looked like we had absolutely nothing to do with it, I think it might just work!" he shot out excitedly. "But God help us though, if Stone and Huxton find out that we've hatched another one of our little conspiracies."

"Hey, not to worry, the man knows more tricks than we've ever even thought of," I assured. "He's a goddamned propaganda genius, he'll know how to camouflage it so that it looks like we had nothing to do with it."

"Yeahhh ... he's a master, all right. But if the stirred-up pot ends up boiling over to the fucking Board of Supervisors, there could be a real problem. 'Cause if downtown decides they just can't send us a deputy and ignore the other sub-offices, and asks for more slots at a time when the system's working properly, our request might look like we've just grown lazy. I mean, you have to appear reasonable with those bastards."

"Okay. But that shouldn't be too hard, the volume here is insane!"

"Absolutely. But politics has a way of twisting definitions, you know?"

"Uh-huh, I do. Just ask Tricky Dick in the White House, he'll tell ya—we're trying to bankrupt the County or raise everyone's taxes, right?"

"Exactly," George confirmed, the twinkle in his eye returning for an encore. "So now that we understand perfectly that our ass could be grass on both sides of the line, what do you say we get on the horn and see what Sills thinks of your brainchild?"

"Sounds right to me, Georgie," I chuckled. "Hell, as the Good Book says: God helps those who help themselves—if you'll forgive me for dragging religion into this fucking mess."

"I'll think about it, stay tuned," he fired back through a widening grin.

Then, after reaching for another cigarette, he picked up the phone, fumbled around inside his desk for a small piece of green paper that held the desired number, and dialed our erstwhile ally. Sills was still in his office, and after a conversation of no longer than ninety seconds, during which I explained to the custodian who had entered and become alarmed at the sound of voices that it was just us who were present, George spun around in his chair and announced, "He's coming over to see us."

"Right now?"

"Yeah ... okay?"

"Well, uh ... sure," I nodded, digesting my surprise. "I'll just give Stella a ring and let her know that I'm going to be later than my normal late."

"Uh-huh," he shrugged through a knowing grin. "Good luck."

"Yeahh, thanks," I snickered, reaching for the phone. "Like I said: sacrifice for breakfast, lunch, and dinner, it's not only nutritious, it's delicious!" I added, shaking my head as I dialed.

Stella was naturally disappointed that we were going to have to forgo our planned shopping expedition to procure me a much needed new suit, and dinner out afterward. But her voice lacked genuine irritation, and after she noted that "my skinny little butt definitely couldn't afford any barbering by a lawnmower!" then followed with a sweetly toned, "No problem, but only because I love you," after I promised that the weekend would be totally work-free, the smile that had jumped across my face lingered well beyond my return of the receiver to its resting place.

"Everything, okay?" George finally asked several seconds later, cutting into my replay of "I love you."

"Uh-huh, sure, Georgie. I was just feeling grateful, that's all."

"You really care for her, huh?"

"Yeah, I do," I nodded slowly. "She's been so good to me, I mean really good. She's cooked and cared for me, and encouraged night and day. And on top of that, she's managed to help me learn a lot about myself, and made that self feel special, a feeling I never ever had before. So I care, all right, I ... uh—Say, speaking of someone special, don't you want to give Marie Anne a call?"

"No, no, I ... uh, she's not at home. She's in class tonight, and won't be home till around eleven, so I've got plenty of time, Matt."

"Oh ... I see," I returned after a slight hesitation, the far-away look that had flashed in his eyes, then disappeared as rapidly as his staccato reply, reaffirming my previously formed feeling that all was not right between them. "Marie Anne's getting her Ph.D., right?" I quickly tacked on before the silence could grow awkward.

"Uh-huh."

"In math, correct?"

"Yeah, right. Boy, you've got a good memory, Matt."

"Yeah? Well when you're short on brains, God tries to make up for it in the recall department. Say, where did a blockhead like you find such a good-looking lady, with major smarts thrown in, too?" I teased, hoping to keep on subject and learn more about their history.

"Didn't I ever tell you how I met Marie Anne?"

"No, as a matter of fact you've been holding out again."

"Well," he chuckled, "I told you how I grew up in Connecticut, didn't I?"

"Yeah ... on a farm near Hartford."

"That's right. And that's where I met Marie Anne—in high school. I started going out with her in our junior year, and we've been together ever since."

"I see ... Did you go to college together, too?"

"Well, not to the same school, but we both went to colleges in Hartford. It drove her fucking mother out of her mind!" he tacked on, a tinge of emotion creeping into his tone.

"How come?"

"Well, she's a real twit, for openers, and she never liked me on top of it. I don't think she really likes anybody."

"Really? I mean, everybody likes someone," I snickered.

"Not this bitch, Matt. She walks around through life with a pole stuck up her ass, if you know what I mean?"

"Oh, I think so. I grew up in Beverly Hills, remember?"

"Yeah, right. Well, this asshole would fit right in. I mean, the only thing she ever thinks of is herself and her social standing. You know the type, the would-be darling of the country-club set—always involved with teas and parties, and being accepted by the right people."

"Yeah, I've had occasion to meet a few."

"Well, she took one look at me, and decided that I was totally unacceptable for her son-in-law. Gotta give her credit, though, she didn't pull her punches, she let me know right off, and always treated me like I had poison ivy from that moment on!" George rapped out through a thin smile that punctuated his frown.

"What did Marie Anne do?"

"Well, there wasn't much she could do, except flip her the bone by continuing to be with me. Hell, she hates her worse than I do. When we were in college, she occasionally would come pounding on the door of my apartment at two o'clock in the morning, crying and carrying on 'cause shithead had yelled at her and called her a bunch of dirty names—and she used to hit Marie, too!" he stressed, his eyes suddenly hardening.

"Sounds like a r-e-a-l sweetheart," I sympathized sarcastically.

"Uh-huh, if you like sickies," he nodded.

"What about the father, or should I even ask?"

"Old Jim?" George quipped, his tone instantly warming, a full smile flushing across his face. "Hell, he's the nicest guy you'd ever want to meet. Why the fuck he ever got married to that piece of shit I'll never know, but he's sure paid for it."

"How so?"

"Well, Jim's an engineer, and—Say, is there any more coffee left?" George interrupted himself, feeling dry and running his tongue over his lips.

"There sure is, I put on a fresh pot after the last refill," I reported, jumping to my feet and heading toward Marilyn's domain, then returning. "Here, enjoy," I muttered, handing him his cup. "I hope it's not too strong from sitting in the pot."

"Can't be too strong for me, Matt—thanks," he grinned, leaning back in his chair and replacing his feet on top of his desk.

"You're welcome, buddy. And you were saying about Jim?" I reminded gently.

"Yeah ... well ... like I said, he's really a terrific guy—and one hell of an engineer, too. The dude just loves to tinker with complicated machines, and he's really good at problem solving, really creative. One time, when his company was working with the navy trying to perfect some kind of special diving bell, he was so enthused he damn near worked around the clock. In fact, I've never seen anyone as excited about his work as Jim was. But, of course," George further detailed, shaking his head in disgust, "there's more money in sales, so slowly but surely old bitch-face henpecked him into switching over. Now, the poor bastard's miserable, and it's really a shame 'cause he's a sweet guy, a really sweet guy. If I live to be a hundred, I'll never understand why he stays with her."

"Well ... maybe he figures it's irresponsible to get out? You know how the older generation feels about divorce?"

"Yeah ... maybe?" he shrugged. "But the kids are all grown now, and on their own. He could tell her to go fuck-off, but I guess he somehow just doesn't have it in him."

"Well, maybe it was different when they started out?" I suggested, glancing at the sad expression that had surfaced on his face. "Maybe he remembers a brighter time?"

"Yeah ... well ... that could be, I guess," he returned sluggishly, hunching his shoulders, then lighting his third cigarette in a row. "Hell," he picked up, the sadness now infiltrating his tone, "sometimes it seems like ages ago that Marie Anne and I started out together, and were close, really in love and all—and things aren't like that anymore, not exactly anyway, so I guess it's hard to figure," he acknowledged, the far-away look reappearing in his eyes as he drew on his Marlboro.

"What do you mean, Georgie? You ... you got problems?" I inquired softly, breaking the silence.

"No ... not exactly," trickled off his tongue as he thought carefully about how to phrase his feelings. "It's just that things aren't the same as they used to be between us, I mean we used to be s-o close, the kind of close that you can't exactly define, if you know what I mean?" he squeezed out, me nodding my understanding as he continued. "It's a kind of togetherness that you just feel. I mean, you can't describe it, you just know it's there, that's all," he added, then smiled and nodded knowingly when I returned it.

"I know what you mean, Georgie. It's new to me, but I understand what you're saying."

Reading my eyes, and digesting the matching sincerity inside my voice encouraged George to further open up, and after dropping his feet to the floor and his cigarette into an ashtray, he leaned forward, placing his elbows on top of the desk as he picked up. "God, but we were close, Matt," he shared. "I mean, we could just look at each other and know what the other was thinking or feeling. When we got married, after our last year in college, we didn't have anything, but it didn't matter. We were together, and that's all that counted!" he stressed, a confirming smile creasing his face. "We drove out to L.A. in an old car that I had, and arrived here knowing no one and with less than a hundred dollars between us. I remember it so well, we checked into a small motel in Westwood, down on Pico Boulevard in the low rent district, and for a week or so we lived on hot dogs and beans, and grapefruit, till we finally got jobs. Say, am I boring you with all this shit?"

"You know better than that, Georgie," flashed my reply. "Go on, I wanna hear."

"Well, okay ... But remember that you asked for it?" he gibed, his smile returning, his need to talk propelling him onward. "Anyway, when law school started a couple of months later, and Marie Anne continued working, and me too, part-time, life was so good that I used to pinch myself to make sure I wasn't dreaming! Once Marie Anne was away from that asshole mother of hers, she relaxed completely, and we had the greatest times together. We went on walks, and had picnics, and sunned on the beach—we listened to music and danced, and even had pillow fights. And best of all, we laughed all the time! You want to hear something amazing, Matt?" he asked with childlike enthusiasm.

"Yeah, sure, Georgie. What?" I returned, matching his grin inch for inch.

"Well, poor as we were, we saved up enough money to go to Europe."

"Really? ... How?"

"Well, we lived on what Marie Anne made, and saved what I brought in part-time—and then with me working full-time the next summer, by the end of my second year we had enough. We took a charter over, and for six weeks we traipsed all over the damn place!" he explained jubilantly. "I mean, God, did we have fun! We didn't stay in fancy hotels, or eat in the best restaurants, but we saw everything—all the places that we'd read about, and dreamed about experiencing. You ever been there?"

"No, Georgie, not yet."

"Well, you gotta go sometime soon, while you're still young. It's great, Matt, believe me, you ought not to miss it. In fact, if I were you, I'd talk to Stella and make plans now. Really, it's something else, you won't be sorry," he rushed at me, his river of enthusiasm threatening to overflow its banks.

"Okay, you've got me convinced," I chuckled in response. "I'll bring it up first thing when I get home, I promise."

"Good. I'll expect a full report, or otherwise I'll have to chat with Stella myself," he kidded, his reminiscing having momentarily freed him from his concerns. "Anyway, as I was saying, we had the time of our lives, and I'll never forget it, ever!" he resumed, a fresh grin appearing. "And after I finished school and started with the PD, Marie Anne—"

"The PD was your first job?" I interjected.

"Uh-huh. First, and only. I never ever wanted to be any other kind of lawyer but a defense attorney, and I knew that this was where the action was. I was right, too, huh?"

"Yeahhh, and then some. Was it what you expected, right from the start?"

"Oh, yeah, it was exactly what I hoped for. And as I was about to say, with me now working, Marie Anne went back to get her Ph.D., and everything was just as we always wanted. I don't know why exactly, but since that time things have sort of gone downhill, as I look back on it," he trailed into a pause, the wheels in his head gradually beginning to spin again as he reached for a fresh cigarette and lighted it, the one in the ashtray having long since died.

"Well ... you can't be on a high all the time, Georgie—right?"

"Yeah, sure, I know," he returned, exhaling slowly. "It's just that the closeness seems to have disappeared. I don't know, Matt, maybe I worked too hard and didn't give her enough time—maybe if I didn't take this place so damn seriously, and didn't treat the job like a crusade, things would be different."

"Doesn't Marie believe in your work?"

"She did. She used to be almost as excited about it as me. But lately, during the last year or so, she doesn't seem to care about it—doesn't even like to hear about it, really. She's just all into her math, and only talks about graduating and teaching," he explained, again choosing his words carefully. "Don't misunderstand, though, I'm real proud of her, and I've tried to show a real interest in her work. Problem is, I don't understand math at her level, so you can't talk it over like you can the war here in Solina," he added, frustration furrowing his forehead.

"Hell, Georgie, I get one and three quarters or four and an eighth when I add two plus two, so you don't have to explain to me," I gibed, trying to cheer him up a bit. He smiled, but weakly, and it faded totally when he picked up.

"I don't know, Matt ... I'm really concerned about it 'cause I love her a lot," he said slowly, sadness infiltrating his tone.

"Have you talked to her about it?" tiptoed off my tongue cautiously.

"No ... not exactly. I mean, I tried a couple of times lately—hinted at it, without making a big deal over it," he shared, the sadness in his voice burrowing deeper. "She just smiled and kissed me, and went right on talking about school and her plans for teaching. I don't know, I'm so tired and fucked over from what's been going on here, that maybe I'm not seeing things right—maybe I'm making a big deal out of nothing. I sure do hope so," he ended, lowering his eyes to gaze at the desktop, his mind's lowest gear still churning in search of an answer.

"This hell-hole almost guarantees it," I offered, again seeking to bolster his flagging spirits, "surest way I know to become deaf, dumb, and blind. It's an extra perk to supplement our minimum-wage salary, did you forget?"

"Uh-huh," he muttered, lifting his eyes, a faint smile forming. "And maybe that's it after all, let's hope so. Anyway, thanks for listening."

"Hey, your memory really is going fuzzy—we're friends, remember?"

"Yeahhh, I do," he smiled, this time warmly. "And next time, it's your turn—okay?"

"Absolutely. In fact, stand by, 'cause the need could arise at any moment," I gibed, matching his grin.

Sills knocked on the front door just as our grins turned into soft chuckles, quickly returning us to the mission at hand as we hurried down the hallway to unlock it. "Say, you fellas really do look exhausted," Marty commented sympathetically as we shuffled back to George's office.

"Brother Sills," I responded as we settled into our chairs, "we're on our proverbial ass—still full of piss and vinegar, mind you, but on our ass nevertheless!"

"Well, now ... Brother George told me you had a problem, but he didn't put it quite as eloquently as you did, Brother Matthew," oozed his reply, accompanied by a broad smile.

As was the case with George and me just a minute or two earlier, laughter followed. Then, after it faded, we settled just as easily into a serious discussion of the unexpected problem that had arisen. "I'm sorry, I should have realized," Marty commiserated, shaking his head as he informed us that while several of his associates who were "keeping an eye on the courthouse" had reported that in general all had been going well for us, they had also noted that we looked worn out. "Jesus, I should've known that five men can't do the work of ten indefinitely, I just got distracted by working on the food bank program the churches are organizing, I'm sorry, fellas," he explained, frowning. "How can I help?"

"No problem, Marty, we wouldn't have the success we've enjoyed without you," George assured him, then detailed what we had in mind regarding the procurement of a sixth deputy. Readily agreeing with George's caveat that whatever course of action was undertaken, it must be patently clear that neither the five of us, nor the Office of the Public Defender, had originated it or was influencing it in any way whatsoever, Marty promised that he would personally supervise the campaign and that special care would be exercised by everyone involved. Indicating that he would immediately have several different reporters prepare a series of articles devoted to cultivating greater cooperation between the local citizenry and our Office, he then articulated practical considerations to be advocated, such as the need to be on time for interviews and making sure that witnesses appeared for trial. These improvements were vitally important, the articles would heavily stress, "to ease the tremendous burden our dedicated Public Defenders were laboring under due to their highly meritorious standard of treating each and every case as if it were the most important one in the courthouse." Moreover, there would be a "special side benefit," Marty explained further, "to catch the attention of the bigs downtown, and lay a heavy load of guilt on them when they learn about the physical toll involved," with the proviso that nothing would be published in the *Bugle* until we had approved it. "Frankly," Marty added, the articles are Plan B. I've got a couple of more expedient avenues to explore, and an IOU or two that I've been saving to cash-in when a special occasion occurred. It shouldn't take long, I'll be back soon," he smiled as he replaced his pipe in his jacket pocket, then shook our hands and drifted back out into the night to attend yet another of his seemingly endless meetings. George and I followed behind him and stood in the doorway chatting about what mysterious political buttons he was going to push until his tall, shadowy figure turned the corner on Hester Street and was lost from view.

 Tragically, that was the last time we ever saw our friend and faithful ally. At one forty-five the following morning, while entering a small neighborhood liquor store to purchase a bottle of milk with which to soothe his ulcer, Martin Frederick Sills was shot and killed by a single bullet that pierced his good heart after leaving the gun of a heroin-crazed youth he accidentally surprised in the midst of a robbery. Robbie brought me the news around nine-thirty, as I sat plea-bargaining with Irene Fisher and Steve Shafer in Judge Austin's chambers. Instantly, a sharp stab of pain coursed upward from my stomach and lodged in my chest, propelling me out of my chair, tiny, tingling goose bumps chilling my arms as I rose. "Honest to God, Rob? There's no mistake, you're sure?" I asked, learning it was absolutely true from the sadness blanketing his face even before he confirmed it, his eyes moistening as he patted me on the shoulder when mine overflowed and tears rolled down my cheeks.

"Now you know how the victims and their families feel after your wonderful clients have done their dirty work!" suddenly knifed through the fog. And numbed as I was from shock, the reality of Marty's death settling heavily inside me, I still recognized the shrill tones of Shafer's voice, and instantly whirling around, exploded at him.

"Listen, here, you pitiful excuse for a human being!" I opened fire. "We all know you have shit for brains—same thing for your heart? Or do I hear an objection on the grounds of assuming a fact not in evidence, you little turd?" I growled ferociously, lurching two steps forward in his direction. His response was to quickly slide sideways on the couch where he was seated, then hurriedly climb to his feet and move to the windowsill behind Judge Austin's desk, fear mapping his thin face as my flaming eyes burned holes in him. When a crooked smile crept out of the corners of my mouth and I took a third step, His Honor quickly intervened.

"Get hold of yourself, Matthew, and calm down!" he ordered forcefully, rising halfway out of his chair.

The hollow sound of my first name, which in the intense heat of the moment seemed like it emanated from an echo chamber, strangely triggered a portrait of a frowning Dr. Frankl into view, and inside the next second, my rage began deflating like air flowing out of a punctured balloon. Glancing sideways at Judge Austin, then at Robbie, and finally with disgust back at Shafer, I retreated the three or four feet to my chair and wearily lowered myself onto its edge. "I'm sorry, Your Honor, and I apologize to you, Sir," I mouthed slowly and sincerely, my voice still quivering with emotion. "But not to that imbecile over there, cowardly hiding behind your robe," I tacked on. "Because anyone who's so damn dumb that he thinks because we represent our clients we're in favor of crime, wouldn't understand anyway!" I ended, my tone firm, but without anger, sadness having swelled up and overwhelmed its remnants.

Austin nodded his head up and down several times, then broke into a faint grin. "That's probably true, Matt ... That's probably true," he repeated, rising to his feet and shuffling over to the coffee pot, granting Shafer's request to be excused while en route. "But only for half an hour or so," he added as Shafer scurried away, joined quickly by Irene Fisher. Then, after Robbie announced that he had to return to Division Four, His Honor poured two cups of coffee and sat down in the chair next to me. "Here, Matt," he smiled, handing me a cup. "You look like you could use this."

"Thanks, Your Honor, I sure could," I murmured, taking a swallow and concentrating on the warmth that drained comfortably down my throat.

"You know, Matt," he picked up in a soothing tone. "I realize that you're upset, and with good reason. But if you don't learn to stop expending energy the way you do, you're going to eventually harm yourself, and I'd hate to see that happen," he smiled, nodding his head ever so slightly.

"You're absolutely right, Your Honor," I replied, returning his smile, then widening it as I thought of Stella and her identical warning. "I'll try to monitor myself more closely starting right now—and thank you for your concern, I really appreciate it, Sir."

"Okay, that's a good idea," he chuckled softly. "'Cause I'm sure that our mutual friend Marty would want you to stay in the fight for a long time."

"You knew Marty, too?" I asked, mildly surprised.

"Ohhh, yes. And I'll miss him, 'cause he was one of the finest men I ever met in all my life—and that's taking in quite a few years, you know?" His Honor gibed low-key, adding a fresh smile to his effort to cheer me up.

"Well, that may be, Your Honor," I responded, the corners of my mouth crinkling, "but you're still at the top of your game, that's for sure."

"Oh, that's because I've had a lot of time to practice fooling everyone. And speaking of making time for important pursuits, have you read any interesting books lately?" he posed, trying to further lift my spirits.

"No, Sir, I'm afraid I haven't had much free time lately."

"Well, I've been reading this new book on Greek poetry. Would you like me to share a little bit of it with you?"

"Sure," I grinned, now fully. "Sounds nice—thanks."

For the next twenty minutes, the two of us just sat there, chattering over coffee and laughing over our inability to fathom the meaning of most of the three poems he read aloud. When the time finally drew near for the resumption of business, I warmly thanked him for making me feel better, then excused myself for a quick visit to the men's room. As I started down the short hallway that led out of his chambers, I stopped and turned sideways.

"Your Honor," I called out to him at his desk, where he had reseated himself and was just opening a court file.

"Yes, Matt?"

"I just wanted to say thanks again, and to let you know that I'm really sorry that we're on opposite sides of this little war that's been going on."

Even at a distance of twenty feet, I could feel the empathy radiating from his bright blue eyes as he fixed them on mine. "We're not, Matt—not really … It just seems that way," soothed his response over the airwaves. "I've got no hard feelings."

"I'm very glad to hear that, Your Honor, very glad indeed," I replied, a smile flooding my face. "'Cause you're not like the others. You're really special in the human being department, and I hope you know it!" I stressed with reawakened emotion, then turned away before he could respond further and hurried back outside into the courtroom.

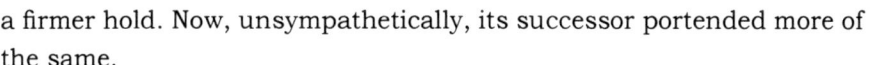

XXI

THE MONTH OF MAY OPENED UNDER hazy skies and a warming sun that harbingered the coming of a long, hot summer holding great uncertainty. April had closed with the five of us clinging desperately to our hard-won share of the embattled turf, and clawing at it like chickens in search of a worm to find a handle on which to grasp a firmer hold. Now, unsympathetically, its successor portended more of the same.

Martin Sills' death had shattered our hope for aid in the immediate future. And saddened at a deeper level by what we deemed a personal loss that far outweighed any professional considerations, the five of us had mournfully attended the simple but crowded funeral on the quiet Sunday morning following his murder. His wife of forty-seven years had granted our request, and George had proudly served as a pallbearer on behalf of the Solina Five as this gentle, loving man who befriended us, as well as countless others from all walks of life, was laid to rest with a dignity that he would have liked.

Afterward, we had returned to battle with an additional sense of purpose born out of our loss, and nourished by the even closer kinship that resulted from the heightened sense of aloneness that it left us with. For a short while, this sad but sustaining booster shot served to foster a false feeling that we enjoyed fresh, new energies, and we went about our business with restored confidence. Nothing had really changed, however, and as April faded away, so did our newfound and short-lived supply of adrenaline-fostered strength. Thereafter, our performance remained remarkable under the circumstances. But beyond tired from trying to do too much, frustrated further by limitations we refused to accept, and with nerves strained to the breaking point by the omnipresent pressure, slowly but surely our efforts slipped beneath our established standard of excellence. Errors were committed, both in open court and during the tedious and difficult plea-bargaining sessions conducted in chambers.

Technical, as well as judgmental in nature, they served to add yet another layer of anxiety to our desperate attempt to avoid surrendering a single inch of ground, which in our harried state, our collective mind raised from prized to hallowed.

Even when we paused long enough to take a deep breath, exhale, and peek outside our personal reality, the conflict, of which we were a microcosm, still occupied center stage and threatened to engulf the entire nation as the tumultuous decade ominously ticked toward a close, one shockwave seemingly setting off another, the struggle for socio-political change surfacing across the length and width of the country and even spilling beyond our borders. On the radio, Creedence Clearwater Revival was moaning and groaning about a "Bad Moon Rising," and it certainly seemed as if they were testifying to the truth, the whole truth, and nothing but. For mirroring our chaotic condition on a grander scale, society was painting a portrait of endless turmoil in bold strokes and vivid color.

Following February's student protests against the Vietnam War in the South, in April the energy of dissent channeled northward to New York City, where a vastly broader cross-section of citizenry numbering in the thousands marched down the Avenue of the Americas in opposition to the ever escalating engagement, only to be answered toward the end of the month by Nixon ordering the largest B-52 bombing thus far. Serving to further incite the steadily growing dissent, as the death toll of American soldiers rose above thirty-three thousand and surpassed the number lost in Korea, in May, student anger led to the occupation of college campuses at Columbia, Queens College, and Cornell in New York, then hopscotched to Harvard outside Boston, and finally broad-jumped to Berkeley on the West Coast. Responding forcefully to this challenge of authority, Harvard's president called in four hundred police to remove three hundred students from University Hall, while in California, Governor Reagan ordered out the National Guard and helicopters, then proceeded to rain skin-stinging powder on Berkeley's dissidents. And when Canada, our friendly neighbor, then added a large dose of highly combustible fuel to the fire by officially announcing that its government was offering American military deserters the right to settle permanently within their borders, an enraged Establishment instantly countered, one hand directing a wide range of authority figures to vehemently condemn the action in every media outlet possible, while the other summoned major corporate advertisers to bully CBS into canceling the *Smothers*

Brothers Comedy Hour due to Tom and Dick's continuous chastisement of the War and Nixon.

Decorating this two-scoop, socio-political sundae with a sour cherry, when Chief Justice Earl Warren, author of the Magna Carta opinion that ended school desegregation, retired, Nixon promptly replaced him with Warren Burger, whose legal philosophy from our point of view harkened back to the Dark Ages. "I warned you," Robbie decried the appointment, sadly shaking his head during a late-afternoon gabfest when we were too tired to do anything else. "And that pig's not done yet, believe me! First, you blackmail the media into submission, then you start packing fascists onto the Supreme Court, the only institution that can protect individual rights, and pretty soon the pigs can control everything!"

"Jesus, Robbie, you're starting to sound like me," Leon teased.

"Well, that may be," Robbie smiled. "But all the same, that's what law and order means to them—their laws, and their order. It's a conspiracy, I tell you!" he tacked on, setting off a round of laughter due to his history of expounding conspiracy theories whenever the opportunity presented itself. "Okay ... Okay ... you laugh all you want," he continued, chuckling himself, then flashing back into serious mode. "But when you're done," he nodded out slowly, "ask yourself this question: Who disappeared from the scene? The pigs? Or JFK, Bobby, and Martin Luther King?"

"Yeahhh, maybe you've got something there, after all," Ron sighed with resignation after fidgeting in his chair for several seconds. "I don't know," he shrugged, shifting venues," even the sports news is bad, what with those damn Celtics beating our Lakers for the NBA Championship."

True, I thought privately during the drive home, the news is pretty much bad, all right. If change was blowing in Bob Dylan's celebrated wind, I mused sadly, it sure was blowing on the chilly side these days. A gnawing thought, it would reoccur many times as May began to turn gray with age. And winking at the good Dr. Frankl when the sad scenario reappeared during my travels, or between cases, or underneath one of the many showers I took to revive myself at day's end so that I could enjoy the brief respite with Stella, I would answer again and again: All you can control is yourself, and your reaction to what the world serves up.

A truly wise philosophy, whose benefits increase exponentially in an ever expanding universe of life situations when coupled with the old adage that practice makes perfect, slowly but surely, it became my bible.

And though my colleagues had not formally studied at the same school, harsh circumstance soon taught them the same invaluable lesson. For though exhaustion had etched hard lines into our pale and drawn faces, fortunately the flip side of being so worn down was that each of us was forced to carefully preserve his supply of energy by daily dialing back our intensity, and then utilizing it only in accord with a specific list of priorities. This necessary discipline not only put into practice Dr. Frankl's dual controls, but also employed the corollary that laughter soothes the psyche far better than anger. When Leon attempted to serve us home-cooked lunches off of the office hot plate, thereby incurring a beleaguered Marilyn's wrath for spattering grease over the pale-green walls she had finished cleaning only hours before, we laughed long and loudly at her scolding "What the hell would Lenin say about this fuck-up?" until she, too, joined in. And when George stormed back from the courthouse screaming about the latest atrocity to justice that had occurred at the hands of Lacy or Steiggerman, we howled at his solution. "You want me to tell you what those blockheads need?" he posed, releasing his frustration into a chuckle as we nodded our collective yes. "They need a scoreboard, a giant, electric scoreboard!" he expounded, stretching his arms wide. "Then, when we've asked the right questions, and cited the right cases, the fucking thing would light up in all different-colored lights and explode with fireworks, like the ones at the baseball stadiums—and at the top, bells would ring and it would flash: No probable cause! ... Illegal arrest! You can now dismiss the case, you morons!" thundered his happy ending, further relaxing George, as well as his cackling audience.

Infrequent and fleeting as they were, these lighthearted moments pierced the veil of pressure we were operating under just often enough to refresh our weary psyches, and in combination with the discipline of conserving our energy for when we needed it most, allowed us to continue the battle while waiting to be rescued by the long-promised sixth deputy. Then, too, an unexpected show of community support, from an even more unexpected source, also helped keep our spirits up. Surprised, to understate our reaction significantly, when twelve members of the local chapter of the Black Panthers showed up in the office, dressed immaculately in black uniforms and armed to the proverbial teeth, we were in turn greatly relieved, then delighted by their offer of help. Explaining that Marty Sills had vouched for us, and that they fully understood that they could not compensate for his loss, nevertheless, their leader, Ed Ward, informed, they wanted to be of service and believed that they could assist us by serving subpoenas, driving witnesses and clients to court, and taking photographs of crime scenes. Accepting their highly useful offer with warm smiles and firm handshakes, we marveled at the fact that our fallen ally was still aiding us, making the long drive home that night shorter. And while purely a psychological lift at the time, within three weeks and in a form not yet conceived, the Panthers' services would prove valuable indeed.

Shortly afterward, and equally unexpected, a most generous pat on the back provided an additional boost to my own personal outlook, when toward the end of the month the mail brought to my desk a copy of the Bankman murder Prelim I had handled several weeks ago. Accompanying it was a handwritten note from Cliff England, the deputy from our Office who had handled it in Superior Court, informing me that with the agreement of the DA, the trial had consisted of submitting the transcript to the judge for a verdict, and that Louise and Robert had been found not guilty. England was one of the Office's most respected attorneys, and his compliments to me for a job well done that filled the remainder of his brief note cheered me immeasurably. Remaining seated at my desk at the end of another long and trying day, his words, "outstanding ... brilliant," and "You belong in Superior Court," shimmered before my tired eyes as I lighted my pipe and leafed through portions of the neatly typed and tightly bound pages, smiling as I silently read fragments of my cross-examination of the deputy coroner that Cliff had starred in red ink in the outside margins.

"Good morning, Doctor Leeder," my eyes picked up, "I hope you will bear with me as I inquire of you, because I don't have your great expertise, Sir, and it's a struggle for a layman like me just to pronounce some of these rather complicated medical terms—okay?"

"Yes, Sir."

"Thanks ... Now as I understand your testimony, you stated to the District Attorney that the proximate cause of death in this case was malnutrition. Is that correct?"

"Yes, Sir."

"All right ... Now that was the underlying cause of death in layman's language, as distinguished from the direct or immediate cause which you articulated as being from uh ... inter ... sti ... tial pneu ... mon ... itis ... Did I get that correctly?"

"Yes, Sir, you're doing fine."

"Well thank you, Doctor. And was I also correct in my layman's definition of proximate cause?"

"Yes, Sir, the underlying cause of death, as you say, was malnutrition."

"And this condition weakened the child and left him susceptible to the inter ... stitial pneu ... monitis, is that right?"

"Yes, Sir, absolutely."

"Okay, thank you, Sir," I read, my eyes following carefully, just as I had proceeded in Division Three to lay a foundation. "Now, Doctor, in order for me to try and understand this case, I read a little bit from this book here which I'm handing to you. Are you familiar with it?"

"Oh yes, certainly, Sir. Doctor Sarkowsky is the most recognized authority in the field of child nutrition."

"I see ... And you've read this book?"

"Yes, Sir, more than once."

"Kind of complicated, isn't it?"

"Well, for a lay person it would be, yes, Sir."

"Boy, I sure thought so, Doctor. I stumbled around all over the place, but I think I learned that malnutrition can result from more than one cause. Am I correct?"

"Yes, Sir, you are."

"In fact, Doctor, aren't there several causes that can lead to the condition?"

"Yes, Sir, there are."

"Okay, thank you, Doctor," read my response, the obvious deferential treatment he was receiving causing me to recall how my humble, friendly tone of voice had relaxed the witness and loosened his trained reluctance to share openly with defense counsel. "Now, excluding the obvious cause of a person receiving no food, or very small amounts of food," traipsed my words onto the next page, "would I be correct if I said that malnutrition could also result even if a person received adequate amounts of food, but that food was of a type that didn't adequately nourish the body?"

"Yes, Sir, that's another reason that could cause it to occur, but it would take a much longer time."

"Okay ... But it would occur, right?"

"Uh-huh … yes, Sir, definitely."

"Very well, Doctor, thanks again. And would I still be correct, Sir, if I said that malnutrition could also occur even though a person received both adequate amounts of food, and of a type that supplied him with the proper amounts of vitamins and minerals, if, by chance, he had something wrong with his digestive tract that prevented the nourishment from the food from being properly absorbed by his body?"

"Yes, Sir."

"I see … So just so I'm sure I understand, you're agreeing that malnutrition could occur if the digestive tract had a problem—right?"

"Yes, Sir, that's right."

"Okay … good. Now you personally performed the autopsy in this case, didn't you, Sir?"

"Yes, Sir."

"And as part of it, you checked out the digestive tract of the deceased child, correct?"

"Yes, Sir, I did."

"And if I understand your report correctly, you found some heavy scar tissue there, right?"

"Yes, Sir, I did find some evidence of fairly heavy scarring inside the gastrointestinal tract."

"All right … Now isn't also true that your finding of this fairly heavy scar tissue in the digestive tract of the deceased indicated to you that there had been something wrong with that system?"

"Yes, Sir, probably a high-grade infection of some sort, but I couldn't say for sure."

"Okay … But didn't you investigate this factor further?"

"Yes, Sir, I sent for the child's medical records at L.A. County General Hospital."

"And did you review those records, Doctor?"

"Yes, Sir, I did."

"And isn't it true that they indicated that shortly after birth, the deceased suffered an infection in his digestive tract?"

"Yes, Sir."

"And didn't they further indicate that the deceased had trouble during his infancy absorbing nourishment and gaining weight?"

"Yes, Sir, there were notes to that effect."

"All right then, Doctor," I read, turning the page again as the heart of the case approached. "If I understand all of what we've discussed here, as an expert, wouldn't it be difficult for you to say which of the three possible causes actually led to the malnutrition the deceased suffered from?"

"Yes, Sir ... it would be."

"In fact, it would be impossible, wouldn't it, Doctor?"

"Yes, Sir."

"And to be specific, Sir, based on the total evidence at your disposal, you couldn't testify that the deceased suffered from malnutrition solely because he didn't receive enough food—correct?"

"Yes, Sir ... I couldn't say that."

"In fact, Doctor Leeder, wouldn't your expertise lead you to the belief that more likely than not, it was one of the other two possibilities, or a combination of both, that caused the malnutrition in this case?"

"Yes, Sir. I couldn't be positive, of course, but that would be my opinion."

"Thank you, Doctor, I have only a few more questions and then we'll be done," my words on the page pointed toward a conclusion, then seemed to slow down as memory intervened to remind that having knocked out the underlying cause, I had paused for several seconds to pick up a second book from the counsel table before focusing on the second hurdle, old Mr. Immediate. "Dr. Reeder," the transcript then continued, "I have here another medical treatise, and in it I read that interstitial pneumonitis is a type of pneumonia that most commonly attacks children between the ages of birth and four years old. Is that correct?"

"Yes, Sir."

"And I also read that it is an extremely difficult type of pneumonia to detect or diagnose. Is that also correct?"

"Yes, Sir."

"And that's because its symptoms are not easily observable, right?"

"Yes, Sir."

"In fact, Sir, isn't it true that with this type of pneumonia, one moment a child looks perfectly okay, and then all of a sudden the symptoms surface and he's not?"

"Yes, Sir, that's true."

"So, isn't it also true, Doctor, that even if the deceased had been routinely examined by you, say a few hours before his death, that you would have most likely failed to detect its presence?"

"Yes, Sir ... that's quite possible. It's an odd illness, and doesn't give much warning. It's what we commonly call crib death."

"I see, Doctor ... And if it would be difficult for you, Sir, a highly trained expert with years of experience, to detect it, in your opinion wouldn't it be next to impossible for ordinary lay persons like my clients to notice it?"

"Yes, Sir ... absolutely."

"Thank you, Doctor ... Thank you very much."

Closing arguments followed. But smiling as I slowly lifted my eyes while recalling that my poor clients had only a sixth-grade education, instead of reading further I gently closed the plastic-covered transcript and placed it on top of the desk. Then, after toasting justice with my coffee mug, I set it down and raised my arms overhead, stretching my aching muscles taut before leaning far back in my chair and gradually going limp.

In the silence that surrounded me, a myriad of thoughts crawled into mind as I sat there feeling good, but also a tiny bit uncomfortable. I had never read one of my transcripts before, and with memory supplying sights and sounds as a backdrop, my printed words on the page had added a third dimension, like I was seated in front of my TV watching a replay of a drama in which I was an actor. A truly interesting experience, for sure, I mused. But while the distance generated a degree of objectivity unavailable during or shortly after the live performance, it also created a feeling of strangeness, like I fit but was out of place all at the same time, like something had changed for the good, but was also too good to believe, not for sure anyway. "Well," I murmured softly, striving to make sense out of my mixed feelings, "one thing is for sure, and that's that forcing yourself to stay up all night reading those medical books certainly paid off. On direct examination, sneaky Irene Fisher had made it seem like food deprivation was the only possible cause of malnutrition, and that interstitial pneumonitis was just like a heavy cold," I snickered, shaking my head. "But you were ready, old boy, and you got the whole truth out of that crusty coroner. So while 'brilliant' may be a bit of a stretch, still your hard work did get a not guilty verdict on a 187 in Superior Court, and that's damn good for a little pisher who fifteen months ago didn't even know what a 187 was," trickled my analysis to a close. "Yeahhh ... not bad at all, counselor. You're not really ready for Superior Court yet, but just keep learning and you'll get there," I tacked on in the returning silence that now seemed to give me a little hug. "And thanks, Cliff ... damn nice of you to make the time to let me know I'm doing okay, I owe you one, man."

As the faint echo of my whispery conclusion faded away, George entered the front door and made his way down the corridor to my office. "Hi, there," he squirted out, dropping his briefbag.

"Hey ... What's up, Georgie?" I smiled back at him, glad to no longer be alone.

"Not too much for a change. I just finished up in Lacy's pit—wasn't really too bad today."

"Yeah, just hell, huh?"

"You could say that," he grinned. "It's all kinda relative, right?"

"For sure," I nodded out as I relit my pipe and he slipped into a chair.

"Everybody else gone home?"

"Uh-huh. Rob was the last, and he left about twenty minutes ago."

"What's that?" he asked, catching sight of the transcript.

"Oh ... it's a copy of the transcript of that murder Prelim I did last month. Remember?"

"The one where the baby died?"

"Yeah."

"What happened?"

"Would you believe it, Cliff England submitted it, and got a not guilty?" bounced my reply, causing a smile to flood across his face.

"Well, I'll be a sonofabitch, that's great, Matt!" he enthused. "Rob told me he heard your closing argument, and that it was one of the best he ever listened to. Did you tell him what happened?"

"No, I didn't know myself till I opened the mail after he left for home."

"Well, wait till he hears. I mean, goddamnit, but that's great news!" rollicked his continuing delight. You ought to be proud of yourself, Matt—really, no bullshit, I mean it. You and I are both going to be a lot older before a 187 goes to trial again on just a transcript. I'd like to read it. Could I take it home this weekend?"

"Sure, of course you can, Teach."

"Well, I don't know about that," he gibed, chuckling, "maybe you ought to be teaching me now, and Robbie, too."

"Yeah, sure, that'll be the day, old buddy," I returned, a smile creasing my face. "But thanks for being so happy for me ... I've been sitting here thinking it over, and I really do feel pretty good about it."

"Well you fucking-A ought to!" he opined, emphasizing the strength of his conviction with one of his notorious fist slams onto the desktop. "Say, how about we go have a drink to celebrate?"

"Sounds great if you're sure you have time. It's already after seven, you know?"

"I've got plenty of time, 'cause Marie Anne's in class as usual. But what about Stella?"

"No problem. She's visiting a friend out at the UCLA Medical Center who just had surgery."

"Well okay, then, let's get moving."

"You got it, my man," I nodded, following him as we first checked to make sure that the front door was locked, and the coffee pot was turned off, then headed to the parking lot.

We had selected a small bar in close proximity to the freeway for our celebration, and amidst its cozy atmosphere, with music playing comfortably in the background, for the next two hours we happily jabbered at each other over our drinks, first about my "momentous victory," as George hailed it, and thereafter about the most unimportant subjects we could conjure up. I wasn't supposed to meet Stella at a restaurant we had decided to try until ten o'clock, so released from time's restraining hands, and relaxed further by the icy gin-and-tonics we slowly but steadily sipped, the two of us quickly put aside our worries, and rambling from one subject to another, we laughed and chattered like two young school boys without a care in the world.

Later, there was the added pleasure of watching the gleam form in Stella's eyes as she read England's note and parts of the transcript out loud at dinner, unwilling as she was to wait patiently for the privacy of home. Then, too, congratulations flowed forth from Robbie, Ron, and Leon the following morning over coffee and donuts, their compliments extended with gibes. And inserting herself into the celebration as soon as the laughter subsided, Marilyn then capped the festivities with her sweetly toned "Guess I'll have to show a little more respect," followed by a kiss on the cheek.

Enhancing my sense of satisfaction, the recognition and respect flowing from those to whom I accorded the same proved momentarily intoxicating. And because the victory was so wholeheartedly shared in by my colleagues, when combined with the Panthers' show of support, the sudden updraft made our load seem lighter as we went about our business that third week of May.

XXII

HINDSIGHT, AS THE OLD ADAGE reminds, offers twenty-twenty vision. And had I even an inkling of what lurked just around time's corner, I would have savored that shared moment of euphoria even more than I had, maybe even tried foolishly to make it last a lifetime. For as the end of May approached, the weight of our burden once again grew frightfully heavy from having carried it such a distance of days, pressing in like a vise and causing us to suffer through nightmarishly long days, one of which for me came complete with the queer experience of nearly fainting at its end.

Beginning at eight-thirty that steamy Wednesday morning, when Division Three's doors swung open and the waiting human avalanche squirmed inside and squeezed forward to fill every nook and cranny of Judge Lacy's domain, it wouldn't end until twelve tumultuous hours later in the cool darkness of an unexpectedly rainy night. And in between, a carousel of concerned faces and controverted events whirled and spun before me like a top whose pace was dizzying when viewed in retrospect, but slow and tortuous on the grainy surface of a single hour's living experience.

Appearing first on the court's calendar was James Alexander. Twenty-five years old, black, and married with four children, he had been unemployed for the past three years, and a heroin addict for the past seven. Nine days ago, at gunpoint according to the arrest report, he relieved the cashier at a Brynhurst mini-mart of between two and three hundred dollars in small bills of mixed denomination. Arrested six hours later, and subsequently identified by no less than five witnesses, he denied committing the crime when I interviewed him an hour earlier. Frightened, he had camouflaged his fear with an assumed arrogance and a genuine display of hostility. Forcefully denying that he had ever been arrested, even when I showed him the court file's CII sheet that listed eleven arrests and three prior convictions for minor offenses, as the interview progressed, he grew steadily more surly, remained steadfast in his defense that he knew nothing whatsoever about the crime he was charged with, and ended on an all too familiar note. "Hey, white motherfucker," he taunted as I closed my briefbag. "When I get to Superior Court, do I get a real lawyer?"

"Absolutely, Jim ... Absolutely," I smiled back at him, then shook my head knowingly to myself as I departed the small interview room near the holding tank.

Objectively, his case was hopeless, what the trade commonly called a dead-bang loser. This discouraging fact, however, did not deter me from doing my job and intensely probing the testimony of the two eyewitnesses that Irene Fisher used to convincingly establish the People's case. Hammering away at them for just over forty-five minutes from every angle that experience had taught me, I accomplished the only objective that I could, that of insuring that no gross miscarriage of justice had occurred. Not as high a priority on Judge Lacy's list, when I had finished, he promptly displayed his annoyance over what he perceived as a waste of the Court's time by raising bail from ten to fifty thousand dollars, in turn provoking Jim into an outburst reiterative of his previously expressed desire to be represented by genuine counsel. Delivered loudly as he was led from the courtroom, his belligerently toned request further piqued His Honor, and instantly turned the battle personal.

"Mr. Harris," Lacy opened fire, his tone bursting with disgust, "I trust that beginning right now you will exercise better control over your people. If not, I will be forced to deal with any similar behavior by adding contempt of court charges to the complaints already filed. Do you understand?"

"Yes, Your Honor, I do," I returned firmly. "And I would respectfully advise this Court as follows: First, that the individuals I represent before it are my clients, not my people. And secondly, with regard to their conduct, you may rest assured that I always instruct my clients to demonstrate full respect for the Court, just as I do. However, I can't control them like they're some kind of machines, and if they become emotional because they're frightened, and feel that the Court is deliberately trying to further frighten them by say, for example, raising a bail setting they already couldn't meet if their lives depended on it by five hundred percent, then there is little I can do. So if you choose to hold them in contempt, Sir, I'll just have to represent them on that charge, too, as best I can."

Scowling, Lacy requested both Irene and myself to approach the bench. "Do I understand, Mr. Harris, that you are threatening this Court?" he picked up after I shuffled over and stood alongside Irene.

"I don't believe my statement to the Court, if read back, could be interpreted that way, Your Honor," marched my response confidently.

"Well, I get the feeling that you were telling me that if I exercise my powers as I see fit, that you might resort to your former stalling tactics—and I understand that as a threat."

"Well, Your Honor," I jabbed in return, "what you understand is something which I also have no power to control. If I did, I'd win a lot more cases in your courtroom. So I'm perfectly willing to stand on the record, Sir, and that's all I've got to say on the subject."

Searching my eyes across the short distance that separated us, Lacy found a calm but resolute defiance, and well aware of the fact that the record would not support his accusation, he broke off his gaze and ended the confrontation abruptly. "Very well, Mr. Harris, very well," he snapped, a crooked smile then squirming to the surface. "We'll just have to see, won't we?"

Leland Jones was next. Employed part-time as a shipping clerk in a warehouse, while attending Solina Junior College on a full-time basis, he had been both pleasant and fully cooperative during his interview. With refreshing candor, Lee had freely admitted having had several marijuana cigarettes in his right jacket pocket while walking home from a girlfriend's house around eleven o'clock in the evening, at which time he had been stopped by two white officers who then searched him and found the marijuana. Now, he sat quietly beside me and shook his head in disbelief as my old friend from the Ginther case, Deputy Sheriff Glenn Hardy, repeated on direct examination the lie he had previously written into the arrest report.

Having been educated on the subject that law enforcement officers cannot legally stop and search an individual just because he's walking down a street late at night, and that if they do, any contraband which they discover by such illegal means will be inadmissible in court, Officer Hardy proceeded to relate one of four alternate stories that the collective police authority had invented and commonly used to avoid having cases dismissed because they failed to comply with the legal requirements of the Fourth Amendment to the United States Constitution. In Lee's case, Hardy presented what our Office sarcastically nicknamed Script Number One, testifying that while on routine patrol he and his fellow officer had noticed the defendant walking down Oak Street, and that when the defendant spotted their black-and-white marked vehicle approaching, he had made "a throwing motion," which caused him and his fellow officer to suspect that contraband was involved. So, ordering the defendant to stop, they recovered the thrown object which turned out to be a Winston flip-top hard pack containing marijuana cigarettes, and then placed the defendant under arrest.

Knowing that the only defense to the simple fact situation laid out neatly before the Court was to make it appear so ridiculous that it could not be believed, and that realistically this tactic was effective only in front of a jury during a full-blown trial, I still harbored serious doubts about the argument that the wisest policy for the defense to adopt at the preliminary-hearing stage of the proceedings was to silently accept the situation so as not to provide the officer with a taste of what awaited him in Superior Court. Feeling that this option was more valid prior to law enforcement's widespread use of the Big Lie, and therefore their subsequent knowledge of the defense's reaction to it, and believing even more strongly that the silent-acceptance posture created an indelible impression in the client's mind at a critical stage of securing his trust that his only representative didn't give a good goddamn about what happened to him, I therefore rejected this strategy and proceeded to cross-examine in detail.

"Officer Hardy, you arrested my client, correct?" I opened perfunctorily while strolling over to the vicinity of the witness box.

"Yes, Sir, me and Officer Bowles."

"But you were the one who actually told Mr. Jones that he was under arrest, right?"

"Yes, Sir."

"And you personally placed the handcuffs on him, right?"

"Yes, Sir."

"Now, Sir, before you placed the handcuffs on Mr. Jones, did you conduct a routine pat-down search of my client?"

"Yes, Sir, it's standard procedure."

"I see. And at that time, did you look at his face?"

"Yes, Sir."

"And did anything appear to you to be wrong with Mr. Jones' eyes?"

"No, Sir."

"They weren't bloodshot?"

"No, Sir."

"Well, were they pinpointed?"

"No, Sir."

"How about dilated?"

"No, Sir, the defendant appeared to be fine."

"It was dark, wasn't it?"

"Yes, Sir. But we had our vehicle's headlights trained on the defendant, and I also used my flashlight to check him out—he appeared fine."

"Really, officer? Fine?"

"Yes, Sir, that's what I said."

"Then he didn't appear to be intoxicated?"

"No, Sir," he answered, a faint smile forming.

"Not even a little bit?

"No, Sir."

"You're sure? No odor of alcohol on his breath? No staggering?"

"Yes, Sir, I'm absolutely positive!" he announced, now grinning visibly and glancing at Irene Fisher as if to say, We don't have any problems here, do we?

Pausing for several seconds, I watched as Hardy smiled broadly at what he deemed my foolish focus on Script Number Two, when he had testified on direct examination to Script Number One. Quite aware that Lee had not been arrested for being intoxicated in a public place and searched pursuant thereto, the scenario I had nicknamed the Fred Ginther Fairytale, a faint smile of my own appeared, then quickly washed away as I turned my attention to Script Number One's fabled theme of Lee having allegedly tried to dispose of the marijuana by throwing it away.

"Officer Hardy," I picked up, now focused on wiping that arrogant grin off his face, "were there streetlights along Oak Street?"

"Yes, Sir."

"And when you and Officer Bowles were riding in your vehicle, did you have your headlights turned on?"

"Yes, Sir, of course. As I already testified, we were on ordinary routine patrol, so there would've been no reason to have them turned off."

"Well, Sir—"

"Mr. Harris," Lacy suddenly intervened, having grown irritated with what he considered useless cross-examination, "the Court does not see the point of your questioning. The witness hasn't testified about the defendant being intoxicated, Officer Hardy said he was on patrol and as he approached the defendant, he saw him throw an object into the street. Now if you want to explore that area, go ahead. Otherwise, stop wasting the Court's time."

"Your Honor, Sir," issued my reply instantly, "is the Court telling me that I cannot cross-examine with respect to my client's physical condition at the time he was arrested?"

"No, counsel, I am not. What I am telling you is that at some point it's irrelevant."

"I've heard no objection from the District Attorney, Your Honor?"

"Well, the Court on its own motion objects, Mr. Harris! Do you hear that?"

"Yes, Sir, I do," I nodded, noting that he had grown visibly more agitated. Standing on solid legal ground, and desiring to bait him into committing judicial error, I decided to continue the confrontation. "Are you ordering me then to cease my inquiry into this area?"

"Would you understand me, if I did?"

"Yes, Sir, I believe so. Are you so ordering me?"

"Yes, I most certainly am!" he boomed back at me.

"Well, that being the case, Your Honor, I would move for the dismissal of the charges on the ground that my client has been effectively deprived of his Sixth Amendment right to cross-examine through his counsel, citing Jennings versus—"

"Your motion is denied!" he cut me off, his tone growing even louder.

"But I haven't even finished making it, Your Honor."

"I've heard it before, and it's denied! Now, do you wish to inquire further?"

"Actually, Your Honor," I replied slowly, smiling inwardly at the now excellent 995 Motion I had set up in Superior Court, "there are a few more questions I'd like to ask the witness."

"All right, then proceed," he growled. "But stay in a relevant area."

"Very well, Your Honor, thank you," I nodded, turning my gaze back to the witness box. "Officer Hardy," I resumed, "how many cigarettes were there in the flip-top box you recovered?"

"Eleven."

"Okay ... And how far from my client was it when you retrieved it?"

"About three or four feet."

"I see ... Now how tall would you say my client was?"

"About six feet."

"And how much would you say he weighs?"

"About a hundred and seventy pounds, give or take a little."

"All right ... Now Mr. Jones was standing in front of a house when you observed him to make this throwing motion that you testified about—correct?"

"Yes, Sir."

"Did this house have a front lawn?"

"Yes, Sir."

"And flowers and bushes?"

"There's a hedge around the yard, and it was dark, so I can't say about the rest."

"There weren't any lights on inside the house, or nearby?"

"No, I couldn't see the yard, just the hedge which was right next to the sidewalk."

"Well, how high was this hedge?"

"About four feet."

"Okay, Officer. Now about this throwing motion you saw Mr. Jones make, was it a motion like throwing a baseball?"

"Yes, Sir, you could say that."

Having meandered politely around John Brown's barn to arrive at a comfortable spot, I suddenly hardened my tone and attacked. "Officer Hardy," I jabbed, "how do you explain the fact that a six-foot, one-hundred-seventy-pound man, trying to get rid of a half-filled cigarette box, threw it the enormous distance of three to four feet?"

Surprised more by my sudden shift of tone than by the question itself, for an instant Hardy looked perplexed, before recovering quickly and supplying the standard explanation of "I don't know."

"You don't know?" I challenged, my tone infused with amazement. "Well I don't blame you, no one else understands how that could happen either! One thing's for sure though, the Dodgers aren't interested, right?"

"Well, I didn't mean that the defendant wound up like a pitcher," Hardy responded, the remnants of his grin having disappeared, "he just made an overhand toss into the street. That's what I thought you meant by a baseball throwing motion."

"Oh, I see, Officer ... Well let's just see if I can make myself a little more clear so that you won't have to think so much about what my questions mean. Now, you did observe my client to raise his arm and place it behind his head, right?"

"He raised it, but only up to shoulder height."

"Okay. And then he brought his arm forward, correct?"

"Yes, Sir, sort of sideways."

"But overhand nevertheless, right?"

"Yes, Sir, it was overhand like you say."

"And it's still your testimony, Officer, that a six-foot, hundred-and-seventy-pound man, who you testified appeared fine, made a sideways, overhand throw of a cigarette box containing eleven cigarettes, and it traveled only an amazing three for four feet away from him?"

"Yes, Sir, that's all a toss would go, especially if a person were in a hurry and didn't take time to wind up so that he might not be noticed."

"Noticed by whom, Officer?"

"By my partner and me, of course."

"Ohhh, yes," I nodded, "you did testify that Mr. Jones looked in your direction before he made his throwing motion, didn't you?"

"Yes, Sir, he did … definitely."

"And if I remember correctly, your vehicle was traveling toward him—correct?"

"Yes, Sir."

"So there wasn't much chance of his missing your sheriff's car, was there?"

"No, Sir."

"So wouldn't it have made more sense for Mr. Jones, if he didn't want the cigarette box to be noticed, to have thrown it away from you, instead of toward you?"

"I don't know what the defendant was thinking, Sir, maybe he was confused."

"I see, his self-preservation instinct just disappeared," I opined sarcastically, my tone remaining placid. "Officer Hardy, have you ever testified before Judge Lacy before?"

"Yes, Sir, several times."

"And he impressed you as being an intelligent, fair-minded person, didn't he?"

"Yes, Sir."

"Then how in God's name," I suddenly lashed out, boring my eyes into his, "can you calmly sit there and expect him to believe that a good-sized person, knowing that he possessed illegal contraband, and observing a sheriff's car approaching, would make an overhand throw that delivered the contraband only three to four feet away from him, and right in your direction so that you couldn't possibly miss seeing it? Especially, Sir, when he could easily have slipped it over the adjacent hedge into a dark front yard that you admitted you couldn't see hardly at all?"

Bolting upright as my accusatory tone steadily amplified into a full-fledged bellow, Hardy flushed with anger as he leaned forward and grasped the witness-box railing with both hands. Only Fisher's ringing objection, which was superseded by Lacy's even louder-toned inquiry, prevented him from shouting his reply back at me.

"Mr. Harris, what exactly are you suggesting?" His Honor snarled.

"That the witness, Your Honor, is purely and simply not telling the truth!" marched my reply in a rock-hard tone, fueled by a storehouse of frustration from having listened to countless police officers confidently relate the identical fact situation just echoed by Hardy, secure in their knowledge that the only other witness was a fellow officer, and leaving the defendant standing alone and helpless in the face of their manufactured testimony.

Already aware of our Office's feeling from having listened to the five of us imply the identical accusation on innumerable occasions, Lacy was still not expecting the terse but graphic indictment which spilled effortlessly off my tongue. "Whaaat?" he cried, articulating his astonishment. "Are you accusing this officer of committing perjury?"

"Your Honor," I replied, now flooding my voice with sincerity and meeting his gaze head on, "formal accusations are the business of the District Attorney's Office, not mine. My job is only to defend my client, and while you and I do not always see eye to eye on many issues, I have always admired the fact that this Court does not take lightly the giving of false testimony. In fact, Your Honor," I continued, now nodding my head for emphasis, "I have always respected the Court's intelligence as well, and I feel that I am only pointing out what you, yourself, would have already recognized if you were not distracted by being so angry and upset with me—which I very much regret, Sir, 'cause I'm only doing the best I know how."

Fully expecting me to respond with additional vituperative remarks, which he fully intended to punish, my unexpected compliments, delivered in a painfully apologetic tone, instantly dulled the sharp edge of

Lacy's anger. And arriving just as his eyes shaded glassy and he reached for his right temple and began earnestly massaging it, the fortuitous combination extinguished the hostile expression mapping his face and replaced it with pure puzzlement. Further softening the intensity of his gaze, he stuttered out a confused "Well ... then ... what are you actually saying, Mr. Harris?" and as a cloudy curiosity settled over him, listened to me intently as I answered.

"Your Honor, all I'm saying is that on behalf of my client I beg you to look at the evidence before you—not glance at it, Sir, but really take a long look and see it for what it is. Now, when all is said and done, Your Honor, what Officer Hardy's testimony boils down to is this: He wants you to believe that a six-foot, one-hundred-seventy-pound man possessing ordinary intelligence observed a clearly marked sheriff's car approaching with its headlights on, and becoming frightened because he knew that he illegally possessed marijuana, stood there dead in his tracks and tossed the evidence of his crime three to four feet away and right smack in front of the officers," I presented slowly and calmly, then paused for a second to let the short summary sink in.

"Now, Your Honor, was this man intoxicated, or otherwise incapacitated so that he could not think or act differently?" I then continued, keeping my tone humbly conversational. "No, Sir, he was not. Officer Hardy testified that he examined him and that he appeared fine, to quote his exact words. And did this man have no other place to throw his package? Well, Sir, the facts show that he certainly did. According to Officer Hardy, there was a hedge just a few short feet away, and beyond that, a yard which was unlighted and which Officer Hardy stated was so dark that even with his vehicle's headlights on, and supplemented by his flashlight, he couldn't see whether there were trees or bushes or flowers in it," I explained, again slowing into a brief pause.

"Your Honor," I then resumed, my tone growing plaintive as I met his now relaxed gaze, "we're not dealing here with some kind of machine named Mr. Defendant. My client, Leland Jones, is a human being, just like you and me, and I beg you to see that and to place yourself out on Oak Street late one night. You haven't done anything wrong, Sir, you're just walking home, when all of a sudden you see a sheriff's car approaching, and you become frightened because you know you've got some marijuana in your coat pocket and you don't want to go to jail. Now fortunately, only a few feet away is a hedge, and behind it a dark, unlighted yard where you could easily hide the marijuana and save yourself. So I ask you, Your Honor," flowed the heart of my plea, as I summoned a touch of emotion into my tone, "would you really take it out of your pocket and toss it right in front of the sheriffs? ... No, Sir, you would not, I submit, because you're a human being, and human beings just don't act that way—and the truth of the matter is, Your Honor, that Leland Jones didn't act that way either!" I stressed, heading toward a close. "And that's why I implore you, Your Honor, to consider the human factor involved in our situation here, when you're being asked to accept an almost impossible series of events as the truth. Please reject that testimony, Your Honor. For even at this stage of the criminal process, where the burden of proof is not beyond a reasonable doubt, you still have the right and the power to dismiss a case where the testimony is so inherently unbelievable that it does not warrant holding the defendant to answer. You should make that finding, Sir. You really ... and truly ... should."

Articulating my last words barely above a whisper, I broke my fixed gaze, and after sitting down glanced back up at Lacy after three or four slow seconds had ticked by. His facial expression mirrored his internal conflict as he lowered his eyes and fidgeted with his notes, trying to decide what to do. Persuaded, despite his preconceived ideas and deeply embedded prejudice in favor of the prosecution, that the evidence was totally unbelievable, and as such dictated a dismissal of the charges, with equal certainty he understood that such a ruling would mean that he officially confirmed my labeling Officer Hardy, and the law enforcement authority he represented, a liar and a perjurer. Such rulings, he also knew, were not the type which led to a promotion to Superior Court. So, after factoring this latter consideration into his thinking, and weighing both sides carefully, he surrendered as always, to the dictates of his ambition, and offered up a sugar-coated compromise.

"Mr. Harris, I have given your argument serious consideration," he opened, his tone sympathetic, "and while I find considerable merit in it, I do not share your opinion of my right to view the evidence in the manner which you suggested. So, I'm going to bind the defendant over to Superior Court, where you can then renew your motion before trial and get a ruling on it from a higher authority. I will, however, grant a motion to release the defendant from custody on his own recognizance until that time."

"So moved, Your Honor ... And thank you," I responded while rising to my feet, pleased that Lacy fully expected the case to be dismissed before trial, and that Lee was out of jail, but inwardly snickering in disgust at his passing the buck on calling Hardy a liar.

"Very well, then, that'll be the order of the Court. Are you ready on the Leans case, Mr. Harris?"

"Yes, Your Honor, I am."

"Well, good. We'll take a five-minute recess, and then hear that one next."

Turning towards Leland Jones as Lacy disappeared into chambers, I returned his smile and walked with him toward the door which led to the lockup. As we passed the departing Hardy, he reached out and tapped me on the shoulder. "Nice try, counsel," he jabbed sarcastically. "But you shouldn't work so hard, it's just a waste of time."

"Oh, I don't mind," I fired back. "If it gets that far, which I seriously doubt, the jury downtown is going to see right through you the exact same way any reasonable person would!"

"Say, you really are a little bastard, aren't you," hissed his reply, his snide grin having disappeared.

"Wrong again, Officer," I retaliated, forcing a grin of my own. "I'm a bigger bastard than you can even imagine."

Bristling, he growled "I'll see you again, prickhead!" before starting to move in the direction of Irene Fisher, who had called out to him.

"Oh, I sure hope so," zinged my retort. "I won't have to work so hard preparing the case, 'cause I'm sure your story will be exactly the same."

Turning back around while he was still searching for an appropriate vulgarity to fling at me, I hustled over and caught up with Lee just as he was about to pass through the open doorway. "Jesus," he muttered, shaking his head. "You better watch yourself, that man was really pissed off at you!"

"Hey, that goes with the job, Lee," I smiled. "Listen, you're going to be released in a couple of hours, and I want you to promise me that you'll show up downtown, 'cause we'll win this for you. Okay?"

"You can count on it," he nodded back. "But I sure wish you were going to be there."

"Don't worry about that," I assured him, patting him on the shoulder, "our lawyers in Superior Court are even better than me. You just be there, you hear?"

"I will ... I promise. And thanks, man, I won't forget you," he tacked on as the bailiff motioned it was time to get moving.

Gideon's Children | 391

"No sweat—Just take care, and good luck to you," I called out to him as the door began closing.

No sweat, huh? I gibed silently as I headed to the restroom. Then would you mind explaining why at ten-thirty in the morning you're already bathed in it? Taking off my coat after I had "made a contribution," as Grampy liked to joke, I tugged at my shirt, then sighed slowly with relief as it loosened from where it was stuck to my back and I felt a rush of cool air from the overhead vent. "Ohhhkay, that's better, Matthew, old boy. Now just settle down and get next to yourself," I chuckled softly as I emerged back outside into the hallway and bumped into Ron.

"Talking to yourself again, little guy?" he tossed at me, grinning.

"Hey, it beats hell out of talking to the pigs in this shit-hole. How's your ass?" bounced my answer.

"Not real good, I think I've got the flu or something."

"It wouldn't surprise me, this fucking place is full of germs. In fact, some of them are so big, that they parade around in black robes, you dig?"

"Uh-huh," he nodded, "I have no trouble at all, and neither would Leon at this moment."

"What do you mean?"

"Well, the jury came in guilty on that stupid trespass case that Steiggie pushed him into trying, and old Arlie Asshole gave the defendant—aged seventy-one, mind you—a hundred and twenty days!"

"You got any other good news for me?" I shrugged, shaking my head.

"Sure ... Richard Nixon loves God, mother, and apple pie, how's that?"

"Can't be," I cracked. "That Nazi doesn't have a mother, he was issued by Hitler and sent over here to undermine us in the last days of the war. And speaking of dictatorial dickheads," I added, glancing into Division Three through the small window in the door, "here comes William the Ball-less Wonder back to his pit. I'll see you at lunch, big fella—feel better."

"Yeahhh ... okay," he shrugged, smiling and shaking his head as he walked away.

Relinquishing my own grin, I quickly pushed through the double doors and returned to my seat at the counsel table and my seesaw battle with Lacy. Not unexpectedly, it resumed in its usual manner. For apparently recovered from the momentary physical affliction that had forced his habitual belligerence and steadfast prosecutorial bias to take a brief vacation, His Honor had now returned to familiar form, with his manufactured arrogance and accompanying sarcasm operating at full capacity. Once again clear-eyed, and massaging his ego instead of his temples, with his need to complete the court calendar resurrected as his number-one priority, it took less than five minutes for us to recapture the maximum level of hostility.

Marijuana was once again the subject, as the People proceeded against Ellen Leans, a moderately attractive, twenty-seven-year-old white woman, whose occupation was listed on my interview sheet as unemployed waitress. Arrested eight days ago for being intoxicated in a public place, as usual the pot had been discovered in her purse during the booking procedure according to the arrest report, though Ellen indicated to me that she had imbibed only two manhattans, and had only been arrested after the officers patted her down and found nothing of interest. Then, with Script Number Two having reported for duty, Number Four checked in and vigorously wagged its tail for attention. This all too familiar fable involved Theodore Knox, a fifty-two-year-old reformed alcoholic and over-zealous welfare recipient, the latter condition having twice led to his conviction for fraud. This time, however, the charge was illegal possession of drugs, after two deputies from the Solina Division of the Sheriff's Department stopped him for failing to have a functioning light over his car's rear license plate, and a clear plastic baggie containing thirty-seven Seconal capsules was subsequently discovered to be lying in plain view on top of the dashboard of his 1949 Ford. Equal in creative content to the set of circumstances comprising the Leans matter, these two recent supplements to the police authority's ever-expanding storybook readily combined to further stimulate my already heavy flow of adrenaline, and for just under two hours I proceeded to cross-examine and argue in like fashion to my efforts in the Leland Jones case. Lacy, having previously decided that he was not going to officially buy the Big Lie argument I was selling, and feeling that he had adequately communicated this to me, watched warily for a short while as I minutely probed the testifying officer in the Leans' case, my reminders every so often that he was under oath finally provoking His Honor to severely chastise me for wasting so much of the Court's time.

Apologizing profusely to protect the record for the contempt hearing that he intermittently threatened me with, I continued to attack the witnesses' credibility. And by the middle of Fisher's direct examination of Deputy Sheriff Morrow in the Knox matter, Lacy was so exhausted from arguing with me, as well as with Fisher, whom I had drawn into the fray by questioning her ethics in supporting the unfolding fictional episode, that he was forced to declare a fifteen-minute recess. Then, after we resumed, I added further fuel to the fire by objecting, on grounds only theoretically applicable in most instances, to every single question that flowed from Fisher's stentorian-toned voice, which tactic quickly inflamed His Honor to within an inch of his breaking point.

"Mr. Harris!" he roared fiercely like a wounded bear. "If I hear one more word out of your mouth—just one—during the rest of this officer's testimony, you are in contempt and that's a promise! Do you understand me, Harris? Do you? Answer me, now!"

"I do, Your Honor," I returned softly after allowing the quivering flesh of his face to settle, "and of course I will obey the Court's order. I would, however, have the record reflect my objection to it, as well as my motion to dismiss this case on the ground that my client has been effectively deprived of his right to counsel. And with all due respect, Your Honor, I do think that it's unfair for you to shout at me at the top of your lungs, just because I'm not as knowledgeable about the legal technicalities of objections as you are, Sir."

Without even bothering to overrule my objection and deny my motion, Lacy requested Fisher to resume. Then, thirty minutes later when I had completed my raking cross-examination, and before Fisher could read her stipulation regarding the chemist's report, he raised the bail from twenty-five hundred to twenty-five thousand dollars, booming out, "That's because your lawyer has a big, dumb mouth, Mr. Knox!"

"Your Honor, Sir," I responded, jumping to my feet the instant he finished, "I urgently request permission to approach the bench to confer with you."

"Very well, Harris, you may come forward," he nodded out slowly, condescendingly.

Bounding around the counsel table, I arrived three full steps before Fisher, and began delivering my message in a low hiss. "If Knox's bail isn't immediately restored to what it was, I won't even stipulate that your name is Lacy!" I informed, meeting his harsh glare with my own.

"Are you threatening this Court again, Harris?"

"No, Sir, just informing it that you agreed to refrain from such arbitrary and vicious tactics, and that if you're not going to live up to your side of the bargain, I'm not going to either. Now the decision is yours, Your Honor, what's it going to be?"

The abject enmity inside Lacy's glare intensified even further, reaching the border of raw hatred, before fading as my reference to the leverage that our Office still held finally penetrated his anger and fully registered. "Very well, Harris," he grunted in an icy tone, "I'll tell Andrea to change it when we're finished."

"You'll do it now, in open court," flashed my demand. "And there's another thing, a word called mister that goes in front of my name, in case you've forgotten that also, Your Honor, Sir," I tacked on with undisguised sarcasm.

Still seething, Lacy just nodded his acquiescence as I turned away from him and returned to my place at the counsel table. Hurriedly he announced the bail reversion in a subdued, barely audible tone of voice, Lacy's obvious chagrin engendering the small reward of a smile from Ted Knox as he was led away. And still rushing, His Honor then called the morning's fifth case before the side door to the lockup had fully closed: a family affair, wherein my client, Sarah Filo, stood charged with one count of assault with a deadly weapon, a second for assault by means of force likely to produce great bodily injury, and a third for mayhem, all of which originated from an altercation with her husband Max, whom she allegedly aimed a pistol at, then when it wouldn't operate, used it to strike him in the head, before lastly chewing off a piece of his right earlobe during the subsequent struggle.

Drained as both Lacy and I were from our previous expenditure of energy, this hearing transpired relatively quickly, and without any further histrionics from either one of us. On cross-examination, I was successful in ferreting out from a recalcitrant Max the fact that the weapon in question was a toy replica of a German Lugar, and that both he and his wife were heavily intoxicated. His Honor, without a trace of emotion in his voice, then dismissed Count One, and in the next breath both forwarded Sarah to Superior Court and recessed his for a thirty-minute luncheon break.

Reeling from the morning's strenuous altercations, I wearily retreated to the interview room adjacent to the lockup and rested inside its silence for a full five minutes before ringing for the next name checkmarked on my calendar. Jesus, fucking-A Christ, I brooded after noting that there were still ten Prelims remaining, then consoled myself by germinating the hope that Ron or George would finish their assignments early and come to my rescue. I was just about to check on their status when Sheriff Moorehouse smilingly delivered the personage of Oral Tucker to me, followed in turn by Edward Williamson and Jean Graham. In between the latter two, he brought me two oranges which I nibbled at as the thirty-minute interval elapsed and I pressed to complete the last of my three interviews.

Upon reentering Division Three, I was pleasantly surprised to find Marilyn seated in my chair at the counsel table. "Hi, Matt," she chirped through her million-dollar smile.

"Hi, yourself," I grinned back at her. "And to what do I owe this unexpected pleasure?"

"Well, George sent me to tell you that he heard you've got trouble here, and that he'll get here to help you as soon as he can. Ron was running a fever and had to go home, and Leon and Robbie are both in trial so they can't help. But George said that he'll get here the second after he's finished the arraignments, okay?"

Reflexively, I chuckled and shook my head. Bye-bye help, flashed a thought, and so much for pleasant surprises followed its sister, provoking a second chuckle. "Hey, what's so funny?" Marilyn asked, slightly perplexed over my response.

"Oh, it's nothing, hon. You tell that red-haired maniac that I'll be here, holding the fort—or at least what's left of me will be anyhow."

My poor attempt at humor produced only a weak smile, her face having grown serious as she studied mine. "Is there anything I can do to help, Matt?" she offered, concerned. "You look even worse than Ron."

"Thanks, you're a sweetheart. But not to worry, I'm all right. You just go and tell George to get here as soon as he can, okay?"

"Sure. You got it!" she tossed back, then departed at a swift pace. As she disappeared through the double doors leading to the corridor, a voice behind me called out my name and cut into my forming resolution to suck it up and hold my ground till George arrived, however long that might take.

"Harris?" I listened to a second time, having failed to respond. "Are you ready on your cases?" Swiveling around in my chair, I looked up into the fat face of Andrea Colari and flashed the thought of how perfectly proportioned it was to the rest of her spongy body. "Listen," she continued when I still hadn't replied, "the judge wants to know how many cases you're ready on. Also, you'll be pleased to know that Judge Steiggerman will be sitting in for Judge Lacy this afternoon." Possessed of a sandpapery voice to match her personality, Colari had an officious manner of pronouncing the word "judge" that attempted to cloak herself with judicial authority, while simultaneously instilling in one a strong desire to assist her in swallowing her teeth. Ignoring her effort at self-promotion, as well as her question, I finally answered by advising her that my name was Matt or Mr. Harris, her choice, then inquired as to the reason for the substitution.

"Judge Lacy is ill with the flu," she informed.

"Ohhh, that's too bad, Andrea, I'm sorry to hear it," trickled off my tongue.

"Yeah, I'll just bet you are."

"No, honestly, I'm really disappointed. I thought maybe the stupid sonofabitch had a stroke, died, and went to hell where he belongs!" I machine-gunned back at her. "I'm ready on three cases, and you can tell Steiggerman that he can start as soon as he wants."

Shaking her head in disgust, she turned away and disappeared into chambers, where she remained till just before Steiggerman took the bench some fifteen minutes later. Wearing his professional smile, His Honor exchanged greetings with the various court personnel, then having been advised by Andrea of my state of readiness, as well as my bellicose attitude, as always he tried to exercise control and prevent disruption of the Court's hallowed calendar by serving up some sugar while holding the arsenic in reserve.

"Mr. Harris," he oozed, "I understand that you're prepared on three cases—any preference for which one we take first?"

"No, Your Honor," I smiled faintly back at him. "Thank you, but whatever suits the Court is perfectly fine with me."

We began with the Graham matter, another marijuana case where Script Number One, the throwing scenario, raised its fictional head once again. Written, produced, and directed by the Brynhurst Police Department on this occasion, it was virtually an instant replay of the Leland Jones case, and ended identically with Jean being held to answer two weeks hence in Superior Court after Steiggerman took some pains to compliment me on the cleverness of my Big Lie argument.

The Tucker and Williamson cases followed, and in that they presented factual situations that left little, if anything, capable of being disputed, the afternoon's first hour and a half passed away smoothly and without any altercation between me and His Honor. Oral Tucker, a black twenty-year-old youth, had been involved in an automobile accident that rendered him temporarily unconscious. Called to the scene, the police had administered first aid, and then while filling out their accident report discovered that the vehicle driven by Oral had been stolen approximately three hours earlier. Oral's defense, related both to the arresting officers and subsequently to me, was the classic *some dude tale,* the essence of which is that some person, known only casually and therefore never by name, had allowed the defendant to use the subject vehicle, which he learned was stolen only after his arrest. Possibly the truth in one out of a million cases, the remainder of the time it serves as the counterpart of the police authority's throwing fable, rivaling it in its quality of incredulity, but unfortunately failing to match its level of acceptance. Cross-examining seriously only with respect to Oral's physical condition, in an effort to establish evidence of intoxication and negate the specific intent to steal necessary to prove grand theft auto, I was able to achieve only negligible results, and the hearing quietly concluded.

To Deputy DA David Ludlow, there is no such thing as an illegal search and seizure. And the fact that he was the deputy in charge of filing complaints on the day the Solina Police Department's Narcotics Division indicated its desire to prosecute Edward Williamson is the only reason why Ed was in custody. Larry Stroble, working an undercover detail for the very first time in his rookie year as a police officer, received information from an anonymous and untested informant that a person named Williamson was selling heroin in Apartment C at 300 North Siler Street. Williamson was described as being white, about six feet tall, and on the thin side, and without any further information or inquiry, Officer Stroble proceeded to the provided address, where after hearing "some suspicious noise" and failing to receive a response to several knocks on the door, he forcibly entered. Crashing inside with his weapon drawn, he discovered Edward Williamson, a twenty-two-year-old service-station attendant, to be toweling off after just having taken a shower. Interrogating the bewildered Williamson while he searched his apartment, Stroble was unable to find any heroin present, but did discover half of a marijuana cigarette in an ashtray on top of a nightstand in the bedroom, for which he promptly made an arrest.

Establishing the almost totally factless basis for Officer Stroble's equally erroneous formation of the belief that probable cause existed within the first ten questions I asked him on cross-examination, I immediately moved Steiggerman to dismiss the case. Shaking his head in disgust, he granted my motion, and then declared a recess to allow me to conduct further interviews. Glancing at my watch, which read five after three, I slowly released a heavy sigh of exhaustion, then turned around to head for the lockup and walked instead into a kiss, lightly placed onto my right cheek by a young woman who was both strikingly beautiful and noticeably pregnant. "Thank you, Mr. Harris," she purred through a wide smile. "I'm Eddie's fiancée, and I really appreciate what you did for us."

"Well, I'm glad I could help," I grinned sheepishly as the bailiff slipped me a stack of court files, accompanied by a teasing wink. "What's your name?"

"Sharon ... And I hope I didn't embarrass you."

"No way, that's the nicest fee I've ever received," I assured her, now looking directly into her enormous brown eyes. "Listen, Sharon, I'd love to chat with you, but I've got to prepare for another case. One thing, though—I don't know who wanted to get Eddie, or why, but someone must not be too crazy about him. I already advised him, but you make him move to a new neighborhood and stay clean, okay?"

"Sure ... I understand."

"Good ... And Sharon, you tell him also that he's a very lucky guy, and that if he doesn't take the best possible care of you and your baby, that you know a good lawyer who's going to make a lot of trouble for him."

"I'll tell him," she nodded through a fresh smile. "And thanks again," she tacked on as I turned away.

Forty-five minutes later, I returned to the courtroom, and pushing aside a meandering thought as to what hellish endeavor was delaying George from assisting me, I began the day's ninth Prelim, snickering to myself that at this point I was doing well to recall the subject matter. Steiggerman's demeanor, which thus far had been model for him, and a welcome relief from Lacy's sour truculence, remained constant through the Guerrera case, a dead-bang loser involving a twenty-nine-year-old Chicano who was arrested by the police while exiting from a jewelry store that he had robbed at gunpoint in broad daylight. However, upon its conclusion, the fact that the large wall clock behind Lacy showed five minutes after four began to prey on his nerves, and midway through my cross-examination in the Myers matter, another marijuana throwing case, his growing impatience surfaced. Denying my motion to dismiss, he rattled off the formulistic language which forwarded Heidi, a twenty-two-year-old Long Beach State senior with no prior criminal record, on to Superior Court, then called for the next case to begin before Lester Burger, an alleged burglar, had even been escorted into the courtroom by the bailiff. With a brief interval necessitated by Burger's absence, His Honor's frustration trickled into a reprimand.

"Mr. Harris, I do hope that you'll confine yourself to relevant areas during your cross-examination in the remaining cases," he scolded. "It's getting late, you know, and we still have five to finish up."

"I'll do my best, Your Honor," I shrugged back.

"Well, I hope that you'll do quite a bit better than the last case, 'cause I'm getting sick and tired of listening to a bunch of endless talk about throwing and the lot!" he chastised further.

"Your Honor," I returned, my adrenal gland reawakening, "I can only reiterate that I am doing the very best that I'm capable of to represent my clients. And I might add, Sir, that I regret the fact that you find it necessary to make insulting remarks about my honest efforts on their behalf."

A wry smile snaked across his face as he responded. "Now, now, Mr. Harris," he intoned patronizingly, "you mustn't take everything I say so personally. The Court is perfectly aware of how hard you work for your clients. All I'm asking is that you try and conserve a little more of the Court's time, all right?"

"As I stated before, Your Honor, I'm doing the very best I know how."

"Well, okay, let's just get on with our business. Your client has finally arrived, and I think you understand what I mean."

You just bet I do, you flaming asshole, flashed a thought as our eyes met and I answered, "Very well, Your Honor, I'm ready."

Having now fully awakened from its nap, my adrenal gland climbed all the way out of bed, and in response to Steiggerman's continuous efforts to crowd my cross-examination into a corner labeled brief and harmless, fueled the most meticulous approach in the opposite direction that I was capable of mounting within the limitations imposed by the virtually defenseless scenario that the Burger case presented. Thoroughly unappreciative of my minutia-highlighted performance, after the matter finally concluded and Fisher promptly requested that the Geiger case be heard next because the testifying officer was suffering from flu-like symptoms, a visibly upset Steiggerman sternly ordered me to proceed immediately to the lockup and to return no later than five o'clock, thereby generously allotting me fifteen minutes to arrive there, interview Neil Geiger, and return. Glancing at the arrest report as I strode briskly from the courtroom, I came to a complete halt and allowqed a smile to widen across my face as I discerned the subject matter to be yet another marijuana-throwing case, with the name G. Hardy appearing in the tiny box at the top of the first page labeled arresting officer. Well, how about that? I mused. It's been hours since Officer Hardy and I have had a little chat about Script Number One, I wonder if the latest fictional episode differs from this morning's, or is just a rerun? I queried sarcastically, suddenly excited to have another crack at him, then winking at Dr. Frankl as he popped into view. Oh, I know, old buddy, I concluded as I entered the interview room, control, control, control—I hear you.

Lighting up my pipe as I introduced myself, when Neil Geiger asked if I by chance had a cigarette for him, I slipped him one from a pack I carried with me and saved for use during difficult or special situations. Special was on tap in this instance, as Neil proved to be instantly likeable. Fifty-three, and recently laid off from his custodial job, he exuded an unmistakable aura of genuine kindness that made his careworn face appear younger as he shyly answered my questions, three times interjecting his thanks for the cigarette. Gifting him with the rest of the pack as I closed my briefbag, I informed him about the smoldering atmosphere in Division Three. "Listen, Neil," I summarized, "we're likely to be in for a rough time, 'cause I'm going to do my job in there, and the pig running the show isn't going to like it, you dig?"

"Yeahhh, but that's all right," he smiled back at me, "I trust you."

"Well, I can't think of a really good reason why you should, other than the fact that you're stuck with me," I muttered, grinning. "But I'm glad you do. Just remember to keep quiet and let me make all the noise. I'll do everything I can for you, okay?"

"Sure," he nodded. "And it's your eyes, Mr. Harris."

"My eyes?"

"Uh-huh ... Black people can tell a lot about a white person by what's in their eyes. Yours tell me that you're okay."

My grin reappeared as I nodded my understanding back at him.

"Well, just remember that black is beautiful, and try not to worry too much. I'll see you inside."

Upon my return to the courtroom, I found Steiggerman already seated on the bench. Chafing at the proverbial bit, he announced the case as Neil was being led in by the bailiff, and began rapidly droning out the ritualistic formalities the law required before he was even seated. Waiting patiently until he finished, I then rose to my feet.

"Your Honor?"

"Yes, Mr. Harris. What is it?"

"Well, Sir, I have become aware of the fact that the Court is in a great hurry, and I would like to make a motion that would most likely shorten this hearing considerably."

"Very well, Mr. Harris, you may proceed."

"Thank you, Your Honor ... My motion is for the Court to dismiss the charges against my client on the grounds that the Court's order to me, to interview him and prepare his defense in less than fifteen minutes, effectively deprives him of his Constitutional right to counsel under the Sixth Amendment—and in addition, violates the fundamental fairness doctrine embodied in the due process clause of the Fourteenth!" I finished with a rush, then watched the color flow into Steiggerman's face while waiting for the expected response.

"Your motion is without merit, and is therefore denied!" he ruled loudly, his eyes spitting fire.

"Very well, Your Honor. I ask then that the record reflect my client's continuing objection to every phase of these proceedings on the grounds previously stated, and thereafter, Your Honor, you will hear nothing further from the defense."

"What, Mr. Harris? Are you telling me that you are refusing to proceed with his hearing?"

"Not refusing, Your Honor. I'm merely advising you, Sir, that I am incapable of proceeding because you have not allowed me sufficient time to prepare a defense, so there won't be one at this time—just a continuing objection and motion to dismiss."

"Mr. Harris, would your position remain the same if I ordered you to proceed? I have the right to do that, you know!" Steiggerman threatened, having lowered his voice but retained the venomous tone.

"My position, Your Honor, would remain exactly the same! It couldn't change even if I wanted it to, 'cause I can't be prepared if I'm not, and that's all there is to it!" I fired back at him, lifting my outstretched palms to emphasize my helplessness. "Now, as for Your Honor's implied reference to holding me in contempt, I certainly realize that you have the power to do so. And if that's what you choose to do, I'll just have to trust that a higher court will judge that while you had that power, you did not have the right to exercise it! Moreover, Sir," I tacked on, softening my tone slightly, "while we're on the subject of moving forward, I haven't heard that the District Attorney is ready either. There certainly hasn't been a request by her for the stipulation ordinarily required in a case allegedly involving marijuana."

"Whaaat?" rolled off his tongue, his head shaking in disbelief. "On top of everything else, are you now refusing to stipulate? Are you starting that nonsense all over again?" he growled, his outrage propelling his tone louder again. "Answer me, now!" he bellowed when I failed to promptly respond.

"Well, Your Honor," I replied slowly and calmly, "my answer is twofold. First, Sir, I would respectfully remind the Court that the Judges here in Solina entered into an agreement with my Office, and if you're not going to live up to your part of the bargain, than my obligation is also null and void. And secondly, if you were in my shoes, and about to be ordered to proceed and then held in contempt because you aren't prepared and can't, would you stipulate as a courtesy to your adversary, who without the stipulation isn't ready to proceed either? ... I rather seriously doubt it, Sir, you're far too intelligent to do that."

Shooting daggers at me, Steiggerman started to respond, caught himself and stopped, and then after three or four seconds had elapsed, attempted an end run around me, measuring his words carefully as he articulated his stratagem. "Very well, Mr. Harris ... In that you insist that you're not ready to proceed, the Court will continue this matter over to another day until you are ready. Any problem with that, Mr. Harris?"

"Yes, Your Honor, there is. My client is in custody, and I could be ready to proceed if allowed just fifteen additional minutes to further prepare. So I strenuously object to any continuance, and my client will not waive his statutory right to have his case heard within ten days from the date of arraignment, which is today, Your Honor, Sir."

Still seething, but having once again regained full control of his unruly emotions, Steiggerman just sat there with his steely gaze fixed on me, the spinning wheels inside his head almost audible in the stony silence. Finally, after what seemed like an hour's worth of seconds had slowly shuffled away, in a gravelly tone he declared, "This Court stands in recess for fifteen minutes," then exited the bench and disappeared into chambers with such alacrity that the door closed behind him before the echo from his order died away.

Smiling sarcastically at his begrudging acceptance of the fact that he was not going to badger me into anything less than a full and vigorous defense, I then had Neil follow me to the jury room where the bailiff locked us inside. Perspiring heavily underneath my blazer, I removed it and entered the small bathroom provided for the jurors, where I took my time splashing cold water over my face. Then, feeling somewhat refreshed, I lit up my pipe and sat down next to Neil.

"Hey, man—you okay?" he asked, concerned.

"Uh-huh ... not to worry, I'm fine," I answered reassuringly. "How about you?"

"No problem, here. You're the one taking all the shit."

"And throwing a little bit back, too—huh?" I smiled, causing one to creep onto his lips.

"That's for sure, and more than a little," he noted. "But aren't you a little scared? That judge hates you."

"Sure ... in a way," I explained. "'Cause power is scary, and the State has a lot of it, what with its cops and DAs, and laboratories and fingerprint experts. So it's tough going up against it all alone, just me and you, especially when bullies like that pig on the bench try to abuse it."

"Yeahhh, I know what you mean," he nodded out, commiserating, "I've been scared of the cops all my life."

"Well, don't you worry too much now, Neil," I responded to the deep sadness embedded in his voice. "'Cause we're going to battle that lying sheriff, Big Time, and make a really good record for Superior Court so that we can win for you."

"You sure you're up to it? You look awful tired."

"I'll be okay, man. You just pull out one of your cigarettes, and we'll just relax a bit and store up some energy—while hopefully, that asshole Hardy is getting sicker and sicker from the flu."

"Hey, that's a good idea, Mr. Harris," he chuckled softly, the worry wrinkles in forehead finally retreating. "Serve'm right."

When we resumed, the clock now read five-thirty. Officer Hardy, looking pasty, took the stand, and on direct examination related a sequence of events virtually identical to those he presented earlier that morning in the Leland Jones case. Only the street where the alleged throwing incident occurred, and the time of night differed. All else remained exactly the same, and after I pushed myself upward and onto my feet, I searched out his eyes and curled a snarly smile across my face to provide him with a sneak preview of what was coming. Then, painstakingly, I struggled against his hostility, and both Fisher's objections and His Honor's chastisements, to paint as brightly colored a portrait of the Big Lie as I could obtain. After thirty-five minutes, the record, if read back, would have also appeared to be an instant replay of the Leland Jones matter. And at that point, with both my adversaries expecting me to initiate my plea for a dismissal on the ground of gross incredulity, instead, I took one additional step forward into the realm of the Impossible Fairytale and drew fresh blood in an amount that surprised even me.

"Officer Hardy," I began, having moved over to within ten feet of the witness box, "in the last three months, Sir, roughly how many arrests would you say you've made or participated in involving drugs or narcotics?"

"I don't know exactly," he shrugged back.

"I didn't say exactly, Officer. How many approximately?"

"Well, maybe ... about a hundred or so."

"All right, Sir. And, approximately, in how many of those arrests would you say the person arrested threw the contraband in question?"

"I couldn't be sure, counsel."

"I'm not asking you for an exact number, Officer, just an approximation?"

"Well ... I'd guess about twenty to thirty. Like I say, I can't be sure."

"Are you really sure that any of those cases actually involved a so-called throwing situation?" I jabbed, my tone suddenly hardening.

"Are you calling me a liar again?" he shot back, his nostrils flaring.

"Well, earlier this morning in the Leland Jones case, you told the exact same, totally unbelievable story that you've just repeated here. So if you're finally hearing yourself, Sir, and the shoe fits, feel free to slip it on, though I think you'll find it pinches quite a bit!" I blazed at him, my eyes radiating contempt.

"Why you little son-of-a-bitch!" rocketed his reply as color flooded his face, his voice rising with rage as he elongated the pronunciation of his emerging expletive, reflex simultaneously propelling him to lurch halfway out of his seat and reach for his gun, before he suddenly realized where he was and slumped silently back into his chair. Glancing sideways and up at Steiggerman in search of succor, he found His Honor wearing an expression of genuine horror, so hurrying his gaze back toward Fisher, he discovered that the picture hadn't improved much, her face mirroring a mixture of amazement and chagrin that caused him to lower his focus downward into his lap.

Inside several scant seconds, Script Number One had added an Epilogue, complete with spontaneous gasps from the individuals seated in the audience. Seizing the unexpected opportunity, I pounced before either of my stunned opponents could react. "Your Honor," I intoned sharply with newfound confidence, "I demand the protection of this Court before we proceed any further!"

Sincerely dumbfounded by Hardy's behavior, which totally contradicted his stockpile of preconceived notions about what a police officer was, and how he acted at all times, regardless of stress, Steiggerman nevertheless recovered rapidly and snapped back at me.

"Just what do you have in mind, counsel, an armed guard? You've provoked this officer for the last forty-five minutes. So what do you expect, that he should kiss you, maybe?"

"What I have done, Your Honor," flowed my reply, "is cross-examine Officer Hardy in an effort to force him to tell the truth, which he categorically refuses to do! I have proceeded in a perfectly legal manner at all times, and if my questions have irritated and upset the officer, that's not only permitted in an adversarial situation, but is part and parcel of the judicial process. Moreover, Your Honor," I rolled on, emotion crowding into my voice, "in no possible way does my cross-examination justify his cussing me out in open court, though that pales in comparison to his movement in the witness box, whereby he lurched in my direction and reached for his gun! He may be an officer of the law, Sir, but I'm an officer, too, an Officer of the Court, and I respectfully demand that it take steps to insure my safety!" I ended, meeting his gaze with steel of my own.

"Now, now, Mr. Harris," he replied, switching gears like a chameleon changes color, fully aware of the serious situation that Hardy had created, and now hoping that sugar might succeed in mollifying me after acid had clearly failed to intimidate. "I understand your concern, and I'm willing to instruct the witness so as to prevent any similar outbursts from occurring. But considering that things happen in the heat of battle to all of us when emotions get involved, don't you think that you're exaggerating the situation a bit for your own purposes?"

"No, Your Honor, absolutely not!" marched my reply, my tone softening slightly in response to his lower volume, but still firm. "In addition to the record, Sir, there are probably fifty people here who heard and saw exactly what you and I did. If I cursed a witness, and made a physically threatening movement toward him, you'd hold me in contempt and have me in custody before I could even take my next breath. And the District Attorney, who's remarkably silent on this incident, would be screaming for my prosecution for assault and any other crime she could conjure up," I argued, enjoying each and every word I threw up to him. "No, Your Honor," I closed, "my alleged purposes are not the issue here. Officer Hardy's outrageous conduct speaks for itself, and I respectfully renew my demand!"

"All right, Mr. Harris ... all right," Steiggerman responded, having decided to protect himself in view of the recorded facts, the large number of witnesses, and just in case Hardy suffered a further loss of control, "without making another speech, what measures would you suggest I take to insure your safety, so that we can complete this hearing?"

"Thank you, Your Honor. My solution would be for Officer Hardy to turn over his weapon to the bailiff, who would then be stationed between us."

"Very well, that will be the order. Bailiff Roberts, will you please take charge of the subject weapon and then place yourself between the witness and Mr. Harris."

Totally humiliated, Hardy slowly removed his gun from its holster and handed it over, then poured a stream of cold hatred toward me as I leaned up against the jury box and resumed cross-examination.

"Now, Officer Hardy, before this little diversion occurred, we were discussing how many of your hundred or so arrests for drugs and narcotics involved throwing incidents, and I believe you stated twenty or thirty, but you couldn't be sure—Is that correct?"

"Yes."

"So if we took a halfway figure of twenty-five, that would be a fair approximation, wouldn't it?"

"I guess so."

"Don't guess, Officer. Is twenty-five a fair approximation, yes or no?"

"Yes."

"And that would also amount to twenty-five percent of the total cases, correct?"

"I suppose so."

"Excuse me, Sir. What was your answer?"

"Yes."

"Thank you. And now that we've got that clear, Officer, how long have you been a member of the Solina Division of the Sheriff's Department?"

"A little over twelve years."

"So you began your career then about 1957, correct?"

"Yes."

"In that first year, Officer, did you make any arrests involving drugs or narcotics?"

"Yes."

"And did you make out arrest reports in those cases?"

"Yes."

"And are those reports still in the Sheriff's Department's files?"

"Yes."

"And also in the County Courthouse files?"

"Yes."

"All right now, Officer," I picked up after a brief pause. "In that first year, approximately what percentage of all those drug or narcotics cases involved throwing incidents?"

"I don't remember, that was a long time ago."

"Of course it was, Officer. And I'm not asking for a specific number, but rather an approximation. Would you say one percent?"

"No, it would be more than that."

"Okay. How much more, say five percent?"

"I can't remember."

"Seven, maybe?"

"I can't remember."

"Can't, Officer, or don't want to?" I queried, sharpening my attack. "Because—"

"Objection, Your Honor," Fisher shouted, cutting me off. "I've tried to be patient, but this line of questioning is irrelevant, and counsel is also badgering the witness."

"Your Honor," I responded instantly, "the credibility of the witness is always before the Court and therefore highly relevant. And it isn't badgering, to suggest possible answers when a witness admits having difficulty rememb—"

"Sustained!" Steiggerman ruled forcefully.

"But, Your Honor, I haven't even finished my—"

"I've ruled, Mr. Harris! There will be no more questions in this vein. Now go on to something else, or sit down and shut up!"

"Very well, Your Honor. We'll just have to get out Officer Hardy's records when we reach Superior Court, and see if before the U.S. Supreme Court began enforcing the Fourth Amendment, whether any of his arrests, let alone one out of four, involved a throwing incident!"

"Mr. Harris," he machine-gunned back at me. "Are you going to proceed, or are you going to stand there like a fool making accusations you can't prove, until I have the bailiff drag you out of here?"

As Steiggerman issued his ultimatum, the muscles in my chest tightened and I suddenly felt extremely dizzy. Grasping the jury-box railing for support, I answered that I had no further questions, and requested a five-minute recess before final arguments were heard. Anticipating the Big Lie plea I would make, and wanting time to think his decision over, His Honor granted my request, and I walked unsteadily back to the counsel table and slid into my chair next to a visibly disturbed Neil.

A glass and a half of water seemed to cure my dehydration. Steiggerman's problem, however, was more complex. Like Judge Lacy earlier that morning, he understood that Hardy was not telling the truth. But armed with much greater vision, he also worried that if he forwarded the case on to the next level and Hardy was thoroughly discredited downtown in Superior Court, an entire jury panel could be infected. Christ, flashed an even more frightening thought as he further analyzed the situation, if that little bastard Harris is telling the truth, which he most likely is, and Hardy's two transcripts prove identical, Hardy could even be indicted for perjury and the infection could spread so that officers from numerous other law enforcement agencies would also be viewed as professional liars. "Fuck!" he hissed into the silence inside his chambers, twisting in his chair as he weighed his options. "If I don't dismiss this case, a huge disaster could occur!" But on the other hand, he mused as his echo died away, if I do dismiss it, I have to call Hardy a liar to his face, and the local sheriff's division has been most supportive of my candidacy for promotion to Superior Court. So, Steiggie old boy, think, think, think: How can you weasel out of this predicament? he challenged himself, then dipped into his carefully compiled storehouse of chicanery in search of the proper escape. Hey, wait a minute, spun his neurons several seconds later, I've got it. I mean, I don't have to take the responsibility, let the judges in Superior Court handle the tricky situation. They'll see the problem, especially if I have the DA's Office call it to their attention. Yeah, let them quietly dismiss the case when no officers are present, that way no one loses face, the potential disaster is avoided, and I score some additional brownie points all at the same time—a great solution! he concluded, breaking into a wide smile.

And that's exactly the way the scenario played out, too. When Steiggerman returned to the bench, he held Neil to answer in Superior Court despite my impassioned plea, and three weeks later both his and Leland Jones' cases were dismissed on motion of the District Attorney. The latter development of course lay in the future. In the present, I was left standing at the counsel table swallowing yet another dose of disappointment. Only the fact that I was able to obtain Neil's immediate freedom from custody by trading my stipulation to the chemist's report for an OR release sweetened the sour taste in my mouth. That, and the smile on Neil's face as he departed the courtroom.

I didn't get to enjoy it for long, however, as before he left the bench Steiggerman had expressed a desire to meet with me and the DA in chambers to discuss the three cases that still remained to be heard. For a minute or so I remained seated at the counsel table, taking stock of myself. The dizziness had vanished, but left me feeling weak, and every muscle in my body ached from exhaustion. My adrenal gland, which had performed heroically, had gone back to sleep, leaving only my wry sense of humor to stimulate me. When JFK's adopted motto filtered into mind, advising that when the going gets tough, the tough get going, it oddly tickled my funny bone. "Uh-huh, great idea, Mr. President," I snickered softly to myself. "Got any tidbits of wisdom on what to do if you're not tough, and you're too dumb to run?" No answer followed, so as I dragged my weary body up out of my chair, I consoled myself with the thought that the good news was that the pig waiting in chambers didn't know it. Besides, he's not really a pig, he's a cockroach, and you've got enough left to fight a little cockroach, don't you?" I tacked on through a smile as I shuffled over to the door marked private, then knocked.

Bailiff Roberts promptly opened it, and Steiggerman greeted me with a curt, "Have a seat, Mr. Harris, you don't look well." The fury that had filled his voice only minutes ago had dissipated, but remnants still streaked his stony facial expression. As I seated myself, a second knock occurred and Stephen Shafer then appeared.

"It's late, Mr. Shafer," Steiggerman barked. "I'm dealing with Miss Fisher, and don't have time for you right now."

"Well ... Your Honor ... uh," Shafer stammered, startled by the rude reception, "Irene has a very important appointment on another matter. But I'm ready on all the cases," he then rushed to assure, "and we've got one less to deal with—my Office is dismissing the Leonard assault matter due to the victim having fled the state."

"Well, that's certainly good news," Steiggerman smiled. "Sorry for the gruffness, Mr. Shafer, but it's been a long day. And as I was about to explain to Mr. Harris when you entered, he looks ill, and in that it's already six forty-five, I think that if it's all right with you gentlemen, we'll just trail the remaining two cases over till tomorrow—okay?"

Shafer had no objection. But I did. "Your Honor," I mouthed slowly, "I appreciate both your concern for me, and the late hour. However, both of my clients are in custody, and while I'd be happy to call it a day, I wouldn't have to spend the night in jail so—"

"Now, Mr. Harris," Steiggerman interrupted, "I understand that you have a very high sense of duty and all, but you're not expected to work when you're sick," he oozed out, trying the sugar approach yet again.

Anxious as I was about my ability to continue to properly function, the cold-blooded ruthlessness with which he changed channels when it suited his purposes, like a dial on a radio, instantly stiffened my resistance. "As I said, Your Honor," inched my reply before picking up speed, "I appreciate your concern, but I've already read the arrest report in the burglary case, which isn't very complicated, and there's only one case after that—so I can make it."

"Not with the way you carry on, you can't. Now reconsider with your own health in mind, and be reasonable, Mr. Harris."

"I already have, Your Honor, and I thank you again for your concern. But I'm ready to proceed as soon as I've interviewed my clients."

"Now you listen here. I'm trying to be understanding, because I know you're nuts!" he growled, the sugar having made an abrupt U-turn and alchemized back into acid yet again. "But if you think that I'm going to sit here all night and listen to your stupid questions and absolutely insane arguments, then you're even crazier than I think! Now, are you going to continue these two cases or not?"

"No, Sir."

"Goddamn you, Harris! What in the hell is wrong with you people?" he rocketed back at me, his anger fully resurfacing, his eyes blazing into mine as he paused for an answer. "All right, all right, Mr. Noble," he picked up when I just stared back at him, "you just go ahead and interview your asshole clients. But you just remember one thing—you're so exhausted that you're sick, and I'm not. So if we start, we're going to finish even if you die out there! And don't you pull any priests out of your little bag of tricks either, or maybe I should say rabbis—that would be more appropriate, wouldn't it?" he roared to a close, color having flowed back into his face.

Having risen to my feet toward the end of his diatribe and turned sideways in preparation for taking my leave, when his last jab fully registered I whirled back around to fully face him. "What's the matter, Jew-boy, jigaboo-lover?" he snarled out through a crooked smile upon catching sight of the pain underlying the agitation on my face, "Did I hurt your super-sensitive little feelings? Well, I guess you haven't learned that all a Public Defender is, is a kike like you, defending your nigger clients from the good-guy WASPs like me!" he ground out with relish, his insidious grin widening further.

Having felt my slumbering nerve endings reawaken when the confrontation began to escalate, I now pushed down heavily on the nuclear-alert button as I stared squarely into the face of everything life had taught me to loathe. "Now *you* listen, Your Honor, not that there's anything honorable about you!" I steamed back at him, molten anger welling up inside me. "It's you, and all the sociopathic shit-heads like you, that cause all the unnecessary problems in this sad, tortured world! 'Cause what you are, is little, selfish worms that crawl around on their slimy bellies spewing out lies, and fear, and hatred in an effort to destroy anything that even smacks of equality and justice, or human goodness and decency!" I continued firing at point-blank range, shock now wiping away his grin.

"What's the matter, pig, lost your smile?" I thrust at him like a jousting spear after a split-second's pause to inhale oxygen. "Not used to being stood up to, you bully-fuck? Hard to hear the insults and hate flowing back in your direction, you shit-eating snake? Well, let me add to your education, Mr. I'm-Better-Than-You, 'cause you need to know that while you may have money, and status, and power, we're not afraid of you!" poured my stream of lava. "And that's right, I said, we, 'cause I'm not alone—there's millions and millions of people just like me who'd rather die than live in the diseased house of elitism you call the American way. So, yeah, I'm tired and sick, all right. But like them, I'll fight you till I drop, or kick your fucking, bigoted guts out!" I screeched to a halt, then watched as he jumped to his feet, the color having so thoroughly drained from his face that he looked ghostly pale.

"You're in contempt!" he shouted, pounding his desktop with this fist. "And your ass is under arrest! Shafer, go call the bailiff!" he ordered, his echo then bouncing back and forth off the walls as several loud seconds ticked by.

"Why, Your Honor?" Shafer finally answered, hunching his shoulders. "I didn't hear or see Mr. Harris do anything contemptuous. All I heard was you call him a kike and a nigger lover, and a lot of other ugly insults!"

"Whaaat?" Steiggerman cried.

"That's all I heard, Your Honor—nothing more. And between my testimony and his, the only one likely to be found in contempt is you!" Shafer stated emphatically. "You see, I'm also Jewish, and damn proud of it! You've made a very serious mistake, Sir. From now on, there will be two of us filing affidavits of prejudice against you—and for cause, too! And while I can't speak for Mr. Harris, I also intend to file a complaint through my Office with the Judicial Council!" he ended, his message falling on Steiggerman's ears like a lead weight.

Just as surprised as His Honor was, though far more pleasantly, I nodded my approval, a smug smile flickering across my face as I turned my gaze back to Steiggerman. Having slunk back into his chair and turned ashen from the impact of realizing the magnitude of the problem he now faced, he struggled to force a grin onto his lips in an effort to recover his judicial demeanor and begin wheedling his way out of his precarious predicament. "Now, gentlemen," he mouthed slowly, his head nodding slightly. "Let's all of us cool off, and not act hastily. I admit that my choice of language was in poor taste, but you mustn't take every word I say literally ... I'm human, too, and—"

"I doubt that very seriously, Your Honor," I interrupted. "Anyway, you can save your breath, 'cause your bullshit won't work on me. And this time, I doubt if there's anything you can say that'll convince Mr.

Shafer that he didn't hear what he heard, and that you didn't mean it, 'cause you and I both know that you did!"

"Nooo, honest, now hold on a minute," he shot back, trying not to show the alarm he felt. "Listen, I know that you're tired and ill, Mr. Harris, and it's easy to misunderstand someone when you're—"

"Tired?" I interjected, cutting him off again. "You just bet your ass I'm tired, and you want to know why? It's because I don't get some afternoons off to rest like you do. When you were out playing golf at your country club yesterday afternoon, I was here in this shit-hole fighting with your fellow tyrant, Judge Lacy, who's an even poorer excuse for a human being than you are!" I streamed, still angry, but having calmed considerably since my volcanic eruption a minute before. "You look surprised, Sir," I tacked on when his facial expression added quizzical to the mix. "Did you honestly believe that people around here actually bought that bullshit story your clerk tells about you being at a doctor's appointment?"

Forced to abandon his soft-soap attempt to extricate himself from the cesspool he'd created, he instantly substituted defiance. "Very well, gentlemen," he grunted. "If that's the way you feel about it, fine! If you won't listen to reason, go ahead and do what you want. But you'll regret it, both of you will. You'll see!" he declared, the weakness of his threat causing me to snicker.

"Don't bet your life on it!" I shot back at him as I turned away, then strode outside without looking back. Shafer quickly followed, and called out to me as I reached the side door leading to the lockup.

"Yeah, Stephen?" I answered, turning sideways.

"I just wanted to tell you to take your time, that's all. 'Cause I don't mind staying late, I'd like to talk with you later, anyway—okay?"

"Sure ... And by the way, thanks for the assist in there."

"Hey, no problem," he grinned, shaking his head. "I don't relate well to anti-Semites."

"Yeah, me neither," I shrugged, returning his grin. "See you in a few minutes."

Still smiling, I shuffled down the hall to the stairway wondering what the hell had come over Shafer. "Must be some sort of divine intervention," I chuckled softly to myself. "Either that, or my hydrogen-bomb blast scared him so shitless that he decided it was best to humor me." The reference to my nuclear attack on Steiggerman triggered Dr. Frankl into mind, thinning my smile and slowing my pace to a shuffle. "Hey, listen, Vic," formed my defense quickly. "I was under control. I didn't kick His Honorless in the balls like he deserves, not even once—right?" I argued, then winked after he smiled. "Well, thank you, I'm glad we agree," ended our brief conference. Then, having reached the lockup, I instantly shelved my private thoughts when Sheriff Moorehouse greeted me with the news that my client, David Hilton, had been causing such a ruckus that he had been placed in a separate, more secure cell. "Sorry, Matt, but you'll have to interview him standing up," he advised, adding with a shake of his head, "That is, if you can even get the ornery bastard to talk to you."

"That's okay, Ed," I nodded, then followed him down a narrow corridor to a cell that I never knew existed, where I waited behind him while he unlocked and slowly slid the heavy steel outer door into its wall pocket and switched on the light. Then, as he walked away, I stepped forward and peered into the small, dimly lit room through the bars that prevented entry as well as exit. As my eyes adjusted to the dusky atmosphere, my nostrils suddenly filled with a putrid odor that caused my face to crumple up into a frown, and still searching for Hilton, I noticed that pieces of a sandwich were lying about on the floor, and that several more were stuck to the wall to my left. An instant later, I was struck in the forehead over my right eye by a warm, moist substance that then dropped down onto my right cheek where I swiped at it as I recoiled several steps backward and banged into the wall, striking my head hard against it. "What do you want, you white motherfucker, huh?" then snaked into ear as I rubbed my head, turning it further right toward the shadows from which Hilton had emerged. The stench, having grown stronger, now combined with the dizziness that had returned courtesy of the head-bang to cause a wave of nausea to sweep over me. Leaning forward, I gagged, then listened to Hilton's low, guttural chuckle as he enhanced his warm greeting. "What's the matter, honky, you got a weak stomach?" he mocked.

"Listen, toilet-mouth, my name's Harris, and I'm an attorney from the Public Defender's Office, appointed to represent your dumb ass!" I stormed back at him, my storehouse of anger still not empty. "And the first thing I want you to know is that I've had all of your shit that I'm going to take. So shut your fucking mouth, before I leave you here by yourself—and I do mean all alone, 'cause in this whole fucking courthouse, you've only got one friend, mister, and that's little old me!" I blazed, my throbbing head adding fuel. "Now I was born white, and you popped out black, and neither one of us had a choice in the matter, so knock off the racial bullshit, and knock it off now! Do you hear me, friend?"

Stunned by my stinging retort, he blinked rapidly several times in succession before muttering, "Mean little sonofabitch, aren't you?"

"Well, let's put it this way, Mr. Hilton ... I've been fighting pig judges, and pig cops since eight-thirty this morning, and I'm tired Big Time—so the very last thing I need is a pig for client!" I clarified, then gradually lowered my volume, but retained the steel in my tone as I continued. "Now my job is to get you out of here if I can, and from the looks of the arrest report that isn't going to be easy, so you'll pardon me if I don't have time to be afraid of you, 'cause I don't! Now, do you want to help me help you, or do you just want to sit here in this shit-hole feeling sorry for yourself?" I asked, boring my eyes into his.

"I'll talk to you man, I'll talk to you," he returned, nodding his head for emphasis.

"All right ... that's better," I nodded back. "Now, the first thing I need to know is—"

"Hey, Matt—you okay?" Sheriff Moorehouse suddenly interrupted, shouting to me from the end of the corridor.

"Yeah, I'm fine, thanks ... no problem here," I returned.

"Well, I heard you yelling. You sure?"

"Yeah ... really. But listen, as long as you're here, will you come and unlock the door so I can sit down? It's awfully difficult to write standing up."

"Well, I don't think that'd be a good idea, Matt," he cautioned upon arriving next to me. "He might hurt you."

"No, I don't think so, Sheriff," I smiled. "I appreciate your concern, but Mr. Hilton and I have reached a little understanding. It'll be okay, really."

"Well ... all right," he replied, acquiescing, and unlocking the door, but still concerned. "Let me tell you something, Hilton," he added, pointing a finger. "You lay a hand on this man, and I'll be back with a lot of help, and you'll wish you'd never been born—you hear me?"

"He hears you, Sheriff," I quickly assured him. "And thanks."

As Moorehouse slowly strolled back down the corridor after wishing me good luck, I entered the cell, and after stepping over a puddle of urine, sat down on the small wooden bench attached to the rear wall. "All right now, Dave, let's get down to business," I instructed, studying his face. "Tell me your side of the story, okay?"

"Sure, Mr. Harris," he nodded.

Charged with forcible rape, Hilton, a twenty-seven-year-old, unemployed jack-of-all-trades, with a prior record for burglary and grand theft auto, readily admitted having had sexual relations with the alleged victim, nineteen-year-old Lois Chapman. In a tone now devoid of hostility, he quickly related to me the story of how he had met her at a party several months ago, had been dating her steadily since that time, and had had "full sex" with her an average of three times a week for the past two months. Puffing on my pipe, I listened carefully as he explained further how just three weeks ago she had informed him that she was pregnant. "I like the girl, man—a lot, really," he stressed, emotion creeping into his tone as his delivery picked up speed. "But I don't want to get married. Hell, I don't even have a regular job, and neither does she. Anyway, when we rapped about it, I ran it down to her about how I felt and all, and about getting an abortion—which is no big deal, right?"

"Uh-huh ... to some people," I nodded. "But not to others."

"Yeah, you got that right. 'Cause she started crying and carrying on about how it's against her religion, and a whole bunch of shit like that. I kept trying to talk sense to her, but ... well ... to tell the truth she's not real smart, if you know what I mean, so she just kept crying about how she loved me and we should get married. Then, about two weeks later, the cops came and got me, and here I am, man," Dave closed with a rush, shaking his head.

"What do you mean, when you say she's not too smart?" I queried, instinct telling me I didn't have the full story.

"Well, she's sorta on the slow side," trickled Dave's response. "Pretty, but kinda dumb—you know the type, right?"

"Yeah, I know," I nodded, neurons flashing that Dave was an asshole, followed with equal speed by my notation that his taking advantage of the situation didn't constitute rape. "All right, now listen, and listen carefully," I instructed. "When we get in the courtroom, I'm going to have to lean on the lady really hard, you understand?"

"Yeah."

"She may start crying and carrying on, like you say, and the pig judge we've got will do everything he can to protect her. Which means that then I'll really have to rip her up, and I don't want any interference from you—absolutely none, you hear? No outbursts, no funny facial expressions, nothing! You dig?"

"Yeah, man, I dig," he nodded vigorously. "I don't care how bad you mess her up, just get me out of here!"

"I'll do my best. You just hold on, and I'll see you in court in a few minutes."

Shuffling back down the corridor, I knocked on the door for Moorehouse, then slowly inhaled and exhaled several deep breaths of the fresh air in his office outside the lockup, before asking permission to use his phone while I waited for him to go lock Hilton's cell and return to unlock the regular interview room. Explaining to Stella inside of sixty seconds that I was fine, but delayed more than usual due to a Prelim calendar from hell, and rushed for time to boot, I was still smiling from her "No problem, sweetie, you can share the details over dinner," when Moorehouse returned, patted me on the back, then went to fetch Raoul Garcia.

Raoul also proved to be a breath of fresh air. After I identified myself and explained that he was charged with burglary and that the arrest report stated that he had been caught inside the premises, when I asked for his side of the story, he simply nodded shyly and confessed, "That's what happened, man, they got me."

"Were you drinking?" I queried, searching for a shred of a defense.

"No."

"On pills or pot?"

"No. I smoke pot sometimes, but not that night."

"Well, Raoul, I'll do what I can," I advised with equal candor, "but the situation doesn't look real good for you."

"I know," he returned sadly. "Listen ... uh ... You wouldn't have a smoke, would you?"

"Oh, yeah ... *that* I've got for you, a couple in fact," I smiled back at him. Pushing two of the four cigarettes I had borrowed from Sheriff Ed through the tiny holes in the grating that separated us, I then stood up to leave, offering a consoling, "Enjoy. I'll see you in the courtroom in a little while."

"Okay, Mr. Harris," he smiled. "And thanks, you're an all-right guy."

Matching his grin, I rang the buzzer to summon Moorehouse, and departed before he arrived, accompanied by the sad thought of how Raoul would like the accommodations in state prison. His parting words filtered back into mind as I pushed open the door and reentered the courtroom, shrugging my shoulders at my helplessness.

His Honor was already perched atop the bench. Staring blankly at me while I took my seat at the counsel table, he slowly turned his head in Shafer's direction without changing his expression, then monotoned People versus Garcia into the record and directed the People to proceed. It took Shafer barely five minutes to have Officer Palmer of the Solina Police Department present the State's case. Testifying that while on routine patrol, he and his partner had received a radio call informing them that a silent burglar alarm had been tripped at a small warehouse on Lester Street, only three blocks away, he then related how they had promptly proceeded to the scene, where after carefully surveying the premises, they had discovered the rear-door point of entry, observed Raoul inside, and arrested him at gunpoint. Improving even further on his demonstrated ability to act swiftly, Palmer needed less than five seconds after I began cross-examination to trigger the ever-festering anger inside me.

"Officer Palmer," I asked perfunctorily, "where were you standing exactly when you first observed my client?"

"On the ground, counsel! Where else?" he rocketed back at me scornfully through a wide grin.

Laughter erupted from the audience, now thinned to twenty or so hardy souls as the clock's hands arrived at seven-fifteen. Smiling, I nodded my apparent appreciation while I waited for it to die down. Then, as I felt yet another rush of adrenaline, I laid my notes down atop the jury-box railing and turned slowly back to the still smiling Palmer.

"Thank you, Officer," I nodded out calmly, "at this late hour a little humor certainly does help. You know something, though," I added, then paused for a split-second to meet his self-satisfied expression head-on, "your remark would be even funnier if it weren't also an accurate reflection of your pitifully low level of intelligence! I mean, I'm having real difficulty trying to decide whether you're a moron, an imbecile, or just a plain ordinary idiot!" I machine-gunned, my tone rising with each barb that blasted off my tongue.

All two inches of his sarcastic smile instantly vanished as we glared at each other across the ten feet of space that separated us. "Now, now, gentlemen, let's not have any more of that!" Steiggerman interjected firmly, reacting quickly to prevent any further problems from arising. To both my surprise and Steiggerman's, Palmer ignored the warning.

"Your Honor," he promptly returned fire. "I've sat in your courtroom all afternoon and listened to this jerk treat my brother officers like they were the criminals on trial, calling them liars and every other ugly name he could think of. I'm sorry, but somebody's got to shut him up and put him back in his hole!"

Stunned by Palmer's blatant insolence, Steiggerman failed to promptly respond, creating a vacuum into which I instantly poured additional venom. "Your Honor, may I inquire where it is exactly that this presumptuous fool thinks he derives the authority to criticize this Court by implying that you're not capable of recognizing improper behavior and correcting it? And may I further inquire where this world-class ignoramus learned that this proceeding is a trial, when it's not? Not to overlook, of course," I rushed to conclusion, "where dumbo learned that there are criminals present, when the persons before you charged with crimes are presumed innocent?"

Tired from the afternoon's seemingly endless series of snarly altercations, and seriously worried about the actions Shafer had indicated he and I would both take in response to what had occurred in chambers, Steiggerman conveniently ignored my further insults to Palmer, and nodding his head slowly, turned in his chair and sternly informed him that my "absolutely correct" view of his conduct matched His Honor's point for point. Then, adding to Palmer's astonishment, he further instructed him that he would do well to answer the questions put to him with a simple yes or no whenever possible, and leave the management of the proceedings to those far more qualified.

Having been startled awake and into full battle readiness by Steiggerman's bigotry, and then further piqued by Palmer's raw contempt, my anger now shifted into overdrive, and for the next fifteen minutes I grilled Palmer like a cheese sandwich, first on one side, then on the other. Bereft of anything resembling a true defense to work with, I substituted creativity, and with virtually a free hand from His Honor, jabbed relentlessly at his still defiant posture at every turn of his testimony. And while the resulting legal effect of this strenuous exercise proved nil, Palmer's obvious relief upon finally being excused from the witness stand was reward enough. You didn't lie in this case, officer, I mused as I watched him depart the courtroom. But just know that if you come back here with one of those scripts you so resented my poking holes in, your ass is going to be in the frying pan, not nominated for an Oscar in original screenplay writing! I chuckled silently, hope, faint as it appeared, a consolation nevertheless.

Raoul thanked me again for the cigarettes before departing, and as the side door leading to the lockup opened to allow his exit, David Hilton was ushered into the courtroom, and the day's fourteenth Prelim began almost before I could catch my breath. The victim of the alleged rape, Lois Chapman, certainly wasn't hard to look at. Tall and slender, she was dressed in an attractive beige pants suit complemented by a pale-green sweater underneath the jacket. Long, dark hair surrounded the soft, sweet features of her pretty face, and jostled about the tops of her shoulders as she seated herself in the witness box and looked nervously over Shafer's head at her parents seated in the first row of the audience. Seconds later, Steiggerman granted my motion for a closed hearing, and as Shafer explained to the visibly upset Chapmans why it was that they could not remain in the courtroom, I turned toward Hilton. "Did you ever meet her parents?" I asked.

"Yeah, a couple of times," he shrugged.

"What's her father do?"

"He's some kind of minister or something."

"What? ... You sure of that?" I pursued.

"Uh-huh ... yeah," trickled his answer.

"Well, why didn't you tell me, man? That's important. I mean, you knock up a minister's daughter and don't want to get married, and you wonder why you're in jail for rape?" I chastised. "Any other little juicy tidbits you forgot to mention?"

"No, no," rushed his answer. "I'm sorry, man, I ... I ... see what you mean," he added, shaking his head disgustedly at himself.

"Well, I gotta say this for you," I quickly offered to repair our sagging relationship, "you can sure pick women, no doubt about that!"

"Thanks," he replied through a forming smile. "Listen, you get me out of this mess, and I'll take care of it."

I didn't have time to inform Dave that he had misconstrued the intent behind my compliment, because Shafer had reseated himself and begun his direct examination. Presented chronologically, Lois Chapman's account of the alleged rape was both short and sweetly articulated by the soft, even tones of her melodic voice. She had met David Hilton at a party, and liking him, had subsequently dated him on several occasions. The last time they were together, about a month ago, they had dinner at his apartment, and after several drinks and much wine during the meal, David had made advances to her. She didn't object, until David began removing her clothes, and when she did, he had just laughed and torn off the remainder of her clothing. Then, despite her protests and physical efforts to resist, weakened as they were by the alcohol she had consumed, he had carried her into the bedroom and had sexual intercourse with her.

Studying her face as she answered Shafer's questions, I noted that even under his painstaking guidance, she had difficulty answering promptly. Nerves accounted for some of the confusion I read in her expression, I reasoned. But the more I listened and watched, the more I realized that David's assessment of "pretty, but dumb" was accurate. She didn't appear mentally disabled, but there was a dullness in her eyes as thoughts formed, and a slowness of delivery when speaking, that strongly suggested her intelligence was below average. Armed further with the belief that she was repeating a story concocted by her parents to validly excuse the unwanted pregnancy when it became necessary in the future, further evidenced by the absence of anger that should have been present when she related her woeful tale, I decided that slow and simple was the method best suited to expose the conspiracy at work. And smiling at her as I walked over to the jury box and leaned up against its railing ten feet away from the witness stand, I devoted a full fifteen minutes to questions calculated to relax her. Times, distances, and physical descriptions of clothing, dinner items, and the scene of the alleged crime were all explored and passed smoothly on into the record, with the date and time of the incident in question having also been firmly fixed so as to later allow for an alibi defense. Then, having further noted the slight lilt that crept into her voice when she pronounced David's name, as well as the sliver of light that slipped into her oversized brown eyes, I decided to first follow my instincts, and hold the traditional full-scale attack on her credibility in reserve.

"Miss Chapman," I offered up with maximum sincerity, "before you and I talk about the horrible things you say my client did to you, which if true will put him in prison for many years, I want to make sure that you understand that my purpose isn't to trick you, but just to get at the truth. 'Cause if David deliberately got a sweet young woman like you drunk, and then tore off your clothes and pushed his penis into your virgin vagina against your will, then I agree with you, he's a monster, and he deserves to be in prison for twenty years! Or even more!" I ended, having suddenly summoned mock outrage into my tone to emphasize the penalty involved.

Having lowered her head when I articulated penis into vagina, she jerked it upward in alarm when twenty years in prison slowly but fully registered, emotion instantly taking charge. "No! ... No ... I don't want that," she blurted out, tears seeping into her eyes. "I ... I ... it didn't happen that way!" she cried, her chest beginning to heave. "David's not a monster ... I love him. It's just that ... I'm—"

"Your Honor," Shafer interrupted forcefully, "the People request a brief recess, as the witness is obviously distraught from her ordeal and—"

"I strongly object, Your Honor," darted my response, cutting him off before he could argue further. "All that's occurred is that Miss Chapman has suddenly realized that this is very serious business we're involved in here, and has decided to tell the whole truth and—"

"Now hold on, gentlemen, both of you," Steiggerman interjected, taking his turn at interrupting. "I'd like you both to approach the bench."

When we arrived, His Honor informed Shafer that he was inclined to let me proceed immediately, unless Shafer could assure him that the witness had been examined at a hospital within a short time after the alleged incident, and medical and lab reports confirmed her initial testimony. Shafer then requested that he be allowed to confer with the investigating officer, and after being granted permission, sixty seconds later he returned wearing a perplexed expression. Advising Steiggerman that no such evidence existed, but that he had just learned that his Office was under heavy pressure to prosecute anyway due to the influence of Miss Chapman's father, who was Chairman of the Southern California League of Protestant Churches, he then stated that it was all right with him if the Court dismissed the case, as long as he was allowed to record the People's strenuous objection. "Very well, Mr. Shafer, that's what I'm going to do in order to spare your Office from being seriously embarrassed in Superior Court," slithered His Honor's unctuous response. "That's a favor to you, Mr. Shafer, as well as your Office, so don't forget it," he stated firmly. "And it's also a favor to you, Mr. Harris, 'cause you get to look like a hero instead of maybe collapsing from exhaustion! Now let's wind this up, okay?"

Glancing at the clock as Steiggerman, on the Court's own motion, dismissed the case, I read through bleary eyes that it registered eight-twenty-seven. For several slow-motion seconds I simply stared straight ahead at the now empty bench. Then, at a snail's pace, my brain stitched together a thought, I-t's ... o-v-e-r, crawling forth drowsily, neurons yawning. Yeahhh ... after thirteen ... hellacious hours, the fucking marathon is finally over! followed the amplified version as emotion added its contribution, the brainwaves' blaring echo still more an anthem of relief than a song of celebration as I slumped down into my chair, exhaustion sweeping over me as my adrenal gland adopted the exact same motto and retired permanently for what remained of the day. Lost inside a cloudy minute of decompression, I didn't turn sideways to face Hilton until he patted my elbow a second time.

"Hey, man—thanks!" he enthused. "You're okay, and I won't forget you. I'll call you later after I've fixed it with Lois."

"Yeah, sure," I nodded wearily. "I hope you work things out."

"No, man," he shook his head, a sly smile forming. "I don't mean for me, I mean for you. I really appreciate what you did for me, and a promise is a promise!"

"Whaaat?" I muttered, the recollection of his having misinterpreted my earlier compliment slowly slipping through the fog of fatigue that still surrounded me.

"You know, man. You liked the lady's looks, and I told you I'd take care of it if you got me out of this jam, so now I'm going to do it," he explained.

"Hey, listen, I was just trying to make you feel better, that's all," shuffled my attempt to clarify the situation. "And besides, that's just not my style," I tacked on when the expression on his face advised that my effort had failed.

"Oh, I know how you feel," he continued undeterred. "But don't worry, she'll put out with her whole heart, you'll see. After I have a little talk with her, you'll have the fuck of your life, I promise. She gives really great head, too, and—"

"What are you, some kind of animal?" I asked, stiffening with revulsion. "Don't you realize that the poor girl loves you?"

"Hey, that's her problem, man," he snickered, no longer misreading me. "She's just a good piece of ass to me! And what's your problem, white-boy, black pussy not good enough for you?" he challenged, heavy sarcasm coating his tone.

As an appropriately scathing retort formed on my tongue, I spied the bailiff approaching and squelched it, choosing instead to end the disgusting conversation by substituting his assistance. "Mr. Bailiff," I growled, fueled by the final fumes of anger from an empty tank, "would you please get this piece of shit out my sight!"

No oral response sounded through the smile of surprise that burst across Bailiff Roberts' face. Instead, he just shook his head and chuckled as he promptly led Hilton away. Stuffing my notes into my briefbag as Hilton's over-the-shoulder "Fuck you, you honky sonofabitch!" echoed loudly, I then exited the courtroom without looking back. As I pushed through the double doors and into the corridor, the dizziness I had suffered earlier suddenly returned, so heavy this time that I lost my balance and fell. Struggling to my feet, I stumbled over to the nearby bench, and after dropping down onto it gagged several times as nausea also paid a return visit. Placing my head between my knees, I concentrated on taking slow, even breaths to quiet the continuing urge to retch, success coming slowly. At the other end of the hallway, Shafer, who was busy trying to deflect Pastor Chapman's outrage, caught sight of my fall, abruptly excused himself, and rushed to my assistance.

"What's the matter, Matt? Should I get help?" he fired rapidly upon his arrival, both his face and tone infused with concern.

"No, no," I sputtered, raising my head and forcing a wan smile. "I'll be all right, Steve—but thanks."

"You sure? I saw you fall down."

"You going to prosecute me for being fucked-up in a public place?" I chuckled, my head having cleared further.

"No way," he smiled. "You'd just figure a way to beat it anyhow, and embarrass me in the process!"

"Yeahhh, right—like you don't win your share, huh?"

"Well ... maybe," he shrugged, shaking his head. "But after that last fiasco, I'm not in the mood to prosecute anyone for anything! I must be getting soft, but I really feel bad about that poor guy spending several weeks in jail for doing nothing!"

"Don't, bother!" I shot back at him. "The sonofabitch is the biggest asshole I ever met! You know what the prick wanted to do? He was going to fix it so that poor Lois was going to have to fuck me to get back in his good graces, just because I told him she was good looking. Oh, he didn't rape her according to the Penal Code," I rolled out, shaking my head with disgust, "but he fucked her over about as bad as anyone gets it in my book. So don't sweat the time he did, I'd like to give him a hundred years, or whenever his cock dries up and falls off, whichever occurs last!" I ended, my smile now stronger.

"Boy, are you the craziest goddamn defense lawyer I ever met, or what?"

he returned amicably, shaking his head again as he sat down on the bench, this time at the apparent contradiction. "I've never seen anyone fight for his clients as hard as you do, then cuss them out afterward."

"I do, when they deserve it, Steve. Like I said that day in Austin's chambers, just because I defend a person's rights and want fairness doesn't mean I'm in favor of crime. But I don't favor lying cops or bigoted judges, either. Hell, you saw both sides, too, earlier this afternoon when you finally took a good look at your ex-buddy, Steiggerman," I tossed back at him.

"Yeah, that's for sure, I could hardly believe him. It was funny, too, you and me being on the same side," he added, joking, but watching carefully, too, for my response.

"Uh-huh ... that's a first all right. But, hey, in this zoo, anything's possible."

"Yeah, right," he nodded, seemingly more comfortable. "And did you see how the slimy bastard tried to make up, by backing you against Officer Palmer, then making a big deal about the favor he was doing me and the DA's Office? You're still going to file Affidavits for Cause, aren't you?"

"Absolutely. You still willing to file a supplemental affidavit that I can attach to mine?"

"You bet I am, he's more than got it coming to him."

"Okay ... thanks—and thanks for your concern, too. I'm a lot better now, so what do you say we go home, so we don't spend what's left of this night in dear Solina?"

"Right, let's do it," he agreed, standing up. "Mind if I ask you one more question?"

"Sure ... What?"

"Well ... the other day when Detective Stillwell was in our office bitching about how we're not supportive enough, he happened to let it slip that you'd told him I was a damn good lawyer. Did you really say that?"

"Uh-huh ... 'cause it's true. When you get your oversized ego out of the way, and just use your smarts and willingness to fight, you're a damn tough opponent," I rolled out, nodding my head for emphasis.

"Well, thanks," spurted his reply through a wide grin. "You know, maybe you're not as big an asshole as I thought you were."

"Oh, yes I am, and don't you forget it either—'cause tomorrow we'll undoubtedly be right back at each other's throats," I chuckled as we began shuffling toward the door. "Meanwhile, have a good night, and I'll see you late tomorrow afternoon about those supplemental affidavits."

"No problem. You bring'em by, and I'll sign'em," he nodded, still pleased as he turned toward the stairs leading up to the DA's quarters.

"Okay. See ya," I flipped back at him, then pushed through the door and walked wearily back across the street to the office, the cool night air instantly adding to my recovery.

Finding it dark, as I expected, I checked the front door to make sure it was locked, then strolled around back and rattled the rear one as well. Approaching my car, I found a note from George fastened to the door handle. He had finished late in Division One, and learned at that time that I had only two Prelims to complete. Then, having received almost simultaneously a "troublesome" telephone call from Marie Anne, he felt compelled to leave immediately, hoping that I would forgive him for deserting me this one time. Staring down at the word "troublesome," I suddenly realized that amidst the total chaos that had unfolded since the raging altercation in Steiggerman's chambers I had totally forgotten about George. You got extra trouble, buddy? I now considered, frowning. Like we don't have enough already? flowed a follow-up thought, causing a wry smile to appear. "Well, I'll just have to see about that later, I gotta get home," I then whispered, breaking the uncomfortable silence after several ponderous seconds had crept by. "You just take care of yourself, Georgie, and don't worry about forgiveness—not after all you've done for me," I nodded, climbing into Old Greener.

As I pulled out of the parking lot, a light drizzle began to fall. Boy, that's unusual for May, I mused, but then it fits all right, 'cause it's been kind of an unusual day—right, Matthew old boy? I queried, breaking into a smile as I drove toward the freeway. "Unusual?" I repeated, answering myself. "Hell, if you had lawyer skills half as good as your gift for understatement, you could bury the pigs all by yourself! What was it you nicknamed this day earlier this morning, Whirlwind Wednesday?" I posed, beginning to laugh. "Well, whirlwind, my ass! It was a goddamned whirlPOOL, old buddy, the kind that slowly sucks you under and drowns you!" I chortled, reveling in the fact that I didn't drown, that somehow, some way I had survived and was about to be rewarded with a warm, delicious dinner after hugs and kisses from the most beautiful woman on earth. Flipping on the radio as I entered the freeway and picked up speed, I chuckled again when the Fifth Dimension crooned out, "Let the Sunshine In." "Yeahhh, you got that right, guys! Sweet sunshine and plenty of peace, as in h-o-m-e!" I spelled out, booming each letter louder and louder, then suddenly feeling overwhelmed with gratitude and falling silent. "Thank you, Adonai ... I sure do owe you one," I whispered after turning down the volume to a barely audible murmur, my smile widening. "Big Time!" I nodded, accelerating Old Greener's speed an additional five miles per hour and nestling back against the seat.

XXIII

WEDNESDAY NIGHT'S REWARD WAS as rich and nourishing as my daydream had promised. For upon sighting my fatigue-mapped face, Stella had instantly gifted extra tight hugs and soothingly sweet kisses that said, I love you, and I'll help you feel better, punctuated by a smile whose warmth made actual words unnecessary.

Having waited dinner for me, Stella further postponed it by insisting that I enjoy a long, steamy shower, followed by a large glass of Merlot. Catch-up conversation then ensued over the cheese and crackers we shared, with my overview of Whirlwind Wednesday quickly whetting Stella's appetite for details. Condensing the more mundane scenarios that had transpired into a short-short story, with relish I then focused on the Leland Jones–Neil Geiger–David Hilton trilogy, chewing over the juicy particulars almost as thoroughly as the scrumptious, cream-sauced chicken and rice I hungrily devoured. Already possessing a full biography on Arlen Steiggerman's personality and modus operandi, Stella was nevertheless as astonished as Shafer had been by the virulent bigotry displayed by his definition of a Public Defender. Having saved this tempestuous tidbit until we were sharing coffee and chocolate-chip cookies, Stella's gape-mouthed response of "As you would say, Jesus ... fucking-A ... Christ!" caused me to break into a broad grin. And even though my mellowing mood prevented me from presenting my profanity-laced retort to "His Honorless" with the same degree of venom that had originally accompanied its delivery, Stella's amazement instantly transformed into approval, forcing a simple "Wowww!" that quickly inspired laughter, soft at first, then sharp and satisfying.

After several more delicious chuckles were digested over the unexpected good fortune flowing from Shafer being Jewish, and therefore harboring a genuinely cooperative attitude regarding the planned filing of Affidavits for Cause, Stella ordered me to bed. With my aching body only too happy to comply, I promptly saluted both demands, and after a lingering good-night kiss and a page-and-a-half read of *SI*, I smilingly slipped into a sound sleep. No interruptions to go to the bathroom, or scribble a note on what to do tomorrow in trial. No nightmares, or even the infrequent happy dream that was still so intense it awakened me. Just seven nourishing hours of lost-to-the-world sleep.

Thursday morning, however, still found me heavily fatigued, as it simply wasn't possible for one good night's rest to offset the debilitating effects from the four months of constant battling that had ensued since the judges employed an attrition-based strategy to regain their prior status, topped off as it was by Whirlwind Wednesday. Hell, it would take at least a week of solid sleep to pay off this accumulated debt! I mused, driving back to Solina, my glance in the rear-view mirror revealing a pale-faced stranger with heavy dark lines etched into the sickly-looking skin beneath his eyes. "Okay, Matty, my man," I summoned sarcastically in a half-hearted attempt to jump-start my body's battery. "You weren't going to win a beauty contest anyway, so suck it up and get going." Chuckling as I flipped on the radio, I continued my efforts to energize myself by trying to siphon off some of the electricity from the saucy sound of the Beatles' "Get Back" through singing along.

Arriving in the office at the late hour of eight-fifteen, I found it almost empty, my fellow defenders having already departed for the courthouse. Except for George, Marilyn informed. He had called in ill, she explained, and had left emphatic instructions that I was "not to go anywhere near a trial court, and just take it easy by working arraignments in Division One." Smiling at George's thoughtfulness, as well as Marilyn's equally forceful, "And you just better listen, Matty, 'cause you look like death warmed over!" I quickly accepted the gift and trundled off to Judge Gelman's domain and the recess from the War's front lines it represented, making a mental note however to check with Ron at lunchtime to make sure he wasn't facing the same onerous overload in Lacy's pigsty that I encountered yesterday. I also worried about George as I settled in at the counsel table and waited for Gelman to take the bench. Was he really ill? I wondered. Or was he embroiled in a domestic crisis at home? The latter possibility made me uncomfortable, and I shifted my weight inside the chair. Hang in there, Georgie, if that's the case, I whispered silently, floating my wishes to where I imagined he was. I'm thinking of you, buddy, and sending good energy your way, I tacked on, a wistful smile playing on my lips.

Thursday then proceeded to peacefully pass by. In stark contrast to yesterday's hellacious fire-fight, the atmosphere in Arraignment Court was amicable, and so tranquil that several times I pinched myself to make sure I wasn't still asleep and dreaming. Judge Gelman's method of proceeding was both simple and efficient. After his bailiff produced twelve inmates from the lockup and seated them in the jury box, His Honor would then promptly advise them of their Constitutional rights and introduce me as their attorney. Thereafter, each defendant would be separately advised of the misdemeanor charge pending, and I would assist him or her in entering a plea of not guilty, setting the matter for jury trial, and requesting a reduction in bail or an OR release when suitable. Busy it was, due to the volume of cases. But, fruitfully, the absence of an adversarial environment featuring constant tension still provided the much-needed breath of fresh air, and inhaling deeply and often, slowly but steadily I could feel the heavy fog of fatigue lift and my energy tank gradually refill. In fact, by noon I was so cheered by my improvement that to make the afternoon even easier, I skipped lunch in the office, opting instead to munch a sandwich that Stella had prepared from last evening's leftover chicken while interviewing several inmates whose cases appeared more complicated. And riding a rising wave of positive vibrations, the self-help booster didn't disappoint. My clients were cooperative, the sandwich quite tasty, and the additional preparation proved highly useful in enabling the court's afternoon session to replicate the morning's smooth operation, a win-win-win trifecta that satisfied my taste buds, provided extra attention for those incarcerated, and eased the calendar's congestion, all of which further enhanced my recovery.

When Division One's business was completed at the early hour of four o'clock, wearing a newfound smile of contentment I shuffled upstairs to the DA's Office to acquire Shafer's signature on the stack of supplemental affidavits that Marilyn had typed. Greeting me cordially, he personally prepared my cup of coffee, then ushered me into his private office where he settled in behind his desk and promptly began signing his name forty times. Upon completing the tedious task, he leaned back in his swivel chair and smiled. "That ought to put a dent in his campaign for Superior Court!" he commented cheerfully.

"Yeah, I certainly hope so," rolled my reply through a grin. "As you pointed out, he's certainly got it coming to him—and thanks again for your help."

"No problem. But, say, can I ask you for a favor?"

"Sure ... if I can do it."

"Well ... I've been thinking a lot about our little conversation last evening, and I really do want to be the best DA possible. You look at the system differently than I do, so I'd like to learn more about that. Would you like to have dinner some night and talk it over?"

"Sure," I answered amicably, "but I think that dinner will have to wait until this little war is over. I certainly appreciate your desire, however, and I think I know what you're getting at, and it's not complicated. You got a good look at gray last night, so just don't boil down the whole world into black and white, to all good or bad, and you'll be fine. Be a prosecutor, but be a human being, too," I said sincerely, smiling at the serious expression on his face as he listened.

"Yeahhh ... hold down the ego, huh?" crawled his response, his head nodding slowly.

"Hey, we've all got'em," I chuckled back at him.

"Uh-huh, that's for sure," he agreed. "It's just that after working so hard to get where I am, sometimes I have a hard time with the lack of respect."

"Yeah, I certainly know that feeling," I shrugged. "And while everyone's story is different, I think I know where you're coming from. The old grapevine says something about you working as a milkman to put yourself through college and law school, and that's highly commendable—as is working your way up to a responsible position in the DA's Office. But honest respect is one thing, expecting to have your ass kissed is quite another," I explained firmly, but without a trace of rancor.

"Ohhh-kay, I hear you," he emitted through a heavy sigh, a smile forming, "I'll have to concentrate on that harder. And thanks for sharing, I appreciate it."

"No problem," I nodded, standing up to leave.

"Say, Matt, what problem do you battle?" he teased, coming around the desk to escort me out.

"Now you don't really expect me to tell you where the holes in little old me are, do you, Mr. Prosecutor?" I chuckled. "You're tough enough to do business with as it is."

"Okay," he nodded. "Maybe you'll tell me when we finally have that dinner."

"Yeah, sure ... At least I'll think about it," I quipped, smiling as we shook hands, and I then departed.

To my surprise, Friday also turned out to be a vacation day in Division One. Virtually an instant replay of Thursday, as the hours flowed busily by, and the morning unwound tranquilly into late afternoon, the healing process seemed to accelerate and it was a rejuvenated me that returned to the office around four-thirty, a slight bounce in my step as I pulled open the front door and cheerfully greeted Marilyn and Robbie. "Hi, you lovely people!" I chirped. "What's happening?"

"Well, not a whole hell of a lot, Mr. Happy," Marilyn responded, the smile that jumped from her lips into her eyes telling me that she was pleased with my improved appearance. "You want some coffee?"

"Well, that would be just delightful, Ma'am. Thanks."

"Heard you had a rough one on Wednesday, Matt," Robbie interjected as Marilyn handed me a mug with my customary cream and sugar.

"Rob," I returned, chuckling, "I now know exactly how they felt at the Alamo!"

"Well, that's not exactly the way I heard it went down," drawled his reply through an exhale of pipe smoke. "Old Roberts says you took a lotta shit, but managed to throw back even more, and Andrea tells me you were a downright prick!"

"Say, that's quite a compliment, considering it came from the world's number-one ranked bitch! Did she crawl out of her own asshole to tell you, Rob?" I quipped, sarcasm dripping.

"Boy, you are kind, Matty," Marilyn dropped into the expanding conversation. "I'd use some much uglier words to describe that witch. You wanna hear what she tried to pull on me the other morning? Let me run it down to you, I ... uh—"

Marilyn's proposed addition to the ever expanding collection of horrors perpetrated by Andrea Colari was lost when George, who unbeknownst to me had returned at noon, suddenly burst into the office beaming with excitement. "Hi, there, troops!" he enthused. "You'll all be happy to know that the team of Harris and Meyerstein have successfully driven that black-robed asshole, Lacy, off his goddamn bench on two successive occasions!" Met with a rapt audience of five smiling faces, George paused just long enough to catch his breath before rolling on. "I'd be only too happy to detail our little tussle, but there's far more serious matters to discuss. So, suffice it to say that when all was said and done, I piled a migraine headache on top of the one Matt left him with, and it warmed the cockles of my heart to see that racist sonofabitch look as fucked-over as us for a change!"

"What serious matters?" Ron posed after the echo of our shared laughter faded away.

"Well, if you'll all follow me to my office, I'll run it down for you," George answered, his smile thinning. "Marilyn?" he then asked, drifting toward the hallway. "Could I please get a cup of coffee with an extra lump of sugar? I'm going to need all my strength for Huxton and Stone."

"Coming right up," Marilyn beamed at his retreating figure, reaching for a mug.

Gathering in George's office, the five of us quickly filled the tiny room with smoke and chatter that soon turned electric. "What's with Huxton and Stone?" Leon tossed out after we settled into our chairs.

"Well, I have a six o'clock meeting with them," George returned. "We've just gotta have help, and I'm going to get down on my hands and knees and beg for it if necessary. There's simply no way that we can keep going on like we've been doing," he explained, concern creeping into his tone. "On Wednesday our man, Matt, did fourteen Prelims, and that's pure and simply insane!"

"Fourteen?" echoed Ron, frowning.

"Uh-huh, that's right, Ron—fourteen! And when it was all over around eight-thirty at night, he half fainted according to Sheriff Moorehouse, who called me at home about an even more serious problem."

"Jesus Christ, Matt!" Ron spurted out. "If I'd have known you had that many to do, I'd have never gone home. I'm sorry, man. I really mean it, shiiit!"

"Hey, don't sweat it, big fella," I shot back at him. "Don't you think I know that?"

"Yeahhh," he grunted. "But, my God, that's gotta be a world's record."

"Yeah, for misery!" George chimed in. "But the good news is that our resident superman also specializes in payback. Lacy didn't have the flu, Matt," George snickered, turning his head so that his eyes met mine, "you gave him a goddamned migraine headache!"

"Well, good!" I responded, flashing on the pain Lacy dished out. "I'd hate for Mother Nature to take the credit. You know, blind and biased is one thing, but hateful and mean-spirited is another, and that sonofabitch combines them better than anyone I've ever met! We really need that scoreboard of yours, Georgie," I gibed. "Honest."

"It wouldn't do any good, Matthew," Robbie interjected. "I read over the transcript of that Bankman murder Prelim you did, and if Lacy held those poor people to answer after what you got that coroner to say, then you can forget the scoreboard—that man is so hopelessly dumb, he wouldn't be able to understand it if he had Einstein for a tutor!"

Once again laughter sounded, this time seeping forth, then feeding further on comments like Leon's "Hell, the Braille Institute didn't vote the asshole Man of the Century for nothing!" so that for over a minute it bounced off the walls and surrounded us with its warmth. Finally, when it subsided, George called our attention to the second matter we needed to address.

"All right ... all right," he nodded, "we needed that for sure. But listen up, guys, 'cause there's another problem coming our way, and it's serious with a capital S!" he informed, his forehead furrowing. "Now I told you that I learned about what happened to Matt from Sheriff Moorehouse, but that's not why he telephoned me. The real reason for his call was so damned important that when I was out of the office ill, he called me at home—and what he told me is really scary, and that carries a capital S, too!" he intoned forcefully, then paused to light up a cigarette.

"Okay, George, we're listening," Leon interjected. "What's up?"

"All right, here's the scoop," George continued, swiveling his head to make eye contact with each of us. "You all know how we've been on a campaign to attack the hell out of the throwing script, along with its brothers and sisters ... Well, on Wednesday Matt drilled old Officer Hardy a new asshole. In fact, he fucked him over so bad that the prick lost it, and called Matt a sonofabitch and reached for his gun while testifying!" George detailed, smiling even as tension infiltrated his tone. "Then, when Matt forced Steiggerman to order Hardy to hand over his weapon to the bailiff, the humiliation was total—so total that after the Prelim Hardy met with his superiors in the Sheriff's Department, and they hatched a plan to do away with us!" George steamed out, then paused to let his message sink in.

"Go on, George," Robbie encouraged impatiently after several slow seconds had slipped by. "What kinda plan?"

"Well," George answered after exhaling, "the Solina Sheriffs, along with the Brynhurst Police, are planning to stop us for some bullshit traffic violation when we're traveling to or from the office, and plant Mary Jane or pills on us! Now how's that for an eye-opener?"

"H-o-l-y shit!" rolled off Ron's tongue as the rest of us just sat there stunned.

"Yeahhh, you got that right," George picked up. "And who wouldn't believe that a bunch of long-haired, left-wing radicals like us wouldn't smoke a joint to relax, or pop a pill to offset the exhaustion from our work?"

"Nobody," jumped Robbie's answer instantly.

"Absolutely," George shot back. "But don't get crazy on me, 'cause while we gotta be careful and watch what we're doing, we have a solution that will totally fuck up their plan. When I got off the phone with Moorehouse, I immediately telephoned Ed Ward, the head of the local Panthers, and after I explained our problem, he quickly volunteered their protection. So here's our counter-plan, and it's a beauty!" George enthused, a twinkle enlivening his eyes. "Beginning Monday, before you leave home or this office, you'll call a number I'll give you and tell the Panther who answers that you're calling regarding Operation Pig-Fuck. He'll then arrange for one or more cars full of armed Panthers to meet you at a designated point and escort you in and out of Solina. Naturally, to expedite matters, we'll try to travel in groups so that the Panthers can use as few cars as possible. Got it?"

"Uh-huh ... And that's great!" Ron answered, breaking into a grin, the rest of us joining him while nodding our heads. "But what about tonight, Georgie?"

"Not a problem, Moorehouse says. The pigs are meeting this weekend to coordinate their plans and make sure that all their superiors back them a hundred percent, so we're most likely safe till Monday. Meanwhile, when you leave tonight, all of you travel together. Now here's the number," George rushed out, handing it to Robbie. "I gotta go, 'cause I can't be late for Hux and Stone. One more thing, though," he tossed out as he stood up and grabbed his briefbag. "On Monday, every single one of us needs to lay a huge thank you on Ed Moorehouse—and while we're at it, we also owe a thanks to God that not all cops are pigs."

Finishing with a smile, and a hurried "Wish me luck with downtown," George strode toward the door to the parking lot. Jumping up, I rushed after him and caught him as he opened it. "Georgie, is everything okay at home?" I queried.

"Not really, Matt," he answered in a hushed tone, a troubled look flushing across his face and thinning his lingering grin. "There's no time now, I'll tell you about it later, okay?"

"Yeah, sure. Listen, give me a call over the weekend if there's anything I can do."

"Right," he nodded, his smile warming again. "And thanks," he tacked on as he passed through the doorway and disappeared from sight.

Turning slowly around, I shuffled back inside George's office. Marilyn had arrived with a fresh pot of coffee, and just-lighted smokes were filling the air as I slid back into my chair. "Rob, what do you make of this?" I tossed at him as he set down his mug.

"It's some serious shit, Matthew," he drawled, "really serious shit. But we'll be okay, we just need to carefully follow George's instructions, that's all. Hell, when the pigs get a load of all those armed Panthers, they'll piss in their pants, and their little conspiracy will dribble down their legs right alongside," he snickered, then sucked on his pipe.

"Well, I gotta give you this one, Rob," Leon interjected. "This time there really is a conspiracy in the works—who would've thunk it?"

"Hey," Robbie smiled wryly. "I don't know why you're so surprised. After JFK, Martin, and Bobby all of a sudden disappeared, which was not exactly a coincidence, and for which we have bullshit answers as to who was really responsible, why are you shocked by what those in authority positions do?"

"Yeah," Ron chimed in. "Why the hell did President Johnson lock up all those reports and all sorts of other evidence in the archives for seventy-five years, when almost everyone who was alive when the shit went down will be dead? Like what are we not supposed to know, huh?"

Time seemed to be suspended as thirty or so long seconds shuffled by, appearing more like minutes as the four of us just sat there in the silence shaking our heads and feeling anxious. Finally, Ron, seeking to break the deepening stillness with a more cheerful topic, turned to Leon and asked how it felt to have won his jury trial yesterday, when the early prognosis had been dead-bang loser.

"Well, it felt great for about thirty seconds or so," Leon shrugged, "until my extremely grateful client thanked me with a most generous, 'Not bad for a PD'!"

"What?" Ron pounced, a smile bursting across his face. "You mean he wanted a real lawyer?"

"Seems that way," Leon quipped, a grin forming.

"Well, wouldn't you, if you were charged with a crime, Mr. Schwartz? How about commie-jew-bastard in the first degree?"

"Oh, yes, Your Honor, I would ... 'cause that's very serious!"

"All right, now to be perfectly clear," Ron spun out, "You mean a real attorney, like one who's already graduated from Public Defender School, and after being a DA is now out in the real world—is that what you want?" he asked with exaggerated sincerity.

"Yes, Sir, that's exactly what I want," Leon returned. "Please give it to me. Please! Please! Please!" he squealed, folding his hands into a prayer-like position.

"Okay ... How about Mr. Jay Mundy?"

"Ohhh ... Your Honor ... you're wonderful!" oozed Leon. "Jay Mundy is the greatest real lawyer of them all! Thank you, Sir. Thank you, thank you, thank you!"

"Now, now ... that's all right, my boy, this Court likes to be fair—and besides, Mr. Mundy has already agreed to plead you guilty, haven't you, Mr. Mundy?" Ron queried, looking over at Robbie.

"Why ... of course ... Your Honor," Robbie joined in, accentuating his drawl, his smile widening. "Being the selfish, slimy, kiss-assing snake that I am, I don't see any need to waste the Court's valuable time. After all, Your Honor, the charge just carries the penalty of death by hanging ... so that being the case, my client is positively happy to waive all his rights and agree to die, but only on two conditions, Your Honor, Sir."

"What's that, esteemed counsel?" Ron asked, squelching his urge to laugh.

"Well, Your Honor, you have to agree to hang him before lunch, so that I can get back to my office. I've got a very important client meeting at that time, a civil matter involving drawing a will for a large estate— you understand, Sir, don't you?"

"Absolutely, counsel, the overhead and other expenses involved in carrying on a real law practice—not to forget profit for a second—is naturally something that you must consider above all else! I understand that with my whole heart, if we can find it. After all, I used to be a real lawyer, too, until I boot-licked my way onto the bench, where I've since become immortal for being one of the world's top-ten pricks!"

Having emulated to perfection the unctuous tone which personified the sycophantic personality of the district's private attorney that we despised most, Robbie finished with a flourish. "Well ... thank you for that understanding and accommodation, Your Honor, Sir ... I stand in awe of your unparalleled ability to empathize, and thank the good Lord that this district is so fortunate as to have your paramount wisdom to guide us," he rolled toward his close, generously oiling his words. "Which, brings me, Your Supreme Highness—I mean, Your Honor—to ... uh ... my second condition. I was wondering, oh, God of the Legal World, if because of my hurry today, I could ... uh ... skip kissing your ass right now, and ... uh ... do it twice the next time I'm here."

"Well ... all right, counsel," Ron nodded out, "but be absolutely sure that you don't forget to make it up. After all, you are getting paid as a court-appointed attorney ... And besides, I just love the way you tickle my asshole with your tongue, it's your cutest trick!" Ron ended, having delivered his final sentence in a falsetto voice before breaking up with laughter.

I was already cackling, and when Leon and Robbie joined Ron, the room quickly filled with our hilarity. Fueled by our need to laugh, so as to temporarily smother our gnawing concerns, the gurgling sounds of our merriment quickly escalated to raucous, booming off the walls of our tiny enclosure to surround us and set off round after round till our sides ached, and Marilyn was finally forced to come to our rescue.

"Do any of you crazy fools want to go home and have a life, maybe?" she interrupted, slicing through the din. "Or do you just want to sit here doing your imitation of a bunch of hyenas on LSD?"

Her sarcastic-toned wisecrack with a message instantly instigated a further outburst. But as she stood in the doorway shaking her head slowly side to side while wearing an expression of bemused disapproval, the roaring river of laughter gradually ran dry, and after atoning with gentle pats on her shoulder as we shuffled single-file to our own cubicles, we packed our briefbags and closed down the office.

Following George's instructions, we caravaned to the freeway. Then, after we waved good-night to each other, I nestled deeper into my seat and pondered the latest sequence of events that had jumped onto Solina's seemingly endless list of surprises. George entered into mind first, and a smile crawled across my face as I envisioned him arguing forcefully to Hux and Stone about our need for a sixth deputy, his blue eyes growing fiery from emotion as words such as urgent and critical rolled off his tongue. "Good luck, Georgie," I whispered out loud, "'cause urgent and critical are right on. I mean, I'm feeling better now, after two days of R & R, but for how long? And how long can you hang on, with trouble now on two fronts, work and home?" I postulated, my smile thinning.

When Officer Hardy's glowering face then suddenly jumped in front of my mind's eye, cutting off my view of George and climbing atop the pile of squirming problems, I winced at the additional worry created by the sheriffs' plot to criminalize us, then squeezed it out of view by replaying Robbie's assurance that they would piss in their pants once they sighted carloads of armed Panthers. The latter image triggered a chuckle, and recalled the still-warm memory of the four-way laugh-fest for a repeat performance, its cackles and chortles bubbling back into ear to keep me company as I steered toward home.

XXIV

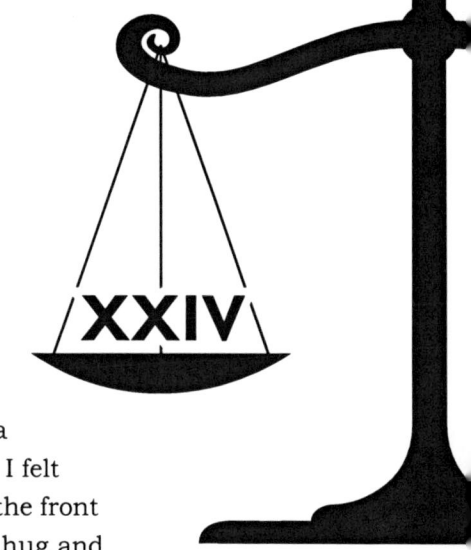

By the time I reached Doheny Drive and parked Old Greener, the echoes of shared laughter had once again died away. Still wearing a faint smile however as I crossed the street, I felt it widen with anticipation as I approached the front door to the apartment and focused on the hug and kiss I was about to receive. After I twisted the lock open and entered, the living-room clock advised that seven o'clock had also arrived. Stella wasn't present in any of the front rooms, so after setting down my briefbag and slipping out of my blazer, I headed toward the bedroom, pulling off my tie as I shuffled down the hallway.

The door was closed, and when I opened it, Stella, who had not heard me arrive, was startled and jumped noticeably upon catching sight of me. "Jesus, Matty, you scared the hell out of me!" she cried out forcefully, hurriedly picking up a small plastic vial she had dropped in her fright and replacing it in the open top drawer of her dresser as she turned toward me.

"I'm sorry, hon, I didn't mean to," I rushed back at her. "You okay?"

"Yeahhh ... I'm fine," slipped out through a sigh after a slight hesitation, a smile squirming over the fading irritation in her face. "Another tough day?" she then inquired.

"Well ... uh ... let's just say it was highly interesting, and—"

"Okay, I know that tone for sure," she interjected. "Go get washed up and into your comfy clothes, then come tell me all about the latest battle on the Solina warfront. Meanwhile, I'll get dinner going and make you a drink," hurried her suggestion at me, Stella then pushing the dresser drawer closed as she shuffled over to me and kissed me lightly on the lips. "Sound okay?"

"Sure, sweetie," I smiled. "Sounds great."

"Okay, then, hop to it so we can be together and I can learn what's going on."

Kissing me again, she patted me on my cheek as she withdrew, then headed for the kitchen. And to this day, I don't know exactly what it was that made me call her back. Maybe it was because I had read something undefinable in her face, something deeper and more serious than surprised fright when I had burst in upon her. Or maybe it was because her agitation seemed to last beyond the initial shock of my entry. Or maybe it was because the door had been closed, something I had never known her to do. Call it paranoia. Or label it instinct, sharpened by courtroom experience. Or both even, working in tandem. But the funny feeling in the pit of my stomach wouldn't budge, instead swelling into an irresistible impulse to call out her name.

"Yes, Matty?" she floated back, stopping halfway down the hallway and turning around.

"What's in the little bottle in the top drawer of your dresser?" trickled off my tongue.

"Ohhh, that," she replied. "Just some pills I take when my allergy acts up."

"Your allergy?" I posed, my premonition that something was wrong remaining firm despite the fact that her answer had been delivered nonchalantly and without hesitation.

"Uh-huh."

"What kind of allergy, Stelle?" I pressed, having unconsciously slipped into cross-examination.

"I'm allergic to wool."

"To wool?"

"Yes, to wool!" bounded her reply, her uncharacteristic irritation with me having reappeared as she returned to the doorway. "Why do you make it sound so strange—lots of people are, you know?"

"Yeah, I know … but—"

"But what, Matty? Don't you believe me, is that what's the matter? Do you think I'm lying to you, is that it?" she machine-gunned, her tone sharpening and her volume steadily increasing with each question she fired.

"Nooo … of course not, Stelle," I mouthed slowly, now certain that her growing annoyance with me meant she was concealing something. "But if you're allergic to it," I tacked on, "why do you wear so much of it?"

"I don't, really," she snapped. "And when I do, it's lined so that it won't bother me. Now, have we finished with our little game of twenty questions?"

Delaying my reply, I snatched the jacket from the pants suit she was wearing up off the bed, then read the label inside the collar out loud. "One hundred percent wool is what it says, Stelle," I pressed. "Now you want to show me where the lining is? 'Cause I sure as hell don't see any."

"All right ... all right, Mr. Smarty-Pants," Stella grumbled, leaving the door jamb she was leaning up against, and walking over to the dresser. "They're pain pills," she tacked on, pulling out the plastic vial and handing it to me. "I've got a little female problem, and the doctor gave them to me for when it acts up."

"Ohhh ... I see," tiptoed off my tongue softly as I flushed with embarrassment. "I didn't know—you didn't mention it, and I thought you told me everything," I added with disappointment, lowering my eyes.

"Well, I do, silly," Stella comforted, suddenly softening. "It's just that you're such a worrier, and with all you've already got on your mind, I didn't want to add to it, that's all," she soothed. "It's just a little problem, nothing uncommon for a woman my age. And besides, what goes on with a woman's organs is entitled to a little privacy, don't you think?"

"Uh-huh, of course," I agreed, smiling sheepishly.

"All right, good," she said, one-upping my grin with the warmth of hers. "I'm certainly glad that little misunderstanding is cleared up."

It would have been, too, except that I noticed her hands were shaking as she reached forward to cup my face and gently kiss me, and that she quickly clasped them together when she saw that I had noticed. That observation quickly mated with a nagging question still lingering in the far recesses of my mind to restoke my anxiety. There had been a long, unpronounceable word on the prescription label, located just to the forefront of the directions and separated from them by three tiny dots. I had seen that word somewhere, and even though I couldn't roll it smoothly over my tongue, I vaguely recognized it and associated it with something ominous. Unable to shake the feeling that something was wrong, and with Stella now smiling at me, I continued the conversation as she turned to head back to the kitchen. "Stelle, are you in pain now?" I asked, concern coating my tone as I placed a search order with my memory bank for where I had seen those fourteen letters that spelled serious trouble.

"No," she answered, "I took a pill just before you came home, so I'm fine," she answered, renewing her smile to assure me.

"Do you have to take one often?"

"No, only when my little problem acts up. So stop worrying, will you, please? You're very sweet, as always, but it's not necessary—okay?"

"Okay," I nodded, my memory's fingers still riffling through files, its eyes sneaking a peek every so often.

"All right, then. Now you climb into your jeans and tennies while I make us something scrumptious to eat, and don't dilly-dally 'cause I want to hear the latest news—okey-dokey?"

"Uh-huh ... okey-dokey," I chuckled as she turned toward the hallway and I took several steps toward the closet.

Suddenly, however, the chuckle died in my throat, and I stopped abruptly when a bomb exploded inside my brain. "Oh ... my ... God!" I groaned as my memory's retrieval system suddenly struck pay dirt, instantly catapulting my partially restored nervous system from vacation status to full alert, goose bumps swelling up my arms and across my chest as I whirled around to catch her before she disappeared. "Stelle," I trickled out slowly, my tongue having trouble forming the words as terror gripped me, spreading across my face and seeping into my tone. "There's a word on that vial ... I saw it in an article I was reading in *Newsweek* a long time ago, and I ... I—"

Already shaking, my voice cracked and I couldn't finish my thought. Dazed, I just stood frozen in place and watched the color drain from her face in sync with her vanishing smile, replaced instead by the far-away, lonesome look she had worn when I had first entered and startled her, and in which I had somehow glimpsed the intense fear that now resurfaced. For several seconds the silence burned with dreadful anticipation as Stella just stood there motionless and returned my gaze. Then, as her eyes filled with tears, she unclasped her hands and clenching them into fists, she raised them up in front of her heaving chest and shook them at me.

"Alll ... right, Matty, alll ... right!" she cried, a tidal wave of emotion flooding over her. "You win ... You win, goddamnit! I have cancer, spelled O-varian, and I'm going to die!" she screeched, slamming her fists down onto her thighs, her anguish-toned message striking me with sledgehammer force, sucking the breath out of me and tightening my chest vise-like.

"W-w-hat?" finally managed to stutter off my tongue, followed by a wailing "Nooo," both sounding as if some stranger was speaking for me.

"Oh—yes, yes, yes!" Stella snapped, bobbing her head. "You dragged it out of me, and now you know—so I hope you're happy!" she fired at me, anger crowning the sadness in her voice.

"But ... but ... there must be something we can do," I offered weakly, tears crowding into my eyes as the body's novocaine numbed the pain enough to allow my defense system to struggle to its knees. "I just can't believe there isn't some kind of help. I mean—"

"Well, you just better believe it, 'cause there's nothing that can help. I'm going to die, and you've got to face it, just like me!" she hurled back at me, her voice cracking, her shoulders suddenly sagging.

Instinctively, I rushed to her side and threw my arms around her. Nestling up against me, she hugged me back, tighter and tighter, her "I'm so sorry" escaping in a tone choked by tears as I ever so gently patted the back of her head. A heavy silence then followed, steadily gaining weight for over a minute as we stood there glued to each other, the only sound Stella's quiet sobs against my chest. Finally, her tears momentarily stilled, she lifted her head and looked into my eyes. "How about we sit down and talk?" she suggested, barely above a whisper.

"Okay, sweetheart," I eased back, "sure."

"Let's go in the living room," she pursued, "I could use a glass of wine."

"Me, too ... C'mon," I murmured, taking her hand, the two of us then shuffling side by side down the hallway and into the living room where we slowly settled onto the couch. "You just sit here and try to relax, I'll get the wine," I instructed softly, a faint smile forming.

"Okay," she returned, forcing a matching grin.

Rising off the couch, I walked swiftly into the kitchen and poured two large glasses of Merlot, my thought process bouncing back and forth between Don't think, don't spill, and This can't really be happening, can it? Returning, I carefully handed a glass to Stella, then slipped down beside her and leaned over and kissed her lightly on the lips. "You want a smoke?" I then asked after retreating a few inches.

"Not yet," she smiled.

"Okay ... Listen, I gotta ask," I began, settling further back to a distance of three feet. "Are you sure, I mean absolutely positive?"

"Uh-huh, Matty, unfortunately I am," Stella nodded back at me. "After Dr. Jeffrey Reiser out at UCLA Med Center came up with the original diagnosis, I confirmed it first at the Fred Hutchinson Cancer Center when I visited Lea in Seattle, then again at M.D. Anderson in Houston during my Christmas visit. Not exactly the gift I was hoping for," she snickered, "but the truth's the truth."

"And there's nothing that can be done?" I asked reflexively. "No way to fight it?"

"No," she answered softly, dabbing away fresh tears. "That's the big problem with ovarian cancer, Matty, there aren't any early warning signs, so by the time you discover it, it's spread."

"I … see," shuffled off my tongue, pain seeping into my tone as I struggled to accept the verdict. "And there's no treatment, no help at all?"

"A little, Matty," Stella offered, squeezing out a thin smile. "There's chemo, and I'm doing it. But it only slows it down, it's not a cure."

"I … I don't know what to say … I … I—"

"I know, sweetie, I know," Stella interjected, the intense pain that forced my voice to quiver causing tears to again surface in her eyes, this time overflowing before she could dab them away. "Sometimes words just won't do."

"Yeahhh, for sure," I agreed, the thought, I'm losing her, burning through the numbness and insisting on being accepted by throbbing with each renewing heartbeat. "How long have you known?" I finally mustered after several excruciating seconds had passed.

"Since just before Thanksgiving," trickled her answer, her eyes fixing on mine.

"But why didn't you tell me?" I squeezed out. "Especially after New Year's Eve when we really got close? Didn't you mean it when you said you always wanted real love based on honesty and sharing?" I asked, doubt suddenly seeping into my tone and accusing.

"Oh, God yes, I meant it, Matty—from the bottom of my heart!" she cried. "And I wanted to tell you, honest I did. But I just couldn't spoil it, I finally had what I'd always wanted, and selfishly I just couldn't spoil it," she ended, muffling a sob.

"What do you mean, spoil it?"

"Well," Stella nodded, straining to make me understand, "I had a terrible conflict in my mind. I wanted to tell you … I knew that you had a right to know. But I didn't want to place any more pressure on you than you already had," she explained, her voice firming. "I told myself to just wait for a better time, like when the war would be over. But it wasn't over for long, and the pressure just got worse, so I didn't know what to do. I wasn't holding out on you, I wanted to share … I needed to share, I just didn't know what—"

"Hey, sweetie, hold up a second," I intervened, reading the anguish that had slowly filled her face, then settled in her eyes where it deepened with each sentence that tripped off her tongue. "It's all right, it's all right ... just take it easy," I soothed, suddenly appreciating her predicament, and feeling like a selfish idiot. "I'm listening ... just take it easy, okay?"

"Uh-huh. But there's more, I only told you the unselfish part. "My other reason for delaying was that I was afraid I'd lose you, that you'd leave me. And even though I realized that this would be good for you, 'cause it would take away a terrible pressure, I just couldn't make me let go of the only real love I ever had—what I always wanted and needed so much ... I know it was selfish, but I just couldn't spoil it—understand?" she pleaded, her voice choking with tears.

"Leave?" I squeezed out, inching over till our knees touched. "I thought you said one of the things you liked best about me was that I don't run from trouble," I tacked on, trying to smile as I slipped my hand over hers.

"Yeah, that's true," she affirmed. "But you didn't sign up for this!"

"Oh, yes I did." I rushed at her. "I said I love you, not I like playing house. And I'm not going anywhere, sweetheart, I'm going to stay right here by your side and take care of you— 'cause real love doesn't run away either."

Stella tried to respond, but couldn't, the swell of emotion simply overwhelming her. Words do indeed fail sometimes. So, in the ensuing silence, we just held each other, tighter and tighter and tighter, in our pain and fear, both of us clinging to the comfort that physical closeness created as seconds slowly ticked into minutes, counting one, two, three, our heart-to-heart hug unconsciously witnessing that we were alive, and together, and more united than ever before. Finally, Stella pulled back several inches and patted me tenderly on the cheek.

"Matthew ... Robert ... Harris," she rolled out, just like she had on the occasion of our first meeting. "I love you, too, you hear?"

"Yeah, for sure," I smiled, noting that she looked tired, the pale skin of her face contrasting sharply with her eyes, still beautiful even though red-rimmed. "Now you just cozy back against the throw pillows and rest for a while, okay?"

"All right, Mr. Boss," she teased, then took a healthy swig at her wine glass before settling back against the pillows. "But you know what? I feel much better already, now that it's all out in the open," she murmured, the muscles in her face finally relaxing, her smile brighter.

"Good ... I'm glad," I tossed back, rising and hurrying into the kitchen to fetch the bottle of Merlot. "Here's to us," I mouthed after returning and refilling her glass, then lifting mine.

"And to Friday night," Stella added, stretching out her arm to clink glasses with me. "No more serious talk tonight, okay? There'll be time for that tomorrow, I want to read the Sports Page with you."

"You got it, pretty lady," I readily agreed, pulling the paper off the coffee table, then nestling up against her.

The hour that followed was both strange and magical. Strange, indeed, for magic to even make a cameo appearance in light of the harsh circumstances that prevailed, but simultaneously magical nonetheless in the surprising degree of pure contentment it contained, and a true tribute to the amazing ability of the human psyche to rebound, especially when aided by a good bottle of Merlot. For somehow submerging the black cloud that now hung over us, and replacing it with a bright sun, we studied the baseball standings, analyzing the various teams, then chuckling over Jim Murray's column, all the while steadily sipping second and third glasses of wine as sixty precious minutes shuffled by, each one unconsciously a baby step we took toward learning how to live our new life. "You know what?" Stella murmured when we finally finished our review and she had bet me five dollars that her Cardinals would best my Dodgers, "I'm hungry—how about you?"

"Well, as Grampy Max would say: 'Food is God's greatest invention, and it's a major sin not to honor it,'" I chuckled. "But you're not going to wear yourself out cooking, sweetie, no way," I hurriedly tacked on.

"No problem," Stella smiled. "I know a cozy little place at the beach with great food and a wonderful view of the ocean. Did I ever tell you how much I love the ocean?"

"No, sweetie, you didn't, but I'm always up for learning more about my best girl."

"You don't think I'm crazy? ... I mean after what I just laid on you."

"Absolutely not!" I bounced back at her. "Though asking a crazy person whether or not you're crazy might not be your best option for objectivity. But here's the deal, pretty lady: A very wise poet named William Blake once wrote that 'He who kisses the joy as it flies, lives in eternity's sunrise.' Now until I met you, I never followed that advice as fully as I should, so how about together we go win a gold medal at it starting right now—okay?"

"Okay," she nodded, her eyes tearing slightly, a smile then forming as she wiped them away. "Let's get into some comfy clothes and go make some joy to kiss."

The Sea Shanty is located on Highway 101, a mile or so north of the City of Santa Monica. A half-hour drive from the apartment, after we washed our faces and climbed into our jeans, we journeyed to dinner holding hands and intermittently interrupting the steady stream of idle chatter to sing along with the Supremes and Jay and the Americans as they serenaded with "I'm Gonna Make You Love Me" and "This Magic Moment," music's spellbinding power energizing our smiles. Once we arrived and were nestled together inside a cozy booth featuring a magnificent view of Father Pacific, the moon casting its glow onto the waves lapping the beach, further baby steps allowed us to enjoy our steaks and onion rings amidst frequent laughter, with an occasional light kiss added to honor the simple joy of the moment, now precious indeed. When Stella suddenly remembered that we hadn't discussed the latest happenings in Solina, my reply of "Not to worry, but as a wise woman just recently advised, no more serious talk today" was accepted with a smile and the agreement to post it on tomorrow's agenda, our conversation then turning to choosing a movie to celebrate afterward.

Arriving home just after Friday night unwound into Saturday's first hour, Stella and I drowsily slipped out of our jeans and into bedclothes, then brushed our teeth side by side before sliding into bed with reading material, unconsciously never losing sight of one another. Stella fell into sleep first, and for another ten minutes or so I lazed over *SI*, forcing away painful thoughts when they infiltrated, and smiling instead at the athletic triumphs so artfully photographed in color. When my eyes finally glazed over, I turned off my light, snuggled further into my pillow, and listened carefully to the soft sounds of Stella's breathing. "Dear God," I mouthed a few seconds later, my lips moving without sound, "I know I mostly turn to you to ask for something, and here I am again. But listen ... please, please listen," my lips formed, a lump rising in my throat, "I need you to make one of your miracles. All I can promise in return is that I'll do anything you say. Just tell me, and I'll do it," I promised, squeezing away the tears as my eyes closed and I drifted toward slumber.

XXV

When I awakened Saturday morning, it was still early. Not my usual five-thirty to five-forty-five, but still only a few minutes past seven, with the blue-gray light outside the window whispering, "New day ... just starting." On weekends, Stella almost always arose first in order to prepare something special for breakfast. However, on this occasion, she was not the early bird, but instead was lying next to me and smiled warmly when I turned toward her. "Good morning, sweetie," she crooned as I opened my eyes wider to welcome the sight of her lovely face, strikingly beautiful without any makeup, her eyes also smiling at me.

"Good morning, yourself, pretty lady," I murmured back at her, feeling so secure from the soft glow of her grin that for a moment I wondered if last evening's painful discovery was just a bad dream, the part of me that knew better instantly reminding otherwise as she cozied over closer to me and nuzzled her head onto my chest.

"I can hear your heart," she informed after twisting her head in tiny movements until she found the comfy spot she was searching for.

"Yeah? ... Is it working?"

"Sounds like it," she answered softly.

"Well that's good," I chuckled lightly. "I really hate it when it isn't, it gets me behind schedule right off the bat and screws up the whole day."

"Sort of inconvenient, huh?" she posed, playing along.

"Very," I confirmed through a widening grin.

"Well, speaking of *very*," she returned, sweetness marrying soft inside her tone, "that's how much I love you, Matthew Robert Harris—and don't you forget it, either."

"I won't," I promised. "Now that I know my heart's working, I can't, 'cause I've got it tucked inside in a special place marked forever. And while we're on the subject," I tacked on, my tone teasing, "I'm kinda fond of you, too."

"Just kinda?" she asked, raising her head and forming a mock frown.

"Well ... that's what one says when there aren't any words capable of saying how much."

"Oh, I see ... And that's the best you can do, that's the best defense you can put up, counselor?"

"Well, if you put it that way ... how about with all my heart and soul, forever and ever, plus one golden day in heaven—is that better?"

"Much," bounced her answer. "So much better, in fact, that it's going to get you treated to a cup of the world's most delicious coffee—sound good?"

"Uh-huh ... sounds great," I returned. "Especially if it's preceded by a kiss," I hurried to add after she slid out from under the covers and slipped into her robe, me quickly following suit.

Fortunately, the two treats were not mutually exclusive. And after Stella's lips had produced a head-to-toe tingle, with coffee then in hand we settled side by side around the kitchen table and eagerly scrutinized the latest baseball scores and attendant articles. Having eaten dinner in Friday's waning hours, we readily agreed to a light breakfast of honeydew and a hard-boiled egg, then turned our attention to the front section of the *Times* and grumbled over the sad events in Vietnam, now protested more and more widely on the home front. Upon finishing our review of the world, complete with several minutes devoted to the Editorial Page, we discovered that nine o'clock had arrived. Stella suggested showers and clothes before we "addressed our agenda," and as she tidied up I headed for the bathroom, an uneasy feeling in my stomach accompanying me.

The anxiety didn't disappear underneath the showerhead. Instead, now that I was alone for the first time since Stella confessed her heart-rending secret, as I cleansed myself, a kaleidoscope of thoughts and feelings cascaded through my mind and psyche like the steady stream of soapy water that flowed over my shoulders and chest. How do you feel? What do you feel? entered first, forcing me to take stock of myself in view of the life-altering situation that had so suddenly developed. "Well, physically I'm all right ... just a little tired," formed my answer slowly. "But God am I scared! I mean, Big Time, and that's an understatement even for me!" I snickered, the sarcastic poke failing to lessen apprehension's hold even as a wan smile wandered onto my lips. "I mean, I'm losing her ... I'm actually going to lose my Stella, my love, my partner—my everything! And, God, I don't know what I'll do without her. I ... I ... can't even really imagine what it would be like, except the world will be so ... so ... empty," serpentined off my tongue and surrounded me, the hollow echo causing the enormity of the situation to fully register, fear swelling so thick I could taste it, the knots in my stomach tightening rock-hard as the bar of soap in my hand slipped out onto the tile floor.

After I picked it up, ten or so silent seconds slid by as the wheels spun round inside my brain, then stopped abruptly when the train rattled into the station marked Super Ego and a question began flashing like a hyperactive neon sign. "Ohhh, yeah ... I know," I answered, shaking my head, "I'm one selfish sonofabitch, all right. 'Cause if I'm scared, just think how she must feel. I mean, she's facing death, so think of how terribly, terribly frightened she must be!" my awakened conscience rolled out, a sourness invading my mouth and stopping the flow of words.

For several more silent seconds that now seemed to crawl by, I just stood still, shivering slightly even though the water was warm, as thoughts bumped into and off each other. Selfish? ... You bet, the prosecution asked and answered. But not totally, 'cause part of me's going to die, too, and I'll be all alone ... all alone, countered the defense. On the other hand, she's the one that's really alone—and not later on, but right this very minute! my better instincts suddenly volunteered. So you just gotta help her, you gotta take care of her, make her days happy, you hear? "Yeahhh ... I hear," I mustered in a barely audible whisper, suddenly crushed by a feeling of remorse as *all alone ... all alone* echoed back into ear, triggering a flash-flood of emotion. Yeah, that's right, I'll still be alive—but why? Why do I get to live and she doesn't? 'Cause she made a mistake with Vicki, is that it? streamed guilt, doubt a half step behind, my mind struggling to intervene and dam the swirling torrent with reason. Hell, she didn't mean to, formed the argument, it wasn't willful, deliberate, and premeditated—she was young and abused, and hurt and confused, that's all. And even if she should've somehow been able to overcome it, the death penalty is a little bit stiff, don't you think? logic posited, anger now jumping into the fray and forcing the dialogue verbal once again. "And while we're on the subject, what did we do to deserve such an awful punishment? Huh, how come?" I asked forcefully. "Is God playing some kind of trick? A dirty trick?" zinged my follow-up. "I mean, first you give us a beautiful gift, then for no reason you take it away. Why?" my heart joined my brain in asking, pain piggybacking anger to squeeze out a seething response.

"Nothing ... absolutely nothing!" hissed the reply with a force that bounced it off the opposing wall. "We've honored our love, we've treasured it, we've been good ... So why would you take it away? I mean, what kind of loving God would do that?" rumbled the acerbic accusation, tears swelling to still my tongue, a feeling of helplessness washing over me as I just stood there underneath the stream of angst and uncertainty pouring forth in sync with the hot water.

Minutes later when I had toweled off and was slipping into my favorite sweatshirt, Stella entered. Her smile returned one across my face, and after she quickly showered and dressed, we retreated to the living room, and armed with our second cups of coffee, settled onto the couch to sort out details and map our future.

"Okay ... I know this isn't going to be easy," Stella eased out calmly, fixing her eyes on me, her concern clearly visible. "But we need to talk, to make plans about how we're going to live with my condition."

"Right," I nodded back, "not easy for either of us. But we're together, sweetie, and together we'll work it out—we're partners, right?"

"For sure, absolutely," she smiled. "And I guess we should start with the time frame."

"Right," I nodded a second time. "How ... much do we have?" I then asked hesitantly, dreading the answer.

"About ... five to six months," she trickled out, then watched closely for my reaction.

"That's all?" I said softly, struggling to suppress the tears that suddenly formed behind my eyes, my expectation, without any foundation whatsoever, having been no less than a year and maybe more.

"Uh-huh," she confirmed sympathetically. "I'm sorry, Matty, but that's all."

"And there's no way to buy more?" I queried reflexively.

"No ... I'm already doing that by having chemotherapy."

"I see ... I see," crawled my reply, as I slowly digested the fresh bite of reality, trying also to swallow my disappointment. "Okay, then, all the more reason to make every minute count," I added, squeezing my lips into a smile.

"Uh-huh ... right, Matty," she soothed, not fooled for a second. "In fact, that's why I absolutely love your poet's quote about kissing the joy as it flies. What do you say we adopt it as our motto?"

"You got it, pretty lady, Blake's motto it is," I bounced back at her, my smile becoming genuine. "And I was thinking in the shower, that to insure we make the absolute most out of our time together, I'm going to resign from the PD's Office so that we'll be together all the time and I can take care of you."

"God, that's sweet—and that's my Matty!" burst her response, her smile flashing, then curling up as her eyes teared. "Thank you, thank you, love," she rushed at me, "but I've had a lot more time to think this out, and what's best for both of us is to keep on living just the way we have been. The—"

"No, wait a minute, Stelle," I interjected. "The best way to maximize our time is—"

"Let me finish, sweetie," she cut in, her smile reappearing. "As I was about to say, the last seven months have been the happiest of my life—like heaven on earth. I had the real love I always wanted, my work was going better than ever, and I had yours to share to boot. So continuing that wonderful life with you, and celebrating every minute of it is exactly what I want and really need," she explained, nodding her head for emphasis. "Besides, you can't quit the PD," she quickly added, her tone growing determined, "not in the middle of a war, you can't, it goes against every grain of your soul. And even if it ended next week, fighting for justice is your life's work, Matty. It's special, and important—damned important—and you've gotta have it to help you go on after I'm gone!" she ended, her lower lip trembling as she fought to control her emotions, her eyes searching mine for a hint of agreement.

In the few fretful seconds of silence that followed, I quickly discovered that I had no answer to the overwhelming logic of her arguments. What she wanted and needed was of course the number one priority, and the sound and unselfish reasoning behind the importance of work in my life was so true as to be irrefutable. So, after swiping away the tears that the echoing "after I'm gone" had caused to finally surface, I just sat there and bobbed my head in acquiescence while a smile slowly snuck out of the corners of my mouth.

"Good!" Stella announced, when my grin widened to full. "I'm glad we agree ... 'cause it helps me, Matty, helps a lot."

"Okay ... okay," I muttered softly, reaching across and gently patting her hand. "That's what matters most, sweetheart, no question. But I'm still going to find a way to spend more time with you, and take care of you—speaking of which, how does the chemo work? Can I help you with that?"

"Sure ... later on," she answered. "The dosage is tailored to the white-cell count in my blood, and so far the count is holding up well and I can keep taking a heavy dose every two weeks. I take a cab back and forth to the med center at UCLA, so you don't need to worry about that. I'll tell you when I need help, okay?"

"Okay ... sure. But you promise you'll tell me if you need help, or there's anything else I can do?"

"I promise."

"And no more secrets?"

"Uh-huh, I swear. And believe me, Matty, the best way for us to live is to not change anything till we have to. As I said, I just love our life together, more than I can tell you, and I want to keep on loving it as long as I can," she smiled, her eyes again searching mine for approval.

"Hey, not to worry, hon, I'm fully into the plan, really—our regular life plus Blake's motto."

"Okay, perfect," she smiled. "Just one other thing, Matty, I don't want any of my friends to know. I told my sister, but not Vicki. I was never there for her in life, and she doesn't deserve this as a final memory—okay?"

"Sure, no problem. I'm not going to tell the guys in the office either."

"Fine," she agreed. "But that reminds me, you still owe me an update on the latest happenings in Solina."

No more than fifteen minutes had passed, though between last evening's revelation and this morning's follow-up, I felt like I had aged several lifetimes. So, when Stella signaled that we could change the subject, I was only too happy to. "Not until I get a hug and a kiss, I don't," marched my snappy toned reply, the just-agreed-to normalcy springing back to the surface. "I mean, you think you can just sit me down here and swamp me with heavy stuff, without a reward? Holy fuckers, is there no justice anywhere? I—"

The softness of her lips interrupted my tease, gently at first, then with a force that took my breath away after she pushed me back against the throw pillows and smoothly slid over on top of me. "Well ... ohh-kay," I sputtered out some thirty seconds later when she withdrew to a distance of six inches. "I guess there's some justice after all."

"Some?" she asked with mock dismay.

"Uh-huh ... I mean that was a lovely down payment, but considering the total weight of what you just laid on me, I think that a great deal more is in order, like—"

"I agree," Stella interjected, smiling. "But if you think you're going to divert me from finding out what's going on with the war, think again," she tacked on, then returned to an upright position.

"Ohhhkay ... all right," I shrugged after sitting up. "I've got three little tidbits for you."

"I'm all ears, counselor."

"Well, first off, at closing time Friday night, George went downtown for a meeting with Hux and Tim—to pressure them face to face for a sixth deputy."

"Great ... Any word on how it went?"

"No, Georgie hasn't called, and I've been somewhat occupied as you know—and so has Georgie unfortunately."

"What do you mean?" Stella queried, concern jumping into her voice as she reached for a cigarette.

"Well, you know how we suspected that all was not A-okay between them? Well it's not. Just last week, Georgie mentioned that they've been kind of drifting apart the last couple of years, but he didn't make it sound really serious. However, when Whirlwind Wednesday happened, the only reason that Georgie couldn't come to help me was because he got a call from Marie Anne that he needed to come home immediately. He was going to give me some details yesterday, but couldn't when he had to leave for his meeting with Hux and Tim."

"I see," Stella drawled, exhaling and reaching for her coffee. "Well, let's keep a good thought that maybe they can work things out."

"Uh-huh, for sure ... And that brings me to another little problem that came up late Friday, which fortunately we've already solved," I spun out in a casual tone, knowing that Stella would learn about our creative commuter-protection plan anyway when it was time to call the Panthers Monday morning, and hoping my deemphasize-as-much-as-possible approach would minimize its worrisome aspects.

"Oh ... what's that?" she inquired nonchalantly.

"Well," I answered slowly, choosing my words carefully. "It seems that Sheriff Moorehouse reported to George that the Solina Sheriffs and the Brynhurst Police were planning to sort of mess with us," I eased out, forcing a thin smile.

"That's not exactly new, they've been screwing with you in court forever," Stella noted through a grin, her forehead then furrowing slightly as instinct suddenly warned that something troublesome was lurking.

"True," I replied. "But it seems that they want to try and get rid of us by stopping us for some bullshit traffic violations and then planting drugs," I added softly, still trying to minimize the impact of my message.

"What?" she cried, the remnants of her smile vanishing at supersonic speed. "A little problem, you say. Well, I'd sure as hell hate to see a big one!" steamed her follow-up.

"Okay, okay, now don't get upset, we've got the problem completely handled," I responded instantly, crowding my tone full of assurance. "We contacted the Black Panthers, and they're going to escort us from the freeway in the morning, and back at night."

"Oh, great, now all we have to worry about is a goddamned shootout!"

"No, no, sweetie, there's not going to be any shootout," I soothed. "First of all, the Panthers are just there as witnesses, lots of witnesses that no traffic violation occurred. And secondly, the pigs don't want any part of a confrontation with them, believe me—not as heavily armed as the Panthers are," I assuaged, reaching out again to pat her hand.

"Oh, my God!" Stella blurted. "I always knew you were in some danger, just from working in such a sewer, and I knew you were making enemies, too, that had to be. But I never ever dreamed that the cops would try to frame you," spurted her concern, her face now mapped with worry. "If anything happens to you, Matty, I'll ... I'll—" she squeezed out, then halted when tears suddenly surfaced.

"Hey ... listen to me, pretty lady ... please," I urged, sliding closer to her. "Nothing bad's going to happen, trust me—okay?"

"I don't know, Matty," she choked out, shaking her head, but trying to smile.

"Well, there's still time to accept my offer to resign?" I chuckled softly, still trying to ease her discomfort.

Like a hastily conceived prayer that's unexpectedly answered, the tease worked. In a tone that mixed stifled tears with a sudden urge to laugh, Stella groused out, "No way, José, we don't run," as she slid even closer and pulled me into a hug, adding over my shoulder when her cheek pressed into mine, "Those pigs can go fuck themselves, and tell 'em Stella said so!"

Growing tighter and tighter, the embrace lasted for over a minute, like last evening, its warmth and sense of safe and secure once again rescuing us by whispering without words: Don't think ... don't focus on cancer or cops ... Just enjoy the moment, and being together ... Just feel the love ... it will make everything all right. And somehow, despite all the accumulated anxiety, the hopeful message was able to find us, and after we finally separated, and patted each other's tears away, for the rest of the weekend we followed its lingering lesson to the proverbial T.

Outside our apartment, May's last day had chosen to exit in bright sunshine underneath a blue sky dotted only occasionally by a cream-puff cloud. And when Stella then suggested that it would "do us both a helluva lot of good to grab a breath of fresh air," the two hours of Saturday morning that remained were happily spent chattering about baseball and the eclectic collection of people we observed during our favorite five-mile walk along Santa Monica Boulevard's former bridle path. Still not hungry, we spontaneously ruled out lunch in favor of collecting our promised reward early by attending a matinee showing of *The April Fools*. A romantic comedy featuring Jack Lemmon and Catherine Deneuve, its lighthearted mood further lifted ours, and over hot buttered popcorn and Cokes, the afternoon floated most pleasurably by, enhanced as it was by holding hands and sneaking an occasional kiss. In fact, the relaxation spawned by totally immersing ourselves in the movie was so complete that it persisted like a hovering halo over the evening we then spent cooking dinner together and dancing barefoot afterward to a parade of tunes, from the bouncy "Build Me Up Buttercup" by The Foundations to the soft sounds of The Temptations' "Cloud Nine," a title that fully lived up to its name as cheek to cheek we gently swayed to its mesmerizing melody.

"Super-Duper Saturday" was the nickname Stella coined for our R & R experience when Sunday morning found us still reminiscing about how the joy from simple pleasures had coaxed us carefree, and it didn't take long for us to jointly agree that an encore was "absolutely, positively essential!" So, after several hours devoted as usual to a leisurely reading of the oversized edition of the newspaper, accompanied by equally oversized mugs of coffee and a steady stream of animated conversation, we revisited Stella's favorite park, this time hiking the steep trails that meandered through the hills behind it. "You know something? I'm out of shape," Stella chuckled out when we finally returned to Old Greener after a two-hour jaunt, a bit achy and winded.

"I don't know," I teased, "I kinda like your shape, the peaks and the valleys are a lot easier to navigate than those hills we just climbed, and a whole lot more enjoyable, too."

"Oh, is that right?"

"Uh-huh ... Want to go home and help me prove it?"

"Sure ... sounds good to me," she purred. "Right after you take me to a movie."

"Oh, I see—no tickee, no washee, huh?"

"Boy, are you smart, or what?" Stella snickered. "I mean, with powers of observation like yours, you ought to consider being a criminal-defense attorney, maybe even a Public Defender?"

"Oh, yeah? ... Do they get preferential treatment in the lovemaking department?"

"Well, one special one does," Stella smiled, pulling open the car door. "Maybe even a double-header if he plays his cards right and throws in a burger and shake after the movie?"

"Hey, that's a deal," I fired back, my grin widening. "But we'll have to go light on the popcorn. I mean, a double-header is difficult to fully appreciate on an overly full stomach, so we need some priorities here, don't you think?"

"Uh-huh, I hear you," Stella murmured, adding a wink as I slid into the driver's seat and turned on the ignition. "But I wouldn't worry about it too much if I were you."

Fortunately, the strenuousness of the hike had created extra room for the popcorn, as well as the burgers, fries, and chocolate shakes that followed. And equally fortuitous, *Sweet Charity*, starring Shirley MacLaine, turned out to be the story of a young woman searching for love, the twin props of circumstance and coincidence thereby combining to set the stage for an evening of lovemaking that can only be described as the perfect ending to a full and satisfying day. For the same sad and fearsome fate that Stella and I now shared had also birthed a heightened intimacy that was crowned by a corresponding intensity. And fully relaxed from the simple pleasures we had enjoyed earlier, in the flickering candlelight, the added closeness created a freedom to give to each other with an almost reckless abandon, melding a union of desire and tenderness into an exquisite joy beyond anything previously experienced. Even the afterglow was different, physical fulfillment slowly surrendering to a vague feeling that together we had created something almost holy, as totally spent, and gasping for oxygen through our knowing smiles, we lay up against each other, neither of us daring to speak a single word for fear of pricking the cocoon of total contentment that surrounded us, the love shining in our eyes saying all that was necessary.

Finally, two or three heavenly minutes later, Stella raised her head off my chest and smiled out, "I know I promised, but after that, I don't think I've got another in me."

"No problem, sweetheart," I murmured back. "One shouldn't try to top perfect, it could piss off the Godperson Big Time."

"Right ... You really are smart after all," she whispered, sliding over onto her pillow. "And we need to sleep, too, 'cause you've got an early call tomorrow."

"Right, yourself," I chuckled, reaching over to kiss her lightly on the lips before falling back onto my pillow and smiling up through the shadows at the ceiling till seconds later my eyes gradually closed.

XXVI

When I awakened Monday morning at five-thirty, Stella also stirred awake. Coaxing her back to sleep with the promise that I'd kiss her goodbye before I left for the office, after I showered and dressed, I nevertheless found her waiting for me in the kitchen, the coffee already poured and the newspaper open to the Sports Page.

"I know I need my sleep," she smiled, anticipating my scold, "but just this once it's okay, 'cause it's the first day with the Panthers involved, and I want to be a tiny part of it."

"No problem, sweetie," I assured. "And I promise I'll call you the second I reach my desk."

"Okay … thanks. 'Cause you can bet I'll be working on my sketches right next to the phone," she mouthed, cheerfulness struggling to overcome anxiety. "Now, how about attending to some serious business right here?"

"You got it," I bounced back, reaching for my coffee mug.

The ten minutes we spent happily scouring yesterday's baseball-game summaries seemed to jump by, and then as planned, at six twenty-five I placed a call to Ron, who in turn telephoned Leon, whose duty it became to immediately contact the Panthers and advise them to expect the three of us to arrive at the Alondra Avenue exit around seven-fifteen. "Well, here we go," I quipped, then hugged Stella tightly before hurrying out the door and across the street to Old Greener.

A few minutes later I met Ron and Leon at the Robertson Boulevard on-ramp to the 405 Freeway, and after a quick exchange of smiles and hand-waves, Ron led the caravan south toward Solina. Lighting up my pipe, I settled in comfortably behind the wheel for the half-hour trek, my mind quickly filling with questions about what possibly lay ahead. Will the sheriffs really be waiting for us? began the parade. And if so, what'll they do when they spot the Panthers? You told Stella that they'd want no part of them, but is that true? Or could there be trouble instead, like what if the first cop car summoned a small army of supporters and that led to a real confrontation? Maybe even a shootout? posed my flashing brainwaves. "Jesus, fucking-A Christ!" I sputtered out in response. "How the hell does a nice Jewish boy from Beverly Hills get his skinny little ass involved in an ugly mess like this?" spilled my sarcasm in an effort to ease the butterflies in my stomach, a grin forming. "Well, the good news is that with such a skinny ass, the pigs will have less to shoot at, right?" I gibed, then halted, my grin vanishing when memory suddenly sprung suppressed desire onto the surface of cold reality. Well, you always did want to get involved like the freedom riders, so here's your chance, Buster Brown. How does it feel? marched the testy taunt along the neurons' highway, then echoed louder and louder.

"Scary," I answered after several seconds' pause to reflect. Scary, indeed, I repeated silently, thinking also that *scary* had become the watchword of the new life that I was now living. Roughly sixty hours had passed since Stella's tragic secret had come to light, having followed closely on the heels of George's revelation that the five of us could be in danger, and even as I steered toward Solina with our painful discussion still vibrating in the backyard of my brain, it was awfully hard to believe that what I faced was real, that in less than three days so much major change could have occurred. "Well, it's real all right," I told myself, my head nodding ever so slightly, "so you just better believe it 'cause you don't have any choice, little buddy—you can't run." Again my words echoed as I continued struggling to evaluate my feelings. "I ... I ... don't want to run," trickled out after several more increasingly sober seconds had shuffled by. "I want to share with Stella for every single minute possible, and I want to take care of her ... It's just that I'm not sure I'm strong enough, I mean I've never been part of anybody dying, I don't even know what to do, and there's sure as hell no book on this. Except, of course, Dr. Frankl's," I suddenly added, a wry grin forming as his lesson on control flashed into mind, followed a second or two later by his friendly face. "How am I doing, so far?" I asked, scrutinizing his eyes for an answer. The slow-paced wink he delivered seemed to say I was doing all right. Well, okay ... okay, I thought. Just keep following your heart, and pay attention so that you don't miss any clues about Stella needing help like you did when you failed to notice her weight loss, or how tired she looked sometimes, or when at Thanksgiving she said, "I don't like wasting time, when no one knows how much we've got."

Yeahhh, right, I mused, shaking my head sadly at how long she had had to harbor her pain all alone. And speaking about doing the right thing, she's sure correct about the war, all right, I do want to finish it. "Hell, I want to goddamn win it!" I ended the churning stream of thought out loud, determination sounding, my right hand pounding the steering wheel for emphasis, then reaching forward and switching on the radio to stifle any further ruminations.

Fifteen minutes later our caravan curved slowly off the freeway and onto Alondra Avenue, Leon then leading us into the lane closest to the curb and gradually slowing to a stop. Within seconds, two vans appeared, one sliding in ahead of Leon, the second behind my third-place position. Each contained six Panthers, and after Leon and I traded smiles and casual fist-pumps with them, the journey to the courthouse began. After three miles, we entered Solina's city limits, and as we dropped our speed to thirty miles per hour, I began swiveling my head slowly side to side to see if I could spot the enemy. I didn't have to wait long, as three blocks later, while we were passing through the intersection, my rightward glance picked up a black-and-white sheriff's vehicle pull from the curb and drop into traffic to the rear of the Panther's van behind me. "Well lookee here—the stupid, fucking game is on!" I hissed, watching through my rear-view mirror to learn what the sheriffs' next move would be. I didn't have to wait long for that either, as within seconds the deputies apparently recognized the identity of our escorts, because they promptly executed a right turn at the very next intersection and pulled over to the front of a second sheriff's car waiting curbside.

"Holy cockamolies—it worked!" I laughed, beeping my horn lightly three times. A triumphant chorus answered me, and ten uneventful minutes later when we reached the office, broad smiles and firm handshakes were enthusiastically shared all around. In fact, I was still grinning when I reached my desk and telephoned the good news to Stella, who was so relieved that she immediately promised something special for dinner. "It's a deal," I chuckled. "Now stop worrying, and really enjoy working on your sketches, you hear?"

"Sure ... I will," she purred. And after we hung up, the suggestion entered into mind that a similar program was in order for me, too, as I picked up the calendar for Division One and made ready to head for the courthouse. Having noted that it bore the date, June 2, 1969, as I strolled across the street I welcomed the new month with a grin and a large dose of caution. "Snuck right in, didn't you?" I whispered through the smoke from my pipe. "Yeah, just tiptoed in and took a baby step like Stella and me, huh? ... Well, Mr. New, if we're going to get along, your offerings had better be a hell of a lot happier than May's," I snickered. "'Cause I can't take too many more body blows, you hear?"

As always, Monday's calendar turned "overcrowded" into a major understatement, having swelled obese with cases during the weekend's hiatus. Work, however, offered the best opportunity to blunt the gnawing angst that still shadowed me despite the success of our early morning commute, so I quickly immersed myself in the steady stream of cases that flowed into the courtroom like a river overflowing its banks. To my further relief, this endeavor was also fruitful, my feverish efforts in comforting my clients, setting their cases for trial, and obtaining OR releases effectively relegating worrisome speculation to a shelf in the far recesses of my mind, and for a bonus, restoring my sense of purpose to its proper place in the front row. In fact, when I telephoned Stella at noon to check on her, she commented that I sounded like my "regular Public Defender Self" and teased that I shouldn't "beat up on old Judge Gelman too much."

The afternoon passed productively by in identical fashion, and when I returned to the office around quarter of five, further buoyed by the absence of stress, I fully enjoyed casually chatting with Marilyn over coffee while waiting for my compatriots to return. One by one, they soon straggled in, each bemoaning some grievous new injury inflicted by the black-robed monsters on the already bleeding body of justice, shared humor and empathy soon filling the air. When George finally arrived however, visibly excited and wearing a gleeful grin, the commiseration session promptly terminated in favor of a meeting in his office.

"Gentlemen, I have a double dose of good news!" he announced in an electric tone, his smile growing Grand Canyon–wide as he pulled off his blazer. "First off, I explained to Hux and Tim about the little problem we're having with the sheriffs, and they took action to help. It seems that old Hux has a lifelong buddy he went to law school with, that now heads the L.A. Division of the FBI—and Hux got him to phone the L.A. County Sheriff himself and let him know they'd heard some ugly rumors of possible illegal goings-on in connection with our Office. You know, the old 'I just wanted to give you a friendly heads-up, so that you could prevent law enforcement from getting a black-eye in case there was any truth to them.' Anyway, when the word comes down to let us the hell alone, there's going to be some very surprised pigs in the Solina Division, don't you think?"

"Holy ... fuckers!" Ron squealed with delight when George paused to light up a cigarette. "You can just bet your sweet ass on it, they'll be shitting in their pants!"

"Well, I certainly hope so," George picked up. "But remember, we can't be sure how long it takes for the word to circulate, and even then there's no guarantee that it'll be followed by every single deputy—like good old Officer Hardy and his hard-ass buddies. So, for the time being, we'll continue our plan with the Panthers, and between them and the threat of being watched by the FBI, we should be A-okay."

"Right-on," Robbie nodded. "And how about our sixth man, any real hope for that?"

"That's good news number two," George fired back. "Tim called me a few minutes ago while I was in Austin's chambers, to tell me that we're getting him."

"When?" Ron flared with eager anticipation.

"Ronald, my man, that's the really good news," George declared, his eyes twinkling. "How does tomorrow morning at eight o'clock sound?"

"Well I'll be a motherfucking monkey! What the hell did you tell them on Friday?"

"Not that much, really. Hux and Tim have been aware of our need for a long time, but internal pressures being what they are, they just couldn't do anything about it. Apparently, however, several of the old guard, like our asshole friend Keyes, have retired in the last month or so, leaving Hux free to finally add staff in the branches—and we were at the top of the list."

"Wow ... that's really great news—all of it," slid off Ron's tongue slowly, relief softening the edges of his enthusiasm.

An accurate reflection of our collective mood, relief-tempered enthusiasm continued to govern during the minute that followed George's momentous announcement, so that oddly, for us, no celebratory explosion poured forth. The War had gone on for so long, with so many up-and-downward spirals, and we were so tired from constantly battling, that the long-awaited news that a sixth deputy was forthcoming was not greeted by screams or shouts as in the past when hoped-for goals were reached. Instead, as the realization fully registered, our considerable happiness was expressed simply in the warm smiles mapping our beaming faces, along with the chorus of "Yeah, right on!" that escaped while we were vigorously sharing a round of handshakes and hugs. "Hey, what's the name of our messiah, anyway?" Robbie drawled when we finally settled back into our chairs, the air of quiet excitement still surrounding us and flowing into our cheerful chatter.

"Ohhh, fuck! Now religion is getting sucked into this hell-hole," Leon chuckled out before George could answer. "And if that happens, I'm getting out. I mean, I can stand all the rest of the shit falling on our heads, but not that, no way!"

"Schwartz," Robbie responded, breaking into a grin. "Go play your piano, will you? I just want to sit here and reflect on our sudden good fortune, without having to be disturbed by one of your Marxist lectures on the ins and outs of Jesus Christ and Company."

"Sensitive little creature, isn't he?" Leon shrugged with mild sarcasm.

"Not really," interjected Ron, playing along. "What you have to understand, is that since Robbie converted to Judaism, he's been under a lot of pressure."

"Robbie turned Jewish?"

"Uh-huh. You didn't know, Schwartzy?"

"No ... When did it happen?"

"Last Thursday, in the afternoon, around four o'clock."

"Well, I'll be damned."

"Yeah, it's really amazing, all right."

"Uh-huh ... But that doesn't quite sum it up," Leon opined, now fully enjoying himself. "I mean, hell, you'd think black would be tough enough to bear. But, now, to add Jewishness on top of it ... well, that's just a little bit much, don't you think?"

"Absolutely no doubt whatsoever!" Ron agreed, stifling his urge to laugh. "And being an experienced Jew myself, with all the scars to prove it, I clearly pointed out the downside. But after he conferred with Steiggerman, there was just no stopping him."

"Steiggerman? ... How did that prick get mixed up in this?" Leon cried, furrowing his forehead with mock concern.

"Why, Arlie Asshole is Rob's religious advisor. Didn't you know that either?"

"No ... I must honestly confess, I didn't."

"Well, for Christ's sake, don't go Catholic on me—not right in the middle of a discussion about Rob's bar mitzvah!" Ron piled on, then watched a look of astonishment jump across Leon's face.

"Bar ... mitzvah?" he howled, raising his arms and turning his palms outward to demonstrate the depth of his incredulity.

"Oh, sure," Ron rocketed back. "Steiggerman thought that that was a good idea, too. In fact, he wrote Rob's speech for him. It started out, Dear fellow kikes, and other assembled scumbags, and then it really got good!" Ron editorialized, then burst out laughing.

George, Robbie, and I were already giggling, so when Ron let loose with his hearty guffaw, followed by Leon's disdainfully toned, "This is a very serious discussion, why are you idiots laughing?" the roar was on. A mixture of glee, relief, and a newly realized but cautious optimism that projected a more fruitful future, five tributaries of merriment quickly flowed into a frothing river of cackling, shrieking hilarity that lasted till our sides ached. And when it finally had run its course, the second round of coffee that Marilyn smilingly supplied tasted even better than its predecessor, as now fully relaxed, we eagerly planned how best to deploy our newest weapon, wondrously scheduled to arrive in just fourteen hours.

Quickly agreeing that if he could adequately handle the stressful duties involved in Division Three, then the five of us could return to conducting an all-out offensive elsewhere, we tabled final discussion of the alternative tactics available to us until we could evaluate first-hand our newest colleague's abilities, as well as his willingness to commit to the cause, then happily made preparations to depart for home. While George contacted the Panthers, I placed a quick call to Stella, informing her of the good news and promising details over dinner, then strolled outside with the others to wait. Before we climbed into our cars, George confided in me that Marie Anne had insisted on a trial separation, and that while it was upsetting, it might be for the best. "I'll tell you more later, but don't worry 'cause I'm okay," he assured as the Panthers pulled into the parking lot and our caravan began assembling.

Well, I mused as we headed for the freeway, good news on the war front, not so good at home. And when that thought was instantly followed by the notion that my gift for understatement apparently knew no bounds, a sad smile snaked out of the corners of my mouth as I slowly shook my head and tried to find a more comfortable spot in my seat while our convoy turned onto Alondra. When I had imparted the positive developments to Stella, I had also told her not to worry if I was a few minutes later than usual, as I was going to stop on the way to the apartment for a quick visit with my grandparents. Conveniently, they were having dinner at my parents' home, so that while sharing hugs and some chatter with Gram and Gramp, I would also be able to rebut my mother's allegation that they hardly ever got the opportunity to lay eyes on me. And as we reached the freeway without so much as spying a single sheriff's vehicle, I pushed away the shadowing domestic worries and focused instead on how I would insure that the visit was short while humming along with Sly and the Family Stone as they warbled "Everyday People."

Adding to the day's good tidings, the visit went well. Everyone was pleased to see me, and after half a glass of wine and some baseball chatter with Grampy Max, I successfully eluded dinner with my iron-clad excuse that I had a dinner date. And I did, too. Not exactly the type that was speculated about after I departed, but a warm and wonderful one nonetheless. Stella greeted me with an extra tight hug, and over the filet mignon and wild rice that followed, I happily supplied the promised details of Monday's propitious happenings. Both lively and reassuring, our conversation carried over to dessert, where the chocolate-cream pie we enjoyed was further sweetened by the optimism we also shared over the prospects of increased commuter safety and the arrival of the "messiah," as Robbie had so eloquently labeled him. And even though our evening closed with the same unanswerable question about his abilities and attitude that the five of us had posed earlier, nevertheless it was a highly contented couple that nestled close in bed for a relaxed read before sleep.

As it turned out, the answer we sought was delivered far sooner than anticipated, and with a bombastic fury that exceeded even our most hopeful expectations. For the following morning, with George looking on, it took Blaine Kraslow less than sixty seconds to initiate the first, faint strains of a migraine headache behind Judge Lacy's furrowed forehead. Setting the stage in the morning's opening prelim, the DA, David Ludlow, had initiated His Honor's frustration with fifteen minutes of his traditionally slow-paced direct examination, made even slower by the alleged victim's tearful description of how during an argument with her fiancé, he had struck her several time with a metal broom handle, cutting her face and head. And like a spark settling into dry brush, Kraslow, naturally gifted with a deep, resonant voice, opened fire on cross-examination while still climbing out of his chair.

"Miss Hagman," he inquired, "isn't it true that prior to the alleged hitting you just described, that the argument you mentioned was about fucking—that you accused my client of fucking someone else instead of you?"

Sledge-hammered into shock by the crude accusation hurled at her in such a loud, ugly tone, Judith Ann Hagman stiffened against the back of her seat, then stammered, "W-w-h-a-t?"

An even six feet tall, lean, but heavily muscled through the chest and arms, Kraslow, with his bushy eyebrows, long sideburns, and shoulder-length hair, was indeed an imposing figure as he strode briskly over to the jury box railing and fixed his dark, piercing eyes on his prey. "What I asked you, Miss Hagman," he then repeated, "was during this argument you've told us about, didn't you accuse my client of sharing his cock with someone else instead of slipping it in that fuzzy little hole between your legs?"

With Ludlow still having failed to object, His Honor rushed to the rescue of the witness before a grimace could fully spread across her flushed face. "Mr. Kraslow, your language is not only highly improper!" he rifled angrily, "but your attempt to frighten and intimidate this poor, young woman is outrageous, and I order you to cease immediately!"

"Your Honor," Kraslow returned with matching intensity. "If the Court so desires, I have in my briefbag the citations to over one hundred cases, all of which hold that the language I couched my question in is perfectly proper! And as for frightening this poor, young woman, as you referred to her, if you will allow me to continue, I will demonstrate that the Court's apparent sympathy for her is misplaced—that in fact, she is nothing more than a jealous, lying bitch, who not only accused my client of being an unfaithful bastard, but was so angry that she attempted to stab him several times with a large butcher knife! Moreover, Your Honor, the only danger she's in is being frightened into telling the truth about what really happened here!"

Wondering what possible sin he had committed to deserve the appearance of the devil himself, at only twenty minutes after nine on an ordinary Tuesday morning, a stunned Lacy shook his head in disbelief at the level of defiance radiating from Kraslow's eyes. Knowing full well though that appellate courts had held such crude language fully permissible, and that he therefore had no choice, he then modified his previous order to Kraslow and allowed him to continue, "but only in a manner that does not badger the witness."

"Very well, Your Honor," Kraslow agreed, smiling smugly as he resumed his cross-examination. And having already suffered the pain of being battered sufficiently to require stitches, Judy Hagman was now subjected to the second most unpleasant experience of her twenty-one-year-old life. For having established the validity of both his probe and style, Kraslow, wearing a scowl across his broad face, proceeded like a highly skilled surgeon to systematically expose every possible nuance of her relationship with the defendant, including the highlights of their sex life, and in the one-hour process reduced her to a sweaty, slobbering shell of herself that finally begged, "No more, no more … please," in a tone that simulated the bleat of a lost lamb in search of its mother.

Highly impressed by Kraslow's considerable cross-examining skills, but absolutely astonished at the degree of ruthlessness he'd witnessed, when the Prelim ended, George quickly conferred with the now relaxed but still angry-looking Kraslow. "That was quite a show you put on," he advised, still surprised by the brutal performance despite his years of experience.

"Glad you liked it, boss," Kraslow quipped. "I didn't have much to really work with, 'cause our dude insists that she attacked him first with the knife, but all the arrest report states is that the neighbors heard them both screaming. No mention of any knife, and she had all the cuts and bruises. So I figured," he continued with a shrug of his shoulders, "that if I could scare the holy shit out her, maybe she won't want to go through it again downtown in front of a jury."

Rarely was George ever at a loss for words. But staring up into the electric smile spread across Kraslow's moon-shaped face, he found himself visited by just such an occasion. Finally, after several awkward seconds had slipped by, he broke into a grin that mixed his lingering surprise with the flashing thought, we've got a new weapon, all right!, and informed Kraslow that he was going to leave him on his own. "That okay with you?" George queried.

"Sure thing, boss," bounced Kraslow's reply, "that fool up there on the bench don't worry me none, he'll just have to learn who's running this place, that's all. Being that he's so dumb, it'll probably take him a while, but I'm a patient man."

"Yeah, I noticed," George chuckled, shaking his head. "Just don't get held in contempt, all right? Otherwise, your *patient* approach is just what Lacy needs."

While he was hurrying outside and upstairs to resume his drunk-driving trial, George's bemusement steadily increased along the way as he contemplated the other judges' painful reaction to Kraslow. And later, at noon, when we collected for lunch, he introduced our new colleague to us with a twinkle in his eye that appeared to be dancing a jig. "Guys, I want you to meet Blaine," he mouthed through a sly smile, "a damn good lawyer, and one of the toughest I've ever seen!"

That terse endorsement, coming as it did from George, was all that was needed to satisfy the four of us as to Blaine's credentials, and after we adjourned to a neighboring restaurant, we promptly began explaining Solinaland to him. To our considerable surprise, he was thoroughly familiar with almost every event that had transpired in our domain during the past six months. "Hell, you guys are famous downtown!" he enthused in response to Robbie's inquiry as to how he had come by such a thorough knowledge of our activities. "And Stone ran the situation down to me detail by detail, when I volunteered to join you. He also said that you were the damndest bunch of hell-raising troublemakers he'd ever come across!"

"Well, from what I saw this morning, you're going to fit in just perfectly," George responded, laughter spilling round the table as George's further seal of approval registered, the four of us trading knowing glances as we leaned contentedly back in our chairs. Blaine then ordered a second pitcher of beer, and an animated discussion of our plans for retaking the offensive was under way before the waiter even reached the bar at the opposite end of the room.

The following morning, June's first Wednesday, witnessed the opening salvo of our escalation of Phase Two of the War—fully assembled by eight-thirty, together the six of us strolled the short distance to the battlefield and one by one began serving notice that Father Time was no longer our adversary. In Division Three, during the latest in the never-ending stream of throwing cases that opened the Prelim calendar, Blaine cross-examined the testifying officer for in excess of an hour, and when a visibly frustrated Lacy ordered him to "speed-up" in subsequent cases, Blaine slowed even further, advising in an acerbic tone that "nowhere to my knowledge is there any legal authority that establishes time limits within which I must perform my constitutionally recognized function." Pressing the issue,

Lacy was soon defeated in the ensuing struggle, as well as those that followed, by Blaine's ability to pull from his briefbag and read into the record voluminous case and statutory authority in support of the various legal positions he assumed as the morning stretched onward. And long before the noon recess, Lacy, grim-faced and embittered by Blaine's blatant defiance, had retreated from interjecting himself directly into the cases, and resigned to the fact that he was legally unable to dam the river of appellate court rulings that energetically flowed back at him through a sardonic smile, contented himself as best he could by simply holding defendant after defendant to answer, regardless of the merits of the prosecution's case. Only once did His Honor vary from his adopted approach to the sticky situation, unable to resist the opportunity to openly chastise a defendant charged with burglary, his most hated crime due to his home having been burglarized three times during the past five years, and double the existing bail. Fuming, Blaine requested a meeting in chambers that quickly turned ugly.

"You wanted to see me, Kraslow?" Lacy queried with obvious repugnance as Blaine entered and approached his desk, studying his face as if maybe he was in fact the Devil.

"Yes, Your Honor, I did."

"Well, then, pull up a chair and tell me what's bothering you."

"I prefer to stand, thank you," Blaine replied curtly. "And what I have to say won't take long, 'cause it's just YOU that's bothering me!" he continued, his voice seething with anger. "Now it suits me just fine if you want to sit up there on the bench all day long holding everyone to answer, including the cases that you and I both know should be kicked the hell out of here. My Office will just run so many 995 motions downtown, that pretty soon the Judicial Council is going to learn that you're one hell of a piss-poor judge—which just might keep you from getting promoted to Superior Court, also perfectly fine with me!" Blaine steamed, his eyes spitting fire. "But raising bail isn't! And if you don't lower it back to where it was in the last case, you're going to have problems that won't quit!"

Grinning sarcastically, a flabbergasted Lacy set his coffee cup down, then slowly lifted his eyes and fully returned Blaine's hostile glare. "Under what type of rock does the PD's Office find blackmailing little snakes like you, Kraslow?" he posed.

"Listen, pig, just remember that the choice is yours!" Blaine growled back instantly. "And I better never hear you speak my name again without mister in front of it!" he tacked on, then whirled and vanished before Lacy could utter another word.

As Blaine returned to the counsel table, and glanced over his notes on the next case while waiting for Lacy to return to the bench, upstairs, in Division Two, matters were proceeding in a routine and orderly fashion. Having fairly instructed the jury upon completion of final arguments in the drunk-driving trial, Judge Austin now served coffee to George and Irene Fisher in chambers, and after complimenting them both on their handling of the case, leaned back in his chair and joked that "it was now time to attend to their pile of dirty laundry." Next door, I had successfully stalled commencement of the plea-bargaining process, while waiting patiently to learn that George's trial had ended. He had requested that I delay filing my Affidavits for Cause until he was free and able to undertake defensive measures on behalf of myself and Blaine in the event that either or both of us were held in contempt, a likelihood whose odds we had calculated at better than fifty-fifty in both cases. Now, having learned from Bailiff Roberts that George's jury had begun deliberation, I proceeded to escalate our offensive by dropping my carefully prepared bombs squarely in Steiggerman's lap.

I had not seen His Honor since our volcanic confrontation a week ago, though so much change had occurred during the interim that it seemed like a lifetime had passed. As Whirlwind Wednesday flooded back into mind however, during my approach to his chambers, once again I listened to his definition of a Public Defender as "a kike like you, defending your nigger clients from the good-guy WASPs like me!" his insidious grin then reappearing as I also reheard his threat upon my refusal to continue the last two cases. "But you just remember one thing," he had flamed at me, "you're so exhausted that you're sick, and I'm not. So if we start, we're going to finish even if you die out there!" Well, I didn't die, pig! I mused, cold anger hardening further inside me as I knocked on the door. And here comes a real, live problem for you that's going to hurt Big Time! I smiled as Roberts opened the door.

His Honor, in the interests of saving time, had been discussing a battery case with the DA, David Ludlow, and had convinced him to accept a plea to disturbing the peace, he explained after I slid into my seat opposite his desk. "Would you like some coffee?" he added.

"No, thank you, Your Honor—to both offers," I replied calmly.

"Why do you feel that way, Mr. Harris?" he queried with sugar-coated sincerity. "It's a good deal."

"Well, Sir," I eased back, "there are two reasons. First, on the battery case, I notice that Officer Hardy is the arresting officer, and in that he's the biggest liar I know of, the only disposition I'd accept is an outright dismissal. But more importantly is the fact that I won't be appearing in your court anymore. I have here," I continued, reaching into my briefbag and pulling out a thick folder, "twenty-nine Affidavits for Cause. And my only question is, do I file them directly with you, or your clerk?"

Watching as the color drained from his face, I waited for the explosion to arrive. "Www-hat?" he stuttered out first, anger churning up inside him as the shock fully registered. "What are you trying to pull off now, Harris?" he then bellowed.

"I'm not trying to pull off anything, Your Honor," marched my steely-toned reply as I met his gaze head-on. "I'm simply advising you that I'm filing twenty-nine Affidavits for Cause, that's all."

"Now you listen here, you fucking little sonofabitch!" thundered his response, the anticipated explosion now having fully arrived. "If you don't put those goddamned pieces of paper back in your briefbag, and I mean right now, I'm going to have you arrested for extortion! Do you hear me, Harris? You're going to be destroyed, just wiped out completely—you understand?"

I understood far better than he could ever have imagined. And struggling to control the rage that boiled up inside of me as once again I read in his face the malicious exercise of power that fortified the injustices I so detested, I snapped my briefbag closed with the force of the punch I wished I could deliver squarely into the center of that evil countenance, then slowly replied. "I most certainly do, Your Dishonor!" seethed each and every word. "And now I'm going to leave, and give you a few minutes to study these affidavits, as well as the supplemental ones attached by Mr. Shafer of the DA's Office. Then, if you still want to add false arrest to the charges against you, Roberts will know just where to find me!"

Turning away quickly, I bolted back outside into the courtroom, where I further squelched my only real concern about being incarcerated, which was the possibility of leaving Stella alone at home. Hell, I assured myself after glancing at my watch, it's only eleven o'clock, and Georgie will have you out by four at the latest. Yeah, no problem, I chuckled silently, then swallowed the sour saliva in my mouth. Advising

Roberts that I was going to make a short visit to the men's room, when I reached it, I promptly splashed cold water over my flushed cheeks, then studied my face in the mirror. "You look okay, buddy," I whispered. "In fact, not bad at all, considering what we have to work with," I gibed, snickering. "Just remember, though," I counseled, focusing on my eyes as I turned serious again, "that this is finally your time for payback. Yeahhh, for sure," I hissed, "I waited a long time, so you sweat, pig, you sweat real good, 'cause this time you're going to lose Big Time! 'Cause your balls are right smack in the middle of that vise that Georgie was talking about a while back, and if it's the last thing I do, I'm going to squeeze them into pulp!" I ended, a sneering smile crossing my face as I subdued the sudden surge of anger that capped my swelling resolve. Yeah, no need to waste energy, I cautioned. Just stay cool and calm, and don't give an inch, I affirmed, nodding my head unconsciously to signal further confirmation, then chuckling softly at the notion that me, myself, and I were in complete agreement, my craving for a smoke suddenly stronger.

Thirty minutes later, while enjoying a second pipeful, I was momentarily studying the cloud-like formations that my smoke was creating as it drifted toward the ceiling when Roberts approached my seat at the counsel table and notified me that Steiggerman had recessed court until one-thirty. It was two-fifteen when he next approached, and this time advised that His Honor wished to confer with me in chambers. Shaking his head with concern when I requested him to inform Steiggerman that I would enter his chambers only if a court reporter was present, I squirmed anxiously in my seat as I watched him disappear carrying my message. A full five minutes elapsed before Steiggerman, dressed in his robe, emerged and slowly covered the forty feet that separated us. "Mr. Harris," he began calmly and deliberately, "I am not ordering you into chambers, I'm politely asking you to come there so that we can discuss, man to man, the problem which has arisen. No one but you and me will be present, so there are no witnesses and no need for a court reporter—all right?"

"Very well, Your Honor," I answered coldly, then arose and followed him, noting that perspiration had begun to form underneath my arms.

When he had taken off his robe and seated himself behind his desk, Steiggerman forced a smile before inquiring, "Would you like a cup of coffee?"

"No, thank you," I eased back.

"All right, then, we'll get right down to business. Now I've been thinking about what happened this morning, and I want to start off by saying that I feel very badly about it, as well as the incident last Wednesday," he offered in a sober tone. "And even though my remarks at that time were intended as dark humor, and not intended to hurt anyone's feelings or impugn their religion in any way," he continued, nodding his head slightly to emphasize his concern, "I want to sincerely apologize for making them, and ask your forgiveness," he ended, studying my face for a reaction. "Are you sure you won't have a cup of coffee?" he quickly tacked on when he found it blank.

"No, thank you," shuffled off my tongue slowly as I enjoyed his discomfort.

"Well, all right ... uh ... As I was saying," he picked up, "I realize that you and I have our little differences, but I think that one remark—admittedly off-base—has caused a situation to develop that has sort of gotten out of hand. Like I said, I sincerely want to correct it, and I feel that if we talk things out, you'll see that the incident last Wednesday resulted from overwork and too much pressure. I mean, I'm sure you'll agree that we've all said things when we're tired and frustrated that we didn't really mean—right?" he ended, then leaned forward to learn my response.

"Right," I replied. "But in this case, I think you meant every single word of what you said last Wednesday, just as—"

"Nooo, now wait—" he interjected, then caught himself in mid-interruption and quickly added, "Excuse me, I didn't mean to cut you off. Please continue."

A faint smile formed in the corners of my mouth as I realized how hard he was trying to evidence an attitude of sincere civility toward me. Wondering fleetingly if this modern-day Machiavelli ever stopped impersonating a chameleon, I then completed my prior thought. "Okay," I nodded, "I was going to add that I also think you meant what you said this morning, as well as all the other times we've had at it. Look, let's face it, and save ourselves a lot of time—peace between us is just plain impossible!" rolled off my tongue firmly, but without emotion.

"Now hold on a minute, please," rocketed his reply, then slowed. "If we talk this out, I'm sure I can convince you otherwise," he stressed, nervously clasping his hands together and squeezing them tightly as he concentrated heavily on not allowing his voice to reflect his growing frustration. "Are you telling me," he posed, "that two intelligent men who have certain little differences of opinion can't agree to keep those differences within reasonable bounds?"

Watching enjoyably as his inner struggle forced the muscles in his cheeks to slightly twitch, I felt a strange sense of power further pique my increasing confidence. The pig was sweating all right. All I had to do now was wait for him to place his testicles just a little further inside the open vise. And more than willing to assist, my simple "Yes," in response to his question, nudged him one inch closer.

"But, why?" he queried anxiously.

"Because those *little* differences you referred to, are in fact as big as outer space."

"Then you're not even willing to try and work things out, is that right?"

"I'm not sure exactly what that means."

"Well … uh … let's say that I was willing to be quite reasonable about disposing of today's cases," oozed his response through a sly smile.

"What's reasonable? You and I define that word differently, you know."

"Well … let's say that I would dismiss outright all of the rotten ones, and give you the courthouse, as we say, on the rest of them."

"Rotten" was a good adjective to describe what sat grinning hopefully across the desk from me. "Putrid," however, was even better, I thought, before leading him a few inches further down the path. "What about the DA? Don't you think he might have some objection?" I asked with feigned interest.

"You just leave the DA to me," he shot back. "Now what about it—will you withdraw your affidavits and accept my offer?"

"No," I answered after a full five seconds of leaden silence had elapsed. "I can't."

"Why not? Isn't that enough?" he countered, anxiety now shadowed by anger.

"Are you kidding?" snapped sharply off my tongue. "If I did what you're suggesting, that would be extortion—and I want no part of that whatsoever!"

"You don't, huh? Well, what do you call what you and the rest of your gang have been doing for the past five months, kissing our asses?"

"No, I wouldn't say that exactly."

"I didn't think you would. Now, if my offer isn't good enough, what is it that you do want, Harris?" he asked, his growing anger now pulling him squarely inside the vise.

"Make that Mister Harris, and I'll tell you," taunted my reply as I began to turn the handle.

"All right ... Mister Harris. Now what in the goddamned hell do you want?" he boomed, his face beginning to flush.

"You know, Judge, I'm glad you're getting pissed at me, 'cause that's at least honest. And now that you've finally reached that point, I'll let it all hang out."

"Go right ahead," he challenged, his anger escaping control.

"That'll be my pleasure," rushed my return. "Do you remember what you said a while back, about what you were going to do to me when this fight was settled?"

"No, not exactly. Why?"

"Well, you said that you were going to hang my ass from the highest tree in Solina—and you know what, you were partly right. I mean, the only mistake you made was that it's going to be your ass that's hanging—and that, and nothing less, is what I want!"

Having barked my last words at him loud enough to create an echo, as perspiration flowed downward from underneath my arms and bathed the top of my ribcage, I glared my full hatred of all he represented across the six short feet that separated us and into the depths of his eyes. Blue, they grew slowly gray with disbelief, and further shaded the paling flesh of his face. Genuinely stunned by the degree of loathing that bore into him like a laser, in turn he surprised me almost equally by failing to lash back, instead wearily lowering his head down onto his folded arms atop the desk. When he raised it, several long and hollow seconds later, the faint trace of moisture in his eyes and the low, quivering tones of his voice when he finally replied raised my surprise to amazement.

"All right ... all right ... you win," he squeezed out, struggling for control. "You win all the way, Harris, and I hope it makes you happy, 'cause I've worked very hard to get where I am in this world that you think you understand so well, but really don't. I've got a wife and two kids at home ... and a mother," he continued, now meeting my somewhat softened gaze head-on, "all of whom are very proud of me, and were looking forward to seeing me promoted to Superior Court. You're going to spoil that now, and I hope it's enough to satisfy you and your friends."

For several seconds after he ended, an ocean of silence threatened to drown us both. Then, simultaneously still outraged, but also feeling a strange sense of sadness swelling up inside me, I interrupted it. "Fred Ginther had a wife and kids, too," I advised. "But that didn't stop you from fucking over the jury's mind, and then sending him to jail for the maximum time for a first offense on a simple drunk charge—not that he was, and you and I both know it!" I tacked on, my voice shaking with emotion as the pain on Fred's face flooded back into mind.

I didn't expect him to remember, but the deepening sadness in his eyes informed me to the contrary and pushed the amazement button for the second time. "Answer one question for me, Harris, if you will, and then you can leave," he responded a couple of seconds later. "What is it that's inside you, that drives you so—that makes you care so much for people, who like you say, we both know don't give a good goddamn about you?" When I didn't answer immediately, but instead rose to my feet and made my way over to the door and pulled it ajar, he added, "Really ... I'd like to know."

My anger had faded considerably, so it was softer tones that carried my answer. "If I have to explain it to you, you wouldn't understand," I said solemnly, the door then clicking closed behind me before my message fully registered.

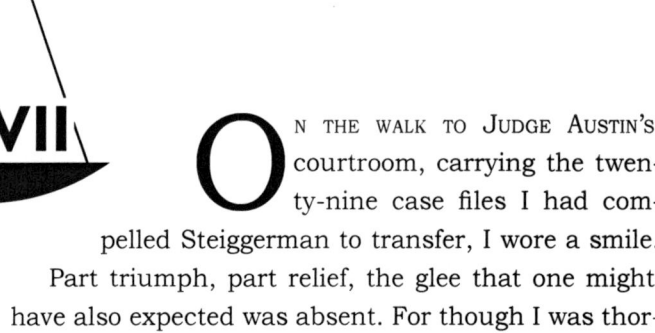

XXVII

On the walk to Judge Austin's courtroom, carrying the twenty-nine case files I had compelled Steiggerman to transfer, I wore a smile. Part triumph, part relief, the glee that one might have also expected was absent. For though I was thoroughly pleased, as well as fully satisfied, a dull ache inside my chest tempered my mood. Why was I not celebrating? I mused. Hell, if I were Vincent van Gogh, I couldn't have painted a more perfect portrait of defeat than the expression on Steiggerman's face when I departed. It was all there, everything I had always hoped for—the crushed remains of arrogance and elitist pride, the complete surrender of power, his personal humiliation, even the anguish I had lusted for! Why, then, was I not ebulliently gloating? And why, instead, of all impossibly possible things was sadness mixing with the sugar spawned by victory? No answers surfaced as I approached the door to Division Two. "Maybe Joni Mitchell's right?" I whispered, listening to "Something's lost but something's gained in living every day," as it echoed into ear. "Yeah, maybe so," I whispered after a panoramic flash of the joy and pain produced by the transformative events of the past week rushed past as I pushed my way through the double doors into the courtroom. "Yeahhh ... maybe so," I repeated through a sigh, then forced a smile onto my face when the following thought entered: It's still a major win, Matthew, my man. You did good! it informed. So don't be too hard on yourself for not having all the answers—Aristotle or Plato you're not.

Judge Austin soon had me fully relaxed and laughing. "Good afternoon, Mr. Matthew," he teased through a smile as I entered his chambers. "It seems that you think we're a little short on business here in Division Two, that we're not pulling our own weight. Any truth to that?"

"No, Your Honor ... absolutely not," I replied. "In fact, I'm very sorry about burdening you with all these extra cases, but I didn't have any choice, I—"

"You most certainly didn't," he interjected, his smile broadening, a twinkle sparkling in his bright blue eyes. "I read your affidavit, as well as the supporting one by Mr. Shafer, and you absolutely did the right thing. Good work—you want some coffee?"

I did. And after thanking him for his understanding and support while settling comfortably into a chair opposite his desk, during the next two hours we amicably disposed of the mountain of cases on highly advantageous terms for my clients. The seven serious ones were continued for a month, to allow for "proper consideration and preparation by the defense," with those clients incarcerated granted OR releases from jail. Next, the least serious were outright dismissed, and the remainder settled for pleas to reduced charges, with time served or a small fine as punishment. And when we were finished, just after five o'clock, upon His Honor's suggestion, we celebrated a hard afternoon's work with fifteen minutes of poetry and popcorn.

Shaking my head and snickering softly at the stark contrast between Austin and the likes of Lacy and Steiggerman while I traipsed back to the office for our day-end conference, as I approached the front door I stopped for a moment to acknowledge the warm, late-spring breeze that stirred gently, then swirled more fitfully before fading away. In retrospect, a tiny harbinger of the tumultuous times that lay ahead, as the six of us settled into our seats to evaluate and plan, little did any of us realize that the long, hot summer waiting in the wings would slowly but steadily transform our days and nights into a virtual tornado of activity on three life-fronts.

For the fires ignited in Divisions Three and Four earlier that fateful Wednesday would soon swell into a full-fledged conflagration, as evaluate and plan we did indeed do, then added a full measure of energetic execution to the fomenting formula. And as June marched into July, and it in turn tailed dutifully into August, phase three of our war soon occupied center stage, with the newly re-nicknamed Solina Six waging an innovative and vengeful campaign. No longer were we undermanned, and thus no longer did physical limitations dictate what we could accomplish. No. No, indeed. For far more than simply reducing our individual caseloads, and thereby vitiating the oppressive exhaustion we had labored under, the addition of Blaine Kraslow sparked a fresh current of energy within the original band of brothers, his omnipresent smile and active sense of humor combining with his super-charged aggressiveness to uplift our worn-down morale to its prior posture of ramrod straight. And once rested, which our youth allowed to occur fairly quickly, we proceeded to unleash a veritable storm of malevolence against our adversaries.

If Lacy had entertained a nightmarish vision of Kraslow as the devil himself, Steiggerman soon declared the pain-induced speculation a reality, as Blaine labored assiduously to turn his judicial day into a living hell. Winning three of his first five trials, and producing hung juries in two other cases, he successfully backed up the calendar to where he, with the intermittent assistance of George, could extract highly favorable dispositions on the remainder despite the howling protests of the DAs. Likewise, in Division Three, Lacy now faced both myself and Robbie. And with both of us renewed and totally prepared, we attacked each and every Prelim, and with particular zeal those involving the four scripts, with a thoroughness that increased the frequency of his migraines tenfold, while forcing him to trail cases dangerously close to the mandated times for dismissal. Almost simultaneously with Lacy's eventual realization that the only way to service his calendar was to dismiss the weakest of the script cases, Leon, in the Arraignment Court, was able to take advantage of Steiggerman's perpetually backlogged calendar by offering to short-circuit the incessant flow of new cases if extremely favorable dispositions were granted, an offer that was soon begrudgingly accepted. Only Judge Austin escaped the full fury of our carefully coordinated assault, as out of respect for him as a fine human being, as well as the only fair-minded jurist in the courthouse, this time by design we excluded him from our unyielding demands and harsh attitude. And exceeding our expectations, this forbearance not only resulted in Ron achieving more than reasonable plea-bargains when the characteristically light sentences that accompanied them were considered, but as a bonus, caused His Honor to refrain from cooperating with his brethren when together with the DAs they attempted to blunt our efforts.

And try they did indeed. But even with the judges hand-picking dead-bang losers for trial in Steiggerman's court, and operating Division Three till seven o'clock in the evening by replacing the exhausted Lacy mid-afternoon with either Judge Burroughs, who had little to do in Division Five, or the Commissioner, who ordinarily heard only small claims matters, their hastily planned efforts to regain control failed to alter our course of action one iota. For inspired by our progress, day after day we relentlessly pursued the permanent reinstitution of those reforms we had fought so hard to achieve just several months ago, only to see them slowly eroded by our adversaries through attrition. In fact, so great was our fervor, that once the lever of power finally tilted into our hands, with its poisonous toxins then seeping steadily into our bloodstreams, unconsciously we moved beyond our original objectives and treated our enemies to an acid bath of revenge. As skillfully alternating our tactics daily, and on occasion hourly, we reopened old wounds and created new ones, then widened and deepened them, no resulting pain great enough to satisfy our hungering need to even the score—to compensate in some small way for all the injustices that plagued the world, and somehow alleviate the sorrowful anguish that leached from them and lay like a festering sore in the pits of our souls. Easing only at the end of a long and arduous day, when time permitted a brief but collegial celebration of our latest victories, like Jesus whose name we profaned daily, the ulcerating ache would resurrect itself and resume gnawing at us the following morning. In fact, mirroring the poverty and prejudice that seemingly cannot ever be totally obliterated, so, too, the raw, throbbing pain that tormented us could only be assuaged, but never completely vanquished. For as the novelist James Baldwin so wisely observed, "Rage can only with difficulty, and never entirely, be brought under the domination of intelligence." This truth, however, did not reveal itself in the dusty pages of the case and statute-filled books we pored over in search of new weapons to launch against our enemies, as together we pursued our endeavor with such sound and fury that years later we had great difficulty in believing that it had been created by only a six-cylinder generator.

In similar fashion, at home Stella and I applied Blake's Motto with a like force, the vigor propelling the heated conflict in Solina spilling over to inspire "kiss the joy as it flies" to seek a wider horizon. For having drawn closer than I ever imagined possible, day by day we broadened the scope of our life together so as to expand the increasingly precious hours that lay between now and the grim darkness that waited patiently at the end of our carefully constructed and colorfully lit carousel of activities. Intermittently increasing its speed when the slightest flicker silently warned us that only too soon it would shine no more, hungrily we explored every avenue open to us. Art, music, and literature were feverishly devoured in both workday and weekend visits to museums, concert halls, and theatres. And when our focus shifted to dining and dancing, we dressed up fashionably to explore a newly opened, upscale restaurant or rock and roll at a trendy club, then picnicked and sipped wine in our jeans on the beach beside Stella's beloved ocean. Playing tennis under warm, sunny skies, under bright stars in the chillier night air, we worshipped the baseball gods in Chavez Ravine's Cathedral. And laughing and crying, we viewed movies, took long walks, talked endlessly into the wee hours of the morning, and savored every sweet second of impassioned sex. Always special since that first, seductive encounter, after Stella's illness was disclosed our lovemaking had not only increased in frequency, but like a slowly blooming flower had steadily opened to the sunshine of greater intimacy and genuine tenderness, thereby transforming into an exquisite effort to communicate the depth of feeling felt, "I love you," escaping in whispers that echoed softly through the conversation that followed as we held each other tightly, as if to ward off the passing of time.

Refusing to be ignored despite our extremely busy lives transpiring in two dimensions, the outside world insistently added a third, crowding into consciousness from time to time to add its tributary of eclectic happenings to the already swollen river of activity. In mid-June, just as time began to spin forward faster like a merry-go-round picking up speed, on the eighteenth, Nixon, in the face of the ever increasing and noticeably more visible opposition to the Vietnam War, announced the withdrawal of 25,000 of our 540,000 troops in a dual effort to placate critics and increase the pressure on the North Vietnamese delegation at the Paris Peace Talks. "Well, at least it's a small step in the right direction," Stella cried, shaking her head sorrowfully. "That is, if it's not another one of Tricky Dick's charades."

"Hey ... listen," I soothed, smiling at how much she cared, "remember old Confucius and his 'longest journey begins with a single step.' So let's just hope for the best, sweetheart, let's hope Big Time."

For obvious reasons, toward the end of the month we quickly passed over the tragic death of tennis great Maureen "Little Mo" Connolly from cancer at only thirty-five years of age. But July then offered up a menu of historical food for thought that was chewed over both at home and in the office. On the seventh, Charles Evers, brother of the murdered civil rights leader Medgar, was sworn in as the first black mayor of Fayette, Mississippi. "Wow!" George enthused to Robbie and me over coffee. "I know it's a small town of only seventeen hundred, and blacks outnumber whites there by three to one—but still, it's fucking Mississippi we're talking about here, so it's still one hell of a ray of sunshine!"

"Hell, yeah!" I chimed in with equal glee, then watched the grin on Robbie's face widen.

"Yeahhh ... it's good news all right," he drawled. "Matt and I will have to make sure we share it with our dear friend Lacy. Who knows? He might just rethink his position as the only black member of the Ku Klux Klan," oozed his sarcasm, shared laughter quickly following.

A week later, however, our conversation was more subdued when the firebrand Stokely Carmichael resigned as Prime Minister of the Black Panthers and was promptly condemned by Eldridge Cleaver, one of the Party's founders, now released from prison and currently living in Algeria. "What do you make of that, Georgie?" I posed, not clear about what conclusion to draw from the rift.

"I'm not sure, exactly," he responded slowly. "Carmichael's always been the extreme hard-ass in the Civil Rights Movement, so I guess it's not too surprising that he's against the Panthers allying themselves with the radical whites of the far left. What do you think, Rob?"

"Well," Robbie replied, sucking on his pipe, "he hates white people so much, and with such ferociousness, that he even scares me."

"Uh-huh, me too," I interjected. "Those eyes of his, they could turn your blood to ice. Wonder what he'd say about the local Panthers helping us?"

"He'd be pissed—damned pissed, is what I think," Robbie snickered. "'Cause only one of us has the right skin color, and even I'm a turncoat in his eyes."

"Well you know what?" George jumped in, a wry smile faintly forming. "I think old Stokely needs to study up on Malcolm X. 'Cause he's a guy who originally believed that blacks and whites could never get along, so they needed to live as separately from one another as possible—in fact, he was the leading spokesperson for Elijah Muhammad and the Black Muslims. But later on, his considerable life experiences, and his major smarts, turned on the old light bulb and changed Malcolm into a huge voice for all of us coming together—for reason and understanding leading to brotherhood amongst all peoples."

"Yeahhh, true enough, all right," Robbie sighed. "And they killed him for it, too," he added sadly, shaking his head.

"Well, the world didn't forget him, though," George consoled. "Nor MLK either," he added with a smile. "You'll see, love and healing will win out over hate in the end. You'll see," he emphasized, his optimism echoing as we finished lunch and prepared to return across the street to resume fighting our part of the battle.

What we saw in the short-run though was just the continuation of the stiff resistance to our offensive, complete with as much enmity and spite as our adversaries could muster those long, stifling hot days of July. On the twentieth, however, a history-making event of such great magnitude occurred that people all around the globe momentarily stopped whatever they were doing, took a deep breath, and then exhaled a deep sigh of relief that transformed into utter awe as Neil Armstrong set foot on the moon. Perched on the edge of the living room couch in the early hours of Sunday evening, Stella and I watched mesmerized as Armstrong carefully lowered himself down the landing craft's ladder one rung at a time until finally one foot tapped, then rested on the moon's surface, and 239,000 miles from Earth he humbly proclaimed, "One small step for man, one giant step for mankind!"

"Wowww!" Stella gurgled through her warmest smile. "I see it, but it's still hard to believe."

"Yeahhh ... for sure," I responded, still listening also to Walter Cronkite's excitement-filled echo, "The *Eagle* has landed! The *Eagle* has landed!"

Buzz Aldrin, Armstrong's co-pilot, then joined him in the Sea of Tranquility, while overhead Michael Collins continued to pilot the mother ship, *Columbia,* as it faithfully orbited the ghostly globe, waiting patiently till it was time to return home. A few minutes later, Stella and I ventured over to the bedroom window to gaze wondrously up at the ivory ball in the sky, the peaceful name of the landing site orbiting inside my mind. "God, but what an accomplishment!" I murmured softly, emotion swelling up inside me, Stella instantly nodding her agreement. "Now if we could only apply that same dedication to learning how to get along with one another down here on Mother Earth, and end war, and poverty, and disease, that would be an even greater accomplishment—a real Sea of Tranquility," I ended, then blew a kiss heavenward to carry my prayer.

"Uh-huh," Stella smiled sweetly, "no question."

At the office, everyone was equally exhilarated of course, and the successful landing and still unfolding exploration dominated Monday morning's coffee klatch before we returned to the courthouse and another week of battle. July, however, already having hosted a worldwide celebration of man's insatiable curiosity and limitless ingenuity, still had one more happy surprise on its calendar, though this one was much narrower in scope, limited as it was to me, then shared with my colleagues. For harboring a private curiosity of her own, and employing her own stock of ingenuity, Stella hatched and executed a plan to surreptitiously visit me in Solina. Obtaining both George's approval and assistance, when July's last Friday afternoon arrived she took a cab, then snuck into Division Three and hid herself in the back row to watch me in action. Fortunately, with an unintended assist from Judge Lacy, who was always willing to share his storehouse of ire and therefore set the stage for a full-fledged confrontation, I didn't disappoint. With His Honor already in a foul mood from having tangled all morning with George, when I calmly but meticulously cross-examined in a dead-bang loser of a burglary case, then followed in the day's last Prelim with my characteristically bombastic attack of yet another marijuana throwing case, Lacy promptly proceeded to paint a portrait of hostile intervention that injected new vitality into the age-old adage that one picture is worth a thousand words. Not that he was in short supply of vocabulary, because he most certainly wasn't. "Mister Harris," he boomed out when his frustration level had peaked some twenty minutes into my cross-examination of a Brynhurst Police Officer, "don't you ever get tired of making a stupid, belligerent ass out of yourself?"

"Your Honor," I fired back, "that's a good point you make. The only problem with it is that your extreme anger has caused you to focus on the wrong target, 'cause it's Officer Wilson here that's trying to make asses out of all of us with his totally fairy-tale version of what actually occurred in this matter!"

"I'm not angry, counsel," he responded, having lowered his volume considerably, "just disturbed by your constant badgering of the witness with your vicious attacks on his integrity."

"Your Honor," marched my reply. "I'm just doing my job, that's all. And I'd also like to point out that the DA hasn't objected to my line of questioning, and Ms. Fisher has a well-established reputation for not only being highly combative, but also not at all shy about engaging opposing counsel. Now, may I please proceed? Or does the Court wish to entertain my Motion to Dismiss on the grounds that my client has been deprived of his right to cross-examine the witnesses against him as defined and supported by Jennings versus the—"

"Very well, Mr. Harris," he interjected, "you may continue. But I warn you, this Court will not tolerate the outright intimidation of a witness, so watch yourself, or you'll find yourself in contempt."

"Thank you, Your Honor, I understand," I nodded back, then returned my attention to the witness. "Now, Officer Wilson," I continued, "I feel compelled to ask whether you feel intimidated by little old me—are you?"

"No, counsel," he smiled defiantly, "not at all."

"I didn't think so," I shrugged, then returned for the third time to the allegedly suspicious behavior that initially caused him to become aware of my client.

I'm not sure whether it was the fact that Officer Wilson finally contradicted himself regarding the circumstances surrounding his stop of my client, or whether it was his firm rejection of His Honor's efforts to assist him by charging me with intimidation that finally registered persuasively with Lacy, but ten minutes later, in a highly irritated tone, he granted my Motion to Dismiss, then rushed off the bench with a speed that called to mind an Olympic sprinter. An unexpected bolt out of the blue, in that evidence and argument rarely dissuaded Lacy to veer from his preconceived opinions, when I turned around to leave, my surprise suddenly swelled into pure amazement as I discovered a beaming Stella standing just beyond the swinging wooden gate that allowed entry to and from the audience area. "Hi!" she bubbled after I reached her. "Congratulations, you were wonderful!"

"Not nearly as wonderful as the sight of you!" I enthused, kissing her lightly on the lips. "What a great surprise, you feisty little devil, you!"

"Yeah, pretty sneaky, huh?"

"Big Time, for sure."

"Well, I just had to see this war zone for myself," she explained. "So having met George, I called and asked him if he thought it would be okay. I would've asked you," she quickly tacked on in an assuring tone, "but I didn't want my presence to add any extra pressure to the situation. So instead, I just hopped into a cab and here I am."

"Boy, are you ever something," I smiled. "And I'm glad you finally got to see it."

"Absolutely. 'Cause it's a big part of my life too, and now it's more real than ever."

"You sure got that right," I agreed, noting that her eyes were smiling too. "But c'mon, we're done here, let's go get some coffee in the office, so I can show you that too."

Hand in hand, we strolled across the street, where Stella was then warmly welcomed by everyone. Having been tipped off by George, Marilyn had purchased an oversized box of donuts to help celebrate "our special guest," and over fresh coffee the eight of us happily chit-chatted away the remainder of the afternoon, our regular meeting having been cancelled by unanimous vote. Finally, around six, it was also unanimously agreed that it was "weekend time," as Marilyn succinctly opined. George then made the routine call to the Panthers, and five minutes later our caravan to the freeway closed out yet another long and tiring, but totally satisfying, workweek, it having ended for me with a memory that would grow more special each and every time I revisited it.

Special was also the perfect adjective to describe the month of August. The war was going well, even better than we expected. As with Blaine's seemingly inexhaustible supply of energy stifling Steiggerman, and Leon taking full advantage of the overload of cases to steal the courthouse in Gelman's court, Ron was able to further improve our relations with the isolated Judge Austin and almost match Leon's success, while Robbie and I continued to wear down Lacy into a state of semi-fairness, and George roamed the courthouse assisting whoever needed help most at a given point in time. Thus, having been carefully designed to provide maximum flexibility and allow us to operate as a smoothly oiled machine, then enhanced by the exceedingly high level of Kraslow's performance, our offensive was finally in high gear and working to perfection, much to the great displeasure of our adversaries. And sweetening the ongoing battle even further, in the middle of August's second week Stephen Shafer reported to me that he had learned from higher-ups in the DA's Office that Governor Reagan had declined to appoint Steiggerman to Superior Court, a result that both satisfied and surprised me. For after promptly sharing the glad tidings with my colleagues and receiving a round of hearty congratulations, I soon discovered that while I remained thoroughly pleased that Steiggerman wouldn't be poisoning the minds of jurors deciding serious felony trials, unexpectedly this success, even though now concrete, still remained tempered by its failure to banish the lingering ache of disappointment I harbored for Fred Ginther and his dear wife and children. "Hell, nothing's perfect, little buddy," I finally concluded, still reflecting on the development a couple of days later while strolling back to the office. "What you achieved is still special, and so is the overall picture—so just be grateful, and hope that the good fortune continues," trickled common sense's prescription, the warm smile that slowly spread across my face confirming that I would do both.

And as if somehow bolstered by my silent vow, *special* continued to rule the month, even spilling its stardust over onto the home front. For still savoring the pinnacle of closeness that resulted from Stella's surprise visit to Solina, when her forty-third birthday arrived two weeks later on August ninth, we decided to celebrate in grand fashion by flying to San Francisco for a weekend of merrymaking. Checking into the famed Fairmont Hotel atop Nob Hill on the Friday evening before the big day, we were instantly charmed by the crimson carpet, pink-marbled columns, and sparkling crystal chandeliers that Stella gleefully noted turned the lobby into a smaller version of Buckingham Palace. A vision that was further magnified when we explored the spacious, elegantly furnished surroundings of our twentieth-floor suite, its splendor was soon topped by the breathtaking panorama of Baghdad by the Bay, as glittering in the dark like ten thousand tiny candles, its moonstruck bridges and sparkling harbor seemingly part of a fairy-tale landscape, it not only caused our smiles to widen, but to silently carry our prayer, Please, God, let this moment last forever!

It couldn't, of course, so for the next forty-eight hours we happily settled into the richly rewarding routine of making more memories. Walking the streets and climbing the hills while holding hands, we explored every nook and cranny of the enchanting city, from Union Square, to North Beach, to Fisherman's Wharf. Lunching on lobster at the latter landmark, as well as devouring the out-of-this-world pasta at Paoli's the following evening, we window-shopped on Candy Cane Lane, then climbed the hill that dropped us into the famous, or infamous, Haight-Ashbury District, depending upon one's point of view. Having gained huge notoriety as a gathering spot for beat poets, then the Flower Children—young people who grew their hair long, dressed unconventionally, and preached the virtues of dropping out of the establishment, hallucinatory drugs, and free love—we found it far more tame than the media portrayed, though fully abuzz with activity, people streaming in all directions, shopping in the eclectic collection of stores, eating food purchased from street vendors, and sharing animated conversation in groups on street corners, or more privately in twos and threes inside crowded doorways, guitars and folk songs sounding in the background.

"It's different, all right," Stella offered up as we shared a smoke and tried to take it all in.

"Yeah, that's for sure," I nodded back. "But you know, sweetie, while I don't exactly feel as if I belong, there's music, and lots of laughter, and somehow I feel sorta comfortable."

"Right ... me too," she agreed after a short pause to make sure. "Wanna take a look inside City Lights Bookstore?"

"Uh-huh, absolutely—we can't miss an icon like that."

Owned by Lawrence Ferlinghetti, who also operated a small press by the same name, City Lights was renowned for having spawned the Beat Generation, a nickname applied to a group of poets and writers, the most famous of which were Jack Kerouac, William Burroughs, and Allen Ginsberg, the latter having created a huge stir within the literary world during the Fifties with his poem, "Howl," while Kerouac and Burroughs birthed the classic prose works *On The Road* and *Naked Lunch*. So, after stepping inside, for several moments I tried to feel the presence of these instruments of change, whose provocative attitudes regarding spiritual growth, political freedom, and sexual liberation had found a firm foothold in the generation that followed, altering world views and helping inspire the continuous clash between new and old that churned so hot and heavy on the revolutionary battlefields of the Sixties. I couldn't feel them. "But I sure can feel the change," I chuckled to Stella as we browsed.

"You certainly should, Mr. Public Defender," she smiled back at me, "'cause you're part and parcel of it."

"Yeahhh ... maybe?" I chuckled, her words spinning around inside my head. "And maybe that's why I sorta feel comfortable here, who knows?" trickled off my tongue as I snuggled up against her and dropped my eyes onto a poem in a thin Ginsberg volume she had opened.

On Sunday, we rented a car and crossed over the Bay Bridge to tour Berkeley, then at Stella's insistence pay a visit to the Boalt Hall School of Law, my alma mater. It hadn't changed much in the three years since I left, but *I* sure had, I mused as we shuffled down the wide halls inside the impressive stone-columned edifice that had been my home for three arduous years. Yeah, you're not near as shy as you used to be, huh? I acknowledged. "And not quite so confused either," I gibed, then recalled how when I had departed the building after my final exam, I had whispered my hope that someday the school would be proud to have their prestigious name attached to me. Well, I'm working hard on it, I advised silently but firmly as we departed this time, my optimism having grown slightly. You won't be sorry, you'll see.

In the afternoon, we traveled over the Golden Gate Bridge to lunch in the artistic community of Sausalito, then visited several galleries before finally the time arrived to motor back to the airport. "God, but that was wonderful, Matty!" Stella enthused, her smile pouring from a full heart as our plane lifted off into the dusk. "The best birthday ever—absolutely, positively magical!" she added, her eyes sparkling with happy tears.

Magical, indeed, I had agreed, then reconfirmed when I revisited our celebration on the drive to Solina the following morning. And one week later, and three thousand miles away on America's opposite coast, magic made another appearance. Not quite as personal, with some 500,000 happy souls gathering on a 600-acre farm near the hamlet of Bethel, New York, but nonetheless, magic flooded the air when on Friday evening next the Woodstock Music Festival sprung to life through the vibrant vocal cords of Richie Havens, Sweetwater, Arlo Guthrie, and Joan Baez.

Having billed their promotion as "An Aquarian Exposition: 3 Days of Peace & Music," the organizers had hoped to lure 50,000 people to attend. Instead, half a million mostly young persons sporting bohemian dress, behavior, and attitudes crowded into the site, camped for three days, and miraculously shared a strong sense of social harmony amidst a continuous menu of music staged by a who's who of performing artists. Following Friday night's appetizer, on Saturday, Santana, The Grateful Dead, Creedence Clearwater Revival, Janis Joplin, Sly & the Family Stone, The Who, and Jefferson Airplane served up an entrée of over nine non-stop hours of their most famous songs to the vast audience that cheered their warm approval and asked for more. And having asked, on Sunday they received dessert from the likes of Joe Cocker and The Grease Band; Blood, Sweat & Tears; Crosby, Stills, Nash & Young; the Paul Butterfield Blues Band, and Sha Na Na, the river of music swelling so great that it overflowed to Monday morning when the one and only Jimi Hendrix, wearing a blue-beaded white leather jacket with fringe and a red scarf, offered up his psychedelic rendition of "The Star Spangled Banner," then morphed into "Purple Haze" to close out the unprecedented assemblage.

Watching clips of the musical marathon on TV, Stella and I could hardly believe it. "All those people braving thirty-minute lines for water or to use a toilet," she marveled, smiling and shaking her head. "And all in the name of peace and love—Wow!"

"No kidding, sweetie, wow says it all," I agreed, my eyes still unable to fully fathom the size of the crowd. "But you can also bet that the establishment will only stress the drugs, and the sex and nudity—and hey, that's not my style either. But I sure do agree with that Yasgur fella, the one who donated his farm," formed my defense, "'cause it really does say a lot when a half-million people get together to celebrate music and peace—just like when MLK spoke peacefully to a like-sized crowd about having a dream that his children would be judged not by the color of their skin but by the content of their character."

"We'll get there, we're making progress," Stella murmured, her tone hopeful. "'Cause more and more people are working for change, just like you, Mr. PD."

"Well," I shrugged, returning her smile. "I'm trying to do my little part, all right. And if more and more people do their little parts, you're right, we can get there—Hey, God willing, we will," I tacked on, the replay of Hendrix's creative interpretation of "The Star Spangled Banner" wailing into ear to further widen my smile.

XXVIII

IN SEPTEMBER, THE SANTA ANA WINDS PAY their annual visit to Los Angeles, often times creating a heat wave. Nineteen sixty-nine proved no different, except that the rise in temperature outside also occurred equally within the conflict-riddled confines of Divisions One, Three, and Four as our adversaries attempted to blunt our offensive by rotating judges and stationing multiple DAs in each courtroom. Calculated to match our energetic attack by providing extra manpower that would allow them to be better prepared to meet each challenge we presented, the tactic did little to alter results, but certainly served well to further escalate the volume of heated confrontations, as well as increase their intensity as the tension steadily accumulated.

Neither my colleagues nor I was surprised, as we had expected heavy resistance to mount. Even August, filled as it was with our successful initiative, and the magical celebrations of Stella's birthday and Woodstock's sweet song, had still signaled troubled times ahead. On the ninth, actress Sharon Tate, who was eight months' pregnant, along with four others had been murdered inside a Beverly Hills mansion, a horrifically bloody crime that would eventually introduce Charles Manson and his bizarre band of followers to the world. Then, eleven days later, Bobby Seale, the National Chairman of the Black Panther Party, was arrested by federal agents for the murder of former Panther Alex Rackley. True, the Tate crime, while certainly catching our attention in that it occurred less than five miles from the apartment, had no direct effect on Stella and me—or the war's continued progress. And while it was also true that Seale's arrest caused no disturbance to the escort service being provided by the local chapter, still, the Dastardly Duo infiltrated our collective subconscious and subliminally warned that we lived in precarious times. Even the music on the radio seemed to confirm the warning, with Creedence Clearwater Revival wailing about a "Bad Moon Rising," the chilly message speaking of the need to keep one's guard up.

All of us did, most notably Stella. For as September began to evidence signs of her physical decline, she camouflaged it as best she could, carefully applying makeup to mask the increasing paleness of her face, and wearing loose-fitting clothing to hide her weight loss. She couldn't fool me of course, but I didn't articulate my growing concern, instead pretending that all was normal and milking each precious moment of every drop of happiness it offered. Likewise, when she occasionally turned our conversations serious and pressed my alarm button, I exercised all of the discipline at my disposal so as to not overreact, once again pretending that the ultimate darkness at the end of the road was still far away. "Tell me about Lanie, Matt," she purred with a purpose after we had made love late one evening toward the middle of the month. "You've mentioned her several times, but never gave any details."

"Yeah, I have. And what do you care about an old girlfriend who's long gone?"

"Well, you've always seemed sensitive about the subject, and with us being so mellow and all, I thought that maybe now we could talk about it, that's all."

"All right ... what do you want to know?" I trickled out slowly, guessing that she was broaching the subject of my need to go on after she passed away, but hoping that maybe she was just curious.

"Well, you said she was very pretty, and very kind, and was crazy about you—so what happened to break you up?"

"Well, the nutshell version goes like this, sweetie. We went together the four years I was at USC, and we really did care for each other, and wanted to make a life together. However, when law school loomed, even though she wanted to go with me to Berkeley and work, my parents wouldn't hear of it," I explained, reaching for my pipe. "Lanie didn't come from money, and so didn't have the proper pedigree for the socially rising Fred and Rosalie. They claimed that Lanie was just a gold-digger, that I didn't know love from a hole in the ground, and that furthermore, if she went along to Berkeley, they would withdraw their support. I didn't know what to do, and neither did Lanie, so we decided to hold off our plans for a year, hoping that they'd come around," I rolled out, shaking my head, then lighting up. "But with me away, Lanie's insecurity gnawed at her Big Time, she worried and worried that I'd change my mind and she'd end up in nowhere-land. So, as the months gradually passed, she finally told me that waiting wasn't going to work, either we get married or we break up—which is what we ended up doing."

"I see," Stella nodded. "Well, is she still available?"

"No, and neither am I, in case you forgot," I returned, now fully aware that Stella was indeed focused on my future love-life, her totally unselfish thoughtfulness forcing tiny tears to creep into the corners of my eyes and cause me to briefly pause. "Listen, you little matchmaker you," I picked up several seconds later through a forced smile. "I know you mean well, but I'm in love with you, and only you, and that's all I want to think about. I'll deal with the future, if and only if I have to—okay, sweetheart?"

"Uh-huh … but time's growing shorter, and I need to make sure you understand," she answered, her eyes pleading, "so only if you promise me that you won't quit on life. 'Cause you need love, Matty, and you're wonderfully good at giving it, so you have to promise me that you'll try with all your big heart to find someone special, and get married, and have a family. Will you promise me that?" she asked, tears also finding her voice.

"Yeah … I promise," trickled my reply. "But only if you promise me that this subject is closed," I tacked on, putting down my pipe and slipping back down close to her.

"Okay, I promise too. But I gottta ask what happened to Lanie, do you actually know?"

"Uh-huh, I do," I answered, kissing her cheek after she nestled her head onto my chest. "A short while after we broke up, she met a guy from one of the wealthiest Jewish families in Mexico City, who was visiting relatives in L.A. He flipped for her, and they got married and had two sons, according to her brother who I used to bump into occasionally. So that's the long and short of it, and I only hope she's half as happy as I am."

Stella chuckled softly in response, and lived up to her promise that the subject was closed. But a week or so later, I learned that the subject of her leaving was still preying on her mind. "Matty, do you believe in God?" she queried softly, looking up from the newspaper she was reading on the living-room couch after dinner.

"Yeah, I do," I answered, "but not in organized religion, 'cause that bullshit has caused more wars and pain and suffering than all the other causes added together."

"Right, I agree," she nodded. "I was raised a Christian, as you know, but I never really believed all the fairy tales—I just sorta hoped that there was a loving something watching over us, that's all. And now, I don't know what to believe."

"No problem," I quickly sought to assure, watching the concern in her eyes swell. "You remember how we heard last week on TV that the famous clergyman Bishop Pike had died?"

"Uh-huh."

"Well, he was a real piece of work. He started out Catholic, then turned agnostic, and ended up as an Episcopalian Bishop—quite a spiritual journey indeed. And, after much searching, what he said was that the fairy tales don't matter, all religions have got'em, from Moses walking up Mount Sinai to meet God face to face and receive the Ten Commandments, to virgin birth and the Holy Trinity. All that does matter, he explained, was that we have the Commandments, and Jesus' Sermon on the Mount, and that we try and lead our lives accordingly. Listen, hon, Jesus was all about love, and you're absolutely full of it, so it's all good," I smiled, reaching over to take her hand and pat it.

"Is that what you believe, Matty, that God is love?" she pursued, struggling to feel what I had hypothesized.

"Uh-huh, for sure," I nodded. "That, and what wise old Ralph Waldo Emerson taught. He said that his religion was goodness, and that his creed was kindness, which to me is part and parcel of love."

"I see what you're saying, I like that," Stella smiled back, growing more relaxed.

"Yeah, me too, sweetie. And while I can't explain how a loving God lets all the shit in the world happen, I do believe that we have free will to choose between good and evil, and if people would just be about love, most of the crap wouldn't happen."

"Uh-huh ... okay ... that helps," she responded, smiling again. "When did you figure that all out?"

"Well, Grampy Max helped straighten me out early on about the organized-religion bullshit, and my high-school English teacher, Eunice Schmidt, turned me onto Emerson—and in between I spent a hell of a lot of time up in my avocado tree thinking things over."

"Yeah, you did, I'll bet you miss that tree of yours."

"You know ... crazy as it sounds, I really do," spilled my words slowly, the thought flashing that so much change had occurred the past ten years that childhood and early adolescence seemed to have transpired in a different lifetime.

"No, it doesn't seem crazy at all," she smiled. "I wish I had such a tree right now, 'cause maybe, just maybe, I could figure out why cancer comes to some, and not others—and why so early," she tacked on, tears seeping into her eyes as the smile paled.

"Ohhh ... you've got me there, hon, I'm ... I'm so very sorry, but I can't answer that one," I strained to squeeze out, having wanted with my whole heart to soothe her anxiety, my limited ability to do so mixing with my own fear and doubt to swell a large lump in my throat.

"Nooo, don't you dare be sorry, you helped a lot," Stella responded when I tried to speak further but couldn't, stretching forward to kiss me lightly on the lips. "No one knows the answer to that, but that doesn't mean your loving God doesn't exist—okay?"

Okay, it was, because okay was all that our best efforts could provide. Which, apparently, was also all that could be said for the outside world that seemed to be spinning its own web of contradictions as the autumn of 1969 unfolded, solid ground dissolving into quicksand, and belief mixing with doubt to weave logic and confusion into a mesh so fine that its components were almost indistinguishable.

On September first, the King of Libya was ousted and a colonel named Khadafy assumed power, the U.S. formally recognizing the new regime five days later. Yet another political occurrence inside a country far away and ordinarily out of mind, what did the development mean? Was it good or bad? And for whom? Equally hard to evaluate clearly were the happenings on the more familiar but still foreign stage in Vietnam. On the fourth, Ho Chi Minh, the leader who had overseen the defeat of France in 1954 in what was then called French Indochina, died. He was the enemy, our government said, because he was the communist leader of North Vietnam, and sought to take the South by force. But why was this man whose political hero was Woodrow Wilson an enemy? Just because he thought a socialistic economy might work better for an agrarian society, one without the natural resources and historical traditions necessary to build a capitalist-based democracy? And why did so many million people, North and South, follow him? Questions. Everywhere questions. But no sure answers. Nixon's response to Ho's death was to order the resumption of bombing in the North on the twelfth, only to announce four days later the additional withdrawal of 35,000 American troops. Why? What was the match of these two contradictory events supposed to signal? And why also did Nixon, who had blessed the creation of a memorial in Washington D.C. to honor Martin Luther King, then treat its development so nonchalantly that Martin's family halted talks with him, citing his indifference to blacks? Yes, more questions. Always more questions. What was a person supposed to think? To feel? To do? And always answers that were vague and uncertain. The only antidote it seemed was to seek something to smile at, to search assiduously for something to nod approval at somewhere on September's cloudy world stage. It wasn't easy, but peeking out of the back pages of the newspaper there was the felicitous fact that Harvard had opened a program in black studies, another small but still significant step in the right direction. And if one turned to the Sports Section, one learned that at age thirty-one, Rod Laver had for a second time secured tennis's Holy Grail, the calendar-year Grand Slam, by winning the U.S. National Championship at Forest Hills to add to his collection of the Australian, French, and Wimbledon titles. "Wow!" I enthused to Stella. "Just imagine how many more titles, and even Grand Slams, he would've won if he hadn't been banned from the Slams for eight years for turning pro after 1961?"

"Yeah, he sure got the Open Era off to a special start, didn't he?" she chuckled in return, pleased to share an "upper" with me.

And though such *uppers* were hard to find and celebrate that sadly serious September, as October arrived and slowly stretched out its fitful calendar in front of us, we had to search even harder to locate them and enjoy an appreciative laugh. Fortunately, in Solina the first week produced only good news, starting with Sheriff Moorehouse's report to George that the Panthers' escort would no longer be needed, "'cause even Officer Hardy isn't a threat anymore, due to some serious fear and worry dropped on his head by his superior advising that the FBI was keeping a file just on little old him!" Greeted by a chorus of cackles, intermixed with Robbie's observation that "Old Hux's buddy must have really laid on the pressure Big Time to have so effectively solved our outdoors problem," this rewarding revelation was equally matched by positive news inside the courtroom, as our well-coordinated attack staunchly withstood our adversaries' countermeasures and continued to produce a high percentage of successful results for our clients. However, as favorably as our smoothly oiled offensive was humming along, still, the cumulative mental strain from the constant struggle began to take a toll, and, complemented as it was for me by Stella's steady decline, created a burden whose weight increased with each passing day.

I'm not sure of the proper accolade to describe Stella's performance as October's shadows deepened, but heroic seems to sum it up best. Never complaining, and always eager to listen to my latest tale of battle and offer encouragement when frustration and exhaustion raised their heavy heads, she struggled valiantly, but with steadily diminishing strength, to stave off the inevitable entrance into the hospital. Returning home, after long, friction-packed days, I would call on adrenaline-fueled reserves of energy to comfort her as best I could, watching closely through increasingly sad eyes that I did my best to hide as Stella began to slip away from me. Losing weight daily, she noticeably turned from slender to thin, and when her medication likewise grew less effective, the constant pain etched cruel lines underneath the hollowing eye-wells of her still beautiful face. As a further consequence, rest also became problematic, and clinging together through the long, sleep-interrupted nights, we desperately tried to mount our own private offensive by choking back tears and laughing and talking endlessly about whatever happened into mind. "You lost our baseball bet, you know," Stella chuckled out in the wee hours of a mid-month new day, an extra pill having momentarily provided some relief.

"I did? ... How?" I played along, holding her close. "I mean, your Cardinals didn't win anything, the Miracle Mets won the whole shebang."

"Yeah, that's true," she admitted. "But my Cards still finished two games better than your Dodgers in the win-loss column, so I win and you owe me five bucks."

"Yeah, you got a point there, counselor, guess I'll have to pony up—you take BankAmericard?"

"Nooo ... Sorry, Buster Brown, cash on the old barrelhead."

"Ohhh-kay, tough guy. What are you going to spend your winnings on? After all, five bucks is a heavy-duty sum to work with."

"Oh, that's easy," waltzed her reply. "Ice cream, lots of ice cream. And we both need it, too, 'cause I don't know which one of us is winning the who's the skinniest contest."

"Sounds like a great investment to me," I chuckled. "Which flavors?"

A subject whose subsequent discussion sweetly soothed us back to sleep, on other evenings the focus turned to music, the two of us chattering about how much we enjoyed the Beatles' tunes, "Come Together" and "Here Comes the Sun," then laughing gratefully at the fact that we were still lying side by side, our chuckles in turn growing ironic when the great golden ball's first streaks peeked through the window. Wine and cheese was a favorite topic, too, always inspiring a search for the perfect combination to kick off tomorrow night's dinner, as was recounting which guests on *The Tonight Show* we found particularly interesting or funny, or some new ad we found obnoxious. It didn't really matter, whatever helped pass the time served as our friend till the extra pain pill kicked in and some semblance of peace combined with the security of hugs and kisses to ease us back asleep for a few precious hours or even minutes.

Time, however, did not favor our private offensive as it had that of the Solina Six. For having metastasized long ago, the cancer now gnawed away at Stella on several fronts, further eroding her already waning strength. Arriving home on October's fourth Friday, I found her lying on the bathroom floor next to a pool of vomit, and struggling vainly through agonizing pain to rise to her knees so that she could crawl back to the bed. Dropping to my knees as she collapsed and fell forward again after God only knows how many tries, I slipped her into my arms and gently held her. Twisting her head backward off my chest, she tried to smile, her eyes tearing as sobs muffled her message. "Ohhh, M-a-t-t-y," she stuttered out ever so slowly, "hhhelp me, p-p-please ... I'm trying ... but I hhhurt s-o-o mmmuch!"

"I know sweetheart, I know," I assured. "And I'm going to help you, don't you worry, I'm going to help you Big Time," rushed the rest of my response calmly even though I didn't have a clue as to what my next move was or should be, thoughts of how best to help her to the bed flashing in and out of mind.

"I'm going, Matty," she continued, her voice somewhat more steady. "I ... I'm still trying like we pplanned ... but I jjust can't ... ." she tailed off, unable to finish her thought when tears crowded into her throat.

Blinking back my own, I leaned back against the bathtub for support, pulling her gently with me and guiding her head down onto my chest with my free hand. "Don't try to talk, angel, please don't try to talk. Just rest," I urged, struggling to keep my voice from cracking, "just rest, and you'll feel better, I promise."

Too weak to reject my plea had she wanted to, she agreed by nestling further onto my chest. Then, lying still, for a full minute she cried ever so softly, tears continuing to trickle down her cheeks, until finally, her exhaustion further increased by this meager effort, she fell asleep. Closing my eyes also, after several slow, deep breaths, I kept them fastened shut and tried to think what to do. As thoughts of the hospital and what entry there meant slipped into mind, a heavy ache swelled up inside my chest and forced them back open. Glancing down at her face, now momentarily relaxed but still shadowed by strain even in slumber, I grimaced as the ache balled so tight that tears finally squeezed out of the corners of my eyes and spilled down my face. Oh, God, please help me help her, escaped my prayer as I struggled to squelch the urge to cry, instinct commanding me to hold on, to remain in control. Somehow, I did, by forcing a smile and ever so lightly kissing the top of her head, then relaxing a degree or two and simply watching over her.

    She didn't sleep long, maybe ten minutes, before she stirred awake. "Hi," she whispered through a weak smile that she forced stronger. "Nice way to welcome your love home, huh?" she gibed, reaching up and patting my cheek.

    "I'll take it," I smiled back, "as long as you're here with me, I'll take it. But I know a better place to nap, lots more comfy and all—do you think you can stand up?"

    "Yeah, I think so," she murmured, "especially if you give me a kiss."

    "You got it," I quipped, reaching down to brush her lips lightly. Then, in one flowing motion, I twisted sideways and out from underneath her, and partially lifted, partially pulled her up after me as I quickly climbed to my feet. Instantly slipping my left arm underneath hers and across her back, I used my right one to cradle her legs, and after a split second to make sure of my balance, I carried her to the bed and carefully lowered her onto its surface and propped her up on two pillows.

    "Wow, pretty cool move, Mr. Strong-Man," she chuckled softly. "Thanks."

    "You're welcome, sweetie," I chirped, cheered by the return of some color to her face. Then, noticing that she looked cold, I grabbed an extra blanket from nearby and tucked it around her. "You hold on here, I'm going to get us a washcloth," I informed, then scurried toward the bathroom.

    Pulling off my tie as I returned, I dropped down beside her and gently rinsed from her smiling face a few dried remnants from her lunch. After finishing, I applied the opposite side to my own forehead and still flushed cheeks, lingering for several refreshing moments beneath its cool umbrella to drink in the comforting vapors.

"Matty?" Stella inquired when I had finished. "I'm feeling lots better, and if you would get me a couple of my pills, I think we could make the pain go away completely for a while."

"Sounds like the best idea I've heard in quite some time," I rapped back at her, already in motion toward the bathroom. "Hey, you still look a little cold to me," I added after she had swallowed the capsules. "How does a nice cup of tea sound?"

"That would be wonderful—just like you," she grinned.

"Okay, now don't go anywhere, 'cause I'll be right back."

Entering the kitchen, after a brief search I located the tea kettle, filled it, and placed it on the stove. Then, after carefully setting out mint tea bags alongside two cups and saucers, I hurried back to the bedroom and started to resume my seat next to her. "Don't sit—lie down next to me," Stella smiled.

"Okay ... Boy, if I get that just for tea, what do I get if I throw in a cookie?" I teased, cheered further by the appearance of a slight twinkle in her eyes as I slipped down beside her.

"Anything you want," she murmured as she shifted her head onto my chest and nestled about until she found the most comfortable spot.

"Well, I don't think you're quite up to that at the moment—maybe after tea—it'll be ready in a couple of minutes."

"No hurry, I need to tell you something."

"Okay, what? You can't decide between honey or sugar in your tea, and need my advice?" I gibed, sensing what was coming and futilely attempting to mask my apprehension.

"Nooo," she answered softly, hesitating for a second or two before adding, "I ... I'm going to go into the hospital."

Even though I had intuited correctly, nevertheless, the dreaded message still struck home like a spike to the heart. Instantly, a sharp pain knifed through my chest, forcing tiny tears to surface as No! formed on the tip of my tongue and waited for me to shout it out. But the flashing recollection of her helplessness and mine in the bathroom, together with the knowledge that the terrible pain which wracked her body could be nullified by expert care, halted the charge, and only a fearful-toned "When?" emerged.

"Tomorrow, sweetie ... okay?"

It was, of course, it had to be, there was no other realistic choice. But that awareness inside both my brain and heart didn't stop my fear from choking tears into my throat and releasing those in my eyes to spill down my cheeks. They were quiet tears, unaccompanied by any sound from me, but when I failed to respond, Stella understood and raised her head to look at me. Smiling sweetly, she slowly lifted her hand to my face and gently brushed the tears away with her long slender fingers. "Sorry, Stelle," I whispered, finally finding my voice.

"For what, silly?"

"For acting like such a child, 'cause the last thing in the world I want to be is a burden. I mean—"

"You're not a burden, dear one," she interjected, "you're the only thing that's saved me."

"But I—"

"But, nothing—you're the one true love of my life, and you've been wonderful, everything I could've expected and more. It's just time, sweetheart, that's all," she soothed. "I know it's hard for you—me, too. But we've gotta go, we can't fight from here anymore—okay?"

"All right, hon … all right," I returned slowly, her words still turning over inside my head. "We'll fight in the hospital."

"Right … that's fine," she murmured, relieved that I had accepted her decision without greater resistance.

Once again, silence reigned, the soundless seconds sliding by while reality slowly burrowed a hole in my consciousness, settled in, and took up permanent residence. Stella, knowing that I needed a little time to let the woeful choice fully settle inside me, nestled back down onto my chest and waited patiently until resolution was finally reached. "Stelle?" I floated out a minute or so later.

"Uh-huh, love."

"I just want you to know that I'm not giving up, 'cause I still believe we'll get a miracle."

"Okay, me too. And before we move on to more pleasant topics, there's also something else I want you to know, which is that you're not a child and never really were—except Gideon's," she tacked on, her tone growing slightly firmer as she raised her head again and looked into my eyes.

"Gideon's?" I reflexed back, suddenly confused.

"Uh-huh," she affirmed. "Isn't that the name of the big case that says everybody charged with a crime has to have a lawyer?"

"Yeah, that's right. But what's that have to do with the price of pickles?"

"Well," she nodded, breaking into a smile. "When that happened, that's when you were truly born. You could've climbed out of that old avocado tree of yours the moment the Supreme Court acted, 'cause you didn't need it after that, you weren't lost anymore, and neither was the rest of your gang."

"Really? ... I never thought about it that way," I returned slowly, surprise now piggybacked on top of the sorrowful judgment I had known was coming but still wanted to deny even after its arrival.

"Well, then, think about it now," Stella encouraged. "'Cause from that moment on, Mr. Gideon gave birth to a whole family of children. They're spread out all over the country, and they come in all different sizes, shapes, and colors, but they're all the same, too—just think about it."

I did, all the way into the kitchen and back. For as Stella rolled to a stop, the tea kettle pierced the air, its shrill whistle not only signaling that it had completed its task, but seemingly saluting Stella's novel proposition as well. Having decided that there was more than a little truth to her discovery by the time I had returned with the tea, I smiled as its validity seemed to increase with each swallow of the sugar-sweetened brew. "You're unbelievable, sweetie, you know that?" I enthused, the idea of Gideon's children continuing to grow on me. "Purely and simply u-n-b-e-lievable!"

"Why? ... Because I really know you?" she quipped, matching my grin.

"Nooo ... that's not the reason, though you're the only one that does."

"You're wrong there, Matty—you do, too."

"Yeah? ... well, maybe?"

"No maybes about it. You know yourself very very well, and don't you forget it either," she responded, concern suddenly returning to coat her tone.

"All right, no problem," I quickly assuaged, "I was just kidding."

"Well, I'm not, I want you to remember just how special you really are—it's very important to me."

"Okay, I will," I nodded, my smile thinning from the urgency that had emerged to project a picture of me having to remember alone.

"Promise me," she pursued.

"I promise, absolutely," sprinted my confirmation, my eyes meeting hers, then watching for her approval.

Finally satisfied, "That's good," slipped out over the edge of her cup as she picked it up, then sipped at her tea. Suddenly spent, I was only too pleased to honor Stella's next suggestion that we snuggle up and read the Sports Section together, then take a nap before dinner.

"You know something, sweetie?" I enthused wearily after a yawn. "That's an absolutely genius idea!"

It wasn't much of an exaggeration. For when Saturday morning arrived, rest, and a bite of dinner, mixed with the healing power of laughter and followed by a miraculous night of uninterrupted sleep, had further improved Stella's color, along with the vitality in her eyes. In fact, for one hopeful moment, I wondered if yesterday afternoon had been just a bad dream. However, by the time we had finished breakfast, the pain had begun to reassert itself, and after Stella placed a call to Dr. Reiser, she packed a small suitcase, and just after eleven o'clock we began driving west along Sunset Boulevard toward UCLA Medical Center.

Of necessity, another chapter of our life together had closed. And while I felt cold and clammy inside, I tried not to dwell on that sad fact, instead flashing on my old friend, Dr. Vic, and forcing a smile onto my face as hand in hand we climbed the stairs to the admitting office.

Once inside, I helped Stella fill out the necessary forms, then rode with her in the elevator to the fourth floor where we slowly strolled down the corridor to Room 405. Some tests were required, so I settled into a chair near the window to await her return. Outside, the scene was postcard perfect—a truly magnificent fall day, with the air clear and crisp, a deep blue sky harboring billowy clouds, and bright sunshine filtering down onto the green lawn and casting early shadows around the fountain below and the trees across the way. God, you sure can paint a pretty picture! I thought, following it by wondering why on such a totally alive day, we had come to this sterile monastery to begin dealing with death? The thorny question caused my eyes to mist, and I momentarily lowered them to search for the comfort of my pipe. Lighting it, I leaned far back in the chair and banished the quarrelsome query by comparing the clouds of smoke I was making with those floating in the brilliant sky, the self-induced therapy soon working to usher in a tidbit of hope. The room numbers added up to nine, it suddenly occurred to me, a faint smile forming in the corners of my mouth, and nine's your lucky number, old buddy. So don't give up—ever, flashed my next brainwave, 'cause a miracle can still happen, and you and Stelle definitely deserve one, you hear me? I did, my smile gradually widening as my imagination magnetically pulled the furthest cloud in the sky closer and shaped it into the number nine.

An hour later, Stella returned, and after exchanging the white smock for her own nightgown, we sat together by the window holding hands and talked the afternoon into dusk. At dinnertime, we shared the provided tray, which was more than enough for our absent appetites. Then, with Stella now freed from pain by the slow-drip, morphine IV, we watched an old John Wayne war movie with a happy ending, and chatted some more until eleven o'clock when Stella drifted into a sound sleep. For the next hour I read *SI*, every so often looking over and listening to her relaxed breathing. Then, pleased at how peaceful she looked, I folded down a page to mark my place, nestled down inside the oversized chair, and eased into slumberland after wafting a silent prayer.

Sunday passed in similar fashion. After breakfast, when Stella departed for additional tests, I rushed home for a quick shower and a change of clothes. The afternoon drifted pleasantly by with us watching a football game, and just as the post-game show was ending, Dr. Reiser visited. Tall and slim, he appeared both confident and caring, and his "we'll do everything we can for her," issued to me in the hallway through a warm smile, made me feel that Stella was in the best of hands.

Dinner showed up a few minutes later, and afterward, we once again settled into TV-land, this time deciding on a musical spectacular starring Fred Astaire and Ginger Rogers. Cheerful talk followed, with the two of us holding hands until eleven o'clock once again approached, and this time I had to leave. For the umpteenth time, Stella denied my plea to take a leave of absence from Solina so that I could spend all day with her. "No, we've already decided that, remember? And I'm too tired to argue it again," she succinctly squelched my request, then quickly followed it with a warm kiss. She wasn't too tired to still mother me, however, calling out my name sweetly as I reached the doorway.

"Yeah, hon?" I floated in return.

"Now don't forget to eat lunch," she hummed at me. "And if you get hungry before you go to sleep, there's some cold chicken in the fridge—okay?"

"Sure thing, sweetie, I'll remember," I nodded. "And I'll call you in the morning, and come here as soon as court's over."

"You just better," she smiled, then nestled further into her pillow.

Tears welled in my eyes when I reached the hallway, and I paused there for several seconds before I finally forced myself to slowly walk away. The drive home was slow, too, and once I arrived, the silence inside the apartment was so painful that I immediately turned around and went for a walk. Returning about an hour later, I forced myself into bed, and eventually fell into a fitful sleep by lying on Stella's side of the bed in an effort to feel her close to me. Like myself, the long, life-altering weekend had finally slipped away also, leaving behind a trail of questions, and the thin hope of a better tomorrow.

Thereafter, October's final days quickly settled into a rigorous routine, spelled with a capital R. Arising early, I would drive to the office thinking about what I would say to Stella first after I arrived and hurried inside to call her. Then, summoning all the discipline I could muster, I would force her out of mind and push and pull myself through the long, bellicose days, amazed when I stood back from myself for a moment that somehow I could still function well inside the acrid atmosphere that pervaded the battlefield. Also telephoning Stella at lunchtime, and again during the afternoon if time permitted, thereafter I fled the office at the earliest opportunity in order to join her for dinner, TV-time, and talk. The nurses, in particular Julia, the floor chief, were wonderful to me, and overlooking rules and regulations allowed me to stay until after midnight. Then, returning to the empty apartment five hours before I had to arise again, I would pray for the miracle I still believed was possible, before falling teary-eyed into sleep that grew increasingly troubled, interrupted as it was more and more frequently by nightmarish visions from which I would awaken riddled by anxiety and soaked in perspiration.

As the end of the month approached, the war appeared to take on a life of its own, one which was seemingly interminable. For even though we had fully achieved the reinstitution of our January Reforms by mid-October, still the battle raged as the six of us labored doggedly to set them in cement, our success to date simply serving to increase our appetite for more, the resistance of our adversaries only evidencing the need for us to widen the wounds to their authority already forged and further cripple their power.

On the twenty-ninth, our cause received a further shot of adrenaline when Smitty, our former colleague, now stationed in the appellate department, notified us that Fred Ginther's conviction for being intoxicated in public had been reversed on appeal as part and parcel of the State Supreme Court's censorious abolishment of Solina's system for selecting jury panels. Encountering Steiggerman by chance in Judge Austin's chambers late that afternoon while waiting to try a Prelim that Lacy had transferred upstairs, I presented him with a spare copy of the decision. After he glanced over it, a wry smile squeezed out of the corners of his mouth. "Well ... congratulations, Mr. Harris," he mouthed slowly and calmly, trying to hide his disappointment over the additional blemish now attached to his record. "And I'm sure you'll be even more pleased to know that you and your affidavits also overturned my appointment to Superior Court. The Governor filled his vacancies just this morning, so it's official now, and you can be very proud of yourself, 'cause you've caused me to lose something I wanted very much."

A portrait of defeat, despite his efforts to deflect his pain by laying a load of guilt on me, the hurt showed in the depths of his eyes nonetheless. Thinking how sad it was that he couldn't even imagine what it was like to really lose in life, and noting that Judge Austin had stirred uncomfortably in his chair, I answered without rancor. "Your Honor," surfaced my succinct reply, "I'm sorry that you don't see the injustices you created. All I did was simply record them."

After he departed without saying another word, I treated myself to a thin smile. When I returned to the office an hour later, however, I was wearing a wide one after Austin had dismissed the throwing case that followed my diplomatic success in chambers. As I entered, Robbie and George were engaged in a serious discussion. "I'm telling you, George," I listened to Robbie say after I dropped my briefbag and began pouring myself a cup of coffee. "If we file my proposed affidavit, we can absolutely, positively, destroy Lacy—and Arlie asshole, too!" stomped his argument, his grin failing to hide the venom in his tone.

"Well, now, I don't know, Rob," George replied, as I turned around and took a sip. "It could work, all right, but it's dangerous, too. I mean, it could also backfire on us."

"How? You just tell me how?" Robbie urged.

"Well, for openers," George fired back, "your affidavit might start out as a strictly legal issue. But as soon as the Judicial Council hears about it and runs lickety-split to the Board of Supervisors, old, ugly politics comes roaring into the situation, and this time we don't have Marty and his newspaper to rally the troops!" marched George's counter, his pace then picking up as he continued. "Moreover, this time we also don't look like the little guy getting beaten down by the big, bad, bully judges for just doing our jobs—in fact, quite the contrary. And to boot, my friend, you can just bet your sweet ass that the big boys downtown don't want to go to war a second time over us!" George steamed to a close, concern creasing his face.

"Okay ... okay, I see what you're saying," Robbie responded, in a calmer tone. "But I think the risk is worth it, 'cause I'm confident that we can keep it a legal matter, and just let the Supreme Court decide. Hell, did you read their language in the jury-panel reversal? Why they did everything but call the judges outright assholes, so they're already sympathetic to our side!"

"Hey, guys, hold up a second or two—what's this all about?" I quickly interjected as the two of them just stared at each other, seeking to lower the level of the electricity in the air before it matched the heat rising from my coffee.

"Well, Matt, to back up a bit," George answered, his volume dropping several decibels, an inkling of a sheepish smile appearing. "Old rebel Rob here wants to file a *blanket* affidavit against Lacy and Steiggerman on the grounds of racial prejudice. It seems that they were the ones who devised the selection process for keeping people of color off of the jury panel, and like Rob said, their scheme was most heartily condemned by our Supreme Court as downright nefarious!" George stressed, nodding his head for emphasis. "Now, it's a great idea, and if it actually works, Lacy and Steiggerman would be finished as judges. They couldn't hear Prelims or preside over cases anymore, and as a result the Judicial Council would have no choice but to force them to resign. But there are some heavy risks, too, so what do you think?" George posed, then reached for a cigarette.

"Well ... I don't know whether our Supreme Court would sustain such an affidavit, even with the strong language I read—and I certainly see the risks you pointed out," I replied cautiously. "But I also can't help but remember that not so long ago a certain group of black-robed assholes tried to get us fired, so I'm willing to try if you guys are."

"You see, George, Matt agrees with me," Robbie enthused, jumping back into the fray.

"Now hold on a minute, Rob," George rushed back, "I heard what Matt said. He agreed that he'd go along with it, not that he thought it would work—and he hasn't had time to fully consider what the consequences might be if it didn't. Now, here comes Ron and Leon, and Blaine's not far behind, so how about the two of us calm down, and then all of us go back to my office and think this through thoroughly before deciding what to do?"

"Okay ... okay, that's the right thing to do," Robbie shrugged, visibly relaxing, a smile wrinkling his lips. "I guess I'm just overly cranky from tangling too many days with that sonofabitch Lacy."

Within a minute or so, the rest of our compatriots meandered in, and after a round of warm greetings was shared, George led the way to his office. Last in line, as I started to follow, Marilyn, who had remained silent throughout Robbie and George's little flare-up, motioned me over to her desk. "Matty, you gotta stop them before this thing really gets out of hand!" she appealed the instant I drew near, concern coating her tone and flooding across her face.

"What? ... What do you mean?" I returned, startled.

"You got a minute?"

"Uh-huh ... sure."

"Well, then, pull up a chair and listen to me. There's something that's been bothering me for some time, and now it just can't wait any longer," she shared, sounding even more ominous.

"Okay," I nodded, sliding a chair over and sitting down next to her. "What's wrong? Tell me."

"All right ... Now I don't want you to misunderstand, so please listen carefully so that you get what I really mean—okay?"

"Yeah, for sure. You've got my full attention, so lay it on me."

"Okay," she nodded, her eyes fastening on mine. "Now when this thing started, you know that no one wanted to knock down those pigs across the street more than me. I mean, I disliked Lacy and Steiggerman, and all they stand for, as much as any one of you guys, right?"

"Uh-huh, I know that."

"And no one has worked any harder at helping beat them, true?"

"Absolutely, no question."

"I mean, I've come in early and gone home late, I've typed motions and affidavits in the evenings and on weekends, and I've tried to encourage all of you in every way I could—'cause I believed with my whole heart in what you were doing, and in each of you as a special person!" she stressed, her voice swelling with emotion as her words tumbled off her tongue. "But I'm sorry to say, Matty, I don't anymore—not now, not any longer. Hell, no!" she tacked on, jerking to a stop.

"But, why?" I asked incredulously, now totally stunned.

"Because we already won the war, that's why!—only nobody around here seems to realize that, or wants to accept it," she explained, straining to help me understand, striations of frustration and anger mixing into her tone. "We're not fighting for our clients anymore, to get them a fair deal. Ohhh, no, instead you guys are over there kicking ass for only one purpose—for revenge, to pay the pigs back for all the shitty things they've done over the years!"

"Now hold on a second, hon, we care about our clients Big Time!" spurted my challenge. And if we fuck over the pigs in the process of doing our best for them, what's wrong with that?"

"Nothing! ... only that's what you *were* doing, not what you're doing now!" she half shouted, then instantly caught herself. "I'm sorry, I didn't mean to yell at you. It's just that you don't see it, none of you do—and it really hurts me to see what you're turning into," she tacked on, tears creeping into her voice, then into the corners of her eyes.

Shocked by Marilyn's assertion, accented as it was by the pain etched across her face and the tears she quickly swiped away, not to forget for a moment my knowledge that she was undeniably one hundred percent on our side, for a full ten seconds I just sat there and let her message sink in, tiny wheels spinning her words round and round inside my head. "All right," I finally muttered softly, "it is hard to see yourself, particularly in the middle of a hell-storm, so if we're doing something wrong, spell it out for me so I can see it better."

"Ohhh-kay," she nodded, her tone softening in recognition that she did indeed have my full attention and an open ear. "Now, first off, hate is an awful thing, Matty. I had to learn that once, and you guys need to learn it right now. 'Cause it's perfectly okay to strongly dislike bad people, and the evil things they do, like what was going on across the street—and it's equally right to fight back hard against it. But when strong dislike turns into hate, well ... after a while you lose control and it takes you over, and before you know it that's all you're doing, just hating, hating, hating. I know," flowed her explanation, "'cause just a few years ago, I wouldn't even have talked to you, just because you're white—surprised?"

"Uh-huh ... I didn't know."

"Well, it's true, believe me. 'Cause I grew up in what I was taught was a white man's world, and it didn't take me long to learn to hate every wrong suffered by black people for four hundred years. In fact, I learned so good, that pretty soon I had learned to hate all white people—to me, there weren't any good ones, all whites were bad, and I wanted to kill every one of them!" she stressed, shaking her head. "Hell, Matty, I got so good at hating that by the time I got out of high school, I had turned into a bigger bigot than George Wallace and the Ku Klux Klan put together!"

"Yeah, that's quite a combo, all right," I shrugged back at her. "And the way you see it, we're doing the same thing? We're letting hate rule our actions?"

"Exactly! ... Listen, Matty, Lacy and Steiggerman are absolutely lousy human beings—mean, and prejudiced, and abusive as hell. But you've beaten them, they can't do anymore what they used to, you've stopped their vicious abuse of power, and the system is working as best it can! Only problem is, you guys are so wrapped up in hating them, that now that's not enough, you want to destroy them—and in the process, you're becoming just as bad as they are! Don't you see?"

"Hey, I see the point you've been making, but a little payback doesn't make us like them."

"A little payback?" Marilyn squealed. "Why a few minutes ago you told George and Robbie that because the pigs tried to run you guys out of Solina, it would be perfectly all right if you guys did the same thing to them. Now if that isn't becoming just like them, and using power just like them, then I'll kiss your backside!"

"Wow, that's certainly a mouthful," I replied when her echo died away, her analogy refusing to join it and instead circling round my brain like a merry-go-round, the truth inside it sinking in deeper and deeper with each silent second that passed. "Jesus, Mare ... I ... I think you've hit on something extremely important, 'cause I sure didn't hear how I sounded," I confessed after flashing again on my response to the affidavit issue. "I gotta talk this over with George and Robbie, and then with the rest of the guys, too."

"Well, good! ... that's what I hoped for, and why I picked you to talk with," she responded, relieved that she had succeeded in reaching me, her tone warming. "'Cause you're the most gentle, and I felt you'd listen and hear me out—and also 'cause the others will listen to you, 'cause they all respect you so much for being fair, as well as a hellion in court."

"Thanks ... I think," I squeezed out, then began to smile after one formed on her lips.

Marilyn's critique wasn't complete, however. "And while we're on the subject of you, Matty," she quickly continued, a motherly tone now creeping into her voice, "you've gotta take better care of yourself. Have you looked in a mirror lately? You look like a walking disaster, what with those bloodshot eyes, and the lines underneath that have even more lines under them. Why God only knows how long it's been since you've had a good night's sleep, 'cause you're always sitting up late, worrying and reading cases on how to screw over the pigs. And you've lost so much weight, you're turning into a scarecrow. Hell, if I didn't know better, I'd think that sweet lady of yours didn't feed you. Now, you better listen to Momma Marilyn on this matter, too, you hear?" she chastised gently, now grinning widely, but serious all the same.

The reference to Stella caused my smile to flicker, then disappear, replaced by an anxious expression as I glanced down at my watch, which read five forty-five. "Something wrong, Matty? You look kind of funny," Marilyn picked up, concern edging back into her voice. "I didn't mean to get overly personal."

"No, no, Mare, that's not it," I blurted back at her. "And the war's not what's worrying me so much, or making me so tired and scarecrow thin, either," I tacked on, the words rolling out before I had a chance to stop them. For the last several weeks I had wanted to share the burden I carried so carefully concealed inside me, to lessen it, at least a little bit. Now, somehow, the serious shock of discovery flowing from Marilyn's observation, piled on top of the terrible fear and hurt I harbored, combined with the totally innocent reference to Stella to create a tiny crack in my iron defense, my secret then sliding slowly through the narrow opening. "It's Stella, Mare ... she's very, very sick, and ... uh ... she's going to die," crawled my confession out of hiding.

"Wwwhat?" Marilyn stuttered, it now being her turn to be startled.

"Uh-huh, it's true, Mare ... she's got cancer, and it's spread all over. In fact, Stelle's in the hospital now, and it won't be long unless a miracle happens," I confirmed, my voice cracking.

"Oh, Matty, I'm so sorry ... I ... I ... don't know what to say."

"There isn't anything to say—or do," I eased back, forcing a pinched smile. "I just had to tell someone, too—okay?"

"Of course, it's okay ... I only wish to God that I could do something," she soothed, her voice trailing into silence as she reached forward and took my hand, tears squirming into her eyes.

Seconds later when George suddenly appeared, she abruptly turned away and swiped at them before spinning back around, but he wasn't fooled. "Hey, what's the matter here?" he queried, focusing on our sober faces.

"Sorry, Matt," Marilyn murmured, tears still in her voice.

"That's okay, hon, I was going to tell Georgie anyway."

"Tell me what?" George queried again, his concern now accelerating.

"I've got some bad news about Stella, Georgie," shuffled my answer, "you better sit down."

"All right, I will," he responded, grabbing a chair and dropping into it, his eyes indicating he was fully focused.

"Georgie," I mustered with only traces of emotion, "my Stelle has cancer real bad, and she's going to die very soon unless we get a miracle."

Whatever possible problems George was anticipating, what I had communicated wasn't one of them. Staring blankly back at me while he absorbed the shock, the muscles in his face tightened, and his eyes narrowed. "Ohhh ... fuck!" he finally growled in a low tone of voice.

"Yeah ... you got that right," I returned through a heavy sigh, then watched as he slowly climbed to his feet and wandered over to the reception counter and slammed both fists down on it.

"Goddamn fucking world! Does the shit ever end?" he groaned out. "I just knew it had to be something serious, for you to keep us all waiting for over ten minutes. But I didn't expect this kind of serious, no fucking way!" he ended, raising his fists again, then catching himself and gradually unclenching them as he shuffled back over to his chair and slumped down inside.

In the uncomfortable silence that ensued, the three of us just sat there feeling helpless. "Listen, both of you, please," I quickly interjected before the feeling gained strength, "I appreciate how you feel, and I'm very lucky to have such good friends. Just knowing that you know, and care, helps me a lot, believe me. So let's not dwell on the subject, 'cause we gotta carry on like Stella wants us to," I rolled out, easing the tension as best I could. "And speaking of the pretty lady, I've gotta run now, I want to get to the hospital in time for dinner—okay?"

"Yeah, sure," George nodded, Marilyn's agreement following in the form of a faint smile. "Listen, Matt, if you want some time off, just take it," George added as I climbed to my feet.

"Thanks, Georgie, but Stelle won't stand for it. It's not my choice, but that's the way she wants it, so that's the way it'll be. I'll see you guys tomorrow," I smiled, picking up my briefbag and heading for the corridor.

"You'll let me know if there's anything I can do?" George called after me.

"Uh-huh," I answered, turning back around to face him. "In fact, Georgie, there is one very important thing you can do. A little while ago,

Marilyn was explaining something to me about our war, and as usual she was making one hell of a lot of sense. You need to discuss it with her, 'cause it's really important for all of us. Then, we could talk it over with Robbie, and later with the whole gang—okay?"

"Consider it done!" he bounced back at me firmly. "And you'll take our best to Stella?" he added, squeezing a sympathetic smile onto his lips.

"You can bet on it," I assured. "See you in the morning," I tossed over my shoulder as I turned and headed down the hallway.

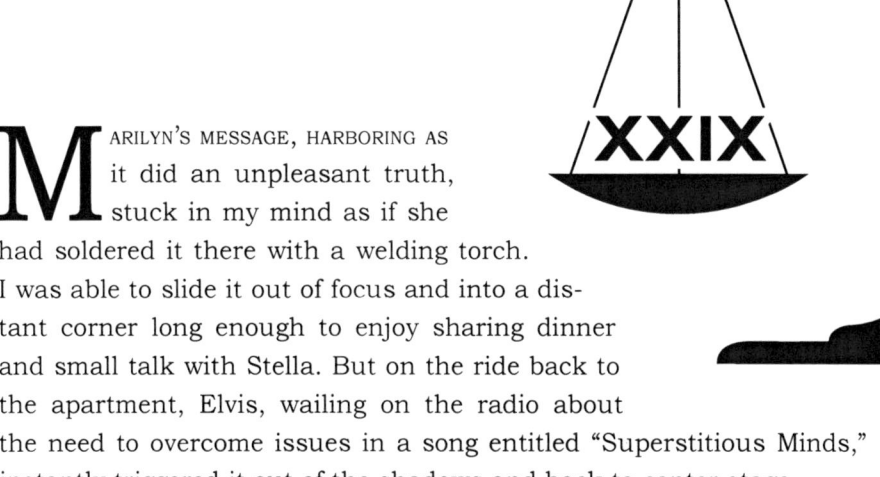

XXIX

MARILYN'S MESSAGE, HARBORING AS it did an unpleasant truth, stuck in my mind as if she had soldered it there with a welding torch. I was able to slide it out of focus and into a distant corner long enough to enjoy sharing dinner and small talk with Stella. But on the ride back to the apartment, Elvis, wailing on the radio about the need to overcome issues in a song entitled "Superstitious Minds," instantly triggered it out of the shadows and back to center stage.

Had we really lost sight of what we started out to achieve? I mused as I steered Old Greener east along Sunset Boulevard. Our goal had been to right the ship, to pressure the Judges and DAs into operating the system fairly, like it was designed. So, were we now engaged in something over and above that? arose the prickly issue, settling uncomfortably into the surrounding silence till Marilyn's opinion once again floated into ear. "Listen, Matty, Lacy and Steiggerman are absolutely lousy human beings ... But you've beaten them ... you've stopped their vicious abuse of power and the system is working as best it can!" she had argued urgently, her message echoing and reechoing as I steered through one of Sunset's innumerable bends into a short straightaway, my response to her that I thought she had hit on something important also recycling to squeeze a wry smile onto my lips.

"I'll give you important, all right," I shrugged out, breaking the silence which had grown weighty. "Old Lord Acton said that power corrupts, so in trying to halt its abuse, and the injustices that flowed from it, have we overstepped and become abusive ourselves?"

"Well ... the system is humming along pretty damn well," I answered myself slowly. "I mean, we can now take cases to trial without fear of our clients being punished for it with a maximum sentence, we're certainly getting fair plea-bargains, and we totally wiped out their prejudicial system for selecting jury panels," flowed my reasoning. "Not only that, but Steiggerman's been punished Big Time for being a bigoted asshole, and Uncle Tom Lacy isn't nearly as blindly pro-prosecution as he used to be ... so how in the hell did filing a blanket affidavit and forcing them into early retirement suddenly become part of the plan? From hating them, as Marilyn said? Is raw hatred now fueling our actions, with pure revenge now our purpose?"

The silence returned as the sound of my voice trailed off, now even heavier than before as I approached the city limits of Beverly Hills and was unexpectedly greeted by the sight of my father's face floating into view, having surfaced from my subconscious. As usual, he was wearing a serious expression, the hint of a smile on his lips only a sign of his unwavering self-confidence. I had lived with that commanding countenance my entire life, just as my resistance to an all-knowing authority, with the power to act arbitrarily, trailed back to my earliest memories. Had I, however, I now asked for the first time, allowed a lifetime of accumulated anger to grow into a rage that sought not just to correct injustice, but to also punish with the same degree of cruelty that I abhorred? The Old Testament says an eye for an eye and a tooth for a tooth, but what about the New One's message of love? You've always believed that love was stronger than hate, but how does a warrior war with love? I mean, I'm all for Gandhi's and MLK's nonviolent resistance, but on the other hand, how effective would that be against Hitler's storm troopers? And speaking of love, Matthew, my man, have you also added to your rage the molten anger you harbor from losing your precious Stella? fired the final salvo of hyperactive neurons as I turned off Sunset and headed south on Doheny Drive with only hard questions for a companion.

"Fuuuck," I finally growled out, shaking my head sadly as *maybe* clashed with *maybe not,* without anything close to resolution. "Are we just lost in a war without end, our offensive flowing into our adversaries' counteroffensive, only to instigate another offensive—just like in Vietnam?" I posed, suddenly struck by how we seemed to be unconsciously emulating the tragic situation. "Hell, just last month we had the Vietnam Moratorium, the largest anti-war protest in the history of the movement, with millions of students, laborers, housewives, and school children from one coast to another demonstrating their opposition in diverse ways, all peaceful, like wearing black arm bands—with seventy-nine college presidents appealing directly to the White House to boot. And what was Nixon's response? He promised not to be swayed by the movement, the fucking sonofabitch! So, on a scale large or small, is peace possible? ... And is there ever one that lasts? Apparently not, if you open up a history book and take a little look? Remember what you read in *Newsweek* the other evening when you couldn't sleep, that peace is like the horizon—you can see it in the distance, but it's always far away and you can never touch it? Well, that's certainly the way it looks in Vietnam, all right—and that's the way it looks in little old Solina, too, goddamnit to hell!" I suddenly shouted, frustration flaring, then dissipating slowly as I slipped into silence for the final mile of the journey.

At home, with the collage of questions still buzzing about in the back of my mind like a swarm of bees, I poured myself a glass of wine and sipped it while I perused the Sports Section. When the Merlot had finally found my bloodstream and quieted the queries, as midnight approached I managed to close my eyes, Joni Mitchell's bittersweet message about having looked at life from both sides trailing after me to swim in circles around winning and losing, her lamentation that "It's life's illusions I recall/I really don't know life at all," then slipping into the picture, my agreement full but silent. You got that right, lady, crawled my confession as I fell into sleep, 'cause I sure can't figure it out.

Driving to the office the following morning, once again I reexamined the issue Marilyn had raised, and the more I thought about it, the more valid her concerns appeared. The opportunity I then sought to discuss it with George and Robbie proved elusive, however, on what turned out to be an extra busy Thursday, though each of my compatriots somehow made the time to express his heartfelt regrets about Stella's condition and gift me with a hug. By late Friday afternoon though, the court calendars loosened up and the three of us were able to huddle together in George's office, where to my surprise the issue was quickly rendered moot, at least temporarily. As it turned out, after I had left George to discuss the troublesome issue with Marilyn, thereafter he had returned to the meeting with Ron, Robbie, Leon, and Blaine regarding the possible filing of a blanket affidavit. Some discussion had ensued, which led to a decision to table the contentious matter for a week or two in order to allow the possible political ramifications to sink in and permit a more thorough evaluation of the risks involved.

Okay, I thought, while the kettle of boiling water is still on the burner, at least the level of heat has been lowered to a simmer. Then, I surmised, when the subject was reintroduced, we could more properly discuss it within the broader framework introduced by Marilyn. Mercifully, however, the testy trial of our behavior was further stalled by another decision reached the following Monday, when as November's first work week opened, we voted unanimously to finally utilize our long overdue vacation time in rotating two-week periods. No plan to reduce hostilities was involved in arriving at this decision. Instead, the governing factor dictating this hiatus was the simple realization that we had expended a tremendous amount of energy over a long period of time, and that it was essential to maintaining the success we had attained for us to temporarily diminish our frenetic level of performance in order to allow refueling.

Robbie was first, due to seniority. And when he returned from visiting his mother and sisters just after the middle of the month, he not only appeared well rested, but in the best humor since when I had first met him. Smiling and joking with each of us, as in previous times, he seemed to have abandoned his plan to remove Lacy and Steiggerman from the bench, at least for the immediate future, in that he failed to even mention it. Instead, with great excitement crackling in his voice, he proposed a new project, "Cracking the cops' throwing game," he drawled, his mischievous grin widening full.

"Sounds like baseball, can I play, too?" Ron teased.

"Ronald, my man, you, and all the rest of us have been playing their sick little game for quite some time now," Robbie returned. "I just think that enough's enough, and that it's time to expose the whole rotten conspiracy!"

At the sounding of the word "conspiracy," smiles quickly appeared, then graduated into chuckles all the way around our table at Alessandro's, where lunch was in progress. Because of his penchant for discovering a conspiracy, evil or otherwise, but primarily the former, Robbie had long ago been appointed our resident conspiracy expert. Now, as soup gave way to salad, he was in rare form.

"All right ... all right, you bunch of jackasses can snicker if you want to. But remember that you also laughed when I first told you about the pigs screwing with the jury panel selection process, and it turned out to be a conspiracy of the first order—just like I told you!"

"Yeah ... that's true, all right," Ron admitted between giggles. "So now you better watch out for another serious conspiracy—the one to smother your exposure of the cops in the spaghetti and lasagna before you can bring it out in the open for everyone to see!"

No one within our close-knit family commanded greater respect than

Robbie, and he was well aware of it. So even as he frowned at the skepticism scrawled across our faces, a smile began to form in the corners of his mouth, which slowly grew wider as the volume of our chuckles increased. "Well, Ronald, what the pigs are doing is shitty, so at least you're hiding the cover-up in an area that will come out the same place," rolled his reply. "But, my friend, when the pigs start making up scripts to explain why it's okay for them to bug your car, and your office, and even your bedroom, YOU better watch out—especially if it's true about all that great but highly illegal oral sex you're always bragging about," he added, still smiling, but serious all the same. "And don't any of you other trusting souls come looking to me either."

Amidst a fresh outburst of laughter, Leon inquired first as to where Robbie would be located, in that it sounded as if he were planning to take refuge in some distant place. Then, following his tease, Ron jumped back in to raise the question of whether or not the local authorities were sophisticated enough to eavesdrop the way Robbie had described, opining that they weren't.

"Well," Robbie drawled, shaking his head, "to answer Leon—as far away as possible from this bunch of howling hyenas, that's for sure. And as for you, Mr. Smart-ass," he added, his eyes darting to Ron, "who said it was just the local cops who were involved? That's where the illegal shit starts, all right. But if you don't think the Feds are involved, especially with that dictatorial dick-head of a President we've got, then you better think again real quick."

"Jesus," Ron shrugged while sinking his fork into his salad. "You make it sound like that asshole Nixon is planning to turn the FBI and the CIA into a Gestapo—you really believe that?"

"Absolutely," Robbie fired back, his smile having disappeared, but his tone still amiable. "Did you ever stop and take a good look—I mean, a real good look at that bunch of goons he's surrounded himself with? Do it sometime. Study the faces of Ehrlichman and that other dude, Haldeman, then just listen to what they're saying, along with that other prick, Mitchell!" Robbie suggested, nodding his head to emphasize the depth of his conviction.

"Hey, now, just hold on a minute, Rob," Leon cautioned, sliding back into the colloquy, his voice swelling with sarcasm. "How about we show a little bit more respect for our government and the dedicated officials serving us. I mean, for God's sake, Rob—such harsh language!" he admonished, his mockery fully intended to spur Robbie on.

"Dedicated?" spurted Rob's reply. "They're dedicated, all right—to abolishing freedom! Hell, they don't like the old First Amendment, 'cause the press keeps telling us what a bunch of cocksuckers they really are. And they don't much care for the Fourth either, 'cause that stops the pigs from breaking into people's houses in the middle of the night and dragging them off to jail. Not to forget, of course, the abominable Sixth!" Robbie hastened to add with thickening scorn, "'cause those goddamned juries made up of common folk have a nasty little habit of seeing the truth! I mean, who needs juries, when you can appoint fine, upstanding people like Lacy and Steiggerman to the trial courts, and even more wonderful people like Haynsworth to the Supreme Court? Christ, if being a card-carrying member of the Ku Klux Klan, and ardent supporter of the John Birch Society, doesn't qualify you to sit on the highest court in the land, what does?" Robbie stormed toward a conclusion. "And as we all know, the Court is the ultimate protector of individual rights in our governmental system, so if you control that, that's all you need to destroy them. Then, anyone who opens his mouth, or does anything else they don't like, can be gotten rid of by putting them in jail on charges they make up—the exact same way the local cops invent the throwing stories! Don't you see?" he pleaded, finally braking sharply to a stop, his eyes swiveling round the table before settling back on Leon.

"Well, I don't know if the conspiracy is as well formed as you say, but I wouldn't put it past them," Leon agreed after swallowing a mouthful of salad. "You'll get no argument from me on that group, Nixon's a Nazi if I ever saw one, and the rest of the group is probably worse!"

"You just better believe it," nodded Robbie. "Why I bet they've got lists of people they consider enemies that they're just waiting to get rid of. And I wouldn't be a bit surprised if the FBI was working overtime to help them. I tell you, you don't realize how really dangerous these people are."

"And what about the CIA?" Ron added, reaching for a roll.

"Them, too. Nobody even knows what the hell they're into, it's all hush hush hush."

"All right ... all right, Rob," Ron squeezed out, finally surrendering on behalf of all of us. "Tell us what we can do to crack the cops' throwing-case script."

"Well," Robbie replied, pushing away his salad untouched. "I want every one of you to start marking with a red star each and every arrest report you read that deals with a throwing situation. Then, I want you to cross-examine every officer, in every case, as to when he first became an officer, how many drug and narcotic busts he makes every month, and what percentage of them were throwing situations—just like I taught Matthew. I also want you to tightly pin down the officers on the details of the throwing incident itself, like we always do. And then, gentlemen, I want you to make notes on each case and turn them in to me at the end of the day—okay?"

All of us readily agreed. And thereafter, Robbie spent long hours after court had ended studying the reports and our notes on the various cases, and carefully cataloguing them according to different police authorities, the frequency with which the individual officers within them reported such incidents, and the times, places, and various other details that accompanied the subject occurrences. Amazingly, toward the end of the month, he had already compiled an impressive list of statistics in support of the planned motions that would later serve to initiate step one of the appeal process. And after he had shared them with us during a late-afternoon meeting, we all promised to faithfully continue our laborious efforts, before finally relaxing and drifting into more casual conversation that was soon spotted with spells of laughter.

The outside world, however, wasn't chuckling much that November. For while our decision to ratchet down our efforts slightly in order to provide the needed R & R was proving most effective, the already contentious debate about the Vietnam War heated up considerably. On the fifteenth of the month, in Washington D.C. a quarter of a million fervent protesters marched from the Capitol to the Washington Monument, where they were then addressed by Republican Senator Charles Goodell, and by Eugene McCarthy and George McGovern representing the dissident Democrats. Followed in turn by MLK's widow, Coretta, and celebrities Arlo Guthrie, Dick Gregory, Leonard Bernstein, and Peter, Paul, & Mary, this distinguished company further heightened the legitimacy of the demonstration, and due to extensive media coverage generated fresh attention from the American public at large, which had grown numb from the six-year length and seeming futility of the conflict that had claimed so many casualties.

Then, only four days later, the media reported that a sergeant in our army reported that he had witnessed fellow soldiers massacre women and children in the Vietnamese village of My Lai. Unbelievable? ... Impossible? No, unfortunately not. For after further investigation, on the twenty-fourth of the month Lieutenant William Calley, who allegedly commanded the massacre, was ordered to stand trial for murder, with the body count of those slaughtered now standing at five hundred sixty-seven. "Jesus, fucking-A Christ!" George groaned, succinctly summarizing our collective horror as the six of us huddled together in our daily meeting after court had ended. Was there no limit to tragedy? we wondered, shaking our heads slowly side to side in our bewilderment.

Searching for something positive to celebrate, for something warm to take the edge off the blood-curdling chill blowing out of Asia, we found little to comfort us. For the only good news that November served up was that the Senate rejected Nixon's nomination of Clement Haynsworth to the Supreme Court, and even that bit of cheer was dampened by the realization that forty-five Senators had voted in favor. What kind of country did we live in, if that many Senators thought a former Ku Klux Klan member was qualified to sit on our highest court? the six of us wondered without answer.

Personally, I didn't have a great deal of time to reflect on either the nebulous state of our nation's morality as displayed in the Senate, or the even more heart-sickening implications created by the atrocities in My Lai. For during my nightly hospital visits, I was painfully witnessing a massacre of a far more personal nature, as during November's second week the cancer cells had begun their final assault on Stella. Since I had discovered her illness on that now seemingly long-ago Friday evening in June, I had never given up hope for the miracle of spontaneous remission. But now as I studied her frail frame and the drawn features of her face, even when her eyes smiled at my appearance, the once luminous pools harbored a light that was distant and hazy, and my hope grew emptier by the day as November stretched past its mid-point.

With the reality of Stella's steady decline marching before my eyes, as the pain increased and higher and higher dosages of morphine were needed to blunt the ravages of the cancer's aggression, I summoned every ounce of strength I had to maintain the smile and cheery tone of voice necessary to uplift her sinking spirits as best I could. Wanting desperately to ease the fear that sometimes surfaced and provide her with peace of mind, I turned for guidance to my former high-school

English teacher and trusted friend for a lesson I could in turn impart to my fast-fading sweetheart. During my three years in her classes, Eunice Schmidt had not only brilliantly and innovatively instructed me in the important aspects of our language, from grammar to the giants who composed its magnificent storehouse of literature, but even more valuably had gifted me with innumerable life lessons, both small and large. Over the years since my graduation, I had remained in steady touch by telephone and the lunches we occasionally shared, and now, I explained, I needed her wisdom more than ever.

Eunice's recommendation was that because of time constraints, I needed to read and digest a collection of metaphysical writings she had compiled over the years. "They're special, Matt," Eunice had advised gently over the phone. "And they make such good sense, if one keeps an open mind and carefully thinks over their teachings. They've brought me much comfort, and I hope they will help you and your Stella as well," she had added sweetly in conclusion. Fortunately, the fastidiously fashioned anthology was only two hundred sixteen pages in length, and I hungrily devoured it the same evening I picked it up on the way to the hospital, beginning while Stella dozed after we shared dinner, and reading through the night when I reached home. To my amazement, the central message of the collection instantly resonated with me, as if I had somehow known its teachings on my own and just needed outside confirmation. And carefully re-exploring the individual spiritual philosophies one by one over the next few nights, as Eunice had suggested, I was able to construct a basic lesson that I hoped would comfort Stella, as to my considerable but happy surprise it had consoled me. "Thank you, Eunice," I whispered, setting her little book on top of the pillow next to me and gently patting it as I tumbled into sleep. "And thank you, brave thinkers, who dare to explore outside the box with other souls that channel knowledge of life from *the other side.*"

As Thanksgiving approached, I waited nervously for the right moment to try and convey what I had learned to Stella. That moment arrived when the evening before the holiday the fog suddenly lifted, and for a few short hours Stella resembled her old self, clear-eyed, alert, and armed with her sharp sense of humor. "See, you're getting better," I chirped. "You're in the old ballgame, sweetheart, so just hang in there—okay?"

"Okay, Mr. Manager," she murmured, glad for the respite, but knowing that it was only temporary. "Matty, I'm so sorry," then trailed off her tongue. "I know how bad I look, and how hard this is for you."

"Hey, what the hell are you talking about? You're still the prettiest lady in the whole world, and I've got it easy next to you—so I've got no complaints, believe me," soothed my reply. "But that reminds me, sweetie," I smiled, inching onto the bed beside her and taking her hand. "You remember how you asked me why some people get hit with illness and others don't, and I had no answer?"

"Uh-huh ... but not to worry."

"I'm not, sweetheart, 'cause I've been doing some reading in a collection of writings by some really smart people, and I learned a little something that I want to share with you—okay?"

"Sure," she smiled. "What's up?"

"Well, now listen carefully, 'cause I think that what I'm going to explain makes a lot of sense if you keep an open mind."

"All right, it's open," she murmured, her smile widening.

"Good, sweetie. Now, for openers, the thinkers I've been reading believe that there are many levels of reality, with our stay on earth just one of them. It's one of the lower levels actually," I rolled out slowly, my tone casual. "It's a kind of schoolhouse that we come to after we've formed a life plan in a higher plane with the help of our guide. That plan is for us to come here and learn some lessons, and if we do, well ... we graduate to a higher plane permanently, and we don't have to come here anymore. Are you following me?"

"Yeahhh ... I sure agree with that lower-level classification, all right," she snickered. "And I think what you're saying is ... that I came here to learn a lesson—right?"

"Exactly, hon."

"Well, that's funny ... 'cause ever since I learned about the cancer, naturally I did some thinking," shuffled her response, the morphine still slowing the pace of her delivery despite her improved clarity. "I've searched back through all the troubles I've encountered ... and the mistakes I've made ... wondering if I was being punished for them. I didn't really get an answer ... but I think all of my troubles and mistakes had to do with abandonment."

"I think you've got that exactly right, hon. But I don't think you're being punished, I think that feeling abandoned, and feeling that you abandoned Vicki on top of it, caused such a great hurt inside you that it made a hole and cancer filled it up," I shared with her, fighting back tears as I met her gaze squarely. "I don't know how that fits in exactly," I continued, "'cause that lesson is only the sub-lesson."

"There's more?"

"Oh, yeah ... and it's the biggie. It seems very odd, considering how all-powerful God is, but the thinkers believe that despite this omnipotence, because God is about love, and gives us so much love, that God, too, needs to be loved by little old us."

"Yeah, I'll give you odd, all right," Stella gibed gently.

"Right, I said it was a different way of looking at things. But think about it, why wouldn't God have needs, too?" I posed softly, then slowed my delivery to emphasize my explanation. "In fact, let's look at it this way, hon—let's start with the idea that God created love, the greatest gift of all. But just because God's the creator of this most special treasure doesn't mean that God doesn't want to share in it and be loved in return. I mean, that's not fair after all the blessings God gives us, is it?"

"No, I suppose not," Stella replied, "though I sure never looked at it that way."

"Neither did I, sweetheart. But that doesn't mean we can't, or shouldn't."

"All right," she smiled, "go on."

"Well, out of that need by God to be loved by us comes the master lesson—which is to learn to know and love ourselves, so that we can better learn to know and love God."

This time Stella didn't respond quickly. Instead, as her head nestled deeper into her pillow, the concept which had instantly resonated within me circled slowly round and round inside her mind for almost a minute, her eyes narrowing and her forehead furrowing as she carefully considered it. Finally, a smile inched out of the corners of her mouth, and she squeezed my hand. "That's really beautiful, Matty," she said softly. "And you know what? You helped me do that—your love ... a real love ... helped me know myself better, and love myself better ... so thank you, dear one," she added, tears creeping into her eyes.

"Hey, me too—we're partners, remember?" I smiled back at her.

"Uh-huh. And that's why I've got to work on loving God more ... 'cause I'm so grateful for you."

"Well, good news, sweetie—you already did that by loving me, remember?"

"I'd never forget that ... ever," she murmured. "Come closer and lie next to me, okay?"

"Sure ... I thought you'd never ask," I teased, watching her inch over to the guardrail, then carefully sliding in beside her.

"That's good," she whispered, "just like old times."

"Yeahhh ... for sure, we should've thought of it a long time ago."

""Uh-huh," she smiled, her eyes searching mine. "And listen, love, I don't mean to harp when you've been so wonderful ... but speaking of remembering reminds me—do you remember your promises to me?"

"Uh-huh, absolutely ... every single one of them."

"Tell me one more time ... please," she asked, fatigue suddenly shadowing her face, the plea inside her request signaling that she was beginning to say goodbye.

"All right, hon, but I'll tell you again later, too," I replied, swallowing the tears that had crowded into my throat and steadying my voice. "First of all, I'll remember that you taught me I'm special and to be good to myself—which your love makes easy," I rolled out through a smile. "Then, next, I'll remember how very important my work is, and to never give it up—'cause I need to help others, while also keeping in mind that I can't right every wrong, that I can only do my part. And finally," I managed to squeeze out, the words coming more slowly, "I promise to not close myself off, that I'll love again when the time is right—okay?" I asked, tears now squirming out of the corners of my eyes and trickling down my cheeks.

"That's fine," she smiled, reaching over and tenderly wiping away my tears. "And just one more thing, love—don't forget me and what we shared together."

"Are you kidding, sweetheart? ... Like I could forget to breathe, maybe?"

"Ohh-kay," struggled off her tongue, tears now finding her cheeks, too. "Now, just hold me ... just hold me," she added, turning slightly so that I could slip an arm around her, then lowering her head onto my chest.

What followed was a much-needed interlude. For just as our emotions threatened to bubble over, one slow-passing hour rescued us, precious minutes crawling by as snuggled close together we chattered in soft tones about baseball, our favorite songs, and the latest news from Solinaland. Dinner then arrived, which I shared from my newly acquired perch. And afterward, we watched TV till Stella finally slipped into sleep around ten-thirty, kissing me sweetly on the lips just before her eyes closed, the peaceful look inside them accompanying me all the way home and into bed.

The following morning ushered in Thanksgiving Day. Arising early, I checked with the nurses' station, and after learning that Stella was sleeping comfortably, I headed over to Gram and Gramp's for a visit. Early risers, too, they were just settling into breakfast when I arrived a few minutes before eight, and after hugs and kisses were warmly shared, an extra place setting was quickly added to the breakfast-nook table. Fortunately for me, my parents were once again spending the holiday in Hawaii, and my sisters were celebrating it together in Palm Springs, freeing me from having to create a believable excuse for why I could not share at length with them and allowing me to fully enjoy the day with Gram and Gramp, then with Stella. Not to forget, of course, my dearly loved Nanny Lou, whose baking apple pies were adding the sweetest of aromas to the air even as we enjoyed her French toast and link sausages, cheerful conversation flowing in a collective stream as steadily as the coffee she poured into our cups.

When time finally snuck up on us and eleven o'clock arrived, I departed, carefully carting one of Nanny Lou's apple specialties to Old Greener, then heading west along Wilshire Boulevard to Westwood. Stella was awake when I arrived in her room, and though looking paler than when I had left her last evening, she greeted me with a full smile and a firm, "Happy Thanksgiving, love!"

"Happy turkey day, yourself, sweetie," I returned as I leaned in to kiss her.

"Yeah ... And you know what that means, don't you? Football!" Stella asked and answered, beaming a fresh smile at me.

"Okay, hon, you got it," I answered as I turned on the TV.

The NFL's morning game was just starting the second half, and after climbing up into bed with Stella, I filled her in on my morning with Gram, Gramp, and Nanny Lou while we watched the Minnesota Vikings' lopsided 24–0 triumph over the Detroit Lions. The hospital had decided to make lunch the main Thanksgiving Day meal, so just after one o'clock we enjoyed the San Francisco–Dallas Cowboys battle while we munched our turkey and stuffing. This encounter turned out to be far more entertaining, with both teams having something to celebrate when it ended in a 24-24 tie. Having saved our special pie until the game concluded and we had managed to find a little additional room in our tummies, we not only savored Nanny Lou's "genius concoction of sugar and love" as Stella nicknamed it, but enjoyed sharing it with the nurses and other hospital staff that drifted in and out during the remainder of the afternoon.

Around six o'clock, Stella, having tired from the day's activities, drifted into a nap, and seated near the window, I enjoyed a pipeful as dusk nudged ever so gently into darkness. Alone for a few minutes, I couldn't help but reflect on how different this Thanksgiving was from the one a year ago. Smiling wistfully as memory's door swung open, I recalled how Stella and I had shared pecan pie during our private celebration after I'd returned from my parents' home, and she from dinner with friends. It was the true beginning of our full relationship, friends, lovers, and partners melding together, a special moment indeed, I mused, tears creeping into my eyes to keep my smile company. And oh what a year it had been, followed my next thought, my mind's eye rushing the long battle in Solina together with dinners, dancing in the apartment, lovemaking, and the joyous weekend in San Francisco, a dull ache swelling up inside my chest as I stared out the window at the sunset's final rays painting the horizon peach-purple.

Several minutes later, the night nurse, Rachel, entered to check on Stella, and I quickly returned to the here and now, offering her a piece of pie after she had completed her notes on the chart at the foot of the bed, then chatting with her for a few minutes until Stella stirred awake and teased us about carrying on behind her back. "Oh, yeah, you got that right," I drawled with maximum sarcasm as I crawled back into bed beside her and kissed her. "After all this time together, it's about time you got a little bit jealous," I added, reaching over and patting her cheek, noting that the faraway look had returned to her eyes.

On Friday evening when I returned, that faraway look had grown even more distant and Stella appeared noticeably weaker. Even her "Hi, love," seemed to struggle off her tongue, and her smile was pinched as she motioned with a finger for me to climb in beside her. Slipping out of my blazer and pulling off my tie and shoes, I quickly complied, wincing when her effort to inch over and provide me with room caused a groan to escape her lips. Kissing her lightly to chase it away, I nestled close to her and softly stroked her hand as she closed her eyes and fell back into sleep, the sour smell of the morphine seeping from her pores causing tears to form, then trickle down my cheeks.

For over an hour I just lay there, listening to her breathe and trying to match her slow rhythm to soothe the throbbing ache in my chest.

Nurse Rachel arrived at six o'clock, and Stella's dinner tray shortly thereafter, Rachel then insisting that I eat it after explaining that it made no sense whatsoever to wake Stella. "If I do," I bargained, tears again creeping into my eyes, "can I spend the night here, I just can't leave her." Permission was granted, and after I managed to eat half a piece of chicken and some rice, exhaustion caught up with me, too, and I joined Stella in slumber.

When I awakened just after five-thirty on Saturday, Rachel informed me that Stella had slipped into a coma. "Now you need to take a break, and go home and shower and change clothes," she instructed with a smile. "This could go on for quite some time, and you need to take care of yourself, so that you can help us take care of your lady—okay?"

"Okay ... sure," I nodded, overwhelmed by her logic, the kindness in her voice also radiating softly from her eyes.

"Now you take your time and drive safely," she added. "Nurse Roberta, who comes on at six, will take the best of care here, and I'll see you tonight."

"Okay, I will—and thanks," I smiled.

"You can thank me by promising to drive slowly and keep alert. You're upset, Matt—remember that, you hear?"

"Yes ma'am ... I hear, and I promise."

Departing after whispering in Stella's ear that I would return soon, I fulfilled both pledges by eleven o'clock. Settling back into my chair by the window upon my return, after I finished the Sports Section, I spent the afternoon carefully reexamining Eunice's little book, breaking every so often to talk to Stella. Rachel had informed me that of all five senses, hearing was the last to cease working, so comforted by the knowledge that Stella unconsciously might still be listening, every so often I'd take her hand and tell her that I was there, that she was not alone, and that God was waiting for her with open arms. "It's all right to leave, sweetheart," I whispered through my tears. "Just tell God how much you love Him, and ask Him to bring you Home to where there is no more pain and no more fear. 'Cause you've learned your lesson, and you deserve to graduate," tiptoed off my tongue soothingly. "So just ask, and don't worry about me, I'll be fine thanks to you."

Sunday passed in similar fashion, the only difference being that Rachel convinced me to sleep at home, arguing effectively that my sleep in the hospital was so broken by my waking every few minutes to check on Stella that "it amounts to no sleep at all," adding that she would telephone me if there was any change in Stella's vital signs. Reluctantly, I agreed, and after kissing Stella good-night and hugging dear Rachel, I headed home. Earlier in the evening, I had watched a TV special on CBS entitled "Songs of America," and during a spliced-in film clip featuring JFK, Bobby, and MLK, the song playing in the background had struck a chord inside me. Now, with the ache in my chest throbbing again as I steered east along Sunset toward the apartment, it replayed in my mind and slowly but steadily eased my pain. "When you're weary," Simon and Garfunkel silently sang to me, their harmonious message that God understood my anguish and would dry my tears if I just turned to him stitching hope into my broken heart, the lullabying lyrics "like a bridge over troubled water" playing and replaying on my brain's turntable until finally a smile squirmed out of the corners of my mouth as I licked away my tears, then squeezed the steering wheel tighter as if I was pulling my Stelle into my arms and holding her close.

"It'll be okay," I whispered, when I could finally speak. "Somehow, some way ... everything will be okay."

XXX

MONDAY MARKED THE BEGINNING OF a new month, as well as the opening page of 1969's final chapter. "Well, hello there, December," I muttered, smiling faintly as I steered Old Greener toward Solina. "Got any miracles in you? 'Cause Stella and I could sure use one," I tacked on, recalling that when I telephoned before departing for the office her condition was unchanged. "No answer, huh?" I shrugged, looking up through the windshield at the overcast sky that hinted of drizzle. "Yeahhh ... well, according to the *Times* we're going to have sunshine and reach almost eighty, so dig deep and find us a miracle—okay?" issued my challenge as I leaned forward to switch on the radio.

The Jackson Five were just finishing up their first Motown hit, "I Want You Back," and for several fleeting seconds, I smiled faintly at the one-in-a-trillion chance that my never-say-die nature was continuing to hope for. But as the Rolling Stones then began sermonizing that "You Can't Always Get What You Want," the notion of farewell implicit in December's swan song also struck a sour note, and together they instantly evaporated my fantasy and sent a twinge of anxiety spiraling upward from my stomach into my chest. An ill omen, to be sure, it soon transformed into reality. For having reached the office at seven-thirty, I had just settled into the chair at my desk with my cup of coffee, when Dr. Reiser telephoned and advised that Stella had died fifteen minutes earlier. His voice was calm, and he tried as best he could to deflect the blunt force of his message, but that didn't stop my heart from delivering trip-hammer blows to my chest. Somewhere I had read a poet describe a like moment as lightning and thunder in the heart, and even though all signs had pointed to this tragic moment for many weeks, still the lightning and thunder struck me full. With tears jumping into my eyes, I squeezed out a muffled "Ohhh ... God," then bolted from my chair, ran down the hallway past Marilyn's cry of "Matty?" and out the front door, where I turned left and headed for the small park behind the courthouse.

Reaching it, I dropped down beneath a large magnolia tree, leaned my head forward into my lap and sobbed out the excruciating hurt which had exploded inside me, slowly at first, then like an overflowing river. For months I had held my emotions in check so that Stella wouldn't see my fear or my hurt, and I could bolster her spirits whenever needed. Now, alone, with no need to protect, I was free to release my storehouse of pain, and a stream of sorrow poured out of me seemingly without end.

I don't know how much time passed before I heard a voice mouth my name. Looking up through my tears, I watched as Marilyn slowly knelt in front of me. "She's gone, Mare," I mumbled. "She's gone."

"Oh ... I'm so sorry," Marilyn replied, reaching forward and taking my hand.

"I know ... I know," I returned. "And I know I'm a big baby, too—only I didn't think anything could hurt this much," I added, struggling to squeeze out the words as the pain stabbed at me. "There's a hole in the sky, can you see it, Mare?" I moaned through fresh tears. "Just like the one in my heart. I ... I ..."

Gasping for oxygen as my sobs choked me to a stop, and the now throbbing pain in my chest threatened to burst through my ribcage, I offered no resistance when Marilyn instantly responded by pulling me into her arms. Clutching her tightly as my muscles stiffened and threatened to spasm, I felt the soft, smooth skin of her face cool against my flushed cheek as she gently rocked me in her arms and murmured, "It'll be all right, baby, you'll see" over and over again as I cried and cried until finally no more tears would come and the tension in my body drained away.

Separating from her, I then leaned further backward and up against the tree trunk. Several additional seconds of silence ticked by before words finally crawled off my tongue. "Thanks, Mare," I mustered, a faint smile finding my lips.

"For what, sweetie? For helping a friend who's just had the biggest hurt there is?"

"Yeah ... that's for sure, but thanks anyway."

"Well, you're welcome anyway. You feeling a little bit better?"

"Uh-huh, I am. But you know what? Only part of me realizes that she's actually gone, the other crazy part still thinks that I'll see her again."

"Yeah, well that's normal, Matty. Facing the loss of a loved one is one thing, accepting it is a whole different ballgame, so don't be hard on yourself. You're hurting a whole bunch, so you've gotta be good to yourself, you hear?" Marilyn smiled.

"Yeah, I hear you, Mare. You're right."

"Of course I am, I'm always right—you know that," she gibed, her tone soft and gentle.

"Uh-huh, of course, I just forgot for a moment," trickled off my tongue through a slim smile.

"Forgot? Hell, you're so tired and worn out, Matty, it's a wonder that you can remember your own name."

"Yeah, well I'll never forget yours. It's very special, you being here for me, and I really appreciate it."

"Hey, what do you think friends are for anyway? Just for sharing the good times?"

"Nooo ... that's why you and the guys mean so much to me, 'cause we've shared so much good and bad together," affirmed my reply, this time accompanied by a wider grin. "You know, Stelle was like that, too, Mare, always there for me. I mean, I don't even have words to tell you how good she was to me," I shared, the lump in my throat suddenly reappearing and my eyes misting. "Sorry," I tacked on, wiping the tiny tears away.

"Don't be silly, you just cry anytime you want to," Marilyn soothed. "Like I said, you've just had the biggest hurt anyone ever gets, and you sure don't have to hide your feelings about it. 'Cause I understand, and so will the guys."

"Okay," I nodded. "It's just that it's so new, so raw. I mean, I just can't imagine never seeing Stelle again—never looking at that super smile of hers, or those lovely eyes, and not being able to hug her or even touch her hand. Hell, I even loved the way she bawled me out," I added, somehow a chuckle gurgling forth. "And you know I'm more than a little sensitive in that area."

"Uh-huh, I've noticed," Marilyn grinned.

"Oh, you have, huh?"

"Yeah, it sorta creeps out every so often—mainly in that building over there," she tacked on, pointing a finger at the courthouse.

"Funny," I shrugged, "but right at this moment I couldn't care less about that place. Stelle would be furious if she heard me say that, but that's the way I honestly feel. I mean, I'm way overdue in Division Three, and I just don't care, 'cause it just doesn't seem so important anymore."

"Don't worry about it, for God's sake—Blaine's covering it for you. And I thought we were in agreement that you weren't going to be hard on yourself, did I misunderstand? Or am I going to have to get tough with you?"

"No, I'll be good, I promise," I smiled, then shook my head as it widened and I added, "Poor Lacy, he's going to have a bad day, too."

"Why? What's different? You gave Uncle Tom plenty of migraines long before Blaine got here."

"Yeah, I guess you're right. But all the same, I'm a little old pussycat next to that tiger."

"Oh, yeah? ... Well Blaine sure doesn't think so," Marilyn spit back at me. "He was telling me just the other afternoon about how he thinks you're the best damn lawyer he's ever seen."

"Well, that's the capper," I shrugged, matching her smile. "Now I know he's crazy, 'cause Robbie and George are the best. But you know something, Mare? I'm going to be, too, 'cause I promised Stelle that I'd refocus, and never let fear of failure stop me from trying to be as good as I want to be. It won't be easy, but I'm going to keep that promise Big Time."

"You sure don't have to convince me," spurted her response, her grin renewing as the firmness in my tone evidenced that I was truly feeling better. "'Cause for openers, you've got the goods, and determination is your middle name."

"Thanks. You taking over for Stelle?" I teased, then climbed slowly to my feet and pulled Marilyn up after me.

"No, but I'll sure get on you if you don't keep that promise."

"No problem ... it's what I've got left," I affirmed as we began to stroll toward the office. "You know, Mare, she wouldn't let me take time off work to be with her more, 'cause she wanted me to have something to turn to after she was gone. Unbelievable, don't you think?"

"Yeah ... But she loved you, Matty—remember?"

"Uh-huh, I know. That's unbelievable, too, but I'm sure glad she did."

"You're what's unbelievable," Marilyn shot back, squeezing my hand tightly as we crossed the street, then entered the office. It was empty, and when I commented on how unique that was, Marilyn laughed. "Not for long, you can be sure of that," she snickered, shaking her head. "But don't you worry none about it, you just go on home and try to rest."

"Well, thanks, I appreciate it, Mare," I nodded, "but I'm going to stay right here with my friends. I couldn't stand to be in the apartment alone, not just yet anyway. So I'll just stay here with you and the guys—okay?"

Having carefully watched over me until I relaxed and regained control, she finally lost the tight grip she had maintained on her own emotions, her large brown eyes suddenly brimming with tears. "Why, sure—how dumb of me. Where else would you belong?" she answered, trying to smile and only half succeeding.

"Hey, no problem, believe me. I'm okay, thanks to you ... and now we're both okay, all right?" I suggested, then kissed her on the cheek and smiled at her till one reappeared on her lips. "Now, if I can get a cup of coffee and a smoke, I'll be ready to make some necessary calls," I added, my hint sparking her smile to widen.

"I'll make a fresh pot and bring you a cup in a jiffy, you just go light-up your pipe," she rushed back at me, wiping away her tears and heading over to the coffee pot.

After pulling my pipe from the breast pocket of my blazer, which was draped over the back of my chair, I settled in behind my desk for the second time that morning, carefully packed my curved Barling, and lighted it. Surprisingly it tasted as delicious as always, and I nodded my appreciation as the smoke curled upward and floated away. Having poured out a sea of emotion during the hour that had passed since Dr. Reiser telephoned, as I now took stock of myself, I discovered that a numbness had settled over me, like somehow I'd received a large shot of novocaine. It wasn't an unpleasant feeling, no, I thought. The terrible ache in my chest had disappeared, and the accompanying anxiety along with it, replaced instead by a dull sense of relief that I faintly recognized and appreciated, but couldn't fully feel. Okay, I reasoned, you're not sharp, but you're still fairly alert and able to function—not bad for openers. So, little buddy, time to make those hard calls. And after Marilyn entered, presented me with a cup of coffee in my favorite mug, then patted me on the shoulder and disappeared, I did exactly that.

Stella's sister, Lauren, was first. And even though Stelle had informed me that like with Vicki, she did not wish Lauren to have illness and a funeral as a last memory, and had discussed this with her, still tiny pin-pricks of anxiety returned to pierce the blanket of anesthesia and lodge in my stomach as I dialed her number. Unexpectedly, they disappeared as swiftly as they had arrived, as after I identified myself and the sad purpose of my call, Lauren treated me with genuine warmth and compassion. Instantly inquiring as to how I was feeling, and then graciously sharing with me how Stella had confided in her that I was Stelle's one true love and had brought her indescribable happiness, Lauren concluded by adding that she, her husband David, and Vicki would all welcome the opportunity to meet me. Not having known what to expect, I suddenly discovered that my pipe now tasted even sweeter, and I immediately responded by telling Lauren that adding them to my list of friends would be very special to me, and that when my vacation-time occurred next spring, I would come for a visit.

Next in line were Stella's closest girlfriends, Lea, Samantha, and Jean, all of whom tearfully thanked me, made me promise to call if they could assist in any possible way, and then advised that they would see me tomorrow at the funeral. Smiling after I hung up, as I listened to the echo of Jean's sweetly toned, "Please don't feel alone—and remember that me and Lou are your friends, too," I took a few moments to savor how good that made me feel while refilling my pipe, before reaching for the phone again and calling the funeral home. Ted Warwick, of Williams and Williams, was both pleasant and professional, and after expressing his condolences, promptly informed me that they had already been contacted by the hospital and had arranged to take charge of Miss Charles at noon. "Well, that's all of the calls, Matty, my man," I sighed with relief after hanging up, then settled back in my chair and attempted to further relax by reading the newspaper I spied on Ron's desk.

Life in the outside world seemed to have taken its cue from the sorrowful event which had begun my day. Freeway accidents had claimed the lives of eleven persons, an airplane crash in Brazil had extinguished a hundred and four more, and to keep the toll rising, two men had been shot and killed during an attempted bank robbery after they had killed a security guard and wounded two police officers. And oh, yes ... several members of the House of Representatives and a handful of Senators—most notably, McGovern of South Dakota and Kennedy of Massachusetts—were again blasting criticism at Nixon on the Vietnam War, while Secretary of State Kissinger continued to secretly negotiate, and our military continued bombing small villages into rubble and napalming young children, women, and other defenseless civilians to death in an effort to recapture territory that had already been won and lost by both sides more times than anyone could remember.

Would it ever end? I mused, shaking my head as I tossed the paper back onto Ron's desk. "And what about the war you're involved in, huh, Buster Brown? How's that going?" I muttered, a wry smile forming. "Well, let's go find out," I answered myself, climbing to my feet and shuffling back toward the front of the office. Several people had entered the reception area, I noted as I reached the front counter, and Marilyn was answering their basic questions and advising them that attorneys would be available at noontime, now an hour away. Over her protests, which I quieted with my argument that Stella would absolutely approve, I took over for her, introducing myself, then interviewing clients one at a time at my desk. Pleasantly surprising myself with how thoroughly I was able to analyze the varied factual situations presented, then patiently advise the individuals involved about their rights and what was likely to occur as the process moved forward, I also discovered that as a bonus the required concentration left no room for sad thoughts to intervene, thus further aiding my recovery.

During lunch, each of my compatriots approached me separately to learn how I was faring. No specific mention of the morning's tragic occurrence was made, the deep concern written in their faces, along with the gentle pats they bestowed on my shoulder as they left to return to their duties, silently saying all that was necessary. Musing about how lucky I was to have such good friends as I returned to my afternoon interviews, I drew strength from the depth of the brotherly bond between us, which warmed both my heart and my smile. Buoyed further by a group of unusually cooperative clients, I then sailed smoothly through the remainder of the busy workday. And when it ended at six o'clock, and our regular after-hours meeting was cancelled "in the interests of a little justice for us, too," as George put it, acting on his subsequent suggestion I then followed him on the return journey to West Los Angeles, where we shared dinner and idle chatter at a coffee shop. Comfortable as always in George's company, I remained relaxed, and even managed to find enough of an appetite to squeeze down a burger, fries, and a scoop of ice cream, the novocaine blanket which had sheltered me since I had departed the park with Marilyn earlier that morning continuing to salve the open wound inside me.

Finally, however, after I said goodnight to George and returned home, the protective painkiller lost strength, and the re-exposed sore began to bleed anew. Standing outside the front door for over a minute while I recollected the first time I had strolled up the stone pathway to have that first drink with Stella, I recalled also how intimidated I had been by her beauty and the aura of mystery that surrounded her. And as fragments of our first real conversation floated back into mind, once again tears returned. Wiping them away, I finally entered inside and turned on the light, my eyes instantly spying the couch where we had sat that first evening spent together, and for so many wonderful hours in the days and months that had followed. "Ohhh ... God," I moaned as the realization that Stelle was gone, that all that had existed was no more, struck home again, tears now overflowing as the throbbing ache returned to my chest and I dropped down onto the couch and cried uncontrollably for what seemed like an eternity. When I finally stopped, drained for the second time in the last twelve hours, I slowly strolled around the apartment turning on lights in an effort to make it seem less empty. Then, seeking refuge from the heavy silence that surrounded, I turned on the TV and let it drone in the background as I returned to the couch, settled up against the pillows, and tried to dull the pain by sorting through the mail, then immersing myself in *Newsweek*, all the while sipping steadily from several glasses of Chablis. The latter remedy eventually provided some relief, and when midnight arrived I slipped into my pajamas, then into bed. Tired as I was, physically, mentally, and emotionally, sleep did not come easily. And only after I read *SI* cover to cover, my eyelids now weighing almost as much as me, did I finally slide into slumber, fitful as it proved to be.

Five hours later my trusty alarm clock jarred me awake, jumbled thoughts twisting and turning before finally falling into a cohesive sequence. Feeling anxious, I quickly made coffee, then fetched the newspaper, noting that Tuesday had dawned clear and sunny, with the *Times*'s weatherman predicting a warm high of seventy-six. At ten o'clock, however, when I arrived at Ocean Park Cemetery in Santa Monica, it was still cool and comfortable, and following Stella's wishes to the last letter, her funeral was simple and without oration calculated to render the bereaved into an even more maudlin state. Joined by Stelle's girlfriends Lea, Samantha, and Jean, I stood silently behind the casket while the Unitarian minister recited the required prayers and the casket was then lowered into the gravesite.

Afterward, hugs, kisses, and promises to get together were exchanged amongst the small band of mourners, the ladies then departing as eleven o'clock approached. I wasn't ready yet, so as a gentle breeze stirred, I just stood alone beside Stelle's final resting place and waited for my heart to unburden itself. "All right, sweetheart," I finally murmured after a minute or two had elapsed, the words crawling slowly off my tongue, "you're lying near your beloved ocean like you wanted—so you rest easy," I tacked on, my voice cracking as tears swelled into my throat and eyes. "You once said that sometimes words just won't do," I continued after I took a deep swallow, "and you were right, hon. Just know that wherever you are, that I love you, and I always will … Always, you hear?" I stressed, the ache in my chest throbbing once again. "We didn't say goodbye, and I'm not going to now either, 'cause we'll always be together. I've got you tucked right here inside my heart, you see, and you'll always be there, forever … and ever," I ended, my voice trailing off as tears once again clogged my throat. For another long minute I just stood there, until the flood receded. Suddenly recalling that I had ordered a headstone which would be installed later, with the words "who is and always will be … love" to be etched beneath her name, I felt a smile slowly join me as I reluctantly turned away and shuffled toward Old Greener in the parking lot. "It'll face toward the ocean, and she'll like that for sure," I whispered, my smile inching wider.

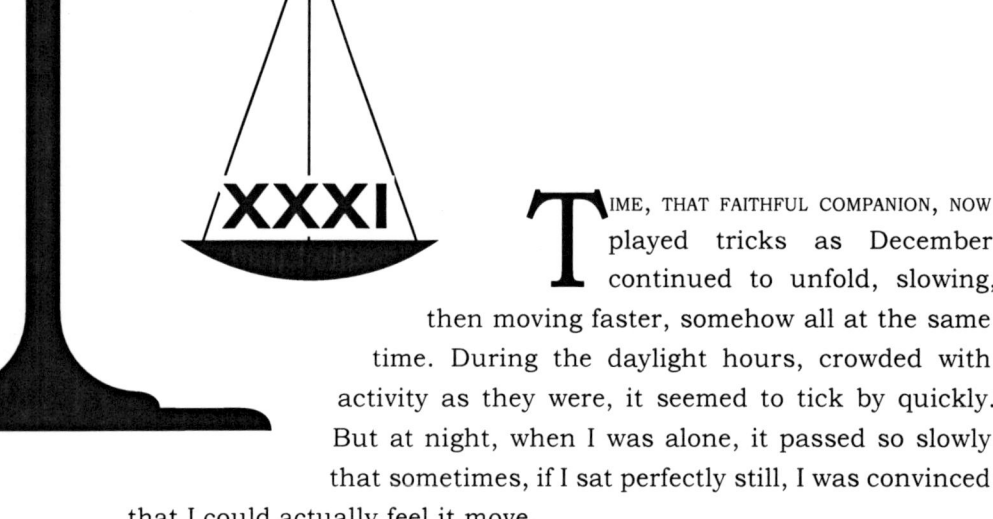

TIME, THAT FAITHFUL COMPANION, NOW played tricks as December continued to unfold, slowing, then moving faster, somehow all at the same time. During the daylight hours, crowded with activity as they were, it seemed to tick by quickly. But at night, when I was alone, it passed so slowly that sometimes, if I sat perfectly still, I was convinced that I could actually feel it move.

Having reduced the intensity of our assault in November, when our tremendous expenditure of energy during the prior five months had produced the need for some R & R/vacation-time, we further moderated the pace of our endeavors when Marilyn's fervent call for some self-reflection was answered. And fortuitously both fallbacks were facilitated in mid-December when once again court calendars were curtailed due to the judges' attendance at their annual state-wide conference. Upon my return to full-time duty after the funeral, George still insisted upon stationing me in Division One, "where your skill in plea-bargaining will continue to be most valuable, while you heal a bit more before engaging in a full-fledged fight," he explained, his tone compassionate, but also firm. I didn't argue strenuously with him, because the struggle to return to normalcy was even more difficult than I had anticipated.

Marilyn had gifted me with a book on the grieving process, and late at night when I couldn't sleep, I studied it. Of the four stages, I mused, analyzing my progress as the days passed, *facing* wasn't a problem. Stella was gone, I slept in an empty bed, and I knew she was not away visiting in Dallas. *Reinvestment* was also not a problem, I acknowledged, as due to my promise to Stelle, I had returned to work on day one. "But *acceptance* and *letting go*? ... Aye, but there's the rub, right, Willie S?" I muttered out loud when the silence grew too heavy. "'Cause I don't know this world without her, the streets look different, the sky and the flowers, too—everything! So that's going to take some time, and all you can do is control your sadness as best you can—right, Professor Vic?" I smiled wryly through the tears that frequently found me.

And try to help yourself, too, I reminded myself when anxiety suddenly appeared, and the ache inside my chest began to throb again. And I did, time after time, day by day. I increased my visits to Gram and Gramp ... I even stopped by my parents' home on two occasions for a drink and some chatter. And when silence threatened to burst my eardrums, I busied myself packing up Stella's belongings for shipment to Dallas, and when that effort resulted in her apartment growing even emptier, I moved back to my own, and pledged to look for a new home outside Beverly Hills as soon as the moving van headed east. Stelle had left me two items that she knew I treasured, an antique bookcase that swiveled on its base, and a Kennedy rocking chair. "You're going with me wherever I go," I smiled as I carefully moved them downstairs. And when I accidentally tipped over a small wooden box atop her dresser, and dried petals from the roses I had gifted her with so long ago spilled out and whispered how much they had meant to her, after I had a painful cry I slowly slipped them back inside and set the precious little box atop my beloved bookcase as a permanent reminder. By the thirteenth of the month, I had completed the sorrowful task, and after the moving van had pulled from the curb, I wistfully wandered from room to room before locking the door one final time and retreating back downstairs while wiping away the tears that once again visited me. Turning on the radio for company, unexpectedly I squeezed out a loud chuckle when irony tickled my sleeping sense of humor awake at the sound of the Rolling Stones belting out "Gimme Shelter." "Boy, I could sure use some of that," I gibed, suddenly feeling a little bit better. "Wonder where I could get some, at the shelter store maybe?" I tacked on with friendly sarcasm, trying to further cheer myself up, then turning the radio off and hurrying back outside into the sunshine to work off the prickly tension that still remained with a long walk.

The five-mile hike helped, just as the judges conference served to lower the level of hostility in the courthouse. In fact, the knowledge that he was leaving the bench for two weeks to attend the convention even softened the attitude of Judge Lacy, who in a fit of gleeful anticipation dismissed two out of six Prelim cases I tried on my return to Division Three the following Monday morning. Neither of them were throwing cases, of course. But, still, I mused, shaking my head in wonderment as we adjourned for lunch, a one-third winning percentage in front of old butt-head Bill was an early Christmas present for sure.

And that wasn't the only gift to arrive prematurely either. For although Christmas still lay ten distant days away on December's hazy horizon, the political powers that be, in combination with the higher-ups in our Office, had in mind a larger bonus to hail the arrival of Santa Claus, one, which while intended to create laughter and celebration, was instead greeted first by silence, then groans of disappointment. As on the fifteenth of the month, a single yellow piece of paper appeared on each of our desks just before noontime. Delivered by messenger, and entitled Memo, its sparse sentences authored by Huxton congratulated us on "an unbelievably tough job well done!" then followed with the news that as a reward, we were being promoted to Superior Court, effective the second full week of the coming January.

"Jesus, fucking-A Christ!" Robbie boomed out, finally breaking the somber silence that suddenly surrounded us, stunning disbelief swirling around inside it. "The bastards are breaking us up," he added as he headed for George's cubicle, the rest of us following lethargically as his message confirmed what each of us was already thinking.

"Now hold on a minute," George cautioned, twisting in his chair to try and get comfortable as he stared at his copy of the Memo. "It doesn't say anything about us being separated."

"You wanna bet?" Robbie shot back. "I've been assigned to Pomona, how about you, Georgie?"

"Downtown," tiptoed George's reply softly, his forehead furrowing as the truth of what had occurred sunk in, the instantaneous around-the-horn check that followed confirming five different assignments. "Well, let me make a call, and see what I can find out—okay?" George then picked up, his voice fully reflecting his disappointment.

The call was made, and what we expected proved to be absolutely true, the only grace-saving factor being that we learned that the judges and the DAs were also being rotated to different courts, though without promotion. That tasty tidbit of information managed to generate a collective chuckle, but did little to disperse the cloud of gloom that hung over the office for the remainder of the afternoon. Already mourning the loss of Stella, I was struck even harder than my kinsmen by the realization that now I was also losing my family of brothers, and despite my best effort to stifle them, tears crowded into my eyes. "It'll be okay,

Matt, you'll see," George consoled after following me out to the parking lot where I had retreated to hide them. "You're assigned downtown, and I'm going to be heading up our office in Juvenile Court, which is only two miles away, so we'll see each other all the time. Hell, we can even have lunch together if we want," he soothed through his magnetic smile, pulling one onto my lips.

"Yeah, that's true … that's good," I nodded back at him. "It won't be the same, but that's still good, no question."

"Right … and listen, I know how you feel," George responded swiftly, continuing to salve my feelings with empathy. "Change is a fucking bitch to deal with, and it ought to be a goddamned felony to drop this on your head after all you're going through!"

"That's a for-sure, Georgie … absolutely," I mouthed slowly, shaking my head. "And speaking of trouble with a capital T, forgive me for being so selfish, and being so wrapped up in losing Stella that I forgot to ask how things are going with Marie Anne. I didn't forget, I just—"

"Hey, no problem at all," George interrupted. "Let's go get some coffee and a smoke, and I'll run it down to you."

"Yeah, sure, I could really use a smoke," I agreed, then followed him back inside.

Marilyn put on a fresh pot to brew. And after our colleagues dispersed early to get a head start on the weekend, and try to find the silver lining in the "conspiratorial cloud hovering over us," as Robbie sardonically nicknamed the highly upsetting decision to separate us, George and I returned to my cubicle and lighted our smokes. "God, but does that taste good," I smiled, inching back in my chair as my pipe smoke swirled around me, then floated toward the ceiling.

"Yeah, you got that right," George nodded back after a long exhale, tapping his cigarette over the ashtray. "And Marie Anne and I tried to get it right, too, but things just didn't work out," he picked up, the light in his eyes dimming as he continued. "I mean, you already know we had a brief trial separation. Well, after a month, we agreed to try being together again, and for a few days life was a little bit better. But, unfortunately, like I told you before, over the years we've grown apart—we just want different lifestyles, with different goals. And on top of that, she's really changed personally, too, grown frustrated and angry," George explained, hunching up his shoulders. "Anyway, she's moved out again, and filed for divorce ... And that's ... that," he ended, smiling to cover up the sadness that crept into his tone.

"I'm sorry ... really," I responded.

"Hey, don't be," George replied instantly. "It was a long time coming, and after the major hurt you've suffered, my little bump in the road is only a misdemeanor."

"Yeahhh ... I understand, Georgie. But all the same, a divorce is a kind of death, too, so I'm sorry, I really am."

"Okay, I hear you," he returned slowly, December's combined losses suddenly weighing in on him, the centers of his eyes darkening. Never one to dwell on defeat, however, when he then focused on the strain etched into the tired lines creasing my face, the optimism that founded him quickly squeezed a smile back onto his, then generated an upbeat tone in his voice as the smile inched fuller. "Listen, I've got a story for you. You wanna hear just how tight-assed Marie Anne has become?" he bounced at me.

"Okay," I grinned back at him, not knowing what lay in store, but surmising that he was trying to alter our gloomy mood.

"Well," he began, excitement filtering into his voice, "let me tell you what that woman tried to pull off the morning before she left. I had just awakened and come into the kitchen for coffee, and bang, first thing to greet me is that she was about to execute Sam!" he rushed out with exaggerated disbelief.

"Sam?" I inquired, getting involved.

"Uh-huh, you know—he's the parakeet we have."

"Oh, yeah, I remember now. What did he do to deserve execution?"

"Well, that's just it ... nothing! At least nothing that was provable!" George stressed, pausing to search my face for an interest rating, the customary twinkle returning to his eyes as he realized my curiosity was fully aroused.

"Go on, Georgie," I encouraged, a chuckle escaping. "Sounds like something I gotta hear."

"Good!" he exclaimed gleefully. "I knew you'd be interested, now dig this. Marie Anne comes into the breakfast room and goes to feed the parakeets, only to discover Tillie, the female, lying dead on the bottom of the cage. And what does she do? Instantly, without giving any thought to the situation whatsoever, she decides that Sam killed her, and that he must die for it!"

"Wow ... sounds serious," I responded, shaking my head and snickering softly.

"Serious?" he boomed out. "I'll give you serious all right. Do you realize that this crazy lady was about to inflict the death penalty on my bird without even giving him a trial? Not to forget, of course, an arraignment or a Prelim. Hell, poor Sam didn't even know that charges had been brought against him!"

"Jesus, what did you do?" I fired back with mock concern, now having forgotten for the moment the serious subject which led to his spoof.

"Well, the first thing I did was demand a trial for my client. And reluctantly, Marie Anne agreed on the condition that she could be the judge as well as the prosecutor. I mean—"

"What?" I interjected in a tone of outrage. "Hell, that's the DAs' and judges' dream come true!"

"Uh-huh," George, replied, the twinkle in his eyes now dancing. "And I'm glad to see that you recognize the terrible handicap under which I had to try the case. I mean, it wasn't easy, believe me," he spun out, his voice continuing to rise. "Hell, there I was, first thing in the morning after only a little sleep, and on an empty stomach, too, trying to defend my poor little bird against a murder-one rap, with the goddamned prosecution also serving as the fucking judge! Think about it—that's one hell of a way to start the morning, right?"

"Oh, yeah, for sure," I chipped in. "That's a high degree of difficulty, all right."

"You got that right," he stormed forward, stifling an urge to chuckle. "I mean, that's purely and simply too much pressure at that hour of the day. A man ought to be eating a goddamned egg or reading the sports page on the crapper—or doing something else civilized!" streamed his exaggerated sense of unfairness in a steadily rising tone of voice. "Nobody ought to be engaged in a knock-down, drag-out war with a female maniac over a bird, first thing out of the sack! It's not only outrageous, it's fucking-A unconstitutional if one considers the prohibition against cruel and unusual punishment!" he thundered into a pause to take in oxygen, then extended it for effect.

"For Christ's sake, Georgie, and Moses' too," I cracked, now laughing heartily. "Tell me what happened."

"Well," he drawled, pleased that he had me totally engaged, "she tried, and I do mean tried, but she couldn't even establish the elements of murder-one, let alone link Sam to the allegation! I mean, she ranted and raved, all right, and carried on like a regular twit. But when it was all over, there was absolutely no evidence whatsoever to support her theory, and Sam was acquitted!" George roared to a close, characteristically slamming his fist down on the neighboring desktop to accentuate his triumph, then joining me in laughter.

"Was Sam grateful?" I squeezed out when our initial round had run its course.

"Grateful?" George cried, the twinkle in his eyes now glittering. "Hell, the poor bird was so upset by the whole incident, and all the yelling and screaming and what not, that he shitted all over the cage, then fainted from the accumulated aggravation! But he's all right now, though," he rushed to assure me, "still a little shook up, but all right all the same," he trailed off as another stream of laughter burst forth, then swelled into a river.

Complete with ripples that curlicued slowly into shallows before surging rapidly again, for a short while our roaring river carried us far downstream from our troubles. And even though it didn't rival the Mississippi in length, nevertheless, its cackling, chortling current still traveled far enough during the slow-ticking minute that followed to allow both of us to savor how truly good it was to laugh. Not just emit a chuckle or a snicker, but actually let loose with a series of full-fledged guffaws that shake both the body and the soul with a pure sense of merriment. I hadn't encountered such a joyous experience in recent memory. And to my happy surprise, the heartfelt warmth flowing from its innocent origin managed to linger clear through the weekend, uplifting my beleaguered spirit, adding a heightened sense of satisfaction to accomplishing routine errands, and making my visit to Gram and Gramp even more memorable than usual.

In fact, I was still smiling and giggling over George's good-natured parody when I returned to the office on Monday. Unsurprisingly, no one had located a silver lining in Robbie's conspiratorial cloud. However, the weekend respite had allowed the disturbing decision to separate us to settle, and as the days then crept closer to Christmas, a begrudging acceptance finally followed on the heels of the collective agreement that regardless of how crowded future schedules became, the Solina Seven, as we nicknamed ourselves in honor of our dear friend Marty, would meet for dinner on the last Saturday of every month.

For me, however, as I continued to struggle with acceptance and letting go in connection with Stella, the additional loss of family lingered longer, and when I wasn't occupied with my caseload, my mind consistently strayed to the subject of change. First, the loss of my pretty lady, then my brothers, the painful sequence would inevitably sidle into view, the neurons then flashing: Why? And what did it mean? When George had attempted to assuage my wounded feelings after the Memo arrived, he had opined that change was "a fucking bitch to deal with." Well, profoundly phrased as it was, it's still a super-sized understatement, I gibed silently to myself with sour sarcasm, searching and searching for an answer as the lonely nights crawled by. In Eunice's little book I had read that "there are no accidents, not with respect to major life events." So ... all right, I reasoned slowly, if these horrible happenings are not accidents, but instead part of life plans—whose? tiptoed my exploration cautiously. I mean, mine and Stella's, sure. But all of the guys, too? I mean, we're all connected, that's obvious. But that's also a lot of individual plans interacting and coming together, then trailing off in separate and different directions, too. And just to complicate matters a little bit more, how the hell does free will fit into the picture? I tossed into the boiling pot of unanswered puzzles, shaking my head even more vigorously when I concluded that accident or no accident, I was still left staring at the same overriding quandary composed of: Why? And what is the lesson or lessons to be learned?

Part and parcel of the excruciating challenge that George had so aptly and profanely articulated, the seemingly unsolvable interrogatories turned over and over inside my troubled mind day after day, no answer ever arriving. No, I would tell myself after each search-session had concluded, I can't really explain the schoolhouse, not yet anyway. I don't know for sure why Stella had to leave. I don't know why the Solina Seven have to be separated. And, hell, I can't even figure out why I've been given the plum assignment downtown, instead of Robbie or George. No, think and reflect, focus and refocus as I did, I couldn't explain, *I just don't know* becoming my constant companion and taunting me until temporarily I would back off. All you can do, Matthew, my man, I would then encourage myself as best I could amidst the confusion that swirled around inside my tired brain, is hope that somehow in the face of closing doors a new one is opening to something good.

"Yeahhh ... something good," I would repeat slowly in a murmur. And oftentimes, in the early hours of a new day, I would close my eyes and visualize the new door. I could see it slide open, but the space beyond was always blank, and I couldn't feel anything, hard as I tried. "See," I would whisper to Stelle, focusing intensely on her eyes as I returned her smile through my tears of frustration, "I'm trying to keep my promises, honest. But it's not easy, hon, not easy at all. I'll keep trying, of course, just like Grampy taught me. So just have patience with me, sweetheart, like you always did, and everything will be all right. Somehow ... some way ... everything will be all right."

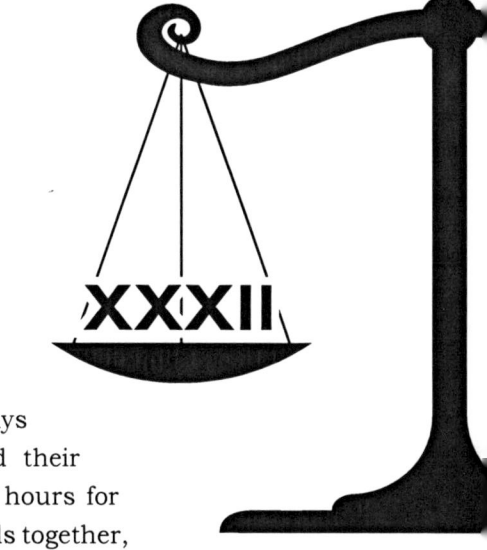

XXXII

As December now began to wane, once again Father Time dipped deep into his bag of tricks. Having slowed to a crawl for several days after Huxton & Company had dropped their Memo Bomb, as if to provide additional hours for internal reflection, now he clicked his heels together, and in full hijinks mode sprinted forward in what appeared to be a mad dash to close out 1969's final chapter.

Despite this rush of hours into fast-fading days, noteworthy historical events were still occurring. But busy, busy, busy, as always, and now frantically trying to meet year-end deadlines, the world at large couldn't afford to pay much attention. With only a sideward glance, it noted that in Chicago, in a pre-dawn raid the police killed Fred Hampton, the Black Panthers' Illinois Chairman, and Mark Clark, its party leader in Peoria. A slight nod of its head greeted the award of the Nobel Prize for Literature to Samuel Beckett, and it mustered only a thin smile and a slight shrug of satisfaction when Charles Manson and four followers were indicted for the Tate-Bianca murders. It wasn't that these happenings weren't deemed important enough to warrant serious consideration. No, the difficulty lay in matching the scarce resource of time to the tenacious demands of work's deadlines. Finally, however, the collective citizenry, weary from its various labors, carefully sidestepped the endless conflict in Vietnam and happily chugged to a stop to celebrate Christmas.

Finding it difficult indeed to personally celebrate after December's multiple losses, I steeled myself and managed to smile my way through dinner and the small talk that fortunately flowed harmlessly around the table at my parents' home, escaping early to meet George at Robbie and Lou's family gathering around eight o'clock and share dessert and coffee. The abundance of genuine warmth and good cheer flowing forth from this convivial conclave not only saved the day, but possessed such staying power that it propelled me energetically through the weekend and the three quickly passing workdays that followed. Add a few additional ticks of the speeding clock, and an exhausted 1969 found itself standing on its last leg, its shoulders slumped from age and activity, its eyes smiling wanly at the promised relief now just twenty-four hours away.

George and I had planned to spend New Year's Eve together at his house, and after court finally adjourned and we carefully closed up the office, we headed there directly. Arriving around five-thirty, after we surveyed the Sports Page while sipping a beer, we adjourned to the patio and watchfully barbecued oversized steaks to perfection. Large as they were, we managed to enjoy every single ounce, along with the accompanying salad and garlic toast, washing our feast down with glasses of Pinot Noir amidst casual conversation. Stuffed, we postponed dessert in favor of a long, slow walk around the neighborhood. And having helped digestion along with our hour-plus stroll, we finally settled onto a couch in the living room with coffee and smokes to continue chatting while we watched Guy Lombardo steadily count down the hours to the birth of the new year.

For the most part our conversation remained casual, dominated by speculation about tomorrow's Rose Bowl outcome and commentary on the musical performances and celebrity interviews on the TV. But around eleven o'clock, when the glittering globe atop Times Square slowly began to mark 1969's final hour, as well as the decade's, bittersweet nostalgia suddenly put in an appearance. "What a ten years, huh, Georgie?" I posed wistfully, lighting up a fresh pipeful, the question drifting off my tongue and momentarily hanging in the air amidst the clouds of smoke.

"No shit, man," George quipped, a wry smile appearing. "First, we had real hope—JFK, the Peace Corps, and growing support for the Civil Rights Movement. Next thing you know, JFK's gone, and Martin and Bobby, too, and for a chaser we get stuck with that slimy shithead Nixon!"

"Yeahhh, I thought we'd seen the last of that asshole for sure," I nodded back. "But with Bobby dead, and Johnson ruined by the fucking Vietnam War, a nice, little power vacuum opened up and old Tricky Dick climbed out from underneath his rock and right into the Oval Office. Too bad, too," I opined sadly, shaking my head, "'cause Johnson got the Civil Rights Acts of sixty-four and five passed, and really had a hell of a good start on his Great Society."

"Uh-huh, for sure," George agreed, exhaling a stream of cigarette smoke. "The War on Poverty was the best idea for a war, ever, and LBJ could've accomplished really great things for millions of people who have shitty lives. But once Vietnam got out of hand, and not only turned into something we couldn't win, but in addition sapped all the money for the poverty projects, it was just a losing proposition for old Lyndon all the way around."

"Yeahhh" emerged slowly through my sigh, "talk about a lot of back-and-forth change, boom, boom, boom. And that's not all either, we've had the Beatles build on Elvis to revolutionize music, the hippies teaching drop-out, drugs, and free love, with society's morals, ethics, and values subject to question every time you turn around. My God, but what a lot of change in such a short period of time!" I stressed, struggling to truly fathom the magnitude of the chaotic train of events even as they tripped off my tongue.

"Yeah, Big Time, as you would say," George nodded back. "The war nine thousand miles away, TV'd right into your living room every night alongside dinner—followed here at home by protest marches, freedom riders, assassinations, and riots all over the country, with good and bad flowing every which way. Hell, you got it, Matty—change, change, and more change. It's the old cardinal rule of the universe acting out, and you can't stop it."

"Yeah, I hear you. But the problem is, not all change is good, Georgie."

"You got that right. Hell, sometimes even the means for getting positive change are bad—like violence. I mean, riots are fucking awful, but sometimes that's the only way to wake folks up."

"Uh-huh ... 'cause most people are so busy with their own lives that they're just not paying attention to how horrible some other people have it," trickled my agreement, emotion then jumping into my voice. "Then, of course, there's the Steiggermans of the world, elitist assholes who think that that's just fine—that that's the way society's supposed to work, and tough shit for those who draw the short straw in life!" groused my indictment.

"Hey, take it easy, Mr. Public Defender," George gently poked. "It's a holiday and you're off duty—remember?"

"Yeah, I do ... And that's what Stelle would say, too," I tacked on, chuckling. "But you know what I can't figure out, Georgie? If ye olde cardinal rule is always changing our lives and the world around us, why now, so much so fast?"

"Well ... I'm not sure ... but there's a tip or two in an essay I recently read by David Halberstam," crawled the preface to George's reply before he paused to sip his coffee, a twinkle then dancing in his eyes as he lighted a fresh cigarette and continued. "Now, after outlining how we fought World War II against monstrous evil, and how the war jumped our society from a rural to an urban-industrial base, he suggested that in 1947, when Jackie Robinson came along, America stood at a kind of crossroads between two contradictory impulses, one composed of darkness and prejudice, the other of an idealism and optimism that believed in the possibility of all Americans being able to raise themselves up in a democratic and meritocratic society, as he called it. So ... I'm guessing," George added after a brief hesitation, "that the two contradictory impulses smashed head-on into each other, like two cars in an intersection—and boom, all the pent-up frustration that had been steadily building since the turn of the century just exploded!"

"Boy, Georgie, that's really interesting," I responded, his explanation then replaying on my mind's screen as I relit my pipe. "I mean, I've been thinking for the longest time about why so much change all of a sudden, with no answer. But now, the more I think about what Halberstam said, and your analogy of a car crash, the more sense it seems to make," I nodded, the proverbial light bulb flickering on. "And like I said before, change comes so much faster these days, it makes it even harder to adjust. I think that's why the older generation has had such a hard time with rock 'n roll and the hippies. I mean, if *we're* struggling to adjust, it's gotta be a hell of a lot harder for them."

"Yeah, I agree," George nodded. "Since things went sour with Marie Anne, I've thought a lot about all the changes we've been talking about, and how a person adjusts, and where he fits in. There's no easy answers of course, even Bob Dylan didn't have one, and he's one smart dude for sure. I mean, first he told us that 'The Times, They Are a-Changin,' and that's good for openers, 'cause if you don't see the problem, you sure as hell can't try to fix it. But answers? ... like how? ... and what is your personal responsibility? ... Well, they may be 'Blowin' in the Wind,' all right, but the wind can be just a little bit tricky to read sometimes, and if we don't watch out, it can just plain blow us away."

"No argument there, 'cause change is r-e-a-l-l-y tricky—especially when you consider that riding that wind is a wave of history," I rolled out, slowly shaking my head at how difficult it was to grasp a comprehensive overview of the complex decade and its tumultuous occurrences. "So what's actually causing the change anyhow? ... the wave pressing in on the times, or the people living in them?"

"Both, I think," George shot back. "That same Jackie Robinson said that times don't change, people do. But I don't think they're mutually exclusive ... I think that there's this long train of events we call history, that keeps building up pressure until finally people are forced to see the problem, and then adjust in order to try and fix it. When it's actually happening, it's kind of like the chicken and egg scenario, hard to see which one comes first. What do you think?"

"I'm with you, I think it's both!" I agreed, excitement suddenly flushing a smile across my face as the light bulb burned brighter and I could see more clearly. "It's like MLK said, there comes a time when people get tired. But, hell, they didn't just get up that way one morning, it took that long train of time and events to make them so tired that finally enough really does become enough, and then that car crash you were talking about happens," streamed my reinforcing analogy to a stop. A short one however, as a similar conclusion, this one hard-earned after much self-reflection on the issue, bubbled to the surface. "You know, I kind of compare it to my own personal situation, Georgie," I tacked on, my grin fading. "All my life, as long as I can remember, my father was putting me down. Naturally, he was the authority figure in our family, and he always had this superior attitude about him that he used to make me feel inferior, especially when I grew older and expressed ideas that ran counter to what he believed," I explained calmly, even as a myriad of nasty incidents flooded into mind. "Anyway, to make a very long story short, after years of growing more and more uncomfortable, finally the pain of being diminished and humiliated grew so great that it outweighed the fear of unknown consequences from openly rebelling against it—and change finally occurred."

"I see ... And that's why you left the real estate world to be a PD?"

"Uh-huh, exactly," I affirmed, the muscles in my face which had grown taut now relaxing. "And while my situation isn't even a pimple on the old elephant's ass when compared to the unbelievable pain and suffering of blacks over a four-hundred-year period, the principle's the same: Someone, or some group, who wants to be on top and stay there, pushes somebody else down, and then creates and enforces a set of social and legal rules to keep them there. The way they see it, a person can't be superior, unless someone else is inferior—and equal be damned!" I stressed, emotion finally creeping into my voice.

"Okay ... that seems to fit right in," George eased out after swallowing a sip of coffee. "I mean, if I read you right, what you're saying is that when the pain of the present situation, while familiar and therefore kind of safe, finally outweighs the fear of change, which has uncertain factors attached to it and therefore might be unsafe, movement occurs."

"Exactly. Only in my case, I got an extra shove from all that was going on in the world around me. I saw what was happening with the freedom riders, and the marchers in Selma, and I said: hey, me too."

"Okay ... I see ... I see," George acknowledged, my illustration sinking in further.

"Uh-huh, right. But what happened to me, Georgie, doesn't solve the chicken and egg puzzle, I'll have to leave that for the heavy thinkers in the world—the psychologists, sociologists, and philosophers. In the meantime, however, I'm sure grateful that I finally made a change and got to be a tiny part of the overall movement."

"Yeahhh ... me, too, I not only picked up a co-conspirator, but a damn good friend to boot!" George shot back at me. "And you know what? I can't even fully express what our little clan's accomplishment means to me. Like you said, it's only a small part of the big picture, but still, we saw the injustices in Solina's judicial system and wanted to change it—and goddamnit, we grew some balls, fought like hellions, and we did it, we absolutely made change happen!" George enthused through a prideful smile, its fullness then constricting slightly when an earlier counterpoint flashed back into mind. "Well, at least for a little while anyway," he added, his exuberance slowly fading. "'Cause the old establishment is still around, and like we said, change is always continuing."

"Yeah, but that's not a problem," I bounced back. "Like you said, Georgie, the judges and the DAs are being rotated, too, so our changes, particularly the jury selection system, are almost certain to remain."

"Hey, good point, counselor, I forgot that little goodie," he readily acquiesced through a fresh grin, his innate optimism resurfacing instantly.

"No problem, buddy," I returned, my grin widening to match his. "Would you like a little icing on the old proverbial cake?"

"Yeah, sure ... What?"

"You know how sports are said to reflect society at a given point in time?"

"Uh-huh ... right."

"Well, in baseball, the Sixties started off with the Pirates defeating the Yankees on Bill Mazeroski's ninth-inning home run, and this year the Miracle Mets, who were picked to finish ninth in the National League, beat the Baltimore Orioles. So, my friend, the battling underdogs stuck it to the lordly establishment on both ends of the wild-and-wooly Sixties! Now how's that for a little odd-ball symbolism?" I posed with a chuckle.

"Well, I'll be damned, that's great!" George heartily agreed. "A regular synchronicity sandwich!"

Truly a miraculous set of circumstances, we were about to further expand on their wondrous properties, when Guy Lombardo suddenly intervened from TV-land to inform us that midnight was about to arrive. Ten final seconds then ticked off, accompanied by the glittering ball sliding slowly to its base and instantly triggering a neon-colored Happy New Year! onto the screen in sync with the band playing "Auld Lang Syne." "Well ... so long to the Sixties," I muttered in response, suddenly feeling overwhelmingly melancholy, goose bumps surfacing on my arms, and tears creeping into my eyes as my mind's projector flashed a fast-forward replay of all the sweet hours of joy and triumph that the vanished era had held for me.

"No, no, Matty," George soothed after catching sight of my reaction. "I know you're hurting Big Time from losing Stella, and the loss of what we all shared together in Solina. But listen, I need to tell you something important, and you need to know it," he urged kindly. "What we were discussing about change caused me to think of something my favorite writer, William Faulkner, taught me. He was one wise dude, you know," George continued, his tone soft and reassuring, "and he said that 'The past is never dead. It's not even past.' So think about that—okay?"

Okay ... okay, for sure! I thought, a smile rushing across my face as his words registered, Stella's beautiful face floating into my mind's eye, trailed by the battle the Solina Six had successfully waged. "Well, I'll certainly shake on that, Georgie," I offered up, noting that his eyes also held tears as I stretched out my hand and he firmly grasped it. "Happy New Year!" I tacked on as he smiled back at me. "And may 1970 be a good one!"

"Amen!" George announced firmly, then pulled me into a hug.

Short, lasting but a few seconds, nevertheless, its silent testimony to unity and hope was the perfect salute to the newborn year. In fact, driving toward the office on the following Monday, I could still feel the warmth and strength of that message. Yeahhh, I mused, a grateful grin sneaking out of the corners of my mouth, Georgie and my other brothers are still with me, and who knows, maybe Mr. Faulkner's right, too? I mean, God, I certainly hope so, hurried my follow-up thought, leading me into a short pause to embrace the comfort I gleaned from his peace-producing hypothesis. The always present lawyer in me having noted also that the adopted adage did have a second side, I quickly nodded my head in affirmation at my judgment that in my case the good far outweighed the bad, then forced my focus away from the past and onto the new year. So, how does 1970 feel so far, old chap? I posed, a moderately contemplative expression creasing my face as I turned off the freeway and headed east on Alondra. "Well," I answered, breaking the silence, "pretty damn good for only being four days old. I mean, for openers, on New Year's Day my mighty Trojans squeaked out a 10–3 victory over Ohio State in the Rose Bowl, and Georgie and I had a hell of a good time watching while we stuffed ourselves with hot dogs and ice cream!" I mustered cheerfully, building my case. "Then, too, the weekend was pleasant enough, what with plenty of time to start preparing for the upcoming assignment in Superior Court, and Sunday's long and joyful visit with Gram, Gramp, and Nanny Lou. And, hey, I've still got them, too," jumped off my tongue, the flashing reminder adding to my upbeat mood. "Okay," I tacked on as I pulled into the parking lot, then exited Old Greener. "Let's go see who we can help today!"

A casual challenge, encapsulating a rhetorical question, both were soon satisfied by 1970's opening calendar. Overcrowded as usual, and followed in like fashion by Tuesday's and Wednesday's, together the dockets' conveyor belt of cases forced a hustle-bustle agenda of interview and plea-bargain that caused the corpulent trio to busily pass by. Well rested from his attendance at the judges conference, Judge Austin returned with his native good humor restored and fully on display, and my negotiations during the three-day whirlwind resulted in a host of advantageous settlements for my mostly pleased clients, with numerous outright dismissals of the minor cases highlighting my final week in Solina. Final still sounded strange to me when it snuck into mind from time to time, but by Thursday I had surrounded it with a smile of acceptance, a grin that grew wider when I realized that Division Two was the easiest platform from which to launch the process of saying my farewells. "I'm going to miss you, too, Matt," Judge Austin responded when I broached the subject. "We've worked well together, and you've not only made my job a lot easier, but sharing poetry with you has been a real joy for me."

"Well, thank you, Your Honor, and for me too," I returned. "And I want you to know that there aren't sufficient words to say thanks for the countless kindnesses you've shown me."

"They were deserved, Matt ... they were deserved," he issued through a spreading smile, his blue eyes gleaming. "It was a pleasure to watch you grow as young lawyer, and if you maintain that strong work ethic of yours in combination with your compassion and the courage of your convictions, great things are in store for you, you'll see."

"I'll give it my best, Your Honor, you can bet some of your popcorn on it."

"I'll just do that, Matt. And one more thing ... I heard about the terrible hurt you suffered in losing your lady, and I want you to know how sorry I am. You take the best of care, and that's an order of the Court, you hear?"

"Yes, Sir ... I promise I will," I mustered, fighting off tears as I shook his hand. "And please know that I'll never forget you," I added before turning away and hurrying back outside into the courtroom, where I regained control of my churning emotions by busying myself saying goodbye to Ray Cline at his clerk's desk.

On Friday morning, I arrived in Solina extra early so that I could pay visits to Sheriff Moorehouse and several clerks and bailiffs in the various divisions. Handshakes and good wishes were shared, and Sheriff Ed added a hug. Fittingly, my final court assignment was in Division Three where I had started eighteen long months ago. Judge Lacy, also rested from his relaxing days at the judges conference, and aware that we would soon be parting company, appeared to celebrate by moderating his usual combative attitude, and four Prelims passed by in routine fashion. The head nods we exchanged as Court adjourned for the noon recess served as our farewells, and I was still shaking my head at the hint of a smile that had accompanied Lacy's nod as he exited the bench when Stephen Shafer approached. "What's up, Matt?" he chirped cheerfully.

"Not much, Steve," I shrugged. "Just winding up and getting ready to leave."

"Yeah, me too—in fact that's what I wanted to talk to you about. Maybe now that we're going to be in different jurisdictions, we can finally have that dinner."

"Yeah, sure ... no problem," I slipped out, surprised that getting together was still on his mind. "We've got each other's numbers, so maybe after we get settled in our new assignments, say in two or three weeks, we can meet—okay?"

"That's fine," he nodded back through a smile. "And I want to wish you good luck downtown," he added, stretching out his hand for a shake.

"Thanks. You, too, of course," I returned, shaking his hand firmly. "See you soon," I added, before we turned away and headed for our respective offices.

Blaine was covering Division Three for the afternoon session, so as I pushed open the double doors that led outside, I was struck by the fact that my official duties in Solina had ended. The bands and the cheering crowd were still nowhere to be found, but I shrugged a smile at the entering thought that the number nine next to January atop today's calendar had once again harbored good luck, and it was a very relaxed me who slowly ambled back to the office. Lunch and animated conversation were already in progress, and after I helped myself to a large breast and some fries from the spread we had all earlier chipped in to purchase from the neighboring Jim Dandy chicken stand, I eagerly joined in the banter and accompanying laughter. Then, when my brothers had returned to the courthouse to attend to the afternoon's abbreviated calendars, I lit up my pipe and leisurely began clearing out my desk and the small bookcase on the far wall. Around three-thirty, after I had sorted what needed to remain behind from what needed to leave with me, and had seated myself at my desk to finalize my interview notes from the morning's Prelims, Marilyn interrupted to advise that I had a "very special visitor." Then, wearing one of her patented smiles that could light up the darkest room, she ushered Fred Ginther into my cubicle.

"H-el-l-o, Fred!" I enthused, then gleefully chuckled as I shook his hand. "God, but it's good to see you—and to see you looking so good, too!" I added, nodding my head vigorously for emphasis as he returned my smile.

"It's good to see you, too," he returned, "I'm glad I caught you."

"There's not a problem is there, Fred?" I shot back, the temporarily retired lawyer in me suddenly awakening.

"Oh, no Sir, none at all," he assured. "I just read in the *Bugle* that you all were being promoted and transferred, and I wanted to see you and thank you again for all you did for me and my family."

"Well, that's really nice, Fred, thank you. I uh—say, did you get the papers I sent you, the ones that said your conviction was reversed, and that your record's one hundred percent clean?" I hastily jerked out after I interrupted my previous thought, a smile following at the same speed.

"Oh, yes, Mr. Harris ... I sure did," he assured, a smile also hurrying across his face, his head now nodding for emphasis. "That was great, and so good of you to send to me."

"Well, good ... And listen, Fred, you don't have to call me Mr. Harris anymore. I'm no longer your lawyer, so we're just good friends—okay?"

"Well, thank you, Sir ... I appreciate that a whole bunch. But you'll always be my lawyer, Sir, and that reminds me—" he tailed off into a brief pause as he reached into his coat pocket before continuing. "I want to return the three hundred dollars you mailed to my wife while I was in jail, you'll never know how much it helped her and the little ones."

"Ohhh ... that's not necessary, Fred," I returned, totally stunned.

"Oh, yes it is," he nodded out. "After I got out, I got a new job, a better one. I'm a manager at the new barbecue restaurant in town. It's called Charlie's, and I started as a kitchen helper, then got promoted to waiter—and then they made me manager just last month," he rushed out, then chuckled shyly.

"Boy, that's fantastic, Fred ... the best news I've had in a long time!" I stressed, taking the money from his outstretched hand, then shaking it. "I'll bet that lovely wife of yours is one proud lady," I tacked on.

"Uh-huh, she sure is, and she made me promise to pass along her thanks to you, too. And that's not all," he rushed to add, "she wanted me to ask you to come for dinner with us sometime soon—she's a real good cook, and it'd be an honor for us."

"Well, I think we'll have to share the honor, Fred, but I'd love to come—providing, of course, that you'll all call me Matt."

"Yes, Sir, we'll do it ... Matt," he managed to squeeze off his tongue after a slight hesitation. "And now I know you're busy getting ready to leave, so I'm going to mosey along."

"All right, Fred. I'll call you soon, just give me a couple of weeks to get settled in the new court," I answered, then shook his outstretched hand with both of mine.

After Fred departed, I carted my two boxes of belongings out to Old Greener, the rich reward of Fred's visit accompanying me and further swelling my emotions to the point of tears. "Now, don't you get all teary-eyed on me," Marilyn teased after I was finished packing and settled into a chair beside her desk for a so-long cup of coffee.

"I won't, I promise," I returned. "'Cause I'm going to see you every month for dinner, and call you in between just because I want to—okey-dokey?"

"You know it is, and I'll be expecting those calls, too," she smiled, then clinked coffee cups with me.

We were still engaged in idle chatter when the rest of the family returned around four o'clock. And for an hour, all seven of us huddled together over coffee one last time, the lively conversation flowing round the circle propelled by the nervous energy we shared from the knowledge that our time together was steadily ticking to an end. When the inevitable departure time finally arrived at five-thirty, hugs were shared all around, and together we closed the office for the final time. George and I were the last to leave the parking lot, our simultaneous callings of "See you for dinner tomorrow night" echoing as we climbed into our cars and headed for home.

As I pulled onto Hester Street, a lump formed in my throat, and when I reached the front of the courthouse, I pulled Old Greener over to the curb and climbed out for one last look. Dusk was settling as I stretched my arms overhead, then relaxed them and stood still and stared up at the tattered letters of Justice high over the entryway, just as I had on that sunny day when I first arrived so long ago. So much had happened during that eighteen months, I mused, my mind flooding with fragments of Prelims, trials, clients, my brothers, and Stella, my eyes tearing over all that had been gained and lost, time ticking slowly by. Finally, the lights flickered on inside the courthouse as the custodians began their labors. And glancing down at my watch which Stella had given me last March on my birthday, "So you'll remember me every time you look at it," I heard her murmur once again, then smiled and wiped away the tears that had trickled down my cheeks, my grin spreading as the five-fifty reading reminded me that I had better get going if I was to be on time for dinner at Gram and Gramp's.

Climbing back into Old Greener, I gently waved a goodbye to the courthouse, then switched on the ignition and inched away from the curb. As I neared the end of the block, my mind still spinning and now melding together the beginning made here in Solina with the one waiting for me on Monday downtown, suddenly the Talmudic adage on the subject rushed into view. "All beginnings are difficult, especially one you make by yourself alone," it instructed from its age-old vantage point. "That's true," I whispered when I reached the stop sign and delayed for several seconds. "But there's truth in what old Bill Faulkner said, too, I added through a forming smile. "'Cause you're still alive in my heart, pretty lady, and I'll never be truly alone ever again," I ended, my grin growing as I then accelerated, heading for the freeway and home.

About the Author

HOWARD G. FRANKLIN RECEIVED HIS B.S. FROM USC AND HIS J.D. FROM THE University of California, Berkeley, then served as a Deputy Public Defender in Los Angeles County in the late 1960s and early 1970s, and currently lives outside Portland, Oregon.

His well-received travelogue, *An Irish Experience*, was published in 2008, and since 1986 his short stories and poetry have appeared on radio and in *A Different Drummer, Razem, The Lake Oswego Review, The Sandwich Generation, Silver, Quill, Nomad's Choir, Single Vision, Poets at Work, Grit, Eureka Literary Journal, PoetSpeak Portland Anthology*, and *Verseweavers, the Oregon State Poetry Association Anthology*.

He has also appeared as a guest poet in PoetSpeak's Reading Series at Portland State University, and in the Northwest Poetry Coalition's celebration of National Poetry Month in Vancouver, Washington.

CPSIA information can be obtained at www.ICGtesting.com
Printed in the USA
BVOW04s1419171014

371206BV00002B/2/P